## Praise for Gabriele Wills's previous novels

"Once in a while a novel grabs the reader's attention from the opening pages to long after the final words have been savoured. Such is **A Place To Call Home**... it is Wills' ability to create believable characters that is most impressive. No two persons are alike and each comes to life through vivid description and convincing dialogue. Wills cleverly weaves several real historical figures into the novel who give the story a strong sense of authenticity.... **A Place To Call Home** is a long but satisfying read. A novel that is so detailed yet not boring is a rare gift. It takes the reader back to that period about which too little is known. It leaves him wishing he could join Rowena and her family for a further 50 years." – *Anne Forrest, NUACHT, Community Newsletter of St. Patrick's Society, Montreal*

"**A Place To Call Home** is a gripping and fascinating saga about an Irish family's immigration to Canada and the building and founding of the [*fictional*] Ontario town called Launston Mills. Wills masterfully traces the development of the town, told through the eyes of Irish immigrant, Rowena, and her son, Keir. The historical facts were flawlessly researched, but rather than it reading like a series of facts, Wills peopled the book with vivid and very real characters whose experiences captivate the reader. .... an exceptionally well-told story. ... **A Place To Call Home** offers a delightful glimpse into Canada's past, told through characters who come to life and jump off the page.." – *Writer's Digest Magazine*

The following are excerpts from readers' comments.
For more, see
**www.mindshadows.com/publishing**

Regarding *A Place To Call Home* :

"Absolutely wonderful! *A Place To Call Home* is so vivid, descriptive and intriguing... I couldn't put it down! You made me feel like I was part of the story from beginning to end. The characters are so real, their lives so intense that it stirred emotion."

"I am not much of a book reader, but your fictional chronology of a pioneering family felt so real to me that I read the entire book in about 2 days."

"Thank you for writing this important book, which I enjoyed immensely.... Apart from the story line, which I believe carries the narrative brilliantly, I was fascinated by the wide spectrum of characterization."

"I was immersed in your descriptive and vivid writing style, which flowed so magically."

"I found it hard to put down... The historic detail and geographic descriptions in your book are clear and, together with the dialogue, help the people come alive in the realistic setting you have so carefully crafted.... It is a rare novel that satisfies the geographer in me!"

"You have a very special gift of relating historical events in a wonderfully interesting manner."

"I found the book to be a fascinating and insightful story about family relationships, romance, and 'roughing it' in Upper Canada. It was a wonderful read!"

"I could go on and on about how much I've enjoyed getting to know the characters, how I've become involved in their struggles, and tremendously impressed by their courage as well as moved by their human frailties."

"When I wasn't reading the book, I was thinking about it."

"I really loved and related to your **A Place To Call Home**. I have read it twice and got much enjoyment out of both reads."

"I was looking for a novel that would bring 19th century Ontario to life for me and your book did exactly that. I am impressed by the amount of research that went into the book and with your skill in dramatizing many of the key themes that went into making pioneer life."

"The characters and the story itself were so compelling, I was reluctant to put the book down once I started to read it!"

"I have just finished reading it for the third time.... Like long-time friends, a good book teaches one something through every reading!"

"My husband and I read **A Place To Call Home** with immense pleasure. It is truly a well written and immensely interesting book. I have not accomplished much in the past two days, as I could not put the book down."

Regarding *Moon Hall* :

"I just finished reading **Moon Hall** and felt I needed to tell you what a beautiful story it is... I literally couldn't put the book down."

"After enjoying **A Place To Call Home** so much, I was really looking forward to reading **Moon Hall**. I wasn't disappointed! Both stories captured my interest immediately and kept me enthralled to the end."

"**Moon Hall** was a captivating read!"

"**Moon Hall** was such a fascinating and vivid story, one often felt one was in the house with Kit and Violet at the same time. Toggling between past and present was something Gabriele Wills did with great ease. Kudos to yet another great Canadian writer! We need more historical fiction like this...."

*A Place To Call Home* and *Moon Hall*
are available online and at select stores, which are listed on
**www.mindshadows.com/publishing**

# The Summer Before The Storm

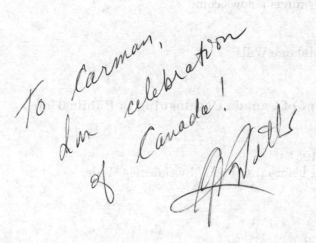

*To Carman,*
*in celebration*
*of Canada !*

*The First of "The Muskoka Novels"*
*by*

# Gabriele Wills

**MIND**
*SHADOWS*

Cover photo by Melanie Wills

**National Library of Canada Cataloguing in Publication**

Wills, Gabriele, 1951–
    The summer before the storm / by Gabriele Wills.

ISBN 0-9732780-2-1

1. World War, 1914-1918--Canada--Fiction. I. Title.

PS8595.I576S94 2006      C813'.6      C2006-905483-5

First edition
Published by Mindshadows
mindshadows.com
Printed and bound in Canada

# Foreword

My fascination with Muskoka began in the 1960s when, as a teenager, I stayed for weeks every summer at my friend's cottage on Mazengah Island on Lake Rosseau. The cottage had been built by her great-grandfather in 1879, so a family compound developed around it over the next century. Hearing wonderful tales of the "old days", I knew then that one day I would write about that genteel time in legendary Muskoka. My deepest thanks to Fay (Patterson) Willsie, her parents, Art and Isla Patterson, and her large, extended family for introducing me to Muskoka and a unique way of life. Thanks to Barb Mason for lending the impressive Mazengah history compiled by her father, Arthur D. Blachford.

Thanks also to the following people for their help with questions relating to law, medicine, physics, finance, and so forth, for editorial comments, and for their generosity and hospitality during research trips: Vic Tavaszi, Laurie McLean, Dr. R.B. Fleming, Dr. Peter Anderson, "Perfessor" Bill Edwards, Dr. Peter, Vally, and Stephanie Wills, Kathleen James, Sue Wills and Lee Salvati, Fay and Frank Willsie, Michael Wills, Anne Vinet, and Annie Morshead.

Special thanks to my dedicated editors – my daughter, Melanie, and my husband, John. Their unfailing love, support, encouragement, commitment, and enthusiasm allowed me to joyfully immerse myself in this project. Once again it has been a thrill to use one of Melanie's evocative photographs for the cover. John has also been instrumental in upgrading my website to allow for online sales. What a team!

I'd also like to thank Melanie for believing that my life is interesting enough for a documentary, which she is producing. Watch for *Not Quite Famous* – the story of a struggling writer.
    See www.DoubleHelixCreations.com for more information

This book is dedicated to my daughter, Melanie Wills. May she find her own Muskoka.

Comments are always appreciated at books@mindshadows.com

# The Islands

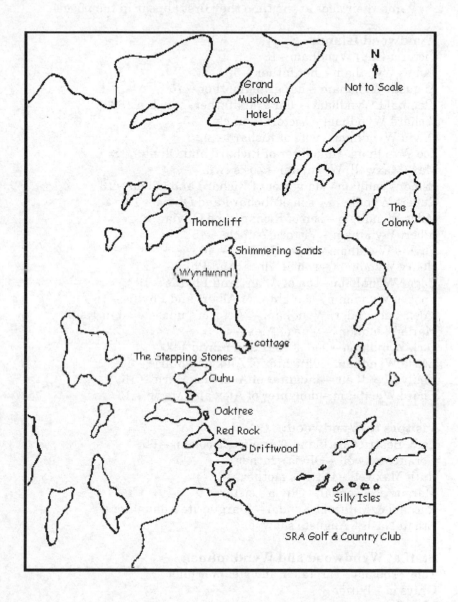

- Grand Muskoka Hotel
- N — Not to Scale
- The Colony
- Thorncliff
- Shimmering Sands
- Wyndwood
- cottage
- The Stepping Stones
- Ouhu
- Oaktree
- Red Rock
- Driftwood
- Silly Isles
- SRA Golf & Country Club

# Cast of Characters

and their ages at the time they first appear in the novel

**Wyndwood Island:**
Victoria (Ria) Wyndham –18
James Wyndham – her father – 50
Augusta Wyndham – her grandmother – 75
[Reginald Wyndham – her grandfather – died in 1896]
Richard Wyndham – Victoria's uncle – 45
Olivia Wyndham – wife of Richard – 42
Zoë Wyndham – daughter of Richard and Olivia – 18
Max (Maxwell) Wyndham – Zoë's twin
Esme Wyndham – daughter of Richard and Olivia – 13
Rupert Wyndham – son of Richard and Olivia – 10
Miles Wyndham – son of Richard and Olivia – 8
Albert Wyndham – Victoria's uncle – 48
Phyllis Wyndham – wife of Albert – 46
Henry Wyndham – son of Albert and Phyllis – 21
Edgar Wyndham – son of Albert and Phyllis – 19
Phoebe Wyndham – daughter of Albert and Phyllis – 16
[Alex (Alexander) Wyndham – Victoria's uncle, died in 1908]
Marie Wyndham – wife of Alex – 41
Jack Wyndham – son of Alex and Marie – 20
Lizzie Wyndham – daughter of Alex and Marie – 17
Emily Wyndham –daughter of Alex and Marie – 15
Claire Wyndham – daughter of Alex and Marie – 13

**Visitors to Wyndwood:**
Lady Beatrice Kirkland – Augusta's cousin – 65
Gerald Maxwell – Olivia's father
Ruth Maxwell – Olivia's mother
Marguerite Kendal – Olivia's sister
Rachael & Millicent Kendal – Marguerite's daughters
Ethan Nash – Augusta's lawyer

**Staff at Wyndwood and Wyndholme:**
Toby (Tobias) – caretaker and steamer pilot
Grayson – butler
Mrs. Grayson – housekeeper and  butler's wife
Mrs. Hadley – cook
Molly Jones – parlour maid
Libby – parlour maid

Tom – footman
Bayley – lady's maid
Will – under-gardener
Mary – laundry maid
Rosie – kitchen/scullery maid
George – chauffeur

## Thorncliff Island:
J. D. (Joseph Davenport) Thornton – financier
Marjorie Thornton – his wife
Chas (Charles) Thornton  – son – 22
Rafe (Ralph) Thornton – son –19
Felicity  (Fliss) Thornton  – daughter – 14

## Red Rock Island:
Edward Carrington – mill owner
Rena (Rowena) Carrington – his wife
Justin Carrington  – son – 21
Vivian Carrington – daughter  22
Lydia Carrington – daughter – 18
Simon Carrington – son – 25
Keir and Megan Shaughnessy – Rena's parents – see *A Place To
    Call Home* for their story

## Ouhu Island:
(Professor) Thomas Carlyle – physics professor
Hannah Carlyle – his wife
(Dr.) Blake Carlyle – son – 22
Eleanor (Ellie) Carlyle – daughter – 20
Daphne & Derek Carlyle – younger children

## Oaktree Island:
Oswald Oakley – Pittsburgh steel magnate
Letitia Oakley – his wife
Louise Oakley – daughter – 15
Martin,  Roger,  & George Oakley – younger sons
Thaddeus Parker  – friend of Oswald
Helena Parker – his daughter
Hugo Garrick – famous New York songwriter
Sadie Burke – singer

**Driftwood Island:**
Ernest Spencer – senator, lawyer – great-grandfather of Kit of
  *Moon Hall*
Kathleen Spencer – his wife
Archie (Archibald) Spencer – son – 22
Freddie (Frederick) Spencer – son – 20
Emma Spencer – daughter – 17
Arthur, Maud, & Hazel Spencer – younger children

**The Colony:**
Edelina Fuerstenberger – artist
Frieda – German servant
Gil – handyman
Anton – Bolshevik
(Father) Paul – Catholic priest

**Others in Muskoka:**
Horace Camford – owner of Pittsburgh Plate Glass
Lionel Camford – his son and heir
Fremonts, Delacourts, and Vandemeers – American tycoons

**In Relation to the *Lusitania*:**
Lady Margaret Dunston – wife of Sir Montague Dunston of
  Montreal who owns the Transatlantic Steamship Line
Oliver Dalvay – American writer
Theadora (Thea) Prescott – American journalist and heiress
Lady Meredith Powell – British suffragette
Alice Lambton – 13
Kathleen O'Rourke – hostess in Ireland

**England:**
Lord Cedric Devenish – cousin to the Wyndhams
Professor Peregrine & Phyllida Milford – Alice's grandparents
Peggy & Sebastian Kendal – own aerodrome and teach flying
Hugh Paynter – Oxford friend of Chas
Percy (Percival) Dunston – son of Sir Montague & Lady Dunston –
  Oxford friend of Chas
Lady Sidonie (Sid) Dunston – wife of Percy and friend of Chas
Quentin, Viscount Grenville – Oxford friend of Chas and Sidonie's
  eldest brother
Lieutenant Philip (Philpot) Pottinger – old schoolmate of Blake's
  convalescing at Bovington Abbey
Captain Robert Armitage – convalescent officer at Bovington

**Antibes:**
Montgomery (Monty) Seaton – American playwright and author
Dixie Seaton – his wife
Liam Sullivan – ex-pat Irish painter
Lieutenant Ponsonby – convalescent British officer

**Real People Mentioned or Appearing:**
Woodrow Wilson – President of the United States – owned an
    island in Muskoka
Timothy Eaton – founder of successful department store and mail
    order business
(Sir) John Craig Eaton – his son, who took over the business
    (knighted in 1915)
Josephine Burnside – daughter of Timothy Eaton – on *Lusitania* –
    survived
Iris Burnside – her daughter – died in the *Lusitania* tragedy
Sir Henry Pellatt – financier – built Casa Loma
(Sir) Joseph Flavelle – Wm. Davis Meat Packing, later Canada
    Packers – was made a Baronet in 1917 for his war work
Sir William Mackenzie – railway entrepreneur – for a definitive
    look at Mackenzie, see *The Railway King of Canada* by R.B.
    Fleming
Tom Thomson – one of the Algonquin Group of painters, later
    known as The Group of Seven, although Tom was already dead
    by then
Herb Ditchburn – world-renowned Muskoka boat-builder
Lieutenant Porte – of the Royal Naval Air Service
Sir Robert Borden – Prime Minister of Canada 1911-1920
Count Jacques De Lesseps – an aviator and son-in-law of Sir
    William Mackenzie
Mary Pickford – renowned Hollywood star, originally from
    Toronto
Pauline Johnson – part Mohawk Canadian poet
Commander Stackhouse – explorer – died in the *Lusitania* tragedy
Sir Hugh Lane – art expert and director of the National Gallery in
    Ireland – died in the *Lusitania* tragedy
Captain Turner – captain of the *Lusitania* – survived
Staff Captain John Anderson – died in the *Lusitania* tragedy
Alfred Vanderbilt – famous American multi-millionaire – died in
    the *Lusitania* tragedy
Charles Frohman – renowned impresario – died in the *Lusitania*
    tragedy

Rita Jolivet – actress – on the *Lusitania* – survived
Josephine Brandell – actress – on *Lusitania* – survived
Dr. McDermott – ship's doctor – died in the *Lusitania* tragedy
Winston Churchill – First Lord of the Admiralty
William Rhodes-Moorhouse – first airman to receive the Victoria
    Cross, 1915, but posthumously
Max Immelman – famous German aviator – killed in 1916
Ivor Novello – singer, composer, actor, playwright
Lord (also Major) and Lady Astor – owned Cliveden which they
    turned into a Canadian convalescent hospital during the war
Rudyard and Mrs. Kipling – on executive committee of the Maple
    Leaf Clubs
Rupert Brooke – poet, died en route to Gallipoli, April 1915
Sir Max Aitken – became Lord Beaverbrook in Dec. 1916
Lady Drummond – from Montreal – established an Information
    Bureau within the Canadian Red Cross in England
Nurse Edith Cavell – executed by the Germans in Oct. 1915
General Haig – Commander-in-Chief of the British Expeditionary
    Force
The Stinson sisters – of San Antonio, Texas, taught Canadian
    pilots
Major-General Hugh "Boom" Trenchard – in charge of the RFC in
    France
Albert Ball – RFC ace with 44 victories – died in 1917
Lieutenant Colonel John McCrae – Canadian doctor and poet who
    wrote the famous call to arms, "In Flanders Fields", in 1915

# Shadow River

from the collection, **Flint and Feather**
by E. Pauline Johnson
1861–1913

Muskoka


A stream of tender gladness,
Of filmy sun, and opal tinted skies;
Of warm midsummer air that lightly lies
In mystic rings,
Where softly swings
The music of a thousand wings
That almost tones to sadness.

Midway 'twixt earth and heaven,
A bubble in the pearly air, I seem
To float upon the sapphire floor, a dream
Of clouds of snow,
Above, below,
Drift with my drifting, dim and slow,
As twilight drifts to even.

The little fern-leaf, bending
Upon the brink, its green reflection greets,
And kisses soft the shadow that it meets
With touch so fine,
The border line
The keenest vision can't define;
So perfect is the blending.

The far, fir trees that cover
The brownish hills with needles green and gold,
The arching elms o'erhead, vinegrown and old,
Repictured are
Beneath me far,
Where not a ripple moves to mar
Shades underneath, or over.

Mine is the undertone;
The beauty, strength, and power of the land
Will never stir or bend at my command;
But all the shade
Is marred or made,
If I but dip my paddle blade;
And it is mine alone,

O! pathless world of seeming!
O! pathless life of mine whose deep ideal
Is more my own than ever was the real.
For others Fame
And Love's red flame,
And yellow gold; I only claim
The shadows and the dreaming.

# Chapter 1

It was the whisper that started their war. That's how many at the table that evening would recall the summer of 1914.

Naturally, Victoria hadn't even noticed the waiter until then. In their black uniforms, the resort staff slipped about unobtrusively, meeting one's needs without being obvious. Without really existing. It wasn't until he boldly bent over her grandmother's right shoulder and whispered in her ear that Victoria thought how handsome he was. And then realized with a shock that he was the trespasser who had spied her swimming naked yesterday.

He'd sported casual white trousers and shirt, his sleeves rolled up as if he'd just finished a winning set in tennis. He'd perched on the rock and begun scribbling on a pad of paper.

"What the devil are you doing?" she had demanded, immersing herself up to her chin in the chilly lake, but wondering if the crystal clear water provided much cover.

With a massive granite slab sliding into the lake next to a broad crescent of pale sand, this was Victoria's favourite place on the island, which she called "The Shimmering Sands". The others never bothered to come to the north end, preferring to swim in the bay behind the house at the point. But Victoria hated the confining bathing costumes, and would sneak away to indulge in the luxury of stripping off everything and allowing the silky water to caress her.

Unusually flustered, she had challenged, "And who the hell are you anyway?"

"My, my, what language! I thought I was in the presence of a lady," he had replied with a mocking grin.

"You, sir, are obviously no gentleman!"

He had winked at her, and continued to draw, occasionally examining her as one might a captured butterfly.

"What are you doing? Kindly take your leave!"

"I believe I'm sketching a water nymph."

"You are trespassing!"

"Am I?"

"If you are a guest of one of my cousins, I'll have him banish you as an ill-mannered lout!"

Although her cheeks had burned with embarrassment and frustration at her helpless situation, Victoria had become thoroughly chilled. The lake had not warmed up yet, despite the recent heat wave. Indeed, the ice had only been out for a handful of weeks.

He had seemed unperturbed by her anger, even amused by it. The nerve of the man!

His nonchalance had just added to his attractiveness. Under different circumstances, Victoria would have delighted in flirting with him.

But her skin had prickled with cold and she had been in no mood for games. "I'll give you one last chance to leave!"

"Indeed? And then what?" He had stopped sketching and regarded her with amusement.

"I will swim back to the cottage and make a scene, and then you won't be so cocky," she had bluffed, knowing that she would suffer the consequences of her indiscretion. Proper young ladies didn't swim naked, even if there were only loons and chipmunks for company.

He had laughed, a delightful, appreciative laugh that rang out through the woods. And when he's stood up, he'd ripped off the sheet of paper and placed it on the rock. "A scene I should like to witness. But you are quite right, Miss Wyndham," he had said with a courtly nod. "I have to admit that it's been a great pleasure to make your acquaintance."

With that he had turned and sauntered off towards the north shore, leaving Victoria fuming. "Cad!" she had shouted, and had heard a faint chuckle in reply.

She had emerged warily from the water, dressed quickly, and stretched out to bask on the glittering, sun-warmed rock. When her anger had been replaced by curiosity, she had picked up the abandoned sketch and been impressed by the masterful strokes that depicted a spirited young woman with a sensuality that surprised her. She had secreted the drawing in her skirt pocket.

Upon her return to the cottage, Victoria had discovered that her cousins hadn't invited any friends, and decided to tell no one about the intriguing stranger just yet. She preferred to keep him to herself, to ponder him at her leisure.

It wasn't unusual that he should have guessed her name. The Wyndhams were well known on the lake, and he must have realized he'd been on their island. She'd wondered if he'd dare to return to the Shimmering Sands, or whether she would soon meet him at some soiree or dance. She was determined to have the upper hand at their next encounter.

But now here he was, making her grandmother blanch. The old lady carefully laid down her knife and fork, and turned deliberately to look at him. He did not flinch under her steely gaze, but merely stared back at her with a self-confidence that Victoria's father would term impudence. Victoria sensed the others — her aunts, uncles, and cousins — holding their breath in anticipation of a lacerating reprimand.

But Grandmother's eyes softened, and she said to the waiter, "You do that," before resuming her meal.

"What the dickens was that about?" Victoria's uncle, Albert, demanded. "What did the fellow want? What impertinence! I'll talk to the management and have the scoundrel dismissed!"

"Do be quiet, Albert," Grandmother said. "You have the bad manners of asking a question and then not allowing one to respond."

"That's rich! That boor has the audacity to address his betters without a by-your-leave, and you don't care to do anything about it, but find fault with me instead!"

Victoria's father, James, ignoring his younger brother's outburst, said calmly, "Really, Mother, what was that fellow on about? You can't mean to leave us in suspense."

"Time will tell. And that is all I have to say on the subject this evening."

As if a royal edict had been declared, Albert, exhaling the breath of unvoiced thoughts, shut his mouth and looked disgruntled. The others slowly took up the dropped threads of previous conversations, although it was evident that all they really wanted to discuss was that odd little scene.

Victoria looked discreetly around, but couldn't see the waiter, and wondered if someone in authority had noticed his breech of conduct and dismissed him. She was surprised that he was, indeed, no gentleman. But Grandmother's astonishing reaction meant that there was something enticingly mysterious about him. How annoying of her to keep them guessing!

The massive dining room of The Grand Muskoka Hotel was two storeys high with two levels of windows inviting the mellow evening light to filter in, and framing a stunning panorama of water and rock. Among the scattering of craggy and tufted islands was the Wyndhams own substantial island, Wyndwood, about a mile distant, reflecting its grandeur in the gilded, tranquil lake.

An orchestra played softly in the minstrel's gallery above so as not to interfere with the conversations of the hundreds of diners. Potted palms were interspersed among the crisply-linened tables. Guests were arrayed in their finest silks and diamonds.

It was hard to believe that they were virtually in the primitive backwoods of Canada.

When The Grand Muskoka had been built at the turn of the century, it had been touted as the largest and most splendid summer resort in Canada, perhaps even in the British Empire. Accessible only by steamboat on a lake more than a hundred miles north of Toronto, The Grand boasted all the modern conveniences of any city hotel, including electric lighting, central heating, hot and cold running water, en suite bathrooms, telephones, and a barber shop, but with the added bonus of good fishing, golfing, tennis, water sports on a pristine lake, and the curative benefits of fresh, pine-scented air.

For the Wyndham family, who had been summering at their island cottage since 1878, the coming of The Grand had added another dimension of entertainment. Although there were many other popular resorts on the lake, The Grand catered to guests from the Wyndhams' own social set.

Grandmother had long ago decreed that they would dine here on Mondays, when the servants had their half-day off. It was the only time during the summers, aside from formal evenings, that they were all required to dress for dinner. Grandmother didn't want them to become too lax or even Bohemian in their habits.

Victoria was surprised to see that the Oakleys, who owned one of the neighbouring islands, were already here for the summer. Oswald Oakley was a Pittsburgh steel magnate – a term that had confused and delighted the children, who still regarded him as a "magnetic" person.

After dinner, the Wyndhams took their customary stroll along one of the three levels of the massive, sweeping verandas that encircled the main hotel rotunda, where they were soon joined by Oswald Oakley, his wife, Letitia, their four children, and some friends.

A big bear of a man with shaggy whiskers, Oswald delicately took Grandmother's hand and bowed over it as he declared, "Milady, what a great pleasure to see you again! Always the highlight of my summer to see you hale and hearty. Allow me to introduce to you a friend and colleague, Thaddeus Parker, and his daughter, Helena. The Honourable Augusta Wyndham."

"Such a great privilege to meet you, Milady!" Thaddeus Parker said, beaming. In contrast to his friend Oswald, Thaddeus was short, compact, and mostly hairless, so his entire head seemed to glow pink with delight.

"Oswald, you really must stop this Milady nonsense," Augusta said, though everyone knew she was amused by it. "A pleasure to meet you and your daughter, Mr. Parker. Is this your first visit to Muskoka?"

"Indeed. Indeed. Our very first to Canada, in fact, but I daresay not our last. Most charming! Why I understand that our President owns an island on this very lake!"

"Yes, Formosa Island. We met Professor Wilson years ago. Before he became President." She turned to Oswald and Letitia. "You've arrived early this year."

"With this infernal heat, the city is like Hades itself. And we can hardly breathe for the soot and smoke," Oswald replied.

Victoria thought that his own factories must surely be spewing those noxious fumes into the air, but he and his family were lucky enough to be able to escape. They usually arrived in late June and stayed until early September, having their own private Pullman coach to carry them, their silver and china, and their numerous trunks to the wharf station at Gravenhurst, while their twenty-seven servants took the regular coaches. The staff and the cargo were then conveyed to the Oakleys' island by one of the big lake steamers, while the family traveled in their own steam yacht to The Grand, where they would stay until the servants had readied the cottage.

"Will you be able to enjoy our wilderness here for a while, Mr. Parker?" Augusta asked.

"A most civilized wilderness, I must say, Milady," he chortled. "We are indebted to the Oakleys for their hospitality. Helena does feel the heat so. We usually go to the seaside in summer — Newport mostly. But I expect that business will soon take us away."

"Surely Helena can stay with us," Letitia said, her toned-down Southern drawl nonetheless revealing her origins as a 'Southern Belle'. "It would be cruel to drag this poor child back to the city."

The "child" must be at least twenty-five, Victoria thought. Helena was no beauty, but she had remarkable poise and confidence. Victoria wondered that she was not yet married.

"Oh yes, you must stay, Helena!" fifteen-year-old Louise Oakley cried. Having three younger brothers and no sisters, she was undoubtedly enjoying some female company.

Helena looked pretty when she laughed. "I do hope that we won't be leaving just yet. This is such a magical place." She brushed a mosquito away from her face.

"Aside from the mosquitoes," James said with amusement. Smudge pots burned to deter them, and as the hotel was on a peninsula, the breezes tended to keep the annoying insects at bay. But they were always worst at dusk.

"This will help," Oswald said, offering Cuban cigars to the men and older boys. They moved away from the women so that the smoke didn't offend them. Augusta eased herself into a rattan chair and motioned for Letitia to sit beside her. With no more vacant chairs, the other women and children stood as if in royal attendance. Victoria wished she could join the men at the railing, as their conversation was surely more interesting than the domestic details that the women discussed.

Like smoke billowing from the fiery sunset, the scorched clouds scraped the bristling treetops and drifted over the molten lake.

Into the encroaching darkness, Victoria whispered to her cousin Zoë, "I saw him yesterday. That waiter. He was sketching at the north end of the island."

Zoë tried to suppress her amazement. "Did you talk to him?"

"I told him he was trespassing."

"What did he say?"

"He was quite blasé. And much too presumptuous to be a servant."

"What are you two plotting now?" their younger cousin Phoebe asked as she sidled up to them.

"We thought it would be fun to paddle over in a canoe next time we come for dinner," Victoria improvised. "I'd love to be on the lake right now. Just look at that sunset!"

"You can't be in a canoe in your evening gowns," Phoebe scoffed.

"Why not? We'd be deliciously avant-garde," Victoria said.

"You're just plain silly," Phoebe declared.

"As always," Victoria agreed, for that was what Phoebe invariably said when she wasn't allowed to participate in Victoria's adventures. "So we won't ask you to do anything so unconventional."

"Grandmother wouldn't let you anyway," Phoebe said smugly.

Victoria stifled a retort, knowing that Phoebe was right. She turned her attention back to the others. Augusta was asking Helena, "Your mother is no longer with you?"

"Sadly, no. She died a few years ago."

"Helena was wonderful!" Letitia jumped in. "Nursed her mother faithfully. Even turned down a marriage proposal from a most eminent suitor because he wouldn't wait for her. Helena would not leave her mother's side."

Augusta said, "So have you taken it upon yourself to stand in, Letitia, and see the girl properly wed?"

"Yes, I expect I shall."

"That really isn't necessary, Letitia," Helena said.

"Oh, but I would love to plan a wedding! With only one daughter still a few years away from marrying, I would deem it a privilege to help. Consider it a kindness to me."

Helena laughed delightedly. "If it pleases you, then of course, Letitia. But I'm in no hurry to marry. Perhaps I shall be content to be an aunt to all my friends' children," she said, hugging the youngest Oakley boy, whom she had quietly maneuvered away from the youngest Wyndham when the restless youngsters started to push each other about. He seemed content to have her arm draped about his shoulder as he was pressed against her silk skirt.

"She's superb with the children!" Letitia exclaimed. "I really won't allow your father to take you away from us too soon, Helena."

"Have you known one another long?" Augusta inquired.

"Hardly any time at all," Letitia replied. "And yet it seems like years."

"So you didn't know Helena's mother?"

"Unfortunately not. Although she was one of the Boston Thorpes, don't you know?" With determination, Letitia added, "I've quite made up my mind that I shall indeed find Helena a suitable husband this summer!"

"You mustn't take on such a formidable task, Letitia," Helena said with a self-deprecating smile.

"Nonsense! It'll be great fun. We'll plan even more picnics and parties than usual." Letitia clasped her hands together like a joyful child. "This will be such a wonderful summer!"

# Chapter 2

"A visitor's coming!" ten-year-old Rupert exclaimed.

All eyes turned to watch the guest stride up the path from the large steamer dock, where a solitary canoe now bobbed gently in the waves.

Victoria recognized him instantly this time, but she was certain that the others wouldn't know him. "Oh, it's that cocky waiter from The Grand," she remarked casually.

"Hello, Grandmother," he said as he joined them on the veranda.

After the initial unanimous gasp, there was stunned silence.

"Who do you think you are, talking to The Honourable Mrs. Wyndham like that!" Henry blustered, walking toward the stranger as if he intended to knock him down the steps.

"Do be quiet, Henry," Augusta said. "Be civil to your cousin, even though I haven't yet decided what's to be done with him."

Both the stranger and Augusta smiled. Victoria felt as if the known universe had just tilted a little. Grandmother rarely smiled these days. Old age did not amuse her, and her family seemed more a trial than a comfort to her.

It was fortunate that her father had gone to Gravenhurst on business this morning, Victoria thought, or there would have been hell to pay. But her uncles said nothing, merely looked surprised and a bit embarrassed, and there was wariness in Albert's face.

"This is Jack," Augusta said. "The spit of Alexander, isn't he?" she asked her sons.

"Indeed," Richard said, stepping forward and graciously offering Jack his hand. "Welcome, nephew."

"I thought Uncle Alexander was dead," Richard's son, Max, said.

"He is," Jack replied. "He died six years ago. Of consumption."

Victoria wondered if anyone else noticed the look that passed between Jack and Grandmother. His, challenging; hers, defiant. And shocked.

Of course they had heard about Alexander, the youngest of the family. But they had thought he had died in childhood, as so many did. Victoria felt a frisson of excitement, for surely here was a family secret about to unfold.

Augusta rose to her feet with even more majesty than usual, a sign that she was pulling together all her reserves. She announced, "I am going to speak to my grandson. Alone. Then he can come back here and join us for tea."

"Really, Mother, you must allow me to accompany you," Albert stated.

"No, Albert. You may have your say later."

He hung his head, probably to hide his annoyance, for Victoria could see the muscles working in his jaw.

Before she led Jack off to the library, Augusta glared at her grandchildren, including twenty-one-year-old Henry, and said, "I won't have anyone eavesdropping. Do you understand?"

It meant that they couldn't linger on the veranda on the west side of the house. But as soon as Augusta and Jack were safely inside, Victoria announced that she was going to "freshen up" and dashed up to her bedroom. She and her three female cousins shared a large room which, like the other bedrooms on the west side, gave onto a long balcony over a section of the veranda below. Next to them was Richard and Olivia's room, and beyond that, the boys' shared bedroom. Low walls divided the balcony so that each room had its own private section. Augusta's room was at the front of the house, with a fanciful screened balcony framed in arched gingerbread. James's room, Albert and Phyllis's room, and two guest rooms were across the wide hall and faced east. They too shared a balcony. The old nursery at the back of the house had been turned into a bathroom and another guest room, with a tin-lined linen and storage cupboard between.

Victoria tucked her hair, which was loosely restrained with a ribbon, into the back of her shirtwaist, hiked up her skirt, and scrambled over the balcony railing onto the veranda roof. She had just lain down when Zoë and Max hissed at her, "What are you doing, Ria?" as they, too, clambered onto the roof. She expected that Albert's children would not be allowed to leave the front veranda. Aunt Phyllis did not approve of Victoria, whom she considered too audacious and undisciplined.

"Hang onto my feet," Victoria whispered as she inched her way to the edge of the roof on her stomach. The rocky ground, studded with trees, dropped away sharply from the cottage on this side, but she ignored that as she hung her head over the edge of the roof. As she suspected, the French windows were open to the veranda, and she could hear Grandmother and Jack talking.

"Do you drink?" Augusta asked.

"Yes. And smoke."

"I like a man who's willing to admit to his pleasures. You can pour me a large sherry and take what you will."

Victoria was imagining the room. Although the two end walls were lined with books, it was more an office than a library. There was a large rosewood desk, where Augusta conducted all her business. Several wing-back leather chairs were strewn about, and a drinks trolley sported crystal decanters filled with various liquors, glasses, and a soda bottle. Victoria could hear the chink of the stopper being replaced in a decanter.

"Thank you. Sit. So... You are bold, I'll give you that."

"Life's been hard."

"Are you blaming me?" Augusta demanded.

"I'm merely stating a fact," Jack replied easily, not answering the question, Victoria noted. "I have no wish to follow in my father's footsteps."

"It's unfortunate that he didn't have your wisdom, or he would never have run off with that slut."

"You're speaking about my mother." Victoria noticed a hardness in his voice.

"I'm speaking about the woman who enticed my impressionable and rather naïve son away from his family and his senses, and ruined his life."

"Things were fine in the beginning. But his health had never been good, so he wasn't always able to work. And you provided no support when he desperately needed it."

"He knew the consequences. He was an adult. About your age. What are you, twenty-one?"

"I will be in October."

"I knew that she was with child..."

"...And offered her money to go away and forget him," Jack finished the sentence. "But they were in love, you see."

"Piffle! People make too much of love! Lust is what it was. And that soon wears thin. He could have made a good marriage and still have had his passions on the side, if he'd really needed to." Augusta seemed unusually flustered, as if reliving the anger at her son's desertion.

"He was an honourable man. He did the right thing by my mother."

"He was a fool!"

"So you disowned him."

"He made his choice. As far as I'm concerned, he's been dead to me these twenty years. I don't want to know anything about his life…. But you intrigue me. So what do you want of me?" Victoria could imagine the piercing gaze now levelled at Jack.

"A chance to do something with my life. I've lived in squalor, and I don't fancy it. I intend to succeed, and will use any means at my disposal. So why not start with family?"

Augusta let out a sound that Victoria momentarily thought was a cry of pain, and almost lost her hold on the edge of the roof. But the old lady was hooting with laughter.

"Damned if you haven't got your grandfather's spirit and candour! At least there's one of you who has inherited the drive that brought us all this."

"Hunger can do that, and desperation. I'm sure my uncles and cousins have never known them."

"Ah, but hunger in a business sense as well. You have to be sharp, observant, clever, take risks. Be ruthless." There was a pause, and then Augusta said, "Yes, I think you can be all that. And perhaps I would be letting a wolf in with my sheep, if I took you on."

"How would you like me to prove myself?"

"You're working as a waiter at The Grand. Get yourself into a better position by the end of the season, and I will consider taking you into the family business. If you have your grandfather's ingenuity and spunk, it should be easy enough for you. In the meantime, you may come to visit whenever you have time off. Give us a chance to get to know you. If you can't get along with your uncles and cousins, then there's no deal. I know that won't be easy. James, for one, will be hostile. He resents not having a son to take over the business. But if you can't charm them and impress them with your intelligence and diligence, then I don't need you."

There was a silence, and then she said irritably, "Well, did you think it would be easy? That you'd just have to waltz in here and lock those stunning blue eyes on me and I would fête the return of the prodigal grandson?"

"Oh, no, Grandmother. I never thought this would be easy. I'm grateful for your offer, and I accept the challenge."

"Just remember one thing, young man. I don't care how you get ahead, but don't dare ever disgrace the Wyndham name!"

"Yes, M'am."

Thinking the interview about to end, and wanting to join the rest of the family before Augusta and Jack returned, Victoria began to shimmy back up the roof, but her skirt stuck to the rough cedar shingles and rucked up. "Let go," she told Max and Zoë as she swung herself around so that she could clamber back up headfirst. But as she moved into a crouch, her foot slipped on some lichen and she slid down the roof. Zoë shrieked; Max dove for Victoria and almost toppled off himself. Victoria grabbed frantically for support and suddenly found herself dangling by her fingertips from the eaves. Jagged rocks loomed below.

Augusta and Jack heard the commotion. Just as Victoria was losing her tentative hold, he dashed onto the veranda and leaned over the railing, grabbing her around the waist and pulling her into his arms. He held her perhaps a moment longer than necessary before lowering her onto the veranda.

Shaking, her heart pounding with shock and excitement, Victoria didn't even notice her ripped clothes or the bloody scrapes and scratches on her arms. Augusta glared at her. "Victoria Elizabeth Wyndham! You were told not to eavesdrop!" To Jack she said, "Bring her in and give her a tot of brandy."

Victoria didn't resist as Jack took her firmly by the elbow and escorted her to an armchair. She accepted the drink gratefully, but coughed when the fiery liquid hit her throat.

Instead of looking angry, Augusta actually seemed to be trying to hide her amusement. "If only you'd been a boy."

"I don't have to be a boy in order to do things," Victoria managed to counter. It was an old argument between them. "After all, you run the business, Grandmother. So could I!"

"Jack, meet your incorrigible cousin, Victoria."

"A pleasure indeed," he said with a slight bow. His eyes mocked her, reminding her of their first encounter, and she couldn't help blushing. Then he took out a clean white handkerchief, squatted down beside her, and gently dabbed at the blood oozing from the scrapes on her arms.

"Oh, Lord, ring that bell and then go and fetch Olivia. She's the blonde. She can deal with these things."

Jack did as he was bid. Augusta turned her eagle eyes on Victoria. "So, what do you think of your cousin?"

"Handsome but arrogant."

"Ha! Two peas in a pod then, you and he."

"He presumes too much."

"As do you, my girl. Which is why I'm prepared to like him. Much as I love my children, none of them can hold a candle to their father. What a man he was! And Alexander was the worst of them. My fault perhaps, for being indulgent with him. He was a sensitive and delicate child." Her eyes glistened for a moment as if tears threatened. "And that is all I will ever say on the subject. So don't pry! ... But Jack, he has the promise of filling his grandfather's shoes."

Libby, one of the maids, appeared and Augusta ordered hot water, ointment, and bandages. Then Olivia arrived with Jack.

"Goodness, child! What have you been up to?"

"Eavesdropping — literally," Augusta cackled at her pun. She seemed in unaccustomed good spirits. "Come, Jack, we will rejoin the others. And the punishment for your disobedience is being confined to your room for the remainder of the day, my girl," she said sternly to Victoria. "She'll be in torment," Augusta said to Jack as she led him out the door, "missing all the excitement of your visit. Can you stay to dinner?"

"Regretfully, not today," Jack replied, giving Victoria a sympathetic farewell glance. "I'm on duty at dinner. In fact, I must leave shortly."

"Pity. That would be punishment indeed for Victoria to miss that."

"You have a few splinters we must see to," Olivia said as she began to clean Victoria's wounds. "And I daresay you'll be bruised and sore. No doubt Max and Zoë were in league with you, so I must have a chat with them."

"They were just trying to keep me from falling off the roof," Victoria said in their defence.

"Then they didn't do a very good job did they? Now tell me what transpired," Olivia said with a grin.

Victoria loved Olivia like a mother, and Olivia reciprocated. Victoria's mother had died giving birth to her, the second but only child to survive. Her brother had died in infancy, before she was born. Her father, James, had never remarried, and had become a bitter man. Victoria had always felt that he blamed her for her mother's death. They lived with Grandmother in her mansion in the upscale Toronto suburb of Rosedale. The others had their own homes nearby, and although they visited one another frequently (Sunday dinner at Grandmother's was an edict), the Rosedale house was a big and empty place, devoid of warmth or much affection.

That was one of the reasons that she loved the summers so. The entire family spent at least three months together here at the cottage.

"Now it's your turn," Victoria said when she had finished her tale. "Tell me about Alexander. You must have known him."

"Certainly. Your Uncle Richard and I were married for a year before Alexander... left. I always liked him. He was much like Richard, only more... vulnerable, perhaps. Less able or willing to defend himself. He loved to draw and paint, and fancied himself an artist. Oh, his work was very competent. Pretty. But perhaps not something that could provide a living. He was never interested in the family business, and was an obvious disappointment to his father, who, I'm afraid, was not kind."

Victoria had never known her grandfather, who had died just before she was born, eighteen years ago. But she had heard enough about him from Grandmother, who idolized him and had probably idealized him over the years, turning him into a legend. He was the yardstick by which every man was judged, and so far, no one else had measured up.

Olivia said, "Alex fell in love with an actress and there was a terrible row when he told his parents that he was going to marry the girl. So he left, and they told him never to come back."

"It sounds as if he asked for help at one time," Victoria said, remembering Jack's accusation. "And didn't get it."

"He should have come to Richard! That's what I mean about him not having the sense to look after himself. He should have known that we would help!" Olivia seemed angry as she finished bandaging Victoria's wounds. "He should have been here, or at the sanatorium in Gravenhurst, if he had consumption. That may have cured him. And I can hardly imagine what his family must have suffered." She shook her head. "The misery that some people create with their pride and stubbornness!"

Victoria wondered if Olivia meant Alexander or his parents. Probably both. She also wondered what Olivia would think of Jack's sketch of her. It had seemed more than competent to Victoria. Perhaps Jack had perfected his father's talent.

"If Father so desperately wanted a son, as Grandmother suggested, why did he never marry again?"

"He almost did – twice. The first one, Charlotte, I think her name was, was quite young and most flirtatious. They became engaged, but then she fell in love with another man – someone, I have to admit, with more energy and humour than your father. It would have been a poor marriage on both sides. Then there was Francis – you must remember her visiting. Her family was more keen on an alliance with James than she was, but I think she wasn't given much choice. When she died of influenza, your father felt that he was somehow jinxed in love. He had married your mother quite late, and by the time he was forty, no young women from 'good' families were interested in him, and Augusta kept any gold-diggers at bay. She nearly disinherited him when he took up with a beautiful young French woman of 'questionable breeding' – her father owned bakeries, and I think has since made quite a fortune."

Although Grandfather had boasted no noble lineage, Augusta was the daughter of a Viscount, albeit it a destitute one until Grandfather had come along. She used her title when she wanted to impress, and had endowed her dead husband with God-like qualities that made it easier to ignore his humble beginnings.

Reginald Wyndham – Reggie or RW to his friends, but never to Augusta – had been the only surviving son of an immigrant farmer trying to scratch a living out of the thin soil of the Canadian Shield. Reggie, tall and strong for his age, had joined the lumbermen at age twelve, and quickly learned all about the trade. He started his own lumbering company at the age of twenty-one. By thirty, he owned lumber and shingle mills throughout the district of Muskoka and the north. By forty, he had business interests in mines, manufactories, and railroads – and was a millionaire. He met Augusta on one of his many business trips to England when he was thirty-five and she, more than a decade younger. At sixty-seven, Reggie died a legend in Canada and abroad, and left his extensive business interests in the capable hands of his wife, not quite trusting his sons to preserve or expand the Wyndham empire.

"And now, young lady," Olivia said, "you'd best get to your room. I'll see that a supper tray is sent up for you. And I'm sure that Zoë will fill you in on your new cousin later," she added, forestalling any protest.

.     .     .

Jack was good at remembering names. He knew that if you wanted to get ahead in life, it was essential to know the right people. And since you never quite knew who would be helpful to you — it could be a butler as readily as a banker — he had trained himself to recall names and useful information about everyone.

So being faced with more than a dozen new relatives was not that daunting.

There was tall and thin Uncle Albert and his plump wife, Phyllis, who looked as if she was sucking lemons instead of sipping the best China tea. Cousin Henry mirrored his mother's sour face. He'd be trouble, Jack knew. Spindly, with protruding ears and a collection of features that seemed to be at war with one another, Henry was not the type to make a girl's heart flutter or an athlete quake. Having no illusions about himself, Jack knew that Henry was bound to resent both of those virtues in his new cousin. Henry's younger brother, Edgar, who was nineteen, looked soft and self-indulgent. He regarded Jack with disdain but also with a curiosity that gave Jack hope of gaining his respect. Their sixteen-year-old sister, Phoebe, Jack pegged as a silly, spoiled pudding of a girl who was already enamoured of him. She kept looking up at him through lowered lashes, and stifling her giggles with cupped hands.

The resemblance between Uncle Richard and his father gave Jack a momentary stab of grief. This was where his father had belonged, where he would have lived a long and happy life. But Jack had to suppress resentment. It was useless to waste thought and energy on the unchangeable past. At this moment he was better off than he had been in all his twenty years. And Richard seemed genuinely pleased to meet him. His best ally, Jack thought, for Richard may well feel some guilt at his own good fortune in the wake of his younger brother's wasted life. He'd have to play on that angle when they were alone, be sure that Richard knew exactly how hellish his brother's life had been. But never seem to be expecting pity for himself. Just a litany of hard facts that would leave little doubt about the hardships and deprivation Alexander — and, of course, his family — had endured.

Richard's wife, Olivia, had Gibson Girl good looks and a pleasant manner. She would be easy to charm. Nice people usually were. Her daughter Zoë might be more of a challenge. At eighteen, she seemed careless of her beauty, and Jack suspected she might be a bluestocking or one of those suffragettes, a girl who was neither flirtatious nor a fool. Max, her twin brother, reminded Jack somewhat of his own brother, Eddie, who had died horribly at twelve in a factory accident, falling into a press. Eddie would have been about the same age as Max now. Richard's youngest children, Esme, Rupert, and Miles seemed intrigued by their newfound cousin.

So this was his family. They lounged with practiced ease on white wicker chairs and rockers and chaise lounges on the broad, pine-boarded veranda that wrapped around the cottage. The youngest children, sitting side by side, swung lazily in the hammock that hung in the bandshell on the southwest corner. A silver tea service and plates of small sandwiches, thick scones, and rich cakes was set before them. To nourish the soul there was the stunning panorama of the lake — rocky islands adrift along miles of shimmering blue water. A few sailboats and the distant smoke from a steamship wafted across the horizon.

This was his birthright, Jack thought, feeling both excitement and anger. Here his brother and sisters should have frolicked, instead of in the gutters of the city.

"How did you come to be working at The Grand?" Richard asked, unaware of Jack's inner turmoil.

"I had experience waiting at table in the Four Seasons Club in Toronto," Jack replied. The Four Seasons was an exclusive men's club that everyone recognized, but not the one to which the Wyndham men belonged.

"I knew about the island, of course. My father often talked about it. 'My soul has an affinity for it, indeed, craves it' he would say." With such poignancy.

"Enough about the past!" Augusta said tetchily. She did not need to be reminded how much Alexander had loved this place, how he had counted down the days until the summer would officially begin with them boarding the train for the journey northward, how he'd had to be dragged away in late September when they had loaded everything onto the steamer for the homeward journey.

"Well, I wanted to see the lake and thought that perhaps it was time to meet my family. I had no intention of just showing up at the door like some sort of supplicant or prodigal grandson." He flashed Augusta a smile. "But I thought that if I happened to meet you, then I would make myself known." He didn't mention that he'd bribed one of the other waiters to switch places so that he could attend to their table yesterday. Although Augusta would surely have approved. "Grandmother acceded to my request to visit."

"You're bloody well spoken for a waiter," Henry said with a sneer.

"And you, my dear Henry, are not – for a boy who's had the finest schooling in Canada," Augusta said. "I won't tolerate cursing."

Henry pursed his lips and Jack thought that Augusta was doing him no favours by alienating Henry even more. He said, "My father was well educated, of course, and made sure that we children were articulate. He would read ... Sorry, Grandmother," Jack said, recalling her edict. And he would never tell them that he, determined to be a gentleman since he was old enough to realize the difference between his family and the one that his father spoke about with such longing and remorse, had read voraciously to improve his vocabulary and general knowledge. They had at least been able to borrow books from the library. And Jack had watched carefully the mannerisms of "his betters". The job at the Club had been particularly useful to him because he had listened intently to conversations, not only to improve his communication skills, but also to pick up tips on conducting business. Gentlemen spoke easily in front of servants, as if the "lower classes" had no thoughts or sensibilities. If Jack had actually had money to invest, he would have known which stocks were destined to rise and which to avoid.

"I also speak French. My mother is from Montreal, so we grew up with both languages. That has come in useful. And I'm not ashamed to be working as a waiter. It is, after all, just a stepping-stone for me. Grandfather is my inspiration, since I know that he worked hard in a variety of jobs which helped him to know his business inside and out," Jack pointed out tactfully, just to remind them that they had not always been what passed for aristocracy in Canada.

"So you see yourself owning The Grand one day?" Edgar said sarcastically, seeing that his brother didn't dare risk Augusta's wrath again.

"Perhaps!" Jack said with a laugh.

"The cockiness of youth," Albert mumbled.

"Would that we had more of that in this family!" Augusta snorted. "It's what drives men to success. You should all take note, as I despair of any of you living up to Reginald's initiative and accomplishments."

Jack groaned inwardly. Was she deliberately making it difficult for him to be accepted by the family?

"You spoke of siblings," Zoë said in a non sequiteur which gave Jack a reprieve. "Who are they?"

"Really, Zoë!" Augusta said. "You have the unfortunate habit of changing subjects so abruptly that one is left dangling open-mouthed. You must learn the art of conversation and repartee. And I have already declared that I wish to have no more information about the past."

"It's hardly the past if we have cousins living and about to pop out of the woodwork at a moment's notice," Zoë responded nonchalantly. "Really, Grandmother, I find this whole situation unconscionable. We had no idea that Uncle Alexander had children."

"So you need know nothing about them now. It won't change anything." Augusta suddenly looked her age, a frail old lady holding herself upright by sheer force of will.

"I'm afraid that I must get back, as I am on duty in an hour," Jack said with some relief at the truth of his excuse. "I do appreciate your invitation to visit at any time, Grandmother. And I look forward to getting to know you all better," he added with a winning smile.

"I'll walk with you to the dock," Zoë said, jumping up and joining him. She threw a defiant glance at Augusta, who ignored her.

It had been a trying day, and Augusta suddenly felt her mortality. She would admit to no one, not even to herself, how much she mourned Alexander, now that she knew he was lost to her forever. She had always hoped that he would return, chastened and regretful and ready to take on the role of dutiful son. That she hadn't even known he was dead, hadn't somehow felt it with a mother's instinct, saddened but also angered her. That harlot hadn't even informed her of Alexander's death! Was he buried in some pauper's grave? Oh, God, she couldn't bear it! It was just another slap in the face from that wicked hussy. She would have to send someone to find out, and have his remains brought to the family vault.

As she and Jack ambled down the wide and shallow flagstone steps, Zoë said earnestly, "Do tell me about our other cousins."

Jack was touched by her genuine interest. "Well, there's Lizzie who's seventeen, Emily, fifteen, and Claire, thirteen. Eddie, Anne, and Isabel all died."

"Oh, how tragic! My brother, Terence, died young, too."

They walked across the granite outcropping that formed the point, to the long and wide dock where the steamships could stop to pick up or deposit passengers. Gas lanterns, bollards for tying up boats, and a signalling flagpole punctuated the dock.

"This is all new to me," Zoë said, "but I gather that you didn't have an easy life. And for that I feel regret and a sense of shame. We all take this for granted," she said, spreading her arms to indicate the island and the lake. "As if we have some God-given right to it. The privileged, the chosen. That my uncle, who is every bit as much my blood as James or Albert, should have been rejected by his family — for surely that's what happened, isn't it? — is criminal, no matter how Grandmother might try to justify it. If there is anything that I can do to help, you must let me know. And some time, I do want to hear all about your family." With that she turned and left him, for once speechless.

He had to admit that Zoë had possibilities. But from the moment he'd met Victoria, he had known that she was the one. His plan was simple. Not only did he intend to wrangle his way into the family business through cleverness and diligence, but also through marriage. It was not uncommon for cousins to marry. What a bonus that she stirred his blood! He had no doubt that he could beguile and seduce her. But a sympathetic soul like Zoë would provide him with a good fallback position should his plan backfire. Jack was always prepared for contingencies.

As he pushed off from the dock, he looked again at the cottage that seemed to grow out of the granite rock and pine trees surrounding it. Built in the popular Shingle Style with broad gables, it was painted a soft green with ornate white trim. With its capacious, enveloping veranda and numerous balconies, it dominated the southern point of this roughly triangular island of sixty acres. He had walked with his father through its spacious rooms many times in his mind. And the reality didn't disappoint. On their way to the library, he and Augusta had walked through the ballroom-sized sitting room, which stretched across the entire front of the house and was anchored by two massive granite fireplaces — one double-sided and open to the dining room behind. He'd had a glimpse of a grand piano, numerous chintz sofas and chairs grouped in different areas, like a hotel lounge, tables ready for cards or other games, and the mounted heads of deer and moose — Grandfather's trophies. The oak staircase rose at the far end, with a landing partway up, overlooking the room like a pulpit. Apparently Grandfather had liked to stand there when conducting Sunday prayers. With French windows on three sides and the pale basswood paneling on the walls and high ceiling, the room was bright and inviting.

To the east of the house lay a large dance pavilion, its pagoda roof dangling with Chinese lanterns. Not only did they hold fancy dress balls here, but also theatricals and concerts.

As Jack rounded the point he could see the extensive kitchen wing, which was separated from the main house by a breezeway — in case of fire, and to keep the house cooler — and then several outbuildings. Here the land sloped down to a sandy bay, and the island itself was cinched like a woman's corseted waist, for he could also see the bay on the east side, where the dry slip canoe house and a five room change and bath house were visible through the trees. On this side there was a massive boathouse — much larger than anything that his family had ever lived in — which accommodated the steam launch and sailboat. There was a new two-slip boathouse at the end of the bay, as ornate as the main house, with window boxes spilling over with red and white flowers, and docks along both sides. The doors were open, so Jack could see a young man polishing the brass fixtures of a gleaming mahogany motorboat, and gave him a cheerful wave. The servant, surprised perhaps, waved back tentatively.

Jack was never one to allow resentment to fester or negative thoughts to disturb his equanimity for long. He deliberately pushed aside the might-have-beens and should-have-dones, which only led to bitterness and inertia. Life had too many opportunities, and he was about to grasp some delightful ones! This inveterate optimism was what made his ready smiles seem to come from the heart. Women invariable fell in love with him, and men generally trusted him.

He thought of Victoria, whose pale, almost fragile beauty belied a plucky temperament.

Jack whistled happily as he paddled. This would be his domain some day. One way or another.

.      .      .

On the veranda, Olivia was saying, "Well, he's certainly a charmer."

"A cunning opportunist, if ever I saw one," Albert spat. "I trust you haven't been enthralled by him, Mother, and promised to put him into your will or, God-forbid, offered him a share of the business!"

Augusta regarded her son with some scorn. How had she and Reginald produced such a poor specimen? Dour and uncharitable, Albert had always resented Alexander, the beloved baby of the family, and his jealously would no doubt transfer to Jack. Her heart lurched again as she thought of the favoured son she had lost forever. Perhaps it was the sudden, unwarranted anger at Albert for being here while Alexander lay buried in some unknown grave that prompted her to say, "Jack has as much right to the Wyndham empire as do your sons, Albert. And he seems to have more determination than any of you. Henry could do with some backbone and charisma, and Edgar needs to take an interest in something other than his own pleasures. So don't dare tell me what to do with my money or how to conduct my affairs!"

Although her sons attended to the daily running of the Wyndham businesses, and each had a princely income, Augusta still had the final say on all major business decisions — and in the disposition of the assets. It was a bone of contention between her and her sons that she relied so much on the advice of Reginald's friend, Sir William Mackenzie. Augusta invested heavily in his various schemes, from hydroelectric power to electric street railways in Toronto and Brazil, all of which had so far paid off. But her sons were concerned about Mackenzie's transcontinental railway, the Canadian Northern, still not completed and still gobbling up vast amounts of Wyndham money, outstripping the profits from the lucrative prairie branch lines.

Before his father could bluster a reply, Edgar said, "Jack's welcome to my share in the business. I rather fancy taking up boat racing," before biting into another buttered scone dripping with jam.

"Don't spout such nonsense, Edgar! Mother doesn't appreciate your wit," Albert thundered.

Edgar shrugged as if to say he wasn't being facetious, but Augusta said, "I know that Edgar has no interest in business or indeed, in working. But think about this, young man. Who do you expect will finance your expensive motorboats and automobiles and lavish lifestyle? Alexander chose to alienate himself from this family by putting his own pleasures above duty and loyalty. I certainly won't hesitate to disown and disinherit any of you who think likewise. I intend to give Jack a chance to prove himself, and suggest that you all remember he is my grandson. That his father

was a fool does not mean that he is one. Quite the contrary, for he
has suffered from the consequences of self-indulgent parents. And
now I shall go and rest," Augusta declared as she rose with great
effort from her chair. This had been a most trying day. She needed
time to come to grips with her grief, and to think about this rather
exciting young man who reminded her so much of Reginald, the
other lost love of her life. "I don't wish to be disturbed for the rest
of the day. Bayley can bring me a supper tray." Bayley was
Augusta's lady's maid.

"Of course, Mother Wyndham. Shall I help you upstairs?"
Olivia asked, jumping up to offer an arm to the old lady.

"Don't fuss, woman! I am quite capable of getting to my
room." But it took every ounce of strength to straighten herself
and glide from the veranda with her usual grace. Except for her
walks around the island, she refused to use a cane, although some
days she could have done with one. Revealing any kind of
weakness or emotion left one vulnerable.

Molly, the new maid, was just coming out with a fresh pot of
hot water when Augusta went through the screened door into the
sitting room. No doubt the girl had tactfully waited until Augusta
had finished her diatribe before intruding upon the family.

The rest of them waited until Molly had left before Albert
exploded with, "That is just too rich! She has the nerve to criticize
us, who have done everything to make the business work, who've
kowtowed to her all these years, and yet has nothing but praise for
some bastard who's come along, claiming kinship! And he probably
is a bastard! How do we know that Alex ever married that whore?
Or that Alex was the father?"

"Albert!" his wife, Phyllis, exclaimed, shocked. "Do watch
your language in front of the children! I've never seen you in such
a state."

Olivia said, "It's time for the children to run along and play.
Go on. You too." She motioned to Zoë and Max.

"Oh, Mother, really. We're no longer children," Zoë protested.

But Olivia would not be gainsaid.

When all but Henry, who was legally an adult, had left,
Albert jumped up and ran his fingers vexedly through his thinning
hair, saying, "She's becoming intolerable! Thinks she's so clever
and knows more than we do about business and yet, if we hadn't
curbed some of her sillier investments, we'd be losing our fortune
instead of increasing it. Now she's all starry eyed for this
conniving upstart who reminds her of Alex and Father. He's no

doubt going to 'save' the company! Christ! Do you think we can have her declared senile?"

"Come, Albert," Richard said placatingly. "Things are not as dire as you make out. The boy is our nephew — you only need look at him to see the resemblance to Alex. Can you blame him for wanting to better himself, for it sounds as if he's not had an easy life. I admire his spunk and nerve in tackling us. We must surely present a formidable challenge. He will hardly have grown up in genteel surroundings, imbibing from birth the ways of society, as our children have. Give him credit. Give him a chance. I think that he could be helpful to us. And I think that he'll give our boys a little more incentive to do their bit with some interest and enthusiasm."

Henry snorted, but said nothing.

"He'll be a snake in the grass, undermining our boys. He's dangerous," Albert said.

"Do you have so little faith in our lads?" Richard asked with a chuckle at Albert's mixed metaphors. "I didn't suggest that we make him a partner at this point, but having a manager who is family for one of the mills, for instance, may be beneficial. If he had some share of the profits, he would work even harder. I think it could be to everyone's advantage. I know that the Eatons employ cousins as store managers, and it's worked well for them. Family loyalty and all that."

"I doubt that James will agree."

"Unless he takes that boy under his wing, as the son he never had," Phyllis said with a frown.

"Well I think that we should be rejoicing that the family rift may yet be healed," Olivia said.

"I daresay you will try to foist all of Alex's by-blows on us," Phyllis grumbled.

"Indeed, and the sooner the better, if those poor children are living in want."

"I will not have street urchins here! This is as much our house as yours, and you do not have the authority to... to ..."

"Do calm down, Phyllis," Olivia interjected before Phyllis could find some unforgivable words to utter. "I doubt that they would feel comfortable here just yet. But I do intend to find some way of helping them. Now I shall go for a swim, and leave you men to think of some way to finally right a grave wrong that was done to your unfortunate brother many years ago."

When Olivia had left, Phyllis blustered, "Well! That's a bit much! Accusing your parents of injustice."

"Yes, Richard, I really think that you should curb your wife's liberal tendencies," Albert pontificated. "It's all very well for women to be sentimental and charitable, but they need our guidance to ensure that these qualities are neither misplaced nor abused."

"And I think that you could both do with a healthy dose of compassion. Excuse me while I join Olivia."

"You'll regret this," Albert said to Richard's retreating back.

Richard turned and said, "I never regret what my conscience dictates is right," and went inside before Albert could respond.

In their bedroom, Olivia was collecting her bathing costume. Richard swung her into his arms and planted a firm kiss on her lips. When he released her she laughed. "What instigated that?"

"You. I'm constantly reminded what a lucky man I am!"

"Ah, had enough of Albert and Phyllis then?" she said shrewdly. "There are times when I just can't face that woman. I really do like your idea of building our own cottage. Oh, nothing as grand as this. Just our own little place to get away from everyone when we want to, but close enough to be with the rest of the family when we choose. I would like so much to invite my own family up for more than a few days at a time. I daresay we wouldn't even have to have any staff, save for a maid. We could take our meals here, so that your mother wouldn't think we were completely deserting her."

Richard gave her a peck on the cheek and said, "I will broach the subject with Mother tomorrow. There's a lovely little bay partway up the west shore. Silver Bay, we've always called it. No cliffs, just a gentle rise above a crescent of sand."

"Oh, yes! Let's go there after our swim." Holding hands like daring young lovers, they strolled down to the beach.

The children were already at the east or "back" bay, as it was known. Sheltered from both the prevailing winds and the afternoon sun, it was a perfect spot for swimming or wading, and building castles in the sand, as eight-year-old Miles was doing. Zoë and Esme were just setting out in a canoe, leaving Max to look after Miles and Rupert. Now that they no longer had a nanny, the children took responsibility for one another.

Before the bathroom had been installed in the house the previous summer, the bath and change house had been used for people to bathe discreetly in a cubicle, like a small boat slip with doors for privacy. A platform allowed for disrobing and a ladder led down into the water. The five small rooms were also used for swimmers to change, for it was unseemly to been seen walking about in skimpy bathing costumes, even if the women were expected to wear black stockings and have skirts down to their knees, ending a few inches above the matching bloomers. Olivia dispensed with the stockings, lace-up bathing slippers, and ruffled cap, and even dared to wear her costume in the canoe at times, thus exposing her calves and bare feet. Phyllis was scandalized, as she herself wouldn't even swim when the men were around. She never emerged from the water, but would swim in and out of the cubicle so that even Olivia and the girls only ever had a fleeting glimpse of her bulky figure.

"You're off duty for a while, Max," Olivia said after she and Richard had changed into their costumes. "Your father and I will look after the boys."

"Edgar's going out in the motorboat," he said, tentatively, knowing that his mother in particular didn't approve of Edgar's racing about the lake in the new and powerful Ditchburn boat.

But Olivia was spared a response, for they could hear the engine being gunned as the boat roared away from the west dock.

A disgruntled Phoebe huffed her way over to them. "Edgar wouldn't let me go along!" she fumed. "I wanted to see him again, too! He likes me."

"He?" asked Olivia. "You mean Jack? Edgar's going to... see Jack?"

"Oh, Lord," Richard groaned. They all knew that it would take Jack at least half an hour to paddle to the hotel, which was over a mile away across mostly open water. And James had taken the steam launch to Gravenhurst, so there was no hope of going after Edgar. "I trust Edgar won't do anything stupid."

.    .    .

Jack was already away from the sheltering effect of the smaller islands north of Wyndwood, out in the rougher open water, when he heard the drone of a fast-approaching boat. It seemed to be coming directly at him, and he felt a moment of panic.

He stuck his paddle up to warn the driver, in case he hadn't been seen, and the boat pulled up abruptly, just short of him. The waves rocked the canoe violently, threatening to dump Jack into the water.

"Don't worry, I saw you," Edgar said. "In fact, I was looking for you."

Jack smiled with relief as well as in greeting.

"You are a smarmy bastard, aren't you?"

It was no time to pretend ignorance, so Jack replied, "I didn't come for handouts, and I have no interest in your inheritance or your job, cousin. But I figure there's always room for one more, if that person has the best interests of the family at heart and is competent enough."

Edgar chuckled at Jack's frankness, and Jack breathed easier, although he knew he wasn't out of the woods yet.

"How do we know that you do have the best interests of the family at heart?"

"Because I am a Wyndham, and even more proud to be one now that I have met the rest of the family. Why would I sabotage the Wyndham empire when I would have so much to gain by helping it to thrive? As to whether I'm competent..." He shrugged. "I guess I'll have to have the chance to prove that."

"Well, if it were up to me, you could start tomorrow. I'd rather you were in the business than a waiter at the resort. That's rather demeaning, isn't it?"

"It's honest work. I can set a good table. And I know that Pittsburgh Plate Glass is doing well and that its owner, Mr. Horace Camford, has a tobacco heiress coming up to visit his island next week."

Edgar laughed. "I could enjoy having you around. You're nobody's fool, are you, Jack?"

"I trust not. Nor do I wish to be used as a stick by Grandmother to threaten the rest of you."

"No one can ever do quite right by her, so that is nothing out of the ordinary for us. We young people tend to ignore her. She's so old fashioned. I say, but it's decidedly odd to hear you call her Grandmother, and to have suddenly discovered a cousin!"

"For me as well. I'd heard about my uncles, of course, and had dreamed of seeing Wyndwood Island one day.... Well, I must get back to work. Beautiful boat, by the way."

Edgar beamed. "I'll bet she's the fastest on the lake! I'm racing her in the regatta next month — the over 15 miles per hour category. It took a hell of a lot of effort to persuade Father and my uncles to buy the boat for the family. Grandmother was totally against it, of course. Claims it's too noisy and the gasoline is too dangerous. Look, I'd give you a tow, but..."

"No, that's quite alright. If the management saw me pulling up to the dock in that thing they'd think I didn't need a job anymore. Thanks all the same."

The canoe rocked dangerously as Edgar sped away, but Jack was too elated to care. One more down.

As he paddled on, he pondered how he could meet his grandmother's challenge. It would be useless to undermine or sabotage the Maitre d' or the dining room manager, for there was probably no chance that he, one of the newest of the scores of waiters, would be offered their jobs. So... how to distinguish himself? How to get ahead?

He had always been resourceful, collecting discarded fish boxes from the St. Lawrence Market for fuel, buying broken cookies cheap from the Christie Brown factory and re-selling them for a small profit to neighbours, pilfering fruits and vegetables from market stands and coal from factory coal piles.

And thanks to his father, he was a more than competent artist, so he had made use of his talent by creating interesting advertisements for shop windows, and doing sketches of holidaymakers on Toronto Island. He would charge according to his estimation of what people could or would pay, whether a quarter or a dollar. It all added up. But he had always known that he would never become rich through his art.

Everyone had a Kodak Brownie these days, but perhaps guests at The Grand preferred a decent watercolour painting of the hotel to the postcards and snapshots. Perhaps the rich young ladies would enjoy having a sketch of themselves — nothing too costly, yet giving him extra money and some accolades. All in his very limited "free" time.

Jack wondered how Victoria had liked her sketch. Remembering the soft and luscious feel of her beneath her thin muslin today, he laughed aloud at the delightful possibilities that life was offering him.

# Chapter 3

After the children had left the breakfast table, Richard said, "Mother, I think that Jack should come and stay with us, to give us a chance to get to know him and to start training him in some aspect of the business."

It was another beautiful morning, so they were on the screened east veranda, where a table was always set up for fine-weather dining. Augusta sat at one end, looking down the length of the table and the veranda to the sparkling lake beyond. The adults all sat in a row, their backs to the French windows of the dining room, and their view, the lake to the east through the dance pavilion. Molly had just brought a second pot of coffee.

"I've given him a challenge," Augusta said. "Let him prove himself at the hotel. Then we shall see." She had spent an almost sleepless night, thinking of Alexander, weeping over him in the privacy of her room, and finally succumbing to exhaustion. And yet she felt strangely invigorated, as if some burden had been lifted and she could move on. Was that Jack's doing, his youthful energy and determination giving her hope? She had to admit that she would enjoy having him here, but she would look weak and indecisive if she changed her mind now.

"I think Richard is right, Mother," James said. "I've been giving this a great deal of thought." He had arrived back late last night, but Albert had soon filled him in on the afternoon's events.

"You can't be thinking of taking him into the business!" Albert said, outraged. "This is preposterous!"

Before Augusta could chime in with a scathing remark, James said, "Look at it this way, Albert. Better the enemy you know than the one you don't. If Jack is here, we will soon learn the measure of him. If he stays at the hotel, we risk his sullying the Wyndham name. Isn't it rather humiliating having a nephew in such a menial position, for all our friends to see? Will you not feel embarrassed having him serve you in the dining room on Mondays? And I think he's clever enough to know that, and may well have been counting on that in order to gain our attention."

"You all make him sound like a scoundrel," Olivia said. Normally she refrained from speaking out about matters that did not directly concern her, but she was incensed. "He is your grandson, your nephew. He is of your blood. He is intelligent, charming, gracious, and hard-working. Why is there such suspicion and hostility toward him?"

"This has nothing to do with you, Olivia," Albert said dismissively.

Beneath the table, Richard gently squeezed her knee, forestalling a heated response. He said, "We're all entitled to voice an opinion, and I agree with Olivia. He is family and we can find a decent job for him in the business. If he proves himself competent, I have no qualms about him eventually sharing responsibility and profits with our boys, as Alex's heir."

"Well I have!" Albert said.

"You never wanted to share your toys with Alexander either," Augusta recalled. "Perhaps you're right, James. I was a bit surprised by him, and hadn't had a chance to think things through. You will go and tell him that I have changed my mind. That the summer is too short to see him only occasionally. That he is to be our guest here this summer, during which time we will have a chance to get to know him, and start grooming him for the business. We will hone his social skills so that he will in no way be an embarrassment to the family — ladies, you will help there. If at any time he fails to meet my expectations, he will be sent away."

"And what about the rest of Alex's children?" Olivia dared to ask.

Augusta brushed her hand in front of her as if swatting at a fly. "I can only deal with one at a time! Jack will ensure that they are not starving," Augusta said tetchily. "We will see how Jack makes out. Then I will consider what to do with the rest. And you will not interfere, Olivia! I will not have anyone going behind my back, do you hear me?"

"And where will Jack stay?" Phyllis asked through gritted teeth. "He will not sleep in the boys' room!"

"Nor would he want to, I expect. But the guest rooms are not available. Beatrice arrives in what, about ten days? And others will be visiting," Augusta mused.

"Put him in a tent," Albert said.

"The upper floor of the new boathouse isn't being used for anything but storage at the moment," Richard pointed out.

"True. Toby and Will can begin clearing that out today," James said. "It's something we've intended to do anyway. Let Jack work out the week at the hotel, and we should have a bed ready for him by the weekend."

. . .

James, with Albert tagging along, found Toby raking the tanbark path near the boathouses. Tobias Wheeler, caretaker, handyman, and boatman, had been captain of one of the big lake steamers years ago. When his ship had run aground on a shoal on a stormy autumn day, it had been suggested that he had been drinking and was dismissed. Reginald, who had needed an experienced pilot to drive his new steam yacht, had determined that Tobias was no drunkard and had hired him. Tobias had lived on Wyndwood ever since, driving and maintaining the boats, looking after the acetylene generating plant for the lighting and the pumps for the water, cutting and hauling ice blocks from the lake in winter, doing general repairs, and tending the gardens. He had his own log cabin, in which he lived year round with his dog, bringing in enough supplies to tide him over the winter, although he occasionally ventured across the frozen lake on snow shoes to visit friends on the mainland or a few other islands. The children had always thought Toby a most eccentric and intriguing person, like a friendly hermit.

"Alexander's son, Jack, will be coming to stay with us, Toby. We need to find a room for him, so we've decided that the space above the new boathouse should be prepared. Let's have a look at it and see what needs to be done. We expect Jack here on Saturday."

"And what's become of Mr. Alex?" Toby asked as they climbed the stairs.

"I'm afraid he succumbed to consumption."

"Shame, that." Alex had often spent time talking to Toby while the old man had gone about his chores. Alex had been fascinated by Toby's life on the island, and had begged his parents to be allowed to stay all winter as well.

Toby must be well over seventy now, and they all knew that once he was gone, they wouldn't find anyone to replace him. Even the steam yacht would probably have to go, as a licensed pilot was needed to run it and they were difficult to find.

The motor-boathouse had been mostly constructed two winters ago, with Toby overseeing the workmen, and doing the painting himself last summer. The upper floor had been left as one large room opening onto an expansive balcony. The idea had been to use this for smaller social events and as a place for the children to play on wet days. But it had turned into a storage room when the old nursery in the house had been renovated into a bathroom and guestroom the previous autumn.

"All this will have to be shifted," James said of the bits of lumber, old toys, cribs and so forth. "Is there a useful bed here somewhere? Get one of the maids to help you set up a bedroom. Take things from the guest rooms if necessary and we'll buy new furnishing for the house before Mother's cousin arrives from England next week. Throw out anything that's broken or not useful. Leave the rocking horse and the playhouse, and any chairs and such. They can just sit in a corner for now."

"He'll have the best room in the house," Albert said scornfully, as the brothers stepped out one of the many French windows which gave onto the balcony. Wrapping around three sides with an extra wide section at the front, it had enough space to hold a dance under the stars.

"I'd forgotten what we'd had planned for this," James admitted. "After Jack leaves, we'll have a soiree here."

"Henry has wanted to use this as his room," Albert said. "But Mother wouldn't hear of it. Since the nursery was converted and Richard's young boys have been put in with the older ones, Henry and Edgar have felt much too constrained. Mother never stopped to think how they would find that arrangement. It's ridiculous that an eight and a twenty-one-year-old have to share a room. Mother always makes decisions that are convenient for her – a modern bathroom! another guest room! – but to hell with the rest of us!"

"Hush, Albert," James said. Toby hadn't followed them outside, but he could probably hear them. "Perhaps Mother would agree to the older boys joining Jack down here."

"Absolutely not! They wouldn't like that and nor would I condone it. He makes me uneasy, James. He hasn't been raised with the same sensibilities as our children. He's virtually a guttersnipe, for God's sake! He's going to bring trouble into this family, you mark my words."

"We'll just ensure that he doesn't. We'll find him a job in one of our mills. Somewhere not too close to either Toronto or Wyndwood. Or Mother. One of our northern operations. Fort William, North Bay, the Soo," the latter referring to Sault Ste. Marie on Lake Superior.

"How do we know that he's even Alex's son?" Albert asked. "I know everyone says he looks like him. But I don't hold with that. What if he somehow knew Alex and is trying this on?"

"I've already decided to ask Ethan to check up on him." Ethan Nash was their high-powered solicitor.

Stepping back inside, James said to Toby, "Perhaps you could get Will started on this while you take me over to The Grand, to talk to Jack. We'll just take the motorboat." Since it took at least half an hour to get up enough steam to run the yacht, it made more sense to take the smaller boat. The yacht was indispensable for hauling the entire family and their many trunks back and forth to the train station, or for large groups taking scenic tours of the lakes, or for picnics, since it had a galley and a full service of dishes and cutlery. But the smaller, fast motor launches were really the way of the future. Anyone could drive them.

When the men went downstairs, they found Edgar, Max, Victoria, and Zoë preparing to take out the motorboat. "I say, Toby, we're just going to take *Dragonfly* out for a spin," Edgar said, since he was required always to check with Toby about the plans for the boat before taking it. Edgar had promised the others that he would teach them to drive, something that Victoria had been pestering him about ever since they'd arrived at the cottage last week. She had already mastered the family automobile, much to Augusta's dismay. The chauffeur had nearly lost his job over that.

"As it happens, Toby is taking me out," James said.

"You see, Father, I told you that a motorboat was a good idea," Edgar said. "Now it's always in demand. I really think we need another one."

"You can take it out this afternoon," Albert said. "James is just going over to The Grand."

"What for?" Henry asked, joining them.

James explained to them.

"I can't believe that he's coming to live here!" Henry said in disgust. "And we'll be expected to treat him as an equal?"

"I've mentioned to Grandmother that I'd like to have quarters above the boathouse, but she's always pooh-poohed it. Now he gets the space," Edgar complained.

"Stop whingeing, you two," Victoria said. "You could always move in with Jack."

"I wouldn't mind!" Edgar said eagerly.

"Out of the question," Albert declared.

"Father! Five of us are crowded into a room smaller than that one up there. And the children need their lights out early. It's a stupid arrangement!"

"We know nothing about Jack," Albert persisted.

"He's straightforward. A decent chap, I'd say. And not about to murder me in the night."

The conversation was terminated when Toby returned with Will, who was normally one of the under-gardeners in Augusta's Rosedale house. He was responsible for chopping wood and helping Toby, who was also teaching him to drive the boats and maintain the engines.

"Let's canoe over to Red Rock and see if the Carringtons are here yet," Victoria suggested to her cousins.

"I want to go too," Phoebe said joining them.

"I'm going with Max," Edgar said quickly. Victoria and Zoë didn't even have to claim that they were canoeing together, as Phyllis wouldn't allow Phoebe to go anywhere without one of her brothers along. The four of them scampered off to the canoe house.

"Henry, you'll have to take me," Phoebe said.

"Oh for heaven's sake! Can't you just sit in Edgar's canoe?"

"You know he hates that. 'Three's a crowd' and all that. Do come along, Henry." She pulled on his arm.

"I can hardly wait to hear about Lydia's trip," Victoria said as she stripped off her stockings and shoes, dropping them in the canoe house. She tucked her skirt up under her waistband so that she could wade unencumbered into the water to push the canoe out. Zoë was already seated in the front.

Lydia Carrington, who was the same age as Victoria and Zoë, along with her older sister, Vivian, had spent most of the year in Europe with their mother and eldest brother, Simon. Lydia was certain it was because her parents had wanted to get Vivian far away from an unacceptable suitor.

"We can find out about all the best places to see!" Victoria was excited about her upcoming year in Europe. Grandmother's English cousin, Lady Beatrice Kirkland, was coming to stay for the summer at Wyndwood, and then taking Victoria and Zoë back to England with her. They were to tour the major European cities until January, after which the girls were to attend a finishing school in Switzerland for three months before returning to England to prepare for their presentation at Court in May. They would be home by mid-June, just in time for summer at Wyndwood.

Zoë was less enthusiastic. "As far as I'm concerned, you could just drop me off at Oxford."

"Don't you want to see the Louvre, the Sistine Chapel, the Acropolis, the Vienna State Opera, the...?"

"Yes, of course, but I don't want to attend a 'finishing school'. I don't need 'finishing'. I want an education." She had argued with her parents about this — Augusta's idea, of course. But they had felt that a few months learning deportment and perfecting French and German wouldn't hurt, and was worth the "Grand Tour" that the girls would have under Beatrice's excellent guidance. It would also give them the poise and self-confidence to enjoy their presentation at Court, which was an opportunity not afforded to many Canadian girls.

"You'll hate it, too," Zoë said as Victoria scrambled into the canoe. "They won't let you run about barefoot."

"It's only three months and at least we won't be there in summer. I wish we could wear sandals like the Egyptians and Greeks did. Do you think we can buy some in Greece? I'd love to have nothing on my feet but a sturdy sole to protect me from the rocks and pine needles."

Overhearing her, Phoebe said, "That's indecent. And Grandmother will be scandalized when she hears you're going visiting in bare feet."

"Be sure to tell her that I don't wear corsets either."

"You're wicked!"

"Don't be so stuffy, Phoebe. It's summer. I want to be able to breathe. And my feet want freedom."

"That's just nonsense! You're a shameless hussy and God will... Oh! You *splashed* me!"

"Sorry, my paddle slipped. Perhaps you'd best not get too close to our canoe," Victoria suggested, hiding her grin.

The lake was still beautifully calm as the three canoes set out. They rounded the point, past the large dock, toward a sprinkling of islands known as The Stepping Stones, which stretched to the mainland and were within hailing distance of one another. Hence the name of the first one, Ouhu, which was painted on one of the rocks. Tourists thought it was an Indian name, but it was actually pronounced Oh-you-who.

"Oh-YOU-who!" Phoebe called out as they neared the island.

"Really, Phoebe," Henry scolded. "Aren't you getting a bit old for that tired joke?"

There was no answering call, so the Carlyles were not yet in residence.

The next "stepping stone" was Picnic Island, which was not big enough for a cottage but perfect for picnics. Its south shore was a narrow beach, the clear water shallow with firm, rippled sand.

Fifty yards beyond that was Oaktree Island, owned by the Oakleys. It was about twelve acres in size and had a tiny island — more a large rock really — about ten feet offshore. For obvious reasons, that was called One-Tree Island and was connected to Oaktree by an arched bridge, lit at night with Chinese lanterns. A large gazebo on One-Tree provided a delightful retreat for afternoon teas.

The Oakley's massive, modern cottage contained not only a ballroom but also a billiard room, along with ten bedrooms and five bathrooms. Gaily painted in yellow, with red and white trim, it demanded attention. The matching six-slip boathouse had a full stable of boats of varying sizes and types, much admired by Edgar. A second one housed the eighty foot steam yacht, *Gloryoak*. An inclined railway from the dock provided an easy way to transfer large trunks and other luggage up to the house. The Oakleys generated their own electricity, which provided much better lighting than acetylene gas. A bowling green lay on a flat stretch behind the house. With stone retaining walls, lush, terraced gardens, a waterfall, rock-edged paths, and scores of Adirondack chairs set invitingly about the property, it looked more like a small resort than a private island. It even had a signalling canon that Oswald would fire on special occasions and before a party, as if to summon all to attend. The Oakley's lavish events were renowned among the cottagers.

A stone's throw beyond Oaktree was Red Rock Island, less than half the size with a large slab of red granite as its dominant feature. The grey and white cottage and boathouse, too, were more modest. The Carringtons had been here for about a dozen years now. Edward Carrington had become successful in textiles, owning several woollen and knitting mills along the Grand River and in Guelph. Carrington carpets were prized by many a household.

"The flag is up," Victoria said. It was the Red Ensign, not the white flag that signalled the lake steamers to stop for passenger pick-ups. "So they are here."

They pulled up to the dock and clanged the big brass bell to announce themselves. Lydia Carrington came running down the path from the veranda. "We just arrived last night," she said. "How wonderful to see you! Do come up to the house. I'm sure we can manage some coffee and cake. The staff already have things well in hand. We have so much to catch up on."

Her enthusiasm was, as always, infectious. Victoria was glad to see that, although Lydia looked older and more sophisticated, she hadn't changed. She took Victoria on one arm and Zoë on the other and led them up the rugged path to the cottage, leaving the boys to tie up the canoes, and Phoebe trudging sourly behind, muttering to herself.

The other Carringtons joined them on the veranda, the parents, Rena and Edward, only briefly.

"Europe was splendid," Vivian said. "But I don't think anything comes close to the beauty of this place. I'm so happy to be back here!"

With her glossy black hair, alabaster complexion, and stormy blue eyes, twenty-two-year-old Vivian had an ethereal beauty that invariably turned heads. But there was a sadness about her, despite her exuberance, that made Victoria wonder if Lydia's theory was true. Was Vivian pining for a love that was denied her?

Henry and Edgar couldn't take their eyes off her, while Max seemed to have discovered Lydia as some strange new creature, judging by the discreet looks he gave her when she wasn't watching. Victoria wondered if the easy friendship they had all shared as children was going to become complicated by romantic yearnings.

She recalled her own infatuation with Justin Carrington when she had been fifteen and he, eighteen and just off to university. She'd spent that summer starry-eyed, and had lived for a word or a glance from him. Of course she still found him attractive and enjoyed their conversations immensely, for he never talked down to her because she was younger or a female. He had always treated her as an intelligent and interesting being, and she loved him for that.

But now that she was older and had enthralled several eligible swains, he was no longer the only man whose company she enjoyed. The memory of Jack holding her, however briefly, in his arms yesterday brought a flush to her cheeks. She found him slightly dangerous and very intriguing. Justin, on the other hand, was wonderfully tame and predictable. The best kind of friend, but perhaps not lover.

Justin, who could not fail to be aware of Victoria's crush that summer, was thinking that she had indeed blossomed into a beauty. But he was glad to see that she was still carefree and unconventional. Although cottage life was more casual, going visiting in bare legs and feet would still be considered indecent. He had to admit that he found her slender feet attractive and sensuous.

After Lydia had raved about Europe, Henry asked, "Is Simon not here?" Simon, at twenty-five, was the eldest.

"He has to make up for having had the year off to be in Europe with us. He's managing the businesses, as Papa wants to have more free time. So Simon won't be able to spend the entire summer here," Vivian explained.

"He has to be here for the Stepping Stone Marathon," Edgar insisted.

He was referring to the annual challenge in which all the young male cottagers in the vicinity participated. They swam from one Stepping Stone island to the next, and on to Wyndwood. A costume ball at Wyndwood later that evening honoured the champion, as well as celebrating Dominion Day, and drew revellers from miles around. It was Wyndwood's big event of the season.

"He'd never miss that," Lydia assured them. "He's determined to break Chas's winning streak." Chas Thornton, another island friend, had won the cup for the past several years.

"I think we should change the rules this year," Victoria said. "I think that we girls should be able to join in. After all, we can participate in regattas. Why not in a swimming race?"

"Ye Gods!" Edgar exclaimed. "You'll be drowning all over the place and then we men will have to rescue all the damsels in distress."

"Don't be foolish. I can swim as well as you."

"I think it's a splendid idea," Vivian said. "We could have a ladies' trophy, as well as the men's."

"In that case, I will beg off the race and bring *Dragonfly* along as the rescue boat," Edgar said.

"We don't want that smelly thing roaring along beside us," Lydia said. Usually the girls followed the race in rowboats, in case anyone got into trouble, and also to cheer on their favourites.

"It's one thing to swim at the bay or off the dock, but quite another to be in the open lake," Henry pontificated. "It's much farther to Wyndwood than you think, and there can be weeds out there."

"They twine around your legs and pull you under," Edgar said. "Or is it just the lake monster trying to drag you into the black depths?"

"I think Edgar's' been breathing too many of those gasoline fumes," Victoria said.

"Speaking of which, we should head back," Edgar said. "Uncle James should be back with the boat by now, and I'm going to give these brats driving lessons."

"Oh, you'll find this interesting," Victoria said. "We've just discovered we have a new cousin. He..."

"Is coming to stay with us for a while," Henry interrupted, throwing Victoria a warning glance. "Our uncle Alexander became estranged from the family many years ago, and his son, Jack, is coming to get acquainted with us."

"He's very dashing," Victoria said, ignoring Henry's glare. "Henry is already jealous of him."

"Don't be ridiculous!" Henry blustered.

"A long-lost cousin." Justin said. "I expect there's a story there."

"A rather sad one, I fear," Zoë said.

"We really must be going," Henry stated, trying to end the conversation.

"You do that, Henry," Victoria said. "Zoë and I will be along later."

"Victoria, there is no need to bore our friends with family matters." It was an order, which Henry should have known would only encourage Victoria to defy him.

"Zowie! I smell a scandal," Lydia said, clapping her hands in glee. "Do tell!"

"Come along, Phoebe!" Henry said, incensed as Victoria began to tell the story, beginning with that audacious whisper.

"But I want to stay!" Phoebe pouted.

"Then you'll have to swim back."

"You're such a spoil sport, Henry! I never get to have any fun!" As she followed Henry, Phoebe mumbled in annoyance, "Nobody ever let's me play. Maryanne says it's not fair."

"What's Phoebe going on about?" Lydia asked. "Isn't Maryanne that creepy doll of hers?"

Maryanne *was* a rather sinister two-headed doll, Victoria thought. One side of her head had a somewhat vacant, smiling face, and the other, a frowning, almost malevolent one. "Yes, and we think Phoebe is old enough to stop treating Maryanne as a real person."

"She's lonely," Edgar said in his sister's defence.

"She's immature," Victoria countered. "A dose of school would be good for her." And getting away from her smothering mother.

Phoebe hadn't been allowed to attend the girls' school that the others did, because Phyllis had thought her too delicate to be exposed to the brashness and "cruelty" of other girls. So Phoebe was being educated at home with tutors, and so had no friends other than her cousins. It was little wonder that her doll had become her companion.

"I don't know why Henry is so upset," Max said. "You can't hide the truth."

"Sometimes the less said the better," was Edgar's criticism. "Henry hates notoriety or anything that could disgrace the family name."

"To me it's much more disgraceful to think that our cousins may be living in want," Zoë said.

.    .    .

James was ushered into the manager's office at The Grand. "Mr. Wyndham, a pleasure! How may I help you?"

When he had seated himself in one of the leather chairs, James said, "I have a rather odd request to make, Mr. Graham. It's a somewhat delicate matter, so your discretion would be greatly appreciated."

"Certainly, Mr. Wyndham."

"Our family lost touch with my youngest brother some years ago. It appears that he is no longer with us, unfortunately, but we've just learned that his son is one of your employees." James looked hard at the manager. "He has just discovered his family, and we wish to take him under our wing. So I must ask you to release him from any contract that he may have with you. I realize that this may leave you short-handed, but I expect that there are able men who could use the job, so that you won't have any trouble replacing him by the weekend." It was more a statement than an assumption.

"Jack Wyndham, you mean? I had wondered. It is not a common name. As I understand it, Jack is an excellent worker, so we will be sorry to lose him." The manager was not about to be too intimidated by the Wyndhams. "But of course I understand your... position."

"I haven't spoken to Jack as yet."

"Then let me call him down," the manager said, rising. "I trust that we will continue to have the pleasure of your family's patronage, Mr. Wyndham?"

"Most assuredly, Mr Graham. We always enjoy our evenings at The Grand."

With the mid-day meal about to be served, Jack was mystified by the summons to the manager's office. For an instant he wondered if he had committed some grave error, but could think of nothing.

"You have a visitor," Mr. Graham said, showing him into his office. "I'll leave you alone for a few minutes."

Of course he had seen him in the dining room, so Jack knew right away who it was, and felt momentary unease. James, the eldest. Aloof and judgemental, his father had told him. He took the initiative. "Uncle James, is it?"

Taken aback by Jack's forthright manner, James stammered, "Yes, indeed," and shook the proffered hand.

Both men remained standing as James said, "Your grandmother has decided that she would like to get to know you more quickly than your working here would allow. So we, the family, invite you to come and stay at Wyndwood. We believe that if you are as ambitious and clever as you seem, then we will certainly have a place for you in the family business. We need to prepare you for that, and your staying at the island for the next month or so would allow that opportunity."

All graciously said, but not with great sincerity, Jack felt. They wanted to keep an eye on him, make sure he didn't create a scandal. Yet his heart leapt at this turn of events. It was, after all, what he had really been hoping for when he'd given up his job in the city to work at The Grand for the summer. "I have a good job here. What guarantee do I have that you won't throw me out tomorrow, and I will be without a position at all? I need to support my family."

James hadn't expected any hesitation. Jack sensed that this earned him some respect.

James took a moment to collect his thoughts. "How much do you expect to make this summer? $100? $200 if the tips are generous? I'll give you $500 on the proviso that you stay as long as you are welcome. You will either have a job in the family business by the end of the summer, or you will be asked to leave. But you will say nothing of this arrangement to anyone."

"I would be most honoured to be a part of the family business." Jack offered his hand in agreement. "Thank you, Uncle James. I won't let the family down."

"Tobias will collect you on Saturday morning. Everything has been settled with Mr. Graham."

.  .  .

"Mother, Olivia and I would like to build ourselves a cottage at Silver Bay," Richard said to Augusta in the library. "Nothing grand. We could still join you here for meals. But it would free up some room here for guests, and give us a chance to entertain our own friends more."

Augusta removed her reading spectacles. "I don't believe that's necessary, Richard. We have ample space above the new boathouse, should we need it."

"As our children become adults, it's not reasonable to expect them to share rooms with all their cousins. And once they're married..."

"Heavens! We'll worry about that when the time comes. You know that I don't have many years left, Richard. It's a great comfort to me to have you all here in the summers. And if I let you build a cottage, then Albert will want to have his own, and this place will become too empty. It was built for a large family. We've made do and will continue to do so."

"Mother, Olivia and I would appreciate some privacy as well. It would make for more harmonious family relations if we weren't living in each other back pockets all the time."

"You have the freedom to wander the island. You need hardly see one another except at meals. You may do what you like when I'm gone, for I'm sure the three of you won't live happily together without me to intervene. But for now you will indulge me."

"I think you're being unreasonable, Mother. You treat us like children still. I believe that there is a little island for sale near Red Rock. I don't need your permission to buy that and build a cottage. I would rather do it here, for then we could still be close to the rest of the family, but if you force my hand..."

"I won't be blackmailed, Richard. You may do what you like, of course. As did Alexander. Just don't expect my blessing." She stared hard at him to make sure that he understood the threat.

Richard shook his head in exasperation and marched out, slamming the door behind him.

He found Olivia in the back bay with the three youngest children. They were building sandcastles. He took her aside. "I swear that if Father hadn't been alive when we were married, she would never have let us move out of Wyndholme either," he said, referring to the family home in Rosedale.

"Ah. She said 'no'," Olivia stated with disappointment.

"She likes to have control, to have us in her sights as much as possible. I threatened to buy our own island, but that just induced the counter threat of being disinherited. Her whip! I'm sorry, darling. It's utterly foolish when a man my age isn't allowed to make simple decisions for his family."

"Perhaps she won't find us so accommodating and agreeable in future. I think I shall speak my mind more. A bit of family discord may just change her mind."

"Or make her more determined to interfere."

"Then we'll have to arrange for Jack's family to come and keep her company. I will not let that matter drop, Richard, despite her edict. I cannot believe that she and the others are so uncharitable to their own kin. I'm tired of always giving in. I feel like a fight."

.     .     .

"Your Uncle Albert tells me that you were gossiping about our family affairs to the neighbours this morning, Victoria," her father said sternly. He had called her into the library where he stood beside the desk, at which Grandmother sat. It was a tableau that Victoria had faced many times, Grandmother sitting regally in judgement and her father looming beside her like the executioner.

"I just told Vivian and Lydia about Jack. Nothing more than the truth. Henry telling tales is he?"

Augusta snorted. "Yes, well, I would have thought that he could deal with this himself, but I don't suppose anyone can curb your impulsive nature."

"Victoria, there is no need to give everyone a detailed account of this situation with Jack," James stated. "Suffice it to say that he is a newly discovered cousin. You will ask the Carringtons to be discreet, and will not mention to anyone else anything about Jack's background. No one will have noticed him at The Grand, so there's no need to explain that. And you will remember that loose tongues can harm good reputations."

"And remember that one's words are forever and continually twisted as they travel from one gossip to another," Augusta said.

"Will you ask Jack to lie about his past?" Victoria dared to ask.

Augusta pursed her lips. "Jack is clever enough to know that dwelling upon his past will gain him neither respect nor advancement."

"You're old enough now to stop behaving like a wilful and thoughtless child, Victoria," her father said. "I would expect some maturity and consideration from you. Learn to think before you speak."

Victoria bit back a reply. No need to antagonize them, because she would only lose out, once again giving up some of her precious freedom to no useful end. "Yes, Father."

"And you will never again leave this island improperly shod," Augusta decreed. "It's indecent. We are neither paupers nor heathens, that we run about barefooted.

"It will be a blessing to have Beatrice take her in hand for a while," she said to James as if Victoria weren't there. "Teach her how to behave like a lady. Lord knows I've tried, but I expect I've been too indulgent."

"One can only speculate at what havoc she might wreak on the Continent," James said. "Beatrice will have to keep a firm rein on her."

"May I be excused now?" Victoria asked, keeping the sarcasm from her voice. She itched to say *so that I can go for a swim in the nude*, but they would probably lock her away for the summer. She could hardly wait to escape to Europe, but also didn't want to wish away her beloved summer at Wyndwood. She could be agreeable and demure. She supposed that that was what being an adult entailed – knowing how to dissemble and cover-up one's true thoughts and feelings.

# Chapter 4

Jack recognized the gleaming mahogany Ditchburn motorboat that awaited him at one of The Grand's smaller docks. But it was still a surprise to think that it was there to whisk him to Wyndwood like any illustrious guest.

"Mr. Jack Wyndham?" the grizzled old man asked. "I'm Tobias from Wyndwood."

Jack grinned with genuine delight as he offered Toby his hand and pumped it vigorously. "Of course! You're Toby. My father told me so much about you. You gave him many happy memories of the island."

Startled by such a warm and sincere greeting, Toby flushed slightly and said, "You have the look of him, alright. I was that sorry to hear about your loss."

"I wish Father could have seen the island once more. He loved it so much here. I can understand why."

"Kinda gets in your blood, alright." Toby loaded Jack's few possessions – his carpetbag, his father's easel and some art materials – and started the engine. "Course, it's changed some since his day. Lots of these fast boats on the lake now, more cottages, hordes of tourists everywhere, plenty of steamers tooting away and spewing black filth into the air. All of it kinda destroying what people came up for in the first place – peace and quiet and clean air."

"But it's better than the city," Jack said.

"I reckon it is that, or there wouldn't be so many in such a danged hurry to get up here."

Jack wondered if any of his co-workers were watching him leave The Grand in such style. He'd downplayed his departure, saying only that he was leaving for family reasons. But somehow word had gotten about that he was related to THE Wyndhams, so he'd been subjected to plenty of good-natured ribbing. "I expect I'll be serving you at table some evening," one of the lads had said. And Jack realized that he was probably right. How bizarre that would feel! "I expect a decent tip, mind," the jokester had added. "'Less you want the soup in your lap next time."

With this being yet another scorching hot and humid day, Jack was especially thankful that he didn't have to climb into his uniform and look composed and efficient as he worked in the liquid air. With the wind in his hair, it was a thrill to watch the majestic white hotel recede, and to think that he would never again be a servant there, but a welcome visitor and part of a tradition. Wyndwood and its people were suddenly part of his history. It was exhilarating.

So was the ride as they skimmed across the water, arriving at the island in only a few minutes. Toby expertly manoeuvred the boat into one of the slips in the boathouse. As they disembarked he said, "I'm to show you your quarters and then take you up to the house."

Jack followed Toby up the stairs to the newly furnished room. He was stunned. All he noticed at first was three walls of windows that surrounded him with a panorama of water and islands. And what was that? His own private wrap-around balcony? The room itself was larger than any that his entire family occupied. The single bed, wardrobe, and dressing table seemed lost in one corner. The other corner housed old chairs and toys, which took little space. And there was plenty of room to set up his easel, inside and out.

"I think I've arrived in heaven!" Jack exclaimed.

"Aye, well, Mister Henry thinks this is the best room in the house, so to speak. And Master Edgar's been trying to move in here, but her ladyship wouldn't hear of it."

Jack realized that Toby was warning him without outwardly betraying the family. So, another reason for Henry and Edgar to dislike him.

"If you're ready then, Mr. Jack?"

"Yes, of course," Jack replied, although reluctant to leave this paradise just yet. He was afraid it might disappear while he was gone.

From the bay they walked past the herb and kitchen gardens, which Toby explained he maintained for himself as well as the family, managing to store plenty of root vegetables to see him through the winter. His own log cabin was tucked into the trees behind, an English sheep dog lying contentedly in its shade.

"This here's Shep." Toby said, stopping to scratch the dog's head. "He won't bark at people he knows or iffen there's someone new with them, but knows who's a stranger. Mostly have to keep him tied up though, for her Ladyship doesn't much like dogs, unless they be chasing foxes."

This flat area lay, like a shallow valley, along the isthmus that connected the two bays, and from its middle the land rose gently to the house along its eastern side. The west side of the house was perched on a small cliff. Jack thought he glimpsed Victoria on the veranda there, but the girl had disappeared.

They passed various outbuildings and clotheslines hung with laundry, flapping in the breeze, and skirted the back door to the kitchen, entering the main house through the roofed breezeway that connected the two.

Toby knocked on the library door. "Mr. Jack, M'am," he announced as he ushered him in.

"Thank you, Tobias."

He closed the door behind him, leaving Jack with Augusta, James, and Albert.

"Grandmother, thank you for the invitation to stay," Jack said. "And for that magnificent room. The views are stunning."

"I expect they are. I have yet to go up there, and may well regret giving you the sole use of it."

"I'd be happy with a closet," Jack said, not completely untruthfully. "As long as it had a window." And it meant that he was still an accepted member of the family.

"Ha! I'll remember that. James, get one of the children to show Jack about the island and acquaint him with our routines. I expect some of them are probably on the veranda, eavesdropping again," she said, raising her voice to be sure that they heard. "We dine at 1:00. I'll see you then," she added to Jack.

It was too lovely a morning for anyone to be in the sitting room, but they did find Victoria, Zoë, and Max uncharacteristically lounging on the front veranda, along with Phyllis and Phoebe, who were doing needlepoint.

Jack greeted them, but Phyllis hardly looked up from her sewing.

"Max, will you show Jack around?" James asked.

"We will, too," Victoria added, including herself and Zoë.

"Mama...?" Phoebe began, but Phyllis interrupted her.

"You will finish your sampler, Phoebe, and do some Bible study before luncheon."

Phoebe, muttering to herself, looked so unhappy that Victoria felt sorry for her. She'd rather have no mother than one like Phyllis.

The girls let Max take the lead as they went back into the house. "Sitting room, obviously," Max said as they walked through it. "We gather there after supper. And here's the dining room." A huge rosewood dining table that could easily seat the family and numerous guests stretched across the large room. Built-in glass-fronted china cupboards, filled with dinnerware bearing the family crest, flanked the two-sided stone fireplace that also gave onto the sitting room. With a wall of French windows and a ten foot high ceiling, this room, like the others in the house, seemed airy and spacious.

"We eat supper here, which we now call dinner mostly, as no one wants a huge meal mid-day because we're out all day canoeing or swimming or sailing or fishing or whatever. Grandmother dresses for dinner, but we just have to be neat and tidy, unless we have guests and then we have to wear evening dress. I say, I don't suppose you have any of that, do you? You're a bit taller, but something of mine might fit. In any case, we have breakfast and luncheon out there on fine days, which is to say when it's not freezing cold, and even dine there if it's devilish hot," Max said, pointing to the screened porch where another long table was set up.

"Oh, and there's coffee, tea, and biscuits on the side-board here from 7:00 in the morning, if you're an early riser. Breakfast is at 9:00, luncheon at 1:00, tea at 4:00 on the front veranda, unless it's cold and then we have it in the sitting room, dinner at 7:00 except when we have guests and then it's 8:00 with drinks at 7:00. And if you get hungry in between times, you can sneak in the back door to the kitchen and talk nicely to Mrs. Hadley, the cook, and she'll slip you some bread and cheese or tea cake. But don't let Grandmother know."

"Always thinking about your stomach," Zoë accused her twin.

"Mrs. Hadley is a better cook than ours, and I *am* always hungry. It's the air here. I swear I eat twice what I do in the city. Oh, and servants. There's Rosie in the kitchen, and she'll give you food as well. Tom is the footman. Bayley is Grandmother's lady's maid. Libby and Molly, the housemaids, Mary, the laundry maid, and Will helps Toby."

He led them back out to the hallway, toward the breezeway. "Butler's pantry on your right, box room and lavatory on your left. That was installed a few years ago, but the outhouses are still in use as well. We have another lav upstairs, and a new bathroom, but only the women and children use it. We men bathe in the lake."

When they reached the breezeway, Max turned left where the broad veranda, which swept around from the west side, ended. Several mirrors were hanging in a row against the back wall of the house with empty porcelain wash basins beneath. "Here's where we shave in the mornings. Hot water is set out and kept warm before breakfast, so just come when you like."

"Sounds very convivial," Jack observed.

"Don't bet on it," Max replied, "Uncle Albert is a bear before breakfast, and Uncle James, mostly uncommunicative. I try to get here either really early or just before breakfast. That way I can avoid them."

They went back through the breezeway and down to the east bay, passing the icehouse, washhouse for laundry, with the male servants' quarters above, outhouses, woodshed, acetylene gas house, and the water tower and windmill used for pumping water from the lake.

"This is where we men bathe between 7:00 and 8:00," Max explained when they reached the bathhouse. "Some of the women, like my mother, still like to bathe in the lake."

"That's because there are too many of us to share one bathroom," Zoë said. "And Grandmother takes an age. So this is for women only between 8:00 and 9:00."

There were half a dozen canoes and two rowboats in the dry slip canoe house next door. Fishing rods and life vests hung on the walls. "Edgar and Henry must still be out fishing – one of the rowboats is gone. I say, you'll have to practice up for the Regatta," Max said. "It's on the first Saturday in August. Perhaps you and I could enter the tandem canoe race and the jousting. Edgar's only interested in the motorboat races now."

"Can you swim?" Victoria asked Jack.

"Father taught us all, although my mother never took to it. We swam in the Don River or at Cherry Beach or sometimes at Hanlan's Point Beach, on the island." When they could afford the ferry ride from Toronto harbour to the popular island, where people flocked for picnics or to the amusement parks and hotels. It could never compare to Wyndwood or Muskoka, his father had said, but it was better than being stuck in the grime and stink of the roasting city. Sometimes they used the last of their meagre savings to go there. "Did you know there's a naturist beach there as well? Where clothing is optional?" he said, looking pointedly at Victoria, who blushed prettily.

"Holy smoke! You're having us on!" Max exclaimed, his eyes wide in shock. "You mean men and... women. Naked?"

"Yes. Not always a pretty sight, mind you." Bare-assed Beach is what many called it.

"You actually went there?" Max croaked.

"Sure." As children they had become used to swimming naked in the Don River, along with other children from their nearby Cabbage Town neighbourhood. Among poor families, who often lived, ate, bathed, and slept in only one or two rooms, modesty was not a concern or priority.

"Well, I'll be damned!" Max said.

"You may well be, if you keep talking like that," Olivia said as she came around to the canoe house. "Jack, how wonderful to have you here," she added, taking his hands in both hers.

"But Mama, Jack has just told us the most extraordinary thing," Max protested. "He said there's a beach on Toronto Island where people swim in the buff!"

"Yes, I had heard that. Goodness, I think that's been allowed there for donkey's years. Quite scandalizes some Torontonians. Actually, Hannah Carlyle was telling me that she and the girls sometimes swim naked at night. Of course no one sees them in the dark, so it's hardly immodest. Skinny dipping, it's called. She says it's wonderful. I think I would enjoy that too." And stirring up a bit of discord. "You girls would join me wouldn't you? I'll invite Phyllis and Augusta, of course, but I rather doubt that they would participate." There was a mischievous twinkle in her eyes.

"Mama!" Max chided. "Grandmother would be appalled!"

"No doubt she will be," Olivia said with a meaningful grin. "But one must move with the times. I've always wanted to go beyond that door in my morning baths. I should feel free to... express myself. Not expose myself, of course," she added with a chuckle.

"I'll definitely join you," Victoria said, avoiding Jack's eye.

"Me, too," Zoë said. "How liberating that will be."

"Perhaps tonight, then, if it stays this hot," Olivia promised. "Although I expect we're in for a break in the weather. So now I am going out for a blessedly solitary paddle in the canoe. Your father is off teaching the children to sail. Jack, I want you all to myself sometime – perhaps tomorrow, after you've settled in?"

Jack thought how comfortable and fun it must have been growing up with Olivia. Of course he loved his mother, but she had grown bitter over the years, and her tongue, wicked. She was all angles and sharp planes, both in her looks and demeanour. Too often she had berated his father, usually over money. His failure to properly support the family. His extravagances, like a picnic on Toronto Island, which might mean that they survived on porridge, and bread and drippings for the week. His lack of ambition and dreamy nature. His dwelling on his magical childhood and Wyndwood. Jack was sure that soft and gentle Olivia had never screamed a demeaning or filthy word at Richard. But then his mother might never have either, if they had lived in luxury instead of want.

They helped Olivia launch her canoe. She had removed her shoes and stockings in the change house and now said with a conspiratorial smile, "I'm not going visiting."

So Olivia had heard, Victoria thought, and was giving her tacit support. An irreverent thought crossed her mind. Once the old people, like Grandmother, died off, life could become less rigid and more amusing. Of course there were always the sanctimonious ones, like Aunt Phyllis. But they could be ignored.

"Now look at the island from here," Max said, as they all turned back to the path. "We call this flat stretch the 'Dragon's Neck'. The land rises and widens and then narrows again toward the point – that's the 'Dragon's Head'. And see how that cliff rises abruptly behind Toby's cottage? That's the 'Dragon's Back'. It stretches about a third of the way along the island. There's a smashing view from up there. It's an easy climb from the west side. We'll take the short route. Grandmother does this walk most fine days after breakfast."

He led them along the tanbark path which ascended gradually from the water's edge. The Dragon's Back, although not close to the shore to begin with, came constantly closer until they reached a spot where its sheer cliff face almost fell into the lake. The path became a narrow shelf for about twelve feet, just wide enough for one person to walk. A rope had been bolted into the cliff at either end to act as a hand railing.

Jack looked down the thirty foot drop to the rocks and lake below. "Wow, has anyone ever fallen off here? I don't suppose the water's deep enough to jump into?"

"No, it's not. There are some big rocks just below the surface. We call this the 'Dragon's Claw'. Not everyone can walk it."

"Some people get vertigo," Zoë explained. "Aunt Phyllis never comes this way."

"And Phoebe isn't allowed to," Victoria added.

They all passed the Devil's Claw with ease. Jack said, "Grandmother really manages to walk along this? Isn't she getting rather frail and unsteady?"

"Tough as old boots," Max said. "But she always comes the other way, starting on the west side, so that she can hold onto the rope with her right hand."

The path widened quickly and sloped down to the water's edge again. A large octagonal gazebo, open at both ends to the path, invited strollers to sit on the benches that lined the low walls

inside. It matched the house veranda in style and colour. From
here they could see past the end of a two mile long island, itself
nearly two miles distant, to the far misty shore of the lake. It was
the longest vista, which was elsewhere broken up with islands of
all shapes and sizes, and gave some sense of the magnitude of the
lake.

"My father told me about this view," Jack said. "He tried
painting it from memory." And every other part of the island.

"Do you have his paintings?" Zoë wanted to know.

"I do actually have a few with me. My mother has the others."
But she had put them away after his father's death. She'd wanted
nothing to remind the children that they had a wealthy family. She
didn't want them to waste their time dreaming, like their father
had. She wanted them to face up to the brutal reality of their lives,
and make themselves a decent and honest living. Working in
factories, sweatshops, and as servants, was as much as she aspired
to for her children.

"Do you paint as well?" Victoria asked, meeting his eyes. She
saw his amusement.

"Indeed I do. I intend to paint when I have free time."

"Will you teach me? The art mistress at school said that I
have a modicum of talent, but I'm afraid that the same could not
be said for her." Victoria was determined to find time – alone –
with this handsome and intriguing cousin.

"I'd be delighted." Particularly with her eagerness to flirt with
him.

"Let's sit for a few minutes," Zoë suggested. "Jack, will you
tell us about your family?"

"Egads! Girls always want to talk," Max complained, but sat
down as well.

"My mother takes in sewing." Which paid a pittance for the
arduous hours that she spent embroidering or sewing beads onto
gowns for ladies like the Wyndhams. "She'd started in the theatre
as a costume designer, so she's very skilled with her needle. My
sister, Lizzie, is seventeen. She works as a maid."

"Oh for whom?" Victoria asked. "We might know them."

Jack hesitated for only a moment. "She's actually in
Montreal." He didn't elaborate, and Victoria wondered if there was
a story there. Had she quarrelled with her family? Run off with a
lover? Been disgraced?

"Emily, who is fifteen, works in a dressmaker's shop." A
sweatshop, but Jack didn't think this was the time to complain
about the conditions of the downtrodden working poor. "She has a

glorious voice and ambition to be a professional singer." His mother wouldn't hear of her trying out for the theatre. Her own experiences had turned her against that way of life. But it was better than Emily ruining her eyesight and health with long hours in the sweatshop. "We're encouraging Emily to try out for the stage." At least he was. "And Claire, who's thirteen, helps Mother with sewing when she's not at school." He had struggled to keep her there, wanting to give her a chance to complete her education, since the rest of them had not had that opportunity. "Claire wants to be a teacher."

"I've heard about sweatshops," Zoë said, surprising Jack. "And they appal me. I expect that your wages are what's keeping the family going. You must let me help. I have some savings which I would like to donate to Claire's fund for Normal School. Perhaps it can earn some interest until she is ready to attend."

"That's most generous of you, Zoë, but I really can't accept that," Jack said.

"Tosh! You will or I will just send it to her as a present from her new cousin. And I expect I can find something for the others as well."

"You might as well give in, Jack," Max said. "When Zoë has set her mind on something, there's no stopping her. Especially when she senses any injustice. She'd be chaining herself to fences along with the other militant suffragettes if we lived in England, but ours, of course, are much tamer. Grandmother is sending these two to Europe because she's afraid that now they've finished school, Zoë will be spending days running soup kitchens and berating politicians, and Victoria will be racing about the city in the motorcar, knocking down pedestrians."

They all laughed.

More seriously, Zoë said, "I wish we could invite them all to come up here, even if just for a week. It would be so good for them to get away from the city, and I would love to meet them. I expect I won't even have a chance before we get sent to Europe."

"It's too much for Grandmother at one time. Perhaps once she knows me better, she'll be willing to accept the others as well. I'll have to be careful not to blot my copybook," Jack said with a grin. Yes, one day his family would be here with as much right as any of them, he swore. But he had to take things slowly.

"We should get back," Max said. "It's almost time for luncheon. "From here the path is no longer maintained, but Toby and Will check occasionally to remove fallen branches and such. So you can walk around the entire island, which is about three miles."

The short path now led inland, across the middle. "The Dragon's Back ends here, but the land does rise and fall and the rock outcropping meanders to the north shore, so we call that the 'Dragon's Tail'."

"There will be a bountiful crop of blueberries here later in the summer," Zoë said. "Berry picking has always been the children's job."

"Yes, I had heard that. And the cook makes wonderful pies and preserves," Jack said, suddenly feeling that he belonged, his father's memories giving him a sense of shared experiences with these cousins.

The path was anchored by a matching gazebo on the west shore, which was more gentle and much less dramatic, the path rarely more than a few feet above the water's edge. Because it actually faced south-west, the sun was beating down here.

But a wind had come up and was whipping the waves into whitecaps. Distant clouds portended rain.

"There's the path to get to the top of the Dragon's Back," Max pointed out after they had passed 'Silver Bay'. "You should go up there when you have time."

They came to the west bay behind the new boathouse. "How do you like your digs?" Max asked Jack.

"They're absolutely splendid! And I'm more than willing to share."

"I'd take you up on that, but I have to look after the boys, and Mama wants them up at the house, since they usually go to bed earlier. Edgar would, but I don't think Aunt Phyllis will allow him."

"Thinks I'm dangerous, does she?"

"She doesn't approve of any of us," Victoria said dismissively.

"In any case," Max said, "Grandmother thinks that gasoline engines and storage tanks are dangerous. Highly explosive. That's one of the reasons this boathouse is at the end of the bay. Of course it's too shallow elsewhere along here, until you reach the other boathouse, but that's too close to the house for her liking."

Jack laughed. "So she doesn't allow any of you to use the new boathouse. Which makes me lucky, I suppose. Or just expendable."

"*We're* not worried about the gasoline," Max pointed out.

They continued past the sandy beach and the large boathouse which sat just below the house. Here the path was narrow between the steep, treed slope and the water, which was lashing against the rocks that edged the lake side like a retaining wall.

When they arrived at the steamer dock, they noticed the supply boat, *Newminko*, just pulling away. A floating general store, greengrocer, and butcher shop, it stopped by three times a week to replenish the kitchen with fresh meats and other essentials. One of the mainland farmers came every morning with milk and eggs.

"You missed your chocolate," Zoë said to Max. "We've always been allowed to go onto the boat to buy a treat when Mrs. Hadley has finished her shopping," Zoë explained to Jack.

"Hell's bells!" Max said. "I keep missing the boat. So to speak." Amid laughter he said, "And speaking of catching boats, when anyone wants to escape from the island and there's no one to take him on *Calypso* or *Dragonfly*, we hoist the white flag and the next southbound steamer that comes by stops to pick him up.... Ah, I hear the tintinnabulation of bells."

"It's a gong, you chump," Zoë said.

"It's a summons to a fine repast," Max replied.

Luncheon was a simple buffet, the table in the dining room laid with trays of cold meats, various cheeses, freshly baked bread, devilled eggs, lettuce, radishes, pickles, relishes and chutneys, apples, oranges, and fruit tarts for afters, iced tea, lemonade, and ale for the men. They helped themselves and carried their plates out to the adjoining veranda.

"You will come and sit by me, Jack," Augusta commanded as she seated herself at the head of the table and pointed to the chair on her right. It was where James usually sat when there was no guest, but if he was annoyed by this displacement, he didn't show it. At formal dinner parties, James would sit at the other end of table, but otherwise that was still Reginald's place.

"This is a dream come true," Jack admitted, trying to keep his voice steady. "The island is everything I had been led to believe and more. Even a child's imagination could not have improved upon it." He knew when to speak from the heart.

They sensed the sincerity of his words and were warmed by them. There is nothing more complimentary than to have what you hold dear, praised by others.

"The family welcomes you, Jack," Augusta said.

"Thank you, indeed. At the risk of sounding too effusive, I have to admit that I am absolutely thrilled to have discovered such a family."

He almost expected a cutting remark from Henry or Edgar, but then realized that they weren't at the table. No one commented upon their absence or seemed concerned.

"So, Jack, I don't suppose that you have any experience in sailing, or tennis, or golf," James stated as if sure of the answer. "Part of succeeding in business is entertaining well."

"I would certainly like to learn, " Jack said.

"I can teach him," Max volunteered.

"We can help," Victoria added quickly, including Zoë in her offer so that she didn't seem too eager. "Zoë and I can teach him tennis." She looked at Jack, who sat directly across from her. His ice blue eyes were mesmerizing.

"We'll wallop you in no time," Max countered. "I expect that Jack is a natural athlete. You'll have to participate in the Stepping Stone Marathon, Jack." He went on to explain it to him. "We'll have to start training. It's only a few weeks away."

"So it is," Olivia said. "And high time we started preparing for the ball, I think."

"Jack will need some formal clothes," Max pointed out.

"Of course," Augusta said. "James, you will take Jack to the city when you go to pick up Beatrice next week. He can be measured for a wardrobe at the tailor's, and Grayson can bring the things when the servants come to help with the ball." Grayson was Augusta's butler at her Rosedale house.

"In the meantime, we have an Eaton's catalogue somewhere, so if you need anything right away, we can telephone an order to the city and have it sent up," Olivia suggested.

"Could you bring me some art supplies?" Victoria asked her father. "Jack is going to teach me to paint."

Phoebe said, "I should like to learn, too."

"You have adequate lessons," Phyllis said.

"But, Mama!"

"You heard your mother, Phoebe," Albert said sternly.

Victoria was relieved, although she couldn't help feeling sorry once again for Phoebe, who was now pouting.

"Well, I make no pretensions to artistic talent," Zoë said, as if to lessen the sting of disappointment for Phoebe. "I rely on my camera."

"But you should see her photographs, Jack," Victoria said. "She has such an eye for composition. That's a talent, too. My shots are always higgledy-piggledy."

"Yes, you can't tell a leg from a lamppost in Ria's pictures," Max said.

"Goodness, you children are rambling on today," Augusta commented. "Do let the adults get in a word or two. And Max, you will refrain from using pet names for people. It is childish and undignified for a boy your age." It didn't occur to her that Max's name was short for Maxwell, his mother's maiden name, which no one ever called him, unless he was in trouble.

There was an awkward silence. Albert and Phyllis were disinclined to talk because they resented Jack's presence, James only spoke when he felt he had something important to disclose, and Augusta seemed suddenly at a loss for words. Victoria stifled a giggle as Max, who sat beside her and was unruffled by Augusta's reprimand, gave her a conspiratorial nudge as if challenging her to break the silence and Grandmother's command.

But Olivia said, "Have you always lived in Toronto, Jack?"

"I was actually born in England. My parents were in France and England for several months, as my father was pursuing his artistic career." Until they had run out of money. "We returned to Toronto when I was just a baby, so yes, Toronto is all that I know." They had never lived more than an hour's walk from Wyndholme, whose carriage house or outbuildings would have been luxury compared to the increasingly smaller and more squalid hovels they had called home. Only once had his father taken him past his childhood home. It had been a dark October night. Although the large property was protected by a stone wall, they had looked through the open wrought iron gates. Music and golden light had spilled onto the lawns from the many arched windows. "My mother's birthday," his father had explained. But Jack had been too stunned by the opulence to believe that his grandmother actually lived in that house.

Wyndholme was a whimsical Gothic confection of towers and turrets, a rambling, fanciful castle that Reginald had built for his aristocratic bride. A warm, honey-coloured brick with cream tracery and gingerbread, it had bold finials crowning steep gables, jutting bays and oriole windows, balustrated sun porches, and a port-cochère, as his father had called it, where carriages were still arriving to drop off bejewelled revellers.

At that moment, Jack had wondered if his father was truly sane, or whether he had just chosen a house and fictional wealthy family to adopt as his own, to somehow counteract the depredation of a disappointing and disagreeable life.

Jack had gone back a few times since that day, always in the dark, always keeping his distance. It didn't do for street urchins or scruffy young men to be seen hanging about a wealthy neighbourhood where they so obviously did not belong and so must surely be up to no good. The coppers on the beat were quick to move you along. And Jack had promised himself that he would one day be welcomed in that house. He even dared to dream that he would live there.

Only once had they ever caught sight of his father's family. He had been about twelve when he and his father had been on Yonge Street, both looking for jobs. They had just come out of Eaton's when his father had spied a carriage. His face had lit up and he had been about to wave when he suddenly turned away and seemed to crumple in upon himself, as if punched in the stomach. When Jack had asked him what was wrong, his father had replied, "Just a ghost from the past," and had gone on to talk about how lucky they had both been to land jobs at the prestigious Eaton's department store. But his job as a catalogue artist had not lasted long, for it was shortly after that that he had fallen ill with the consumption.

"Strange that we've never run into you in the city," Zoë said, as if she had been reading his mind.

"Hardly a surprise, as you didn't know him and we don't move in the same circles," Augusta snapped. "And now I do insist that we NOT discuss the past!"

"But Mother Wyndham," Olivia said sweetly, "it is only common courtesy to inquire about a guest's life. We all want to get to know Jack. How can we do that without talking about his childhood and family?"

"You are defying me just to be difficult, Olivia. And that distresses me greatly. Is this some sort of ploy to convince me to approve a new cottage?" Augusta said shrewdly.

"What new cottage?" Phyllis asked immediately.

"The one that Richard and Olivia would like to build," Augusta said. "But I have refused the request."

Phyllis's shoulders sagged even more than usual as she uttered, "I should like my own cottage as well."

"Ha! What did I tell you!" Augusta cried. "Everyone is anxious to desert me."

"Don't upset yourself, Mother," Albert said, glaring at his wife. "We have no intention of moving out. However, I don't think it a bad idea if Richard and his brood did. It would certainly free up space here."

And leave her with only Phoebe and her repulsive doll, Maryanne, as room-mates, Victoria thought in horror.

"Your boys will just have to put up with their younger cousins for the time being," Augusta said. "And speaking of Henry and Edgar, what can have happened to them? I'm quite casual about luncheon, as you know. I realize that when one is out in a boat, one often loses track of time, and thus we have a buffet where one can join in at any time, if one can't be prompt. But they are now nearly an hour late."

Phyllis, who had been looking about anxiously for a while and had begun wringing her hands, burst out with, "I'm sure something dreadful has happened to them!" She jumped to her feet, as if Augusta's words had unleashed a dam, and cried, "Albert, you must send out a search party! Oh, I can't bear it!"

"We saw them near the Silly Isles just before we returned from sailing," Richard said. "They waved to us."

Olivia put her arm about Phyllis's shoulder and said, "Yes of course the men will go and search for them. Surely they've just lost track of the time. You mustn't think the worst, Phyllis." This in response to a heart-rending wail. "They are competent and sensible young men, and quite able to look out for themselves."

Phyllis shrugged her off as if she were a bothersome fly. "They are *never* so inconsiderate! Something dreadful has happened to them! A mother always knows! Look at the waves, and the clouds are gathering. We're in for a storm. They wouldn't be fishing in those conditions. I knew today was ill-omened!" She glared at Jack as if he were to blame.

They all felt she was right to be concerned, for Henry and Edgar were invariably on time, not only because of their upbringing, but because, like Max, they loved their food.

Zoë had run upstairs and fetched a couple of blankets. "You may need these," she said as she handed them to her father. Max and Jack offered to go with the men, but were told they were not needed. As they watched *Dragonfly* speed away, Jack said to Max, "The Silly Isles?"

"That's just what we call them. You see those dots over there, just before the mainland?" He pointed to the east of the Stepping Stones. "You can't see them all because some of the larger islands are blocking the view, but there are a few tiny islands, some no larger than a rock, and the largest only just big enough for a cabin. Grandmother once made a reference to the Scilly Isles in England, and we children thought it a perfect name for these, since they are rather silly, as islands go. Great fishing there and a fun place for picnics, though."

Richard put his hand reassuringly on Albert's arm but said nothing as the runabout sped away. In the high waves, the boat bounced and crashed on the steely water. The wind was definitely cold now, blasting in with what looked like a savage storm on its tail.

The Silly Isles were within a few hundred yards of the mainland, and they saw the rowboat as soon as they entered the channel. It was overturned.

"Dear God!" Albert cried.

"They must have swum to one of the islands," James said with conviction. "The boat has undoubtedly drifted in this wind, so let's start with the nearest ones," he instructed.

Toby had already powered down to a slow crawl and was scanning the rough, black water carefully before him.

"There!" Richard shouted. "On the fourth island. There's someone on the beach!" Someone who rose and started waving wildly. Those on the boat could suddenly breathe again.

Toby edged *Dragonfly* as far as he could up to the beach, and Henry grabbed the rope that Toby threw him. "I think Edgar's broken his leg," he shouted into the wind. For a ghastly moment it looked as if Edgar was dead and buried, for Henry must have covered his brother with sand to keep him warm, and only his head was really visible.

The men jumped into the shallow water. Richard draped a blanket about Henry, who was shaking with cold and shock, and silently thanked Zoë for her quick thinking in supplying the blankets. Albert and James rushed over to Edgar, who was as pale as the sand that buried him.

Albert fell on his knees and began brushing away the sand. "Edgar, thank God! How are you?"

"Hurts like hell," Edgar managed to grunt. He cursed as they got him up and carried him to the boat. There was a distant rumble of thunder as they deposited him on the leather bench along the back of the motorboat.

Lightning knifed into the water and impaled the islands behind Wyndwood; a wall of rain, like a charcoal curtain, drew ever closer. The wind was fierce and the water so choppy that Toby had to take several approaches to the front dock before finally being able to land. It would be easier to carry Edgar to the house from here than from the boathouse. Victoria and Zoë steadied the boat as best they could while Max and Jack supported Edgar when the men lifted him onto the dock. Phyllis's frantic cries pierced even the roar of the wind as she grabbed hold of him and nearly toppled them all over. Phoebe was holding herself and rocking back and forth as she shook with gasping sobs.

"Mama, I'll be alright," Edgar said, grimacing in pain as he tried to keep his good leg from buckling under her maternal assault.

"Run along and fetch some of your chloral, Phyllis," Albert ordered as he and James linked their hands to carry Edgar.

"I'll fetch Dr. Rumbold from Port Carling," Toby shouted above the wind. "I had Will fire up *Calypso*, just in case." The large and stable fifty-foot steam yacht had a glassed-in wheel-house and mid-section with a canopy over the rest, and was reliable in all kinds of weather. It should have had a chance to build up enough steam by now.

"Good man," Richard shouted back. "But take care."

Toby, already pulling away towards the boathouse, waved his hand in acknowledgement.

Richard helped to steady Edgar's injured right leg as the men carried him up the stone steps toward the house. Olivia put her arm around distraught Phoebe and said, "Hush now. Edgar will be fine. Your mother needs you to be strong, and you don't want to worry Edgar." As if stung by Olivia's touch, Phoebe suddenly jerked away and ran shrieking up to the house.

Henry was left standing on the dock with the blanket about his slumped shoulders, looking momentarily lost. Victoria grabbed his arm and steered him toward the house as a blinding flash of lightning was almost instantly followed by ear-splitting thunder which seemed to break open the liquid clouds. Phoebe, who was terrified of storms, screamed even louder as she bolted into the house. The rest of them, not far behind, got only slightly wet.

"Phoebe! You will stop this caterwauling or you will go to your room," Augusta ordered.

"He's angry," Phoebe shouted, ignoring Augusta's command. "I had evil thoughts. He will smite us. But I will stop him. I'll apologize for my impure thoughts. He always listens to me."

"Stop your jabbering, girl," Augusta said. "Go up to your room until you can pull yourself together."

"Go and pray," Albert said sternly to Phoebe, who walked away obediently. But before she reached the stairs another clap of thunder shook the cottage. As had been her habit, she dove under the grand piano, folded herself over her knees and wrapped her arms about her head, her face pressed to the floor. They all knew that she couldn't be touched or comforted until after the storm had passed.

"That child needs some backbone, Albert. She's not six anymore. Now what's all this?" Augusta demanded tetchily. She didn't like dramas at her time of life. What had the silly boys gone and done now? Surely no one was seriously hurt?

Edgar yelped as the men deposited him onto one of the sofas. Zoë plumped up the pillows behind him, and he lay back gratefully. Although he was damp and covered in sand, she draped him with one of the many thin quilts scattered about for cool evenings.

Phyllis bustled to his side and offered him a glass with the sedative, which he drank obediently.

"Now you must have some yourself, Phyllis," Albert suggested. "Libby, go and fetch the chloral from our bedside table, and a glass of water," he said when the two maids came into the room.

"You can shut all the doors," Augusta said to Molly. She shivered against the ferocious, intrusive wind that howled about the rafters and sent a fine spray of rain in through the screened French windows on the west side, whipping it sideways across the broad veranda which normally never got wet. Thrashing trees were bent nearly double under the lashings of the wind, as heavy black clouds roiled menacingly across the lake. "And turn on the lamps."

"I think some strong tea for everyone would be helpful. And bring a basin of hot water and towels, please," Olivia added, "so that we can make Edgar presentable."

"That is the least of our worries now!" Phyllis exploded. "Really, Olivia, you are heartless!"

"Don't carry on so, Phyllis. I was only trying to lighten the mood."

"This is NO time for jest! Edgar may be crippled. He may even lose his leg!"

"Really, Mother!" Edgar protested, blanching even more at that thought. "It won't come to that."

"The bone's not sticking out," Henry offered.

"Perhaps you will now oblige us by telling us what happened, Henry," Augusta said.

Max handed Henry a snifter of brandy, which he gratefully accepted, and Victoria led him to a chair.

"Edgar snagged his hook on something. He stood up in the boat and pulled with all his might. I was surprised that the line didn't snap. But suddenly a deadhead came shooting up out of the water. It must have been lodged under a rock or caught on something else. It slammed into the boat, which was already rocking as Edgar had lost his balance when the line suddenly came free, and knocked us overboard. It or the boat must have caught Edgar a sharp blow to the leg. I didn't see him at first. He may have been unconscious for a moment. But then I grabbed hold of him and pulled him to the overturned boat. We held on for a while. But no one came and Edgar was in pain and the waves were getting high and the churned up water is frigid.. So I grabbed him and swam us both to the island, which, thankfully, wasn't far away."

"And Henry cleverly decided to cover Edgar with sand to keep him warm, as I'm sure he was in shock, to say nothing about soaking wet," Richard added.

Victoria startled Henry as she threw her arms about his neck and declared, "Henry, you are a hero!" She rarely held grudges long, and had already forgiven him for tattling on her. After all, propriety was Henry's nature.

"Well done, old boy," Max agreed.

The others all added their praises, and Henry grinned suddenly.

Although she had taken the chloral that Libby had brought, Phyllis burst into fresh tears as she realized how close she had come to losing her sons. Albert patted her shoulder and said, "I think we should give thanks to God for sparing our boys. Calm down my dear while I pray."

They all bowed their heads as Albert said a brief but heartfelt prayer of thanks. While Henry's tale had been punctuated by thunder and constant flashes of lightning, a violent explosion suddenly shook the house, making everyone jump and look about anxiously. Still under the piano, Phoebe began screaming again.

"Good Lord!" James exclaimed. "That sounds like it hit something nearby."

The men rushed onto the veranda, with Victoria and Zoë close behind. Hissing and smouldering in the torrential rain, a massive split pine tree bowed its shaggy head into the water beside the dock.

"It's our big Jack Pine!" Max said. "It was one of the few old trees that Grandfather's lumbering business didn't cut down," he explained to Jack. "One of the very few trees left from the ancient forests."

"Which may well have saved the house, since it took the lightning strike," James said. "Well, you've certainly had an eventful introduction to life on Wyndwood," he said to Jack.

Back inside, Olivia said, "Henry, my dear, why don't you go and have a hot bath. You must be chilled to the bone. Phyllis and I will make Edgar comfortable, so the rest of you will give us some privacy. Max, kindly fetch some clothes for Edgar."

Augusta, shaken by the savagery of the storm and her grandsons' near escape, went to her room to rest. Her recent loss of Alexander made her feel vulnerable and fragile. Much as she constantly criticized her children and grandchildren, the thought of losing any more of them upset her more than she would ever admit. Her comments were, after all, designed to make them better people, not a sign of disaffection.

The men, mackintoshes and umbrellas at the ready, went out to the dry east veranda to keep a lookout for the doctor. They watched in awe the power and destructiveness of the storm. "I expect there'll be more trees down on the island," James said.

"I hope that this storm hasn't caught too many people out on the lake," Richard said. "I expect that a lot of the tourists are not used to canoes and sailboats at the best of times." But they all knew that there were bound to be some mishaps and perhaps tragedies this day.

Zoë coaxed a pale and quivering Phoebe out from under the piano, and the children, including Jack, went to the dining room. Victoria brought packs of cards and announced, "Let's teach Jack to play Racing Demons."

They all loved that wild and energetic game. Jack caught on quickly, and there was soon uproarious laughter and delighted shrieks that drowned out the fading thunder. Phoebe, calm enough to join in after the second round, became quite excited as the game progressed. They didn't hear Dr. Rumbold arrive, but would not have been allowed back into the sitting room in any case.

When Phyllis and Olivia had stripped off Edgar's wet clothes, they had seen the redness and swelling near his ankle. "Perhaps it is merely bruised," Olivia said reassuringly. She had applied cool cloths to reduce the swelling

Albert ushered in Dr. Rumbold, saying, "It was most kind of you to come out in this beastly weather."

"Not such a hardship in that yacht of yours. The boy, Will, even made me a cup of tea. Now let's have a look at the patient."

Dr. Rumbold was a thin, wizened man of indeterminate age – anywhere from a decrepit sixty to a sprightly eighty. His small winter practice to the few year-round residents of the area was amply augmented by busy summers on the lakes. Although sympathetic in sentiment, his handling was rather rough, so when he started to examine Edgar's leg, the boy howled, despite the tranquilizing effects of the narcotic.

Dr. Rumbold straightened up and said, "A simple fracture at the lower end of the tibia. I'll immobilize the leg and he should be back to normal in about eight weeks."

"But that's most of the summer!" Edgar moaned.

"You were lucky, lad. Looks like it could have been worse. Ladies, I require some water to make up the Plaster of Paris. He'll have to stay off the leg – absolutely no stairs – for at least four weeks, and then only minimal pressure on the leg for another few weeks. So no golf or tennis, eh?" he said with a chuckle. "Keep it elevated as much as possible, and best get yourself some crutches, lad. Then maybe you can still go dancing or enter the three-legged race." He chortled, amused by his own wit.

As he applied the cast, he asked how the accident had happened.

"One of yours then, was it? That deadhead?" he said when Albert had finished the tale.

The winter cuttings of logs were floated through the lakes to Gravenhurst, but not all the logs stayed in booms. Even in early summer there were log jams or congestion in the waterways, which made boating on the lakes not only difficult at times, but treacherous. The deadheads were the worst, since they were submerged and not expected or noticed in places that should have been free from obstacles. And the hardwoods were the most difficult to transport, since they tended not to float. The Wyndhams' planing, shingle, and hardwood mills at Gravenhurst alone exported more than twenty million feet of lumber per year, all of it still taken out of the Muskoka forests.

"Some of the other loggers are not as careful as our gangs and drivers are," Albert said.

"Ah well, a bit ironic, anyway. Give him some laudanum or chloral if the pain becomes too much. I expect it will take a few days for things to settle down."

"Thank you, doctor. May we offer you some tea or coffee?" Olivia asked, since Phyllis seemed numbed and stupefied by her sedative. "Or perhaps something stronger?"

"Wouldn't say no to a Scotch. Her Ladyship maintains a fine cellar, and it will help to keep out the chill. Downright cold it feels after this early heat wave we've had. A relief it will be though, for I've had quite a few, ladies especially, almost perishing with the heat."

"Do come through to the library," James offered, and the men went off with the doctor. Augusta thought him a rather common little man, and doctors, in general, much below her station, but her sons knew that they needed to keep the doctor happy in order to get good service.

"Well, we'll have to make some arrangements for Edgar to sleep down here," Olivia said to Phyllis who stared blankly back at her. Edgar had drifted off, and Phyllis threatened to topple over.

With a sigh of exasperation, Olivia went into the dining room and said to the children, "I need to muster some troops. Come along." They followed her into the sitting room, Phoebe staring at Edgar as if she was afraid he was dead.

"He'll be just fine," Olivia said. "His leg is broken, but will mend. Now, you'll want to get your mother settled down for a nap, Phoebe. Max, could you help Phoebe take Phyllis upstairs?"

"The rest of you need to get your thinking caps on. Edgar won't be able to manage stairs and must stay off his leg completely for a month. So where should he sleep?"

"In the library?" ten-year-old Rupert suggested.

"Perhaps, although I expect Grandmother wouldn't be best pleased."

"Could we screen off an area of the sitting room?" Esme asked.

"That might not offer Edgar enough privacy."

"What about the box room?" Victoria said. "It has a window, and we could move all the trunks to…." She was at a loss.

"My room," Jack said.

"Let's have a look," Olivia said.

They all trouped along with her. The box room, which was between the library and the loo, was a very large closet that contained the dozens of trunks and boxes in which they brought the entire family's supplies for the summer – clothes, hats, the silver, linens, staples, wines, and spirits. It also stored all the winter shutters for the house, extra chairs for parties and beds for visitors, and trunks of costumes and paraphernalia left here for balls and theatricals.

"It would certainly be large enough," Olivia said. "We couldn't move much before the storm stopped."

"We could move things onto the east veranda for now," Zoë said. "It's dry. We can all help."

The others agreed and Jack liked them all the better for it. They made no pretensions that this was servants' work and therefore beneath them.

"I'll talk to Albert," Olivia said, knowing that she could make no such arrangements for Edgar without his father's permission. Oh, to have her own cottage!

She knocked on the library door and walked in. The men were enjoying cigars as well as drinks. Now that the rain no longer pelted against the windows, they had opened one of them again, but the room was still thick with smoke. Dr. Rumbold looked most comfortable and quite content to stay for a while. Richard winked at her. "Excuse me, gentlemen. Albert, may I have a word? And Richard, if I could have your help?"

They followed her next door, where the others waited, explaining their idea. "Phyllis has gone to rest, as this seems to have been a bit overwhelming for her. So the children and I put our heads together and have come up with an idea for a bedroom for Edgar. There will be space enough once we have all this cleared out, and the children have offered to help. Edgar will have everything close to hand, and will certainly benefit from some privacy during his convalescence."

Although Albert did not seem either pleased or grateful, he was at a loss for another solution. "And where will all this go?"

"Above the boathouse. Jack doesn't mind sharing his space."

"You seem to have things in hand. As usual. Yes, by all means go ahead," he muttered ungraciously before he went back to the library.

Olivia was by no means upset by Albert's dig at her. He was undoubtedly as annoyed by Phyllis's lack of control as the fact the Olivia was making decisions for his family.

Richard put his arm about her waist and planted a swift kiss on her cheek. "Thank you, darling. And now I suppose you want me to pitch in as well?"

"The children and I do so love to spend time with you," she said with a grin. "All right, let's get started!" She rounded up some aprons – eight year old Miles insisting he needed one too — from the maids, who joined in after they had finished their other chores, as did Tom, the footman, who had been cleaning the silver in the butler's pantry across the hall.

Victoria noticed how Jack was quick to help them when he thought that she and Zoë were carrying too heavy trunks. "They can manage," Max said to him as he struggled with his own load. "They're strong as oxes."

"Oxen," Zoë corrected.

"And obviously smarter than me."

"'Than I'," Zoë corrected again. "The 'am' is understood after the 'I'."

"Are your sisters such a nuisance?" Max asked Jack.

"Oh yes," he replied.

Molly, who had been lifting a box behind Jack suddenly lost her balance and fell against him, almost knocking him over.

"Oh, I do beg your pardon, sir," she said in her soft, lilting Irish accent.

"No harm done," Jack replied, eyeing her carefully. "And are you alright?"

"Ah sure, sir. That I am," she replied, avoiding his gaze.

Victoria wondered if Molly was flustered by her handsome cousin. Although she had her dark hair pulled tightly away from her face and tucked under her mobcap, Molly was quite a pretty young woman, Victoria realized. Good bones and a flawless English complexion, as Grandmother would say. Well, she would have to make sure that the girl didn't get any ideas above her station. Jack may well have come from poor beginnings, but he was a real Wyndham now.

When they finished, the doctor had long gone and the storm had abated.

The men moved Edgar's bed, dresser, and wardrobe downstairs. While Olivia and the girls organized Edgar's clothes, Molly and Libby made up the bed and strung curtains.

'There! Doesn't that look splendid?" Olivia asked.

"Sure, but it looks like the room puked on the veranda," Rupert said.

While the others giggled, Olivia, hiding a grin, said, "Rupert, really! What language!"

Richard said, "I expect it will be difficult to dislodge Edgar from here once his leg heals. I think you should take some time to rest and freshen up before dinner, darling."

"Oh, do I look so bad?" she asked, her eyes twinkling as she gave herself a cursory once-over.

"Not at all – if you discount the smudge on your brow, and your skirt, and the cobwebs in your hair," Richard teased, as he pulled the latter from her dishevelled curls. "The boys and I can help Tom and Will move these boxes now that the rain has stopped. And you girls can go and fuss over Edgar. He is awake and, I think, thoroughly bored. When Toby took Dr. Rumbold back to Port Carling, he telephoned Pringle and asked him to buy crutches and send them by the next train. So I expect that Edgar will soon have some mobility." Pringle was Albert's butler, who looked after Albert's city house throughout the year.

Dinner that evening was a very fine roast of renowned Muskoka lamb with all the trimmings. Jack could hardly believe that he sat here at the gleaming table set with sterling silver, gold-crested china, and cut-crystal wine glasses in the witty and delightful company of his newfound family. Hothouse flowers shipped from Wyndholme on a regular basis decorated the table along with silver candelabra. The rain had begun again, the sky now so dark that it threatened never to stop, so the gentle candlelight was welcome. As was the warmth from the fragrant fires that burned in the fireplaces.

Max and Jack had offered their shoulders as crutches, and pretty well carried Edgar into the dining room. He was absolutely delighted with his new bedroom, which they showed him en route. They had placed him at the end of the table so that he could rest his cast on Reginald's vacant chair. Although he was still pale and obviously in pain, Edgar seemed to prefer joining the family to lying in the sitting room on his own.

Victoria had taken particular care with her appearance this evening, choosing one of her best informal muslin dresses. She felt excited at Jack's presence, which was reflected in her radiance as well as her animation. Augusta was shrewd enough to notice, and thought she may well have to trounce any flirtation between her impetuous granddaughter and charismatic grandson.

After dinner they returned to the sitting room, where coffee was served. Olivia was prevailed upon to play the piano. Her skill astounded Jack. "She's amazing," he said to Max.

"She studied at the Toronto Conservatory. She could have been a concert pianist, but, well..."

"Being a woman," Zoë cut in, "it wasn't an option for her. She was only expected to play to her guests. Once she married well, of course."

"Mama's not bitter about it, so why should you be?" Max challenged his twin.

"How do you know she doesn't have regrets?"

"Because if she were giving concerts all over the place, she wouldn't have had a chance to marry Papa and have us. And she loves us and Papa dearly."

"Your logic..."

"Is logical."

Zoë laughed. "I hope they can teach you something at university."

When Olivia had finished, she said, "Max, why don't you play and the girls can sing for us."

The four girls were obviously well practiced, for Jack thought they sang beautifully in harmony.

When they had finished, Max started to play *The Red Rose Rag*, but Augusta said, "That's enough of that, Max. I won't have that vulgar music played in my parlour."

"But Grandmother, ragtime is all the rage." And had been for years, he wanted to add.

"It's indecent."

Max switched to another tune. "Irving Berlin," he told Augusta. "*If I Had You*." He started singing, "'I never envied the rich millionaires, I never wanted to have what was theirs, I never bother about their affairs'..."

"Ridiculous," Augusta said. "If you won't play something sensible, we just won't have any more music from you, young man. Phoebe, I would like some Chopin, if you please."

"You are wicked," Zoë whispered with a suppressed grin to Max when he rejoined them. The young people were all sitting near Edgar. Augusta was warming herself by the fire at the other end of the room.

"Just trying to liven things up," he explained. "And prepare Grandmother for the new gramophone records I've brought for the party."

"Oh! We haven't told Jack about our Midsummer Night's Dream party," Zoë said, and turned to Jack to explain. "It's an annual event, and all the neighbours come and perform. Well, at least the younger ones do. It's very casual, and then we have a dance on the pavilion afterwards to celebrate the longest day of the year. Grandmother said it will have to be next Saturday instead, because Midsummer is Sunday, and of course, we can't have any theatricals or dancing then. I've written a play. There's a part for you, if you're willing."

Jack was apprehensive. Although he felt he could hold his own in social situations, acting was a different story altogether. His cousins had undoubtedly grown up staging plays, but he would be stiff and awkward.

Sensing his reluctance, Zoë said, "Oh, it's not long and you won't even have to say anything. It's mostly a pantomime. We've been working on the costumes, and will have our rehearsal next Saturday afternoon. There really isn't much to practice. You'll pick it up in no time."

"And if you don't participate in that," Max threatened, "then you'll have to do something else, like sing, or recite a poem. Zoë's play is a cake walk. The girls are going to sing as well, and I'm going to accompany them, so you'll be getting off easy. Henry's in the play, too, but maybe we can get him and, let's see — how about Vivian? — to demonstrate the Turkey Trot or the Bunny Hug."

"Those are just common and disgusting," Henry said of the modern dances. He turned suddenly and walked out, leaving his cousins bewildered.

Victoria followed him out onto the veranda, glad that she had a shawl to wrap about her shoulders.

"You're becoming very prickly, Henry," Victoria said as she joined him. "You've lost your sense of humour." What little there was of it, she thought.

"I've put away childish things. And childish attitudes."

"It's not childish to enjoy yourself. You're turning people against you – no one finds gloominess attractive, or congenial company."

"Don't bully me, Victoria!"

"I'm trying to help you, you oaf! I saw you smile today, and I realized I hadn't seen that for a very long time."

Henry pursed his lips and ran his fingers agitatedly through his hair.

"What are you so unhappy about?" she asked, putting her hand on his arm to reassure him of her support.

It seemed to be his undoing, for he blurted out, "Today, in the cold, black water, I didn't care if I survived! If it hadn't been for Edgar, I would have gratefully surrendered to the pull of the lake."

She was shocked by his words. "But why?"

"Because I hate what I do! I hate the business! I hate what I see of my future!"

"What would you rather do?"

"I don't really know. Study something." He shrugged. "Philosophy, theology, history? I don't want to deal with businessmen, with contracts and investments and accounts and employees."

Henry had attended the University of Toronto for one year, but had done so poorly in his economics classes that it hadn't been considered worthwhile sending him back. But Victoria could imagine him in a roomful of books, puttering away at his own quiet pace, perhaps spending his life writing a treatise on something esoteric.

"You should just tell them."

"Don't be so naïve, Victoria! Edgar has no aptitude at all for business and even less interest. Max, if he can ever stop being flippant, or the boys may, but if not, who's going to run the family empire? It's like being born to be king. I have no choice."

"Jack might be able to help."

"Oh yes! He has it all, hasn't he? Looks, charm, ambition, cunning. And probably talent."

"Instead of being jealous of him, you might consider making him an ally. If he were to do all the things in the business that you detest – while you still maintained control – he could allow you to pursue your own interests. Anyway, it will be years before our fathers give up control, so you should insist upon doing some things to please yourself. You can take part-time courses at the university, you know. You can even get a degree eventually, if you care about that. And for what it's worth, I would be willing to learn the business and help out."

He seemed to be about to say something snide, but looking carefully at Victoria, said instead, "I expect that you would do well."

"But because I'm a woman I'm not allowed, so I will also make the best of that limitation."

Henry took a cigarette out of his silver case, and Victoria said, "May I have one?"

He frowned as he said, "I don't approve of women smoking. It cheapens them."

"You shouldn't have double standards, Henry. I enjoy a gasper as much as you. That doesn't make me a fallen woman."

"Grandmother wouldn't approve."

"Then we shan't tell her." Victoria perched on the veranda railing, wrapping her right foot around her left knee in a very unladylike manner. She drew deeply on the cigarette and exhaled with evident pleasure and experience.

"So what do you want to do?" Henry asked her.

"Go down the Nile and up the Amazon. Ride a camel to the pyramids. Fly aeroplanes. Run an empire. I just don't want to be confined to a life of domestic concerns. I expect I won't make a good wife."

"A suffragette then."

"No, I don't have the political dedication. Not like Zoë. I don't want to change the world too much. Just enjoy it. Perhaps manipulate it."

They looked out over the sodden landscape growing ever darker and Victoria said, "But I certainly always want to come back here."

As she turned to go back inside, Henry put his hand on her arm and said., "Thank you, Victoria. I may heed your advice." He gave her a rusty smile, and her heart went out to him. Henry had never been easily lovable, but he had always seemed just and honourable. She hoped that he could find something that brought him joy.

Inside, Zoë asked her, "What was that all about?"

"Henry needs adventure. Or to find some romance," Victoria said with sudden conviction. Surely love, or at least a happy flirtation, would lighten his mood. "He's not very good at it on his own, so I think we should help him along."

"Egads! Plotting females are dangerous creatures," Max said to Jack. "Our dear cousin is not exactly Prince Charming, so who do you have in mind as your victim?" he asked the girls.

"Shh! Edgar will hear," Victoria cautioned.

"I know he likes Vivian," Zoë said.

"But she's a goddess," Max said. "Too classy for him. Anyway, isn't she potty about someone else?"

"How about that American woman at the Oakleys. Helena. One of the Boston Thorpes," Victoria said, imitating Letitia Oakley's drawl.

"Too old," Max said.

"Only by a couple of years. That makes no difference, if they suit."

"Well, she's no Cinderella either," Max said, falling into the game.

"Then perhaps you can give Henry a bit of a nudge, and we'll try to provide opportunities," Victoria said.

"And the whole thing will undoubtedly blow up in our faces," Zoë predicted.

# Chapter 5

Jack woke early, the uncurtained walls of windows allowing the dawn to seep into his room. His father's gold pocket watch, given to Alex by his parents on his twenty-first birthday, showed it was just past five. But Jack rose eagerly and gazed out at the gossamer mist that danced across the mirror-smooth water and sometimes shrouded nearby islands so that they seemed to be adrift on the lake.

He felt such joy at the sublime beauty of his surroundings and at his good fortune that he thought he would surely burst. His own magnificent room, on his family's island, on this wondrous lake – what an amazing beginning to his new life. And many of the family already seemed to accept him. When they had played cards and games last evening, he had felt a part of the group. There had been no awkward silences or stiff formalities. The younger children had been eager to regale him with tales of island life, as if he were a cherished cousin who rarely came to visit and so must be brought up to date on family lore.

How he longed to bring his sisters here! They would be embraced by their cousins and soon blossom. His mother might be an embarrassment, for seeing all this opulence would raise her bile which would spew forth and foul the beauty. But she would have no wish to come anyway, and Augusta would never allow her here.

But one day. He wanted his mother to know what his father had given up for her, why his soul had yearned so for this place. Not out of hate, but out of justice, did Jack want her to realize that she had been too harsh and unkind to her husband. Jack had been convinced that his father had gladly embraced death. It had been his only escape. And his mother had felt that her husband had yet again let her down by deserting her.

But he would not dwell on that while a glorious day beckoned. After the violence of yesterday's storm and the steady rain that had lulled him to sleep, this day promised to be perfect. Already the mist was thinning to reveal the first blush of sunrise. The cry of a loon echoed across the water, a haunting sound, like a disembodied soul in search of its mate. There was nothing like it to stir one's own soul.

All the transplanted boxes and trunks now piled along one side of the room served to screen this room from the main house.

The wide roof overhang and the railings along the veranda also gave some privacy. Jack dressed quickly and grabbed his towel, intent on having an early morning swim. But first he would climb to the top of the Dragon's Back to watch the sunrise.

As he went out into the fresh morning, he noticed smoke from Toby's chimney and from the kitchen wing, but saw no one. He climbed onto the path behind the boathouse, followed Max's instructions, and soon found himself at the top of a granite outcropping overlooking the point, with the cottage and outbuildings looking small through the treetops, and the lake beyond, immense. A multitude of shaggy islands awakened through the sun-tinged haze. It was a stunning vista. One he would be sure to paint. And one that he recognized from his father's attempts to recapture the lake.

Jack smoked a cigarette, lost in the beauty of the moment, not wanting to move in case it should all shatter, like some dream upon waking.

Realizing that an early morning coffee and biscuit could be enjoyed on the veranda, while he drank in the view from there, Jack finally decided to go for his swim. Wanting to be on the morning side of the island, he looked for another path that might lead him directly there, only to find himself at a cliff's edge, overlooking the Dragon's Claw. His foot dislodged some loose stones that tumbled down the sheer face. He hoped that no one was walking below, and thought that he should be sure the path was clear of debris so as not impede Augusta's walk, or even endanger her.

Because of the rugged rocks and increasingly dense shrubbery, Jack decided to backtrack and take the path that cut across the island at the gazebos. At the east one, there was a strip of sandy shoreline that was inviting. As no one was likely to be coming along here so early, Jack stripped naked and plunged into the water. After the initial cold shock, he welcomed the silky smoothness of the water. Still elated, he felt he could swim effortlessly to the distant islands, his strong, confident strokes claiming the lake as his own domain. He felt invincible, god-like, unstoppable.

So wrapped up was he in his joy that he didn't even notice the silent canoe approaching from the north.

Victoria was amused and slightly shocked to see Jack's bare buttocks skimming the surface. The sloshing of the water as she manoeuvred the paddle to slow down finally alerted him.

His momentary surprise gave way to a welcoming smile. "You're out early."

He seemed unabashed by his nakedness, and Victoria didn't avert her eyes as any modest and well-bred young woman should. It pleased her that this time the tables were turned and he was at her mercy. Although the water was clear and calm, the way the sunlight reflected from it prevented her from seeing into its depths. But Jack wouldn't know that.

Determined to keep him there, treading water, she said, "I love the mornings here. And Sundays I like to go out in the canoe before Grandmother rises. She doesn't approve of most activities on the Sabbath. We go to church in Port Carling after breakfast, and come back to our dinner at 1:00. Then it's quiet time on the veranda or in the sitting room. No cards, dancing, theatricals, golf, tennis. Only books that improve the mind or the soul are allowed to be read, nothing 'frivolous'. No ladies magazines, for instance. Swimming is permitted after tea, if we're not too 'rambunctious' or obviously enjoying ourselves. The servants go to the evening service, so we have a cold supper laid out for us. Afterwards we usually have some music but it has to be solemn, and of course, nothing modern. So Sundays can be rather a bore, but is usually saved by visits from neighbouring cottagers."

From Jack's viewpoint, the light hit the water so that it seemed completely transparent, making it appear as if the canoe were suspended in mid-air with Victoria a slightly dishevelled and still dripping Aphrodite emerging from the depths. With an exotic hair ornament.

"You have a dragonfly in your hair," he told her, and was surprised she didn't shriek.

She smiled, "Dragonflies seem to like me." There was another one fluttering about her, which landed on the hand she offered as a perch. "Especially these iridescent blue ones."

"You've been for a swim at your special bay," he said astutely.

"Yes. But you mustn't tell anyone, or they'll all want to go there as well."

"I don't think it's safe for you to be swimming on your own, especially so far from any help."

"You've been my cousin for only a day and already you're badgering me!"

"I'm just concerned about you."

"And you haven't been here long enough to know that I do what I please!"

He grinned. "Oh, I think I have. But now you may want to head back, as I intend to get out of the water."

"I recall making that request myself once. To an impertinent trespasser who wasn't about to oblige me," she shot back, challenging him with her forthright gaze.

"But I, dear cousin, won't hesitate to emerge from the lake, whether or not you choose to stay. Don't forget that I've swum at nudist beaches."

She thought his smile mocking, and wanted to prove him wrong. She would call his bluff.

Jack weighed the risk of shocking her so much that she would report him to Augusta — who may well decide he lacked good sense as well as morals and send him away — against showing Victoria that he was a man of his word and no pushover. He swam to the shore and walked out unashamed.

Victoria gasped at his boldness, but also at the sight of his firm body. She had never seen a man naked. She blushed with embarrassment and excitement at the power and magnetism of his maleness.

As Jack began to towel himself, he said, "Did no one ever tell you that it's rude to stare?" Although he had his back to her, her eyes seemed to burn his flesh, arousing him so that he wrapped the towel about himself before he turned to her. He wanted nothing more at that moment than to seduce her.

Not allowing herself to be goaded she replied, "I'm told that it's even more rude to expose yourself in public. Grandmother would be scandalized."

"Then we won't tell her that you watched."

She laughed, much to Jack's relief. "So, I shall expect to see a little less of you at breakfast," she quipped as she paddled away.

Jack admired her aplomb. She was no prissy miss given to tears and vapours. He couldn't imagine a dull moment in her company, and was already planning their married life as he walked back to the house, but not getting far beyond the bedroom at this point. At the Dragon's Claw, he remembered to clear away the loose stones that had fallen, realizing how treacherous they made the narrow path and wondering if Toby regularly kept it cleared for Augusta's walks.

As it was still early, Jack shaved alone and then fetched himself a coffee and a warm biscuit with a dollop of melting butter and plenty of blueberry jam from the sideboard in the dining room. These he took to the front veranda where he sat in a cushioned wicker chair and felt as if he owned the world.

Although his mother was a remarkably good cook, her mother having been one to a wealthy Montreal family, she had very limited scope for her talent on their meagre funds. In the one day that he had been here, Jack had eaten better than ever before in his life. Although the staff food at The Grand had been good and plentiful, it had not been of the gourmet calibre served to the guests or in this house. So he savoured every bite, and thought he would ask the cook, Mrs. Hadley, if he could send a bottle of her excellent jam to his family.

He had just finished his second helping when Olivia came out with her own coffee in hand. "Good morning, Jack. I'm so glad to find you on your own. Perhaps you would walk with me down to the front dock. I find mornings even more exquisite there."

"Do you always rise so early?" he asked as they walked down the stone steps and path to the wide dock that jutted out far enough for the large lake steamers. He had his reasons for asking.

"Oh yes. The summer days here are too beautiful to languish away in bed. It is my time for myself, before the children and the others are up and about. I like to come down here, sit on the edge of the dock, and dangle my feet in the water," she said, as she did just that, having walked down barefoot.

Removing his shoes and socks and rolling up his trousers, Jack sat down beside her.

"Isn't this glorious?" Olivia said, splashing her feet in the water. "I can't imagine a more beautiful spot on earth."

"I know now why my father loved it so."

"Did he talk about it?"

"Oh yes. As much as my mother would allow. She thought it wrong to dwell on the past. It made him melancholic. And yet, there was always this remembered happiness in his face. I wish he could have seen it once more." As if with the pang of opened wounds, Jack said, "In his last months he talked of bringing us all up here in the summer, to take a cruise on one of the big steamers, one that would take us past the island. Of course we didn't have the money." That was when they had been at their lowest, living in squalor in the Ward – Toronto's notorious slum. They'd had barely enough to eat, and that had been pigs' swill. "But he died in June, just as he said it was time to go 'home'."

Olivia put her warm hand on his and said, "I'm so sorry, Jack. I wish we could have spared you all that. We should have done more to stay in touch with Alex. Richard had told him to write, to let us know if ever he needed help. We gave him as much as we could afford to when he left, because he had little money of his own. We had one postcard from him, from Paris, and after that, not a word. We thought that he must have settled abroad, when we stopped to consider what had become of him. Why didn't he come to us?"

"He wrote to Grandmother when Grandfather died, asking permission to attend the funeral. She wrote back to say that her son Alex, lost to her, could only be restored to the family if he returned unencumbered by wife and family, whether legitimate or bastards. She added that her selfish son had broken his father's heart and surely contributed to his early demise, that Alex could expect nothing from his father's will nor from his family through any other means, at the present time or in the future. And that he was certainly not welcome to attend the funeral service. It was written so impersonally, as if by a lawyer. Maman said that was just what she had expected, and never wanted to be humiliated and treated so shabbily again. So he never tried to contact any of the family after that. Not even when he was dying. Although Maman finally did. She wrote it in Papa's name, saying only that his family needed help as he was ill and unable to provide adequately for them. I helped her to write it and signed his name. I know that it cost her much pride to do so. There was no reply – perhaps Grandmother recognized that it was not his handwriting – so Maman felt vindicated in her hatred of the family. But that didn't help us." They hadn't even had the money to bury him, so he had gone into a pauper's grave. Although from the time he was ten, Jack had worked every hour in the day and evening that he could, he had finally had to quit school then, at fourteen, and find full-time employment to keep his family fed. Eddie, too, had quit school and gone, much too young, to work in a factory.

"But we would have done anything to help! If only he and your mother had approached us instead of Augusta."

"Perhaps, because you had already given him money and he couldn't repay you, he felt he couldn't ask for more financial help. He was sensitive about that – owing money, repaying debts. And I think he was embarrassed by his failure. He had expected to become a renowned artist of whom Grandmother would have been proud, and would eventually have forgiven, admitting that she had been wrong all along."

"Then he didn't know his mother well enough," Olivia scoffed. Shaking her head she said, "How can we right such terrible wrongs? For so many it is too late. I find that infinitely sad. However," she added brightly, "we can change things now. Where is your family living?"

"On the lower floor of a small row house in Cabbage Town." Although it had no central heating and the walls were paper-thin, it had an inside lavatory and was a far cry from the tumbledown wooden shack in the Ward where his father had died. Cabbage Town was a working class area of the city where he had spent most of his childhood, some of their homes and landlords better than others.

"Richard and I have discussed this and are determined upon it. We wish to buy a house for you so that your family can live comfortably and with a sense of security. I'm sure that you will be able to   provide the necessary funds to keep the household running, but should that ever become an issue, we will be there to help. So I want you to consider where you think that house should be."

Jack was stunned. He had not expected such wholehearted, unbridled generosity after the years of neglect by the family. He couldn't help but curse his father just a little for his stubbornness in not contacting this obviously loving and caring brother, with his equally kind-hearted wife. "I'm overwhelmed. I never expected this!"

Olivia, realizing how deeply and genuinely he was moved, patted his hand and said, "It is only fair. We live well, but would not sleep well if we knew that our brother's family was in need. It is no hardship to share some of our good fortune. Indeed, it lightens the spirit! So tell me if you have any thoughts on the matter. But first, perhaps you would kindly bring me another cup of coffee — one spoon of sugar, and cream. And may I have one of your cigarettes? I rarely indulge, but I do so enjoy them." She knew that he needed a moment to compose himself. Poor lad! Thinking about the past made her incredibly angry, so she would think only of how to change things, not what could and should have been.

And she almost hoped that Augusta was looking out her window, which had a full view of the dock, to see her smoking. It was what young women did these days to rebel and to show their equality with men, but was still considered 'fast' by the older generation. Just what she needed to shake things up. Perhaps she should take to an after-dinner smoke, like Hannah Carlyle.

Augusta was indeed watching from the screened porch off her bedroom. Still dishabille, she was enjoying her early morning tea and toast, which Bayley, her lady's maid, always brought promptly at 7:30.

Augusta had not been pleased with Olivia's behaviour lately. Undoubtedly Olivia had been adversely influenced by Hannah

Carlyle, who was tastelessly *modern*, a vocal suffragist, and not of their class. Hannah was a pharmacist who had helped her physician father in his practice, and had continued to work even after her rather late marriage. Her husband, Thomas, was a professor of physics at the university. The family even verged on atheism, attending church only sporadically, and the professor spouting off about space as if he weren't taking about the heavens but something that need to be explored and explained. Every summer the Carlyles mounted their telescope on the upper veranda of their tiny cottage on Ouhu to seek answers in the stars. Utter nonsense! One of the vicissitudes of rustic cottage life was that one's neighbours were a mixed bag. Of course, one put up with them in the summers, for life here was rather more casual than in the city and one couldn't really ignore one's neighbours. But Augusta drew the line at mixing with them once they were back in Toronto.

But it seemed that Olivia and Hannah had become close friends, not only sitting on some of the same committees and volunteering for the same organizations, but often meeting socially. Something Augusta would have to discourage. Olivia was too easily impressed, and led astray by emotion and a misplaced social conscience. Take her work at the settlement house affiliated with the university, for instance. It was one thing to give money to the poor – who Augusta felt just squandered it on drink anyway – but to actually go and work among them was carrying social responsibility too far. God only knew what pestilence Olivia might pick up from them and bring into her own home! And they were mostly ignorant, non-British immigrants, to whom Olivia was teaching English, and everyone knew that this class of people invariably turned whatever once-respectable neighbourhoods they took over into teeming slums. As far as Augusta was concerned, the poor had only themselves to blame for their condition. With hard work and sound morals, a man could achieve anything. Just look at her Reginald, or men like Alexander Mackenzie and Henry Pellatt, both knighted – as Reginald would surely have been had he not died so young.

So Augusta could guess what it was that Olivia and Jack had been discussing so earnestly – his family. And no doubt Olivia would be doing something to undermine her orders not to interfere. She would have to come up with a way to keep a tighter rein on Olivia. And find out what it was that had just made Jack's step so light and chipper.

Jack was grateful for the time to gather his thoughts, to still the thrumming echoes of 'if onlys'. He bounded back to the dock, hardly spilling any of the coffee in the two cups. "I feel like an urchin in a candy store with a king's ransom in my fist," he said as he handed her a cup.

"High praise indeed for Mrs. Hadley's coffee," she quipped.

As he sat down again he said, "I had been thinking about what would be ideal. It's what I have been working towards. My mother is a very capable person – organized, thrifty, hard working, personable, when she chooses to be. And a good cook. I thought that it would suit her to run a boarding house. Perhaps for young women come to the city to work or to attend university. I had thought the Annex a good place."

It was an area just north of the University of Toronto, in a middle-class suburb of the city that had been annexed not that many years ago, and was where the Carlyles lived.

"That does sound ideal. We will have our solicitor scout out possible properties, and then you and Richard can go to the city some time – using the excuse of business – and make a decision. But you must keep this to yourself. Not a word to the others, not even my children, who may blurt things out, and especially not to Augusta. She expects you to earn your way into the family. We don't feel that is necessary, but are in no mind to argue the matter with her. Although she has no right to tell us what we can and can't do with our money, she may yet decide to punish us for 'disobedience'."

Jack knew that she was inferring disinheritance, and was even more astonished at their generosity.

Olivia said, "So let it be a *fait accompli*." And if Augusta wanted to contest that, she was in for a fight! "I will tell Zoë and Max in good time, for I know my daughter will not be happy until she sees some justice done to your family."

Thinking, earlier that morning, that he couldn't be happier, Jack now found it even harder to contain his joy. And his sense of triumph. It also augmented his confidence so that when he met dozens of neighbours and friends after the church service that morning, no one had any doubt that he was a Wyndham, born and bred.

"Your cousin is divine!" Lydia Carrington whispered to Victoria and Zoë.

"Mm, luscious," twenty-year-old Eleanor Carlyle agreed. The Carlyles had arrived at Ouhu Island late on Friday. "We'll certainly come over to visit this afternoon," she added meaningfully.

"So will we," Lydia said. "After all, it's only polite to see how poor Edgar is getting on, and cheer him up."

Henry had opted to stay with Edgar that morning to see to his needs. With the help of Augusta's walking stick and a shoulder for support, he could hobble to the lavatory or onto the veranda. They had left him in the hammock there, with Henry reading to him from the scriptures, at Phyllis's behest.

Augusta had not asked Jack about his religion, probably assuming that he was a good Anglican. But his mother was Catholic, and had raised her children in her faith, with no objection on Alex's part. Alex had rarely gone to his own church – and never, of course, to St. James' Cathedral, which the Wyndhams and the rest of Toronto society attended. Jack was not convinced that there was a God, at least not of the breed spoken of from pulpits, so he attended church only to please his devout mother and only when necessary. Jack could already see, however, that as a businessman and future pillar of society it would be important for him to be seen at the Anglican church.

. . .

The Carlyles were the first to arrive that afternoon. The professor was a favourite of the children, if not Augusta. As well as his wife, Hannah, and daughter, Eleanor, there was twenty-two-year-old Blake, sixteen-year-old Daphne, and thirteen-year-old Derek.

"Professor," Rupert said after the formal greetings, "have you found more stars? May we come and look through the sky watcher?"

"Oh yes, please," Esme added. The children were sometimes allowed to stay up late to scan the heavens through the professor's telescope. Those night outings were highlights of the summer for them.

"Of course," Thomas Carlyle said. "Whenever you please. Have you decided if you will come to study astrophysics at the university, and help us prove Albert Einstein's Special Theory of Relativity?" he asked them with mock seriousness.

"I should like that," ten-year-old Rupert said.

"You won't have time for such nonsense, young man," Augusta countered, not amused by the professor's teasing.

He, in turn, did not take offence, but did share a sympathetic look with Richard, who was forestalled from speaking by Olivia. She was quite fed up with her mother-in-law's rudeness and imperiousness. "Rupert shall be free to study whatever takes his fancy. We encourage our children to use their talents and interests to create happy and fulfilling lives for themselves."

Augusta, surprised by Olivia's attack, especially in the presence of guests, could only conclude that in the Carlyle's presence, Olivia was reduced to their code of conduct. But her hesitation in delivering a cutting reprimand gave Blake the opportunity to declare, "A sentiment that I should like to endorse wholeheartedly, except that my talents don't go far beyond playing tolerable tennis and outwitting the occasional fish."

"So says the man who just finished medical school and is going on to study psychiatry," Zoë said amid the laughter. Blake, a brilliant student throughout his schooling, had started his medical studies at seventeen.

"Well, one does need to earn a living, which neither tennis nor fish are bound to give me," he said.

"There are easier ways than dealing with lunatics," Max pointed out.

"But lunatics are endlessly fascinating," Blake explained. "Especially when one applies Dr. Sigmund Freud's analysis and methods."

"Isn't he the one who says everything comes down to sex, or the lack of?" Max said.

"That's quite enough, Max!" Augusta remonstrated.

Zoë quickly intervened. "Well, I know that you have to be very clever, and I applaud your sentiments in trying to help those poor souls."

Augusta thought the entire Carlyle family slightly mad, so did not wonder that like turned to like. Hannah Carlyle was very tall and slender and wore her ill-fitting department store clothes rather unflatteringly loose. Her reddish hair, with naturally tight curls, did not lend itself to a fashionably smooth upsweep, and stray strands corkscrewed around her face, which most would have called handsome. But to Augusta she just looked untidy and frumpy. The professor, though clean-shaven, also looked as if he had been carelessly thrown together. The three oldest children were all redheads, like their mother, and the youngest boy took after his father, with thin, wispy, mousy hair and an ascetic face.

"What about you, Ellie?" Max asked Eleanor.

"I shall be just a run-of-the-mill doctor," she replied.

"How was your second year at university?" Zoë asked eagerly.

"Fine, now that I'm accustomed to the puerile humour of some of the *boys*, who are still playing pranks on us. Many are not comfortable with the idea of having classes with women."

"Quite right," Augusta said. "It's not respectable for women to learn about, well, bodies and diseases and depravity."

Zoë said, "Women are expected to deal with sickness all the time, so we may as well be doctors rather than unpaid nurses. We are quite capable of learning the science."

"You modern girls!" Augusta snorted. "Why must you feel that you should or even can challenge men's domains?" Out of consideration for her guests, she didn't go on to say that professional careers, like doctors and lawyers, were not laudable occupations for anyone, let alone women. Only her solicitor, Ethan Nash, with his shrewd grasp of business and his humble manner, was neither a parasite nor a failure.

"Quite right, Grandmother. I intend to be idle, flirt with every handsome millionaire, and leave a trail of broken hearts throughout Europe," Victoria said wickedly.

"Piffle! Don't you mock me, young lady!"

"Times are changing," Victoria said. "Women who have the intellect and ambition can be what they like and may want more than to be an adjunct to a man. You yourself run an empire, so don't think that becoming a doctor or lawyer is any different."

"Business is different from trade and professions." Which, by Augusta's tone of voice, implied "more respectable". "And a woman's job is to run a household, which in my case included taking over your grandfather's financial interests. Of course, I have sage advice from Reginald's old friends, and I let the boys deal with the mills. Women have no place in the actual day-to-day operation of industry. Now how is it that you young people have managed to monopolize the conversation?" she said, casting blame in order to change the subject.

"Young people are our future, Mrs. Wyndham," the professor said, not addressing Augusta by the false but flattering title of 'Your Ladyship' or 'Milady' as so many, especially the lower orders, invariably did. It was another reason she didn't take to him. "We need to heed them."

"They demand too much attention and express themselves too freely for those who have but half-formed ideas and no experience of the world," she countered.

"I find that we can all learn much from their idealism and their uncluttered view of the world," he stated.

"I have no qualms about lady doctors, and would be most happy if Ellie were to tend to me," Edgar quipped. He was stretched out on the hammock in the bandshell corner, somewhat away from the mainstream of the conversation, and pain kept him from fully participating in or enjoying the company

"Of course. Poor darling," Eleanor said, going to his side. "But all that I can do at this point in my career is to offer you sympathy."

"I'll settle for that," he said with a grin.

Jack thought that Edgar rather fancied Eleanor, and could understand the allure. Despite being a bluestocking, she exuded an unconventional sexuality which hinted that she would not be averse to having an affair just to please herself, and to hell with what others might think. He had caught her examining him quite boldly, assessing him as a specimen of manhood rather than in a flirtatious manner. He found it slightly disconcerting, and yet stimulating. But Jack was not prepared to jeopardize his relationship with Victoria for a bit of a fling, no matter how tantalizing the creature. Not at this point.

"I'd even consider going to university just to be near you, my ministering angel," Edgar said, but only so that Eleanor could really hear.

Edgar, like so many young men of wealthy families, hadn't even tried to go to university, especially after Henry's failure, but had gone straight into the family business.

Eleanor boxed Edgar's shoulder. "You wouldn't like my beside manner," she bantered.

"Oh, but I would. And you'd like mine."

Eleanor laughed, not at all taken aback by his insinuation. She had heard far worse from male students. She was spared a reply as the Carringtons streamed boisterously onto the veranda.

Although still close to their industrial origins, the Carringtons were deemed acceptable friends by Augusta. Their wealth put them into the upper class economically, and their refined manners, socially. Although Augusta knew that Rena Carrington's father was merely a newspaperman and had been a popular mayor in the small town of Launston Mills, he had, nonetheless, made a modest success of a life begun in a log cabin. Not the calibre of her Reginald, but then few were. Edward Carrington had expanded his father's small woollen mill on the Grand River into an internationally successful business. So the Carringtons were readily welcomed by Augusta, and especially now that she no longer had only the unconventional Carlyles to entertain.

"Edgar, how thoughtless of you to injure yourself before the marathon and ball," Lydia said as the young people gravitated to Edgar's side. They perched themselves on the veranda railing and on chairs that had suddenly appeared thanks to Tom, the footman. "Now I shan't be able to dance with you."

"I shall practice with my crutches, so be prepared," Edgar said.

"You can start a new dance craze – the Broken Leg Shuffle," she retorted gleefully. "And soon everyone will want a cast on. Does it hurt very much?" she added with a frown of concern.

"It's beastly. But I'm being brave."

She laughed again. "So I suppose that your cousin will have to take your place in the race?"

Victoria felt unaccustomed pangs of jealousy at the flirtatious way Lydia was eyeing Jack, and was surprised at her proprietary feelings toward him.

"I've been told that I need to start practicing," Jack said, revelling in the obvious adulation of the girls.

"We haven't had the Cup for years," Max said disconsolately.

"So we girls will have to do our bit, Zoë, to restore the family honour," Victoria said. "Edgar can cheer us on."

"You've gone to great lengths to have an excuse to use the boat rather than swim, Edgar," Vivian said.

"And you will be glad of it when I have to fish you out halfway through the race," he replied.

"And how, pray tell, do you expect to do that? Jump into the lake with that anchor you have glued onto your leg?"

"Just mock me! I thought you came to cheer me up?"

"With our plans for tennis matches and canoe picnics?" Vivian asked.

"*Dragonfly* can whisk me to the picnics, but I'd prefer not to go to the Silly Isles." Edgar shuddered in remembrance of the previous day's events. He was easily prevailed upon to relate the incident, and gave a fair accounting, allowing a blushing Henry his moment of glory.

When everyone had accepted a frosty glass of lemonade from Molly, Blake said, "So, Jack, where have you been hiding all these years?"

The question was asked innocently enough, but rang out on a suddenly quite veranda, so that almost everyone except the Carlyles seemed to be holding their breaths. Of course the

Carringtons knew some of the story, but Victoria, obeying Augusta's wishes, had asked them not to say anything when she and Zoë had visited again last week.

Having anticipated this would eventually happen, Jack replied easily enough. "My father, who was the youngest son, left to follow his dreams, and embarked on a rather Bohemian life, which estranged him from the family. He's been dead for several years, and I thought it was time to acquaint myself with my family." Said so simply and sincerely without casting blame on anyone, his explanation not only seemed reasonable, but earned him gratitude and respect from those who knew the truth.

"We're so happy that Jack has come to stay with us for the summer," Olivia announced, proud of Jack and wanting to ensure that he wouldn't be sent away on a whim from Augusta. It would be harder to dismiss Jack now that their friends knew of the supposed plan. Olivia didn't miss Augusta's searing look, but just smiled and said, "And Jack's three sisters will undoubtedly come for a visit some time as well. Now do tell me, Rena, about your trip to Europe. I envy our girls the opportunity they will have under cousin Beatrice's guidance."

As the adults once more became absorbed in their own conversations, Eleanor Carlyle asked Jack, "Bohemian as in artist-living-in-a-garret?"

Jack laughed. "Yes, I suppose you could say that. But he was never a great painter."

"So you must have had an interesting life." Which seemed to pique Eleanor's fascination.

"Certainly different. Although I must say that Wyndwood is eminently preferable to a garret."

Justin Carrington had to admit a grudging admiration for Jack, although his initial and instinctive reaction to the man was that his charm was calculated and he couldn't be trusted. Perhaps it was because all the girls seemed enthralled by him, even Vivian, who he knew was madly in love with someone else. Well, it might do his elder sister good to take her mind off a hopeless love affair. It might give her a chance to realize that Blake Carlyle, who had loved her for years, was by far the best man.

"We have more company," Victoria said. "Looks like Letitia Oakley and her guest. In a canoe!" Victoria said. "Henry, do run down to help them."

They all looked out to see two ladies, barely identifiable beneath enormous hats that were gaily plumed and beribboned. Letitia waved. She had long ago asked them to call her by her first

name, probably because "Mrs. Oakley" made her feel too old among
the smart young set.

"It will be interesting to see them getting out," Victoria said.
"Do hurry, Henry, before they fall into the water."

"Why should I go?" he asked.

"Because Tom seems to be occupied elsewhere, and someone
should help them, and you're the eldest." The excuse sounded lame
even to her, but she had to throw Henry and Helena together
somehow.

But James had already noticed them and hurried down to the
steamer dock, with Henry following rather hesitantly.

"Letitia, Miss Parker, what a pleasure," James said.

"Oswald and Thaddeus are bringing the children, because I've
been teaching Helena to canoe. Be a dear, James, and give us a
hand getting out. I haven't yet mastered the art of disembarking a
canoe gracefully. I'm as likely as not to flip us over!" She laughed
delightedly.

Helena looked slightly alarmed, and seemed relieved as
James steadied her so that she could manoeuvre onto the edge of
the dock, where he then helped her to her feet. Henry held the
canoe to keep it from rocking too much, so he also earned a warm
smile.

When both women were safely on the dock, Letitia said, "My,
that is a major feat. I think that's enough of a lesson for today,
don't you, Helena? We'll tow the canoe back behind the boat." She
put her arm through James's and ambled up the path with him.

Henry and Helena fell in together behind them and Henry,
striving to make conversation, managed, "How did you like
canoeing, Miss Parker?"

"She's a natural," Letitia threw the comment over her
shoulder, seeming to have the uncanny ability to participate in two
conversations at once.

Helena suppressed a grin and said, "I think I would like it
just fine if I were dressed in something a little more forgiving than
a tea gown. And a smaller hat perhaps?" She seemed to be mocking
herself.

"Quite right, Helena. Goodness me, but these narrow skirts
are really not suitable for canoeing," Letitia was saying as they
reached the veranda.

Olivia had always thought that Letitia was too much of a
fashion plate, Oswald taking her to Paris nearly every spring to
have a new wardrobe created. So she said, "The hobble skirt was
certainly not designed to be practical."

"Oh, but Monsieur Poiret's fashions are the latest word," Letitia declared.

"Monsieur Poiret wasn't thinking of women paddling canoes," Olivia pointed out.

"Then someone should design clothes for us sporting women," Letitia declared.

The idea of Letitia being a "sporting woman" almost made Olivia burst into laughter, but she contained it with a smile.

"Will you and Miss Parker be entering the canoe race at the regatta?" Hannah Carlyle asked Letitia after the introductions had been made.

"Good Lord, I shouldn't think so," Letitia said. "That's for young people. Helena and Louise may wish to try."

"Why, that's August, isn't it? I don't expect Dad and I will be here. We can't possibly impose upon Letitia and Oswald that long," Helena protested.

"Nonsense! I'm quite determined that you shall stay. If your father has to leave for business, then so be it. He can fetch you from Pittsburgh in September."

Rena Carrington asked, "Do you not have any other family, Miss Parker? Brothers and sisters?"

Helena looked down into her lap as if to compose herself and then said, "I had a brother. Edwin. He was on the *Titanic*."

There were gasps of horror and expressions of sympathy, the sinking of that "unsinkable" modern ship only two years earlier still fresh in people's memories. It was also a stark reminder of the *Empress of Ireland*, which sank just a few weeks ago in the St. Lawrence River.

"Oh, how ghastly for you, my dear!" Rena said. "I am most dreadfully sorry."

Helena nodded, as if not trusting herself to speak. So Letitia did it for her. "And poor Thaddeus lost not only his son, but much of his fortune as well, can you believe it? Edwin had been in Europe on business for his father, buying diamonds and other precious stones. They were also lost, of course. Helena's mother had been poorly for years, but the loss of her beloved son finally broke her spirit, and she, too, was lost. So Helena and Thaddeus have had a frightfully bad time of things these last years."

And been very careless to lose so much, Victoria thought, amused by Letitia's choice of words. Of course it was a tragic tale, so she chided herself for her flippant thoughts. And wondered if Henry was moved by it. Perhaps because she was petite and demure, Helena seemed somehow vulnerable and fragile – the kind of woman that men and motherly women wanted to protect and please. Helena might indeed bring Henry out of his funk.

She was saying, "We are so grateful to the Oakleys for being such good and kind friends. And having a chance to be here is just too delightful. I'm awed by the beauty of it all. It's so... healing. I can't imagine anything more wonderful than being able to be here every summer. You must all so look forward to that." Her face glowed with pleasure, and the sombre mood was lightened.

"Helena was even impressed by the storm yesterday," Letitia said. "But I surely thought it was a hurricane! Do you know, it knocked a big tree down right across our bowling green. It'll take the groundsmen days just to cut it up and haul it away. Oh look, here comes Oswald."

Tom had noticed and was already hurrying down to the dock to help. Oswald took pleasure in driving his own motorboats, but was not very experienced at docking yet. He drifted too far out, but Tom managed to catch the rope that Thaddeus tossed him, and pulled the thirty-six foot Ditchburn launch alongside the dock, dwarfing the Carlyle's rowboat in front. Letitia's canoe and the Carringtons' Minett motorboat were tied up on the opposite side, leaving the end of the dock free.

"See you had a tree come down as well," Oswald said as he, the children, and Thaddeus joined them. "Had to go over to The Grand to make a telephone call. And take the children to the ice cream parlour," he added with a fond smile at his offspring. "Heard that several of their guests were caught on the lake when the storm hit. They sent their motorboats and steamers out to bring them back, and, although no one was seriously hurt, there were a few shaken people. But they said guests at the Westwind Inn weren't so lucky. Two young women in a canoe."

"How tragic!" Hannah Carlyle said. "I think that too many tourists are inexperienced with watercraft and some can't even swim. And imagine falling into the water with heavy or restrictive clothing and not having life vests to hand. Even a strong swimmer would have difficulty staying afloat."

The point hit home with Helena who blanched and said, "I can't swim. We always holidayed by the seaside, but I never fancied invading the territory of all those sea creatures, who I've heard can sting and bite."

"There's nothing to harm you in our lake," Victoria said. "We can teach you to swim, if you'd like to learn."

"Yes, do, my dear," Letitia said. "I'm not a strong swimmer, so Oswald taught the children."

"Come tomorrow afternoon, if the weather is suitable," Victoria suggested.

"We'll put one of the boats and boatmen at your disposal," Letitia said to Helena. "Now let's all plan a big picnic. My treat!"

Letitia's picnics were lavish and seemed to require about half her staff, but were always an event that no one wanted to miss. The Wyndhams own picnics were comparatively simple affairs with hampers of sandwiches which were enjoyed right from their waxed paper wrappings, not served on china and eaten with silverware. It was settled that they would await Lady Beatrice Kirkland's arrival later that week.

"Beatrice will be pleased," Augusta said. "She was last here eighteen years ago, and was surprised then that we managed to live so well in the wilderness. She'll be astonished at how civilized we've become, especially with The Grand at our disposal. Beatrice is an avid golfer."

"Of course it will be even better when we get the Golf and Country Club going," James said. They all belonged to the Summer Residents' Association, which not only ran regattas to encourage water sports, but more importantly, concerned itself with preserving the beauty, character, and integrity of the lakes. Several years ago, the SRA had pushed to force the Muskoka Steamship Line to stop dumping raw sewage into the lakes from their steamers, and encouraged residents to install septic systems or ensure that outhouses were properly managed and maintained. With Oswald currently at its helm and James as Past President, the SRA had bought a marginal farm on the mainland, within sight of Wyndwood and not far from the Stepping Stones, in order to build a clubhouse with billiard and ballrooms, tennis courts, and a golf course. Construction was well under way, so this would probably be the last summer that the SRA's popular Annual Regatta would be held at The Grand.

A lavish tea appeared with little sandwiches, cakes, and the inevitable tea biscuits served with fresh strawberries and cream. As soon as they had had their fill, Rupert and Miles asked if they and the two Oakley boys, Roger and George, could go to play at the pavilion. The boys were much of an age, and always enjoyed getting together.

"As long as Esme and Louise tag along," Olivia said, not completely trusting ten and eight-year-olds to play wisely.

"We'll come, too," Daphne Carlyle said, dragging her brother Derek along after a subtle nod from their mother.

Phyllis motioned to Phoebe to join them, and she shuffled along, disgruntled.

They heard the blast from one of the large steamers and watched as the elegant *Medora* pulled up to the front dock. Tom was there to greet it. A parcel was passed to him and the ship glided away with a farewell toot.

"My crutches!" Edgar said, when Tom handed him the parcel. "Help me up," he said to Henry and Max. Much to Victoria's disappointment, Henry had drifted back to their section of the veranda, instead of staying near Helena. He seemed much more interested in Vivian than Helena, so he would be doomed to disappointment.

Blake helped to adjust the crutches and supervised Edgar's attempts to use them. Edgar stumbled about on the west veranda for a while, then went into the sitting room and collapsed onto a sofa, his entourage following him. "Enough for now," Edgar said, looking pale and drawn.

"Is it throbbing?" Eleanor asked.

"What?" Edgar asked with a suggestive grin.

"Your leg, oaf!" Turning to her brother she said, "I think Edgar can be one of your first patients for psychoanalysis. He seems to have a fixation on sex."

"Maybe he's already gone mad from indulging in the 'solitary vice'," Blake said. "They say that up to half of those in asylums do. It'll be blindness next."

"Look at his pallor," Eleanor said to Blake. "And he tires easily. He must be in decline. Do you have headaches? Heart palpitations?"

"I don't...! You're kidding me, right?" Edgar said, looking worried.

Brother and sister burst out laughing, and the others joined in more tentatively.

"Isn't it true, then, what they say in those books?" Max asked.

"You mean the Self and Sex books?" Blake said. "*What a Young Man Ought to Know. What a Young Husband Ought to Know*. And so forth. All saying more or less the same thing – the evils of masturbation and excessive intercourse, even with your wife, cause the depletion of the life force, leading to the shrinking of the intellect, eventual insanity, and even death. Hogwash!"

The girls tittered at Blake's candid vocabulary.

"I don't think that this is suitable conversation for the present company," Henry reprimanded.

"Well that's precisely the problem, don't you see?" Blake said. "People not wanting to talk about sex, or be honest about it. It's sexual repression that causes neuroses, not over-indulgence."

"I take it that's Dr. Freud speaking?" Justin Carrington said.

"Yes, and he has case studies to back up his claims."

"So what does he advocate? Free love?" Edgar asked hopefully.

"Not promiscuity. But also not guilt for having natural feelings and desires. More openness. Taking enjoyment and fulfilment from sex. Accepting it as a wholesome and healthy part of life."

"Hot dog! So get married young and have an active sex life," Edgar said. "Sounds good to me. How about it, Ellie?"

Eleanor laughed. "Not on your life!"

Edgar feigned a broken heart by crossing his hands over his chest. "You're so cruel!"

"No, darling. Just honest."

Jack was enjoying the difference between this unconventional conversation and the one he usually heard about sex, which was men bragging about their conquests or complaining that the wife was about to drop yet another brat and where would the money come from to feed it. The streets taught you young about the realities of life and sex, and few there worried about depleting their energy and much more about how to prevent another pregnancy. Abstinence wasn't a consideration.

The thought struck him that his own encounters with women gave him a distinct advantage over these probably inexperienced young men who needed books to tell them what's what. Written by preachers no doubt.

He knew how to make a woman feel good. There was nothing like having a whore instructing him. Of course he hadn't paid. She had been a neighbour, a former mistress to a banker until he had tired of her. But she had done well enough out of him, had managed to buy herself a house and run a discreet brothel. She had liked the look of Jack, and he had run a few errands for her in appreciation.

Looking at all the pretty young women in the room, Jack thought he wouldn't mind introducing any of them to the delights of sex. Perhaps his pick of useful women wasn't just limited to family.

He wondered if the Carringtons were as wealthy as the Wyndhams.

# Chapter 6

"I'd like to see you in the library, Jack," Augusta said after breakfast the next morning. She had gone to her room after tea yesterday, as was her wont, to spend the rest of the day relaxing on her chaise lounge, taking her supper on a tray. Jack had thought it unfortunate that despite her absence, the mood had still been dictated by her restrictions on games and music. The young people had gone out to the veranda to smoke and make plans for the week, all retiring early. Max had offered to teach Jack to sail today.

"You seem to have charmed some of the family and our friends," Augusta said when they had seated themselves.

"Some of them have made me very welcome."

"Like Olivia. What has she promised you?"

Jack realized that Augusta must have seen them on the dock, and that to prevaricate would just make the old lady more suspicious. He met her sharp gaze without flinching as he said, "She has concerns about my family. She is going to help my mother secure a better paying position so that she can become more self sufficient." Which wasn't a lie. "With what I hope to earn, my family could move into a more respectable neighbourhood."

As he had hoped, Augusta was distracted by his last statement. She chortled. "And what do you hope to earn? I certainly don't recall mentioning a salary as yet."

"But surely you can't expect me to give up a job, at your pleasure, and not compensate me? I expected that during my training this summer, I would receive at least what I would have at the hotel, otherwise my mother *will* be out in the street."

"I applaud your loyalty, much as I might dislike the object of it. Well, if that is the extent of Olivia's interference, I will ignore it for now. It is preferable that your mother fend for herself, rather than rely upon you for support, especially when it will be my money that you send her." Which rankled more than she could say. She wouldn't go beyond a fleeting and painful thought that if she had sent money years ago, then Alexander might still be alive.

"As for a salary... I think $300 for the summer is generous. And I'll pay your tailor's bills for now. Once – *if* – you work for us, things will be different, although I suspect that your salary would be better than any you've had so far." She wrote out a bank cheque and handed it to him.

"Thank you, Grandmother. I am truly grateful. Now may I make one more request of you?"

She gave him a look that warned he had already had more concessions than were warranted.

"I would like to paint your portrait. Would you sit for me?"

Taken aback by this unexpected change of subject, she chuckled. "Think you have talent, do you? I already have a portrait that Reginald commissioned, by John Singer Sargent. You've no doubt heard of him?"

"Of course! But my idea wasn't for a formal oil painting, but a watercolour. I envision you on the veranda, looking out into the distance. I promise not to impose upon you too long."

"I suppose I could manage a bit of time to sit still and reflect."

"Thank you."

"And now I am off for my daily constitutional."

"Would you like me to accompany you?"

"No. I prefer to go on my own." Not only because it gave her time to herself, but also because she didn't want anyone to know how often she needed to stop to rest. "I've asked the boys to spend some time with you every morning to begin teaching you the rudiments of business. I think Richard is starting you off today with some accounting. Stay here and I will send him in."

Olivia slipped in with Richard and said, "Augusta just made a cryptic comment that she hoped I knew when to stop interfering. Do you know what she meant?"

Jack could remember his conversation with Augusta verbatim, and told her.

"Thank you for not lying," Olivia said. "And yet for not being too forthcoming. I really do resent not being able to speak or act freely. And Augusta is becoming more autocratic as she ages. Perhaps it is her attempt to control her life, as her physical frailty becomes more apparent."

"It worries us that she does have so much control over the finances," Richard said, "and that she relies so heavily on the advice of Father's old friends, like Mackenzie and Thornton. Some of the investments are even a bit dodgy, 'privileged' information and... Well, here, let me show you what I mean."

Not wanting to hear about stocks, bonds, debentures, equities, and securities, Olivia left them to it. By lunch time, Jack already had a much better grasp of stock dealing, something which had intrigued and excited him ever since he had heard mèn speak of it in the Four Seasons Club. For the past couple of years, he had been "investing" fictional money and checking the stock market reports regularly. He usually chose well, and would have doubled his money by now, had he any to invest. And that was precisely what he intended to do with the cheque that seemed to burn in his pocket, once he got to the city. Some of the $500 that James had promised him would go to his family, but the rest he would invest as well, for he knew that he would never get rich by saving money.

"I just realized that I won't be able to go to The Grand tonight," Edgar said as he tucked into his lunch. "Too many stairs there." For The Grand sat atop a bluff, accessed by numerous stairs from the wharf or a long, if gentle, slope that would tax him on the crutches, since he wasn't to put any weight on his leg yet.

"Oh, dear! The servants have already gone. We'll have to find you something to eat," Phyllis said.

"I'll stay to keep Edgar company," Jack offered. "I'd feel rather awkward dining at The Grand without the appropriate attire."

"Edgar doesn't need any help now that he has crutches," Phyllis said quickly, obviously not wanting her precious son left alone with Jack. Most of the staff would be away on their half-day off.

"I say, that would be good of you, Jack," Edgar declared. "We could have a game of chess."

"You could teach me," Jack said. He looked at Augusta as Phyllis was gathering her thoughts to launch another protest.

"Very thoughtful of you, Jack," Augusta said. "Yes, we do need to outfit you properly. It wouldn't do for you to show up looking like a poor relation, would it?" She chuckled. He was certainly clever, she thought with admiration. Go back in style or not at all. "Now, where shall we go for tea today?" Since the servants were off for the rest of the day, Mondays were Augusta's visiting days, so that she could get afternoon tea. Sometimes they went to The Grand to golf, and had tea there as well as returning later for dinner.

"When we were out canoeing around the island this morning, Zoë and I noticed that the Thorntons are here," Victoria said.

Joseph Davenport Thornton – known to everyone as J.D. – was one of the most affluent and influential financiers in the country. Already a financial whiz in his twenties, he had become a friend and advisor to Reginald. On one of his visits to Wyndwood, he had decided to purchase his own island close by. J.D. was one of Augusta's favourite people.

"How lovely," she said.

After lunch, Zoë asked to speak to Augusta in the library.

Although the servants were off duty, one of them was always required to stay around for security reasons, since the cottage was never locked. Although not her turn, Molly had pleaded a headache and chosen to stay behind from the excursion to the Pinegrove Lodge. It was a modest hostelry with lots of activities – the young people particularly enjoyed the roller skating rink – and reasonable food. Mrs. Hadley and Prudence Bayley just enjoyed the freedom to sit in the shade sipping tea, and later indulge in a hearty meal prepared by someone else. Because of his diminished duties in the winter, Toby was the only one who never had official time off in the summer – not that he minded, for he liked to keep busy. He had run the rest of the staff over to Pinegrove and would fetch them before bringing the family back from The Grand later that evening.

Molly, broom in hand, was on the west veranda, but made no pretence of actually sweeping it. She could hear every word between Augusta and Zoë through the open French windows.

"Grandmother, I know that you don't wish to discuss this, but please hear me out," Zoë said when Augusta started to purse her lips. "We must do something to help Jack's family. I can't in all conscience enjoy myself when I know that members of the family may be in want."

"You're too soft and naive, my dear Zoë. Jack is certainly enjoying himself. I doubt that his family is starving in the streets."

"But they have so little and we have so much."

"All well earned, I assure you."

Off the backs of workers who barely make a living wage, Zoë wanted to say. "You tell us that philanthropy is an obligation of our position in society. We give huge sums to endow university chairs and cultural buildings. Surely charity begins at home, by looking after one's own. That would require only a fraction of what you regularly donate. Surely charity is not just done for the sake of show." Although Zoë felt that was certainly a large consideration. Having a building or scholarship named after you gave you prestige and a type of immortality. It also let everyone know that you were wealthy and noble enough to spread your good fortune.

"It is vulgar to discuss money," Augusta said dismissively. She had no intention of telling Zoë about her arrangement with Jack, since it was none of the girl's business. She needed to learn not to interfere, like her mother was wont to do.

"And even more vulgar, or dare I say, appalling, for a child to die a horrific death by being crushed in a machine because he must work scandalously long hours in order to eat, and because the wealthy factory owners didn't put proper safeguards into place. Owners who have sat at your table, Grandmother. That's what happened to your grandson, Edward."

Augusta was waving her arms as if to fend off the words, but Zoë didn't stop.

"And you have two granddaughters who died but three more still living, Elizabeth, Emily, and Claire Wyndham. They are as much your blood as I and Victoria and the rest. You like Jack. Why would they be any less likeable? Why are they any less deserving of your affection and support?"

"Enough! I will not be berated by a chit of a girl!"

"Grandmother, I have no wish to criticize you, but do you think it fair to punish his children because Alexander disappointed and defied you?"

"I said, enough!"

"I'm afraid that is not a good enough answer," Zoë said boldly.

"Do NOT be impertinent with me, young lady!"

"Grandmother, please, at least assure me that you will leave them some bequest to keep them from penury, from an evil life of subjugation."

"I owe you no explanations and I certainly will not tell you the contents of my will. The unmitigated cheek!"

"May I make a request then? If you were planning to leave anything at all to me, would you leave it instead to Elizabeth, Emily, and Claire?" Zoë could, of course, just give them any money she might inherit, but she wanted to keep pressing upon Augusta that these girls were not some ephemeral idea, but living, sentient people. "Otherwise Elizabeth will be forever someone's skivvy. Emily will ruin her eyesight and health working in a sweatshop. And Claire may never realize her ambitions to be a teacher. They have already inherited something from you and grandfather. They may even resemble you. Don't you think you owe them more than indifference?"

Looking almost apoplectic, Augusta said, "I may well decide to leave you nothing at all, after your inconsiderate display of rudeness!"

"I'm sorry that you consider voicing one's opinions and caring about family as bad manners. If your affection is so easily lost, then so be it." Zoë turned to leave.

Augusta was startled by this quietly spoken indictment. "I have not yet dismissed you, Zoë." She composed herself while Zoë turned back and stood patiently before her. Augusta was almost afraid of her granddaughter's quiet tenacity and determination, and the disappointment in her eyes. Disappointment not at failure, but at her grandmother. It was a novel experience for Augusta to realize that she wasn't living up to someone's expectations. "I have given Jack a sum of money to compensate him for his lack of employment this summer. As for inheritance, I have left each of my grandchildren a small legacy. Enough to provide a little independence but not enough to ruin the character. Since I haven't specified any names, I realize now that Jack and his sisters also qualify. Unless I change my will."

"On no, please don't! Oh thank you, Grandmother! Surely the greatest legacy you can leave the world is grandchildren of whom you can be proud."

"I do hope so, although I sometimes despair of that. But I do approve of your strength of character, Zoë. It will stand you in good stead. As long as it is not misdirected. Now you will no longer pester me about Jack's family," she stated dismissively.

"Only to ask if they may not have their legacy from you now, rather than waiting?"

"They may not. Jack will see to their welfare in the meantime. And you will not wish your grandmother an early demise."

"Of course not!" Zoë said, rushing up to give Augusta a quick hug.

Augusta was not one for displays of affection, and said, "Get along with you then!" although she was pleased by the sentiment.

Molly, the unnecessary sweeping not done, went quickly off to remove the food from the sideboard in the dining room, and the dishes, to the scullery.

⁕

Wanting to avoid Phyllis, Olivia had escaped to her room after lunch, picked up her novel, and gone out onto her balcony. But the book lay unopened beside her as she gazed out over the treetops.

That was how Zoë found her a while later. Coming onto the adjoining balcony from the girls' bedroom, Zoë said, "You seem lost in thought." She perched herself on the low wall between them.

"I was thinking how lovely it would be to have our own cottage. Something small and cozy. More like the Carlyles' place." Which they could see from here.

"Why do we always have to do what Grandmother wants?" Zoë asked. "Surely you and Papa are old enough to make your own decisions."

Olivia laughed ruefully. "More than old enough, I should think! Augusta likes to have control."

"And we allow her to because she's old?"

"Because she still controls the purse strings."

"We wouldn't be poor, like Jack's family. Surely Papa has made investments that have given us some measure of wealth."

"Indeed he has. But after working in the family business for twenty-five years, he's not about to lose our share of the inheritance for want of a few more years of concurring with her wishes."

"Subservience, you mean. But do we need that much?"

Olivia smiled. "It will ensure that you children have secure futures. And the money can be put to good use elsewhere. There are many charities that are close to my heart, as you know. Oh, and I must tell you! We are buying a house for Jack and his family, but, of course, you must say nothing to anyone, not even Max and Victoria as yet, or Augusta is bound to hear." Olivia went on to tell Zoë about the plan.

"That is wonderful, Mama! And what a perfect idea that Jack's mother should run a boarding house for students." She mentioned the conversation she had just had with Augusta.

"I am glad that she's left them something in her will, even if it is inadvertent. Well done! I expect it wasn't easy to extract that information from your grandmother." Olivia regarded her daughter with deep admiration and affection.

"Mama, you know how yesterday you said that your children should be free to use our talents to create fulfilling lives for ourselves?"

"Yes." Olivia knew what was coming.

"Why must Max go to university, when he doesn't really care at all, and I'm not allowed to, when it is what I want more than anything in the world?"

"Max still needs to grow up a bit, before he starts to work in the family business. We hope that the university will give him a good balance of exercising his mind, body, and social skills. Augusta has convinced your father that you are already too much of a bluestocking and will endanger your chances of finding a good husband if you pursue any further education."

Zoë fought hard to contain her anger. "What makes a *good* husband? Do I need a husband? Do I want a husband? Or more to the point, would I want a husband who doesn't respect my thoughts and opinions? Is getting married the only option for a woman? What if all I wanted was a career? Why does everything become Grandmother's decision?"

Olivia smiled at her daughter's vehemence. "You have a fierce intelligence, Zoë, so I expect that you don't need further education to scare away men of lesser intellect anyway." She put up her hand to forestall a protest. "I'm inclined to agree with you. I don't believe that anyone can have too much knowledge. Augusta thinks that women can become dissatisfied with their true vocations of wives and mothers if they know too much."

"But that doesn't make sense at all! That sounds as if she believe that only idiots would become wives and mothers. Sorry, Mama."

Olivia laughed. "It serves some men well not to have to compete with women, for surely they would lose out. So they make it seem as if women who have a career are undermining family and society. Who, after all, will have and nurture the children if not women?

"But even those of us who willingly choose to follow the proscribed path feel rather powerless at times, because we are dependent upon our husbands. Hannah Carlyle, as a pharmacist, could quite easily fend for herself should she ever become widowed, for example. You and I have to rely on whatever money your father has managed to put aside for us, or we'd have to find you a *good catch*, like Augusta did. Oh, she talks now as if Reginald was the love of her life, and I think that she liked him well enough, but certainly married him for his money. He treated her like a queen and so, of course, she thinks of him as her hero."

"Do you ever regret not pursuing a career as a concert pianist?"

"Oh, I doubt I would have been good enough. But I do sometimes wonder what it would have been like," she said wistfully. "And I always come to the same conclusion – I wouldn't give up my husband and family for it."

"Were you in love with Papa when you married?"

"We were fortunate, for we were both deeply in love with each other, as well as being *suitable*. That doesn't often happen, I've realized. And what about you, my chick? Is there no young man who warms your heart?"

Zoë hesitated. She had told no one, not even Victoria, that she was in love with Blake Carlyle. He would not be intimidated by her getting a degree. In fact, he probably wanted an educated wife. But he didn't seem to think of her any differently than usual. "There are boys I like to talk to, of course, but I'm more interested in improving my mind than worrying about my heart at the moment."

"Let me work on your father. Your year in Europe will be good for you in many ways, and then we'll see about next autumn. I'm not going to allow Augusta to have her way in everything, especially when it comes to my children's happiness."

"Oh, thank you, Mama!" Zoë swung herself across the banister and ran over to give her mother a hug.

"What do you want to study?"

"Modern languages, literature, history, philosophy, psychology!" And yes, her Grand Tour would give her an advantage. She would see the ancient arenas of history, the great works of art and architecture, and learn about the cultures that went along with the languages she wanted to perfect.

"Goodness! Perhaps you could impart a bit of that enthusiasm to your brother."

"Perhaps you should let him take a year off and come to Europe with us. Oh, Mama, it just makes everything so much more wonderful! And if I decide that it isn't for me after all, that I somehow don't fit in or am not clever enough, then I will be the first to admit it."

But Olivia doubted that would be the case.

.       .       .

James was enjoying a pipe on the veranda when he saw Helena arrive in one of the Oakleys' smaller motorboats. Edgar, who was lying in the hammock, had been complaining of boredom. Phyllis and Phoebe were doing embroidery, while Albert and Henry were both reading books. Max had taken Jack out for a sailing lesson; Richard and Olivia had gone to the beach with the children. Augusta was resting. James had no idea where Victoria was. How typical of his daughter to invite someone and then not be around to receive them.

He went down to the dock and helped Helena alight.

"Thank you, James. That was much easier, and, I daresay, more graceful than yesterday," she chuckled musically. By the end of tea yesterday, the Parkers had already been on a first-name basis with the others.

Helena was dressed in a more sensible skirt and shirtwaist today, and was clutching a hold-all that probably contained her swim suit.

"I think you'll find canoeing more fun in forgiving clothes, and once you feel comfortable with swimming."

"I do feel rather foolish, not being able to swim. Why, all the ladies here are so accomplished with their athletic pursuits."

"Most of them have had the advantage of growing up here, and enjoying summer means spending plenty of time on the water, in one form or other. I recall when Oswald and Letitia became summer residents just five years ago. Although they had spent a couple of summers at The Grand, Letitia didn't really master the canoe until that first summer at Oaktree. And not without mishap, I'm told."

"Well, it is very kind of Victoria to offer to teach me to swim."

"Let's see if we can find her," James said as they reached the veranda. But no one there had any idea where she was. They saw Richard and the boys in one canoe and Olivia and Esme in another, just rounding the point.

"Perhaps Victoria and Zoë are already down at the back bay," James said. "Let's go and see."

Phyllis said quickly, "Helena, dear, you may appreciate some moral support, so Phoebe and I will come along. It's so frightfully hot again, I'm sure a swim will be most refreshing. We'll just fetch our bathing costumes and meet you at the bay."

When James and Helena arrived at the back bay, there was no sign of Victoria. "I can't think where she's gone," James said, irritated. "I'm afraid my daughter is somewhat irresponsible and impulsive. With no mother, she's had too much freedom. I do apologize for her rudeness, Helena."

"Not at all! She has undoubtedly become caught up in some other activity. One does rather lose track of time here. Actually, I envy Victoria her carefree life. My mother's illness was long, and rather a strain on us all. One does have to grow up more quickly in such circumstances."

Victoria and Zoë had been hiding behind the east veranda when Helena had arrived, hoping that Henry would greet her and perhaps spend a few moments becoming acquainted with her. Once they had seen James accompany her to the veranda, Victoria thought that James would ask her to sit and wait there, giving Henry another opportunity to talk to her. But when they had seen James and Helena go out past the pavilion, they had rushed down to the bay and were hiding behind the change house. So Victoria had overheard this conversation, and was feeling rather miffed by Helena's insinuation that she was somehow immature and unreliable. She had already regretted making the offer to teach

Helena to swim. Why should she spend time with someone she wasn't really sure she liked, so that that moody Henry might just have a chance to woo her? He was obviously not interested. Perhaps with good reason. And now she, Victoria, would have to follow through with her offer.

She and Zoë came out from behind the change house. "Oh, Helena, you're already here. I do apologize for being tardy. Zoë and I were out for a walk, and I'm afraid I twisted my ankle on a rock."

"Oh, dear! Let me have a look at it," Helena said with concern.

"It's not that serious. It's just slowed me down a bit. I'm sure the cold water will be good for it. But you will forgive me if the lesson is perhaps a bit short?"

"Of course, Victoria. Are you up to it at all?"

"Certainly! I'll let you know if it becomes too painful." Trying to keep sarcasm from her voice she said, "Thank you, Father, for taking care of my guest."

"I think I should take a chair and be available if Helena gets into any difficulty, seeing that you are incapacitated," James said, scrutinizing her as if he didn't believe her excuse.

But Victoria looked back innocently and said, "Perhaps Helena wouldn't welcome an audience, Father. After all, learning anything can make one look and feel awkward. Zoë is a strong swimmer. We won't let Helena drown."

Helena, who didn't look that reassured, said, "I don't mind if you stay, James. And I shan't be offended if you find some mirth in my endeavours."

While James settled himself in one of the many rattan chairs set on the lawn about the bay, Victoria made sure to hobble to the change house, where each of the girls took a cubicle. While Victoria and Zoë now had the thinner and lighter silk bathing suits, theirs were still in the old-fashioned navy, trimmed with white. Helena's stylish silk suit was pink, its tunic a reflection of the current fashion. Even the matching cap was flattering. Victoria and Zoë never bothered to wear theirs.

"How lovely!" Victoria couldn't help saying when they all emerged from the change house into the shallow water. With the newer, skimpier style of suit it was quite obvious that Helena had an admirable figure.

"Letitia insisted on buying me this when we were in Paris," Helena explained. "Even though I told her I couldn't swim. She assured me that I would need it at the cottage."

"It's almost too elegant to get wet," Victoria said.

Phyllis, who was coming down the path, would, on the other hand, still be wearing her voluminous black Victorian wool costume, that would be sure to drown a person of lesser size by its sheer weight.

Although annoyed with her task, Victoria was nonetheless thoughtful and thorough in her instruction of Helena. Zoë demonstrated and Victoria guided Helena, teaching her first the kick and then the breast stroke, holding onto her in chest-deep water. Phyllis, staying out at shoulder depth, called words of encouragement, while Phoebe, thrilled to be included in something for once, splashed about them like an eager puppy.

Her resentment now faded, Victoria forgot that she had planned to cut the session short. Helena was a determined student, and they were all impressed by her quick grasp of the rudiments. After half an hour, Victoria was letting Helena paddle about on her own. She sank the first time, but just laughed when she resurfaced. But then she was able to gauge the movements required to stay afloat. "This is wonderfully exhilarating!" she said with delight.

"Well done!" James called, and clapped his hands.

"Now you just need to practice," Victoria said.

"I'm so grateful," Helena said. "Thank you both. And Victoria, how is your ankle?"

She had forgotten, but said casually, "Not bothersome at all. Water must be the best therapy."

When they had changed back into their clothes, Victoria said, "It's the servants' afternoon off, so I'm afraid that we can't even offer you tea. But I'm sure I can find some lemonade or barley water."

"Please don't worry about me. I've imposed long enough on your hospitality today, and should be getting back."

"Nonsense!" James said. "After all that exercise you must be parched. Victoria can fetch something from the larder." He fell into step with Helena as they ambled back up to the house.

Victoria remembered to limp behind them as she and Zoë followed reluctantly. She hoped her father wouldn't insist on her entertaining Helena until they were to go to the Thorntons' for tea at four.

She and Zoë went into the kitchen from the breezeway, while James led Helena through the house to the front veranda. Molly had put the food away to keep it from spoiling, but the lunch dishes awaited the return of Rosie, the scullery maid. They found a tray and clean glasses, and a jug of lemonade in the ice box. When they carried them to the veranda, Victoria was disappointed that only Edgar, snoozing in the hammock, and Augusta were there with James and Helena. Henry was hopeless!

"That was so liberating," Helena enthused as Victoria handed her a glass. "Isn't it odd that one can feel such a sense of accomplishment simply by not drowning?" She laughed. "I think I shall enjoy swimming."

"You're a natural," James said.

She didn't demure but said, "Victoria and Zoë are good teachers. The children will be delighted that I can now venture into the water with them. I was beginning to feel quite stupid, watching them darting about like fish and unable to join in the fun."

"You're very fond of the children," James observed.

"I'm fond of all children, but the Oakleys are particularly adorable. I was beginning to think that I might make a good nanny, when Dad lost most of his assets when... well, you know about my brother. But fortunately, he's made some wise investments, and has good friends like Oswald to help him out, so I don't have to earn a living just yet."

"Perhaps I should talk to him as well," James suggested. "I might be able to steer him in the right direction with a few other investments. The economy is rather tricky right now, what with this depression."

"Oh, that would be kind!"

"Do you live in Pittsburgh, Helena?" Augusta asked.

"No, we're mostly in New York, although we've been all over the country and in Europe. We gave up our house in Boston after Mom died, and have been going wherever Dad needs to be for his business."

"Which is?"

"I'm afraid that I don't know anything about business, Lady Augusta. All I know is that he invests in various ventures, some more successful than others. He met Oswald through one of them, and the Oakleys have since taken us under their wing. I don't know how we will ever be able to repay their kindness. But for us it's like having a new family. And now I really must leave and let you get on with your day. Bless you, girls, for all your help."

Victoria didn't bother to hobble down to the dock with Helena, as James took it upon himself to see her aboard the boat. She was rather surprised to hear Augusta give voice to her own vague feelings of disquiet when the old lady said, "She's sharp, that one."

. . .

Twenty-acre Thorncliff Island was about a quarter mile from the north end of Wyndwood. J.D. had also bought the three closest islands to Thorncliff, which were smaller, at only a few acres each, to ensure his privacy and also as an investment.

The cottage, although every bit as grand and luxurious as the Oakleys', was less ostentatious, more in keeping with the sentiment that wealth should be tasteful and discreet, and not flaunted as the Americans were wont to do. Although massive and sprawling, with acres of verandas and balconies, the tan and white mansion seemed to blend into its rustic surroundings. The tennis court was a popular gathering place, especially for the young people, and the Thorntons held a yearly tennis tournament for the neighbours in mid-July, with a ball the following day.

A liveried footman greeted them at the dock. Edgar had insisted upon coming, and they managed to disembark him from the steam yacht without too much difficulty. Victoria remembered to favour her right ankle. J.D. hurried down to meet them on the path. "Augusta, how delightful." He gave her his arm. J.D. was not an imposing figure, standing only slightly taller than Augusta, with a thin, heavily bearded face.

"Joseph, I am glad that you have managed to get away from the city. What a summer we are having, and it's only mid-June."

"These days, with a telephone nearby, I can do much from here. The city is becoming quite unbearable."

"I trust Marjorie is well?"

"Tolerable, thank you. You know how it is with her." His wife was a semi-invalid, although no one was quite sure what was wrong with her. Something with her heart, it was thought, as short walks, even with the help of a cane, left her breathless and pale. And she, only in her forties.

In contrast, her two sons, Charles and Ralph — who never answered to anything but Chas and Rafe — were robust and athletic, one or other of them always winning prizes and accolades in some sport. Daughter Felicity, at fourteen, was a spindly, mousy little thing, quite in the shadow of her exceedingly handsome brothers, one dark, the other fair, although she might yet blossom. It rather surprised everyone that two rather ordinary people like J.D. and Marjorie could have created such stunning children. Especially blonde-haired, blue-eyed Chas, with his long eyelashes and transcendent beauty.

But if he was aware of it, it never showed in his behaviour. He had a rather self-deprecating humour that made light of all his assets. Which made him all the more lovable.

The rest of the family joined them as J.D. made the Wyndhams comfortable on the veranda. Jack was introduced, his story now becoming accepted and acceptable lore.

Of course Jack had heard of J.D. Thornton! Who hadn't? To think that he was a welcome guest of this financial titan, who either owned or sat on dozens of boards of banks, trust and insurance companies, mining, utilities, and railway companies, was almost unbelievable, even to someone who had seemingly impossible dreams and ambitions. So how could he make use of this connection, Jack wondered.

"Come to the music room," Chas said to the young people. "We'll leave the aged ones to their chatter and listen to some new music I've brought." Felicity Thornton, Esme and the boys knew they were not included, and Phyllis motioned Phoebe to stay.

As they passed through the cavernous sitting room strewn with trophies and hung with medals, Victoria asked Chas, "How many awards did you end up with this year?"

He and Rafe had been attending Oxford University, the idea being more to make important connections than to get a useful education. Chas had recently — and barely — graduated. Oxford, of course, was in a different league from the University of Toronto, as far as Augusta was concerned, Oxford being more a rite of passage for the wealthy and titled than a training ground for a middle-class career.

"Not that many — tennis, rowing, fencing, cricket. Oh, and debating," Chas replied.

"So you're planning to become a politician?" Victoria said with a grin.

"Good God, no! Oxford has accustomed me to a hedonistic existence. I intend just to contemplate and enjoy life. Starting with a Grand Tour this year. I say, would any of you chaps like to come along?"

While the others shook their heads, Jack said, "I hope to one day, but I need to learn some business first. Start earning some money."

"Time enough for that. In any case, Lord Devenish and I are leaving in September, and you're welcome to come along."

"Perhaps Zoë and I will," Victoria said, and told him about their plans.

"I say, that would be smashing! We can work around Lady Kirkland's itinerary. In fact, it will be a relief not to have to plan anything, but just to tag along. Life doesn't get much easier, I expect," he said with a beatific look on his face.

"And what will you do once you return? Start working with your father?" Zoë asked.

"Actually, I don't see the point of working at all, once you have money. It has a wonderful habit of multiplying all on its own, when you put it into the right hands. I would just make bad investments and lose it all. So I intend to let someone else look after it," Chas said as he riffled through a stack of phonograph records.

"But what will you do with your life?" Zoë asked.

"Do with it, darling girl? You mean how do I intend to enjoy myself? Well, I thought I would take up flying. Perhaps I will circumnavigate the globe in an aeroplane. And I think I will spend my winters on the Riviera. Rafe and I spent the Christmas hols there. Smashing! So I expect I'll do some sailing." He chucked Zoë under the chin as he said, "I can see that you don't approve. A waste of talent, you're thinking. I had considered trying out for Wimbledon, but quite honestly, it's too much work. Believe me, darling, I have nothing useful to offer the world other than my charming company."

He put *Row, Row, Row* on the Victrola, the suggestive chorus eliciting a few smirks and titters.

Chas said, "Now, Edgar, I have to tell you that you are going to lose the motorboat race at the regatta, for I've just bought a bigger and faster boat than yours."

"You rat!"

While they discussed the relative merits of their boats, Rafe requested a drinks tray from one of the footman, saying, when it was delivered, "Can't abide tea. Let me mix you some cocktails. What's your poison? Pimm's, Singapore Sling, Gibson?" Although he was Edgar's age, Rafe seemed older and more dissipated. He was fanatical about horses, and into polo, jumping, and racing – the latter becoming a drain on his and the paternal purse.

Where Chas seemed somehow innocent and honest, if lacking in ambition, Rafe seemed driven, but in a destructive way. Victoria had never warmed to him. She was glad that he still had a couple of years at Oxford, and no intention of joining them in Europe. But having Chas along would be great fun.

Chas turned from Edgar and grabbed Victoria by the hand, pulling her into his arms, saying, "Dance with me, darling."

She laughed as they began a dramatic Tango, and said, "I'm not really sure how to do this."

"Just press your body close to mine and follow my lead," Chas said. Although the Tango had been refined from its rather sleazy origins and was now popular with the upper classes throughout Europe, it still occasioned debate about its sexual implications. Augusta would not have been pleased to see Victoria so closely entwined with Chas.

"So glad to see that your ankle has healed," Zoë said with a grin.

Victoria laughed again and said, "I'm terribly wicked, aren't I?"

"Mmm, I do hope so," Chas said, pulling her suggestively close. Gladly playing along, she snuggled her head against his shoulder, and their dance became slow and sensuous.

Suppressing a pang of jealousy, Jack decided that Chas would make an excellent ally. Not quite sure what he wanted from him yet, he resolved to cultivate a friendship, which shouldn't be too difficult. Jack, too, was good at games.

· · ·

Before the family left for The Grand, Phyllis and Olivia scoured the pantry to put together a meal for Edgar and Jack. Through her friendship with Hannah Carlyle, Olivia was not a total stranger to a kitchen. Hannah could afford to employ only one general maid, who could cook basic meals when necessary, but Hannah preferred to do that herself. So Olivia sometimes joined her in the kitchen when she visited, watching her friend bake bread or scrape vegetables as they talked.

So she sliced some ham and bread, decanted pickles onto a plate and chutney into a bowl, while Phyllis put a variety of cheeses onto a tray along with biscuits and butter, and half a cherry pie. They added a pitcher of beer and took it to the sitting room, where Edgar and Jack sat alone, the others still dressing for dinner.

"It's not much, I'm afraid," Phyllis said, wringing her hands.

"Not Grand fare," Edgar agreed. "But I expect it will keep body and soul together."

Jack said, "It looks 'grand' to me." Not adding that he would have thought this a king's banquet many times in his life.

"Oh, a picnic," Victoria said as she seemed to fly down the stairs. She looked stunning in a blue satin sheath with jet-beaded tunic, and Jack wished he could spend the evening gazing at her across the silver and crystal and candlelight.

Victoria could see the admiration in his eyes, and regretted that he wouldn't be coming to add spice to the evening. It was hard to believe that it was only a week ago that he had served them at The Grand.

There was a flurry of activity, the swish of silk and rustle of taffeta, and then they were gone.

Edgar and Jack had their cigarettes on the veranda, and Edgar suggested that Jack bring out one of the chess tables. Looking for an excuse to go to the kitchen, Jack said, "I could use another ale. Why don't I fetch another pitcher?"

"Good idea. We have no women looking over our shoulders telling us not to drink too much. I say, this leg of mine is still beastly painful, but the beer does help."

Jack went through to the kitchen, put the jug down on the table, and went into the room behind, which was the servants' dining and sitting room, with its own small veranda overlooking the valley behind the house.

Molly was sitting in a chair, her feet up on a table beside a discarded book.

"How's my favourite girl?" Jack said, leaning over and giving her a hug.

She pushed him away. "Favourite girl, is it? I've seen how you look at those rich bitches!"

"Jealous, are we?" Jack said with a chuckle.

"It's alright for some, prancing about like the lord of the castle. While I get to clean slops and sleep in a stuffy closet above the kitchen."

"I can't dally or Edgar will wonder what I'm up to. I said I'd raid the larder for more ale."

"I try to listen at keyholes as much as possible," Molly said as she helped him. "But you don't need me to tell you who's on your side and who isn't, do you? But you will be interested in this," she said with satisfaction, and related the conversation she had heard earlier that day between Augusta and Zoë.

"I guess I'll have to watch my step so that the old lady doesn't change her will. Now how about this? Richard and Olivia are buying me a house! No one's to know, especially Augusta. She'd disown them, stupid old cow. I'd better get back. Leave notes under my pillow when you do my room. Take early morning walks when you can, and meet me on the hill behind the boathouse. I'm going to be painting there, and you might just be exploring and happen to run into me, should anyone see us. Olivia is often about early." He told her how to find the path up the Dragon's Back.

"I'll keep Edgar busy. Why don't you go and look through the library to see if there is anything interesting among Augusta's papers? Her will, for instance. I'd like to know exactly how much she's leaving and who gets what. And one day, sweetheart, you'll look just as glamorous and be just as pampered as the 'rich bitches'. I promise." He gave her a swift kiss, and carried the jug back to the veranda.

# Chapter 7

Jack was sorry to be leaving Wyndwood. He and James were off to the city for a few days, which would give Jack an opportunity to make some investments, so he was surprised at his own unwillingness to leave. But he didn't want to miss a moment of this magical summer life at Wyndwood.

What would Victoria be up to while he was gone? He knew that the young Wyndhams were planning a picnic with the Carlyles and Carringtons today, a tennis afternoon at Thorncliff tomorrow, and a golf day at The Grand with the Carringtons and Thorntons on Thursday. He couldn't imagine any man resisting Victoria's charms, and there were too many eligible men in her sphere, with Chas Thornton by far the most compelling. For a moment Jack wondered what *he* had to offer her – even his good looks and cultivated charm were nothing special – when there were men like Chas around who had everything, including phenomenal wealth. But he pushed that dark and defeatist thought away. He hadn't come this far by thinking negatively.

After an early breakfast, Toby and Will took them to Gravenhurst in *Calypso*, Will keeping the boiler fed while Toby piloted the steamer. There was barely a channel for the boats to get through the thousands of logs that cluttered the large bay, feeding the hungry and noisy mills that made this harbour look like a wasteland. But the name "Wyndham" was emblazoned on many of the mills, and this is what had originally fuelled and kept providing some of the Wyndhams' fabulous wealth.

They had a couple of hours before the train left for the city, as planned, so that James could take Jack to one of the sawmills. Jack had to admit that he didn't like the squealing, screeching cacophony of the saws. The men, toughened by years of hard, physical labour, touched their caps to James but seemed a surly bunch.

James took Jack into the office and introduced him to the mill manager, Roger Edwards, who, despite the sawdust that seemed to mist the air even here, wore a suit.

"I'll just go through the books, Roger, while you show Jack around," James said, settling himself in Roger's chair.

"Certainly, Mr. Wyndham. I expect you will find everything in order, as always."

"Indeed, we count on you, Roger, to run a tight ship. And to see that nothing goes astray."

Roger gave Jack a tour of the sawmill, talking about the process right from the delivery of the logs in early spring by the lumbermen to the loading of the planks onto the railcars at the end. Jack wondered who could work in the perpetual noise of the mill without going deaf. Or losing a limb, for it looked a dangerous business to him. It was why he had chosen to work as a busboy first and then, a waiter, rather than in a factory, like Eddie. His brother had been fascinated by machinery, claiming he could design and build all kinds of useful machines if given the chance. And he would have done a damn sight better job of making them safe than the one that had crushed the life out of him!

"Everything looks fine," James said when Roger and Jack returned to the cubicle of an office. Windows on all sides overlooked the yard as well as the interior, so that the small space seemed larger than it was. "We'll be issuing our usual yearly bonuses to those managers who show good results. And Christmas hampers to the men on his team."

To Jack he said, "We value capable and honest people, and they appreciate having a share in the profits."

"Indeed, Mr. Wyndham. Our mills are renowned for treating men fairly," Roger said with pride, as if he had a stake in them all.

They shook hands, Roger seeming very pleased with the visit and the approval from James.

As they walked back to the wharf station, James said, "Roger is one of our best managers. He'll be training you in the business. If it works out, we'll give you your own mill to run. I'm not sure where that will be yet. We're thinking of expanding into British Columbia."

Jack was stunned. He hadn't expected to be working in a mill, even as a manager. It seemed like hell itself, all the noise and dust, which you couldn't escape even in the office.

"I had thought that the mills were no longer a major part of the family business. I had hoped to be more involved in the financial side. I think that's where my strengths lie – in evaluating the potential of investments. I did some mock investments on paper and managed to double them in a year, despite the current depression."

"There are enough of us in the family already doing that. It's just a small part of the day-to-day business. We need to find new markets, cheaper ways of shipping, new timber limits. We look for less profitable mills to buy or places to build new ones, set up lumber camps, hire capable and trustworthy men to run the camps and the mills, to improve productivity, reduce waste, keep the workers from trying to unionize or agitate for shorter hours and higher wages. We make deals with men like Mackenzie to build railways where we need to go. And, as I said, we may be starting a major logging operation out west. Eventually, you could be responsible for the entire enterprise out there. It has huge potential – for the person in charge as well. Your grandfather began as a lumberjack in the woods. You don't think you're up to following in his footsteps when you're being handed a productive business?"

Jack hid his disappointment. "I know that gives me a tremendous advantage over what he faced. I expect I'm up to the challenge."

As if reading his thoughts, James said, "But you think it unfair that your cousins don't have to actually work in the mills. Just remember that my brothers and I have been working at this for thirty years. Our children take over from us, from what we have built up. You don't have that advantage. But at least you don't have to start at the bottom."

"I do appreciate that," Jack managed to say, but it was hard to seem enthusiastic. He would be expected to spend his life in some remote part of the country. No endless summers at Wyndwood, or winters in the city where there were clubs, entertainments, and like-minded people. Victoria would never stand for it. But then, if he married her, he wouldn't have to be a mill manager.

Cheerful again, he said, "So will Victoria take over from you? She seems to be interested."

James said, "I haven't yet given up on the idea of having a son. In fact, that's been on my mind lately. But, if I didn't have a son or grandson to pass it to, I expect that her cousins might buy out Victoria's share."

Which would be a third of whatever vast fortune the Wyndhams had amassed. Enough for him to live a life of luxury and have the opportunity to become a financial tycoon, like J.D. Thornton. The fact that James was only fifty and might well live another fifty years didn't occur to him.

On the long train ride to the city, James started teaching Jack about wood – the different kinds, their properties, their problems, their prices. And Jack became interested despite his determination never to actually work with the product. But as a commodity it presented great potential, as James had said. With the west opening up, there were untold riches waiting to be plundered, including oil and minerals. With subtle questions, he got some good tips from James about investments, although Jack already had his own ideas. Richard and Olivia were fulfilling his first priority – real estate – and he would invest some money in automobile, steel, and oil stocks.

If only he could get hold of some more money now – like his inheritance – he would show them all how well he could do without having to dirty his hands in the mills.

•   •   •

Wyndholme was even more impressive than Jack had imagined. Sir Henry Pellatt might be building himself a castle in another part of the city, but Wyndholme had the essence of a castle, at least the kind described in the novels that Jack had read as a boy.

From the moment he stepped through the wide oak door into the roomy vestibule, Jack was awed by the magnificence of the place. The bevelled glass in the double mahogany doors sparkled with light from the great room behind it. This massive hall had an enormous stone fireplace at the far side with overstuffed sofas and easy chairs strewn about.

James took him on a quick tour of the house.

Off the great hall, tucked away under the stairs, was a small jewel of a Moorish room that had once been the cloakroom, James explained. Augusta had converted it in the 90s when this exotic style had been fashionable. It was surprisingly sensuous and mysterious with it's scalloped, gilded arches, bright, rich colours, ornate brass tables inlaid with mother-of-pearl, and plush sofas with red and gold pillows inviting one to lounge decadently against them.

There were so many rooms – dining room, morning room, billiard and smoking room, library, ballroom, music room, sitting room, palm room – also known as the conservatory – eight bedrooms, four marble bathrooms and two downstairs lavatories, and of course, the kitchen and all the servants quarters.

There were vaulted and coffered ceilings, oak and mahogany panelling and wainscoting, watered and brocaded silk wall panels, Italian tooled leather walls, oak and marble floors, leaded and Gothic arched windows, some with tracery and others with stained glass, and a domed skylight edged with ruby glass.

And then there was the tower. Steep spiral stairs led up to two levels of rooms, the lower one bumped out with an oriole window which embraced a cozy window seat. Jack was sure that Victoria spent time here, gazing out over the city or reading a book. He suddenly thought of her as a princess waiting to be rescued from a dull and tedious life of luxury. The higher room had a broader view with windows on all sides.

When it had been built for Reginald's young bride in 1863 as their country estate, there had only been four houses in this hilly and wooded area, which had since become known as Rosedale and was now one of the enclaves of the wealthy.

Molly had told him a little about the house, but it hadn't prepared him for this. By God, his father had been a fool! He had thrown away everything for a woman who had come to despise him, precisely because he had nothing. And Jack blamed her as well, for seducing his father away from this life. Selfish, stupid people!

Jack had agreed with Augusta, although he hadn't wanted her to know it. Passion was temporary madness; love, a fragile thing that could only survive if it were nurtured on a full stomach and with a cheerful heart. Marriage should be a business decision.

They had dinner on the balustraded stone patio that overlooked the extensive rose and formal gardens that were protected by a low stone wall from the steep drop into the lush ravine. There was an orchard on one side of the house, and tennis courts on the lawn at the other.

James explained that Richard's cook had come to prepare meals for them, the three households sharing staff as necessary when some were up at Wyndwood.

First thing Wednesday, James took Jack to his tailor, where Jack was measured for a variety of suits. A rush would be put on a couple of items; he would have a fitting tomorrow and some formal attire would be shipped to the cottage Monday, just in time for dinner at The Grand.

Then James took Jack to the Thorntons' bank, The Canada Investment Bank, to set up an account, and started him out with the promised $500. James had business to do, and Jack said he needed to pick up some items from Eaton's and visit his mother, so they would meet back at Wyndholme for dinner. James, of course, had the chauffeur-driven automobile, and Jack would take the street railway – which was another of the Wyndham's investments.

When James had left, Jack returned to the bank to deposit Augusta's cheque. Then he went to a brokerage house – also owned by the Thorntons – and arranged for his investments.

Picking up a small bunch of flowers from a roadside vendor, he went home.

The bottom floor of the house that was his family's flat would easily have fit three times into the great hall of Wyndholme. Jack knocked on the door to alert them, and walked in.

"Jacque!" his mother cried in surprise. "Qu'est-ce que tu fais ici?" Marie Wyndham was thin and pinched, but remnants of her former beauty were still visible in her large dark eyes and fine cheekbones.

"I can't stay, Maman, but I wanted to bring you this." He hugged her and handed her the flowers and a hundred dollars in cash. His sister, Claire, beaming with delight, ran and threw herself into his arms. "Hey, poppet. You've grown again!"

"Jack, we miss you so!" thirteen-year-old Claire said.

"Well, I hope that will change soon. Let me tell you the good luck I've had. I've met Papa's family and they have invited me to stay at their summer home. They are not all bad, Maman," he said quickly, seeing the frown cloud her face. "His brother, Richard, is kind and generous, and he is giving me – us – a house!"

"Non! I will not accept charity from that family!"

"It's not charity, Maman. Richard feels that the family owes it to us, since his parents treated us so badly. This is nothing for them. If you saw how rich they are, you wouldn't worry about this. They are giving it to *me*," he said pointedly, so that she had no misconception of who was in control. If she chose not to live there, then she would have to fend for herself. He knew that Lizzie and the others would be delighted to have a real home of their own. "I thought you could run a boarding house, rent rooms to young women attending the university. You could probably charge five dollars a week. We're looking for a house in the Annex with at least six bedrooms, so that you can rent out four. That's twenty dollars a week, Maman!" She was making about seven or eight now, working long and tedious hours.

"Tu es fou! The Annex! That is where some of my clients are. It is for rich women that I make these dresses," she said, pointing to the yards of silk she was beading so intricately. "Me, live there? Tu es tombé sur la tête, ou quoi?"

"You won't need to make dresses anymore, Maman. And Emily can stop working in the sweat shop. The girls can help you. You can show off your cooking skills, and take life a lot easier.

You'll be a respectable widow. The Wyndham name is highly esteemed."

Still she frowned. "It's not right."

"Oh, yes it is! And it's only the beginning of making things right and fair."

"What do you mean?"

"That we are going to get our share of what should have been Papa's."

"How?" she asked.

"I'll be working in the family business. I mean to make a success of my life. Now let me tell you about the family."

Claire was fascinated by her unknown relatives and the legendary island, which Jack said was even more beautiful than Papa's paintings. "One day, maybe soon, I'll take you there," Jack said.

"Oh, but I would feel so awkward," Claire said.

"Your cousins will love you. Just be yourself. And you can think seriously now about becoming a teacher, if that's still what you want to do."

"Oh, yes! Oh, Jack, this is too exciting!" She clapped her hands in glee.

"Your brother is perhaps blinded by the glitter from all the gold," Marie said with disapproval.

"Au contraire, Maman. It's opened my eyes to all kinds of possibilities. I can promise you one thing. I intend never to be poor and hungry again. Only a fool would pass up the opportunities that are within my reach."

Jack was sorry to miss Emily, who wouldn't return from work until the evening, sometimes very late if they had a rush job on.

"Have you heard from Lizzie?" Marie asked him. "She's only written once, and she knows I don't have time to write. I can't imagine why she had to go to Montreal with that family. She had a perfectly fine job with the Duponts."

"But they didn't have enough staff and worked her too hard. She can come back when you get settled in the house, and she won't have to work for others anymore. She now has a lot of knowledge about how things are done in a larger establishment. I expect that will be helpful." As well as the fact that she, like he, easily picked up the mannerisms of the upper classes through their interactions. Lizzie was a great mimic. He wondered if any of the rich young men he had met so far would make a good husband for her. Perhaps Chas Thornton. She could certainly give Victoria some competition.

Jack felt slightly guilty going back to luxurious Wyndholme and leaving his mother and sisters behind in their tiny flat. But his job now was to establish himself firmly in the life and business of the family, which also meant being familiar and comfortable with a different lifestyle.

James took him to his club for lunch the next day, following Jack's fitting at the tailor's. This was the first time that Jack dined formally in a restaurant, and it felt both odd and wonderful to him. If it hadn't been for his temerity last week, he would still be serving at table rather than sitting at it. He wondered why he had waited so long to get in touch with his father's family. It had all been so easy.

But would they have been so welcoming before he had polished his charm and manners? He had learned well from his gentle father, but also from the mean streets of the city, where a rough tongue and a quick fist earned respect. It was through being in daily contact with gentlemen that he had developed the poise, restraint, and confidence that impressed Augusta.

There were few diners in the club, James explaining that many of the members would already be at their summer places or travelling abroad. But Jack was introduced to Ethan Nash, the family's solicitor. Jack had heard of Nash, who was one of a new breed of corporate lawyers who were helping their clients – and themselves – to amass fortunes.

"So Mrs. Wyndham has finally relented," Nash said, as if he knew the full story.

"She's giving me an opportunity to prove myself," Jack explained.

"To prove what exactly?"

"That I'm a hard worker and fast learner, and have ambitions to help expand the family empire."

Nash laughed. He had already reported to James that Jack was indeed Alex's son. "If your abilities match your enthusiasm, then the family will be well served. Good to have a strong succession in place, James, for when you and your brothers want to retire. Poor Flavelle just lost the young man he's been grooming, and can't count on his son."

"Speaking of Flavelle, the pork business hasn't been giving us such good returns lately. Do you think we should pull out?"

"Give him another six months or so to turn things around. He's been having problems with his British markets. I expect he'll find new ones. And so, gentlemen, I'll bid you good day. I'm off to a meeting."

"I expect that Mother will want to see you at Wyndwood some time."

"I shall look forward to it, as usual," Nash said. "Do give her my warmest regards."

James said he had various errands to run before picking up Lady Beatrice from the train station, so Jack said he could find things to occupy himself for the afternoon. He wandered around the Annex, to see if there were particular streets or even houses that he thought would be suitable. He was excited at the possibilities. Of course this house would be just for his mother and sisters. Once he and Victoria were married they might live at Wyndholme, or else he would build a grand house in Rosedale or on the escarpment near Pellatt's Casa Loma and John Craig Eaton's new estate, Ardwold.

So Jack was even more cheerful than usual when he wandered back to what he was already thinking of as home.

James and Lady Beatrice Kirkland were having tea on the patio under the shade of an old maple tree when Jack arrived. Although sixty-five, Lady Beatrice looked a decade younger and exuded vitality, even when sitting still. She had probably never been a beauty, but she was a handsome woman, perhaps one of that rare breed who improved as they aged.

"I was sorry to hear about your father," she said to Jack. "I'd always felt that Augusta and Reginald had been too hard on him. Lord, if every eminent family disowned sons who took up with actresses, there would be plenty of dispossessed blue-bloods roaming about Britain." What she didn't say was that most, of course, didn't marry them. "But I am glad to see that you have taken the initiative to heal the rift." She eyed him carefully as she said, "I expect that wasn't easy."

"I've never been afraid of a challenge. But as it turns out, the family has made me most welcome."

"Nicely said. But I expect that you've not had an easy life, which makes you interesting. I will regale you with my own interesting tale at dinner, for I expect that Augusta hasn't mentioned it even to you, James. But remember that you have aristocratic blood that can be traced back to William the Conqueror. Of course they were robber barons all, but it was a brutal world and only those who had brains and brawn survived well. Nothing to be ashamed of there."

Jack was pleasantly surprised by this revelation, for his father had never talked about his family's history. Jack knew only that Augusta's father had been a destitute peer, so he had never considered his lineage much beyond that, only wondering, ironically, if they had lived in a draughty, leaking mansion, their lives perhaps not much more comfortable than his own.

"I say, but it's dashed hot on this side of the ocean," Beatrice declared.

"We've had an early start to summer this year. It will be much more enjoyable at the lake," James said.

"I look forward to that. Now I intend to indulge in a bath and will see you both at dinner. I'd be most grateful, James, if you could send me up a gin and tonic."

Dinner was served in the intimate atmosphere of the conservatory, beneath the shade of palms, with a breeze wafting in from the rose-scented garden through the open doors.

As if reading his thoughts, Beatrice said to Jack, "One of the benefits of having had a difficult childhood is that one can take joy in things that others take for granted. I think it is the person who has always had everything, without effort or thought, who is the impoverished one. How can you truly appreciate an epicurean feast or a fine wine if you've never known anything but that?"

"You endure a bad cook for a while," James jested. "We've had our share."

"But a good wine cellar can make up for that." Beatrice chuckled. "So now let me tell you something about your family history. Augusta's mother, Julia, and my mother, Caroline Chalmers, were sisters, and daughters of the Earl of Leamington and Viscount Devenish."

Jack was startled. "Chas Thornton told me that he and Lord Devenish were doing a Grand Tour this year."

"He's a relative," Beatrice said. "Only the eldest son of the Earl is referred to as Lord Devenish. Two of my uncles, Bertram and Granville, survived childhood. Bertram was the heir and Granville had an illustrious career in the church, eventually becoming a Bishop. So I expect your Lord Devenish is Bertram's great-grandson, which makes him your third cousin, I believe. I can't keep track."

Jack was thrilled. Here was one easy way to impress Chas Thornton.

"Our grandmother had been the daughter of the Marquess of Abbotsford, so there are long lines of illustrious ancestors on both sides, some more noble and deserving than others. But we needn't delve too deeply into that.

"Julia and Caroline married relatively well, if beneath them, both to Viscounts. Things were fine in the early days, but both men made bad investments or poor decisions. Julia died when Augusta was fifteen, and her husband rather lost his will to revive his fortunes. He had no surviving male heir – both Augusta's brothers had died in childhood. I think his only goal was to get Augusta married as well as possible, but she didn't have much of a dowry, so Reginald was a godsend. He met her at Uncle Bertram's, fell in love with her, and was happy to help his father-in-law out of debt. Augusta's father eventually remarried, quite happily, but to a woman past her child-bearing years, so his title and estate went to a cousin.

"My mother, however, had no intention of ending her life in penury. Of course, divorce wasn't at all easy in those days, and quite scandalous. When her sister Julia died, she decided there was nothing to keep her in Britain, and ran off to Italy, where she met and eventually married a Count. I was only five. Mother thought it best not to take me away from what little we had to a Bohemian life abroad. In other words, she didn't want to be encumbered with a child. That's when Augusta and I became close. She became my older and wiser sister. Father was lost, felt betrayed, drank too much. He sold our city townhouse and some of our land and heirlooms. We had only a few loyal servants who stayed with us. Food was sometimes scarce, even though the wine cellar lasted for years."

She spoke without bitterness, but with regret. Seeing her so comfortably elegant in silks and diamonds, Jack found it hard to believe that she, too, may have gone hungry as a child.

"Augusta and her father did what they could for us, but they had little to spare. Uncle Bertram finally took pity on me and sent me to a boarding school. I spent holidays with Augusta. Father died when I was twelve. What was left of the estate went to a nephew, along with the title. And that was when Mother, herself now a rich widow, decided that I should go and live with her. That was when my formal education ceased.

"Although we spent most of each year in Italy, we also travelled to all the places popular with her circle of friends – Baden Baden, Paris, Côte D'Azur, Vienna, and so forth. But the only time we went to England was briefly for Augusta's wedding. So I had a very liberal education, and am consequently fluent in German and French as well as Italian.

"I was a rather plain little thing, which both disappointed and comforted my mother, for it meant that I was no competition for her when it came to men. Of course, she had countless affairs, and

I was happy to be left in the shadows. I took up sports, and quite excelled at tennis and golf and equestrian events.

"Then I met Russell, the Earl of Kirkland, at Cannes. He was an avid sailor – won all kinds of races at Cowes and so forth – and was surprised that I was a competent one as well. We got on splendidly, and I was delighted to become independent of my mother and her busy social life. I was also happy to return to England.

"Russell arranged for me to have everything except the hereditary title and estate, which has gone to his nephew. He was a very clever and capable man, so I have a townhouse in London, a country estate on the Thames near Henley, a villa in Antibes, and enough money to do as I please."

"That's a remarkable story. I wonder why Mother never told us any of it," James said.

"She didn't like to dwell on the fact that our families had fallen on hard times. And, of course, my mother created a scandal that all the relatives wanted to ignore and hoped society would soon forget. But doesn't it make one a more interesting person, when one hasn't lived an ordinary life?" She looked at Jack.

"If you can speak from a place that is better than what you have overcome, then I think you have a point," Jack said.

"True enough. And one has to have a bit of luck, as well as resourcefulness. Russell was somewhat hesitant about popping the question, so I gave him a bit of a nudge. Oh, we were never madly in love, but we liked and respected one another, and were well suited in temperament and in our various athletic pursuits. We had great fun. My only regret is that we were never able to have children."

Another wealthy relative, but with no family of her own and a fondness for Augusta and perhaps her family. Jack wondered how he could take advantage of that. Perhaps the old lady would like to "adopt" a grandson. She was obviously interested in him. And who else would she leave her fortune to? He would have to be careful how he ingratiated himself with her, for she was nobody's fool.

He said, "You've made me feel less ashamed about my past. We can't be held responsible for our parents' mistakes and failures. How we overcome those is a test of our own character."

"Well said," Beatrice replied, smiling with approval.

"I have to admit that I'm also thrilled to discover that we have noble ancestry. That's a tremendous boost to one's confidence." With such a distinguished lineage, who would really know or care that Jack had known poverty? Obviously it was not unusual for even eminent families' fortunes to fluctuate.

"It also opens doors and creates new opportunities – perhaps not so much here, but certainly in Europe. Although impoverished aristocrats are often sought out by rich Americans hoping to trade cash for a coronet."

"Yes, the Americans are particularly impressed when Mother gets introduced as 'The Honourable'," James said. "Your presence at the cottage will delight them. What is your formal title?"

Beatrice laughed. "It all sounds so pompous. 'The Most Honourable, the Dowager Countess of Kirkland', but I refuse to be called 'Dowager' – it's so aging – so I am referred to as 'Beatrice, the Countess of Kirkland' to distinguish me from the wife of the present Earl, who is just 'the Countess of Kirkland'. In casual speech, I'm addressed as Lady Kirkland, but referred to by others as Beatrice, Lady Kirkland. Such ceremony!"

"We'll have to apprise the servants," James said with a grin.

"Lord, 'Lady Kirkland' will suffice! No need to confuse everyone."

"Oh, but we don't want to deprive Oswald Oakley of the thrill of hearing your full title," James said, and told her briefly about the Oakleys.

"Now you must tell me all about the other people I will be meeting," Beatrice implored. "I like to be somewhat prepared when there are so many new people to meet. Of course, Augusta has occasionally mentioned names in her letters. Quite a society you seem to have up there."

So they spent the rest of the evening discussing the cottage neighbours, which also helped Jack know more about them, including several he had yet to meet.

They caught the early train the next morning after the formidable task of transporting all of Beatrice's trunks to the station. Her lady's maid, Mason, went ahead with most of the trunks, and the chauffeur managed to strap the rest onto the Rolls Royce Silver Ghost, when he drove the family on the second trip.

They took the Canadian Northern Railway to the Lake Joseph Station, which was closer to Wyndwood than the Gravenhurst wharf station on Lake Muskoka, and didn't require having to lock through at Port Carling. James explained that the family owned substantial shares in the Canadian Northern, so of course they preferred to support that one of the three rival lines that serviced the three large connected lakes.

Toby picked them up with a welcoming committee aboard *Calypso*. Jack was secretly delighted to see Victoria, Zoë, and Max. He wondered if Victoria had missed him, and had brought the other two along for show.

Beatrice had last been in Canada after Reginald had died, eighteen years ago, when these children had been babies.

"Ah, Victoria and Zoë! What a pleasure to meet you. I have to tell you that I am so looking forward to our little jaunt around Europe," Beatrice said. "You two will make me feel positively young again! And Max, I think it's a pity that you won't be joining us, but I understand you have to complete university studies before you're allowed on a Grand Tour."

"I don't see why university couldn't be postponed for a year," Max said. "I say, Cousin Beatrice, you couldn't persuade them, could you? Chas Thornton and some British toff are thinking of tagging along with you as well."

"That British toff, Lord Devenish, is your third cousin," Beatrice said, and laughed at the surprised expressions on Victoria and the twins' faces. "Jack told me, but he didn't mention that they wanted to come with us. Well, I shall begin to feel like the Pied Piper soon!"

They took to her instantly. Victoria thought her a vibrant, no-nonsense kind of person. Beatrice was interested in everything around her, exclaiming with delight at the scenery and asking them intelligent questions about themselves with genuine interest, and not merely idle chit-chat. More than ever, Victoria was looking forward to spending time in Europe with this fascinating cousin.

It was obvious that Augusta and Beatrice were deeply happy to see one another again. Augusta had always been sparing with her shows of affection, a hug often being no more than a light touch on the shoulders. But she embraced Beatrice vigorously.

Jack and Beatrice were introduced to Olivia's parents, Ruth and Gerald Maxwell, who had arrived yesterday and would be staying until after the ball.

The Maxwell carriage works in Kingston had been renowned in Ontario for more than half a century. Gerald had just that morning been discussing with Richard the idea that his son-in-law buy him out, as Gerald felt it was time he retired but had no sons to take over. But Richard was convinced that automobiles were already sounding the death knell of the horse and buggy, and thought it best that Gerald find another buyer, and soon. Gerald may well have been disappointed – wanting to see his grandsons carry on the family business, for instance – but knew that Richard was a wise investor. Gerald himself had recently bought an automobile.

While they had tea on the veranda, plans were made for Beatrice to go golfing with James and Richard tomorrow at The Grand. In the evening, of course, there would be the Midsummer Night's Dream party, when Beatrice would meet many of the neighbours. Letitia Oakley had already sent an invitation to a special Summer Solstice picnic on Sunday, which Augusta had accepted, since a picnic usually didn't involve any frivolous entertainments, and they could dispense with their customary cold supper while the servants went to church.

"And now I should really enjoy a swim," Beatrice said. "James, you were right that the heat is more tolerable here, but it still entices one into the water. Will you join me, Augusta?"

"I have given up swimming, but I shall come and watch."

"We'll come," the children said, running off the fetch their suits, and racing to see who could get to the change house first.

As they ambled down to the beach together, Beatrice said, "You are indeed fortunate, Augusta. Your children and grandchildren are delightful. How I envy you! And how glad I am that you asked me to shepherd Victoria and Zoë about Europe."

"I wonder if you'll still feel that way after you've dealt with them for a while," Augusta snorted. "Stubborn and opinionated, the pair of them."

"And beautiful. Which will be more of a challenge for me, since I shall have to keep hordes of amorous men away from them," Beatrice laughed.

"If you can't, then be sure that you land them young men wealthy enough to keep them in luxury and strong enough to keep them in line. No socialists or adventurers, if you please! And what do you think of my prodigal grandson?"

"Charming, with the hunger and determination to succeed. I wouldn't underestimate him."

"Meaning you don't quite trust him," Augusta said.

"I never fully trust charming men. Unless they are richer than I. But I feel rather sorry for the boy as well. I remember all too well how crushing poverty is, and how it undermines one's feelings of self-worth."

"It's given him more spunk than the rest of them put together," Augusta declared. "Except perhaps for the girls."

"Yes, well they need that just to survive well," Beatrice declared as they reached the back bay. The children were already cavorting in the water, which daily grew warmer, as the sun was now at its strongest.

Everyone went swimming except for Augusta and Edgar, who was becoming proficient on his crutches and had managed to hobble down to the bay to watch. The pain had eased, although his foot was often numb.

"Oh, Grandmother," Victoria said. "I forgot to ask if you would sponsor a Ladies' Cup in the Stepping Stone Marathon."

"What's that?" Beatrice asked before Augusta could respond. When it was explained to her she said, "Oh, do allow me to sponsor it. Does 'The Countess of Kirkland Ladies' Cup' sound prestigious enough?" She chuckled at their delight.

"It will make it even more of a prize," Victoria declared.

"I can't say I approve of you girls swimming such a distance," Augusta said.

"I'll follow in the boat," Edgar assured her, "and fish them out with a grappling hook if they start drowning."

"More likely they'll pull you in and you'll sink to the bottom," Augusta chortled.

"We'll be fine, Grandmother," Victoria said. "In fact, we'll practice now by swimming around to the other bay and back."

Phoebe and the younger children weren't allowed to participate anyway, so Victoria and Zoë set out with Max, Jack, and a reluctant Henry, who also needed to practice, and who wanted to keep an eye on Jack.

The water was calm on the east side, but after they rounded the steamer dock at the point, the lake became choppy. They were swimming into the wind, which made it sometimes difficult to keep one's head above the waves.

Although the girls swam the breaststroke, the boys kept pace with them, occasionally speeding ahead with the faster front crawl, and then coming back.

Max suddenly disappeared underwater and popped up right in front of them, amid surprise and laughter. Just at that moment, a particularly large wave hit them, and Victoria gulped in water rather than air. She began coughing violently and struggled to keep her head above the wind-whipped waves, but breathed in another mouthful of water as she was gasping for air.

Zoë and Max, frightened now, tried to hold her up, but just sank themselves. Jack was beside her in an instant, flipping her onto her back, grabbing her about the neck, and hauling her toward shore. As soon as he could touch bottom easily, he pulled her onto his shoulder and pounded her back, using the pressure of his shoulder to help expel the water from her lungs.

Choking and spluttering, Victoria was shaking violently, but Jack held her tightly. He could feel her soft breasts against his shoulder. With his arm cradling her slender waist, they would have been considered to be in a most compromising position had this not been such a dire situation. He felt her relax against him as she could breathe again. Slowly he lowered her so that her chin rested on his shoulder. "Are you alright?" he said into her hair. He could feel the rapid pounding of her heart.

She nodded, but couldn't yet speak. She needed to feel the comfort of breathing again, and was not ready to let go of Jack.

The others, who were beside them, also breathed easier. Zoë smacked Max on the arm. "That was a stupid thing to do!"

"I didn't mean for that to happen! But I'm terribly sorry, Ria! Holy smoke, you put the wind up me!"

"I've thought it a stupid idea from the start," Henry opined, "you girls swimming the Marathon. You haven't even gone half the distance to Ouhu, and look what's happened. It's even rougher out in the open lake, you know."

Victoria coughed again, but then managed to say, "I'll refrain from laughing when I swim across. And it wasn't Max's fault. You mustn't tell anyone about this. Promise, Henry!"

"Suit yourself. You always do," Henry said with resignation.

"I know you mean well, Henry," Victoria said. She moved away from Jack reluctantly. She enjoyed the feel of his strong arms about her, but no longer had an excuse to cling to him. And she was annoyed with herself for having had to be rescued twice already by her dashing cousin. It was surely no way for her to earn his admiration. "Thank you, Jack," she said simply.

"I think Henry's right," Max said, frowning. "About the last stretch from Ouhu. Why don't you girls have a shorter race that ends there? It's enough of a challenge. Anyway, you don't want to tire yourselves out and not be up for the ball."

"We frail little flowers wouldn't want to wilt too soon," Zoë said. "But perhaps for this first year we could do a shorter race, just to see how it is."

"We wouldn't want to discourage other competitors who may need their beauty rest," Victoria added.

"Try to be thoughtful and caring and all you get is sarcasm," Max complained.

"We did agree with you," Zoë pointed out.

"Your gratitude overwhelms me," he retorted. The girls began splashing him, and he retaliated to much shrieking and laughter.

When Victoria recovered from another coughing fit, Jack said, "We could walk across to the back bay."

"No. I just want to rest on the dock for a few minutes, and then we'll swim back," she replied. "It should be easier going with the wind. And we'll stay closer to shore."

They clambered onto one of the docks that bracketed the new boathouse, where she lay down gratefully.

With a seemingly irrational urgency, Victoria said, "Do you ever think that perhaps one day we'll look back at this moment and think how lucky we were. And how easy life was?"

"Is this a near-death experience making you sentimental?" Max asked.

"Perhaps. I feel suddenly cold, as if someone has walked over my grave," she replied, rubbing her arms.

"That will be shock," Zoë said with conviction. "You'll be your usual carefree self before long."

But Victoria wanted to cling to this moment when they were basking in the sun, just enjoying each other's company and with a promise of more good times to be had.

She was to recall it as a premonition.

# Chapter 8

Zoë said, "Ria will be dressed in black and white, and her hair will be flowing loose and rippled, like water."

Rupert snorted. "A ghost isn't black and white."

"She's not a ghost, you chump. She's a spirit," Esme said.

But Rupert ignored her and said, "What's my wolf costume going to be like?"

"You'll see soon enough," Zoë said. "Now can we get on with this rehearsal? Alright, Edgar."

Edgar, because he couldn't do anything else, was the narrator of Zoë's play. He read the script as the others took up their positions under Zoë's watchful eye. *"The Spirit of the Lake paddled her canoe through crystal waters under a vast canopy of sky."*

"I've never seen anyone paddling a canoe standing up," Rupert said, referring to Victoria's miming the movement.

"I suppose you should get down on your knees, Ria," Zoë suggested.

Edgar continued. *"She lived in harmony with the creatures of the land. The eagle was her messenger, circling high above to watch the lake and all that lay beyond."*

Esme, the eagle, spread her arms and swooped about.

*"The deer took her swiftly across the islands."* Victoria and Blake Carlyle burst into laughter as she leapt onto his back and he carried her piggyback across the 'stage'.

Phoebe said, "Victoria, your legs are showing! Grandmother will be horrified!"

Zoë said quickly, "I think that you should just walk behind Blake and put your hands on his shoulders, Ria."

"But that's not half as much fun. Oh, alright."

*"The squirrel shared his nuts, and the bear, her berries."* Eight-year-old Miles was a squirrel and Daphne Carlyle, the bear.

Rupert said, "What? That's all she ate? Nuts and berries?"

"You could be a fish and throw yourself into the canoe," Blake suggested to Rupert amid laughter.

"Wolf eat deer so you'd better watch out," Rupert said to Blake, who then attacked him, his hands, pretend antlers.

Zoë grabbed her little brother and swung him around beside Victoria.

Edgar took the cue and continued. *"The wolf was her companion."* Victoria patted Rupert on the head.

*"Men sometimes passed through, but they took only what they needed from the land."*

Max and Eleanor Carlyle, who would be dressed as Indians, fished and hunted, made a fire for cooking, and then moved on.

"How come there's a girl when you said 'men'?" Rupert wanted to know.

"Men in the generic sense. Like *mankind* means men and women," Zoë explained patiently. "It would sound too awkward to say 'men and women'."

"That's just dumb! Why don't you have Max as an Indian, and let Ellie be a raccoon or something," Rupert said.

*"The Spirit of the Lake was happy with her friends,"* Edgar continued pointedly. They all danced about.

*"One day a handsome white man appeared. He was enchanted by the land and the Spirit of the Lake."*

The others retreated to leave Victoria centre stage, smiling as Jack approached and sank to one knee before her, as if awestruck. It was Victoria who was spellbound as his eyes held hers with such promise. She felt weak kneed as he took her hand and gently brought it to his lips, and had a sudden urge to throw herself into his arms. She remembered all too well the feel of his virile body against hers. It had kept her awake for much of the night. The others were silent for once, caught up in the tension between them.

Edgar broke the spell. *"So enamoured was the man that he brought his many friends."*

A disgruntled Henry joined Derek Carlyle and Phoebe, who all ignored Victoria and pulled Jack away from her.

*"But while they exclaimed at the beauty, they plundered the riches."*

"You're making a mockery of the family," Henry said to Zoë. "Grandmother, especially, will not be amused by the implied criticism."

"You mean showing how the lumbermen clear-cut the land and then burned what was left?" Zoë said. "Perhaps the truth should jolt the conscience a little."

Before Henry could argue with her, Edgar continued. *"The eagle circled about and said to the Spirit of the Lake:*

"There are no branches where I can rest. I must fly to the far north," Esme said.

*"The squirrel said:"*

"There are no trees to make a home. No nuts to find. I must go north."

*"The bear and the wolf said:"*

"They fear and loathe us. They hunt us down. We must flee northward."

*"The deer said:"*

"Run away with me, darling," Blake pleaded melodramatically, breaking them up. He grinned at Zoë and said, "Sorry. I couldn't resist. I promise I won't do it tonight. OK here goes... They hunt me too. I am a trophy for their walls, to show how man is superior. So I must leave you. But what will you do?"

*"The Spirit of the Lake climbed into her canoe. She paddled and paddled until she transformed into a loon. Now she forever guards the lake. She sings her haunting song to remind Man that he is a part of nature, but is nothing without it."*

Everyone clapped, and Rupert said, "But I want to hear Ria call like a loon."

"I don't think you would," she replied.

"Ellie does a wonderful loon impression," Blake said. "Give us a tune, Ellie."

She did a commendable imitation, so Phoebe said, "You should be the Spirit, Eleanor."

"Oh, no. I don't think I could compete with Ria." She gave Victoria a sly grin, suggesting that she was referring to Jack and not the role. "But I'll do the call from off-stage."

Which worked well.

"Alright," Zoë said. "Let's put on our costumes and do it again – without interruptions, Rupert."

The play that night was a success, despite Henry's misgivings, for no one contested the underlying sentiment. Letitia Oakley said, "I'll never think of the loon the same way again. What an imagination you have, Zoë."

It was another stifling hot evening. The pavilion was lit softly with Chinese lanterns, although the daylight still lingered. The piano had been rolled onto the platform, chairs had been set about, and smudge pots burned to deter the mosquitoes.

Albert's butler, footman, cook, kitchen maid, and parlour maid had arrived on Thursday to help prepare for the party. Trays of drinks were passed around, while platters of food set out in the dining room would later entice the revellers to a late night supper.

The Oakley children performed a short piece from the play, *Peter Pan*, obviously under Helena Parker's direction. Justin Carrington on piano, Vivian on cello, and Lydia on violin, gave a stirring performance of the Allegro movement of Beethoven's Trio No. 1 in E Flat. Chas and Rafe Thornton recreated a compelling and well choreographed fencing scene from Shakespeare's *Romeo and Juliet*, with Chas as Mercutio, dying a dramatic death. Felicity Thornton sang *Scarborough Fair* with great poignancy, belying her young age. Victoria, Zoë, and Esme – with Max on piano – delighted the audience with their perky rendition of Gilbert and Sullivan's "Three Little Maids From School".

The Spencer family had arrived at their Stepping Stone island, Driftwood, earlier in the week, and knew from previous experience to have some entertainment prepared.

Ernest Spencer, now a Senator, had established a highly successful law firm in Toronto before turning to politics and eventually becoming a cabinet minister in Sir Wilfred Laurier's Liberal government. Augusta, being a staunch Conservative, looked more kindly upon him now that his party was no longer in power. His wife, Kathleen, was from old Toronto money, which Augusta considered an incestuous community of jumped-up tradesmen and professionals who owed their position in society to having been the first to settle in Toronto, gaining power early, and their easy wealth, through having acquired huge tracts of land – often as grants from the government – which had since been expensively gobbled up by the ever-expanding city. But she had to remember that Toronto had been just a muddy outpost a hundred years ago, so its aristocracy was still young and constantly being infused with the newer, more dynamic members like themselves and the Thorntons.

The Spencers' six children put on a play that seventeen-year-old Emma had written, called "The Trial of Goldilocks". Nine-year-old Hazel played Baby Bear, twelve-year-old Maud was Mama Bear, and fourteen-year-old Arthur was Papa Bear. Emma played Goldilocks, while twenty-year-old Freddie was the defence lawyer and twenty-two-year-old Archie, the prosecuting attorney. Archie had actually just graduated with a law degree. The play was clever and very funny, and required the audience to be the jurors. Amid much laughter and debate, the defence won its case and Goldilocks was acquitted.

"That doesn't bode well for my law career," Archie commented. Freddie, the "defence lawyer", was studying architecture.

Olivia, appropriately enough, ended the entertainment with a Chopin Nocturne.

The adults and youngest children returned to the house, while the others prepared for the dancing. The breakfast table in the screened veranda had been removed and the chairs set up there so that the older generation could supervise the younger, although some, like Augusta and Marjorie Thornton, ensconced themselves in the sitting room. Later, everyone would gather round the bonfire on the point.

Victoria was glad to see that Helena Parker had decided to join the elders, for she was now convinced that Helena was not the right person for Henry.

Edgar was in charge of the gramophone and kept them hopping with ragtime tunes and popular songs, interspersed with waltzes. They changed partners regularly, and everyone danced with everyone else. Esme and the other children were included this time, so there was a great deal of merriment amongst that age group as they imitated their older siblings in learning the dances.

Zoë sensed that there was a change in Blake's attitude toward her when they danced.

"That was a clever panto you wrote," he said to her. "Simple, but effective. Are you planning to become a writer or playwright?" He said it as if it were natural that whatever she would desire, she could achieve. And she loved him all the more for it.

"Perhaps," she replied. "I haven't examined all the possibilities yet."

"You mean you're waiting and see if some handsome European Count is going to sweep you off your feet, and then you'll spend your life lolling about on the Riviera."

She laughed, and wondered if he cared. "Never! I couldn't stand to live in idleness. You know me well enough by now."

"True enough. You'd spend his fortune rescuing fallen women and educating orphans."

"Not a good enough reason to marry him, I'm afraid."

He danced another, slower dance with her, and Zoë felt that she couldn't be happier than at this moment, when so much was possible. She was sure that he was somewhat reluctant to move on to another partner, as was she.

Zoë had always liked Freddie Spencer. He was easy-going and thoroughly nice, so she tried not to long for Blake while she danced with him. Dark haired and fresh-faced, Freddie was very tall and thin, and seemed angular and somehow awkward. But they danced well together.

"Freddie, can I hire you to design a cottage for me?" she asked.

He guffawed. "By Jove! I hadn't expected my first job offer to come from a pretty girl on a dance floor. You always surprise me, Zoë."

"I am serious. I don't mean detailed drawings ready for construction. Not yet, anyway. Just a concept. I'd like to give it to my parents for Christmas. Mama wants a small cottage, nothing grand like this or the Thorntons'. But it is a secret, and Grandmother doesn't approve of the idea, so you mustn't tell anyone. And I insist upon paying for it."

There was a softness in his face as he said, "Of course I'd be delighted to design it. You'll have to tell me what you want. Shall I come over later this week to discuss it?"

"Oh yes, would you? I have all kinds of ideas that I'm sure they'd like."

Victoria, meanwhile, thought that being in Jack's arms legitimately while they glided about to *By the Light of the Silvery Moon*, was nonetheless seductive. He held her closer than propriety dictated, but not so close that the chaperones would notice. Unfortunately not the languid way Chas had done that day at Thorncliff. As if her senses were heightened, she was intensely aware of Jack – the softness of his hand, the firmness of his muscles, the fresh yet masculine smell of him. They didn't speak, but still communicated their attraction to each other.

She would have stayed with him had Chas not grabbed her for the next tune.

"Mmm, Yum Yum, you were delicious," Chas said, referring to her character, Yum Yum, in the Gilbert and Sullivan song. "Although I should like to taste you for myself."

He sang to her as he swung her about energetically to the current tune.

*By the sea, by the sea, by the beautiful sea,*
*You and I you and I, oh! How happy we'll be,*
*When each wave comes a rolling in,*
*We will duck or swim, and we'll float and fool around the*
*water.*
*Over and under, and then up for air,*
*Pa is rich, Ma is rich, so now what do we care?*
*I love to be beside your side, beside the sea,*
*Beside the seaside, by the beautiful sea.*

"You are an outrageous flirt, Chas," Victoria said as he dipped her backwards and pulled her up into a quick hug.

"I know. But only with you, darling."

"Applesauce!"

"Of course, I love all women. But, like Goldilocks, I do discriminate. Zoë is too serious, Eleanor, too clever, Vivian, too much in love with someone else. But you are just right!"

Victoria laughed.

"We could have a beautiful life together beside the sea. Or the lake, as the case may be."

"Is that a proposal?"

"I'll let you know after we've spent four months together travelling through Europe."

"In case you find yourself a princess who needs rescuing?"

"In case your beauty has blinded me to your true character."

"I can be quite a witch first thing in the morning."

"You wouldn't be if I were beside you," he whispered suggestively. "Shall we give it a try some time?"

Victoria was never quite sure if there was an element of truth behind Chas's flattery – whether he was slightly in love with her or not. She liked him enormously. He always made her laugh, and she imagined that life with him would be great fun. It would definitely add a certain piquancy to their trip if Chas went along as well.

Justin Carrington, on the other hand, always meant what he said. While they danced to *Let Me Call You Sweetheart* he said to her, "Lady Beatrice seems an interesting person."

"Oh yes! I am so looking forward to our trip."

"I shall miss you." The softly spoken statement carried a weight of meaning.

Justin often came to dinner and sometimes joined them for outings to the theatre or symphony, since he was at the university and rarely went home to Guelph. More so this past year, she realized, suddenly wondering if Justin had become enamoured of her. Was it significant that he had asked her to dance to this particular song? That he, who had been so kind and indulgent during her obvious infatuation, should now take her seriously was rather disturbing. She loved him as a friend, but felt none of the sheer delight she did in Chas's company or the shiver of excitement in Jack's.

She refused to meet his eyes because she was afraid that she might read something there that she couldn't ignore. She most certainly did not want to hurt Justin.

She said, "How do you think Lydia and Vivian will take to being back home? I expect it would be a bit of a letdown after their adventures. An experience like that changes you." She wondered if he would take it as a hint.

"Lydia will find her last year of school immeasurably dull, I expect, though she always knows how to make the best of things.

And Vivian is trying to convince our parents to let her attend university."

"Is she?" Victoria was truly surprised, for Vivian hadn't mentioned it or ever seemed so inclined.

"It does rather seem out of character, doesn't it?" he said, as if reading her thoughts. "I expect she's plotting something, although I don't know what."

"She's planning to elope!"

Justin laughed, "She could do that from home. She's not imprisoned there."

"Then I shall just have to sound her out," Victoria declared.

Which she did when she saw Vivian take a break for refreshments. After picking up a glass of lemonade from the sideboard in the dining room, Vivian strolled out into the hall and down to the breezeway. Victoria followed her to the west veranda, but hesitated for a moment when Vivian seemed relieved to find herself alone. She was looking pensively off to the distant islands.

"You've been very secretive, Vivian. Justin tells me you want to go to university."

If she was annoyed by the intrusion, Vivian didn't show it. "My parents haven't agreed, so I thought it best not to say anything as yet."

"What do you want to study?"

"General arts, I suppose. Perhaps I could become a teacher."

"And what's the real reason?" Vivian hesitated, so Victoria said, "You might as well tell me about the fellow you're in love with."

"Is it so obvious?"

"Yes."

"My parents don't approve of him."

"Hence sending you off to Europe for a year."

"I was supposed to get over him, find someone else, grow up, come to my senses."

"But it didn't work?"

"I'm in love with him, Ria! It's not just a pash. Love is not so easily forgotten or dismissed. I don't want to be with anyone but him."

"Then spill. What makes him deserve such devotion?"

"His name is Peter. He was one of our stable boys." The Carringtons had a large country estate on the edge of Guelph where they bred race horses as a hobby. "He's brilliant with horses and was working to earn enough money to attend the Veterinary College at the University of Toronto. Which he's managed to do."

"That's why you want to attend the university."

"Yes. So that we can see each other. And so that I can have a career and can become independent of my parents. I hate being so powerless! Papa threatened to disinherit me if I didn't stop my *liaison* with Peter. Although I don't understand why he's not *good enough* for me. My grandfather was a bastard." At Victoria's raised eyebrows, Vivian continued. "Oh, yes, it's a family secret that we children aren't even supposed to know about. I think it almost kept Papa from marrying Mama, but her family was most respectable by then. And his father was just a simple miller, so Papa wasn't the cat's whiskers that he thinks he is now. Grandfather Keir was richer and more successful at that time. But he had started out dirt poor and living in a log cabin, and Grandmother Megan had been an orphan living on the streets when Grandfather Keir found her."

"It sounds like a romance novel! So what's he like, your Peter?"

Vivian's smile lit her face. "He's dashing! Smart, kind, gentle, dedicated."

"How can I help?"

"Would you?"

"Absolutely. But how?"

"Well, I was going to ask that you let my parents know that I can come to dinner once a week or something like that, to make it look as though your family is keeping an eye on me. Justin is still there for another year, so he can look out for me until you're back."

"Of course. But if you want to convince your parents to let you go, then you might need to employ a bit of subterfuge," Victoria suggested.

"What do you mean?"

"I mean that you need them to think that you are over Peter, that you don't care a toss for him. Stop moping about. Enjoy the summer. Flirt with other fellows. If they see you back to your old self, your parents will relax and perhaps even let you have your way as a sort of reward for being an obedient daughter."

"You are devious, Ria!" Vivian laughed.

"I have to be, living with Father and Grandmother."

"But it's not fair to string fellows along."

"It's all just fun. You don't have to give them too much encouragement or you'll have all of us girls casting kittens."

"*You* have nothing to worry about. But I do think you have a point. Thank you, Ria."

Victoria left Vivian smiling and enjoying a moment of solitude. She walked along the breezeway to the east side of the cottage on her way to the pavilion, and gasped as she was suddenly pulled into the shadows of the kitchen wing.

Jack said, "I didn't mean to frighten you, but I've been longing to do this." He drew her into his arms and kissed her, gently, tentatively at first. When she relaxed against him and moaned, his kiss became hungry and forceful. She pushed him away, startled.

"You've never been French kissed," he said with secret delight.

"You surprised me!"

"You needn't be ashamed of being inexperienced. It makes you all the more desirable."

She started to move away, confused by her yearning to kiss him again and her trepidation at the strength of his passion. Of course she had been kissed before, but those had been chaste in comparison.

He drew her back into his arms. "Can we take things more slowly, and just start with this?" He kissed her again, softly tasting her lips, moving his hands caressingly along the nape of her neck.

He felt her lips part beneath his, and gloried in how easy it was to seduce her. But he knew when to stop. While she was longing for more. She was trembling when he released her.

"You are irresistible. May I have another dance?" he asked.

It didn't seem right to Victoria that they had to return to the bustle of the dance floor after their moment of intimacy. And while she could make it seem outwardly as if nothing had happened, being in his arms made her long for more.

She was reluctant to dance the next tune with Rafe Thornton. He said, "I saw you sneak back with Jack. Where you off necking? Or petting?" He held her in a firm grip, preventing her from escaping.

"Don't be a swine!"

He grinned. "Methinks the lady doth protest too much. What's the big secret about your long lost cousin? Is he a bastard?"

"Of course not! Are you squiffed or is this your usual charming self?"

He laughed. "Then why haven't we seen him before?"

"My grandparents didn't like his wife, so they stayed away. It's as simple as that."

"I wonder. He seems furtive to me. Somewhat cold and calculating beneath all that charm."

"Why Rafe, are you jealous because we girls all like him? You could do with a heftier dose of charm yourself."

"Chas got it all – my share as well. I just don't want to see you get hurt, Ria."

"Hell's bells! I can look after myself!" And in fact it was Rafe who was making her uncomfortable with his intense stare and his vice-like grip.

She was relieved when Justin insisted on the next dance.

He sensed her discomfort and spoke lightly of inconsequential things. He, too, had seen her, looking rather flushed, return to the dance floor with Jack, and had wondered what had transpired between them. Although he couldn't find any fault with Jack, he didn't trust him. But he had never really liked Rafe, and hoped that the boy wasn't going to bother Victoria, who obviously had no interest in him. Justin was somewhat unnerved by how protective he had become of her. He had been such a frequent and welcome guest at Wyndholme this past winter that he felt as if they were already courting.

Because the Midsummer Night's Dream party was just a casual affair, it always ended before midnight. Augusta and Marjorie Thornton stayed inside as the others headed down to the point where Toby and Will had built a bonfire in the stone-edged fire pit. As the new moon was only a few days off, it was a dark night, lit only by the vast spill of stars and the odd light from a cottage or dock shimmering across the water, as well as the lucent necklace of gas lamps that encircled the entire point of the island.

"Does the bonfire have any significance?" Jack asked as he sidled up next to Victoria.

"It's actually an ancient pagan ritual, to give the sun energy as it starts its decline into winter. And the fire is also supposed to guard against spirits that are thought to roam the earth while the veil between the two worlds is thin," she replied. "But we tell Grandmother that it's to celebrate St. John the Baptist – that's what the church prefers us to think. She doesn't believe in mischievous fairies and evil witches anyway."

"And you do?"

"It's fun to pretend."

She shrieked as something seemed to crawl up her spine, and Chas said from behind her, "So you do believe."

"Who needs Puck when you have Chas being mischievous," she retorted, slapping his hand as it came, spider-like towards her.

"As long as he doesn't turn me into Bottom," Jack said, surprising Victoria by his knowledge of Shakespeare's *Midsummer*

*Night's Dream.* She felt ashamed of her reaction, assuming that someone who had grown up poor was necessarily ignorant of culture and literature. But also impressed.

"Now that would be amusing, making an ass out of Jack," Chas said. "For then he'd be a..."

"Oh please spare us the witticism," Eleanor Carlyle said.

"Jackass!" Rupert said with delight as he got the joke.

"That will be enough out of you, young man," Olivia said. "Esme will take you and Miles up to bed now."

"We'll come, too," Ruth Maxwell said to her youngest grandchildren, who seemed delighted by their grandparents' attention.

When they had gone, Beatrice said, "Some European cultures consider bathing in streams or lakes, or gathering the dew before Midsummer sunrise to be beneficial for health and beauty."

"That's an excellent idea," Olivia said. "Girls, remember I said we'd have a midnight swim some hot evening?"

Victoria and Zoë knew what she meant.

As Max started to say, "Do you mean sk...," Zoë trod hard on his foot and said, "Perfect! Oh, sorry, Max, but your foot was in the wrong place." He got the message and grunted.

After they had seen the guests off at the dock, Olivia took Beatrice aside and said, "The girls and I are going skinny dipping, if you're interested in joining us. It means..."

"Oh, I do know. And yes, I'd love to."

Olivia said to Max, "We'll have no monkeying about, young man. No sea monsters, ghosts in the woods, or disappearing clothes. Understood?"

"Yes, Mama. But I think it jolly unfair that it's only for the women."

"You can use the other bay," Victoria suggested.

"Yes, why not? What do you say, Jack? We'll strip down in the boathouse. I don't think we'll ask Henry." He was already up at the house, having a cigarette on the veranda with Edgar.

They went to fetch lanterns which hung on the back wall in the breezeway. Seeing them heading off to the change house, Phyllis said, "Are you going swimming? I think I might join you."

Olivia said, "As you please. Bathing costumes are optional."

"That's disgusting! What can you mean by exposing yourselves like that? Have you gone quite mad, Olivia?"

"It's dark, Phyllis. Even the fish won't see anything. Skinny dipping is becoming quite the rage," Olivia exaggerated.

"Beatrice, surely you don't condone this sort of immoral behaviour!"

"My husband and I often swam naked in the Mediterranean. Our villa has a secluded cove. It really is most delicious."

Beatrice suppressed a chuckle at Phyllis's grunt of horror and indignation.

"I expect we haven't heard the last of that," Olivia said as Phyllis stomped back into the house.

"You mean you think she'll tell Augusta, who will give you a wigging? I'd be surprised, actually. If Augusta's become prudish, then I'd say it's the forgetfulness of old age, and that perhaps she has been too long without a man – like our old queen, Victoria."

Olivia laughed at Beatrice's unabashed candour.

"When I was about ten, and Augusta was twenty, we were out for a walk on her father's estate. It was a blistering hot day and when we came to the river which bordered the property, we were so hot that we just couldn't resist going in to cool off. Swimming was not really a pastime in those days, especially for women, so we didn't even have bathing suits. Not that we could have afforded them anyway. So we stripped down, I, to my shift, and Augusta, to her bloomers and camisole. We had a glorious splash about in the shallow water – it only reached to my waist – and once we were dripping wet, our smalls were pretty well transparent. I, of course, in my scrawny child's body, had nothing particular to hide, but Augusta was a fine figure of a woman and the clothes were moulded to her body. Nothing was left to the imagination."

Victoria and Zoë, fascinated by the tale, crowded around Beatrice as she continued. "A farmer owned the land on the opposite side of the river. It was quite a large and successful holding, and the son was a handsome young devil, Oxford educated. He just happened to arrive at the river to water his horse. You might think that Augusta would have shrieked, grabbed her dress to cover herself, and run off. But she did nothing of the sort. Just stood tall and proud in the stream and said, 'Good day, Stephen. We haven't seen much of you lately.' He replied with a grin, 'I'll have to remedy that, for it's always a pleasure to see you, Augusta.'

"When I was older, I looked back at that and wondered if they had been lovers. Of course she wouldn't have married him. He wasn't rich or important enough. But Augusta was no shrinking violet. She has always been strong and taken what she wanted out of life. He was certainly a prize. And actually ended up doing quite well for himself. Became a cabinet minister and has been knighted."

Victoria and Zoë were both amazed at this anecdote about their stern and critical grandmother. It was hard to picture her as a flirtatious, even brazen young woman. Victoria had a sudden vision of Jack standing so boldly and nakedly in front of her.

"So I may have to remind her about that when I tell her of our midnight swim. Best to forestall Phyllis, don't you think?"

They left their lanterns glowing softly in the cubicles as they swam out into the calm and sheltering darkness of the night. For Victoria, only the darkness was a new and rather thrilling sensation. Being immersed in blackness, gazing up at the infinite stars, made her feel as if she were drifting among them in some timeless space.

"This is glorious!" Olivia enthused. "I never thought it would feel so... so... wonderful."

"Almost sinful, isn't it?" Beatrice said. "I must say that it's a relief not to have to worry about sea creatures. Russell was once stung by a jellyfish, right across his bottom. Dashed painful it was." But she laughed in remembrance.

In the other bay, Max was showing Jack how exceptionally well sound carried over open water at night. They had watched the lantern in the Carlyles' rowboat as they had made their gentle way home, the bobbing light spilling across the black water. They could hear the creak of wood on wood as the boat bumped against the dock. Max called out in a slightly raised voice, "Oh-you-who!"

"Go to bed," came the reply from, undoubtedly, Eleanor.

"So you see," Max said to Jack, "you have to be careful not to say anything nasty about the neighbours when you're down by the water at night."

"Or they might never forgive you," echoed the amused voice across the darkness. "Good night!"

Molly, who was sitting on the servants' veranda, could hear the laughter from the two bays, although the trees and buildings absorbed much of the sound. She was savouring a forbidden cigarette – Augusta considered women who smoked of questionable morals and refused to employ them. Molly had nicked this from the humidor in the library.

She wished she could join Jack for a refreshing dip in the lake. She had been well and truly cooked in the black maid's uniform that covered her from neck to wrists and ankles, with a white bibbed apron and cap to add another smothering layer. She sat now in her thin shift and dressing gown trying to get cool, but the night was humid and there seemed to be no relief anywhere.

Certainly not in the small, stuffy and stifling staff bedrooms above the kitchen. There were no high ceilings there, as there were in the main house, where the bedrooms had glass transoms above the doors that not only allowed light into the upper hall, but were usually open to promote cross ventilation. And their screened French windows to the balconies were rarely closed.

But the six bedrooms above the kitchen could fit into Jack's room above the boathouse. Each was only large enough for two single beds, a small wardrobe, night table, and wash stand, with barely enough room to get around them. Fortunately, the women servants each had their own rooms, although Rosie, the kitchen maid, and Mary, the laundry maid, had doubled up to allow Lady Beatrice's maid, Mason, who was higher in the echelon of servants, her own quarters. And right now, with the extra staff up from the city, Molly had to share her room with Albert's kitchen maid. They all kept their doors open to encourage breezes, but that allowed for little privacy. And Mrs. Hadley snored.

So it was no paradise for the servants to be at the cottage. They didn't even have a staff bathroom here, like they did at Wyndholme, and were expected to bathe in the lake in the early morning before their own breakfast at 6:00. And Molly detested the outhouse, which was always crawling with spiders and bugs she had never seen in the city. She thought she had left the backyard privy behind her years ago.

There was nothing to stop her from going to a spot further along the shore for a swim now, but Molly found the deep darkness of the woods and the night sounds of the skulking creatures much more terrifying than any city streets. No feeble lantern light would penetrate that fear. She wouldn't even use the outhouse at night, preferring the chamber pot.

With long, hot days of work and not many places to spend free afternoons, it was little wonder that it was hard to find servants willing to come up for two or three months. It was partly how she had landed this job.

It had been Jack's idea, of course, that she try to get taken on at Wyndholme. And it had taken a year to finally make it work. She wished he could have seen her performance the day she had boldly knocked on the tradesmen's entrance and asked to speak with the housekeeper. Truly, she should be on the stage!

She had chosen a time when she reckoned that the staff were having a tea break in the afternoon, and had guessed well. She had

wanted to be sure of an audience. She had not waited at the
entrance while the footman had gone to fetch the housekeeper, as
was expected, but had found her way to the servants' hall around
the corner where she had said to the assembled and surprised
staff, "Good day to you. What a warm and welcoming room it is.
Sure, but it must be a pleasure to work here."

Mrs. Grayson, the housekeeper and wife of the butler, had
hurried in and said sternly, "Yes? What is it you want, young
woman?"

"Begging your pardon, M'am. I'm looking for a new position as
a parlour maid and was passing in the street when I happened to
see this grand house and me thinking, 'Well, Molly Jones, if that
be'n't the very place for you!' so I thought I'd come and see if you
needed help. I apologize for not waiting in the hall for you, M'am,
but I did have to come into the house to see if it suits. My present
place of employ, grand though it is, gives me the creeps, that it
does." She shivered dramatically.

As expected, this had intrigued the rest of the staff, if not
Mrs. Grayson, and Mrs. Hadley had said, "Join us in a cup of tea,
Molly Jones, and tell us more."

"Really, Mrs. Hadley," Mrs. Grayson had said. "We don't need
any more staff at the moment, so there's no point in encouraging
the girl."

"No harm in letting the child have a sit-down and a chat."

"Thank you, M'am. I'd be most grateful. I'm that worn out,"
Molly had said, quickly finding herself a seat. "I have a very good
letter of recommendation from my previous employer, and have
been trudging about the city looking for a likely new place. It's my
afternoon off, see. Will you take a look at my letter, M'am," she
addressed Mrs. Grayson, "in case anything should come up some
time and you can see that I'm a hard worker of good character and
clean in habit?" She handed it to the housekeeper and then
accepted a cup of tea from the kitchen maid, Rosie.

Without waiting to be prompted she said, "I could feel it as
soon as I walked in here. It's a peaceful house. No murders or
violent deaths here, I'm that certain. Can't say the same about my
present place."

There was a gasp from some of the women. "You mean
someone was murdered there?" thirteen-year-old Rosie had
croaked.

"That I don't know, but what I know for certain sure is that
an unhappy spirit wanders about. I've seen it."

"What nonsense!' Mrs. Grayson had said.

"Oh no, M'am. It's maybe on account of me being Irish and sensitive and all, but I can sense things that most others can't. I'll be polishing the grate or carrying a tray and suddenly I come over all goose flesh and feel as if someone is behind me. When I look around I see a... well it's like a shadow, only more like white mist, just out of the corner of my eye and then it's gone. But there's a coldness in the room, as if the spirit had sucked out the heat. Most of the staff don't notice anything, although some are spooked at times, not really knowing what it is that makes them shiver suddenly and want to hurry back to the servants' hall. But like I said, I have this gift. I've even felt the presence in my room. Fair gives me the creeps it does! I'd really like to find a cheerful house, like this one."

"You poor child!" Mrs. Hadley had said. "And who is this family you work for now?"

"M'am, if you don't mind, I'd rather not be saying. I don't want to be thought of as gossiping about my employers, and they wouldn't want people knowing that their house is haunted." Mrs. Grayson had seemed impressed by her discretion. As Molly had intended.

"This is dated last year. Why did you leave the..," Mrs. Grayson checked the reference, "Alderson household?"

"I was poorly, Ma'am, and they were certain sure I was dying. I went home to my Ma and she nursed me back to health. It took months and by that time, of course, I had been replaced. But Mrs. Alderson had always been pleased with me."

"So I see. Yes, an excellent reference. And what was your illness? Not consumption, I trust?"

"Oh no, M'am. A chest cold that turned into pneumonia after I caught a chill. But I'm hale and hearty again, and I am a hard worker, M'am."

"Well, I will keep you in mind, Molly Jones, should the need arise. Where can I get in touch with you?"

"Well, M'am, it's a bit difficult, see, with me not wanting my present employer to know that I'm looking for a new position, and my Ma lives out in the country and I hardly ever get home. Might I just come by to ask occasionally?"

"Yes, that would be acceptable."

When Mrs. Grayson had left the room, Mrs. Hadley had poured Molly another cup of tea, and said, "I'll wager you didn't tell us half the story. What else have you seen?"

"I thought your housekeeper might think me daft, so I daren't tell everything." Molly had lowered her voice as if imparting some secret, and the others had leaned closer so as not to miss a word. "But once, when I was in bed – and I hadn't been asleep yet, mind – I felt the mattress sag ever so slightly, as if someone very light had sat down on the edge. Well, there was no one there, and I near died of fright!"

She'd had them spellbound and wide-eyed in horror. And before long she had known everyone's name and something about them, how the household ran and that they sometimes had trouble finding maids willing to spend summers up north.

"Sure, but this has been a great treat for me," she had said when she left, and knew she'd receive a warm welcome the next time she dropped in.

Which she did at least once a fortnight at first, and then on every free afternoon, so that she soon seemed like a member of the staff. She had a gift for story-telling that ensured an audience eager for her visits. Mrs. Hadley always gave her the largest piece of teacake.

With naive amazement, Molly spoke of colleagues who had opted to work in factories, where the pay was much better, the hours, shorter, and with freedom to do what you pleased with the rest of your time, but meant that you had to find and pay for your own lodgings, hopefully with meals included, and make your way to work, either by streetcar or on foot every day, rain or shine or snow. And weren't factories dirty, noisy places? Although one of her friends had come back to show them her lovely new clothes, which she could never have afforded on her maid's salary, and anyway, when would she have had a chance to wear them? Now she went to tea dances with young men from work. And there was no one to say she couldn't. Wasn't that just a recipe for disaster, as Molly's mother would say?

It was becoming harder for even people with the Wyndhams' wealth to keep good servants, so Molly knew it was only a matter of time before a position would become available.

And it was only natural that Molly Jones should be offered a job when the youngest parlour maid quit to work in one of the Eatons' factories, where no one disapproved of her 'stepping out' with her young man. That had been in April. But Mrs. Grayson had made it a condition that Molly be willing to spend the summer at Wyndwood. Everyone had played into her hands.

It would be one thing to be a guest here, but she'd had about enough of being a spy. As it had turned out, they needn't even have bothered with their elaborate ruse, since Jack had been accepted so easily by the family. Molly had little to contribute now. She hadn't even found anything useful among Augusta's papers in the library.

"Well, well, well," Tom, the footman, said as he sloped onto the veranda with a drink in his hand – a crystal glass from the library half filled with whiskey. He had his jacket off, and vest and shirt unbuttoned. "You look like you're waiting for a fuck."

"Bugger off, Tom," she said lightly, for he often made lewd comments to her. She had to admit that he was a handsome lad – footmen usually were – but she had no intention of even flirting with him.

"Ah, but Molly, me love, it's such a waste not to use that lovely cunt of yours."

"Your prick's never going to see it, so leave off, or I'll tell the old lady you're a horny beggar."

"Christ! Then *she'll* be wanting a fuck."

"Then I'll tell her that you're drinking all her whiskey and she'll kick you out on your ass."

"Do you think I care if I lose this sodding job? Shit! What kind of life is it when we work from dawn to midnight, making things magically appear and disappear without being noticed or thanked, while they swan about having fun. I'm surprised they don't ask us to wipe their fat arses. 'Yes, M'am, no, M'am, you're an ugly cow, M'am'. Dick-all time off, no stepping out with girls. And for what? A lousy two hundred bucks a year?"

"You get two hundred? I only get a hundred and fifty."

"Yah, well, you're just a woman. So I say we take what we can. A little whiskey here, a smoke there."

Although she agreed with him, she said, "And then what? A silver spoon? A gold necklace?"

"They wouldn't miss them. Christ! They shit gold around here."

"So why do you stay in service?"

"Plenty of food, nice clothes, a big house I can run when I get to be butler. Christ, it's like running a business! They couldn't manage without us. So I pretend I'm lord of the manor when they're all in bed or away. Look at Grayson, living in luxury all summer like the fucking house in Rosedale is his. 'Sides, I'm not going into the factories or mines like my brothers did. Nah, I'll stay. Grayson and his wife are saving to buy a place back in England so they can run an inn. So I expect I'll be the butler before too long." He drained his glass, and said, "Want one? I'm getting another."

"No."

"Suit yourself. But you and me could at least be having a bit of fun. I might even marry you and you could be housekeeper."

"I'd say 'kiss my ass', but you'd think that was an invitation."

"You used to be a lot nicer when you first come here, Molly Jones. Shows you can never tell."

"Doesn't it just?"

When he had gone, Molly thought that perhaps it was unwise to stay at Wyndwood much longer, with people like Tom paying her too much attention. And she and Jack had to be careful that no one saw them together. It was important for Jack to keep his nose clean.

But she also wondered if she could be useful in some other way. Like hastening the old bitch's death. Maybe adding some spoiled food to her Sunday supper tray. That might make her sick enough that she wouldn't recover. And it wasn't exactly murder.

# Chapter 9

A downpour before dawn cleared the air, and although the morning was grey, the sky was a clean blue by the time the Wyndham party set out for the Summer Solstice Picnic at five o'clock.

They heard Oswald's signalling canon as they stopped to pick up the Carlyles for the short trip to Oaktree. The Carlyles had only their rowboat for transportation, and since no one knew where the picnic was to be, it was thought best that they join the Wyndhams, although they suspected that everyone would end up going in the Oakley's eighty foot steam yacht.

But when they approached Oaktree a few minutes later, they knew they wouldn't be going anywhere. It looked as if it had snowed on the island. White flowers hung, clung, dripped, and clambered everywhere. The gazebo on One-Tree Island was festooned like a June bride; the humped bridge to it was a glorious train. Trees sprouted roses, daisies, and carnations from their trunks and branches. Balustrades and posts were living vines. White-linened tables, placed strategically about, had edges scalloped with garlands. Adirondack chairs were flower thrones. A twenty foot long pergola, completely smothered in blossoms, straddled the path from the main dock toward the house.

There were thousands of planted flowers as well, hot-house forced, in formal gardens, rock gardens, along paths, and in pots. And amongst all the whiteness was a planting of red and blue blooms in the shape of the American flag..

None of them had ever seen anything like it. Beatrice said, "By God, you people know how to impress!"

Augusta said, "It's the Americans. They tend to be ostentatious."

"What a shame to think that all those flowers are already dying," was how Zoë expressed her dismay at such excess.

Eleanor Carlyle was not so diplomatic. "Especially when you think of how many poor people could have been fed with the money."

That had been Jack's first reaction as well, but then he had marvelled at the kind of wealth that supported such extravagance. And approved. What was the point of having so much money if you couldn't do things to please yourself and to amaze and delight others?

"You girls must learn to enjoy the finer things in life instead of looking for ways to criticize your elders," Augusta declared, thinking once again that the Carlyles continually proved that they didn't fit into their society, and wishing that Zoë and Olivia were less influenced by them.

Hannah Carlyle said, mostly to the girls, "I expect that there are plenty of flower growers and vendors who can keep their families well fed now."

A beaming Oswald greeted them, along with a footman, on the dock. "Takes your breath away, doesn't it?" he said with pride.

"Absolutely spectacular," Beatrice replied amid murmurs of agreement from the others.

"Countess, what a great honour to have you join us today," Oswald said, bowing over her hand.

"My pleasure, I assure you, Mr. Oakley."

"Oswald, please, dear Countess."

"And I am Beatrice."

"Forgive me if I prefer Countess," he said.

She laughed and replied, "If it pleases you, then by all means."

"You've outdone yourself this time, Oswald," Augusta stated with approval.

"Anything to please the ladies. Letitia and Helena contrived it all."

"I wonder that you were able to find so many flowers," James said.

"Cleaned out Toronto, Montreal, and Pittsburgh," Oswald replied with glee. "You know that Horace Camford gets to host the Fourth of July Ball this year, so this is our little *do* instead."

Letitia and Helena awaited them on the other side of the arbour with corsages for the ladies.

"This is just too splendid!" Phyllis enthused.

"Magical," Victoria said.

"That's it exactly!" Letitia said with gratitude. "We were trying to create a fairyland. Wait until you see the lights in the evening." She was dressed in a wondrous white silk gown overlaid with a gossamer silver and gold-threaded tunic. Instead of a large picture hat, her pale hair was entwined with flowers and studded with diamond clips, so that she seemed to sparkle and glow in the sunlight like a fairy queen.

The rest of them were more casually dressed, as befitted a picnic. But no one begrudged Letitia her self-indulgence.

"You've done a marvellous job, Letitia," Augusta said.

"I couldn't have done it without Helena. She has the most wonderful imagination. And she's been supervising the staff for two days to get all the flowers strung up."

A footman offered them champagne, while a maid tempted them with delectable hor d'oeuvres from a silver platter.

Letitia said, "The usual crowd will be arriving, although some are bringing guests. We're having a croquet tournament – with a trophy! – on the bowling green, and there will be a treasure hunt for the children. And we're having a real Southern barbecue. The pig has been gently roasting in the fire pit since last night. Do enjoy yourselves. I'll join you later."

"I really think that I shall become a vegetarian," Zoë declared when they had moved away. "I don't want to see an entire pig roasting – gently or not."

"Squeamish, Sis?" Max asked with glee. "You eat bacon and ham. How is this different?"

"I've been examining my diet of late. And you may have noticed that I don't eat bacon anymore, or much other meat. I hate the thought that a creature has to die to feed me when I could perfectly well survive on other foods. And I've heard that the animals are cruelly treated in the slaughterhouses."

"No need to become graphic," Victoria said.

"That's the point, isn't it? We completely ignore the process as if these aren't sentient beings, as if by not seeing, not knowing, we are not implicated in their mistreatment and can enjoy a clear conscience as we feast on their flesh. It bothers me to think that some of our money comes from the Flavelles' pork packing business."

"Egads! I can see another cause emerging," Max said. "*Save the animals from dinner-plate death!*"

"And why not?" Zoë challenged. "George Bernard Shaw said something to the effect that our indifference to our fellow creatures is the essence of inhumanity. He's a vegetarian."

"Well I'm not giving up sizzling steak, crusty lamb, crispy chicken," Max teased, drawing out and savouring each tasty word.

But Zoë ignored his taunting. "I suspect Grandmother wouldn't allow me to request vegetarian meals, since it would cause more work for the kitchen staff and perhaps put Mrs. Hadley back up. I tried to persuade our cook, but she claims that there has to be meat at every meal. Perhaps I'll just have to learn to cook myself."

Victoria said, "Or you could just eat lots of Corn Flakes," referring to the advertising from Kellogg's that advocated people eat much less meat and much more of their healthful cereal.

"I think I'll need more than that to survive," Zoë said with amusement.

"You have to choose your foods properly to ensure you're getting enough protein and other nutrients," Eleanor advised.

"You haven't sworn off meat, have you, Ellie?" Max asked.

"Good God, no! Although our family does eat a lot of vegetarian meals. It's good to vary your diet."

"Yes, beef one day, pork the next," Max quipped.

People were strange, Jack thought. That anyone should choose to live on vegetables and cereals when they could eat proper meals, tantalizingly prepared, was beyond his comprehension. He had spent too many years craving meat but subsisting on stodgy porridge and thin stews that might have a few tatters of flesh left on the bones. It appeared that Zoë would not make a good wife after all.

A string quartet played on the extensive stone terrace off the veranda of the house. A long reflecting pool cut through the centre of the terrace and disappeared over the edge, the water cascading through artistically placed boulders and gardens into the lake not far below. An exquisite sculpture of Aphrodite dominated the other end, and a stone bridge arched shallowly over the pool. Grecian pillars standing sentinel along one edge of the terrace supported nothing except ribbons of flowers. These decorative columns seemed rather out of place in the pine and granite wilderness that was only just being kept at bay by Oswald's army of gardeners.

Augusta laid claim to one of the tables on the terrace while the rest of the family went to mingle with the other guests, who were fast arriving. Marjorie Thornton joined her, sitting down heavily and saying, "You've chosen well, Augusta. This is about the only place that isn't completely overwhelmed by the cloying odour of flowers." She sneezed. "Oh, I can't tolerate all those scents! Especially the lilies. We come up here for clean, fresh air. This is rather excessive."

Augusta tended to agree with her. Beautiful as they may initially appear to the eye, the flowers were oppressive. To Augusta, there was also an underlying whiff of decay and death. Something she had been thinking of more and more lately. It was the destruction of the prized old Jack pine that had brought these morbid thoughts to consciousness. She had even wondered if it was a sign from Reginald that she was to join him soon.

Jack was introduced to American banking, shipping, and industrial barons, including Horace Camford of Pittsburgh Plate Glass, whom he had once served at The Grand, and the tobacco heiress who was spending a month visiting. He eyed these new women carefully, but decided that he was out of his depth with them. With that kind of money behind them, they would be obliged to choose husbands from within their own elite society. Besides, they seemed somehow more self-assured and outspoken even than Victoria. They would be demanding and expensive wives.

But having met them, he could now bandy about names of American tycoons like Vandemeer, Fremont, Delacourt. It always helped to have connections.

The younger people soon moved off to the expansive bowling green where two sets of croquet hoops were arranged in the double diamond pattern.

"String quartets and croquet. How plebeian," Rafe Thornton scoffed.

"What would you prefer?" Henry asked.

"Ragtime and archery. Skeet shooting," Rafe replied.

"Yes, well, since there's a trophy involved, I plan to win it," Chas Thornton said, "so the rest of you had better beware! If you're any good, Ria, you may be on my team. What about you, Vivian? Ready to make mincemeat of those Yanks there?"

Since there were well over two dozen of them and only twelve could play at a time, some of them sat and watched while others wandered back to the terrace or about the grounds. Edgar, whose leg was bothering him, found a spot by the reflecting pool and was joined by the young Spencers as they awaited their turn. Rafe demanded a whiskey from one of the footmen and started chatting to the tobacco heiress.

Two of the groundsmen were on hand to keep score, and the peace, in case of dubious points. Each winning team would go on to the next round. Jack, who had never played, soon realized that there was a great deal of strategy involved. The games were lively and fiercely competitive, with laughter and cheering from the sidelines.

Augusta, who could hear them and just see some of their antics from her vantage point said, "A bit too much levity for a Sunday, I think."

"Do you think so?" Marjorie Thornton asked. "I do so like hearing young people having fun."

"Quite right," Beatrice said. "Joy is a gift from God."

Augusta grunted. "They'll be dancing next."

"Would that be so bad?" Beatrice asked. "Sundays shouldn't be dreaded, or bore one into questioning one's faith. I prefer a God who enjoys hearing laughter."

Augusta was annoyed that Beatrice didn't concur with her, and wondered now if she would be a bad influence on Victoria and Zoë. She had gone rather Bohemian in her years living abroad in foreign cultures with her mother. Beatrice had already confessed to their skinny-dipping last night, but hadn't allowed Augusta to protest, reminding her of that day in the river all those years ago. Fancy her remembering that! And imagine Stephen being knighted. For only an instant she wondered *what if*, but quickly closed her mind to that. She would not even admit to herself that she had loved him. Just a farmer's son.

"Did you read in the paper that someone tried to assassinate the Czar and his family a few days ago?" J.D. Thornton was saying to James as they sauntered up to join the ladies.

"I missed that," James said.

"It didn't make the front page. They always have a passenger train precede the royal train, and it was bombed. Several coaches were shattered and people were injured, but no one was killed. They say the Czarina collapsed from the stress of constantly living in fear."

"I can't pretend to know – or really care, I must say – what goes on in Russia and in the Balkans. There's always some civil unrest. I'm more concerned about my mining stocks after that explosion out west," James said.

"Yes. About two hundred dead, weren't there?"

"And one helluva mess to clean up."

"If you're just going to discuss disagreeable things, then you may go elsewhere," Augusta said to the men.

"Sorry, Mother."

"In that case we won't discuss the upcoming provincial election either," J.D. said to Augusta. "Politics are always disagreeable."

"But there's nothing to discuss, is there?" Augusta stated. "We're all Conservatives, and Whitney will be re-elected."

"I rather like Rowell's intention to abolish bars," Marjorie said rather sheepishly.

"Then it's a good thing that we women can't vote," Augusta replied. "There are too many sanctimonious and controlling women out there who try to force their views on others. We'd have all those strident Temperance creatures voting for the Liberals."

"You don't approve of Temperance?" Marjorie asked.

"Only since 'Temperance' came to mean 'prohibition'. I enjoy my sherry and wine and don't begrudge men who indulge in moderation. It's not alcohol that's the problem. It's the low character of some men that causes them to become despicable drunks. So why should everyone have to stop drinking because of a few?"

"Besides which, Mother has plenty of shares in Gooderhams' distillery," James said to appreciative laughter.

"A good investment then, you think?" Thaddeus Parker asked as he, Helena, and Oswald joined them. No one except Augusta and Marjorie were seated, as people were constantly milling about.

"A certainty, I would say," Augusta replied.

"Countess, I'd like you to come and meet to a good friend of mine, Eugene Vandemeer," Oswald said. "He's visiting the Fremonts, and we're trying to persuade him to buy an island and join our little summer community. Nothing like some royalty to convince him."

Beatrice laughed. "Hardly royalty. But I'd be delighted to meet Mr. Vandemeer."

Augusta was annoyed that Beatrice was getting all this unwarranted attention. So her own 'Honourable' was no longer good enough now that there was a 'Countess' present. Not that Beatrice encouraged Oswald – the foolish man didn't even address her properly. 'Countess', indeed! It should be 'Lady Kirkland'. But then, of course, she herself was only 'Mrs. Wyndham'. Yes, that did rankle.

"I understand that your Dominion Day Ball is rather an impressive event, Lady Augusta," Helena said, trying to smooth ruffled feathers. She had noticed Augusta's pressed lips.

"I rather think that after this picnic, the other events this summer will seem tame by comparison," Augusta said tetchily, feeling that everyone was upstaging her. And Helena had perhaps engineered this extravagance, for Letitia would be easy to persuade and Oswald was quite free with his money.

"Surely not. Yesterday evening, for instance, was delightful. And Letitia has raved about your fancy dress ball and made sure that we had costumes made specifically for it in Paris."

"And will you enter the first girls' swimming marathon?" James teased.

"Heavens, no! I'm now actually able to stay afloat for a while, but I very much doubt that I will ever be good enough to participate in that. But it does sound rather exciting. However did you think of the competition?"

James said, "It started as a dare. When we were young, my brothers and I noticed how close all these islands are to one another, so we called them The Stepping Stones. There were no cottages here then. We thought it was possible to swim from one to the next and finally over to Wyndwood. So Richard dared me, and we decided just to make it a race among us all."

"Who won?"

"I did the first year. Some of our neighbours joined in after that, especially once these islands were sold. We're lucky to have such good neighbours who didn't mind our using their islands, and have enjoyed participating. Soon there was a Cup and then it was decided to hold it on Dominion Day so we could combine it with a ball. Now we have people from all over the lake join in."

"You are fortunate to have such a history here, in this enchanting place. I can't imagine a better way to spend one's summers. Even Europe pales by comparison."

"That's why we do Europe in the spring or fall," Letitia said, joining them, along with a matronly woman. "Augusta, Marjorie, I'd like you meet Ada Vandemeer. I've been telling her all about your ball next week, Augusta."

"Of course you and your family must join us, Mrs. Vandemeer," Augusta said graciously. "The invitation is open to all our friends and their guests."

"We'd be honoured, Lady Wyndham. It seems to be one of the premier events on the lake, so I understand."

"Hardly that," Augusta replied, her good humour restored. "Just some old-fashioned fun. Do you have older children who might wish to participate in our Marathon?"

As Ada began to talk enthusiastically about her offspring, Helena said quietly to James, "I'm going to see how the children are getting on with the treasure hunt. Would you care to walk with me, James?"

"I'd be delighted. But wouldn't you prefer to be with the younger crowd? I believe they've all gone to the croquet lawn."

"How thoughtful of you, James," she replied warmly as they sauntered off. "But I do find them a bit... frivolous, perhaps. Oh dear, that does make me sound stuffy and staid. Of course I like to enjoy myself. And I love to play with the children. But I think that perhaps I was born middle-aged. I'm much more comfortable in mature company."

Helena chose her words carefully for she knew exactly what she wanted. She had decided that the Wyndham fortune was adequate, and that James was a lonely old man who would be flattered by the attention of a woman almost half his age. She also suspected that he wanted a male heir.

"Has Letitia not been trying to set you up with some young chap?" James asked.

"Indeed she has tried. But I'm afraid I disappoint her with my reticence and expectations. I've told her that I won't even consider anyone under thirty-five. Can you imagine me with Chas Thornton?" She laughed delightedly. She had deliberately chosen the most beautiful young man to show that she did not want even the most desirable of them, and also because she knew it would seem an absurd coupling. "I know that I am not much of a catch. I have no dowry to speak of and am quite outshone by all the beautiful young women here."

"Beauty of the flesh is all too fleeting. Beauty of the soul is what truly counts."

"Why, James, how poetic! But you see, that proves my point exactly. A young man would not think that way at all. Wisdom is not given to the young, but it is something that I value. I think that a man who has had some experience of life knows his own mind, and is reliable, thoughtful, sincere. Spare me the false earnestness and shallow promises of youth."

They heard a child scream and, after a shocked gasp, Helena hitched up her skirts and ran along the path. James was right beside her when they came upon Felicity Thornton just standing there, holding a prized treasure box from the hunt. Shocked and pale, she was looking in horror at the blood trickling along her white-stockinged calves below her childishly short white skirt. Helena understood at once. She put her arm around Felicity and said, "It's nothing to worry about, pet. Get down on your knees."

To James she said, "Sometimes a little deception is necessary."

Helena made sure that there were dirt stains on the girl's dress and said, "James, would you mind picking Felicity up and carrying her to the house. It seems she has fallen and skinned her knees."

To the frightened and confused girl, she said, "This is quite natural, pet. Your mother will tell you all about it. It just means that you are becoming a woman. Not always a pleasant prospect." She whispered these last statements into Felicity's ear.

Others had come running, including the Oakley's nanny, who looked even more terrified than Felicity, as she was in charge of all the children. Helena took her aside and quickly explained the situation.

The nanny told the nursery maid and the two under-gardeners who were helping with the treasure hunt to take the rest of the children to the music room and keep them entertained until she returned. Then she and James, who was carrying Felicity, went towards the back entrance of the house.

They had to skirt the bowling green that stretched pretty well across the island behind the house. Chas, who was awaiting his next match, rushed over with some of the others following. "What's happened, Fliss?"

She turned her face into James's shoulder and began to sob quietly. She was scared and highly embarrassed.

Helena said with authority, "She's fallen and cut her knees, but will be just fine. We'll take her inside and clean her up." She ushered them away.

Phoebe started giggling. "Did you see the blood? She's all bloody! She's got the curse." She laughed hysterically.

Victoria slapped her lightly across the arm and said, "Shut up, Phoebe!"

Phoebe turned angrily to her. "Ouch! You're wicked!" she hissed as she stomped off, rubbing her arm.

"I barely touched her," Victoria said.

Blake Carlyle watched Phoebe assessingly. She was muttering to herself as she picked up a mallet and whacked the croquet ball as if she were driving a golf ball. The hard wooden ball flew like a cannonball across the green and bounced off a tree trunk, knocking off some flowers and barely missing the American shipping heir, whose group was still playing. They were all stunned by this violent display of temper.

Henry marched over to her and took the mallet away. "What the devil are you doing, Phoebe?" he demanded.

She looked at him coldly. "I'm playing croquet!" She noticed the others standing nearby, looking puzzled. "What's the matter with all of you?" Phoebe asked. "You always hate it when I'm winning, don't you? He said that you were mean and nasty!"

Blake went up to her. "Who's 'he'?"

"God, of course!" She shook her head in disgust. "You all make it seem as if *I'm* silly and that *you* are all so clever and perfect. Well, He says you're all liars, so he doesn't care to talk to *you*!"

"You talk to God?" Blake asked casually. The rest stood about, uncomfortable with the way the conversation was going. It was as if Blake was trying to open a door that no one wanted to see behind.

"Of course."

"And what does He tell you?"

"I think that's enough," Henry said.

"I'm not telling *you!*" Phoebe said to Blake. "None of you heathens deserves to know! Sodom and Gomorrah, " she muttered before rushing off toward the terrace, leaving the others speechless and embarrassed.

Except for Blake, who said, "Henry, I think your sister needs some medical attention."

"Don't be ridiculous!" Henry replied. "She's a bit temperamental and hasn't developed the maturity for dealing with frustration yet. I apologize for her behaviour, but would appreciate it if you wouldn't make it seem more dire than it is."

He went off to the terrace to join Edgar, who had missed the little drama on the green.

Chas Thornton said, "I expect we've had our excitement for today. I say, Ria, come into the woods with me so I can make wild and passionate love to you."

"Don't be daft!" Victoria laughed, pushing him away as he put his arm about her waist.

"I'm desolated! If that's a word. So I need some fortification before the next exciting match," Chas said, and a group of them headed toward the terrace while others resumed their game.

As they walked along, Jack said casually to Chas, "I almost forgot to tell you. Your friend, Lord Devenish, is my third cousin. Cousin Beatrice has brought me up to date with my relations."

"Well, I'll be jiggered! I say, old man, you'll just have to come along on our European jaunt and get to know Cedric. He's a good egg."

Justin Carrington fell into step with Victoria, and said, "Your conversation with Vivian seems to have had an effect. She's taking an interest in things and seems happier. But I wonder if you two haven't plotted something."

"Your law studies are making you suspicious, Justin," Victoria replied with a grin.

"No, just observant."

Zoë and the Carlyles went back to resume their croquet game. "You think Phoebe has a mental problem, don't you?" Zoë asked Blake.

"I think that Phoebe should be seen by a psychiatrist."

"You know that Phyllis and Albert would never allow that."

"Mental illness is a taboo subject. No one wants to admit that there's madness in the family. It's shameful, and a blight on the family name. So afflicted people are called eccentric or moody or sensitive. But she'll only get worse, and then they won't be able to ignore it."

"They may well keep her locked in the house," Eleanor said. "The madwoman in the attic, like in *Jane Eyre*, is not uncommon, I'm afraid."

"What do you think is wrong with her?" Zoë asked.

"My guess is dementia praecox. More commonly called schizophrenia now. I should have realized earlier. She still talks to her doll, doesn't she?"

"More importantly, Maryanne talks to her," Zoë said.

"Precisely. She hears voices. The doll's, God's, and probably more."

"Poor Phoebe! That must be frightening."

"At times, I expect so. But they are also her friends, aren't they?"

"Did she develop this because Phyllis keeps her a virtual prisoner at home, not allowing her to go to school or have friends?"

"Or perhaps Phyllis suspects, and wants to keep Phoebe away from others who would notice," Eleanor suggested.

"Did anything traumatic happen to her when she was young?" Blake asked.

Zoë thought for a moment and said, "She and her sister, Sarah, both had scarlet fever. Phoebe was about seven, I think, and Sarah must have been five. She died."

"Were they close?"

"I think so. Poor Phoebe. What can we do to help her?"

"I'm certainly not advocating that she be admitted to a lunatic asylum. I don't hold with the old-fashioned treatments or any sort of restraint, so I think she could be looked after more humanely and effectively at home – as long as they acknowledge that she has a problem and are prepared to get help to deal with it. I would like to see her given some psychotherapy."

"Could you do it?"

"I'm not qualified yet, and, as you say, her family probably wouldn't allow me to, in any case."

"So what *can* we do?" Zoë asked with concern.

"Watch that she doesn't hurt herself. Or others. She could think that people are out to humiliate or harm her. Paranoia can be quite severe. The voices could become more nasty as she gets older. They might even tell her to do things that are self-destructive. If she gets to that stage, she may have to be institutionalized. There's a private Sanitarium in Guelph that bears checking out. I believe they take a holistic approach to healing."

Meanwhile, Helena had found Marjorie Thornton, who was still sitting with Augusta.

"Do excuse me, ladies. Mrs. Thornton, Felicity is in need of your assistance for a moment."

"Oh, dear. What's happened?" Marjorie Thornton rose with difficulty as she said, "I can't tolerate any upsets. My constitution won't take it."

"It's nothing serious," Helena assured her. "But the child is a bit distressed and need some motherly advice."

Rather a bit too late, Helena thought scornfully, for it was obvious no one had told the child about menstruation. Of course it was shocking and frightening for a young girl not to know why she would suddenly start bleeding from a private place that was never to be mentioned. And to have this happen in public must be mortifying.

Helena explained the situation to Marjorie as she led her to the nursery. "But surely she's too young," Marjorie said, embarrassed that Helena should even mention such a thing.

"Not at all. Isn't she fourteen? Nanny or I could explain the situation to Felicity, if you don't feel up to it."

"Oh no! I will talk to her."

"And perhaps someone should fetch her a change of clothes," Helena suggested.

"No, no, I will take her home to rest."

"It will be difficult to get her down to the boat without everyone seeing the blood stains on her dress, Mrs. Thornton."

Marjorie practically wrung her hands in agitation. "Oh dear! Of course. Perhaps she could borrow something of Louise's."

Felicity burst into fresh tears when she saw her mother. "Mummy, Mummy! I think I'm dying!"

"No, no, angel! Mummy will tell you all about it when we get home."

"But Helena said that it's part of becoming a woman, and I won't be a woman for ever so long – at least another three years – and if I keep bleeding like this I'll be dead in a month!"

Helena would have laughed if the girl had not been serious and completely distressed.

"No, no, angel, it stops in a few days, but comes every month until you are very old, like Mummy," Marjorie managed to say.

"How horrible! Does every woman have this?" Felicity asked through her tears.

"Yes. Once they're about your age."

"But why? Is God punishing us? It doesn't happen to men, does it?"

"It's all part of having babies."

"But I don't want to have a baby! Make it stop, Mummy!"

"You won't have a baby now, pet," Helena intervened when Marjorie seemed speechless. "Your body is just going through growing-up changes. All the girls you know have gone through the same thing, and they seem quite happy, don't they? You'll soon get used to this. Why not talk to Louise about it, some time. Or Eleanor – she's going to be a doctor."

"They all have this? Every month?" she squeaked.

"We all do."

"But I've never noticed."

"There, you see! So it can't be that terrible."

Marjorie was rubbing her brow as if she had a headache coming on. "Nanny, can you find something for Miss Felicity to wear?"

"Certainly, Mrs. Thornton."

Helena joined James, who had been waiting for her outside the nursery. He had realized soon enough what was going on, and had overhead some of the conversation with Marjorie. With obvious admiration, he said, "Well, it's fortunate for Felicity that you are so quick and resourceful."

She smiled. "It was nothing really. Heavens! I should check on the children in the music room. I'm not sure that the servants quite know how to entertain them." She liked children well enough, but knew that James would be impressed by her seeming devotion to them.

James stayed with her, and realized that Helena had been right. When they saw her, the Oakley children rushed up and said, "Helena, may we go back outside? There's nothing to do here!"

"We'll just wait for Nanny. She'll be here soon. Then you can finish your treasure hunt and have fresh ice cream that chef has made especially for you. In the meantime, let's play musical chairs." She ordered the servants to set up chairs to number one less than the number of children, and had the children stand in a circle about them. Then she sat down at the piano and played 'Oranges and Lemons'. When she suddenly stopped, there was squealing as the children dashed for a chair, with one child and one more chair being removed from the game each round. By the time Nanny appeared, the game was just about over and the children, in high spirits.

James said to her, "I think you deserve a break. Perhaps the gazebo is a quieter spot at the moment."

"Oh yes, that would be lovely."

They grabbed glasses of wine from a passing footman before ambling across the humped bridge to One-Tree Island. A couple of young people were there, but decided to leave when Helena and James arrived.

"I love this spot," Helena said as they sat in the gazebo. A round wrought iron table and four chairs were set up there, all, of course, entwined with flowers. "I usually have coffee here in the early morning. I secretly like to think of it as my place."

"So would you consider living in Canada? Marrying a Canadian?"

"Oh yes." Especially since there was less chance that her fictional life would be exposed here. "Although I think I would have to make it a condition that we have a summer home on the lake." She laughed to keep the tone light, so that he wouldn't think her mercenary, but merely so enamoured of the summer life here that she would fit in easily and happily.

"Helena, I don't know how things are done these days, but.... Would you consider being courted by an old fellow like me?"

"You're not old, James! Why, yes... Heavens! I'm flattered!" She tried to seem surprised and flustered, and managed to blush prettily. She felt triumphant.

"The summers pass so quickly and we won't have much time to get to know one another if we don't see each other often. I'm sorry if it all seems a bit abrupt."

"Not at all. You're quite right. I do enjoy spending time with you, James," she said, looking meaningfully into his eyes as she placed her hand over his.

"And I find you a remarkable young woman," James replied with an unaccustomed grin. He took her hand in both of his and felt absurdly happy.

He had had something of an epiphany today. When he had held Felicity and she had turned her face into his shoulder, he realized that he missed that physical closeness that bound one with another being. He had never held or comforted Victoria. She had killed his beloved wife, and he could never look at her without at first anger and later, bitterness. He had tried to tell himself that that was wrong, that Susannah would have wanted him to love and cuddle their child. But he couldn't get past his grief. So he had rejected Victoria's childish hugs and she had soon learned to find affection from her nanny and from Olivia. And now it was too late to change their relationship. But he wondered if he might have a chance to start afresh with a woman who would give him physical and emotional comfort, and hopefully children, whom he would not push out of his life this time.

"You must have loved your wife dearly, not to have remarried. Will you tell me about her?" Helena asked carefully, implying that she understood if he chose not to.

"You have only to look at Victoria to see Susannah." Which was heartbreaking for him in a different way. It had been one thing to reject his daughter when she had been a squalling red infant, but to see how much like her mother she was now, he felt that he had rejected Susannah as well. "We were only married for three years. It was a good match, contrived by Mother. But I did actually love her. She was so vibrant and vivacious. But you mustn't think that I've been in mourning all these years. I just haven't found another woman I cared to spend my life with." He'd had mistresses, but those had been purely therapeutic business arrangements.

"I'm afraid you might find me dull company in comparison with your wife, if she was as lively and lovely as Victoria."

"I'm not looking to replace Susannah. I think she may have found me dull company before long. It's easy to think that the excitement of a young marriage will last a lifetime, but I've come to realize that people grow apart as they have different responsibilities and needs. Friendship and respect can grow old, but I think that passion rarely does."

"How wise you are. I'm overwhelmed, James! I can hardly believe that a man of your stature and accomplishments would be at all interested in me."

"You mustn't underestimate yourself. You have a good heart. You're sensible and strong, and know how to laugh at yourself. I expect that everything within your sphere would be calm and orderly, and yet warm and cheerful."

"I would like to think so." For a moment she felt almost sorry that she had to deceive him, but she had a stronger sense of survival. And Helena intended to survive well. Being in charge of Wyndwood and a grand house in Toronto were the least that she expected from life.

She was also shrewd enough to know that confessing to some lies would insulate her somewhat if others were discovered in the future. Humbly she said, "James, before our affections become too deeply engaged, I must confess something. Oh dear, I have never been comfortable with this, and you must understand that it wasn't intended to hurt anyone!" She looked at him anxiously.

James patted her hand reassuringly and said, "My dear, it cannot be so bad as to distress you so."

"My brother, Edwin, didn't die on the *Titanic*. He died of meningitis when he was twelve. It was what started my mother's decline." Which was true as far as it went. "Papa perpetrated this *Titanic* story to explain his embarrassing loss of our fortune." An exaggeration, for they had never had much. And it had been her idea. "He didn't like to admit that he had made some very bad investments. So when he read in the newspaper that one of the *Titanic* passengers who had died was named Parker, he thought it would be an easy way to explain his failure to new friends. But unfortunately, small lies can become almost legendary, and now I'm ashamed to have to tell the lie over and over again, as people seem fascinated by the tragedy." She hung her head.

James squeezed her hand and said, "Thank you for your honesty, Helena. It makes me realize just how wonderful you are. I think it very loyal of you to support your father, if perhaps a bit misguided."

"Thank you, James. But you must realize that it is now impossible to take back the lie without losing credibility with our friends. Papa is most distressed with how it has gained a life of its own."

"We shan't pass it on then. Perhaps it will eventually die of neglect," James said with a reassuring smile.

"You are so generous and understanding, James! I hardly feel I deserve such kindness after deceiving you."

He took her hand and kissed it. "But you haven't deceived me. I hope this has taken some of the burden of guilt from your shoulders."

"I feel immeasurably better!" Especially since her gamble had paid off. She smiled warmly at him, knowing that she looked pretty when she smiled, for she was blessed with good teeth and a generous mouth.

Which was precisely what James thought. One did, after all, want to have attractive children. And it wasn't as though she was ugly – her nose was perhaps a bit large for her face, but her skin was unblemished and pale, and her grey eyes were interestingly flecked with blue and green. Her thick and glossy auburn hair practically invited him to explore its richness.

"May I tell Letitia of your interest? I would dearly love to have her stop urging me towards every young man she thinks would suit me." She chuckled.

"By all means. But perhaps you might wait until after the party, so that I have a chance to let Mother know. She doesn't take well to important decisions that are not of her making, so you must be prepared for some opposition from her. She'll say that you are too young or not suited, but please be patient. We are, after all, just trying to get to know one another better."

Helena could imagine the old biddy trying to turn James against her. But she was determined that nothing would stop her from marrying him. Especially no domineering old woman. "Of course, James."

A group of young Americans came over to the island, so James and Helena decided to return to the terrace, where most of the guests had congregated. James offered Helena his arm, which she took firmly in hers. Like an eager bride, she thought, to let him know that she was not a shrinking young maiden who shied away from physical contact, and yet not so bold as to appear to be a vamp or a floozie.

"She's a gold-digger," Augusta said to Beatrice when she noticed them rejoin the crowd.

"You mean she has no money?" Beatrice replied. "Like us, at one time?"

"Not at all like us. Aristocracy has its ups and downs, but we come from noble stock. We didn't put on airs and chase rich men just for their money."

"No, we came by our airs naturally," Beatrice said with a laugh. "But neither one of us wanted to continue to live in poverty either. I've hardly spoken with the girl, but she seems to be sensible and know her own mind. Perhaps just what James needs. He looks happy enough."

"They both do, which worries me. Surely he hasn't proposed to her! I think she's a consummate actress who knows how to manipulate people. And I for one dislike being manipulated, and will not have my son made to look a fool. And I doubt that you would trust her if she looked like her namesake, whose beauty launched a thousand ships into battle."

"You mean Helen of Troy? Well, quite honestly, James is no longer a prize for beautiful young maidens."

"Precisely! And because she's a plain little thing, you think she's harmless. Have you ever seen a photograph of Lizzie Borden?"

"The American woman who supposedly murdered her parents? Wasn't she acquitted? In any case, how did we get from gold-diggers to axe murderers?"

"You seem to think that only beautiful women have ulterior motives."

"What I'm saying is that neither of them is a great catch. But she probably wants security and he wants to recapture his youth. It's understandable. And quite a good enough reason for marriage, if they get along."

"Well I wouldn't trust her not to murder me in my bed, once she realizes that James lives in my house, under my rule."

Beatrice laughed. "Really, Augusta! Aren't you rather over-dramatizing? Anyway, he could always move out."

"Never! It is his duty to look after me. I won't be shunted aside."

"Augusta, you look much too serious for such a lovely day," Letitia said, joining them.

"I'm feeling my age," she replied.

"I think you need refreshment. So, I'd like you ladies to do us the honour of beginning the move to the buffet tables."

"By all means," Beatrice said, as Letitia escorted them to the house. "The air here gives me quite an appetite."

"Doesn't it just?" Letitia replied. "And I trust you won't be disappointed. Chef has been slaving over this for days."

The picnic was a sumptuous affair with lamb and partridge as well as the roasted pig. Long tables lining the ballroom were spread with oysters and caviar, poached salmon and lobsters, pâtés and truffles, galantines and salads, scalloped and roasted potatoes, vegetables swimming in cream sauces, biscuits and breads, a variety of cheeses, elegant patisseries, rich cakes, strawberries with thick cream, and fine chocolates. Delicate bone china and heavy silver cutlery complimented the food.

"I suppose the 'picnic' part is having to help yourself," Beatrice said with amusement to Augusta. "Russell and I would take a basket with cheese, pâté, bread, and wine, plunk ourselves down on some hillside, and think it all heavenly."

"That's more or less how our picnics are as well. The children enjoy canoeing over to an island with a basket of sandwiches. They don't even get wine," Augusta added with a chortle.

It was evident that Oswald employed an expensive French chef, for the food was exquisite, if somewhat rich. Champagne and wine flowed freely.

"Worth coming to after all," Rafe Thornton said after the meal, well into his cups after having downed several large whiskeys and countless glasses of wine.

"Especially since my team won the croquet cup. Well fought, ladies! I salute you," Chas said and raised his glass to Victoria and Vivian, who were at his table along with Zoë, Blake, and Jack. "Ria, do you want be my partner in the tennis tournament?"

"Of course! Oh, Chas, we have to teach Jack," Victoria said. "May we come over tomorrow afternoon to play?"

"You may come and play with me anytime, darling girl," Chas said lasciviously.

"Do stop!" she laughed.

"Tennis it is then," he replied with a dramatic sigh. "You can come every day if you wish. No need to ask. Jack will have a lot to learn in the next few weeks if he's going to be a contender in the tournament."

Thousands of fairy lights began to twinkle among the multitude of flowers as a torrid sunset ended the longest day of the year. The tables of food were cleared from the ballroom, and some people moved inside to dance or to avoid the mosquitoes. Augusta announced it was time for the Wyndhams to leave.

Wyndwood seemed dark and desolate in comparison to the scintillating fairyland they had just left. James spoke for them all as he said, "Well, back to reality. They did a marvellous job of making it seem... magical."

"A bit too bewitching," Augusta declared. "James, I'd like to see you in the library."

He had intended to talk to her tomorrow, and was puzzled that she didn't go straight to her room. When she had seated herself regally behind the desk, she motioned him to sit. He ignored her peremptory gesture and poured himself a cognac. "You must be tired, Mother."

"More distressed than tired, James. You seemed to spend a rather inordinate amount of time with that American woman, Helena." She made the "American" sound like a filthy word. "And she seemed to be clinging to you like a barnacle. What's going on, James?"

"That really is my business, Mother. But I had intended to tell you that I'm courting Helena, with her full consent."

"Don't be absurd! Do sit down!"

"I'm serious, Mother. She has all the virtues I seek in a woman, and we enjoy one another's company. If I still feel the same way at the end of the summer, I shall ask her to marry me."

He walked over to one of the armchairs and leaned against it casually.

"Out of the question! She's half your age. You'll look ridiculous."

"On the contrary, I will be the envy of all other men with old and wrinkly wives."

"Do you think she'll marry you for your youthful looks or charming manners? She's after our money."

"You were poor when Father married you, so you can hardly criticize, Mother. I'm fifty years old. You have thwarted several of my attempts to find happiness with another woman. I have found someone I want to spend whatever time I have left with, and I will not allow you to interfere."

"You won't *allow* me! We'll see just how eager she is to marry you when you're cut off from the Wyndham fortune."

He looked at her sadly. "You're always threatening to disinherit us. Is that the only way you can deal with us? Look at what you did to Alex. You know that there would not be such a fortune if Albert, Richard, and I hadn't been running the business so well all these years. We could prove that in a court of law. We could probably even prove that you are senile now, and no longer in a fit state to be the nominal head of the business."

"How dare you speak to me like that! You have wounded me deeply," Augusta said, truly shocked by his words.

He went up to her and placed his hand over hers. "That was not my intention, Mother. But I'm too old to be told what to do, how I'm allowed to live my life. I want to have more children. This may be my last chance."

She snatched her hands away. "You do what you must, if you won't listen to reason. But I can tell you now that I will not have that woman living in my house, trying to wrest control from me. I don't trust her, James, and if you weren't such an old fool, you'd see through her yourself. But we'll see what happens before the summer is over. You may well regret your unkindness to me."

It seemed like a threat, and he wondered what she was plotting, for he knew she wouldn't leave this alone. Through his own investments, he had already amassed what most would consider a small fortune. But he would fight for his share of the Wyndham empire. And he was damned if he was going to spend any more of his life being controlled by his mother.

# Chapter 10

Augusta's humour was restored by the time Jack asked her to sit for a portrait late the following morning. She had already penned a letter to her lawyer, Ethan Nash, and made sure that Tobias would post it.

Jack had had his morning business briefing, and had told Victoria that she could have her first lesson with him by watching him paint. James had bought plenty of art materials in Toronto, enough for Jack as well as Victoria.

Jack posed Augusta on the veranda so that she was looking out at the lake, but the viewer would see her slightly from the side, with the gingerbreaded veranda and the lake in the background. He explained to Victoria and Beatrice, who had come to watch, the various steps in the process. They marvelled at how quickly he sketched the scene in pencil. As he began apply the watercolours, the portrait gained life and character.

"Paint what you see," he said. "Not what you think you should see. For instance, look at the shadows. They're not grey, but rich with colour."

"You've used green and purple," Victoria said in amazement.

"And burnt sienna and cobalt blue. And here, a touch of carmine."

By the time he had finished an hour and a half later, Zoë, Max, their grandparents, and Olivia had all come to watch.

"That's remarkable!" Beatrice said. "He's caught the essence of you and this place, Augusta."

After his initial sketch, Jack had allowed her to talk, but not to move too much so that he could get the light right.

"I should hope so. I feel as stiff as a board, sitting here so long. Let me see it."

She was astonished. It was softly painted, but the woman in the portrait looked proud and strong, if somewhat bowed by age.

"You're very talented, young man," Ruth Maxwell said.

"Grandma, we should get Jack to paint a portrait of you," Zoë said to Ruth.

"Indeed!" Gerald Maxwell said. "And we should pay him handsomely for it."

"Not at all!" Jack replied. He could hardly charge Olivia's parents, since she was doing so much for him.

Olivia thought that if Alex had been as talented as his son, he would have done well. She said, "I hear you've been painting the island already. May I see some of your pictures? I would dearly love to have a few."

"Of course, but I'd also be happy to paint some for you specially, if you have a particular scene in mind."

"A couple, actually."

"Put me on that list of portraits and landscapes," Beatrice said.

"We all want some, Jack," Zoë said. "So I expect we'll keep you busy for the entire summer."

"It'll give me a chance to teach Victoria."

"I obviously have a lot to learn," she said, as much to have an excuse to spend time with him as in awe of his abilities.

"Get used to carrying the small sketchbook and your paint box, and do plenty of studies of things that interest you. A tree or a rock. Eventually, you can work on an entire scene."

Which is what she did when the two of them set out in a canoe after lunch to go to Thorncliff.

Beatrice, Olivia, Richard, and Henry were spending the afternoon golfing at The Grand. Edgar took them over in the Ditchburn and would relax at the hotel while he waited for them. Tobias had taken the servants off in *Calypso* for their half-day outing. Molly had chosen to stay behind again, pleading exhaustion and swearing that all she wanted was an afternoon of sleep. She didn't want to socialize more than necessary with the servants, particularly Tom, the footman. She had also felt sorry for young Rosie, whose turn it was to stay behind, for the young girl was terrified of being on the island by herself, especially once night fell.

Phyllis and Phoebe were doing their endless needlepoint on the veranda, while Albert worked in the library. The Maxwells were spending time with their young grandchildren, while Zoë and Max were meeting with Freddie Spencer at the proposed cottage site to discuss the secret plans for the design. Augusta had declared an afternoon of rest for herself, so she was lounging on her private, screened balcony, and had decided she would even forego tea that day, since she had no inclination to go visiting. James had gone off in a rowboat without saying anything, but Augusta had suspected he was calling on Helena.

So Victoria and Jack found themselves alone together. "Let's stop at the Shimmering Sands," Victoria said. "Chas won't be expecting us yet, and I want to try painting something."

Barefoot as usual, she jumped into the shallow water as Jack manoeuvred the canoe onto the sandy shore.

"I like the way that granite outcropping slopes into the lake," she explained. "And the crescent of sand. So where do I start?"

"By finding a good aspect to paint from," Jack said. And when she had found it, she started sketching tentatively. Jack sat on the rock beside her, giving her advice on how to do the washes and choice of colours. "You should be painting as well," she said.

"Perhaps next time. I want to be sure you know the techniques. Then you'll know how to express yourself, and we can compare styles."

Victoria was pleased with how the watercolour turned out. "I'm going to enjoy looking at this in the winter."

"You should do a full size painting some time. The sketch book is just for quick studies."

"Let's both do that."

"We really shouldn't be here alone like this," Jack said.

"And why not, pray tell?"

"Because I'm tempted to do this," he replied, pulling her into his arms and kissing her softly on the lips.

She was momentarily taken aback, but then succumbed to the pleasure of his kiss.

"And this," he murmured, trailing kisses along her neck, and then again finding her now-eager lips. She moaned when he touched her breasts and felt her nipples harden beneath her thin blouse. It took all his willpower not to take her right then and there. But when he let her go, he was sure that next time she would be ready for more.

"Chas will be expecting us by now," he said reluctantly, gently brushing a stray curl from her flushed cheek.

Shivering with delight, although her body seemed to be on fire, Victoria was barely aware of how they arrived at Thorncliff.

They found Chas and Felicity on the veranda, along with several contented cats. Felicity was lying in a hammock, looking unhappy and bored, a discarded book across her stomach. Chas put down his newspaper and said to them without preamble, "Did you see that Lieutenant Porte's preparing to fly across the Atlantic in a Curtiss hydro-aeroplane? I say, that would be a gas! London's *Daily Mail* has offered a £10,000 prize for the first direct crossing by air. That's what, about $50,000? Not a prize to thumb one's nose at, although the glory is worth more. I really think that I shall take up flying. Darling Ria, will you fly away with me?"

"I'll let you know when I've seen whether you can land as well as take off, " she jested. "What's a hydro-aeroplane?"

"A flying boat."

"You mean it can't make up its mind whether it wants to be in the air or on the water?" Felicity said.

"No, muggins, it means that it can take off and land on water without sinking. I think I shall take up flying when I get back from Europe. Get Pater to buy an aeroplane – perhaps a flying boat and then we can breeze about the lakes. Just think how quickly we could get down to Toronto. What do you think?"

"I think flying would be thrilling," Jack said, suppressing his envy at how easily Chas could make grandiose plans for his entertainment. He had no doubt that if Chas took up flying, J.D. would buy him an aeroplane.

"Then you must learn to fly as well. You and I will do an Atlantic crossing if Porte doesn't snatch the prize."

"You mean if he crashes into the ocean?" Victoria said. "Charming!"

"Where's your sense of adventure, Ria? I'd ask you along as my co-pilot, but I don't think girls can fly," he said dryly with a twinkle in his eye.

"We'll just have to test your theory when you have your aeroplane."

"And let you break my new toy? Edgar says you're a reckless automobile driver, and not much safer in the boat."

"Edgar has already dinged up their Cadillac, and I haven't put a scratch on the Rolls. That's just envy speaking."

Chas laughed. "Well, I see you're dressed for tennis. Almost. Did anyone ever tell you that it was inconsiderate to go about with your feet unshod, arousing the desires of lesser mortals like me?"

"All the time," she replied with a grin. "But I hate wearing shoes in the canoe." Victoria sat down to put on the tennis oxfords she had been carrying. "Is your mother here? I should pay my respects."

"She's resting. Pater's gone off to the city for a few days of work, and Rafe's gone along so that he can get to the hunt." Rafe, who was passionate about fox hunting, belonged to the Toronto Hunt Club. The Thorntons owned a large estate in the country north of Rosedale, along the Don Valley, where they had stables of prize thoroughbreds and hunters.

"Come along, Fliss, and we'll watch Chas teach Jack how to play, and then you and I might challenge them to a game." Felicity, like Chas, was an accomplished player.

"Mummy says I must rest for a few days," Felicity replied miserably.

"You two go ahead," Victoria said to the men.

When they had left the veranda, she went to sit next to Felicity, absently stroking one of the cats. She loved cats but Augusta didn't. "Did you hurt yourself badly yesterday?" Like Phoebe, Victoria realized what had probably happened at the picnic, and wanted to give the girl a chance to talk about it.

Felicity turned bright red. "I didn't. I mean. Oh, it's too awful!"

"I think I know what the problem is. Sometimes it's easier for girls to talk about it amongst themselves than with their mothers." Of course she wouldn't know, but that seemed a safe bet.

"Is it true that this horrible... *thing* happens to women every month?"

"Your courses? I'm afraid so. Messy and inconvenient, sometimes a bit crampy, but we can just carry on doing what we like. Except swimming."

"But Mummy says I mustn't exert myself until it stops. I don't want to lie around for a week every month!"

"Nor should you. It's an old-fashioned notion. But we modern girls know differently. Look at Zoë and me. We go canoeing, play tennis and golf, dance. You just have to be a bit careful."

"But those things are so uncomfortable," Felicity said, referring to the rubber "serviettes", like boats, with the removable cotton pads that were euphemistically and falsely referred to as 'ladies' comfort".

"Oh, I know. So it's best to do things that take your mind off it and you'll soon get used to it. Do come along. We might just be able to beat Chas if Jack doesn't pick up the game too quickly."

But Chas was a good and surprisingly patient teacher and Jack, an apt pupil. After an hour lesson they had a lemonade break, and then played doubles. It was a very close match, but Chas and Jack won.

"You did remarkably well, Jack, for your first time," Chas said as he wiped the sweat from his face and neck with one of the towels a footman had brought.

"I had excellent instruction, thank you, and I enjoyed it immensely. But I can see I have a lot of practicing to do, particularly with serves. You girls are quite a challenge!"

"Especially Fliss," Victoria said. "You should think about training for Wimbledon, if your lazy brother won't. Your shots are almost as powerful as his."

"Oh, I couldn't do that!"

"I think you could, Fliss," Chas said. "Although I expect Mumsy wouldn't approve. But we'd all come and cheer you on."

"You can fly us all over to England in your aeroplane, Chas," Victoria teased.

"You mock, but I think one day people will be able to fly overseas. You wouldn't have to spend weeks on a ship."

"I'd rather dine and dance on a ship than be crammed into a tin can for days."

"No imagination," Chas said. "Think of a ship, but in flight."

"We can't even get ships to stay reliably afloat on water. Imagine the havoc if they started to take to the skies." They laughed at the absurd image her words conjured up.

Chas began to sing *Come Josephine in My Flying Machine* and Victoria joined in as he took her in his arms and waltzed her energetically about the tennis court.

*Come Josephine in my flying machine*
*Going up, she goes! Up, she goes!...*

Whenever they sang that line, Chas lifted her so she could kick up her heels in a graceful arc as they whirled about. After a few enthusiastic choruses, they collapsed with laughter onto some chairs.

Jack envied their carefree gaiety. How easy and fun life seemed for them, with no shadows to haunt them or dull their pleasure.

"Let me see your scribbles," Chas said to Victoria, referring to the painting she had been doing while he had been teaching Jack. She had focussed on a tall pine that leaned out over the water and then turned to reach the sun.

"Not bad," Chas said. "You'll have to go and join The Colony now."

"Surely not!" Victoria laughed. At Jack's puzzled expression she explained, "The Colony is what people here call a cottage on Mortimer's Island. That's Mortimer's over there." She pointed to the huge island more than two miles long that dominated the centre of the lake at this point. Cottages and small lodges were lost on its extensive meandering shoreline. "The Colony is in a bay on the east side just around that point. It's owned by a woman artist – what's her name? Edelina something – who always has at least half a dozen other artists, writers, and the like staying in tents on the property. They give poetry readings and invite speakers to give lectures. Professor Carlyle gave a talk on astronomy once."

"Most of them are as poor as church mice and some of them are terrible poets, but still think themselves intellectually superior. A Colony of lame ducks and the disenfranchised," Chas said.

"You've been there?' Victoria asked.

"For a lark once. Too much posturing for my taste. Some people try to make a virtue out of poverty. Although Edelina is quite a scorcher."

"Perhaps you should become a patron of the arts, Chas, and keep them out of poverty. Or you could buy my painting," Victoria teased.

"When you've had a bit more practice perhaps. I say, Ria, we should all go to The Colony. Don't they have events on Wednesdays?"

"I think so. Oh yes, let's do! We'll ask the Carlyles as well, since they actually know Edelina. I think the Professor buys her paintings."

"I've heard there's nudity and free love and all kinds of delicious goings on there," Chas said. "Should be interesting."

.    .    .

Having finished their golf game, Beatrice, Richard, Olivia, and Henry wandered back to The Grand's rotunda to have cool drinks on the veranda with Edgar. Olivia fell into step with Henry, having warned Richard earlier that she needed to talk to Henry alone.

"I heard that Phoebe wasn't quite herself yesterday at Oaktree," she said.

He seemed annoyed. "I wish people wouldn't make such a fuss about it! She just lost her temper, and did something foolish and rather childish, I agree."

"Blake thinks that there is some reason for concern."

"He'd like to label everyone mad, since that is his career. But Phoebe is harmless."

"But if Phoebe is hearing voices, Henry, that is not normal. Surely that worries you?"

"She's very religious. Perhaps those of lesser faith can't understand that," Henry said somewhat scathingly. "Because she says she talks to God, she is surely more saint than sinner."

"We're not taking about sin or evil, or that Phoebe is somehow responsible for what may be a mental illness. What I'm concerned about it that she receives help before the illness progresses, and she becomes a danger to herself. She is probably confused, and may get to the point where she can't tell reality from the voices and images in her head. I think you should discuss this with your parents, as I expect they won't appreciate my telling them. But I will, if you'd prefer." Which meant that if he didn't, and Henry knew it.

·   ·   ·

Jack's formal suit had been delivered by steamer that afternoon. Dressed and ready to head out to dinner at The Grand, he checked himself once more in the mirror, and marvelled at how dapper he looked. How wealthy. It really was amazing how clothes could make you feel the part. He had no qualms now about returning to The Grand. With illustrious ancestry, powerful acquaintances, and a wealthy family, he was already a different person, though he had been away for little more than a week.

He belonged here, and no one would take that from him again.

# Chapter 11

"I'm not taking you if you treat this as a circus sideshow," Eleanor warned Chas. He was picking her and Blake up in his thirty-two foot motor launch. Freddie and Emma Spencer, the three Carringtons, Victoria, Zoë, Max, and Jack, were already in the boat. "Edelina is a friend, and a thoroughly nice person."

"I'm desolated that you don't trust me, Ellie," Chas replied. "Anyway, it seems to me that *I* am taking *you*, so I don't quite follow your logic."

"I'll disown you if you mock her friends or lifestyle."

"Then I shall be on my best behaviour!"

"Edelstein" was the name painted on the end of the dock at The Colony. "It means 'precious stone' or 'gemstone' in German," Eleanor explained. "Edelina considers this place her jewel."

It reminded Victoria of the Shimmering Sands but on a much larger scale. The bay was a crescent of champagne-coloured sand anchored at one end by a massive granite shelf that rose in a series of steps resembling an ancient amphitheatre, and a more gently sloping rock at the other. Here was perched a dry slip boathouse sheltering a rowboat and a couple of canoes, with a birch bark canoe lying upended on the shore beside. A dock stretched out to deeper water, and a couple of rowboats and small motorboats were already tied up there. Chas's boat would take up most of the remaining space.

No attempt had been made at landscaping or even cutting down the grass, but a well-trodden path led up to the cottage, which was just a small log cabin with a broad veranda. On the sparsely treed grounds around the cottage squatted several white tents, looking like an army encampment, an Indian wigwam, and a tiny cabin. Here also was a large fire pit equipped with a tripod for hanging pots, and fat logs, drawn up like benches, surrounding it.

Several easels were set up in various locations, with some in use. A violinist was perched partway up the cliff playing a soulful tune. On one of the lower 'steps', a man sat in an odd cross-legged position, his hands resting on his knees, palms up, fingers touching, and eyes closed. Even from here they could see that he had terrible scars on his face, as if he had been carved up with a knife.

"Eleanor! Blake! What a lovely surprise!"

It was Edelina Fuerstenberger who was a surprise. Tall and lithe and in her early thirties, she had a commanding presence that went beyond her Aryan beauty. She was dressed in a thin linen shift that was unfashionably short, ending well above her bare ankles and feet, and would have looked shapeless on any other woman, but on her, it looked like art. It had an Oriental flavour, with wide sleeves cut open halfway to the shoulders and draped like folded wings. It was white with a dramatic, diagonal slash of black that resembled a curling wave. Her waist-length flaxen curls were restrained by a matching headband tied on one side and hanging down to her breast.

"Edelina, we'd like you to meet some friends." Eleanor introduced them as others sidled up to the group.

One of them, a short, scruffy man with a peaked cap, sneered and said in a heavy Russian accent, "Carrington Carpets. Wyndham mills. Capitalist dogs!"

"I feel rather left out having nothing named after me," Chas quipped. "Please don't forget The Canada Investment Bank. I expect it deserves some disdain as well."

The man spat on the ground in front of them and moved away in disgust. Edelina did not apologize for her guest's rude behaviour, but said, "Anton is a Bolshevik. Life is very harsh for the workers in his country."

"He's a Marxist?" Justin Carrington asked.

"Oh yes. He is passionate in his belief that communism is the only way for society to advance. He's in Canada to gather support for the cause."

In response to their quizzical expressions, Justin explained to the others, "Communism is a political ideology that believes that capitalism exploits workers, and that private ownership should be replaced with communally-owned businesses. Communists want to create a classless society in which – how do they put it? – each person gives according to his abilities, and receives according to his needs."

"That's naïve," Chas said. "You'd have people like me doing nothing at all and expecting to be paid handsomely for it."

"The only difference with the present state being that you now make the salary of a thousand people for doing nothing," Eleanor mocked.

"Surely more than a thousand," Chas bantered.

"If you have money to spare, I have paintings that are looking for homes," one of the artists said.

Edelina introduced some the painters and poets who were visiting "to regenerate themselves," she explained. "Like me, they find it very inspirational here. Come and I'll show you around."

"What is that chap over on the cliff doing?" Max asked as they walked toward the cottage. "The one who seems to have turned into stone. I haven't seen him move or even blink."

Edelina said, "That's Gil. He's meditating. It's part of the yoga that he practices. I introduced him to it to help him cope with his mental anguish. You can see that he is terribly scarred, but not just physically. He doesn't mind my telling people, since he would like others to realize the benefits. He was maimed in the Boer War, and now he helps me about the place. I studied yoga when I was in India and have found both the philosophy and the practice of it helpful."

"How exotic!" Lydia said.

Edelina laughed. "I suppose it does seem so. I inherited some money when my father died, and so I spent a year travelling through Europe, northern Africa, the middle east, and the winter in India. I had set out to try to connect with my heritage. My father had come to Canada from Germany as a young boy. So I managed to find some relatives, but still felt that something important was missing in my life. It wasn't just that my parents had both recently died. I felt empty somehow, disconnected from the world. It wasn't until I was introduced to Buddhism and yoga and other ancient philosophies that I realized I was spiritually bereft. In India, I regained my sense of self and reclaimed my soul. So now I practice Theosophy." She laughed and said, "I can't explain that in a moment, but in essense we believe in the spiritual unity of all things, that we are all part of a greater consciousness, and that the divine can be found in nature. In practice, I believe in living as naturally as possible, without artifice and empty social strictures."

She ushered them into the cottage and said, "You see I live rather simply."

The sitting room with its low, beamed ceiling was cozy, its log walls left raw but hung with dozens of paintings. Mismatched chairs were set about a large stone fireplace, and a single bed under a window seemed to double as a sofa.

Jack took a closer look at the paintings.

Edelina said. "These are all gifts from friends who have stayed here, and they are all views painted here. Interesting to see the different styles, don't you think?"

"Jack is an artist," Victoria said.

"But not a practicing one," he added, thinking that some of these were exceptionally good.

"Probably wise, unless you enjoy a simple life," Edelina said with a grin. "I know how fortunate I am to have enough money to live as I choose."

"And support other artists," Eleanor said. "Surely it can't be inexpensive to have to feed so many visitors all summer?"

"True enough! Especially when they all enjoy their wine. But I provide only vegetarian meals and have no objection if any of them care to augment their diet by catching some fish."

"May I talk to you some time about vegetarian cooking?" Zoë asked eagerly.

"Of course. I've collected recipes from all over the world."

"Then you should probably put them into a book and sell them," Blake advised.

"Good idea."

Two tiny bedrooms opened off one side, and a door at the back led to a large kitchen that had obviously been added later, for the walls were panelled in white pine. A long refectory table with at least a dozen chairs set about it seemed to be the gathering place.

A gnome-like woman was busy at the stove. "This is Frieda. She looks after me wonderfully well, so that I can work. She can do anything, from baking all those delicious cakes and pastries my grandmother used to make to sewing the clothes I design for myself," Edelina said, giving the woman a warm smile that was instantly reciprocated. "She's German, and her English is not very good yet."

They went out the back door and found two men around the side of the house who were busy carving. One of them was dressed in traditional native buckskins and was introduced as Chief War Eagle, "who spends a few weeks with us every summer, teaching wood carving and taking guests on excursions."

When they were out of hearing, Max said, "Is he really an Indian?"

"Yes, he's Ojibwa. Whether he's actually a chief, I can't say," Edelina admitted. "His tribe used to hunt and fish in this area generations ago, but they're on a reservation now, over near Parry Sound. And Paul is actually *Father* Paul," Edelina added, referring to the other man. "He's a Catholic priest who is having a spiritual crisis and is finding it helpful to discuss theology and philosophy with us. I have no idea whether he'll eventually return to the church, but he's decided to come to India with me this winter."

They walked toward the cliff, where others were now gathering. The violinist bounded down to meet them. Gallantly he bowed at each young woman as they were introduced. "You've probably already heard Laszlo play. He's a genius on the violin, between jobs at the moment, but rarely unemployed for long. Will you start us off today, Laszlo?"

"My pleasure, dear lady." With a flourish, he walked down to an open area, much like a stage, and faced the cliff.

"He claims to be the bastard son of a Hungarian nobleman," she told them as they seated themselves on the rocks.

"You have an interesting collection of people here," Freddie Spencer said.

"It makes *life* interesting," Edelina responded. "Oh, here comes Tom to join us." She motioned him over. "This is Tom Thomson, a dear friend of mine and an artist to be reckoned with. He's just here for a couple of days, on his way to Algonquin Park. He doesn't find our scenery wild and beautiful enough."

"It's too civilized," Tom said. "I need to go to places where only a canoe can take me, not where hordes of pampered people amuse themselves. Look at all the black soot in the air from the steamers. And what do you hear so much these days? Not the cry of the loon, but the roar of motorboats. Not for me, thank you. But you know that I still envy you being able to spend all summer here, Ede."

"Tom and I have very similar ideas about our art – that you can't paint the Canadian landscape in the pastoral European tradition. But Tom has to find the most out-of-the-way, untouched places just to prove his point. I think the technique works just as well here."

They stopped talking when Laszlo began to play. He knew his instrument intimately and was able to coax sounds from it that sent shivers of delight through the audience. Next was a well-known poet who recited the work he had just created, his words liquid and evocative. Another writer amused them with a few pages from his satirical novel-in-progress which mocked the wealthy cottagers who came north to find nature, and then spent a fortune taming and subjugating it. Chief War Eagle, now wearing a feathered headdress, entranced them with a dramatic telling of a native legend. Anton, the Bolshevik, was next. In bad English he ranted about the evils of capitalism. When the audience was beginning to squirm, Edelina motioned to Laszlo, who edged Anton off the stage with a lively gypsy melody.

Then Edelina took over. "Thank you all for joining us today to acknowledge those who strive to create a unique Canadian voice and vision. We welcome free and open discussion, and appreciate tolerance from others for ideas they may not share. Paintings and books are for sale, should you wish to help support the artists. We certainly appreciate your patronage. I shall be in my studio above the boathouse, where my own work is on display."

"How did you begin painting? Jack asked Edelina as the Wyndham crowd walked to the boathouse with her.

"I was always drawing as a child, but never considered art as a possible way of life. Not until I was in Paris. So I spent a few months studying there, and realized that I did actually have some talent. And then I couldn't get enough. I did hundreds of sketches and watercolours during the rest of my trip that year. But I think I'm only just finding my own style now."

There were stacks of oil paintings leaning against the walls of her studio and several displayed on easels. The colours were bold and laid down broadly, the brushstrokes, strong. This was not soft, misty Impressionism or rigid, classical realism. This was something new and exciting.

"That's powerful," Jack said in awe. "You really have captured the spirit of the scenery."

"Muscular Impressionism," Chas announced. "I adore it! I will definitely buy some. I started collecting art when I was in Europe."

"The large paintings are now selling upwards of $100," she warned, but Chas waved that aside, and began looking among the stacks while Edelina explained her technique to Jack, who marvelled at the prices her work was fetching. If only his father had had such talent and success!

"Tom has influenced me greatly," Edelina said. "And he has a lot of like-minded friends. They're trying to create uniquely Canadian art."

"Jack told me to paint what I see," Victoria said.

"It's important to learn the basics that way," Edelina said. "You need a strong foundation in perspective and composition. But art should be more than a coloured photograph. It should be the artist's interpretation of what he or she sees, capturing not just the visual, but also the emotional impact of a scene. Our country is rugged and vast. A light touch doesn't fully convey the grandeur, at least not for me."

Victoria found Edelina's art rather crude and primitive. Nowhere in nature were colours laid on in such huge swatches, or so intensely. Yet she had to admit that they were strangely captivating, especially from a distance.

Zoë and Emma helped Freddie choose a small painting to remind him of Muskoka during the long winters. Justin also picked one, but as none of them had much money with them, the paintings would be put aside for them to collect later.

Jack looked at the framed watercolours on the wall. "These are quite different in style."

"That's India," Edelina said. "It's a different landscape. For me the country has a soft, watery feel. These aren't for sale."

"May I come and watch you work some time?" Jack asked her.

"By all means."

When they were on their way back, Chas said, "I say, Jack, you have a good excuse to see more of Edelina. I'll never be an artist, but maybe I should take up poetry so that I can visit my Nordic goddess."

"You are fickle, Chas!" Victoria accused. "I thought it was me you loved."

"Of course I do, darling girl. But I love all women, and Edelina is so luscious. I swear she wasn't wearing anything under that dress."

"She's too mature for you, Chas," Eleanor said. "And by that I don't mean in age."

"You are cruel, Ellie."

When some of them returned the next day to pick up the paintings, Max said to Edelina, "Was that a naked woman I just saw heading into the woods?"

She laughed. "Indeed you did. It's Dorothea Liveley, the poet. She is a naturist. But she doesn't like to upset visitors, so she decided to go for a walk when she saw your boat arrive."

"Too bad. I should like to meet her. I mean, I've actually read her poetry," Max said.

"Oh, sure. We know where your mind is, lad," Chas said to him.

Max blushed.

Today Edelina wore an aquamarine blue cotton dress, accented with black, scandalously short again, reaching only to mid-calf , with a soft, dropped waist and no sleeves. Augusta would definitely not approve. The dress was the same colour as her eyes,

Jack realized, and set off her pale hair. Chas was right to think that she was a stunner.

"Will you take a glass of wine?" Edelina asked. "We can sit on the veranda and have a chat."

When they had all accepted a glass of very fine and refreshingly cool white wine, Justin Carrington asked, "Are you related to the Fuerstenbergers of *Sausage King* fame?"

Edelina laughed. "Indeed, I am! So you'll wonder how I could be a vegetarian. I had more than my share of meat when I was a child. My grandfather was a butcher, and so my father and his brothers also became butchers. My grandfather's sausages were very popular, especially with the large German population in Berlin[1], so they went into mass production, and made a fortune."

"And very fine they are too. We grew up with them, because Guelph isn't that far from Berlin. Now you can find them everywhere."

"I grew to detest them, but it's thanks to sausages that I have such freedom. Which makes me feel like a hypocrite, since I believe in the sanctity of all life, and here I am enjoying the profits from slaughtered animals."

Father Paul joined them with a nod of greeting, poured himself a glass of wine from one of the bottles keeping cool in a bucket of ice, and sat on the veranda steps. Probably in his mid-thirties, he was much too good looking to be wasted on the church, Victoria thought irreverently. She wondered about his relationship with Edelina. Had he broken his vows of celibacy? If not, how could he resist her, being constantly in her company? Was that a test of his faith and commitment to his church? With unmarried priests and nuns, Latin services and confessions, Roman Catholicism seemed rather medieval and mysterious to her.

"You have good Karma," Chas said to Edelina. When they all stared at him in stunned silence he said, "Well you needn't look so shocked. I *am* an Oxford graduate after all. Ergo, I can punt a boat *and* discuss comparative religion."

"Simultaneously? Imagine!" Eleanor mocked.

"For you disadvantaged philistines, Karma is a tenet in eastern religions, like Hinduism and Buddhism, that maintains that everything you have done and are doing will affect your future experiences, even into the next life, for those who believe in reincarnation. So you are responsible for the good or bad in your

---

[1] Berlin Ontario was renamed Kitchener in 1916 because of anti-German sentiment during The Great War.

own life, and there's no such thing as luck or chance. And after that dissertation, I'd be most appreciative of another glass of that excellent wine."

They all looked at Edelina for confirmation. She smiled as she poured another glass for Chas. The others had barely touched theirs. "You're right. You can also think of it in Christian terms as reaping what you sow. Theosophy maintains that all religions share common themes and truths, which may therefore be universal truths. What appeals to me about the eastern religions from which Theosophy draws so heavily, is the idea that our souls are not condemned to a fiery everlasting hell or banished to an impotent heaven, but have a chance to return, and having learned from previous mistakes, redeem ourselves, lead better, more spiritual lives, work to improve the world and strive for universal brotherhood. Think of it as the evolution of the soul."

"You'd better start doing something useful, Chas," Eleanor said, "or you'll come back as a slug."

They laughed, and Edelina said, "Theosophy believes that you've already passed through the stages of mineral, plant, and animal in your many incarnations, and can't regress to a lower form of life. But some religions believe otherwise."

"I'm not sure that a slug *is* a lower form of life than Chas," Eleanor said. "At least it does something useful."

Amid the laughter, Chas said, "You're all determined that I shan't rest on my laurels. After all, I must have good Karma, or I wouldn't be so happy and carefree."

"Karma isn't as simple as just doing a good deed and being rewarded," Edelina said. "All things are made of karmic energy and can affect one another. So your thoughts and feelings as well as your deeds have power as you send them into the universe. Bad karma or negative energy can come from anger or selfishness and so forth. Positive energy can come from creating something or loving someone. We're all part of a vast, universal consciousness which includes a divine essence – call it God or Buddha or whatever. That's why, when I look at a sunset or feel the pine-scented breath of wind on my skin, I feel a spiritual joy, and I know that I am communing with a greater spirit. But not a Santa Claus-like God who sits up there on a cloud and judges us." She threw an almost apologetic look to Father Paul.

"So you believe that a divine spirit exists in everything around us?" Victoria asked. She found Edelina's philosophy much more appealing than conventional Christianity.

"Yes."

"I'm still back at that comment about loving someone," Chas said. "Now I know I can improve my soul!"

"I don't think Edelina meant having sex with every woman who takes your fancy," Eleanor said.

Amid the laughter, Chas offered his wine glass for another refill. "Bringing joy and fulfilment to others is surely a good deed," he said.

"And arrogance surely negates that," Eleanor countered.

"Can we recall our previous lives?" Victoria asked, ignoring the banter.

"Not as vivid memories, like you have from this life," Edelina replied. But I think we can sometimes sense things from the past. For instance, I had no feeling of familiarity with Germany when I went to find my relatives, no sense of connection to my ancestors or the soil in which they were buried. But when I was in Rome, I stepped into the coliseum and instantly felt such a breath-snatching fear and horror that I began weeping uncontrollably. Someone kindly escorted me outside, and I was fine."

"You must have been empathizing with those poor Christians who were thrown to the lions," Justin said.

"I think I *was* one of them, in a previous life," Edelina said. "I felt nothing like that when I wandered about the catacombs, and surely there was age-old misery all around me. And when I set foot in India, I felt as if I had come home. I knew what the air would feel like, smell like, although I had never before smelled some of those spices. But I *knew* them. I even recognized the taste. I think we all have times and incidents in our lives which resonate with our past existences."

"So that accounts for Chas being stuck in a somewhat vegetative state," Eleanor said.

"Just mock me! I'll show you how *lazy* I am when I pulverize you at tennis. I say, Edelina, you must join us for the tennis tournament and the ball afterwards."

"And our Dominion Day Costume Ball next week," Zoë added.

"I'm not much of one for balls. My needs and entertainments are simple."

"Surely you don't deny yourself the pleasure of dancing?" Chas asked.

"Not at all. We often have impromptu dances, especially when Lazslo is here to play for us."

"I think what Edelina is politely trying to say is that she doesn't condone the extravagance, the ostentation, the pretentiousness, the pomposity, the affectation of society affairs," Eleanor said. "Not that ours are like that at all, of course."

"Hell, no!" Chas said. "It's all about having a good time. But here's some advice that I *can* give you. If you're hoping to promote your art and your friends' creative endeavours, then you should meet the potential patrons who could keep you all working lucratively. You may be disdainful of the rich, but that needn't interfere with business. Or pleasure."

"I'm hardly disdainful, as I myself am well off," Edelina said with a smile. "I leave disdain to Anton. But you are right that I shouldn't isolate myself  because I have a different philosophy of life. It would be a poor way to live if I felt challenged by other lifestyles. Sometimes it is easier to continue along a well known path than to diverge and embrace new experiences."

"I hope that means you're coming," Chas said.

Edelina laughed. "I shall try."

Father Paul had said nothing throughout their discussion, and his expression had betrayed no clue to his thoughts. Now, with a nod, he left them.

"A man of few words," Chas observed.

"But deep thoughts," Edelina said. "And a troubled soul."

Later, when they were speeding back in the boat, Chas said to the men, "There is something irresistibly alluring about older women, don't you think? There's this smoldering sensuality and sexual self confidence that only comes from experience. Not that I don't appreciate your virgin charms, Ria. I am, after all, more than willing to introduce you to the pleasures of the flesh, so that you too, can blossom into a seductive siren."

"You are incorrigible, Chas!" Victoria laughed.

"Look out!" Zoë screamed, bringing Chas's attention back to his driving and to see a canoe right in their path. He swerved violently, just missing the canoe, but the wake from the motor boat slammed into it and capsized it. Chas spun the boat around. Freddie and Justin already had their shoes off and dove into the water.

There had been two women in the canoe. Only one of them was visible, and she was struggling to stay afloat. Freddie grabbed her and pulled her over to the boat where Blake and Jack hauled her out, but with some difficulty, since her sodden skirts weighed her down. They had to be careful not to upset their own boat.

Justin had dived underwater but came up empty handed. He took a huge breath and went under again.

The others held their breaths in fear. The rescued girl was crying hysterically and shouting, "That's my sister! Oh my God, you must find Annabelle! She can't die! You mustn't let her die! She can't swim! Annabelle!"

Eleanor had found a jacket, which she draped over the girl's shoulders. She held onto her to give her support and comfort.

When Justin surfaced this time, he had the unconscious girl in his grasp. But the tension didn't ease. They didn't know if she was alive.

As soon as Blake had her in the boat, he turned her onto her stomach and kneaded her back, trying to force the water from her lungs. An agonizingly tense moment later, water trickled from her mouth and she coughed and gasped.

"Oh, thank God!" Zoë said.

The other girl fell on her knees beside her sister and wept silently.

Chas was pale and visibly shaken. "They seemed to come from nowhere," he mumbled. "I didn't see them." They had probably come from behind one of the nearby islands, but he should have seen them if he had been paying attention.

Victoria said, "Here, let me drive. I *am* capable, you know. This is no different from *Dragonfly*."

Chas didn't protest.

They grabbed the canoe with a grappling hook and secured it to the back of the boat. Having ascertained that the young women had come from The Grand, Victoria drove them – more sedately – to the hotel.

Driving the boat was easy enough, but docking was trickier. That was what she really needed to practice. But it was a calm afternoon, with no wind to buffet the boat and complicate the approach to the dock, so Victoria managed admirably. They were all vastly relieved when the girls had been safely delivered, explanations given, and apologies – and heartfelt thanks – accepted. No blame was cast. It was an accident. No real harm done. The girls would be sure to wear life vests next time.

But once they were underway again again, Eleanor was the one who stated what they were all thinking. "Perhaps quaffing four glasses of wine is not a wise thing to do before driving a boat. You must have good Karma, because there could have been a tragedy today."

There were no quips in response..

# Chapter 12

Richard's Rosedale home, Rosemullion, was a pleasant, rambling Queen Anne house which whispered comfortable affluence, but didn't shout ostentatious wealth. It had no ballroom or billiard room, and only a small conservatory. But Jack's family would have considered it a palace.

Because the Wyndholme servants had already gone to Wyndwood in preparation for the Dominion Day Ball, Jack stayed in Richard's guest room, while James stayed with Albert. Tomorrow, Monday, was election day in Ontario, so the men had come back to the city today. Although Jack couldn't vote, his excuse for going along had been to help his mother, but he didn't even stop in to see her. He and Richard spent a companionable evening, Richard asking questions about his youngest brother's life and family with great interest and sadness.

Jack didn't have to exaggerate their hardships to appal Richard. Just the descriptions of the deaths – Anne from typhoid, Isobel from diphtheria, his father from consumption, and finally, Eddie's horrific accident – brought them both to the edge of tears. Of course they knew that even the wealthy succumbed to diseases, as had Richard's infant son, Terence, but surely living with inadequate food, shelter, and sanitation had played a role. Richard was thin-lipped with anger when he realized that Eddie's accident could have been prevented had there been proper safeguards on the machinery. Knowing the owner of the factory, he was only too well aware that it made huge profits.

As soon as Richard had voted the next morning, they met with a real estate representative and looked at two houses that Richard's solicitor, Gilbert Cummings, had found.

The first was a comfortable six room house on Brunswick Avenue, but the larger one on Lowther seemed ideal to Jack. It was in the Richardson Romanesque style so popular in the Annex, with ornate bays and gables. Built of stone and red brick and with the typical round-arched windows and entranceway, it looked solid and substantial. The rooms were spacious and bright, and Jack could envision their uses.

The front parlour, with a coal-burning fireplace and large windows in the bay, would be the boarders' dining and sitting room. The dining room behind it, with a bay jutting out to the west side and separated from the front room by pocket doors, would serve as the family's domain. The small office behind the main staircase could be his mother's bedroom. In the "L" between this room and the well-equipped kitchen was a delightful sunroom with a door to each room and the back garden. There were four good-sized bedrooms on the second floor, the master suite at the front so roomy that it could sleep an entire family, and thus could easily accommodate two boarders. There was also a three piece bathroom on this floor. In the attic were three cozy bedrooms, probably designed for servants, but certainly large enough for his sisters – and better than anything they had ever had. One had a small balcony opening off it, overlooking the tree-lined street of other genteel houses. There were oak floors, a built-in china cabinet, electric light fixtures, a combination coal and gas furnace that supplied hot water and hot water heating throughout the house, back stairs from the kitchen, and a narrow but deep lot with a garden.

At $8000 it seemed an impossible sum to Jack, who worked hard to earn a tenth of that in a year.

"What do you think?" Richard asked.

"This one offers more potential for my mother to take boarders," Jack replied carefully, as this house was $2000 more expensive than the first.

"My thoughts precisely. So it would do?"

"Splendidly! But I can hardly believe this could be our home! My mother would faint if she knew that she lived just down the street from the Timothy Eaton family." The founder of that great department store had lived a few blocks west on Lowther, at Spadina Avenue. Although he had died years ago, some of his family still resided in the house.

"If you're happy to stop looking, I'll have Gilbert Cummings make the purchase and put the deed into your name. Your family should be able to move in before the end of the summer. Oh, and you'll need to furnish the house, so I'll give you $500 to get started, so that you'll at least have what you need for the boarders."

"Uncle Richard, I truly don't know how to thank you for this! It's all a bit overwhelming."

Richard patted him on the shoulder. "You can repay me by making the most of your talents, now that looking after your family should no longer be such a struggle for you. I only wish to God I could have done something sooner!"

Their business concluded, they were able to catch the noon train to Muskoka with the others. At Union Station they also met up with the Professor and Blake Carlyle, as well as the three Carrington men, back from voting in Guelph. Jack was introduced to Simon, the eldest, who was as handsome and energetic as the rest of his siblings.

They chatted and read newspapers on the train, James pointing out that the Austrian Archduke, Franz Ferdinand, and his wife had been assassinated in Sarajevo yesterday.

Because it was Monday and Toby would be busy taking the family and servants to their various destinations, the Wyndhams had decided in advance to catch one of the steamers from the Gravenhurst wharf, and dine aboard. They had an excellent meal in the elegant dining room, with a changing panorama of lake and islands to enthral the soul, and interesting conversation, the intellect.

When they arrived at Wyndwood shortly before eight o'clock, Jack decided that a paddle in the canoe and a swim – for the city had been stifling hot – were all that he desired. He canoed up to the Shimmering Sands where he stripped naked and luxuriated in the cool water. Afterwards, as he lay boldly on the granite outcropping and watched the changing colours of a burning sunset, he swore that one day he would build his own cottage mansion on this spot. It would be a present for Victoria.

.        .        .

"Simon, how lovely to see you!" Victoria said. "I think it's jolly unfair that work is keeping you away so much this summer. But aren't we lucky that you haven't had a chance to practice your swimming!" They were gathering at the Ellis's cottage on the mainland, bordering the SRA golf course that was well under construction, as was the club house. It was a perfect day for the Stepping Stone Marathon.

Simon laughed. "Don't count me out of the race just yet. I've decided that Chas can't possibly win the Cup five years in a row. Although I can see you Wyndhams are determined to win it."

"And the new Ladies' Cup," Victoria said. Because this was a public event, she had to wear her stockings and bathing slippers, which she hated, but which Max had told her was better than running barefoot across the loose stones and prickly pine needles on the islands.

Jack marvelled at all the fit and beautiful young people who congregated for the races, with many new faces from other cottages around the lake. There was some good-natured ribbing, and an air of excitement. A flotilla of canoes, rowboats, and motor boats waited for the event to begin, the ladies in large picture hats or carrying parasols to keep the blistering sun at bay. Some of the boats would follow the race to keep an eye on the contestants, in case anyone should get into difficulty. Edgar, as promised, was piloting *Dragonfly,* with Richard along to help if needed. The rest of the family, including Olivia's sister and family, who had arrived yesterday, were watching the proceedings from the shady comforts of the steamer, *Calypso.*

The men's race would begin five minutes before the ladies', to avoid congestion and confusion. Jack felt strangely nervous, as though this was a test of his suitability for his new role as a member of this elite society.

Max had told him that there was strategy involved in choosing the most direct route. Max had even drawn a rough map for him and the girls, although he and Edgar had argued over the best routes. Edgar had taken them around the islands in the Ditchburn yesterday to reconnoitre. It was serious business.

The objective of the race was to land on every island and be the first one to reach the sandy west bay at Wyndwood, where James and Edward Carrington waited to declare the winner. The girls would stop at the dock on Ouhu.

Victoria wanted to throw her arms about Jack and wish him luck. Instead, she smiled and said, "I'll see you on the winner's podium."

"I'll prove you wrong, and take a kiss as forfeit," Chas Thornton said to her. "*En guard*, you Wyndham men!"

Benjamin Ellis waved a flag and yelled, "Positions, gentlemen." After they had lined up along the shore, he went over the rules, which included no interference with other swimmers. Then he fired the starter's pistol and they ran or dove into the water. The girls cheered them on.

The first island was small, and less than a hundred yards away, so there was only one obvious way to get across it quickly. There was a bit of playful jostling for position here. The next island was trickier, since it was long and broader at the north end. Here people's strategies changed, some swimming less and choosing to run along most of the length of the uninhabited, but overgrown island; others, like Max, having figured that swimming half way up the east side and then crossing diagonally to the north west was fastest. That route would bring them close to the west side of Driftwood; from there it was a short swim to the eastern tip of Red Rock; then on to Oaktree, where they could use the maintained path along the north east shore. It was a stone's throw to Picnic Island and again to Ouhu. Jack was up there with the others as they started out on the longest stretch to Wyndwood, about a third of a mile away. Chas and Simon were in the lead, Rafe was beside him, and Max, Justin, and Blake were right behind.

Although they were all strong swimmers, none of them was driven by the same desperation as Jack. If he could win the Cup back for the family, he would be a hero. He concentrated on his breathing and long, bold strokes, and soon found himself passing Simon. Chas was still ahead of him as they neared the bay, so he put on an extra push, surprising a flagging Chas as he passed him, staggering onto the sand and collapsing at James's feet.

"Well done, lad!" James declared.

A cheer went up from *Dragonfly* and more distantly from *Calypso*.

Chas rolled up beside Jack and gasped, "You were determined I wasn't going to get that kiss, weren't you?"

"Absolutely."

"Well fought, old man. But I may steal that kiss anyway."

The girls meanwhile were getting close to finishing their own race. Victoria had decided that she would never win using just the breast stroke, so she'd had Max teach her the front crawl over the past couple of weeks, and had streaked ahead of the others, except for Eleanor. But fortunately, Victoria reached Ouhu ahead of Eleanor, who had a home turf advantage as they raced across the island to the dock. Victoria just beat her out. The Professor and Oswald Oakley declared her the winner, while Hannah Carlyle offered welcome glasses of lemonade.

Edgar sped over in the boat and raised his arms in a victory salute to Victoria. He yelled, "Hooray, Wyndhams! Jack won the men's race!"

"Hot dog!" Zoë called as she stumbled to the finish, and gave Victoria a hug. "That was enough for me. I may actually be able to nap this afternoon." The ball began at nine o'clock and would last until dawn. Everyone usually rested before dinner.

But Jack was too excited to sleep. The family was delighted that he had reclaimed the Cup for Wyndwood. Even Henry had grudgingly congratulated him. Surely they would all realize now that he meant to do his bit for the family honour.

There was a knock on his door and Molly walked in saying, "I've brought some fresh towels, sir." When she had deposited them, she ran over and gave him a big hug. "You showed them, alright! Snooty beggars!"

He spun her around in glee. "I wish you could come to the ball."

"Oh, I'll be there, sure enough. Dressed as a maid." They laughed.

"You'd best not linger. If anyone saw you come in, they'll wonder what we're up to if you don't leave right away."

"At least give me a fag. Maybe I can have a quiet smoke before this hellish ball begins. They have us working in shifts with the rest of the Wyndholme staff and Richard's servants" who had arrived yesterday, "but can you see me getting any sleep with the music and noise going on until dawn? So when you go to bed, I'll be at work again, cleaning up the mess. It seems bloody unfair to me!"

Jack gave her a cigarette and a kiss and said, "You won't have to stay much longer. By the way, I got my house on Monday. Wait till you see it! We'll be having tea next door at the Eatons'."

"Bullshit! You are a dreamer, Jack."

"And if I weren't, we wouldn't be here now. So run along before we're caught."

But as Molly headed for the door, she looked out the window and saw Victoria coming toward the boathouse. "Crap! It's Miss hoity-toity Queen Victoria. Coming for a tumble, is she?" Molly said snidely.

"Behave yourself. Hide behind those boxes."

Molly scrambled behind the mountain of stuff that now lined one wall.

Victoria knocked tentatively. Jack considered pretending he was asleep, but couldn't resist her daring approach.

He startled her when he opened the door. "Oh! I thought you might be asleep. Everyone else seems to be."

"You're not tired?" he asked.

"I expect I'll lie down for a rest soon, but, no, I'm still too wound up. I wondered if you wanted to go and paint?"

"I'm not really in the mood, but we could scout out a spot for our next lesson, if you like."

"Yes, alright." She felt a bit awkward now, thinking that he was just indulging her. But he dispelled that thought a moment later with a warm smile that promised more than a walk in the woods.

They had already congratulated one another, but Victoria reiterated, as they walked out, "You really were marvellous today, Jack! Max, Edgar, and Henry have tried hard over the years, but we haven't had the Cup since Uncle Richard won it some twenty years ago. Of course there were years when we didn't have any Wyndwood contestants, not until the boys were old enough," she said, referring to her cousins.

"And you didn't let anything stop you from being the first one to win the Countess of Kirkland's Cup."

She laughed. "How could I let someone else win that? Do you know what I feel right now?" Without waiting for a reply she explained, "That I can do anything that I set my mind to. And yet, I'm also afraid that events are beyond my control, that something cataclysmic will happen and neither I, nor you, nor anyone we know can change the prescribed course of our lives.

"So I rather like the concept of Edelina's Theosophy, of Karma. It's better than my odd notion that Greek or Roman gods are toying with us. As if we're part of a giant chess game. Some of us get lucky and are the kings and queens rather than the pawns. But eventually, we could all fall."

"That's rather gloomy talk for such a glorious day," Jack said as they walked along the west shore past Silver Bay.

"You're absolutely right!" she said, taking his hand and becoming light-hearted again. "We need to enjoy the moment."

Jack said, "Shall we go up onto the Dragon's Back?" When they reached the top, he said, "My father tried to paint this from memory. But it's never the same, is it?"

Victoria squeezed his hand in sympathy, and he suddenly pulled her into his arms and kissed her. She melted against him. It was as if all the pent-up emotions between them ignited. They sank to the ground as he unbuttoned her shirtwaist and reached under her camisole to caress her breasts.

She was shocked at first, but it felt so delightful that she didn't want him to stop. He trailed kisses down her neck and when his lips found her nipples she moaned.

Jack had to restrain himself from taking her, knowing it was too soon for her. But he reached under her skirt and stroked her through her bloomers until she cried out in ecstasy. Breathing hard, she said, "Oh, my God! Was that sex?"

He chuckled. "That was just the beginning. Petting, it's called. It's just a taste of the real thing."

"I've never felt anything so... so intensely pleasurable. So intoxicating."

He gave her a quick kiss on the lips and said, "Next time it will be even better. Now we should probably get back before we're missed." He helped her to her feet, brushed the dead leaves and pine needles from her back, and pulled a twig out of her hair.

Victoria felt suddenly shy with him as they started down the hill. He had made her lose control, to explode with pleasure deep inside her, in a place that she hadn't even known existed, but that he knew how to reach. But when he took her hand, she realized that he was not gloating or feeling somehow superior, only happy to be with her. And if that was just a taste of sex, she wondered that anyone could ever do without it for even a day.

Surely this overwhelming desire diminished as one aged, for she couldn't imagine how her father had managed without a wife all these years. And yet, she couldn't imagine her father ever having sex at all. Of course he had to, or she wouldn't be here, but it was impossible to believe that he had been so lovingly intimate with her mother. He was so cold and unemotional. And she almost burst into giggles when she tried to envision Albert and Phyllis doing that.

Maybe sex was only so wonderful for certain people, like her. People who were easygoing, like Chas, or devastatingly romantic, like Jack. It was harder to believe that she could have such rapturous intimacy with Justin.

They stopped holding hands before they came in sight of the boathouse. "I shall look forward to dancing with you tonight," Jack said, his eyes burning into hers so that she wanted to go up to his room and curl up beside him on the bed. She remembered all too well his virile nakedness, and imagined herself pressed against him with nothing between them, nothing to dull the sensuous feel of skin on skin.

He left her reluctantly and she scampered back to the house, tiptoeing quietly upstairs to her room.

Victoria and Phoebe had beds on one side of the girls' dormitory, with bedside tables in between and chests of drawers and wardrobes along the other sides. Zoë and Esme had a similar arrangement on the opposite side of the room. But Olivia's sister, Marguerite Kendal, and her family were visiting for a week, so two extra beds had been set up for Zoë's cousins, Rachael and Millicent, making the room rather crowded.

The others seemed to be asleep, so Victoria crept to her bed where she stripped off her skirt and shirtwaist and was about to lie down on top of the thin blankets. She noticed a movement from

Phoebe's bed and looked over to see the horrible doll, Maryanne, sit up with her nasty face glaring at Victoria.

"You've been naughty!" the doll seemed to hiss, but of course it was Phoebe.

For a panicked moment Victoria wondered how Phoebe could know what she had been up to. Phoebe often claimed to be able to read their thoughts, and they laughed at her, thinking that assertion an idle threat or a fanciful boast. But sometimes Victoria wondered about Phoebe's strangeness. People believed in communicating with the dead through mediums and séances. Was Phoebe perhaps one of those clairvoyants, who was still discovering and developing her powers? It was a chilling thought. But she challenged, "What are you talking about?"

"You're supposed to be resting. Where have you been?"

"Just for a walk. Now shush before you wake everyone!"

"Maryanne says you've been up to something. You're all flushed."

"I've been running."

"You've done something wicked. We know, don't we, Maryanne?"

The doll nodded.

"I'll do something wicked to you if you don't stop this nonsense," Victoria threatened, although she felt uneasy about Phoebe's serious conviction and the way she used the sinister doll to spook her.

"Maryanne won't let you," Phoebe said matter-of-factly. Then, as if they had been discussing nothing else all along, Phoebe suddenly said eagerly, "Do you think people will know that I'm Alice?" referring to her costume as the Wonderland character.

"Yes," Zoë said from across the room, "because, like Alice, you don't know when to keep quiet!"

"'Off with her head!'" Victoria quoted the Queen in the story.

"I meant the costume, silly!" It was a crinolined blue dress with a white pinafore, and a large blue bow partially tying back her hair. "I do so love Alice. She's so clever!" Phoebe had read the Alice stories countless times.

"You'll look fine. I think I shall go and luxuriate in a bath," Victoria said, "as I'm certain I'm not going to get any sleep."

As she lay in her lavender-scented bath, Victorian relived her encounter with Jack. She ran her hands across her breasts, remembering all too vividly the feel of his mouth, teasing and sucking until she had wanted to cry out. And then touching herself so that her legs wanted to open in invitation. And suddenly experiencing another paroxysm of pleasure, so that she realized that Jack didn't have a unique touch. But how much more fun it was when he instigated the pleasure! And surely there was more. She could feel it, like an emptiness in that private place that wanted to be invaded. And when she recalled the look of him naked, she realized just how they would fit together. And shivered in anticipation.

.        .        .

Molly was startled as she opened the door to leave Jack's room and found Tom, the footman, standing there. "What are you doing here?" she asked.

"Come to see what's been taking you such an age."

He looked around the room, but Molly said, "Mr. Jack's not here."

Lounging against the doorjamb, Tom said, "I saw the queen sneaking out of the house. So she's not in bed with him then?" He always called Victoria "the queen" when he was speaking to the junior staff, but would, of course, never say that in front of Mrs. Hadley or the Graysons.

"You have a dirty mind, Tom."

"Nah, just realistic. So they've gone off somewhere, have they?"

"I don't know. I haven't seen them."

"So what have you been doing?"

"Delivering towels."

"I saw you leave ages ago. Been snooping about, have you?" He pushed past her into the room and started looking among Jack's few possessions, taking a couple of cigarettes from Jack's pack of Black Cats and sticking them into his pocket. He fingered the costume that was hanging there in preparation for tonight's ball. "Thinks he's a fucking lord now, does he? Bloody hell, I don't get it. He just waltzes in here and goes from being a fuckin' waiter to a member of the family. I should have such luck."

"He *is* a member of the family, bone-head."

"So *he* says. I'll bet there's more to the story. Who's to say that he's not a bastard?"

"The family," Molly replied, not happy with the way Tom was rifling among Jack's papers. She trusted that Jack had destroyed all her notes, but what if he had been careless?

"I think you like him, the mysterious, long-lost grandson. Think he'll want you when he can have rich pussy instead?"

"Mine's neither free nor for sale." Molly started to walk away, but Tom grabbed her by the hand and swung her about so abruptly that she would have fallen had he not pulled her into his arms.

"What's your hurry? The others don't know where we are. There's an inviting bed, just waiting for you and me. You'd be more than just a fuck to me, Molly Jones. I really like you."

He was strong and she couldn't pull away from him. "Let go of me, Tom, or you'll be sorry."

"Oh, yah?" He laughed and began kissing her cheek. He chuckled as she relaxed against him, and loosened his hold. He was pleasantly shocked when she grabbed his groin, but yelled as she viciously squeezed his balls. He released her and cradled his crotch in both hands. "You fuckin' bitch! You bloody stupid cunt!"

"Just keep your hands to yourself next time!" Molly knew that she had to get rid of Tom somehow. He was obviously watching her, if had taken note of when she had left the house with the towels. And he seemed oddly jealous of Jack, so he might be looking for ways to sabotage his relationship with the family. They couldn't risk having someone like Tom hanging about, watching.

. . .

Jack marvelled at all the imaginative costumes. Augusta was an effective, if rather thin, Queen Victoria, probably wearing something from her own ancient wardrobe. James, with deerstalker hat and pipe, was Sherlock Holmes. Henry was a convincing monk. Edgar, with a peaked cap and his crutches was a large Tiny Tim. Beatrice was striking in a midnight blue Moroccan caftan embroidered with silver and gold thread. Max was a black and white medieval court jester, complete with bells on his six-pointed hat.

Zoë was fetching in a silk kimono-style gown which was elaborately embroidered with cherry blossoms, and which her mother had worn at the turn of the century when the Aesthetic Movement had been popular with the artistic community.

Victoria was stunning as a Greek goddess, draped in loose, flowing white chiffon over lemon yellow satin. The short tunic top was attached only with large gold buttons at the shoulders, leaving her arms bare, and draped to the hips, but cinched at the waist with a golden girdle. The chiffon overskirt was slit almost to the waist on both sides and edged with a gold-embroidered classical design all along the hem. Her pale hair was piled high and intertwined with gold braid.

Jack himself felt rather dapper as a Regency gentleman in a blue frock coat and tight yellow breeches. The others had helped Jack rummage through the many costume trunks to find something suitable. Apparently Richard had worn this years ago.

The Mad Hatter arrived with his gypsy wife, otherwise known as the Professor and Hannah Carlyle. Eleanor was a surprise, dressed as a man, but Blake's clothes looked incredibly sexy on her, Jack thought. Blake was a frighteningly good Dr. Jekyll and Mr. Hyde. One side of his outfit was a doctor's laboratory coat while the other was a battered old suit. Even the two sides of his face were different, with Mr. Hyde looking quite sinister.

Medieval and Renaissance kings, queens, knights, wenches, lords, and ladies danced with Vikings, leprechauns, Romans, fairies, Puritans, and characters who had stepped out of novels, plays, and fairytales.

The Carringtons made quite a splash dressed as playing cards – the kings and queens of hearts, diamonds, and spades. They simply wore square white tunics with large appliqués sewn onto the front and back, over regular white clothes, and sported playful crowns.

But it was the Oakleys who left everyone speechless. With his red and white striped trousers, blue, star-spangled frock coat, and tall striped hat, Oswald made an imposing Uncle Sam. Louise was a charming young Statue of Liberty; Thaddeus Parker, a rather short Abraham Lincoln. And Letitia and Helena were resplendent as the sun and moon.

Letitia shimmered in gold from head to foot, her wide, metallic-brocaded skirt radiating out from her waist like light beams. An elaborate headdress also seemed to emanate sunshine while it dripped a curtain of bejewelled golden strands down to her shoulders.

Helena, as the moon, looked like liquid silver, her silk gown narrow but flowing, pooling in a small train behind. Her dark hair was tucked beneath a silver threaded cap with a half moon shape standing up at the back.

"I'd forgotten that they'd had their costumes made in Paris," Augusta said dismissively to a dumbfounded James. His rather plain mouse was regal and beautiful, like Cinderella come to the ball. He was afraid now that other, younger men would be attracted to her. But he was more sure than ever that she was the right woman for him.

He was quick to reach her side, and fulsome in his praise. She blushed prettily and said, "Heavens, clothes really do make the man – or woman – don't they? I could hardly recognize myself."

"I hope I may claim as many dances as my role as host will allow, although I would that they could all be with you," he said earnestly.

She was pleased. "Why, of course. I'd much rather dance with you, James, than with Romeo or his piratical brother," she replied, referring to Chas and Rafe Thornton, who had just swaggered in.

Augusta did not believe in elaborate decorations at the cottage, feeling that the setting itself needed no embellishment. But the staff had brought along boxes of flowers and fruits from the Wyndholme greenhouses, so there were plenty of discreet floral displays, arranged by Olivia, throughout the house, and pots of enormous pink and blue hydrangeas gracing the veranda. Exotic and early fruits like pineapples and peaches were among the light refreshments in the dining room, where later a substantial supper would be laid out.

An orchestra played under a marquis behind the pavilion. Torches, carefully placed between the gas lanterns but away from overhanging trees, since everyone feared fire, conjured up an ambiance of romantic days of old.

The dancers switched partners regularly, as was the custom, and Jack tried to be suave and witty with women with whom he would normally not care to waste time. He managed a dance with Victoria. As if they were both reliving their encounter earlier that day, their limited physical contact now left them both craving more. Feeling the softness of her beneath the thin costume, Jack was jealous of all the men who would be touching her tonight, and thinking lascivious thoughts.

They were all pleasantly surprised to see Edelina, with Father Paul, who looked priestly now in his robes and dog collar. Was he wearing them because it was how the world should always see him, or was there some mockery intended, Victoria wondered.

She thought that Edelina would probably look dazzling in a potato sack, but was even more so in a gorgeous silk sari, the colour of a summer sky, trimmed in gold.

"I hope you don't mind my bringing Paul," she said to Zoë and Victoria when they greeted her. "But I only have a row boat, and felt it would be too much for me to try to come on my own. Especially dressed like this."

"I didn't even think about that," Chas said, having joined them with some of the others as soon as he spotted her. "I can drive you back later."

"Oh, we managed quite well," Edelina said. "It's only a couple of miles."

"And Paul is most welcome," Zoë said. He nodded to her and then drifted off to the dark fringes of the dance floor, leaving Edelina to amuse herself. Chas immediately grabbed her for a dance.

Around eleven o'clock, James and Beatrice silenced the orchestra and called for attention. James said, "Thank you, Ladies and Gentlemen, for joining us this evening in celebration of our Dominion, and our Stepping Stone Marathon winners. I'm absolutely delighted to be able to say that the Wyndham Cup has finally returned to Wyndwood, thanks to Jack Wyndham." Jack went up to shake James's hand and accept the trophy.

Beatrice said, "Ladies, well done on your first race. I applaud you all for your enthusiasm and determination. It bodes well for the new generation of women. And I would especially like to congratulate today's winner, Victoria Wyndham." Victoria was thrilled to hold the new silver cup.

James said, "Now let us migrate to the front dock for fireworks, after which there will be a supper awaiting you in the dining room. And the orchestra will be playing until dawn, so please do enjoy yourselves."

While the others wandered down to the dock, Jack and Victoria took their trophies into the house and placed them on the mantel of one of the fireplaces. "Don't they look splendid," Victoria said.

Taking a peek around and seeing no one watching, Jack, buoyed by his success and the adulation of the others, boldly gave her a swift kiss on the lips. "They're a good match," he said meaningfully.

Hearing someone coming, Victoria said, "I must go freshen up."

"Of course. I'll see you at the dock."

Phyllis came in from the veranda and ogled them suspiciously, but said nothing as she headed for the downstairs loo.

After she had used the lavatory upstairs, Victoria ambled out onto the veranda, where she already heard the explosion of fireworks, and the "oohs" and "ahhs" of the spectators. She hesitated just for a moment to absorb the scene, once again overcome by a fatalistic dread that this would never come again, even though they had held this event for over thirty years. If, as Edelina believed, there was some sort of global consciousness, then she seemed to sense the world holding its breath.

Then she chided herself and set out to enjoy the rest of the ball. She had just stepped onto the path when Rafe, the pirate, appeared out of the shadows. "I saw that kiss," he said. "Do you really fancy that upstart?" He pulled her into his arms, grabbing her breast. "I thought you weren't wearing much under that."

She slapped him but could muster little force because of how he held her. "Let go of me, Rafe!"

"If you don't fancy a fuck, you shouldn't go around half naked." He pulled her hard against him. She could smell the whiskey on his breath as she dodged his lips.

"You're behaving like a drunken swine!" she accused, struggling to push him away.

"Stop playing the demure little virgin." His mouth caught hers and he gave her a punishing kiss.

She managed to free her lips, but he held her fiercely. Scared now, she said, "Let go of me or..."

"Big brother will knock his block off," Chas said matter-of-factly. He had come up the path unnoticed amid the noise of the fireworks.

"And big brother always gets what he wants," Rafe said nastily, but suddenly released Victoria, pushing her into Chas. "You can't have *all* the women, you know."

"And you won't have any if you can't behave like a gentleman," Chas replied. He had caught Victoria and had his arm protectively around her.

When Rafe stomped away, Chas said seriously, "I trust he didn't hurt you, Ria, or I *will* do him some damage. I'm sorry you were subjected to that. I worry about Rafe. He's becoming rather dissolute."

She rubbed her arm, certain she would have bruises from Rafe's vice-like grip, but said, "I'm alright. Thank you, Chas."

He looked at her solicitously, and ran his hand gently along her arm. "Are you sure?"

"Yes." She was grateful for his concern.

"Then allow me to escort you to the dock, my darling girl. It's a good thing I came back to fetch Mumsy's wrap. You just never know what wild creatures will emerge from the woods here at night."

Victoria laughed. She waited while Chas went up to the veranda to collect a shawl. Then they walked to the dock arm in arm.

Phoebe had witnessed the scene from the shadowy bandshell of the veranda. Loud noises frightened her, and although she loved the sparkling, glittering lights, the fireworks were too much like thunder, so she hadn't gone down to the dock with the others. Her mother would be back in a moment to watch with her from here.

Phoebe, too, had seen Jack kiss Victoria, for she had seen them go inside and peered curiously in through a French window. But she had said nothing to Phyllis. She thought that she would like Jack to kiss her.

Dancing resumed after the fireworks, although people began helping themselves to supper, and sat at the many small tables set up on the veranda and in the sitting room. The Wyndholme staff had come well supplied with extra furniture, china, and silverware, but the supper still had to be taken in turns to accommodate the two hundred guests. Some of the older people left shortly afterwards, but there were still plenty who stayed to enjoy themselves.

Phoebe finally managed to have a dance with Jack. "You even look like a hero, Jack."

Distracted by watching Victoria, who was having a gay time with Chas at the moment, he said automatically, "And you look lovely as Alice, little cousin."

"I do, don't I? And isn't it fun that the Mad Hatter could come? And the playing cards!"

"You seem to be enjoying yourself."

"Oh yes! I'm actually in Wonderland! It's where I belong, you see. Mama has me sitting on the veranda forever doing needlepoint when all I want is to visit with my friends."

"How tedious for you."

"I knew you'd understand! Maybe now that you're a hero, Mama and Papa won't dislike you so much. Would you kiss me?"

She suddenly had his full attention. "That's not a question that polite young ladies ask, Phoebe."

"Then pretend I didn't and do it anyway."

"You're too young, and a kiss should just happen naturally between people who love each other."

"Well, I love you."

"As a cousin. That's not what I mean."

"I saw you kissing Victoria! Why is she special?"

"You must have seen the congratulatory kiss I gave her. That's all," he said, trying to sound dismissive.

"I suppose you want to fuck her, too?"

Jack was shocked. "Phoebe! I don't think you know what you're saying. Girls don't talk like that."

"It's what you want to do, though isn't it? Fuck her." She didn't know what the word meant, but by Victoria's reaction to Rafe, and now Jack's shocked face, she knew it was somehow deliciously evil. "Fuck, fuck, fuck!"

Blake, who was dancing next to them with Vivian, heard, and looked over in surprise. Jack gave him a quizzical, dumbfounded look.

He had stopped dancing, and looked at her as if she had turned into a worm or a spider, Phoebe thought. "You're just as hateful as the rest of them!" she cried.

She stomped away from him and almost collided with Dr. Jekyll and Mr. Hyde, whose eyes turned black like coal, and then red hot, burning into hers as if trying to bore into her brain. With a frightened gasp she ran, bumping into other creatures, being tossed back and forth amongst them, amid shrieks and laughter.

*Silly Alice! Where will you run to? We won't let you! Off with her head! The time has come, the Walrus said, to talk of many things, like silly billy Alice.*

The voices were dizzying. Phoebe ran to her bedroom and slammed the door behind her. She sat on her bed and hugged Maryanne tightly.

*You're evil, Alice. You can't be Alice. Alice isn't evil. You mustn't be evil or I will punish you. I will punish all the evil people. I will send them to burn in hell. You don't want to burn in hell, Alice, Phoebe, Phoebe, Alice.*

Meanwhile, Blake said to Jack, "What was all that about?"

"I haven't the faintest idea! How would she even know such a word?"

"She obviously doesn't know what it means. But I think she needs some help. I'll get Zoë."

Jack offered to dance with Vivian, while Blake interrupted Zoë's dance with Freddie Spencer. As they walked to the house, he said, "Phoebe seems quite upset. I think she's having a psychotic episode. I think I may even have frightened her with my two-faced disguise, but if you think I can help, let me know. By the way, do you know the word 'fuck'?"

Zoë blushed. "I've heard it, and I think it has some reference to sex, but I know it's terribly rude and vulgar."

"Would Phoebe have heard it?"

"I doubt it. I heard some of the girls at school tittering over it. Did Phoebe use *that* word?"

"Yes. But that's not what worries me. It was how she looked at us, as if we had turned into monsters. Look, I'll wash my face, so that I don't scare her, and wait for you in the sitting room."

Zoë found Phoebe rocking back and forth on her bed, muttering, still clutching Maryanne to her chest.

"Phoebe, are you alright?"

"Don't let them get me! They're vile. They put evil thoughts in my head. Where's Mama? I want Mama!" she cried frantically.

"I'll get her."

Phyllis was resting on the screened east veranda talking with some of the other matronly women. Zoë told her, "Phoebe is unwell."

"What's wrong with her?" Phyllis asked anxiously as she lumbered up the stairs behind Zoë.

"She seems frightened."

"Oh, Mama! There's a terrible creature with two faces who's trying to get into my head! He's trying to find evil. I don't want to have evil thoughts, but he put them into my head when he kissed me."

"Who? Who kissed you?" Phyllis asked indignantly.

"Jack."

"No!" Zoë said. "You must be mistaken, Phoebe. You just had a dance with Jack."

"He said that I must fancy a fuck."

Phyllis shrieked as if the word had stabbed her. "Go and fetch your uncle! I'm taking Phoebe into our room!" Phyllis was livid with rage.

Zoë went reluctantly, certain that Phoebe had things muddled. This would be a trial for Jack, since Albert and Phyllis already disliked him. But how unfair if they believed Phoebe's mad fantasies.

Several groups of people were scattered about the sitting room, where the extra tables had been removed, but not the chairs. One of the fires had been lit, as it was a comfortably cool night. Augusta and Beatrice were sitting by it with the elder Carringtons and Spencers. Richard and Olivia, with a rather tired Esme leaning against her, were chatting with Olivia's parents and sister and her husband in another corner. Edgar, who was resting his leg, had Eleanor, Henry, Max, and Lydia Carrington for company. Blake, divested of makeup and costume, had just joined them.

Zoë went over to him and whispered, "She's saying the most odd and dangerous things! I'm supposed to fetch Albert. Phyllis is outraged."

She found Albert in the library, where several of the men were drinking cognac and smoking cigars. He followed her out, but just as they were coming into the sitting room, Phoebe came tripping down the stairs with Phyllis trying to catch her up. "Phoebe, come back here!"

"I'm not Phoebe. I'm Alice," she announced with none of the hysteria she had just shown upstairs. "And I won't go with you, because I have friends waiting for me, and you'll just want me to do boring needlework."

"What's all this about?" Albert asked, stopping her at the bottom of the stairs.

Just at that moment, Victoria, Jack, Chas, Vivian and Justin Carrington, Freddie and Emma Spencer, and Edelina, with Father Paul following like a body guard, all came in from the veranda talking animatedly.

"Phoebe just told me the most appalling things!" Phyllis told Albert in distress. "She said that Jack kissed her and put evil thoughts into her head, and said the most *vulgar* and *filthy* thing to her! I can't even repeat it!"

Phoebe said, "I don't know what you're so upset about. It's just a word, and I've decided that words can't be evil, only if there is an evil thought behind it. I'm not evil, so what's the problem? It's just a bunch of letters, like 'luck' only with an 'f' instead."

Some of the others had heard, and it took only a moment for Henry to reach Jack's side and plough his fist into Jack's face as he hissed, "Bastard!"

Jack instinctively moved to fight back, but Chas restrained him, while Justin and Freddie pulled Henry away before he could land another punch.

Augusta rose imperiously to her feet and said loudly, without the bad manners of shouting, "Enough! What is the meaning of this?"

"I don't know what's going on," Jack said, rubbing his sore jaw. Henry might look meek, but anger gave him strength.

"He has interfered with my sister!" Henry accused, white with fury.

"I've done no such thing! I merely danced with her."

"Henry, you shouldn't hit Jack. He might not love me anymore now," Phoebe complained.

Blake went to Phoebe's side. She seemed anxious to get away from her parents.

"Phoebe, can you tell us what happened?" he asked her solicitously.

"Leave her alone! I won't have her badgered!" Phyllis said. "The poor child has been assaulted!"

"I beg to differ, M'am," Blake said. "I was right beside Jack and Phoebe when they danced, and it was she who shocked us."

"How dare you!" Phyllis cried. "Albert, you cannot allow this."

"Tish tosh," Phoebe said. "I don't mind talking to Blake. He's so nice, not like that two-faced man who was reading my thoughts."

Albert seemed about to protest, but Augusta had come over and said, "Let's hear what she has to say. We can't have people making accusations without proof."

"She's already told me what happened," Phyllis said. "Do you think Phoebe would *lie*? Do you trust Jack's word over hers?"

"I want to hear the story from Phoebe's own lips. It's unfortunate that this couldn't have been done in the privacy of the family." She glared at Phyllis, who she felt had not taken proper control of the situation. She didn't believe for a moment that Jack would be stupid enough to insult Phoebe in any way, to say nothing of that fact the child was not particularly attractive, and so would not earn his attention as Victoria had. Perhaps that was the problem. Phoebe could be jealous and be trying to get revenge on Jack for spurning her. Augusta was surprised at how strongly she wanted to defend Jack, and hoped that he was innocent. "But now that everyone present has heard the accusation, we owe it to Jack to hear his version as well."

"If I may just ask Phoebe a few questions?" Blake said to Augusta, who nodded.

"I won't allow my daughter to be interrogated!" Albert said.

"Are you afraid of the truth?" Augusta demanded. "Go ahead, Blake."

"Phoebe, you're really enjoying your role as Alice this evening, aren't you?" he asked.

"I *am* Alice! Did you see that even the Mad Hatter has come to my party? And Humpty Dumpty!" With her ringlets and childish dress, Phoebe looked more like a child playing at being grown up than the other way around.

"Did someone kiss you?"

"Oh, yes. Jack."

"When?"

"When we put our trophies on the mantle. We're King and Queen of the Ball, you see."

There was a noticeable relief of tension in the room as people realized that Phoebe was imagining things.

"And then what happened?"

"He danced with me, and said that he wanted to hug and kiss me. Isn't that what fuck means?"

There were shocked gasps from the others. The room went completely silent.

"No, it's not. It's a word that polite people don't use, especially to people they like."

"Then he didn't say it," Phoebe replied nonchalantly. "Jack is my hero. He wouldn't be rude to me."

"So where did you hear that word?"

"Oh, it was floating around in the air, and it sounded a like a good word for kissing. 'When *I* use a word,'" she quoted Humpty Dumpty in an odd crackly voice, "'it means just what I choose it to mean – neither more nor less'. I know Jack wants to kiss me, but Victoria keeps distracting him."

"I heard you ask Jack to kiss you. Were you angry with him when he refused?"

She pouted. "I expect he'd kiss Victoria without being asked twice!"

Augusta, with a sigh of relief, said, "You've let your imagination run away with you, young lady, and have caused a lot of bother." She turned to Henry and said, "I believe you owe Jack an apology."

Henry glared at them. "I think not. I don't believe there's smoke without fire. Phoebe didn't know *that word* before he came along."

Victoria said calmly, "I overheard one of the guests say it just this evening. I expect that Phoebe did as well."

Henry stared at her as if assessing the truthfulness of her words, before turning and marching away.

"Who would have said that?" Augusta demanded.

"I don't know. I just heard it in the crowd," Victoria lied, although she wondered why she was defending Rafe. Probably because Augusta wouldn't believe her. The Thorntons were unassailable as far as Grandmother was concerned. Chas looked at her with sudden understanding, as he hadn't overheard that part of her contretemps with Rafe. He gave her a rueful smile.

"I apologize to you all for this unfortunate misunderstanding," Augusta said to the room. More quietly to Albert and Phyllis, she said, "I think you need to control Phoebe's flights of fancy."

Blake said, "She may not be in control of her thoughts, Mrs. Wyndham. I suggest she seek medical attention."

"Nonsense!" Augusta said. "She's a silly girl who needs to be less coddled." She looked meaningfully at Albert and Phyllis. To Blake she whispered, "If you're suggesting that my granddaughter is not sane, then you are not only impertinent, but overstepping your relationship with this family."

Phoebe was rubbing her hand across her mouth as if frantic to wipe something off, and muttered to herself, "He's not supposed to kiss me. It's sinful."

Blake just looked at Augusta with raised eyebrows, and replied, "It does no one any service to ignore an illness," before walking back to join the others.

Zoë was relieved that the situation had been so easily resolved, and immensely proud of Blake for the compassionate way he had enticed the truth from Phoebe. She wanted to throw her arms about him and tell him how wonderful he was, but it was Vivian who wrapped her arm about his and said, "Well done, Blake. You seem to have a gift."

Blake, who had been in love with Vivian for years, glowed in the warmth of her praise. At Victoria's suggestion, Vivian had been less aloof with the men recently, and so Blake's hopes had been rekindled. Zoë couldn't fail to see the adoration in his eyes when he looked at Vivian, and felt as if she had been punched in the stomach. She had been so sure that Blake was beginning to warm to her. She wanted to run from the room and weep, but steeled herself.

Jack felt some awkwardness among the others. Edgar refused to meet his eyes, and Jack wondered whether Edgar, like Henry, thought him guilty to some degree, although surely he had been exonerated.

But it had given him a scare. He realized how tentative his situation was, how fragile his bond with the family, and how easily one's reputation could be tarnished. All because of a chippy who was either batty or vindictive. He'd have to avoid ever being alone with her or she might accuse him of even worse deeds.

Victoria said quietly to Edelina, "Phoebe hears voices. Could she be tapping into the universal consciousness you mentioned? Or hearing spirits?"

Paul seemed horrified, and spoke for the first time, "She could be possessed by demons. She may need an exorcism."

"Surely not!" Victoria said. "She claims that God speaks to her."

"He no longer speaks to me," Father Paul said with infinite sadness. "But perhaps she is blessed."

"Her family would prefer to think that, than that she is mad," Victoria said.

"What is madness but a label for those who are different?" Paul said. "Who are we to judge them and think them unsuitable for our company, fit only to be locked away from the world? If it is demons, then she needs help to be rid of them. If God speaks through her, then we would do well to listen."

Edelina said, "There are many mysteries that we cannot yet explain, nor may we ever be able to. I think that we all have psychic powers that most of us are unaware of, or don't know how to use. As a simple example, think of intuition, or the feeling that someone is watching you, a sort of sixth sense. But then there are those who seem to anticipate our thoughts, have premonitions, perhaps in dreams, feel the presence of spirits, even communicate with them. They call it a gift. Or a curse."

"So you think that Phoebe might have tapped into these powers, and just not be aware of it?"

"It's possible."

Blake had joined them earlier and now said, "Edelina, much as I love and admire you, I have to tell you that you're wrong. That girl has a mental illness and needs treatment, not encouragement to consider herself a medium or spiritualist."

"Ah, so speaks the certainty of science," Edelina said with a grin. "Are there more verifiable facts in your Dr. Freud's assertions? Or are his speculations just more interesting than mine?"

As they got into a discussion about Freud, Victoria thought about Phoebe, who was either mad, blessed, possessed, cursed, gifted, or just silly and spoiled. She hoped it was the latter.

• • •

Because Olivia liked to run her own household, and didn't care to share her home with others, Rosemullion had a minimal staff consisting of a footman, parlour maid, cook, scullery maid, chauffeur-coachman, and gardener, the latter two, living above the carriage house. The indoor staff had arrived at Wyndwood on Tuesday to help with the ball. So as Molly, Libby, Mrs. Hadley, and Rosie came into the kitchen from a short and restless night of sleep, the others were preparing to go to bed, first feasting on a light supper of leftovers and ale.

Grayson, the butler, said, "Well done, everyone. Another successful ball, I'd say."

The last guests had departed as a rosy glow appeared on the horizon. Although the staff had been washing up and tidying throughout the night, there was plenty to do before everything was back to normal for the family's breakfast at 1:00 o'clock.

Tom, recovered from her assault, surreptitiously groped Molly's backside as she passed him with her plate of eggs and bacon. She looked daggers at him, but he just chuckled before saying, "Bit of a tense moment in the sitting room at one point, though. Thought there was going to be a blooming great dust-up when Mr. Henry clipped Mr. Jack a good one on the chin. Didn't think he had it in him, Mr. Henry."

"What was that about?" Molly asked, trying not to show any concern.

"Seems Mr. Jack insulted Miss Phoebe. Said he wanted to fuck her."

There were gasps of horror and Grayson said sternly, "We'll have no more language like that here, Tom! That's grounds for dismissal."

"Sorry, Mr. Grayson," Tom said, although Molly could sense no contrition. "I was just reporting what I heard."

"Seems you hear that word a lot then," she said, getting a dig in.

Before anyone could respond to her insinuation, Tom said smoothly, "But it seems that Miss Phoebe was imagining things. Wishful thinking maybe."

"That's enough of that!" Mrs. Grayson, the housekeeper, said. "I think you've had more ale than is good for you."

"You have to admit that girl is a mite strange," Mrs. Hadley said as she sat down at the table with her breakfast. "Her grandmother's a bit eccentric, so they say. Swears she'd been the Prince of Wales's mistress." They all knew she was referring to the old King, Edward VII, better known as Bertie, during his long wait to ascend the throne. "Says she has love letters from him. Of course no one really believes her. They think it's just some harmless fantasy to make up for her early widowhood. Mind you, that family never lacked for money. Always was a bit of mystery, that, with no man about for years before the eldest could take over running the factory. But of course, none of us found out about that until they was well and truly married – Phyllis and Albert, I mean. Or I'll wager her ladyship would have put an end to that match!"

"I wouldn't have thought that anyone would boast about being a mistress," Molly said.

"A king's mistress now, that's another kettle of fish," Mrs. Hadley said. "That would put her into the illustrious company of rich society women like Lady Randolph Churchill and Alice Keppel."

"The aristocracy do things differently," Mrs. Grayson said dismissively. "You, on the other hand," she addressed the staff, "will behave with propriety and decorum." Looking directly at Tom now she added," And if I hear any reports of foul language being used, even among yourselves, you'll have me and Grayson to answer to."

She and Grayson would come to Wyndwood at the beginning of June to open the cottage and organize the staff. Aside from the ball, they also came again at the beginning of each month to make sure everything was going smoothly, and then would supervise the closing of the cottage at the end of September. Their main duties were running the substantial household at Wyndholme, with Mrs. Hadley nominally being in charge at Wyndwood. But should any problems or difficulties arise, one or both of the Graysons were immediately on hand.

As the tired night crew drifted off to their beds, Molly began the massive cleanup, starting in the dining room. Tom slunk in behind her. Picking up a half-finished glass of whiskey that some guest had abandoned, he downed it in one gulp. "You're a bitch, Molly Jones," he said, leaning against the sideboard next to her. "Trying to get me sacked, are you?"

"Sure, you're doing a good job of that yourself, so don't go blaming me." She caught a movement reflected in the mirror above the buffet table. Quick to seize opportunities, she added, "But if ever you grope me again, so help me, I'll tell them," guessing the warning would only incite him to do just that.

He chuckled as he put his arm about her waist and tried to draw her close. "Ah now, Molly me love, you're just so irresistible. Give us a kiss then, and I'll forgive you everything."

"Get away with you!" she said, struggling ineffectually.

Mrs. Grayson's voice bellowed out, "Tom! You will accompany me to the kitchen."

Molly tried to look scared as she stammered, "Oh, Mrs. Grayson, I never did nothing to encourage him!" She was even secretly amused at her double negative, which put a lie to her words, but which Mrs. Grayson would attribute to bad grammar.

"So I see," the housekeeper replied before following a visibly shaken Tom out of the room. Molly allowed herself a triumphant grin.

When she was called into the kitchen a few minutes later, Tom was nowhere to be seen.

If she had liked Tom, she would have told Mrs. Grayson that she was well able to look after herself and felt it had just been a bit of tomfoolery, so to speak. No harm meant. Instead she said when questioned, "Sure, Mrs. Grayson, I've been that uncomfortable around him. Always touching me, he is." She shivered dramatically.

"And why didn't you say anything about this to Mrs. Hadley?"

"I didn't like to rat on a fellow servant, M'am." Besides, she knew that Mrs. Hadley had a soft spot for Tom, who always buttered her up and made her laugh. "Sure, didn't I think that he'd get the message that I wasn't that kind of girl and just leave me be! But then didn't he..." She blushed.

"Go on," Mrs. Grayson urged. Mrs. Hadley had stopped working to listen.

"It was just yesterday, it was. I was taking towels to Mr. Jack's room. He wasn't there, but Tom surprised me and he said... Sure, he made... rude suggestions! Sure, wasn't I that scared when he grabbed me that I had to do what my Ma always said I should when a boy got too close." She hung her head as if ashamed. "I hit him where it hurts."

Mrs. Hadley let out a guffaw. "Kicked him in the privates, did you, girl? No wonder he was looking so sorry for himself then. The boy is high spirited, but he is a good worker."

"But we can't have him molesting the female staff."

Tom was packed off that afternoon with his pay but no reference. Grayson would stay in his stead until Mrs. Grayson could find a replacement. That wasn't easy these days, as young men did not readily give up their freedom for the prestige and relative security of being in service to the rich and powerful. They preferred slaving in factories that made those people rich and powerful, where the pay was better and at least their evenings – and their lives – were their own.

Molly, meanwhile, was relieved that a potential danger had been eliminated. What else might she need to do this summer to protect Jack? And her own future.

.          .          .

When the young people had left the table after the late breakfast, Albert said to Augusta, "If you are determined upon Jack having a job with us, then I suggest he stop wasting time here, and start training with Roger Edwards at the Gravenhurst mill. He just seems to be developing habits of indolence and self-indulgence here. No need for him to think that this is how his summers will be spent from now on."

Olivia wanted to jump in with a rejoinder, but paused to let Augusta respond. "It seems to me that we are doing a rather good job of grooming Jack as a Wyndham of whom we can be proud. He is well spoken, personable, liked by our friends, and making important business connections. And I enjoy his company. So, for now, he will stay." Shrewdly she added, "Jack has been exonerated, Albert. He's no danger to Phoebe."

"But I worry that she might be a danger to herself and perhaps others," Olivia added quickly, thankful for the opportunity to raise the subject.

"What the hell do you mean by that?" Albert demanded.

The guests — Olivia's family — diplomatically excused themselves from the table.

"Did Henry not tell you what happened at the Oakley's Summer Solstice party?" Olivia asked. At their blank expressions, she said, "Phoebe behaved strangely and, in a fit of temper, almost smacked one of the other guests in the head with a croquet ball."

"It was undoubtedly an accident," Albert said.

"She hears voices, Albert."

"She has a vivid imagination."

"She believes that God talks to her. Her doll tells her what to do."

"What's the harm in that? She's still a little girl."

"Extremely immature for her age," Augusta added. "But you shouldn't allow Blake to put ridiculous ideas into your head, Olivia. I expect he thinks we're all mad. God help us when he actually finishes studying. But at least then he'll have dealt with real lunatics, and not just silly girls. You might consider talking to Phoebe about the difference between lying and daydreaming,

Albert. I don't want to have any more scenes, like the one this morning, played out in public." She stared at Phyllis. "It's highly embarrassing that a girl of that age can't comport herself properly in society."

"That's rich!" Phyllis snapped. "The poor child is suddenly the one who is in the wrong, when it's people like Jack who've somehow instigated all this!"

"Nonsense! If Phoebe is beginning to develop romantic feelings for boys, then she should learn how to deal with those feelings, and not go about pretending to be kissed and accusing people of bad things," Augusta said, much to Olivia's relief. "I shall be most distressed if I think she is becoming like her maternal grandmother."

Phyllis could say nothing in defence of her mother, and her claims of having been a royal mistress. Although Augusta might deny that there was a problem with Phoebe, she wanted Phyllis to know that should the girl's odd behaviour continue, she would take it more seriously. Phyllis's mother, though harmless, was surely more than merely eccentric. And madness ran in families.

Phyllis had been a bad choice for Albert, despite her wealth. Augusta would be sure never to allow that to happen again.

.    .    .

When they were alone, Olivia said to Richard, "What did Albert mean about Jack training in the mill?"

Richard seemed uneasy. "James and Albert are determined that Jack not have any real influence in the business. They consider making him a mill manager as much as we owe the boy."

"That's just not right! I can't see Jack working in a mill. I think he hates all that machinery, especially after what happened to his brother."

"I know, darling. James claims that once Jack is thoroughly trained, he may let him run the lumbering business out west, if we start an operation in British Columbia. They want to get him as far away from the family as possible. That would be a very responsible position and Jack could do well for himself."

"But I think he would hate being so far away from his family and from Wyndwood. After the hard life he's had, I think Jack should spend as much time on the island as possible. And his sisters. He just seems so happy here. Now if we had our own cottage..."

"I know darling. I'm determined that we shall have one by next summer."

"But how?"

"I thought we might risk Mother's wrath and just go ahead with it. I've spoken with James and Albert about it. Neither one has objections to our building at Silver Bay. In fact, they both think it's a good idea. This house will be less crowded, with more room for visitors. James even encouraged Albert to think of having his own cottage. In any case, the three of us have decided to stick together. I don't think she can completely disinherit us in any case."

"I wonder. She might leave it all to charity."

"I think not. She's not overly generous with her charitable donations as it is. And she has too much pride in the Wyndham name and success to want her empire to end. I'm certain that when she sees we are united against her, she'll back down. I'm not saying she won't try to make us feel miserable and guilty about it. But we'll manage."

"What's prompted all this?" she asked. "No, don't tell me. James is planning to marry Helena Parker, and Augusta doesn't approve."

"Really?"

"Oh, Richard, haven't you noticed?"

"I suppose I have noticed that James is more cheerful these days. Well, that would explain a lot of things. Including our mutiny."

# *Chapter 13*

It was just after seven o'clock when Jack set out in a canoe for Thorncliff. He'd had his morning swim, and a cup of coffee and biscuits, but hadn't seen anyone else up yet. He loved this time of the day when the lake was as smooth as glass and the only sounds were the occasional cry of a loon or squawk of a gull. He felt as if the fresh new day belonged just to him.

Jack had been invited to use the Thornton's tennis court whenever he chose, so the groundsmen at Thorncliff weren't surprised to see him. They were raking paths, clearing away broken branches and aggressive weeds, and had just finished rolling the clay court.

Jack had bought himself a tennis racquet and proper shoes when he had been in the city with Richard. He felt absurdly proud to have been able to splurge on something non-essential. Another sign that he was moving away from his impoverished past.

The tennis court lay amid formal terraced lawns and gardens to the east of the house. Between the house and court perched a long enclosed pavilion in the style and colour of the main house, with a cupola, walls of screened French windows, and broad verandas all around. From here, spectators could watch a match from the comfort of the shade, or a croquet game on the west lawn, or sit inside away from wind and bugs to have afternoon tea or pre-dinner cocktails. There was even a fireplace at one end.

Netting hung from trees at the ends of the court to catch the balls. Jack practiced his serves, shooting the odd ball beyond the net, which didn't extend far down the sides of the court, but placing most of them in the service court. Now if he could only manage the blistering speed and hard spin of Chas's serves, he might feel confident playing in the tournament.

An amused voice behind him said, "Well, I am impressed by your determination, Jack."

He spun around to see Chas standing there, a towel around his neck, his hair dishevelled, his shirt unbuttoned. "I didn't think anyone would be up yet," Jack said.

"*Et tu, Brute?* You all think that I do nothing all day but lounge around. That's Rafe, when he isn't within sniffing distance of a horse. Or a woman. I actually have my morning swim at seven, so I'm a little late today. I have my breakfast served at eight, and then I'm either off sailing or rowing or whatever takes my fancy, until all the lazy bones are up and ready for some sport or adventure." The young crowd had spent busy afternoons playing tennis, sailing, canoeing, golfing, horseback riding on The Grand's trails – something else that Jack had had to learn – taking excursions to cliffs, waterfalls, and up rivers, so hardly a day went by when the island friends didn't do something together. Chas had taken just Victoria, Zoë, and Jack to The Colony so that Victoria and Jack could watch Edelina paint, and Zoë could get vegetarian recipes from Frieda, the cook. Then he had commissioned Edelina to paint Thorncliff, which gave him more opportunity to see her as he chauffeured her back and forth.

"You give a good impression of indolence," Jack said, "but I've never thought that you could achieve what you have by actually subscribing to it."

Chas laughed. "Very astute of you. It's how I fool my opponents into thinking that I'm a pushover. I'll give you a game if you like." He went into the pavilion to get his racquet and tennis oxfords.

They played a vigorous match. Although Jack didn't win a game, he scored a few points off Chas. "Well played, old chap," he said warmly. "You've become a strong opponent. Now if you can serve some aces, you might have a chance of taking a game from me." It wasn't said with conceit, but with such complete confidence in his own obvious skill, that no one could take offence. "I'm off for my swim. Come along if you like, and then you can have breakfast with me."

"I don't have a swim suit."

"Neither do I. But there aren't any women around to see us. Not that *I* would mind if there were, but one doesn't want to shock the fair sex."

They sauntered over to the change house on the east side of the island – there also being one on the west side. Encountering one of the groundsmen en route, Chas asked him to inform the chef that he would be half an hour late for his breakfast and that there would be two this morning.

"I often swim over to Wyndwood and back," Chas said as they struck out from shore. "I figure that half a mile or so a day will keep me in form."

Chas swam with the dedication of an athlete, focussed on a steady but quick pace. They only stopped long enough in the shallow waters of Wyndwood to take some deep breaths. When they returned, Chas stretched out in the strengthening sun on a granite slope by the change house, unabashed by his nakedness. He had the hard muscled body of a Greek statue. Jack remembered reading that ancient Greek men wore very little, athletes exercising and competing stark naked. As he sat down beside him, Jack could well imagine Chas striding about confidently naked in some previous sun-drenched lifetime.

"No better way to start the day," Chas said, cradling his head in his hands as he contemplated the morning sky. "Gives me all kinds of energy. I think I shall go and visit the goddess Edelina after breakfast. I think I'm in love, Jack"

"I thought you were in love with all women. What about Victoria?"

"Of course I love her. She beautiful, witty, fun to be with, adorable. But I'm smitten by Edelina. Madly in lust with her."

Jack laughed. "So you're not thinking of marrying her."

"Good God, no! We are, after all, quite different. I could no more live with her lame ducks and vegetarian diet than she could live without them. So if Edelina is the kind of woman who takes her pleasure where and when she finds it, I may be fortunate enough to experience her charms. I plan to enjoy what lots of women have to offer before I think about settling down.

"Just think about that expression. 'Settling down'. It implies that you're already doing something wild or audacious and definitely fun. And then you give it all up to become staid and undoubtedly bored. Perhaps I'll never get married. What about you, Jack?"

"I need to establish myself with some sort of career before I think about that."

"Oh, yes. I forgot you were the poor relation. You just need to find a rich wife, like all the other impoverished aristocrats."

"Unfortunately I don't have a title or estate to offer in exchange. My uncles want to banish me to some God-forsaken place to run a mill. I think I have a talent for investing. I practice it all the time and would have doubled my money in the last year, despite the depression, if I'd actually had money to invest."

"Pater started us off with an allowance of $1000 a month when we were fourteen, and tried to teach us how to invest money wisely." Chas laughed. "I always chose the wrong stocks. So after a year of losing money with great reliability, Pater decided that he would invest it for me and show me why he made his choices, but I have to admit that my eyes would glaze over and the numbers would dance around in my head like they wanted freedom. Pater soon realized that I really didn't have a head for finance. I know both Rafe and I are a great disappointment to him in that respect. I say, we should get Pater to take you on and train you as a broker."

"That's actually my dream," Jack said cautiously.

"If you have the drive and dedication you've shown in learning tennis and in scooping the Stepping Stone Cup from me, *and* have a head for business, then you'd do well. Leave it with me."

Jack was almost giddy with excitement but didn't allow himself to rejoice just yet. J.D. might well think him unsuitable from some reason, or be dissuaded by one of the Wyndhams.

"But first you should definitely come to Europe with us. No excuses about money. I can easily pay for you, and you needn't feel beholden. Think of it as part of your commission for all the money you're going to make for me when I put my fortune into your hands." He sat up. "I say, why don't I give you $1000 to invest right now. If I've made a good profit by the time we return from Europe, I expect you'll have a job waiting for you, and you'll have earned your trip. And now I'm famished. Come along."

It was a scary, if exciting, proposal. Jack was so accustomed to working hard that he couldn't imagine taking a year to do nothing but enjoy himself and spend money – even if it was someone else's. And what would the family think of him going off to amuse himself when he should be learning the lumbering business? He didn't expect that there would be a job waiting for him *there* when he returned. He didn't want to alienate Chas, but he couldn't risk his entire future. It was too easy to become seduced by this lifestyle, to never have to worry about money, to think of himself as one of the privileged. But he had to keep his perspective and constantly be prepared to seize opportunities.

So he pondered the idea of putting together an investment portfolio to show J.D. If he liked Jack's thinking, then there might be a job there now. He was determined not to go into the mills, and had only a few weeks left to find an alternative – short of marrying Victoria, of course. He was pleased that Chas didn't have designs on her.

So what had he to lose by approaching J.D.? He would consider the European jaunt if everything else fell into place and he had J.D.'s blessing.

The main house rested on a stone foundation, the granite rising skyward as pillars to support the massive veranda roof. At the south-east corner of the house, the rock grew to knee height, with glass and screens between the pillars enclosing a large room. Breakfast and other informal meals were served at the table, or one could enjoy the views from the many wicker chairs without being exposed to the elements.

A footman brought in fresh pickerel, caught and delivered early that morning by some of the Indians who fished the lake, as well as poached eggs, French croissants, and a fruit platter. Chas said, "We order what we like for breakfast. Mumsy takes hers in her room about 10:00, which is when Rafe arises from the dead. Pater and Fliss are down by 9:00. When we have guests, chef does quite a spread, but my tastes are simple."

But good. Jack had been stuffing himself on whatever Mrs. Hadley put on the buffet table, from porridge, fried potatoes, baked beans, and eggs, to sausages, ham, kippers, and bacon, as well as pancakes with maple syrup and a variety of biscuits, breads, and fruits. He approved of Chas's more refined selection. Here was surely another lesson – to make a wise choice of foods rather than try to eat everything available. It was perhaps what set apart those who had known hunger and those who had not.

"Speak of the devil," Chas said when Felicity walked into the morning room. "You're early."

"You're late," she replied, joining them at the table. "Hi, Jack."

"Jack and I have already had a tennis match and a swim. What are your plans for today?"

"To tag along with you."

"Hardly, darling child! I'll play tennis with you later. We have to practice for the tournament."

"We have to choose partners," she reminded him.

"I have. Ria." To Jack, Chas explained, "We have only two restrictions for choosing partners. You can't play with a family member or the person with whom you played the previous year. Ellie and I won last year."

"Good rules, or you and Felicity would always win," Jack said.

"Jack is becoming a formidable opponent," Chas said to Felicity. "I don't think we should let him practice any more."

"Would you be my partner?" Felicity asked, trying not to show her trepidation and excitement. She thought Jack the handsomest, dreamiest Prince Charming imaginable, and was sure she was in love with him. He had nice manners and Chas liked him, so that was alright. She was even glad now that she was becoming a woman and hoped that she would soon have proper breasts. More than Zoë had and less than Vivian, whose looked like they would get in the way of good tennis strokes. In fact, she wanted to be just like Victoria in every way. She hoped and prayed that Jack wouldn't get married before she had a chance to grow up and impress him. She would find some way to make him fall in love with her.

Jack was momentarily surprised, for he could sense her girlish interest in him. He thought of her as a child, but she *was* a terrific player. And he wondered what she would be like in a few years. The Thornton fortune quite outshone the Wyndhams'. He always kept his options open. "I'd be honoured!"

She blushed and smiled as she looked down into her lap, and barely acknowledged the footman who put a plate of creamy scrambled eggs and buttered toast before her, along with a cup of tea.

"Will you come and practice with me some time then?" she asked.

"Certainly. We have to learn to work as a team, don't we?"

"Yes, we do. I don't mind getting up early, if you want to come over in the mornings."

There was a week until the tournament. "Good idea."

"And how exactly will you practice being a team if you're going to play against one another?" Chas wanted to know as he sipped his coffee.

"You can play against us," Felicity suggested.

"What, poor little me, all by myself against you two?"

"You'll manage," Felicity said. She didn't want to suggest that Victoria come over with Jack, for then she would fade into the background as just a little girl. She wanted to be the centre of Jack's attention. "It'll be good practice for you, too."

"Have you ever noticed how girls can sweet-talk you into getting their way?" Chas asked Jack playfully.

"And boys have to be flattered into doing things," Felicity shot back.

"Actually, what *are* we doing this afternoon?" Chas asked Jack.

"And they change the subject when they're losing an argument," Felicity stated while she spread jam on her bread.

"Golf, I think," Jack replied with a grin. "And there's the moonlight cruise tonight." The young people were going for a trip around the lake in *Calypso*, as it was going to be a full moon, and promised to be a clear night. The adults and children were going out on the Oakley's eighty foot yacht.

"Oh, surely I can go with you rather than with the old people!" Felicity said. It would be so romantic to be with Jack on the boat, in the dark.

Chas shrugged. "I don't see why not. There's plenty of room."
Felicity glowed with joy.

"Good God, I just had a scary thought," Chas said dramatically. "I suppose by the time I return from Europe next summer, you'll have metamorphosed from a tadpole into an alluring young woman and I shall have to take you along everywhere and keep love-struck men at bay."

She giggled. "You are silly, Chas!" But was thrilled by the idea and the fact that even Chas realized she was growing up. She would be fifteen and half next summer – almost sixteen – and Jack would surely fall in love with her. She was determined to become a poised and beautiful young woman, not too smart, for girls like Eleanor and even Zoë were not the sort that men – at least her brothers – seemed to fall in love with. She would be fun-loving and bold, like Victoria.

.     .     .

It had been an amazing summer so far – too hot for those working in the city and too dry for the farmers. They'd had an occasional storm burst that cleared out the humidity, and a day when it had been grey and rainy, and they had been forced to stay indoors playing games and cards, or reading. The young people had gone to Thorncliff to play billiards and dance.

So the night of the July full moon was just the end of another perfect day on the lakes. People from cottages and resorts were out in canoes, rowboats, motor launches, and steam yachts. Even one of the large passenger steamers was hosting a moonlight cruise.

The fiery sunset inflamed the distant horizon, igniting the still lake, as *Calypso* picked up her last passenger, Edelina, for Chas had persuaded her to come along. As they headed away from The Colony, Chas handed her a glass of champagne, saying, "To a magical night," as he clinked glasses with her. Jack wondered if Chas's desires had been consummated, for he seemed even more besotted by Edelina.

They did a leisurely tour along the east side of the lake in the twilight, past bustling resorts, a scattering of cottages, and vast stretches of wilderness. By the time they reached the north end of the lake, the night was burnished by the rising moon.

"That's Kawandag." Chas pointed out  John Craig Eaton's huge summer estate to Edelina.

"Impressive," she replied.

"John always does things on a grand scale." John had been president of the Eaton department store empire since his father's death a few years earlier.

"Yours is hardly shabby. Anton would be putting a dozen families into this place. And yours," she said with a grin.

"Not if he owned it, and had earned it."

"Does anyone really earn *that* much in an equitable way?"

"Meaning that our employees should be living as well as we are?" Chas asked. "We're the ones who take the risks with investments, new ventures, expansions, building infrastructures, stocking inventory, and whatever. Who knows, one day we may make mistakes and lose everything. And then we may be renting out rooms. Meanwhile, I am going to enjoy a guilt-free evening at your service, milady." He gave her a mock bow.

Edelina laughed.

Rafe had brought his gramophone, but they kept the music low since sound flowed undiminished across the night time water, and Augusta had threatened to curtail the outing if there was excessive boisterousness or other unseemly behaviour. The Oakley's steam yacht, *Gloryoak,* hovered like an overprotective parent, never far away.

Some of the young men were smoking cigars and discussing Irish Home Rule, which was daily in the newspapers and becoming rather a bore. The others sat or stood about in loose groups, but leaving Felicity feeling somehow superfluous. All the younger children, including a disappointed Phoebe, were with their parents on *Gloryoak*.

It should have been wonderfully romantic in the rippling moonlight, so this was *not* how Felicity had imagined the evening unfolding. She thought that Chas should be spooning with Victoria, whom she would love to have as a sister, and not that Edelina, who didn't even know how to dress properly and was much too old, and really wasn't of their class anyway. And Jack shouldn't be constantly at Victoria's side – she was only his cousin after all – but with her, Felicity, talking about his hopes and dreams, and realizing what a good listener and friend she was, and developing some inkling of how attractive and desirable she would become. At least he didn't seem interested in any of the other girls.

Despite her disappointment, she was caught up in the beauty of the night. Thinking she might write a poem about it, Felicity sought words to describe it. *Islands suspended in a phosphorescent sea... Moonlight quivering like a lover's heart...*

They were about halfway back along the west side of the lake when Max suddenly said, "Listen!"

Rafe turned off the music and everyone fell silent. They could hear the shouts for help. Max told Toby, who said, "Could be from Gull Rock. That's just off the peninsula over there." He proceeded slowly, edging closer to the shore, while the others kept a sharp lookout. As it was a bright night, it was easy enough to see the darker islands and shorelines against the luminescent lake.

So they spotted the waving arms and heard some hysterical sobs as they came closer, and could see a thirty foot motor launch sitting at a bizarre angle, as if it were diving into the lake, its stern up out of the water.

"Yup. Gull Rock," Toby said. "People as don't know the lake shouldn't be speeding about at night. But they were lucky. They drove up the sloped side of the rock. If they'd hit it from another angle, they could have smashed the boat and themselves, and I reckon we'd be pulling some bodies out of the lake."

"I suppose that's one of the problems now that anybody can drive a boat," Max said. "Can we get close enough to help them?"

"We'll just inch in."

*Gloryoak*, being much larger, kept her distance, but also trained her lights on the grounded boat, so the people on board were now spotlighted. As *Calypso* floated up beside them, the Wyndham crowd recognized the Camford heir – to Pittsburgh Plate Glass – Lionel, as the distraught driver. Of the dozen on board, several looked as if they were injured, with blood streaming from cuts on faces, a girl holding her wrist, someone else, their nose, and one person seemingly unconscious.

"Thank God!" one of the girls cried. "We thought that no one would find us and there's water coming in!"

"We'll have you safely on board in moment," Simon Carrington said. "And you're fortunate that we have a couple of doctors here."

*Calypso* bumped against the large rock which lay mostly below the surface – named Gull rock since gulls usually stood on it – as she edged up beside the disabled craft. Henry, Archie, and Max secured the boat, while Simon and Justin braced themselves across the boats and helped people board *Calypso*, where Blake and Eleanor took them into the cabin to examine them. Zoë and Victoria took the others in hand as they boarded. Jack and Chas climbed into the shattered boat to lift out the unconscious man, passing him to Simon, Justin, and Freddie. They laid him out on a bench in the cabin where Blake examined him immediately, and declared that he probably had a concussion.

Emma Spencer and Daphne Carlyle passed out glasses of water or wine to the shaken group, while Vivian and Lydia had located blankets. Edelina was comforting a distressed girl who couldn't stop crying, and Rafe was reassuring a pretty young woman who seemed uninjured but shocked. Felicity marvelled at how they had all taken on roles almost instinctively, without discussion, but working together efficiently as a group. She was the only one who didn't seem to know what to do.

"I don't know what happened," Lionel Camford muttered, looking confused. He had a large gash on his forehead that Eleanor was cleaning, and had said would need stitching. "We were just moseying along and suddenly the boat lurched upward and over and we ground to a halt."

"That's Gull Rock. But it looks like you were lucky," Max said, explaining what Toby had told him about the angle of impact, but not going into details about what might have happened.

But the girl with the injured wrist said, "Lionel, you idiot! You could have killed us!"

"There should be a buoy there," Lionel said.

"And we were *belting* along, not *moseying*," the girl complained, ignoring his protest.

"The rock's marked on the navigation charts," Edgar said. "And the top is visible in the day. It's like an underwater mountain range just there, so we always give it a wide berth."

"Dumb cluck!" the girl said, glaring at Lionel.

*Calypso* sidled up to *Gloryoak* and it was decided that *Calypso* would see the young people safely to the Camford's island and then head home, while *Gloryoak* would return now.

The young man with concussion had regained his senses by the time they landed, but Simon and Justin escorted him to the house. Since Blake and Eleanor didn't have any medical equipment, other than the first aid kit in the boat, a doctor was sent for to do stitches and confirm Blake's diagnoses that there were no broken bones or cracked skulls.

The incident had put a bit of a damper on the evening's enjoyment, although when they were once more underway, Edelina said, "It's still a beautiful night. Perhaps even more so knowing that there wasn't a tragedy."

"How wise you are," Chas said. "And here I was blaming Lionel for spoiling our outing."

"I expect that Lionel's not only up the pole with his father, but with his friends, especially that girl he seems to fancy," Eleanor said.

"Does he? You mean the one who thinks he's an idiot?" Max said.

"Exactly. The tobacco heiress, isn't she?"

"Ah, well. A love-struck, heart-broken, and boatless Lionel should be no competition in the Regatta race then," Chas said to appreciative laughter.

By the time the Wyndhams had dropped off their friends and returned to Wyndwood, the rest of the family had already retired. Jack went out on his expansive private balcony for a cigarette. As the moon shimmered across the water on this still and glorious night, it seemed a shame to go to bed. He decided to do a watercolour sketch of the moonlit scene, which, surely, was rarely so perfect.

He smelled it first. Just a whiff of smoke, different from a cigarette. Then he saw the flickering glow through the windows of the large boathouse where *Calypso* was sheltered. Instinctively he shouted, "Fire!"

Jack ran down to the boathouse, but realized it was too late to save *Calypso*. The boathouse felt like a blast furnace. It would be suicidal to go inside. He pounded on Toby's door, although Shep was already barking, then roused Grayson and Will, who slept above the washhouse. He dashed to the house and banged the dinner gong wildly to alert everyone. It had been such a dry summer that a fire could spread quickly. Grabbing a couple of buckets from the kitchen, he raced down the path to the boathouse, where the hastily dressed staff were gathering.

Flames were greedily licking the dry walls. With more buckets from the washhouse, Jack organized bucket brigades, the women standing in the water to dip the buckets into the lake and pass them along to finally reach Jack and Grayson, who tossed the water onto the fire. As the family joined them, more lines formed beside them. But the bucketsful of water seemed as effective as spitting on a bonfire, for the entire building was fiercely ablaze, the flames shooting through the roof, the supporting timbers of the building now visible, like a skeleton.

"We can't douse this," Richard shouted above the roar of the fire. "We need to wet down the trees and watch for sparks landing on the cottage roof."

They all realized that if the fire ever caught on the cedar shingles, or in the dry undergrowth and dead leaves of the slope, there would be little they could do to save the house.

"We should wet blankets," Jack suggested, "and I'll take them onto the roof along with some pails of water. Is there a ladder somewhere?"

Grayson ordered Mary, the laundry maid, to collect blankets.

"We can get onto the veranda roof from our room," Max suggested.

"We could start there," Jack agreed.

The bucket brigades had to move away from the intense heat of the conflagration, and were desperately trying to water the shrubbery and trees behind.

As if by magic, the Carlyles were there to lend a hand. The men carried the heavy, dripping blankets into the house and through the boys' dorm to the balcony, where Max, Henry, and Blake climbed onto the roof. Toby brought a long ladder and set it against the east wall, so Jack clambered onto the second storey roof with a wet blanket to beat out any sparks that might land. Justin and Simon Carrington soon joined him, while Archie and Freddie Spencer hauled pails of water onto the roof for them.

Suddenly there were numerous people to lend a hand – Oswald Oakley had arrived with his entire staff and a hand pumper, which three of his men set up and operated, spraying water onto the hillside. More bucket brigades were formed, while some people took a few minutes to rest and catch some fresh air away from the dense smoke. Mrs. Hadley decided that refreshments would soon be called for and went to her kitchen where she rekindled the fire in the stove, and set the kettle on for tea.

Fortunately it was a calm night, but the fire created its own wind and sparks shot high into the air. Jack and the others on the roofs managed to beat out those that tried to gain hold. Meanwhile, the rest were barely winning the battle against the encroaching flames, mindful that the resinous pines were quite flammable.

Augusta watched in stunned horror from the west veranda. Esme had been given strict charge of her younger brothers, and ordered to stay with Augusta. They could feel the searing heat of the fire from where they sat. The voracious crackling, the hissing and snapping, were terrifying sounds. Flames and sparks shot skyward in a gigantic, never-ending fireworks display. Fortunately, most of the thick smoke blew out toward the lake, but the stench of burning leather, canvas, and varnished wood swirled about the veranda.

"Will the fire eat up the house too?" eight-year-old Miles asked as he pressed closer to his sister.

"No," Esme said. "Everyone is helping to put it out."

"I should be, too," ten-year-old Rupert stated, getting restless.

"You're supposed to look after Grandmother," Esme explained. "If we need to move, we're to go to the big dock, and you are to make sure she gets there safely."

"It won't come to that," Augusta declared.

When they had built the cottage, the second growth forests were only just taking hold, and there had been no trees tall enough along this western bluff to block the view of the lake. Pines, maples, birches, and oaks now loosely screened the veranda, but Augusta had not wanted the view obstructed, so many trees had been culled.

And now, through this open canopy, they watched an ember floating up, avoiding the branches and drifting in to land on the railing, like a butterfly come to rest a moment. Fascinated, they watched to see if it would burn out, but it took strength from the dry wood and flared hungrily. Esme dashed into the library behind her, grabbed the soda siphon, and sprayed the little fire that had taken hold.

"Well done!" Augusta said. "Go to the kitchen and see if you can find a bucket or a bowl and fill it with water. Miles, you help your sister, and Rupert, you take charge of the soda siphon. We'll keep that fire at bay."

They did as they were bid, and all were relieved to be doing something other than watching helplessly. Rupert felt rather important to be standing guard with the bottle, and scanned the veranda carefully for any more rogue sparks. Esme and Miles returned with a basin and a bowl. They soaked the veranda railing along its length, and fetched more water. Rupert proudly zapped a fading ember in mid-flight. Augusta cackled and said, "That's the ticket!"

Phyllis, with Phoebe clinging to her skirt, came onto the veranda. She was dressed as if going to a formal tea and had a large carpetbag in her hand. She said, "Mother Wyndham, I suggest that you go and collect your jewellery and anything else you intend to save from the fire, and then come down to the front dock to await rescue."

Augusta regarded her as if she were mad. "Don't spout nonsense, woman! You would have done better to go and help, than pack your belongings and prepare to desert."

Phyllis drew herself up. "It's bad enough that my men are in danger, but I refuse to subject myself and Phoebe to it."

Phoebe, who had been gathering Phyllis's skirt in her frantic hands and trying to disappear behind her, started whimpering as she watched the blaze and heard the cacophony of the fire, the shouting voices, the thumping feet on the roof above.

*That's hellfire, Phoebe. You brought it here. And it'll get you if you've been bad, sinful, evil. Evil devil. It will roast you and toast you, but your screams won't make it stop. Can you feel the heat? Can you hear them, Phoebe? Hear the cries? Hear how it will sizzle your flesh?*

"Stop it! Stopit! Stopit!" Phoebe screeched, burrowing her face into her mother's back.

Phyllis turned around and took the terrified girl into her arms, saying, "There now, Beebee, everything will be fine." Beebee was what Phoebe had called herself when she was a child, before she could say her name properly. "We're going to the front dock," Phyllis announced. "You see how this has upset Phoebe. She has a sensitive nature and a delicate constitution, and this is all too much for her."

Augusta didn't approve of the way Phyllis babied the girl. Despite what she had said to Blake and the others about Phoebe, she was not at all certain that Phoebe was normal, but refused to dwell on that thought or allow it to grow. So she just grunted and said, "Do what you feel you must. But this ship is not sinking yet." Although the rats were ready to desert it, she thought.

A few minutes later, Mrs. Hadley came out to the veranda with the silver tea tray. "I thought you could use some tea, M'am, and I'm brewing a kettleful for the others."

"Mrs. Hadley, you are a treasure. Even with soot on your face," Augusta added with a chortle.

"Ah, well, I reckon I did my bit, but now I'm of more use in my kitchen. I'd say a tot or two of rum in that tea wouldn't go amiss."

"Indeed. Esme, would you kindly fetch me some? And Mrs. Hadley, be sure to be generous with it in your kettle."

"Yes, M'am."

The children took theirs without the rum, of course, but it did seem rather bizarre to be sitting on the veranda taking tea like any leisurely afternoon, while an inferno raged below them.

It was nearly dawn before the fire had burned down to a smouldering mess that no longer threatened the island. People had taken breaks throughout the night, to be fortified by strong, spiked tea and plates of sandwiches. Oswald's chef had felt that his talents were put to best use in the kitchen, so he had helped Mrs. Hadley prepare the food.

But as the first streaks of celestial fire scorched the sky, only Toby and Will were left to watch the fire and douse the ashes, while the staff congregated in the servants' hall and the others, in the sitting room. Platters of food had been set out in the dining room, along with a variety of drinks, and everyone helped themselves, the servants being as exhausted as the rest and not expected to perform their regular duties just at the moment.

James went into the servants' hall to address them. "Thank you all for your hard work tonight, for your courage and fortitude. Take the rest of the day to rest. We'll try to fend for ourselves somehow," he quipped to mild laughter. "And there will be a generous bonus for each of you, including those of you in Mr. Oakley's employ. Thank you, and God bless you all!"

Tired as they were, there was a cheer of triumph and joy.

In the sitting room, the exhausted firefighters wearily took some sustenance. They were soot-blackened, dishevelled, and wet. Many of them were coughing, but no one had been overcome by the smoke. Although the windows had been closed, the pervasive stench of a wet fire lingered everywhere, but especially on their clothes and in their nostrils. Victoria thought her arms would drop off from the punishing weight of the hundreds of buckets she had passed along.

James returned from the kitchen and said, "Well, I – we – don't know how to thank you all for coming to our aid. We couldn't have survived this without your help. You were all so quick to respond!"

The Professor said, "I was on the upper balcony examining the heavens through my telescope when I thought I heard someone yell 'Fire'. A few minutes later I heard your gong, and by that time I could see the glow of the blaze. So I telegraphed it to the others. I happen to have an old speaking trumpet."

"What causes the sound to travel so much better at night, Professor?" Max wanted know.

"At night, the air near the lake cools faster than the air well above the lake. Since the velocity of sound is smaller in a lower temperature, we therefore have a slow layer of air blanketing the lake level at night. It tends to trap sound waves. It's all a consequence of Snell's Law…"

"Thank you indeed, Thomas," James interrupted before the Professor became too technical. "And Oswald, what a Godsend your pump was. I think we shall have to get one as well."

Oswald said, "We have a waterworks system on the island for the gardens as well as the house, but this is a backup, in case of fire. What are neighbours for, if not to pull together in times of crisis?"

"Do you have any idea how the fire started?" Edward Carrington asked.

Richard replied, "None at all. Toby and Will went through their usual procedures when they put the boat away. The fire wasn't out, of course, but that shouldn't have caused a problem. After all, they fire up the boiler for at least half an hour in the boathouse before it's ready to go."

"It's been such a hot and dry summer. Maybe all it took was a stray spark," Edward suggested.

"So it seems. There were no gas lamps left on or anything else inside that could have started a fire."

"Any sort of fumes, gasoline, or something flammable, like an oily rag left about, and with everything tinder dry and a hot boiler, you could have the recipe for fire," the Professor said.

"It couldn't have been set deliberately?" Ernest Spencer, the lawyer, suggested.

"I can't imagine it," James said. "Who would want to burn down the boathouse?"

"A careless servant, then," Ernest said. "Smoking in the boathouse."

"Toby smokes a pipe, but never while he works," James said. "He's careful."

"But getting old," Albert said.

Richard said dismissively, "Well, I doubt that there's any way we'll ever know. Everything is thoroughly destroyed."

"Poor *Calypso*," Victoria said. "She was such a gallant little ship."

"*And* the sailboat," Max added. "I guess we'll be out of the races this year."

"We'll have to replace them both, I suppose," James said.

"But with a motor yacht," Edgar said eagerly. "Then we won't have to rely on Toby and Will to take us places."

"That won't be done instantly," James said. "I'll talk to Herb Ditchburn and see if he can build us one. Perhaps he has something he can rent us in the meantime."

"You need only bang the gong or send out smoke signals, and we'll be happy to put *Gloryoak* at your disposal," Oswald offered, knowing that the entire Wyndham family didn't fit into *Dragonfly*.

"How kind, Oswald," Augusta said.

"My pleasure, Milady."

After they had seen their friends off, the family bathed in the lake and then dropped into their beds. Despite her exhaustion, Victoria couldn't sleep. Her lungs felt raw, her shoulders burned, her skin felt blistered, her hands, swollen, and the pervasive reek of smoke was revolting.

Although Phoebe hadn't needed a bath and so had been in bed for a while, her doll, Maryanne, suddenly sat up and stared at Victoria with her vile face. "It's my fault. The fire and the boat crashing."

"What are you talking about, Phoebe?" Victoria asked wearily. She was annoyed that Phoebe and Phyllis hadn't done a thing to help, especially when all the neighbours had rallied round.

"I was SO mad that I couldn't go on *Calypso* with the rest of you. I felt like I was going to explode. Or burst into flames. So I wished that something bad would happen, so that I could be glad that I wasn't on *Calypso*. But it was the Camfords' boat that crashed. And now poor *Calypso* is dead and it's all my fault!"

Victoria was surprised at Phoebe's candour, and felt a measure of sympathy for her, always being left out of the older crowd's activities – even though Phoebe was so immature that she really couldn't be trusted to behave appropriately. "Don't be silly! You can't make things happen just by wishing for them."

Maryanne cocked her head sideways as if questioning Victoria's sanity, as Phoebe said, "You really don't understand, do you? Of course I can." It was said with such conviction that Victoria felt a shiver down her spine. At that moment Phoebe didn't look like a giddy, witless child. "You're so naïve, Victoria," she stated before rolling over and hugging Maryanne to her chest.

Victoria thought that Blake was probably right about Phoebe. Sleep eluded her.

.    .    .

But Victoria must have slept deeply for she awoke at noon feeling refreshed, if rather stiff. The others were just stirring. She washed and dressed quickly and slipped downstairs.

"Ah, Sleeping Beauty arises," Chas said. He was lounging across one of the wing chairs, his legs thrown over the arm, his head lolling against the broad back. He discarded the *Maclean's* magazine he'd been reading. Felicity sat demurely in another chair reading a recent *Vanity Fair* issue. "A pity I didn't have a chance to awaken you with a kiss."

"Good morning! What are you two doing here?"

"We come bearing gifts. Chef has prepared a breakfast luncheon for you. I suppose we should call it a bruncheon. Our footman, Leonard, is laying it out in your dining room as we speak. We took the unmitigated liberty of inviting ourselves in, as there was no one around to ask." And the doors were never locked. "Chef sent enough food for your staff as well."

"How marvellous! I'm quite famished," Victoria said.

Chas went to her side and kissed her on the cheek. "Darling Ria, I'm mightily relieved to find you in such fine fettle, although I detect a fragrance of Eau de Smoke."

She laughed. "I was sure I'd scrubbed my skin off, and washed my hair twice, but it seems to get into your pores."

"Indeed it does," Beatrice said, coming down the stairs with Olivia.

"Good day, ladies. A pleasure to see you both so well," Chas said.

Beatrice chuckled. "It's a good thing you can't see how I feel! Rather as if I've been run over by a steam roller."

"Was it very ghastly? I'm afraid we slept through it all." Which wasn't surprising, as Thorncliff was off the long north end of Wyndwood, and so not in the line of sight or sound.

"Heartbreaking. And frightening," Victoria said, and described the night's events. "We weren't sure we could keep the fire from spreading to the house and the rest of the island."

Awestruck by the account, but rejoicing at Jack's bravery, Felicity said, "That's horrid! Mummy is terrified of fire."

"Apparently it's why we don't have many trees near the house," Chas said. "And why they chose to build on an island. Because forest fires can spread rapidly on the mainland," he explained to a puzzled Beatrice.

"You know that the Fremonts built their boathouse on a tiny island just off theirs, with a drawbridge over to it, which they can pull up in case of fire," Victoria said.

"That seems quite sensible," Beatrice said. "I was envisioning the entire island ablaze last night."

"It would have killed Grandmother if that had happened, or even if the cottage had burned down," Victoria said.

Although it would have been the perfect time to propose that each family build a separate cottage, Olivia thought, and chided herself for her uncharitable thoughts. Of course she didn't want Augusta to be shocked to death. She merely wanted her own place.

"Do let's go eat." Victoria explained the Thorntons' generosity as they all moved into the dining room.

"How kind and thoughtful," Olivia said.

"And you're invited to dinner tonight," Chas said. "We'll send the yacht over around seven."

"You are fortunate with your friends," Beatrice said to Victoria and Olivia.

"Indeed we are. But how did you find out so quickly about the fire?" Olivia asked Chas.

"I was canoeing around your island this morning after breakfast, and couldn't believe the devastation. I noticed that the trees closest to the boathouse were singed, so I realize how close you came to losing more. I wish we had been here to help."

"This is a big help, believe me!" Olivia said.

When most of the others had drifted in, Chas said, "Pater says he'll put one of our runabouts at your disposal until you have another boat." The runabouts were two sizable Ditchburns, the newest being the one that Chas planned to race in the Regatta. "Do you have room for a thirty-six footer in the new boathouse?"

"Yes, we do," Edgar said. "I say, but how will you manage?"

"We still have my new boat, and the yacht. Rafe rarely goes out. I think he has trouble docking and doesn't want to show his ineptitude. Horses he understands. Machinery he doesn't."

The men got into a discussion about the ideal size of boat to replace *Calypso*, everyone agreeing that steam had had its day.

"We'd best be off," Chas said. "We've been instructed to invite everyone else who spent the night fighting the fire, as they, too, will want to give their staff a chance to recover." He winked at Victoria before he left, and she thought how wonderfully loveable he was.

.    .    .

As soon as Helena spotted James that evening at Thorncliff, she rushed to his side, her face suffused with concern. Laying her hand on his arm, she said, "Oh, James, I was so frightened for you! Oswald insisted that Letitia and I stay behind with the children, but it was an agony not knowing what was happening. I watched all night from the gazebo on the little island. It was a horrifying sight! Like an inferno. As if even the sky was ablaze. I am *so* relieved to see you well, and although I'm sorry about your boathouse and yacht, I'm delighted that things weren't worse."

"Dear Helena," James said affectionately, putting his hand over hers and squeezing it. He drew her away from the others, who were sitting or standing about the lawns and verandas of the tennis pavilion, where hors d'oeuvres and drinks were being served. "Oswald was right to insist you stay at Oaktree. That way I had one less worry."

She blushed and smiled coyly. "Surely you wouldn't think of me in such a crisis."

They were now out of hearing of the others, strolling along the lakeside path toward the eastern change house. "In fact I was hoping that we could preserve the cottage so that you could be its mistress one day."

"Oh! James!"

"Forgive me, Helena. That was a rather abrupt way to propose marriage, and I expect I should have approached your father first. I know that I said we should take the summer to get to know one another, but last night, while we struggled to save the cottage, I realized that I wanted to do that for you. I don't think we should waste valuable time, if we know our own minds. I love you and wish to spend the rest of my life making you happy." They had walked around a small point and were no longer in sight of the others. James stopped and turned to face her. "If you need more time, I shall understand."

She dropped her gaze, pretending to be flustered, and then looked him squarely in the face. "I would be honoured and delighted to be your wife."

He beamed with relief and gratitude, and took her into his arms. His kiss was ardent, but not unpleasant. "You have made me so happy, my dear! Will your father approve?"

"Yes, indeed. He thinks most highly of you."

James drew a small silver box from his pocket and handed it to her. "I bought this when I was in the city last week."

It was a large square-cut emerald flanked with sizable diamonds. "How exquisite!" Helena enthused, as she tried to estimate its value. It could easily be over $1000, which was more than the average working man's yearly salary, so enough to keep her going for a while, should anything go wrong. She would be sure that she showed her appreciation for jewels, so that James would be encouraged to shower her with frequent gifts. "Oh, James, I feel like a princess!"

"You deserve to be treated as one. Now I have to ask you quite foolishly not to say anything to anyone at the moment, except your father, as I need to break the news to my mother. She does not take kindly to change, and considers any woman I would marry a threat. She has been ruling her castle for over fifty years, and is not about to let another woman take any sort of control."

"Oh, but I shan't want to usurp her position, just make a cozy space for us. Is there not a wing or a suite of rooms we could have for ourselves? Or perhaps a small house nearby?" A dower house for her. Wasn't that what the British did with superfluous widows?

"I'll see what I can do. In the meantime, I beg your indulgence, but do start thinking about the wedding. In a few days you can begin making firm plans. And don't worry about cost. I shall foot the bill. I know that your father is in straightened circumstances at the moment. The depression hit a lot of people hard. Would it be completely unrealistic of me to wish for a wedding by summer's end?"

"I expect that Letitia will want to whisk me off to Paris to buy a wedding gown and trousseau, but I am happy for a simple wedding, if that is to your liking," She wanted to be sure he realized what most women would insist upon. "Do you know what I would dearly love? To have the ceremony in the garden at Oaktree, on a glorious summer day, with just our closest friends in attendance."

"You are an extraordinary young woman!" James said, convinced even more that she was the right choice. "Most girls take a year to plan an extravaganza."

"But that isn't what I desire, James. I want it to be an intimate ceremony. I want just the two of us to toast our marriage in the gazebo, like we did that day of the picnic. A month or six weeks is sufficient time, and we can still have a summer wedding." And there would be less risk of something interfering with the nuptials. If James discovered her lies after their marriage, he would just have to learn to live with them. Or pay her handsomely for a divorce settlement.

Back at the pavilion, Eleanor Carlyle said, as if in disgust, "He's even good with children." She, Victoria, and Zoë were leaning on the veranda railing watching Chas, who was teaching the younger children to improve their tennis skills, and appearing to have as much fun as they were. Although they were all in formal evening dress, Chas had thrown off his dinner jacket, rolled up his sleeves, and now looked as cool and relaxed as if he were in his sporting clothes.

"Don't tell me you're in love with him?" Victoria said in surprise.

Resignedly Eleanor replied, "It's absurd, I know. I detest his lifestyle and his lack of ambition. I think he has more money than is good for him – or anybody, for that matter. But he's so generous and witty, guileless and fun to be around that I want to spend every moment with him. And he's absolutely beautiful," she said on a sigh. "It's ridiculous, isn't it? We wouldn't even be good for each other. I expect I would badger him to do something useful, and he would irritate me with his laissez-faire attitude. I may as well be in love with the Prince of Wales for all the good it does me. Love isn't sensible, rational, or logical."

"But it's painful nonetheless," Zoë said.

"Are you speaking from experience?" Eleanor eyed her sharply. "No, don't tell me. I'm really not that blind. It's Blake, isn't it?"

Zoë blushed hotly.

"I thought so! And the fool is in love with Vivian, who's in love with someone else. Pathetic, isn't it? So I think that you, Ria, are the only one of us who has any chance of real happiness." Eleanor took a big gulp of wine.

"How do you figure that?"

"Chas is obviously in love with you, you're fond of him, and you two know how to enjoy life."

"Chas is in love with Edelina at the moment. And tomorrow it may be someone else."

"So he says, but I think that deep down you are his true love. Letting the two of you loose in Europe will be romantically dangerous. You'll have to be sure they don't elope, Zoë, as I intend to be a bridesmaid. In the meantime, what shall *we* do? I think I could fall in love with Jack. Or Simon. Or Justin. Or Archie. Or even Freddie, although I think he's got a pash for you, Zoë."

"Surely not! We're just good friends."

"Ah, but that's what they all say. I'll try to make Blake see reason."

"Ellie, don't you dare tell him!" Zoë said in alarm.

"Never fear. I am discreet and reliable." Eleanor took another mouthful of wine. "I think all this unrequited love is bloody pathetic!"

"You *are* down in the dumps today," Victoria said.

"Don't mind me. Unrequited love can do that to the most resolute soul. But do look. Here come your father and Helena looking almost like naughty lovers who've been canoodling behind the bushes."

"Ellie!" Zoë protested.

"No, she's right," Victoria said. "Good God, you don't think that Father's actually interested in that woman? She's young enough to be his daughter. Surely he wouldn't *marry* her! She's too young to be my stepmother. And I don't even like her."

"She seems pleasant enough," Zoë said. "Anyway, it was your idea to get her and Henry together."

"That was before I knew her. I don't trust her. She seems phoney, somehow. Unctuous."

"Oh, good word," Eleanor said.

"If he does marry her, I *will* elope with Chas," Victoria said. Or Jack, although he wouldn't be able to support her. And he seemed so serious and driven, while Chas enjoyed life and radiated joy.

With their busy social schedule and no time to sneak away by themselves, she and Jack had had little opportunity for more than a quick kiss recently. She wanted more. But she was no longer certain that she wanted it from Jack.

# Chapter 14

"What's this? A delegation?" Augusta asked, putting down a letter and clasping her hands as her sons walked into the library and stood in front of the desk.

The brothers had discussed things and agreed to stand firm. James said, "Mother, I'm delighted to inform you that Helena has consented to be my wife. We will have a small wedding at Oaktree in late August."

Before she could say anything, Richard added, "With James hoping to start a new family, and the possibility of a nursery being needed by next summer, Olivia and I are going ahead with building a cottage at Silver Bay."

Augusta recognized the rebellion. She turned haughtily to Albert and said, "Well?"

For someone who had sworn only weeks ago that the idea was out of the question, Albert said reluctantly, "We are going to build a bungalow on the east side, just past the back bay. Phyllis is finding the stairs a challenge, and that will only get worse as we age. Also, we want our children to have their own rooms. Phoebe, in particular, is disturbed by the others. And look at Edgar, stuck in a closet."

"I see. So you are behaving like wilful and defiant children, deliberately going against my wishes."

"Mother, it is not our intention to distress you. We care for you no less by wanting to change things to suit our own families. All we seek is happiness, but on our terms," James said.

"You will remember that the island belongs to me."

"Not quite," James said. "I checked with Ethan Nash when I was in the city. You are the executor and trustee of Father's estate. You have some discretion with the assignment of assets, but Father left the bulk of the estate to the three of us, upon your death or remarriage. And that includes the island." So even if she disowned them, and they had no access to Wyndham funds while she was alive, she was not able to disinherit them. And a large part of the estate was tied up in trusts, from which she could use only the interest.

She stared hard at them. "You do what you feel you must. And so shall I," she said dismissively. When they didn't move she said, "You have made up your minds, and won't entertain any discussion. So leave me to my correspondence."

When they had closed the door behind them, Augusta unclenched her shaking hands. How dare they? Of course she couldn't disinherit them, as she and Reginald had Alexander. But she would make them regret this. She would not be discarded like some useless old relic, or made to endure a bleating, manipulative young wife who was determined to gain control.

Out in the hall, the brothers looked at one another. Richard said, "I'm not sure that went as well as we had planned."

"You think there'll be retribution?" Albert asked.

"Of some sort, I'm sure," James said as they walked away. "I think it's time to enlist some help to smooth things over. Perhaps Oswald and Letitia can convince Mother that Helena will be a suitable wife. Why don't you try Beatrice, Richard?"

He found her swimming at the back bay with Olivia and the children. It was another stifling day, with dismal clouds sagging over islands which seemed to materialize out of the thick air. The water was perfectly still, so that the sky and lake melded in seamless grey. Just then the sun broke through between distant, ragged islands, glinting off the water like a string of brilliant diamonds.

Another day when it would be too hot to do more than play in and around the water. Richard changed into his swim suit and joined the others.

"Glorious, isn't it?" Beatrice asked. She had had her swim and now sat in the sandy shallows letting the cool water embrace her.

"I can't imagine what it must be like in the city this summer," Richard said.

"Think of all those poor people sweltering in factories," Olivia said. "I even feel badly for Mrs. Hadley, having to have the stove burning all day to cook our meals."

"We should do a cook-out for dinner," Richard said.

"That would be fun," Beatrice said.

Olivia said, "I'll go suggest it to Augusta, shall I?"

"Perhaps not at the moment, darling. She's rather miffed with us, I'm afraid." He went on to tell Beatrice about their plan to build a cottage.

"But that seems entirely reasonable," Beatrice said. "I don't blame you a bit for wanting to have more privacy, and frankly, I'm surprised you haven't done it sooner."

"There was sufficient room initially, so I suppose we rather drifted along. But now that the children are no longer in the nursery, they, too, need more privacy," Richard said.

"But we don't want to upset Augusta too much, and have said that we will still share meals and evening entertainments here," Olivia said.

"Very thoughtful and more than most people would expect. And you wouldn't mind if I mentioned that to Augusta?" Beatrice said shrewdly.

"Would you? She might listen to you," Richard said.

Beatrice laughed. " I doubt that! But I shall certainly try. Now do tell me what it will be like."

Zoë and Victoria, who were also swimming, had heard the conversation. Zoë said, "Are we really going ahead with the cottage?"

"Yes we are," Richard said. "Your grandmother will come round."

"Max and I were going to give both of you this as a Christmas present, but perhaps it could be early birthday presents instead," Zoë said, as Richard and Olivia had birthdays in September. "We've asked Freddie to design a cottage, and he's been working on the plan."

"How wonderful!" Olivia exclaimed. "I can't imagine a better present. Oh, do tell us about it!"

She gave them a brief description and added, "We showed him the location, so he's made some suggestions that we think you'll like. Including a matching boathouse with a sitting room and a balcony above. Imagine reading a book or playing games just above the water on a rainy day when it's always so gloomy in the house. Or on the balcony on a sunny day."

"It sounds delightful!" Beatrice said. "Do let's go and look at the spot after our swim, and Zoë can set the scene."

"I shall hate it," Victoria said glumly. "You'll be leaving me with Phoebe and that freaky Maryanne."

"In fact, Albert will be building a cottage as well, just a hundred yards up from here," Richard said.

"I know I'm being terribly selfish," Victoria said, "but at Wyndholme there are just the three of us and I always look forward to the summers when we're all together. Silver Bay is at least a ten minute walk from here. You won't always want to come for meals or evenings, especially when it's raining. Gradually it will become a weekly visit, like in the city. So I do understand why Grandmother doesn't want you to go."

"You can always come and stay with us, Ria," Zoë said.

"Yes, of course," Olivia said. "You mustn't think we're abandoning you. We'll be sure that the girls' room is large enough for guests."

"In any case, it will be you girls who will soon be deserting us," Richard said with mock despair. "First Europe, then marriage."

"Don't forget university," Zoë said.

But Victoria didn't listen to the lively discussion about that. She was thinking how empty the cottage would be without her cousins always about. She would have half a dozen children to fill her own home! She loved the constant activity, the plotting and scheming, the teasing. And even the squabbles were better than the sterile silence of Wyndholme.

But there was worse to come when James announced at lunch, "I'm absolutely delighted to tell you all that Helena Parker and I will be married in August at Oaktree."

Victoria dropped her fork with a loud clatter, which would normally have earned her a reprimand from Augusta. "You can't mean that?" she demanded.

"Indeed I do. I trust you will be welcoming to your new mother." His tone was severe.

"It's disgusting! She's young enough to be your daughter! I refuse to accept her as a *step*mother!"

James scowled. "You have no choice, young lady! As my wife, she will deserve your respect and obedience."

"*That* she has to earn! She's playing you for a fool, Father. Has she promised you the son you've always wanted?"

"That's enough of your impertinence! Or you will leave the table."

Victoria jumped up and threw her napkin onto the barely touched food on her plate. "You've never been much of a father to me. I'd be happy to leave more than your table!"

With that she ran from the dining veranda.

Augusta said wryly to Beatrice, who sat on her right, "So the pigeons have come home to roost." When Zoë got up, the matriarch barked, "You will sit down, Zoë."

Zoë hesitated, but then said, "No disrespect, Grandmother, but I'm needed elsewhere," and marched away.

Augusta's eyes nailed each of the others to their chairs. Both Max and Jack had been tempted to follow, but realized that Victoria was best left to Zoë's ministrations at the moment.

And Jack was pondering what James's marriage meant for Victoria financially. If James was able to father a son, Victoria would no longer be the heiress to a fortune. He needed to rethink his strategy.

Phoebe was holding her hands over her mouth, giggling, and rocking in barely restrained excitement.

Phyllis broke the embarrassed silence by saying, "What a good thing that we're building our own cottage then." She threw a defiant look at Augusta. "I, for one, am too old to be disturbed by squalling infants. You'll have your pick of rooms for the new nursery, James."

Beatrice said, "I think it's exciting for you to be building your own cottages. I wonder that you haven't done it before, as you seem to be bursting at the seams here. How lucky you are, Augusta, to have such a loyal family always at your side. I understand that they don't plan to change the routine at all, just the sleeping arrangements, in essence."

But Augusta was not fooled. "So they've recruited you, have they?" she said.

Victoria was already heading out in a canoe by the time Zoë caught up to her. "Ria, come back and we can talk!"

Victoria was fiercely ripping her shoes off, almost upsetting the canoe. "There's nothing to discuss! I knew that everything was going to go to hell! I could sense that this would be the last summer, that everything was going to change! But how could he just announce it like that in front of everyone? He didn't even have the decency to tell me first! I hate him! And I hate her, the scheming bitch! She'll want to be rid of me, just wait and see. And they'll have children that he will fawn and coo over and expect me to do the same. And I'll be as welcome as dog shit on a shoe."

Zoë realized just how upset Victoria was because of her swearing. "Come back and take me with you. You *do* need to talk."

"Thank you, Zoë, but I really need to be alone right now." She paddled northward along the shore.

Zoë was tempted to take out another canoe and follow her, but Victoria was upset enough, and she didn't want to annoy her. Sometimes one did need to think things through on one's own. But she felt so sorry for Victoria. How alone she must feel! Zoë couldn't imagine being without her siblings, especially her twin. She had always been close to Victoria, and would make sure that Victoria knew that she was loved like a sister. With James getting married, it might be a good idea if Victoria moved into the new cottage with them. Zoë returned reluctantly to resume her lunch.

Victoria's anger gave way to tears, so she could barely see where she was going. Not that it mattered. She just struck out across the vast expanse of lake, with no destination or plan in mind. She just wanted to get as far away from Wyndwood as possible.

The morning clouds had burned off under a blistering sun. Victoria stopped to splash water on her face and hair, to pull her skirt defiantly above her knees and soak her legs. Her own anger burned as fiercely as the sun. She wanted to throw herself into the lake to put out the fires, but there was nothing but water around her for miles in every direction. She'd never get back into the canoe. So she kept going towards Mortimer's Island. There was a lovely, secluded cove around the northern point that was out of sight of Wyndwood and most everything else. Pirate's Cove they had named it when they had first picnicked there years ago.

She beached the canoe on the sand and jumped out. There were no cottages anywhere nearby, so she took off her clothes and immersed herself in the lake. It had always felt comforting, even healing, but this time it only refreshed her body and not her spirit. Even the loons swimming nearby, a mother with a tiny chick upon her back, didn't make her smile. It only made her realize that she had no one who had ever nurtured her thus. With an acute stab of pain, she found herself weeping for the mother she had never known.

Victoria sat, naked, for a long time on the beach, oblivious to the sun, just going back into the water whenever she was too hot. Dragonflies danced around her.

How glad she was that she was going to Europe in September! She would be spared the domestic love scenes between her father and Helena. She could just imagine his solicitude, trying to please his young bride. And her demure and obsequious manner until such time as she had him properly trained. Poor Grandmother. *She* couldn't run away.

Realizing she was getting sunburned, Victoria dressed and decided that, as she was not far from The Colony, which was just around the large headland that helped to protect the cove, she would go there. She had no wish to return to Wyndwood just yet.

When she arrived, Edelina greeted her warmly and said, "Your cousins were here looking for you. I think they're getting worried."

It had been Zoë, Max, Jack, and Edgar in *Dragonfly*.

"Because I didn't show up for tea? Have you ever thought how much of our lives is dictated by and revolves around food and its consumption?"

Edelina laughed. "Yes indeed. And some of our best discussions and ideas have occurred around a dinner table. So can I offer you anything?"

"A large glass or preferably bottle of wine would be most appreciated. And perhaps a bed for the night."

"The wine I can manage. The bed I would, but not at the expense of your family's peace of mind. At least let me send word to them."

"What, and have some poor fellow paddle four or five miles to do so? I'll return in my own good time."

"Are you trying to make your father anxious?" Edelina asked as she settled Victoria on the veranda. "To teach him a lesson?"

"No. I honestly don't think he cares. He has never liked me, only tolerated me. He blames me for my mother's death." She brushed away a tear, annoyed at herself. "I just can't face going back there yet."

Frieda brought wine and a plate of cheeses and biscuits. Victoria nibbled absently on the food, but gulped down the wine, and found herself talking freely to Edelina. She had no desire to join the rest of the Colony for the vegetarian meal served in the kitchen, but urged Edelina to leave her on the veranda with another bottle of wine. Edelina brought her own plate out and sat with Victoria, in silence now, as the dying sun tainted the sky.

"You really should get home before dark," Edelina urged. "I shall ask Paul to row you back."

As if she hadn't heard, Victoria said, "I'm frightened. I feel as if the world I love is falling apart, and the destruction isn't over yet. Foolish, isn't it? Everyone thinks I'm so adventuresome, fearless even. I'm easily bored and I do love new experiences, but I want everything to be the same when I get home. I'd even prefer my father's indifference to me than to witness his affection for someone else." She poured herself another brimming glass of wine from the bottle between them.

"That's all part of growing up," Edelina said, "moving away from your childhood and all those familiar things that have made you feel secure. That is your family's world. Now you must find your own way, make your own life."

"Yes, of course. I'm being silly, pathetic even."

"Nonsense. You've had a difficult day. Perhaps tomorrow is a good time to start thinking about what *you* want to do, and then make plans for your future. I expect it's hard to imagine your father as a man with his own heartaches, needs, failures, regrets, hopes, and dreams, but he, too, has to find his way to happiness and fulfillment. He doesn't have as much time left as you. Don't be too hard on him for the choices he makes. We all have difficult journeys through this life, but are blessed with those who make them bearable, as well as wonderful."

Victoria couldn't stop the tears that streamed down her face.

That was how Chas found her. Without a word, he took her into his arms and held her while she sobbed and hiccupped. She clung to him, feeling his support and strength as he stroked her hair and back. Eventually he said, "You don't know how relieved I am to find you well, if tipsy."

"Do *you* love me Chas?"

"Of course I do, muggins. Even though you gave us all a scare."

"I'm sorry," she stammered. "I don't want to be unhappy."

Chas rubbed his cheek against the top of her head. "I didn't realize you were."

"Not when I'm with you. But things will never be the same again."

"No, because we'll make them better. So let's go. You can come home with me tonight."

"Truly?"

"Yes."

"Alright."

As he guided her down the path toward his boat, she suddenly felt a wave of intense nausea and ran off the path, where she threw up violently. She realized that Chas was holding her as her body stopped heaving. "I'm so sorry," she said with great embarrassment.

"I've done it before, too," Chas said. "So I think I've now seen you at your worst, and I still love you. Come along."

The trip to Thorncliff was surreal. She sat beside him, skimming over the moon-gilded water, sober enough to know that she wanted forever to be beside him. Jack was exciting in a naughty sort of way, but Chas was her soul-mate.

.　　.　　.

When Victoria regained consciousness, she was aware of three things in quick succession – that her head was threatening to

explode, that her bladder was threatening to explode, and that she
had no idea where she was.

The sky was just beginning to lighten and she could see that
she was in an elegant bedroom with large, screened windows,
uncurtained and open to the early morning air. Confused and
bleary memories filtered back to her. Of course! She was at
Thorncliff.

When she sat up, her head pounded even more, and she was
overcome by nausea. Thankfully, she noticed an open door that led
to a private bathroom, and rushed inside to relieve herself, and
then hung over the wash basin and splashed cold water on her face
until the nausea passed.

Returning to the bedroom, she noticed a jug of water and a
tumbler, with a bottle of Bayer Aspirins sitting next to them. Chas,
of course. He would know that she would have a shattered head.
She drained two glasses of water with two pills, and crawled
gratefully back into the immensely comfortable double bed.

She was dressed only in her camisole and bloomers and had
no memory of arriving at Thorncliff or getting into bed. She had a
hazy recollection of Chas picking her up from The Colony and – oh
God! – throwing up and Chas saying that he still loved her and
being on the boat in the moonlight realizing that she truly loved
him. More than anyone else. Which was reassuring as the rest of
yesterday's events came back to her.

Perhaps she had over-reacted. Having a room like this to
oneself was delightful, and preferable to her narrow bed in the
cramped dorm at Wyndwood. Would it really be so bad for her
cousins to live in a different cottage close by?

And what did she care about her father's life, when she was
going to Europe soon with the people she loved best, and would
probably marry Chas when they returned? Hadn't he promised as
much at the Midsummer dance?

As the pain in her head subsided, Victoria became aware that
her skin was on fire. She looked at her arms to realize that she was
badly sunburnt. Not being able to get back to sleep, she rose and
went into the marble bathroom. The big, claw-footed tub looked
more inviting than the lake this morning, for she could rest her
poor head as she soaked in the tepid water. She couldn't make it
too warm because of the sunburn. Her face was red, her shoulders
livid, even her breasts were burned. An oversized, fluffy bath
towel, a fresh bar of lavender soap and bath oil, a new toothbrush,
and Colgate dental cream had been set out for her.

So Victoria luxuriated in the bath, trying to follow Edelina's sage advice. Planning what to do with her life. She didn't get further than Europe with Chas and Zoë. It was all she cared about at the moment.

She wished she had fresh clothes to wear, but by the time she was dressed, she felt much better. It was still early, so she went quietly downstairs where she encountered a maid, who asked, "May I get you anything, Miss Wyndham?"

"Coffee would be lovely, thank you."

"Where would you like it served?"

"Oh. The pavilion, I think."

"Certainly, Miss. I'll bring it right down."

The morning was fresh but promised another hot day. The dew glistened on the lawns, the birds chirped merrily, and the lake worked its usual magic. So Victoria realized she was remarkably happy. She liked the pavilion with its three walls of windows, the fourth wall sporting a fireplace. From here she could see the sun rising over Wyndwood.

When the door opened a few minutes later, she was surprised to see Chas bearing a silver coffee tray with two cups and a large glass of orange juice.

"You're up early," he said. "I thought you'd sleep until noon."

"Be unconscious, you mean. I don't remember arriving here last night."

"That's because you weren't fully in the land of the living. Here, drink this freshly squeezed juice. It'll make you feel human again."

"Oh, dear. What must your parents think of me?"

"Mumsy was in bed, having taken rather a lot of her potent patent medicine, which is mostly alcohol. Pater and Rafe went to the city yesterday, which no one in their right minds would do in this heat, but Rafe can't stay away from his beloved horses, or the races, and Pater can't stay away from his new mistress."

"Surely not!"

"Rafe followed him one day and discovered his paramour," Chas related casually as he poured coffee for them both. "Now he's using that information to blackmail Pater into paying his gambling debts. We have a generous allowance and most of mine sits in the bank multiplying, but Rafe continually gets into debt. As for Mumsy, I expect she knows about the mistress anyway, but doesn't care. She's probably relieved not to have to perform that wifely duty. Theirs was not a love match you see, but a marriage of convenience. She was spared spinsterhood, and he received a big boost to his career with her fortune."

"You're being very frank," Victoria said, sipping the delicious coffee.

"I just wanted you to know that no family is perfect, and in fact, most are not anything like they appear to the outside world."

"You are thoughtful, Chas. So was it you who put me to bed?"

"Alas, much as I would have liked to, Mumsy's lady's maid and Fliss did, and both are sworn to secrecy."

She laughed. "I do love you, Chas. Will you marry me and give me lots of beautiful and happy children?"

It was his turn to laugh. "We're too young to have demanding little nippers curtailing our fun. Let's enjoy life before we settle down to domestic bliss. But I'm glad we're going to Europe together." He looked at her meaningfully. "Are you up to breakfast now?"

"I expect I can manage some dry toast."

When they rose, she turned to him and said seriously, "Thank you, Chas. I truly don't know what I would do without you. You make me feel as though I'm not alone in this world."

They stared at one another, the playfulness gone. He took her into his arms and gave her a tender, lingering kiss that made her weak-kneed. It was so unlike Jack's forceful, probing kisses.

When he released her, he stroked the still-damp hair away from her brow, and said, "You look painfully sunburnt."

"I am. You should see... other parts of me."

"Oh, I do intend to."

She laughed and the spell was broken. He took her hand as they walked back to the house.

Felicity joined them at breakfast. "Oh, Ria, I'm so glad to see you looking better. When Chas carried you into the house last night, I thought you were dead!"

Victoria regretted that she had no memory of being in Chas's arms. "It seems I've given a lot of people a lot of bother."

Chas said, "There was a search party out for you. *Dragonfly*, of course. Justin and Vivian were out in their boat. Freddie took Eleanor in his, while Blake stayed back in case his medical skills were required. Then there was Oswald with James and Helena. And Henry walked the island in case you were hiding out somewhere there. We went as far as Port Carling, Eleanor thinking that you might have abandoned the canoe and hopped onto one of the steamers there, even though Zoë assured her you had no money with you. But of course, there are countless islands and inlets and bays that you can easily paddle to."

"So why did you go back to The Colony? Edelina said that Zoë and the others had already been." She hoped it wasn't because he'd wanted to see Edelina.

"I just applied a bit of logic. A process of elimination. Because you didn't have any money, you hadn't run off to New York and weren't living it up at The Grand. All your friends were out looking for you, so you weren't hiding out with them. If you'd been playing Robinson Crusoe, you probably weren't planning to stay marooned on an island all night. So where would you seek sanctuary, where you wouldn't immediately be reported or hauled back to Wyndwood to be clapped in irons? Besides, I just had a hunch."

"Oh dear! I expect I'll catch it when I get back. Chas, you wouldn't like to elope with me right this instant?"

"I would, darling girl, but we do have the tennis tournament next Thursday."

"At least promise you'll come and visit me when Father and Grandmother lock me up and throw away the key."

"Of course. Even if I have to climb up the drainpipe."

So it was with great trepidation that Victoria boarded Chas's boat after breakfast. As soon as they arrived at Wyndwood, Zoë, Max, and the others came rushing down to the dock, throwing their arms about her – which was painful on her sunburn, but part of her celestial punishment, she felt sure.

With tears quivering on her lashes, Zoë said, "Oh, Ria, I'm so happy to have you back. I shouldn't have let you go by yourself!"

"Don't you dare blame yourself, Zoë! I think I went a little mad yesterday. I'm so sorry I caused you all such bother and anxiety."

"We're just delighted to have you back unharmed," Olivia said emotionally. "You don't know how much you mean to us, child."

"Please don't do that again, Victoria.," Richard said, "I'm not sure my heart can take it."

Their kindness and concern almost brought her to tears again.

Even Henry gave her a quick hug. But Albert and Phyllis were not so forgiving. When they greeted her on the veranda, Phyllis said, "Of course we're glad that you weren't hurt, Victoria, but it might have been better if you had been, for then there would have been an excuse for the trouble you've caused everyone. Quite unforgivable! And they complain that Phoebe is immature."

"Your father's waiting in the library," Albert said.

James sat in Augusta's chair behind the desk. He made no move to get up to embrace her. "Victoria, I'm thankful to see that you didn't do anything *really* foolish."

Like kill herself? she wondered.

"But you have caused inordinate trouble and distress."

"I'm truly sorry, Father. I didn't mean to. I wasn't thinking..."

He interrupted. "Precisely! You are utterly selfish, inconsiderate, disobedient, and wilful, and I should confine you to the house for the remainder of the summer. But you're fortunate that Helena has asked me to be lenient. Which is more than you deserve."

But still not going to ingratiate herself to Victoria. "Yes, Father."

"So you may not leave the island until dinner at The Grand on Monday, except for church on Sunday morning, and you will write me an essay about what you did wrong and how you will resolve to improve yourself and become a dutiful daughter. Your grandmother is still in her room, recovering from the strain and shock of yesterday. Go and apologize to her."

"Yes Father."

Well, that hadn't been quite as dreadful as she had thought, but Victoria had to steel herself before knocking on Augusta's door.

She was reclining on her chaise lounge in the screened porch, a blanket over her legs.

"Grandmother, I'm so terribly sorry! I know I shouldn't have run away like that! I didn't mean to upset you or anyone else. I was just so miserable I wasn't thinking of anyone but myself, which I know is terribly selfish of me."

Augusta hadn't realized how much she loved Victoria until she feared that she had lost her. She had not truly thought her capable of committing suicide, but she might have had an accident, or even run away with a stranger in her fit of anger.

"I've been trying to think of a fitting punishment for you. Perhaps you shouldn't be allowed to go to Europe after all."

Victoria was horrified. She dropped to her knees beside the chair and looked beseechingly at Augusta, taking her frail hand in both hers. "Oh, no, please, Grandmother. It would surely kill me to be left behind!" Tears started to roll down her cheeks. She laid her head on Augusta's lap, as she had done occasionally as a child, when she had been deeply distressed.

"I couldn't face being with Father and that woman at Wyndholme. He didn't even tell me about her before he broke the news! I know he has no affection for me, but I couldn't bear to watch them together, day after day, him showering her with smiles and compliments, and her, trying to befriend me or treat me like a child. It would kill me! I know that it's not fair on you either, Grandmother, and I wish you could come away, too, but please, please don't take away my escape. Perhaps I'll be mature enough by next summer to deal with it all, but right now, I can't."

Augusta felt her anguish, and knew that Victoria was right. It bothered her, too, that James had so little love for his daughter. She stroked Victoria's hair.

"It just feels like everything I cherish is in danger of disappearing," Victoria sobbed. "When I was little I longed for brothers and sisters, like Zoë and Max, but now I couldn't stand for Father to have a new family, because I know that I won't be wanted. I won't belong. Even Wyndholme will reject me."

Augusta felt her heart breaking. This was no melodramatic performance to gain her sympathy, she knew, but genuine sorrow, perhaps something that had been bottled up far too long. It was more than she could bear at the moment. She said, "I suppose it wouldn't be right to deprive the King and Queen of your presence at Court."

"Oh, thank you, Grandmother! I promise to behave myself, and to make you proud!"

"You run along now and come back after lunch. I want you to read to me. That will be your punishment. We'll start on, let's see – *Bleak House,* I think."

Victoria groaned inwardly, for it was a mammoth novel and would take the rest of the summer to read. But nothing could diminish the happiness she felt at being able to go to Europe with Chas. She washed her tear-stained face in the bathroom, and took a moment to pull herself together. All she longed for right now was that solitary bedroom at Thorncliff, where she could rest undisturbed for a little while and think about Chas.

But of course she was happy to be with her cousins and friends, who rallied round and kept her company, foregoing some of their own activities. It seemed as if they were afraid to leave her alone, so it was Saturday, after her reading session with Augusta, that Victoria actually found herself alone. She took her sketch book and paints down to the back bay, set a chair at an angle, inviting the observer to sit and look out at the lake, and began sketching.

"Hello, Victoria," Helena said, coming up behind her.

"My father's not here. He's gone to Gravenhurst to arrange for a new yacht."

"Yes, I know. I thought I'd take the opportunity to have a chat with you. You don't mind if I sit down?"

"As you please." But Victoria didn't stop painting. She resented Helena, but would try not to be rude or otherwise create more problems for herself. She needed to show that she was mature. But she cringed inwardly at Helena's presence, and wondered what smarmy or patronizing things she would say. If she started out with *Oh you're so talented*, Victoria would be hard put to be civil.

"I expect you're rather annoyed with me at the moment," Helena said. "And understandably so. It's all happened a bit quickly, and I do think it's unfair that you had no warning."

Victoria said nothing and kept painting.

"Shall we go for a walk?" Helena suggested. She had known this was going to be difficult, but also knew that she could handle the girl.

Helena was obviously trying to get her full attention, so Victoria's initial reaction was to say no. But she thought that a walk along the Dragon's Claw might be a good idea. "Yes, alright. There's a path along here to one of the gazebos."

"How lovely." They walked for few minutes in silence, then Helena said, "I would be shocked if my father suddenly announced his marriage to a woman I barely knew. So I'm sorry we haven't had time to get to know one another first."

"I wonder that you and Father have had time to get to know one another," Victoria replied, failing to keep the sarcasm from her voice.

"Sometimes one just knows from the first moment."

When one realizes that a fortune was to be had, Victoria thought, agreeing with Augusta about Helena's motives. Because what on earth could she see in James otherwise?

"Your father has had a rather lonely life. I hope to make him happy."

Again the cold silence, which Helena found unnerving.

"I won't try to be a mother to you." She forced a laugh. "That would be too silly! But I do hope that we can be friends."

"We shall have to see, shan't we?" Victoria said. "Friendship, like love, is not something you can force, but has to happen naturally. Usually over a period of time."

"You're right, of course. I know that you are fair-minded. So I ask only that you not close your heart to me arbitrarily."

"I don't dislike people for no reason."

This ambiguous reply wasn't what Helena had hoped for, but she said, "No, of course. Oh!" They had come to the Dragon's Claw. "Goodness, but that's a narrow path. It looks quite dangerous." Helena had a moment of panic. She disliked heights, although she wasn't petrified like some. She had a horrible thought that Victoria might want to push her off, but then chided herself for that uncharitable idea. Probably the girl was testing her.

"There's a rope to hold onto. And Grandmother does this walk every morning after breakfast, so it's really not as dangerous as it may appear. The gazebo's just a little way beyond, do you see?" Victoria enjoyed Helena's discomfiture. Which was probably immature of her, she knew, but one had to snatch moments of pleasure out of these trials.

"I'll watch how you do it."

Victoria walked along, barely touching the rope. She waited on the other side, hiding a smirk.

Helena grabbed onto the rope tightly as she took the first step along the narrow ledge. *Don't look down*, she kept telling herself, and focussed on her steps. The sheer wall of granite on her left felt threatening, as if it would nudge her off. She tried not to seem too relieved when she reached Victoria's side. She marvelled that Augusta could do this every day, for the old lady was surely rather tottery on her feet.

From here it was an easy amble to the gazebo. They sat down inside. At the vast stretch of sky-mirrored lake before her, Helena had to force down a bubble of glee. This would be hers very soon! This island, this view, and much, much more.

"Not to presume upon any fledgling friendship, but I did wonder if you might be interested in being in the wedding party. As Maid of Honour?"

"I think that Letitia is better suited to that role, as she *is* your friend."

Helena was relieved.

"Why have you waited so long to get married?"

"Because I never found the right man," Helena replied, happy to be back in her element. "I'm no beauty, and lack a fortune, so that hasn't helped," she said with a self-deprecating chuckle. "But there was someone a few years ago for whom I began to develop a fondness. That was in Newport – that's where the really wealthy have their summer homes. Some are literally palaces, like the Vanderbilts' Breakers and Marble House. This gentleman, Carter Jenkins, wasn't in that league, although he was wealthy enough. We once attended a ball at Marble House, which Carter said quite dwarfed his mansion, although I found his lovely enough. I think it would be uncomfortable to actually live in acres of cold marble, no matter how opulent. Anyway, you can't imagine it! It has to be seen. Vast gilded rooms of various types and shades of marble – the dining room, an exquisite pink – a ballroom that looks as if it had been dipped in gold, frescoed and carved ceilings. They say it cost eleven million dollars to build and that was over twenty years ago!" Helena *had* actually been in Marble House when the former Alva Vanderbilt, now Mrs. Belmont, had opened the house to the public to raise money for the women's suffrage movement a few years ago. But Victoria wouldn't know that.

"In any case, Carter and I got on well enough, and he soon asked me to marry him. My mother was ill – we had hoped that the sea air would do her good – so I told him that I couldn't commit myself yet, because I needed to be with her, and that would give us time to discover if we were truly suited. He said that as he was getting close to thirty, he couldn't wait any longer to start a family, and so we parted ways. I wasn't really in love with him, although I thought that might have come over time. I wasn't aware then that love could strike quickly." She left it at that.

Victoria wondered how embellished the tale was, but Helena did seem to know something about Newport. Although it was no secret that the Vanderbilts and others had built castles that made even Wyndholme look like a gatehouse.

Wanting to get back to her painting, Victoria rose.

Helena, not caring to risk the Dragon's Claw again said, "Does that path go across to the other shoreline?"

"Yes."

"Perhaps we could go that way, so that I can get a sense of the island."

And avoid the Dragon's Claw, Victoria thought, feeling pleased to have discomfited Helena a trifle. To keep her from talking about James or any plans she might have for their future, Victoria explained the dragon anatomy of the island to her as they walked across the baking, windless interior. They came upon a deer, carelessly grazing. It looked up at them without concern.

"How delightful!" Helena said.

"Yes, it is lovely to see the deer. They come over in the winter and sometimes get stranded when the ice goes out." Wickedly, she added, "It's the bears we have to worry about."

"Bears?"

"If you see one, you must play dead. Don't try to climb a tree, since they can outrun and out-climb you. They particularly like the blueberries, so you do have to be careful when you go picking."

Helena wondered if Victoria was having her on, but wasn't savvy enough about this kind of life to take a chance. She kept close to Victoria as they sauntered across the island.

They didn't stop at the other gazebo, and Helena was glad to see Olivia, Richard, Max, Zoë, and Freddie at Silver Bay.

"Hello, Helena," Olivia greeted her warmly. Victoria thought how trusting she was, and always nice to everyone, even sometimes those who didn't deserve her kindness. "We're just looking at the plans for our new cottage. Freddie has done a marvellous design! Come and see. I expect that one day we can boast that the famous Frederick Spencer designed our cottage."

Freddie, who was pink with pleasure, said, "Gosh, that *would* be spiffing! And you're absolutely sure you like it? It's a big decision, and I wouldn't want you to feel obligated. I am still just a student."

"But a talented one," Olivia said. "I'm absolutely sure and absolutely thrilled. How soon could we start building?"

"I have to draw up the detailed plans for the builders," Freddie said. "I could have them for you by late August, I expect. Or perhaps sooner."

"You mustn't spend all your holidays working on this, Freddie," Richard said. "We'll need time to find a builder in any case, so as long as we can start in the fall, everything should be finished by next summer."

"I can hardly wait!" Olivia said.

"It must be quite exciting, " Helena said.

"Not unlike planning a wedding," Olivia said.

"Indeed! And which I should really get back to doing."

While the others had been talking, Victoria had looked at the drawings, and thought the conceptual watercolour of the cottage exterior very handsome. She tried to mentally walk through the rooms in the layout, and suddenly felt another surge of sadness. "Then I think we should be on our way."

"And hope that no bears have followed us," Helena added slyly.

"Oh, we don't have bears on the island," Olivia said dismissively. By the look that Helena threw Victoria, Olivia suddenly realized what must have transpired between them. "We are concerned about the wildlife that gets stranded here, but there's no evidence of bears," she added, giving Victoria an admonishing look.

"What a relief!" Helena said with feeling. Victoria really was a nasty little bitch.

"Isn't it just?" Victoria agreed. Helena shouldn't be put out by a bit of teasing. They continued on their way.

Victoria felt a wrench when they came to the bay to see the blackened void where the boathouse had been. Toby and Will were still clearing away the debris.

Helena said, "I'd like you to feel welcome to participate in the planning of the wedding, if you feel so inclined. I don't want you to feel left out, and neither do I want you to feel obliged or expected to do anything. Friends like to give advice on the flowers, or the gown, or the music." Helena felt herself stumbling against the haughty look in Victoria's turquoise eyes.

"I have no suggestions."

When they reached the front dock, Helena said, "I've paddled over in the canoe, as I know that I must become *au fait* with cottage life. And getting around so easily certainly gives me a sense of independence. But getting in and out of the canoe without tipping it is still a challenge for me."

"It's easier to beach it," Victoria said, holding the canoe fast as Helena prepared to lower herself into it from a sitting position on the dock. She shrieked. A spider the size of a splayed hand suddenly appeared on the edge of the dock, but dashed away with lightning speed.

"What was that?" Helena cried. "Some huge creature!"

Victoria contained her mirth. "A dock spider. They're actually called fishing spiders, since they eat small fish." She thought that Helena was about to jump into the lake, but she seemed to pull herself together with supreme effort and said snidely, "Is this another bear story for the gullible?"

"No. They do bite and are venomous, but, fortunately, they're skittish, so we don't often encounter them."

Helena shuddered. With forced humour, she said, "I expect I'll have to get used to the wildlife here, bears, fish-eating spiders, or whatever." Resentful step-daughters, she wanted to add. "Thank you, Victoria, for the tour and for hearing me out."

As Victoria watched her paddling away with some awkward strokes but determination to learn and venture out on her own, she had to admit some grudging admiration for the woman. So Victoria decided to give Helena a chance.

When she reached the back bay, Victoria saw Jack looking at her partly finished painting. He had on his tennis things, so he must have just returned from Thorncliff.

"This is good," he said. "You do seem to have talent, especially an eye for setting a scene."

"Thanks to you. But I know I shall never be an artist, like Edelina. I just find it an amusing pastime. Oh, do you know, I've just decided what to give Father as a wedding gift. I'll do him a painting of the island."

"That's a great idea." Jack hadn't had a chance to be alone with her since she came back. "I'm sorry you took the news so hard." He stroked her arm lightly, and said suggestively, "I should have been there to comfort you."

"I had Chas," she replied, not meeting his eyes, which worried him. Had Chas made love to her after all, even though he had sworn he was obsessed by Edelina? And did he, Jack, really care, now that Victoria was no longer a sure ticket to easy money?

He'd found himself more disturbed by her disappearance than he cared to admit. But he hadn't fallen in love with her. Love had no place in his schemes. Wasn't it more disturbing that his careful plans seemed to be disintegrating?

He was damned if he was going to be banished to a mill in some heathen backwater full of ignorant, rough characters. Of course it wasn't totally pointless to marry Victoria. James would surely settle a decent dowry on her. But would he even allow the marriage? It didn't matter how compliant, determined, and rebellious Victoria might be if they didn't have James's blessing and backing.

So his options were dwindling, and he felt that his only salvation at this point was to convince J.D. Thornton to take him on. He would get that portfolio to him within the week. And it wouldn't hurt to keep Felicity infatuated with him. Even if she was no beauty in a few years, she would still be a considerable heiress. And if he had a job with J.D., he could afford to wait for her to grow up.

.    .    .

It felt odd to Victoria to be the only one in the cottage, aside from the servants, of course, but they were in their hall at the very back, which wasn't even a part of the house. The others had all gone to Oaktree, including the children, who would play in the nursery with the young Oakleys. Oswald had hired a troupe of actors to present Oscar Wilde's *The Importance of Being Earnest* to a hundred of his closest friends in his ballroom. So she felt rather bereft.

She had done the sketch for her father's painting, much larger but similar to the one she had completed that afternoon. But this time she set up a rattan rocker on the front dock. She chose an angle from the shore that took in the end of the dock, the chair pointing out to the far horizon, with the Stepping Stone islands in the background. But it was getting too dark to do any more, especially among the trees on the shore. And the mosquitoes were out.

So she sat at the piano practicing *The Aviation Rag*. She didn't have the syncopation down pat like Max did, but her grandmother would never let her practice ragtime tunes. With her back to the door, Victoria didn't hear anyone enter.

"This is nice. I'd much rather spend time with you than Oscar," Chas said, suddenly standing beside her.

She jumped in surprise, but her face lit with a smile. He was in his tails, and looked exceedingly handsome and debonair. "Have you come to rescue me from my tedious concert?"

He sat down on the bench beside her, nudging her over. "Let me see if I can recall one of the first lines from the play tonight. Act 1 Scene1. Algernon at the piano: 'I don't play accurately – anyone can play accurately – but I play with wonderful expression.' Your wonderfully expressive music drew me in like a butterfly to a flame."

"It's a moth, not a butterfly."

"You can't liken me to a moth, surely?"

She laughed. He gave her a peck on the brow and started playing *Come Josephine in My Flying Machine*. "I pictured you locked up in a tower, and thought you could let down your tresses and I'd climb up to rescue you. But then, of course, we'd both be locked in the tower. Not that we couldn't find a way to amuse ourselves."

"Did you get bored with the play?"

"I saw it last year in London, but I had to take Mumsy and Fliss. Pater and Rafe aren't back until tomorrow. But amongst all the beautiful people there tonight, there was no Cinderella. Her fairy Godmother forgot to send her carriage." He looked at her with a grin. "No one will miss me. I'll just be sure to return before it's over. So tell me what you've been doing."

When she showed him the drawing, Chas said, "That's generous of you, considering how you feel about the marriage. Especially when a shoe horn or a hat rack is easier to procure."

Victoria wondered if she ever stopped laughing when Chas was around. "I'm trying to be mature about this. It's something Edelina told me."

"I like the suggestion of the chair waiting for someone to plunk himself down and admire the view. But shouldn't it be two chairs? One for each of them?"

"No."

"One looks so lonely."

"I'm making a statement. That's what art does. Helena came by today, trying to win me over. What do *you* think of her, Chas?

He shrugged as he started playing *By the Beautiful Sea*. "I don't have much of an opinion about her. She fades into the wallpaper rather, doesn't she? She's some indeterminate age, although not young in demeanour. I'd peg her as a spinster aunt or a governess if I didn't know better."

"Do you think she's honest? Sincere?"

"Is anyone truly? Even if she's not in love with your father, she could still make him a good wife. They could be happy."

"Would you marry for anything but love?"

"Of course not." He changed the tune to *Let Me Call You Sweetheart*.

"But as you claim to be perpetually in love, that isn't saying much, is it? Can you really fall in and out of love so easily?"

"There are different kinds of love. The burning kind that demands instant gratification, the heroic kind that fights dragons, and the abiding kind that requires that second chair on the dock."

She laughed. "And true love is all those rolled into one?"

"I expect so." He started singing the chorus to the tune.

*Let me call you 'Sweetheart', I'm in love with you.*
*Let me hear you whisper that you love me too.*
*Keep the love-light glowing in your eyes so true.*
*Let me call you 'Sweetheart', I'm in love with you.*

Victoria had laid her head on his shoulder while he crooned, but straightened up instantly when Grayson walked into the room. He said, with a note of censure in his voice, "I see we have a guest. Good evening, Mr. Thornton."

"Hello, Grayson. I just popped round to entertain Miss Victoria."

"Indeed. May I offer you some refreshment, sir?"

"Thank you, no."

"What about hot cocoa?" Victoria suggested.

"I say, I haven't had hot cocoa in years. Splendid idea."

"Very good," Grayson said and left.

"Oh dear," Victoria said. "I'm in his bad books now."

"Because you're spooning, unchaperoned, with a known womanizer?"

"You're a gentleman. He trusts you to do the right thing, even if I were to tear off my clothes and fling myself at your feet."

"What a tantalizing vision!"

"But he's probably more annoyed that I didn't send for him as soon as you arrived so that he could offer some Wyndham hospitality."

"I have all the Wyndham hospitality I need right beside me."

*Honey dear, Want you near,*
*Just turn out the light and then come over here;*
*Nestle close up to my side,*
*My heart's a fire, With love's desire.*
*In my arms, rest complete,*
*I never thought that life could ever be so sweet.*
*Till I met you, some time ago,*
*But now you know I love you so.*
*Oh! you beautiful doll, you great, big beautiful doll!*
*Let me put my arms about you, I could never live without*
*you...*

"You're incorrigible!" Victoria said.

"So you've told me. Many times. Would you prefer this?" Chas asked as he changed to *I Wonder Who's Kissing Her Now*.

*You have loved lots of girls in the sweet long ago,*
*And each one has meant Heaven to you.*
*You have vowed your affection to each one in turn,*
*And have sworn to them all you'd be true.*
*You have kissed 'neath the moon*
*While the world seemed in tune*
*Then you've left her to hunt a new game.*
*Does it ever occur to you later, my boy,*
*That she's probably doing the same.*
*I wonder who's kissing her now.*
*Wonder who's teaching her how.*
*Wonder who's looking into her eyes*
*Breathing sighs, telling lies...*

"No, I don't." But it was how Chas probably felt, she thought dejectedly. Love was just a game to him. But she would rectify that. She would make him fall really and truly in love with her.

He seemed to sense her sadness and switched to *By The Light of the Silvery Moon*.

When they'd had their cocoa Chas decided he should get back to Oaktree. Victoria walked down to the dock with him. He took her in his arms and waltzed her along the length and breadth of it as he sang softly, "I *won't* wonder who's kissing you now, Or wonder who's teaching you how, Or wonder who's looking into your eyes, I'll tell no lies. Because... you let me call you sweetheart, I'm in love with you." They stopped dancing, and it was so natural for them to kiss. She didn't care that they were spotlighted by the moon or wonder if Grayson or other servants were watching. At that moment there was nothing but the intoxication of his lips tasting hers. She wanted it never to end. Reluctantly he said, "I really must go, before I forget that I *am* a gentleman. Goodnight, sweetheart."

She helped him untie his boat and pushed him off. She stood beside the lonely rattan rocker, waving and watching the boat skim over to Oaktree, which was ablaze with lights. The moon-gilded wake rippled away and washed against the dock. She felt suddenly forsaken. But hopeful.

The full moon had been only four nights ago. What a lot had changed since then.

# Chapter 15

Augusta began her letter.

Monday, July 13, 1914
Mr. Ethan Nash, Barrister and Solicitor,
Dear Sir,

Kindly incorporate the following into a new will:

As these are mine to give, I leave Wyndholme and its lands, the cottage, all its outbuildings, and the five acres of Wyndwood upon which they sit, and known as The Point, to my granddaughter Victoria Elizabeth Wyndham. The cottage and Wyndholme are to be available to James for his use during his lifetime. Upon his death, neither his wife nor any offspring of that union will have any interest in or entitlements to these properties.

I leave Victoria $100,000 upon the earliest of her reaching the age of 25 or upon her marriage to Justin Carrington or someone approved by her uncles, Richard and Albert, or their eldest male offspring if they are deceased, provided she does not marry her cousin, Jack Wyndham, who is the son of Alexander. I suppose there should be a third opinion in case my sons don't agree, so let us put Joseph Davenport Thornton as the arbitrator, should a problem arise, and let's have the three of them as her trustees. Since Victoria will be a substantial heiress, I want to ensure that she is not the victim of an unscrupulous fortune hunter. Should she find herself in love with an impoverished aristocrat, however, it will be up to the trustees to decide if he is worthy of her affection and fortune. Until she receives her inheritance, ample monies should be available to her through a trust fund for all her expenses, for the running and maintenance of the properties and for her personal use. I leave that to your discretion to recommend how much is advisable and available. Be generous.

To Jack Wyndham, I leave $5000 immediately, and $2000 per year for 10 years, providing he does not marry any of his Wyndham cousins. To Jack's three sisters – you will ascertain their names – I leave $2000 each immediately, and $1000 each per year, once they attain the age of majority, for 10 years, also providing they do not marry any of their Wyndham cousins.

Augusta had not been unaware of Jack's interest in Victoria, and was shrewd enough to realize what his intentions might be. She had to give him credit. He was certainly ambitious and resourceful. But ruthless. She did not want Victoria to be used or hurt. Now if only the girl would take her advice...

*To each of my other grandchildren – whom you know – I leave $25,000 upon reaching the age of majority.*

Their parents would leave them financially sound in any case. But she could not rely upon James to do the same for Victoria, especially if he succeeded in fathering a son with that gold-digger. So it was important for Victoria to be independent.

*The legacies to servants will remain the same as previously, as well as the minor bequests to charities. So I suppose that still leaves a sizable fortune, which must be divided equally among my three sons according to Reginald's wishes. But if you can give Victoria any more of the discretionary funds, please do so. I know that you will provide, as always, an irrefutable document.*

*Kindly come at your earliest convenience, as I am anxious to have matters settled as quickly as possible. I am also anxious to hear the results of your inquiries, as discussed previously. Be advised that James is affianced to Helena Parker, the wedding to take place in late August.*

*As always, we look forward to your visit to Wyndwood.*

·     ·     ·

The day of the tennis match was perfect. A fierce storm the previous evening had cleared the humidity out of the air, but also brought branches down, which kept the groundsmen at Thorncliff busy all morning. By the time the players arrived at one o'clock, the grounds were immaculate, with extra chairs set out in the shade, and a marquis erected on the croquet lawn. Tables and chairs and refreshments were arranged inside, including cold drinks, wine and ale, hors d'oeuvres, ice creams and sorbets, and later there would be tea and pastries. For those who didn't care to wander up to the marquis, maids and footmen offered drinks and canapés from trays.

J.D. greeted Augusta at the dock and escorted her to the pavilion. "I've kept the best seat for you," he said.

"How thoughtful, Joseph. And as always, you seem to be fortunate with the weather." Only once in the past ten years had the tournament needed to be postponed.

"Chas maintains that the middle of July is the reliably best weather we have."

"So far this year, almost every day has seemed like the middle of July," Augusta said. "I'm sorry you've had to go to the city so much, Joseph. It must be unbearable there."

"Fortunately, I only need to go for a few days at a time. It makes me appreciate the cottage all the more."

Victoria, who had been walking behind them, heard the conversation, and thought what a hypocrite J.D. was. If Augusta knew about his mistress, she would no longer consider him such a paragon. Or was that just how things worked in society? As long as the affair was conducted in secret, it was acceptable? Would Chas feel the same way? She hadn't really been able to tell whether he had been appalled or indifferent or accepting when he had talked about his father's mistress.

But her heart leapt when she saw Chas, and she chided herself for thinking that he was somehow different, that every ready smile or warm glance was more meaningful than before. They had always flirted easily, so she shouldn't think that he had fallen in love with her, as she had with him. And yet, those kisses had promised so much. The modified lyrics that he had sung to her on the dock drifted back. *I don't wonder who's kissing you now*...As if he had declared himself hers. Well, right now she needed to keep a cool head.

"Are you all set to show them how it's done?" he asked her.

"Absolutely!"

"You and I are starting things off. Let's see who we're up against."

A board had been set up for people to sign up for matches. They were mixed doubles matches of only one set each, since there were so many players and just one court. The winners of each match were listed on another board and paired off with the subsequent winners.

"Looks like we're not very popular," Chas said, as the space opposite their names was still blank.

"Anyone who wants to get in more than one set is not going to start with you two," Eleanor said, joining them. She and Justin were playing against Beatrice and Senator Spencer in the next match.

Max and Lydia were starting against Zoë and Freddie. Jack and Felicity were up against Blake and Vivian.

Lionel Camford and the tobacco heiress, as the last arrivals, were Chas and Victoria's first opponents. The Camfords had sent a substantial basket of goodies from Eaton's to the Wyndhams as thanks for rescuing Lionel and his party. It seemed the boat would take weeks to repair, but Victoria wondered if Lionel's' relationship with the heiress was already mended.

They were competent players, but Victoria and Chas won the match handily, six games to nothing.

Going off the court, the heiress slapped Lionel's arm and said, "If we'd arrived earlier, *as I'd suggested*, we might have had a chance to play for more than ten minutes! You knew that Chas has won every year!"

"I definitely think that Lionel should look elsewhere for love," Chas whispered to Victoria. They watched the other games as they sipped lemonade in the shade. Eleanor and Justin advanced, as did Zoë and Freddie, and Jack and Felicity.

Wanting to stretch her legs and talk to Justin, Augusta waylaid him. "Justin, would you kindly walk with me?"

"Of course, Mrs. Wyndham," He offered her his arm, which she took, and they ambled eastward along the lakeside path, which was quite level at this point. Although he was curious about the reason for the invitation, he made light conversation. "Lady Kirkland is a formidable opponent. And the Senator, of course." He and Eleanor had fought hard to win the match, six to four.

"Indeed. Beatrice has always been athletic and competitive. I believe she played against some of the best in the world when she was younger." When they were away from the others, she said, "How do you feel about Victoria?"

Justin was surprised by the question. "She's a very engaging young lady."

"Has she touched your heart at all?"

Justin hesitated. He didn't wish to be rude, but thought that Augusta's question was rather impertinent.

She noticed his reluctance to answer and said, "Forgive my bluntness. I sensed in your many visits to us last winter, an affection for my granddaughter. I'm hoping that you might consider marrying her."

He stopped in surprise. "She seems to prefer the company of Chas and Jack these days." He knew that she was young and adventuresome, and needed to flirt and have fun with a variety of people. He himself was only just recognizing how deeply he had fallen in love with her. Eventually she would know her own mind better, and hopefully, would recognize his merits and accept his love. But he wasn't sure he could compete with Chas. He sensed something new between him and Victoria.

"Jack is her cousin and practically destitute. A liaison between them is out of the question. In any case, he could not afford to keep her in the style to which she's accustomed, and I trust that she would not be foolish enough to sacrifice a comfortable, secure future for ephemeral love. And she and Chas are like two wayward and reckless children. Much as I like the boy, a marriage between them would be something of a disaster. They are too much alike. Victoria needs a sensible man who will exercise some control over her impetuous nature. Someone reliable and steady."

Although he wasn't entirely flattered by this assessment of his character, Justin said, "Thank you for your confidence in me, but surely marriage should be prompted by two people's love for each other."

"Nonsense! Friendship and mutual respect are far better than passion for building a good marriage. You young people are constantly falling in and out of love with each other. It would ease my mind if I knew that you would take care of her, Justin. I worry what might happen to her once I am gone. She's really very much alone."

"I must confess that I am extremely fond of Victoria. I haven't given much thought to marriage yet myself. Victoria is young and I have my studies to complete. Of course I'm not sure that she would even have me, but I would like to court her. And I will certainly look after her as much as I am able, even if she'll have nothing to do with me."

"I am going to steer her in the right direction, don't worry about that. I just wanted to be certain that you would be willing to marry her."

He smiled at her. "Indeed, I would." He wondered what machinations she had in mind, and hoped it wasn't something that would actually spoil his chances with Victoria. She could be quite contrary if someone tried to manipulate her. But he was also pleased to have Augusta's blessing.

The final match was exciting – Chas and Victoria against Jack and Felicity. Everyone was amazed at how well Jack played, including Jack himself. Felicity was almost as strong a player as Chas, and Victoria was probably the weakest of the four, although her careful placement of shots outweighed the fact that they didn't have the blistering speed and power of the others'. The set went to five all, but then Chas and Victoria's experience began to show as they didn't allow themselves to get rattled, like Jack did, and managed to win the next two games easily.

"I think we taught Jack too well," Chas said as they left the court. "And you've never played better, Fliss."

She was thrilled. Now Jack would be sure to realize that she wasn't a child anymore. They had almost beaten Chas and

Victoria! Hadn't they played well together, knowing how to cover for one another almost by instinct? She could hardly contain her joy when Jack said, "You really are a fabulous player, Fliss. I'm so fortunate and pleased to have been your partner. Shall we get some ice cream?"

"Oh, yes, please!"

Chas said to Victoria, "Well played, partner. I knew we'd be good together."

She hoped he meant something more as she said with a laugh, "You win no matter who you play with."

"But I'd much rather play with you," he said suggestively. "Before we go for our swim, I want to show you something. Grab some lemonade and come along."

He escorted her into the house and upstairs. She was puzzled as he led her into the bedroom that she had used just a week ago. It was scandalous for them to be alone together like this. But exciting. What was he up to?

"Come and look." He pointed to the bed. A fluffy calico cat lay upon the covers with four tiny kittens nuzzled up against her.

"They're adorable!"

"Cally – that's the mother – decided that she liked your Karma, I suppose, for she moved in here right after you left and had her babies. They're just starting to open their eyes. The maids weren't pleased when Cally took over the room, but you know that Mumsy is dotty about cats, so Cally now gets waited on hand and foot. I thought that since she seems to like you, she would want you to have one of her kittens when they're old enough to be adopted."

"Oh, Chas, I would love to have a kitten, but Grandmother detests animals." Victoria was almost moved to tears by his thoughtfulness, and the fact that she couldn't have one of these soft little bundles to love.

"Then suppose you choose one and name it, and I'll keep it for you, and you can see it whenever you visit. Perhaps your grandmother will change her mind."

"Truly you will?"

"Yes. Of course, the others will have to look after it until we get back from Europe. But it'll be your cat."

Victoria petted Cally, but didn't disturb the sleeping kittens. Two were ginger, one was coal black with white socks, and the other was a calico. "I think I'd like the calico one. But give me time to name her. Or him."

"Calicos are female, Mumsy says. Come back and see them in a few days and they should be more playful."

"Oh, how exciting! Thank you, Chas." She threw her arms about him, almost spilling her lemonade.

He kissed the top of her head and said, "We really should go before you become a fallen woman."

Fortunately no one, except one of the maids, saw them coming downstairs, so Victoria's reputation was intact, although she wouldn't have cared a whit.

All the island friends had been instructed to bring bathing costumes and a change of clothes, and prepare to stay for a picnic supper. The rest of the participants and spectators went home, but would return for the ball tomorrow night.

After they had changed into their swim suits, Chas led the young people to a cove on the east side, with a rocky bluff at its mouth that provided a good diving platform. There was a deep pool of water below, although the cove itself had a beautiful sand beach. The adults chose to stay at the beach by the eastern change house, Olivia not wanting the younger children to be tempted by cliff diving. Phoebe was allowed to go along with strict instructions for Henry not to leave her side or allow her to jump.

"This is torture!" Edgar complained, sitting down on a rock. "Watching everyone have fun while I hobble about with this blasted cast. Do you know how bloody hot it is, wearing this thing? And this is the hottest summer ever."

"Are you talking to anyone in particular?" Eleanor asked him, coming out of the water.

"Anyone and everyone, including God. I have a bone to pick with him."

"Seems he's already picked one with you," she replied in amusement.

"Very droll."

"Shall I cool you off?" Eleanor asked, wringing water from her hair onto his head.

"Picking on a cripple now, are you? I can't even get up and throw you in."

"Poor darling. Why don't you be the judge for a diving competition? No playing favourites, mind. I want to win legitimately," she teased.

"Yes, alright."

Eleanor suggested it to the others who were starting to clamber up the bluff. The ledge was about fifteen feet above the water.

Chas went first. It was a graceful and controlled dive. Everyone cheered. Rafe, Simon, Archie, Justin, Freddie, and Blake all did well. Jack had never dived from such a height, but could hardly back down in view of how the others had done. He tried not to show his trepidation. After all, wasn't he constantly doing things now that he had never done? He landed a clean dive. Max over-rotated and slapped the backs of his legs on the surface of the water. Everyone groaned in sympathy. Eleanor was the only girl who had ever dived before, and did a commendable job, so Edgar proclaimed her the winner.

"Fixed!" Lydia accused, and splashed Edgar.

They did various jumps, Max and Freddie vying to raise the largest splashes. Henry had his hands full trying to keep Phoebe off the cliff, as she declared that she wanted to fly too, and everyone was so mean not to let her.

Victoria decided that she wanted to learn how to dive.

"Not from the top right away," Chas said with a chuckle. "Just around here is a lower ledge. I'll teach you there." It was far enough away from where the others were jumping, and out of sight of the beach.

"But that's only a few feet above the water," Victoria complained.

Chas laughed. "It's far enough to seem challenging when you first learn. It's where we did. And see that ledge above your head? That's the next level. You have to work your way to the top. Here, I'll show you how it's done."

Now that she was actually looking down at the water about three feet below, she realized that it was a bit scary to go in head first. But she screwed up her courage and dove. The first one was a painful belly flop.

"Ouch," Chas said when she surfaced. "Had enough?"

"No!" She scrambled out. "What am I doing wrong? You all made it look so easy."

"We've all had practice. The chaps have been here with me before. Eleanor learned in the university pool, although she was jolly plucky to dive from the cliff." Chas held her waist and said, "Bend more. Concentrate on leading with your hands. And keep them above your head and glued beside your ears. Your legs are springs. Bend your knees before you push off."

She did it! Chas clapped as she surfaced. So did Max, who had just come up from a thunderous cannonball jump which had sprayed them with water. Victoria managed several more, with

Chas making suggestions for improvements. "Now try to keep your legs together, toes pointed."

After a few more, Chas said, "You're doing well. A bit more practice and you can graduate to the next ledge. Let's try it together now," he said, standing beside her.

When they both surfaced he drew her quickly around the bluff, out of sight of the others. He pulled her into his arms and kissed her. Their wet swim suits provided little resistance between them. Victoria moaned as she wrapped her legs about him and felt his answering hardness pressing against her, while his tongue explored her mouth. Once again she had that explosion of sensation deep inside, and had to stifle a cry of pleasure as she clung to him. But as they had both stopped treading water, they sank, and came up laughing.

But a moment later Victoria cried out.

"What happened?" Chas asked with concern.

"I've hit my foot on something."

Chas put his face into the water to peer into its clear depths. His expression was bleak when he looked up at her. "It's a deadhead. Floating. And heading for the pool."

They looked at each other in stunned silence, both realizing how deadly it could have been had that log been only a few feet farther along on its journey. Chas had been the first to dive. And now Victoria had been nearest to it.

"We must have good Karma," she said.

"What are you two doing here?" Eleanor asked, coming around the promontory. "No canoodling. You two really need a chaperone."

"We've found a floating deadhead, Ellie," Chas said.

Her expression turned to one of horror. "Oh my God! Somebody could have broken their neck!"

"You girls go and get help, and we'll pull this monster out," Chas said.

They managed to push and pull the heavy, soggy log out on the far side of the bluff. Then they each took a section to search underwater for more obstacles, although no one seemed much inclined to continue diving off the cliff anyway.

"Today's life lesson is to always check the water before diving in," Blake said.

"Figuratively and literally," Zoë replied, earning an approving look from Blake.

Both Justin and Jack wondered with some unease how Victoria and Chas had found the log that was around the bend from where they had been diving.

So it was a more sober group that returned to the pavilion for drinks before the picnic. Rafe put records on the Victrola, and some of them danced while the footmen served wine. Victoria didn't want to dance with anyone but Chas, not even Jack. He seemed to hold her possessively, and she backed away from him slightly. Of course he noticed, and cursed Chas for stealing her from him. He didn't like losing.

When *Come Josephine in My Flying Machine* came on, Chas said, "This is our song, Ria. Let's show them how it's done."

Laughing, they ran out to the tennis court and re-enacted the dance they had created just a couple of weeks ago where Chas helped her to fly.

"That looks like great fun," Max said, "Come along, Lydia. Let's shake a leg."

Freddie asked Zoë, while Blake and Vivian tried it. Seeing her downcast look, Jack said to Felicity, "Would you like to give it a go?"

"Oh yes!"

They had such fun that Rafe had to play the tune over and over while everyone got involved and changed partners with each round. He finally pleaded for mercy and put on *By The Beautiful Sea*.

"Also our song," Chas whispered to Victoria, reclaiming her.

The picnic was a cook-out, supervised by the chef, at Sunset Point on the west side of the island.

Victoria managed to stay close to Chas as the sun set brilliantly over the distant mainland and turned the calm lake into liquid fire.

.     .     .

Victoria felt she truly was Cinderella when they arrived at the ball the following evening. When Chas had come to see her the other night she had not exactly been in rags, but also not formally dressed as he had been. Now she wore a peacock blue silk taffeta gown with a beaded and metallic embroidered fine black Chantilly lace tunic. A glittering headband sprouted a small black plume.

She could hardly wait to see Chas. Over and over she had relived those few passionate moments in the lake. She knew that she would give herself to him completely at the slightest encouragement on his part.

But she was devastated to see him arrive just behind the Wyndham party with Edelina in his boat. She liked Edelina, so it was hard to be angry with her. But easy to be jealous, for she was so beautiful.

"Good evening, Victoria," Edelina said. "You look enchanting. And so much better," she added with a smile.

Edelina's simple black satin gown was stunning because of how it was draped, and the way it undulated when she moved. Undoubtedly another of her own designs. She wore no jewellery save for a plain gold necklace. Her flaxen curls were piled on her head with a black band across her forehead. Of course she wouldn't wear any feathers.

"How beautiful you look, Edelina," Victoria said brightly. She knew that she mustn't succumb to despondency. Chas loved her in part for her light-hearted gaiety. She had to maintain the playfulness in their relationship. She had to act as if those melting kisses meant nothing.

Edelina took her arm as they sauntered up to the house, leaving Chas to escort Augusta. "I feel completely out of my element," she confided. "But I agreed to come for a while so as not to insult my hosts. Two society balls in one summer are about as much as I can handle of this kind of life. And how are you?"

"I'm trying to take your advice and be mature about things. I'm doing a painting for Father and Helena."

"What a splendid idea! You must let me see it."

"Perhaps you could give me some advice."

"Certainly."

The ball began with the presentation of the tennis trophies to the two winners, who then had to lead off the first dance. Victoria felt odd to be in Chas's arms and yet the focus of all eyes. But as they whirled about in perfect unison, they gazed at each other as if there was no one else in the room. So they didn't see the bent heads whispering to one another. Once they had done a circuit of the room, J.D. with Beatrice – for Marjorie was never well enough to dance – and then others joined in.

"Have I ever told you that you have the most stunning eyes?" Chas asked Victoria. "Like azure pools. A chap could drown in them."

She laughed, her jealousy forgotten. Chas was being his usual self that she had known and loved forever.

Jack succeeded in getting the next dance with her. He made sure to practice his most courtly manners, which put her at ease, he realized. He would show no anger or jealousy, for that would surely alienate her. He had thought long and hard about his relationship with her, especially after reading the note that Molly had left for him the other night, which had read, "Saw Queenie and Chas kissing. Mmm, nice. So have you lost your touch? I wouldn't mind the delicious Chas for myself."

If he really wanted Victoria, he would have to win her back with charm and wit. But not at the expense of jeopardizing his friendship with Chas. That was his best chance of getting ahead at the moment. So he wouldn't pursue Victoria, but he would keep her enthralled enough that she might yet capitulate if he needed her.

And it was easy enough to keep Felicity sweet on him.

Victoria was pleased that Jack seemed more relaxed and friendly, and that their relationship was no longer so fraught with sexual tension. She had felt rather guilty that she had so easily transferred the desires that Jack had awakened in her to Chas.

She danced with all her friends as well as other guests, like the sweaty-palmed Lionel Camford, who kept telling her what a crackerjack tennis player and swell dancer she was. But not enough with Chas. As a host, he had to dance with all the girls, of course, but she was disturbed to see him leave the ballroom with Edelina.

Outside on the veranda, Edelina said, "I think I should go home now, Chas. And I think it's time you examined your heart. I saw what happened between you and Victoria the other night. You both realized that you loved each other."

"I've always loved her, as a friend…"

"But it became more that night. I saw your tenderness and compassion. I feel that our souls go through various incarnations together. We recognize one another on some level. We're easy friends. But there's only one other soul who makes you feel complete. And we don't always get to spend a lifetime with them. Only if we're really lucky. But I think that you and Victoria might be soul-mates. Don't let that opportunity slip away from you."

"I'm sorry, Edelina. I feel a bit of a cad."

"Don't. What we've had, however brief, has been fun. But that's all. I knew it wouldn't last long. I enjoy pleasure, and I don't believe in convention. But I also don't believe in destroying other people's happiness."

"Have you ever been in love?"

"For ten years, and always will be. But I can't marry my soul-mate. He's Indian, of a superior caste that wouldn't accept me in any case. His was an arranged marriage, when he was a child. So I have to be content with a platonic relationship, although we rarely see one another." She put her hand on his arm. "I envy you and Victoria. You have a chance that is given to so few. Don't ruin it by fear of commitment."

"You're very understanding."

"I'm a decade older than you. I've come to know some things in that time. Gentleman that you are, I don't want you to feel any obligations towards me, other than friendship. I wouldn't want to lose that."

He gave her a brief kiss.

"Please ask your boatman to take me home. And you return to the ball."

Victoria, meanwhile, was dancing with Rafe, who had also seen them leave. He said, "Chas is certainly stuck on her. Goes to visit her at least once a day. I don't see the fascination myself. She's rather a pleb, but I suspect she knows how to satisfy men."

"Edelina is my friend!" Victoria said. "You shouldn't talk about her like that."

"You should be careful who your friends are. The Colony isn't all that well liked around here."

"I suppose it's only appreciated by thoughtful people who want to expand their horizons."

"La-di-da! But you might as well stop batting your eyelashes at Chas. He's obviously engaged elsewhere."

"I don't know what you're talking about."

"Come off it. You should have heard the murmurs when you and Chas danced. 'Don't they look splendid together? Don't they look like they're in love?' Got tired of Jack already, have you? Or did you just realize that he's a pleb, too?"

"Don't be so despicable!" She knew he'd already had plenty to drink, but that was no excuse.

He laughed. "I just like to call a spade a spade."

As soon as she could, Victoria slipped out of the ballroom, unable to keep up a cheerful demeanour while her heart seemed to be breaking. She needed a few quiet minutes to steel herself, and managed to sneak upstairs without being seen, but would have used the pretence of needing to find a lavatory.

Cally's kittens were awake and stumbling about on the soft bed, a ginger kitten getting a thorough washing from its mother. Victoria knelt on the floor beside the bed and picked up her kitten.

"You're so sweet," she cooed to the mewling, squirming little bundle. "What shall I call you?"

*Let me call you sweetheart...*

Victoria thought only of how thoughtful and kind and funny and irresistible Chas was, and couldn't stop tears from escaping.

She barely heard the door open and close. She dashed the tears from her cheeks as he came up to her and said, "What's the belle of the ball doing on her knees playing with kittens when she should be downstairs keeping all the young swains in thrall?"

"I had to come and visit Josephine," she said, not looking at him. The kitten's name had come unbidden.

"Well, Josephine, it's time for you to see Mummy." He took the kitten from her and put it beside Cally, who immediately stopped washing the ginger one and started on Josephine. He gave Victoria his hand to help her to her feet. When he turned her to face him he said, "It seems that the azure pools are overflowing."

She managed a strangled laugh.

"What's wrong, my darling?"

"I'm just being silly. You really mustn't mind me. I'm..."

He stopped her with a kiss, which made her weep again. She pushed him away. "Please don't, Chas. I expect I'm not very sophisticated, but I can't bear for you to kiss me like that and not mean it. Not when it makes me feel like I'll die if you never do it again."

"But I do mean it, and I will do it again," he said, brushing a tear from her cheek.

"It's not fair to love two of us."

"There's only you."

"What about Edelina? Rafe says you can't stay away from her."

"She's just a friend, and wiser than we are. You know the boy who cried wolf?" She nodded. "If I tell you this time that I truly love you, will you believe me?"

He brushed away another tear as she looked searchingly into his eyes. "Oh Chas! I didn't know that love could hurt so much. I don't ever want to be without you!"

They kissed deeply, passionately. Chas finally said in frustration, "I can barely touch you for fear of disarranging your hair or your gown. In any case, we really should return to the ballroom before we're missed. We'll continue this later."

She smiled. "I can hardly wait."

# Chapter 16

Victoria marvelled at how quickly love had possessed her. It was as if one day Chas was a dear and cherished friend like the others, and the next, she loved him with such abandon, euphoria, and longing that she couldn't bear to be separated from him for an instant. She sought any excuse to see him.

They all slept late after the ball, and the friends had made no plans for the rest of the day. After their lunchtime breakfast, she told Zoë and Max about her kitten, swearing them to secrecy.

"Would you like to come to Thorncliff with me to see Josephine? It'll also give us practice for the canoe race in the Regatta. That's just two weeks away."

They agreed, and as Max and Jack were to enter the men's canoe race, he was asked along.

"I want to talk to J.D. anyway," Jack said. He had spent hours pouring over the newspapers, checking the stocks and deciding upon which of them to risk his entire future.

Victoria was also apprehensive, wondering if Chas truly meant that he loved her with that all-consuming passion that she felt for him, which left room for no one and nothing else. So she was relieved to see that same tender look in his eyes when he saw her.

"What a delightful surprise," he said as they interrupted his reading of the newspaper on the veranda. "I say, Jack, Porte still hasn't done his transatlantic crossing. Seems they've had some problems with the Curtiss, so they're doing more testing. If this keeps going on, we might yet have a shot at that prize."

"You're not still considering that?" Victoria said with some disquiet. How could he even think of going anywhere without her?

"I've decided I'm definitely taking up flying," Chas said, his eyes mocking her as he added, "I have to take Josephine up in my flying machine."

She laughed. "Not without me."

"Of course not."

"I told them about the kitten, so may we go and see her?"

"By all means."

"And may I see your father?" Jack asked.

"I'll take you to his study. Ria, you take Zoë and Max and I'll meet you upstairs."

Jack's heart was in his throat as they walked down the hall. Chas knocked on a door. They heard a muffled, "Come in."

"Pater, Jack has a proposal to make to you. As he has a head for business and I haven't, I shall leave you to it," Chas said, and did.

"Yes, Jack?" J.D. motioned him to sit down.

"Mr. Thornton, my ambition is to be a stock broker. I've been doing some paper trading for the past year and would have doubled my investment."

J.D.'s eyebrows shot up.

"Chas suggested I invest $1000 for him to prove myself. So I've come up with a list of instruments that I think would do well. If you'd care to have a look?" He handed over his document. He had also included his reasons for his choices.

"So you don't fancy going into the family business?" J.D. asked as he skimmed the paper.

"I don't think that lumbering is my forte. But I haven't dismissed it."

"Impressive," J.D. said, looking up at him. "Let me examine this more closely, and I shall let you know. We're always looking for bright and ambitious young men with vision. Coming from a good family doesn't hurt. Does Augusta know about this?"

"No, I haven't mentioned it to anyone, other than Chas."

"He certainly thinks highly of your character and abilities, and not just on the tennis court. You've settled well into your new life, Jack."

"I've been fortunate that my family and all their friends have been so generous and welcoming. And I work hard to achieve my goals."

"Yes, I expect it doesn't hurt to be a bit hungry. I wasn't content to be a clerk either. Leave this with me."

"Thank you, Mr. Thornton."

Jack felt as if he could breathe again as he returned to the veranda, and he was ecstatic. It had gone well, surely. J.D. had been impressed!

"Hello, Jack," Felicity said, joining him on the veranda. "You look cheerful."

"And why not? It's another beautiful day in paradise, the future looks bright, and I have delightful company."

She giggled. "The others are upstairs looking at the kittens. You wouldn't like one, would you?" she asked hopefully. If he had one of Cally's kittens, it would give her a bond with him.

The idea of feeding an animal when they'd barely been able to feed themselves was not something that Jack had ever considered. "I can't really care for one just now. I have no idea yet where I'll be living."

"Won't you be at Wyndholme?"

"I don't think so. I may have to be in Gravenhurst, and then perhaps even in British Columbia."

"So far? It takes days and days on the train to get there!" When would he ever come back? When would she see him? "Chas says that you want to work for Daddy. Then you'd have to live in the city, and there's ever so much room at Wyndholme, and it's not that far from Thornridge. That's our house. It's on the Don Valley, too."

"I would like nothing better than to work for your father. He's a financial genius! I'm a great admirer of his, and hope to be just like him."

She was pleased that he liked her father. She really, truly, sincerely hoped her father would take him on. Of course it was no use her saying anything. She was just a girl.

The others meantime had been laughing over the kittens' antics. "They are dear little things. Do you think Mama would allow us to have one?" Zoë asked Max.

"We could ask."

Chas came in quietly and pulled Victoria into the hallway where he gave her a long, slow kiss.

"Are you two spooning out there?" Max said. "I have to warn you, Chas, that it is my duty to defend my cousin's honour. It'll be swords at dawn."

Victoria laughed as they stepped back into the room. "I appreciate your concern, dear cousin, but I'll remind you that Chas is a fencing champion, and I'll not have your blood on my conscience."

"Then you'd best behave yourself," Max said with a grin.

"She's behaving splendidly," Chas said.

Zoë threw Victoria a glance that said, "We'll talk later."

When they returned to the veranda, Victoria said, "We're practicing for the Regatta."

Chas immediately replied, "Let's do the ladies and gentleman's canoe race, Ria."

"Yes, let's!" Another excuse to see each other.

Although they hadn't actually talked about who was canoeing with whom, Jack had thought that she would probably ask him. Well, things had certainly changed. But then he had already decided that he'd give up Victoria easily if it meant that he retained Chas's friendship and influence. He needed to remember his priorities.

"Jack, perhaps you could take one canoe back, and Ria and I will race Zoë and Max back to Wyndwood. Come down to the boathouse, Ria, and help me choose a canoe. We'll meet the rest of you at the main dock."

"Sounds like a lame excuse to me," Max said. Zoë nudged him.

"For what?" Felicity asked.

"Nothing important," Zoë said.

When they started to leave, Felicity detained Zoë, whispering, "Are they finally spooning?"

"I think they like each other, but…"

"I'd be ever so happy if Chas married Ria!"

They were indeed spooning. As soon as they entered the boathouse, Chas took her into his arms, his kiss hungrier, his hands caressing her. They were both breathless when he let her go. "How will I keep my hands off you all through Europe?" he asked.

"Please don't."

He kissed her again, gently this time. "We'd better launch this canoe before Max comes after me."

The others were already waiting for them. "Must have been a difficult decision," Max quipped.

"Not all canoes are created equal," Chas replied. "This Peterborough is a superior craft, as we shall now demonstrate."

"Just a minute," Victoria said. "I have to take off my shoes." She had found some 'barefoot sandals' in the Eaton's catalogue, which were canvas Mary Janes, and so not exactly her idea of sandals, but at least she could get away without wearing stockings, as long as Augusta didn't see her going visiting like that.

"You are a temptress, Ria," Chas whispered to her.

They had a lively race to the back bay at Wyndwood, with Victoria and Chas beating the others. He, of course, had been on the Oxford rowing team.

Later that day, when Victoria and Zoë were alone, she said, "So you've both finally realized that you're in love?"

"Oh, Zoë, I'm desperately in love! And I know that Chas is always teasing about it, but I think he truly feels the same way now." She twirled about happily, hugging herself. "It's the most intoxicating, delirious, exquisite feeling in the whole world!"

"I am happy for you, Ria," Zoë said, and envied her terribly. She knew that she would be as elated as Victoria if Blake loved her.

"I wish that Blake would come to his senses, Zoë. I want you to feel like this. I didn't know it was possible to be so happy! I want to spend the rest of my life feeling like this!"

"Oh, dear, I can see Europe is going to be a challenge for poor Cousin Beatrice, trying to keep you two apart," Zoë said with a grin.

Victoria and Chas managed to see each other every day, even if they didn't often have a chance for more than a brief kiss or meaningful touch, or to hold hands when no one was watching. The night that they all went to Ouhu to look through the telescope at the stars, for it was a new moon and a brilliantly clear night, Chas whispered to her, "I'm longing to hold you in my arms and smother you with kisses."

"I sometimes canoe up to the Shimmering Sands for an early morning swim. About seven." She had stopped doing it now that they often went skinny dipping at night. She told him where it was.

He was already waiting for her the next morning. She beached her canoe next to his, and he gave her a hand out, pulling her into his arms and fulfilling his promise of the night before. "God, I've missed you!" he said.

It had been just two weeks since their first kiss, and a week since Chas had declared his love for her.

"And I've missed you," she said, laying her head against his shoulder. He ran his hands provocatively through her loose curls and down her back.

"We shouldn't be doing this," he said. "It's much too dangerous."

"Are you afraid that Max will come after you?" she asked with a laugh.

"That too, perhaps. I was thinking how irresistible you are."

"Don't resist then," she said trailing kisses along his cheek.

His mouth sought hers hungrily. He finally groaned and held her close, saying, "I do love you, my darling, but if we don't stop now, I'll be hard pressed to remember that I'm a gentleman."

She was quivering with desire. "I want you to make love to me, Chas."

"Not like this. We'll do it properly. When the time is right."

She couldn't understand his reluctance. He hadn't even touched her like Jack had. She wanted to rip off her clothes and have him truly smother her with kisses. Did that make her terribly wicked?

"Come along, my barefoot temptress. I've brought something for you." He took a picnic basket out of his canoe and they walked hand in hand over to the rock where Victoria liked to bask in the morning sunshine. He spread out a cloth and brought out a Thermos vacuum bottle and a plate of croissants with a pot of jam. "A good French breakfast for you to get used to. Café au lait and croissants."

"How delightful! Our own romantic breakfast picnic." It *was* wonderful and thoughtful. She was so happy to be sharing her special place with Chas. They sat down on the sun-kissed, sparkling pink and black granite that slid gently into the water.

"I used to come here to skinny dip."

"I wish I'd known. I swim over from Thorncliff most mornings *au naturel*, but to the north shore. Just around the bend really."

"What would we have done if we'd met?" she said with a laugh.

"Said 'Good morning' politely and decided we'd discovered the Garden of Eden?"

"As I recall, that ended badly."

"Yes, I suppose you're right. Except that Adam and Eve did have a good time while it lasted."

"I want this to last forever." A dragonfly landed on her hand, and two on her head, while others played in the air around them.

Chas laughed. "You're like a fairy princess, whose adoring subjects are flitting about in attendance."

They talked easily about themselves, about the places and things they would see on their Grand Tour. It was already well after eight o'clock when Victoria decided she must really get back before she was missed. Meeting Chas alone like this was highly inappropriate. If anyone discovered them, they would both be in serious trouble.

Their kisses were more restrained when they parted, as if they couldn't bear to inflame each other and then just return to the mundane world.

They had already arranged that a group of them would go to The Colony that afternoon. Victoria wanted to show Edelina her painting.

She was slightly uneasy, wondering whether she would see any signs of smouldering desire between Chas and Edelina, but was quickly reassured. Edelina was delighted to see them all, but had no special glances for Chas, nor did he seem to be pining for her. She did wonder if Chas had made love to Edelina, but decided that she really didn't want to know.

"I do like your painting," Edelina said. Beautiful composition, and well executed for a beginner. I'm glad to see you have your own style. You haven't been indoctrinated by formal art training to adhere to certain conventions."

"Oh dear, that sounds like a polite way of saying I've done it all wrong," Victoria said.

"Not at all! Art shouldn't look like everything's been turned out by the same factory. This is truly lovely, and I think your father and Helena will like it and appreciate the effort you have put into it. You must keep painting, Ria."

Zoë posed them for a photograph, asking them to sit on various levels of the cliff steps, glasses of wine in hand.

Anton, the Bolshevik, came by. "You imperialists are ready for war?" he asked with a sneer.

"Anton, this isn't the time," Edelina said.

"Not the time! Hell is in Europe and you say 'not the time'! You think this not affect you? The assassination is only Archduke. Who give shit?" he mocked.

"What's he on about?" Max said.

"The Austrian Archduke, Franz Ferdinand, was assassinated back in June," Blake explained. "That was when we were coming back from Toronto after voting, wasn't it?"

"Will be trouble!" Anton said, flailing his arms about expressively. "Big trouble. Russia go to war. Austria go to war. Germany go to war. Europe go to war. You, you British go to war."

Chas said, "My dear chap, the Balkans are always a source of trouble. There may be a skirmish perhaps, but it won't make a ripple in most of the world."

Anton threw up his arm in disgust as he said, "You blind and stupid!" before marching off.

"I am sorry about that," Edelina said, for once embarrassed by her guest.

"Does he really think there'll be a war that would affect so many? Us even?" Zoë asked in alarm.

"Yes, he does. He's worried that Russia is going to war. Worried about his family and friends back home. Wondering how he can get back there."

"I'll pay for his passage," Chas said dryly.

"But surely he's blowing things out of proportion," Victoria said. "I haven't seen anything in the newspapers about the possibility of a war."

The *Toronto Star* headline the next day, July 25th, read, "The Austrian Demand That May Bring On The War".

The headline that really floored Jack was "Local Financiers Exceedingly Nervous" due to stocks in Toronto and New York plummeting because of the rumours of war. What did that mean for his chances of getting a job with J.D.? He discovered that J.D. hurried off to the city right away.

"It won't affect us," Chas reassured Victoria when they met at the Shimmering Sands again on Sunday morning, although it threatened rain. They sat side by side with a blanket draped around their shoulders to keep off the morning chill.

"Not even our Grand Tour?"

"We may have to modify it. Perhaps we won't get to lovely Vienna this time."

"And even if there is a war over there and we can't go, it won't affect us here, will it?"

"We're an ocean away from it all," he said reassuringly, stroking her cheek and stopping further questions with ardent kisses.

With the Prime Minister happily holidaying at The Grand, none of them thought that there was anything to concern Canadians. Sir Robert Borden was going to be presenting the prizes at the annual SRA Regatta, which would be held at The Grand on Saturday, August 1st.

It poured rain all Sunday, but Monday was sunny and hot as usual, and their activities resumed. Victoria dared to sneak away again in the early morning to be with Chas. He came by after breakfast in his canoe, so that they, along with Max and Zoë for respectability, could ostensibly practice for the Regatta.

The Wyndhams were invited to tea at the Carringtons, it being well known that Monday was Augusta's visiting day. Rena's parents, Kier and Megan Shaughnessy, were visiting from Launston Mills for the week, as they had made it a tradition to attend the Regatta.

Victoria had always found them personable. In their seventies, they seemed more energetic than Augusta, and were a handsome couple. Victoria hoped that when she and Chas were that old, she would still see that affectionate look that passed between them.

Megan Shaughnessy had known the Wyndhams for years, but she looked at Victoria more closely this time. When she had said to her grandchildren yesterday, after they had told her about their summer, "You seem to have such active social lives! Any romances in the air?"

Lydia had said offhandedly, "Justin is sweet on Victoria."

"Where did you get that idea?" he'd asked her.

"Just by watching you watching her. But she and Chas seem to have a pash for each other at the moment."

"What about you and Max?" Justin had responded.

Lydia had blushed. "We have fun together. That's all!"

So two of her grandchildren were entangled with the legendary Wyndhams. Megan still felt awkward among these titans of Canadian industry and finance. Keir wasn't bothered, but then he had attended the best boy's school in Canada and had learned well from his wealthy Launston family. But if Augusta Wyndham knew that he was a bastard, she undoubtedly would not be taking tea with them.

It had been different when their youngest daughter, Rena, had married Edward, for then they had been wealthier than the Carringtons. But Edward was shrewd and had done extremely well for himself. So much so that the Carringtons moved in the most illustrious circles. The Thorntons, The Wyndhams, Senator Spencer, American tycoons like Oswald Oakley and Horace Camford, to name just a few. Hadn't they and their family come a long way from their humble beginnings when Kier had been an outcast in his community, and she, a starving orphan on the brutal streets of Toronto?

She thought that Victoria was certainly a beautiful young woman with expressive eyes and a cheerful demeanour. She didn't seem haughty, like her grandmother, or vain, for she had a summer tan that no proper young lady would have allowed to happen. She was bright and spirited, but perhaps a bit capricious. Megan wondered if she might not be just too much for Justin to handle. She hoped he hadn't fallen in love with the girl. A disastrous liaison had almost destroyed Keir and their chances of happiness once.

Zoë seemed much more the kind of sensible and amenable girl who would be good for her grandsons. And Max, well, he was rather young yet, but held promise for infatuated Lydia. It was melancholy Vivian she was most concerned about.

"I understand that you girls are going to be presented at Court next spring," Meagan said to Victoria and Zoë. "How exciting for you!"

"That's assuming there's no war," James said.

"Do you think there will be?" Rena asked with concern.

"There are some who do," James said. "Although I don't see it myself. Not on the scale the fear-mongers are talking about."

"And what exactly is that?" Olivia wanted to know.

"That Germany and England could get involved. Not on the same side."

"Family relations are not so good these days," Richard said, meaning between the King, George V, and his German cousin, Kaiser Wilhelm II. "They say that Bertie," he referred to the old King, "managed to keep Kaiser Willy's imperialist ambitions in check. But apparently, the same cannot be said for cousin George."

"And if England goes to war... we go to war?" Olivia asked.

"God save us!" Phyllis cried.

Seeing her mother's distress, Phoebe shrieked, "What does that mean? What does war mean?" She clutched herself as if trying to keep from flying apart. "What's going to happen?"

As if in unspoken agreement among the adults that this was a topic best not discussed in front of the children, Albert said casually, "Nothing to concern us, my dear. The soldiers may have to go and fight somewhere far away, but that's their job. It won't affect us. The Prime Minister isn't worried – he's going to be at the Regatta Ball on Saturday – so why should we be?"

"And what events are you entering in the Regatta?" Olivia asked the Carringtons, the talk of war pushed aside, although many of them were uneasy.

After their usual Monday dinner at The Grand, the Wyndhams spoke briefly with Sir Robert Borden, who of course knew them, and was also a good friend of Sir William Mackenzie's. They didn't raise the subject of war, that not being a social or easy topic to engage in for a casual encounter.

Chas surprised them when he showed up with the young Carlyles and Spencers, the Carringtons staying home to entertain their grandparents. They had come for the nightly dance. The adults were persuaded to let the young Wyndhams stay – they had come in two boats in any case, with Edgar driving *Dragonfly* and Toby, the one loaned by the Thorntons. Phoebe, of course, was not allowed to stay. Beatrice happily volunteered as chaperone, since Augusta insisted upon one.

"What a lovely surprise!" Victoria said to Chas as they danced a waltz.

"Any excuse I can think of to hold you in my arms."

"I don't want to be anywhere else. I wish I could lay my head on your shoulder, that you would unpin my hair and run your fingers through it, press your body close to mine, your lips to mine."

"Stop! You're torturing me with seductive visions," he laughed.

"They don't have to be visions. We could go for a walk along the promenade, and who knows where that leads?"

"Can we sneak away from under the watchful eye of our chaperone?"

"We'd best practice, because we'll have to get adept at it in Europe. Don't you think it odd that as soon as it gets dark, we're expected to have a chaperone – meaning someone old – whereas during the day, we're allowed to go out together as a group? It's as if we're not capable of keeping each other morally sound beyond the daylight hours."

"Very odd. It must be all those songs that talk about spooning by the light of the moon. The moon has a lot to answer for."

"Poor moon. I like to spoon at sunrise as well. Or anytime."

"How about now? It's been at least twelve hours. I can't wait any longer to kiss you."

They walked down to the promenade, a lakeside boardwalk that stretched along the entire long waterfront from the docks and boathouses at the west side, around the headland to the beach on the east side. It was lit with electric lamps and there were dozens of strollers taking the evening air after yet another fine meal. But Victoria and Chas continued along the unlit woodland path past the beach.

"A quick kiss before the mosquitoes carry us away," Chas said. "They're never this bad on the island."

They ended up laughing more than kissing, as the hungry mosquitoes buzzed about them, Chas trying to shoo them off. "My hands are spending more time playing with the mosquitoes than with you," he said. "I suppose we should get back."

But even holding hands and walking together was heavenly. And so was dancing. Of course they had to dance with their friends, but no one was in any doubt now that they only wanted to be with each other.

Eleanor said to Zoë, "Isn't it a bloody bore when your friends fall in love? Especially with the person you love. And now I'll be lucky to get a dance. I suppose it was all my fault for pointing out to Ria that they were made for each other. I never did know when to keep my mouth shut!"

•   •   •

The headlines on Tuesday, July 28th read, "Austria Formally Declares War" and "Toronto Stock Exchange Closes in Panic".

The men talked about how this would affect business, but didn't think it would take long for Austria to teach Serbia a lesson for assassinating their Archduke. Russia was just sabre rattling and surely wouldn't go to war for Serbia.

On Wednesday they read that the Russian troops had been mobilized, but predictions were that the war would have few effects here, except that wheat prices would undoubtedly go up.

It wasn't until the headline of July 30th informed them that Germany had given Russia a twenty-four hour ultimatum, and they heard that Sir Robert Borden had cut short his Muskoka holiday to return to Ottawa, that they began to get concerned.

That was the day that Ethan Nash arrived at Wyndwood in time for tea, having sent a telegram to that effect the previous day.

He was sequestered with Augusta until it was time to dress for dinner. She called for Grayson and Mrs. Hadley to witness her signature on her new will, well pleased that Ethan Nash had managed to fulfil her wishes, and indeed, had found another $45,000 for Victoria. When that was out of the way, she said, "Well, what news have you with regard to your investigations?"

He pulled a file from his briefcase. "Agnes Helena Parker, born, Boston 1885..."

"Ha, so she's older than she's letting on. Do go on."

"To Thaddeus and Hazel Parker, nee Thorpe – but not related to the moneyed Thorpes. One brother, Edwin, died when he was twelve of meningitis."

Augusta grunted, "*Titanic*, indeed!"

"Agnes Helena Parker married Carter Jenkins in Boston in 1904. Divorced 1905."

Augusta was stunned. This was even worse than she had imagined! A divorced woman. It was utterly scandalous! She would not have such a creature marrying into her family.

Ethan Nash continued. "Thaddeus Parker, a telegraph clerk, did well with investments early in his career, but has lost most of his fortune on bad speculations, as well as expenses for the care of his wife. Hazel Parker was hospitalized in a private clinic near Boston in 1903. For the insane. She's still there."

Augusta tried not to show how appalled she was. "You have done well, Mr Nash. I am indebted to you for your thoroughness. It can't have been easy following a trail of lies."

"Indeed, Mrs. Wyndham. Fortunately, people who dissemble often tell half-truths. Would you like me to inform James of this?"

"Thank you, no. I will inform Helena and allow her the opportunity to do the honourable thing. If I tell James he will just think that I am trying to destroy his happiness. The old fool! And he's likely to marry her out of spite. He is a man obsessed, Mr. Nash, and cannot be reasoned with in his present state. He would not be pleased with you for looking into this matter any more than with me."

"And you feel that this information warrants a stop to the marriage?"

"Indeed, I do! It is bad enough that James is affianced to a divorced woman, and also one who may bring madness into the Wyndham line. But she is also a liar, Mr. Nash. And I no longer have any doubt that she is a gold-digger."

.  .  .

That Thursday evening the Wyndham crowd attended a musicale evening at the Fremonts', who had a famous opera diva visiting, and she had agreed to give a private concert to their friends.

J.D. had come back from the city earlier that day. When he saw Jack after the performance, he took him aside and said, "I did have a chance to look at your portfolio, Jack. I think you could do well in the business, and would be prepared to take you on. But this is not an opportune time. We're not even sure now when the Toronto Stock Exchange will reopen. But I will keep you in mind. Let's hope it doesn't come to war, eh?"

The July 31st headlines read, "A Black Friday – Kaiser Proclaims State of War – All Exchanges Close, First Time in 50 Years" and "Hope of Peace is Abandoned in Great Britain".

And there was talk of mobilizing the Canadian militia.

.  .  .

Jack didn't have his heart in the Regatta competitions the following day. All his careful planning was coming to naught.

He had no hope now of seducing Victoria. She was so obviously besotted with Chas, and he with her, that Jack expected an engagement to be announced at any moment, despite Chas's contentions that he would marry late, if ever. Love really made fools of people.

It bothered him more than it should have, but he was sure it was only because Chas had won that particular prize and not he. Not because he was in love with Victoria. Of course she was incredibly alluring, and he would have enjoyed fucking her – and probably should have when he'd had the chance, damn it! – but now that she was of no more use to him, he should just forget her. Move on to a different strategy.

Yet what hope had he now but to get his hands on his inheritance? He had been concerned when Ethan Nash had come to Wyndwood, for if Augusta had changed her will, had she left him more money, or less? Molly had had no luck finding out as yet.

Despite the bleak news of the possibility that Britain would go to war, the Regatta, as usual, had drawn thousands of spectators and hundreds of participants. People from the resorts and cottages on the three large interconnecting lakes, as well as people from the city, came to enjoy the day. There was even a special boat leaving The Grand at midnight to connect to a special overnight train to Toronto, for those who couldn't get accommodations or needed to return to the city.

A flotilla of yachts, motorboats, rowboats, sailboats, canoes, and hotel launches, many decked out with colourful bunting and fairy lights, lined The Grand's docks and shoreline three and four deep, and rode at anchor offshore. All around the grounds of The Grand and neighbouring islands within view of the activities, people were spread out on blankets or lounging in deckchairs, with picnic hampers and parasols at the ready. Of course it was another perfect summer day.

The Wyndhams were aboard the Oakley's *Gloryoak*, along with the rest of the island neighbours and a feast of food and drink. Various canoes were tethered to the yacht while the young people awaited their races. No one had looked at the papers yet that day, nor did anyone bring up the grim subject of a possible war. But there was a forced gaiety among them. This was not the usual boisterous, carefree day that had been the highlight of previous summers.

But Beatrice exclaimed, "This rivals the Henley Royal Regatta. That's not far from where I live, so I usually attend. But there are so many different events here."

Like the canoe jousting, where one man tried to keep the canoe steady and the other stood up with a padded pole and attempted to upset the opponents in the other canoe. It made for great hilarity and lots of wet participants. Max and Jack lost, but had brought a change of clothes. The sailboat races were underway, the many white sails on the horizon looking like a flock of gulls bobbing on the waves. There were rowing races – Chas won the men's single sculls, and the doubles with Rafe – and a variety of canoe competitions, which were the most popular, with heats having to be run. All the friends got through their first heats. Simon and Justin won the men's doubles, with Max and Jack a close second. Victoria and Chas won the mixed, Eleanor and Daphne won the ladies', just beating out Victoria and Zoë, and Chas won the men's singles. Freddie won one of the sailboat races.

Edgar was surprised that Chas didn't enter the motorboat race.

"Is your boat not as fast as you bragged?" Edgar asked. "I was looking forward to beating you."

"Oh, but she *is* fast," Chas responded. "I just didn't think it fair to compete against a cripple."

"If I had my crutches in hand, you'd be regretting that statement."

"Why didn't you compete?" Victoria asked Chas, when Edgar went off happily to the starting line in *Dragonfly*.

"I wanted Edgar to have a chance to win something, since he can't compete in anything else this year."

"You're so confident that your boat's faster?" she asked with a grin.

"She's newer with a bigger engine, so yes."

"That's kind."

Chas whispered in her ear, "I also wanted to spend more time with you. Suddenly winning all these trophies isn't so important. But I am glad that you and I won our race. I'll give you a congratulatory kiss later. We'll sneak away at the ball."

"I'll hold you to that."

Edgar was ecstatic at winning the race.

Now that they no longer had the Prime Minster to present the prizes, Oswald, as SRA president, had to do it. Balls were being held that evening at The Grand and other resorts, for even The Grand couldn't cater to the thousands who were present. SRA members could choose to attend the ball at Oaktree, which the Wyndhams and their friends did. Next year, the Regatta and SRA Ball would be held at the new Golf and Country Club.

Victoria and Chas did escape from the ballroom that evening, but as so many other couples were strolling about the grounds, there was no privacy to be found. Fairy lights were strung along the paths around the entire island. They were near the waterfall when Chas drew her into the shadow of a tree and kissed her.

He lit cigarettes for them both as they stood gazing out across the lake. The moon was tumescent.

"You seem preoccupied tonight," Victoria said, wrapping her arm around his and leaning against him. "Are you thinking about the possibility of war?"

"And spoil this perfect evening? Not at all," he reassured her, kissing her forehead. "But I am thinking how lucky we are and have been. And you know it's not like me to have deep or profound thoughts."

"You've created a convenient myth about yourself," she said shrewdly. "And I don't believe half of it. I know that you are intelligent, and caring, and sensitive, and thoughtful, and..."

"Stop!" he laughed. "Or I shall get an inflated opinion about myself."

"So what is your conclusion? About your perusals?"

"That we haven't done enough dancing and spooning tonight. So I figure if we stand in front of that fat pine there, then we can't be seen from most angles, and to hell with the other lovers who might see us but are too wrapped up in each other to care anyway."

Victoria stifled her giggles as they moved into the protection of the pine. Chas took her reverently into his arms and lavished tender kisses on her. "I do love you, Ria," he said.

They swayed together as he sang softly in her ear,
*Dreaming of you, that's all I do,*
*Night and day for you I'm pining.*
*And in your eyes, blue as the skies*
*I can see the love-light softly shining;*
*Because you love me there it seems,*
*Pray meet me in the land of dreams.*
*Meet me to-night in Dreamland, under the silv'ry moon.*
*Meet me tonight in Dreamland, where love's sweet roses bloom;*
*Come with the love-light gleaming, in your dear eyes of blue,*
*Meet me in Dreamland Sweet, dreamy Dreamland,*
*There let my dreams come true.*

•   •   •

"Helena, I'd like to have a private word," Augusta said. It was nearing midnight, and they would soon be leaving as it would be the Sabbath. James was dancing with Beatrice.

"Of course, Mrs. Wyndham."

Helena led her into the empty morning room. Augusta turned to her and said, "I don't approve of adultery, Mrs. Jenkins."

Helena faltered. She tried not to show her shock and dismay. She needed to stay calm and in control. "I'm divorced, Mrs. Wyndham."

"I don't believe in divorce, Mrs. Jenkins. As far as I am concerned, you are about to commit bigamy."

"According to the law, I am unencumbered and free to marry. Divorce is not uncommon. Alva Vanderbilt divorced William almost twenty years ago. It is done all the time in society now."

"You are not a Vanderbilt! You are morally an adulteress. And you are a liar, Mrs. Jenkins. A very clever web of lies you've spun to gain sympathy and try to claw your way into society, to which you never did belong. Certainly not the Boston Thorpes. And what about Edwin, hardly old enough to be on the *Titanic*, especially as he died a decade earlier. And then there's your mother. Are you not ashamed to have already confined her to a coffin?"

"My mother is, in essence, dead to us and to this world." Helena tried to control her rage. How had the old witch found out so much? "It grieves me, but there is nothing we can do for her. It is simpler to say she is dead. And I cannot be held responsible for misinformation that may have been spread about me. I never claimed to be from the *Boston* Thorpes."

"But you never denied it!"

"Do you think anyone tells the complete truth about themselves? Do you think that James hasn't had a mistress, that he's been living like a monk all these years? Do you suppose that I care any less for him because of that? He has fallen in love with *me*, not my past nor my family. And I've already told James about Edwin. He knows what our motivations were in concocting the *Titanic* story, and he understands. Things are not always as straightforward as they seem."

Augusta was surprised, but said, "James will not tolerate a litany of lies, Mrs. Jenkins. He would not marry a woman he could not trust. Nor will he be pleased to know that your children could be tainted with madness. I shall give you a week in order to do the honourable thing and leave before I expose you to James and the Oakleys. I believe that is more than fair."

A week gave her time for a plan. Perhaps she could manipulate James and Letitia's sympathies with a few modified truths, and play James off against his mother. She was damned if she was going to let the Wyndham fortune slip through her fingers because of a vindictive, arrogant old woman!

She thought back to her brief marriage to Carter Jenkins when she had still been Agnes. She had met him in Newport, just as she had told Victoria. But Carter's wealthy façade had crumbled as soon as they were married. He had spent the last of his money in search of an heiress. Helena's substantial dowry, which had never existed, was sadly lost on a bad investment. They had tried to con each other and had eventually laughed about it, agreed on a divorce, and wished each other luck. And Helena had sworn she would be more careful next time. But few opportunities had come along as their money had dwindled. It had been a stroke of luck that they had met up with the Oakleys, who had taken them under their extravagant wing. That patronage she could not afford to lose. She wondered if there was something with which she could blackmail the old bitch.

Already her mind raced to tell James and Letitia how devastating it was to have a mother who didn't recognize you or speak to you, who sat vacantly in a chair as if she were already dead. It was the truth, which could be embellished to bring tears to their eyes. She would take James to visit her as proof. They couldn't be angry with her for not wanting to think about her mother in that state. As for the divorce, she could play that lightly, saying she didn't think it of any consequence, as everyone was doing it these days. Well, at least in society. Sorry that she had forgotten to mention it. She didn't like to recall her disastrous marriage – Carter had beaten her in drunken rages, or something that would be sure to arouse James's protective instincts. She would be the wronged woman that Augusta further wanted to destroy. So now she needed to think carefully about how she would stage this tearful confession.

# Chapter 17

It seemed to Victoria as if the world had suddenly gone mad. Tourists were scrambling to return from the war zone. While summer revellers had enjoyed the Regatta, the Canadian government had sent a cable to Great Britain formally offering Canada's support in case of war. Canadian regiments and nurses were already volunteering.

On Sunday, Germany declared war on Russia, and on Monday, on France, and began invading their territories.

The men spent the best part of Monday, the Civic Holiday, at The Grand, ostensibly golfing, but waiting to hear updates as phone calls were put in hourly to the Toronto newspapers.

That day, Belgium appealed to Britain to protect her, so Britain sent an ultimatum to Germany. On Tuesday, Germany declared war on Belgium. And according to the Toronto papers, people were excited, almost eager about the war that now seemed inevitable for Canada as well.

"They're like squabbling children," Victoria complained to Chas on Wednesday morning at the Shimmering Sands. They were sitting on a blanket that Chas had spread out on the beach. Victoria was wriggling her toes into the sand in the shallow warm water as she sipped her café au lait. Chas, who had his shoes off as well, and trousers rolled up, entwined his feet with hers and played with her toes. "The countries, I mean. Did no politicians sit down to discuss diplomatic ways to resolve issues? And what are their beefs, anyway? The assassination of an Archduke?"

Chas said, "More like, 'my army is bigger than yours, so let me just take over your little country'. So the little countries get their bigger friends to stop the bullies."

"Well, they've ruined our trip! Father says I'm naïve and silly to think that we can still go to Europe when so many countries are at war, with more joining in all the time. I'm so disappointed!"

"We'll go next year, after the war is over," Chas promised.

"Will it be?"

"Some are wondering if the Canadian troops will even have a chance to get over to Britain, but they think it will be over by Christmas for sure." He paused as if searching for words. "Did you read in the paper yesterday that Count Jacques De Lesseps has left for France to join the aviation corps? He flew across the

English Channel in 1910 in a Bleriot, did you know? He was only the second aviator to do that."

"But isn't it only the first one who'll be remembered?" Victoria asked with a chuckle. "You only know that because you're acquainted with him through his marriage." The Count was the son-in-law of Sir William Mackenzie, a friend of both their families. "I did read that, and also that the Countess... how was it that they put it? ... 'undaunted by the terrors of the war and capture on the high seas' has gone along with him."

Chas took one of her hands in his, stroking her fingers, as he said, "I've decided what I'm going to do until we can go on our Grand Tour."

Victoria's heart skipped a beat. She knew what he was going to say. She could see it in the regretful yet tender look in his eyes, feel it in his soothing touch. *I do love you, Ria*, he had said only a few nights ago. But not enough to want to stay with her, was the implication.

"You know I've been saying that I'm going to take up flying. Well this is the perfect opportunity. I have a friend from Oxford whose uncle is a brass-hat in the Royal Flying Corp. I've already wired him. He's certain I won't have any difficulty being accepted."

"No! Chas, you can't go! It's too dangerous. How will an aeroplane help against guns?"

He combed his fingers through her hair and said lightly, "I'll be high above the guns. Aeroplanes are going to be useful for surveillance. I won't actually be fighting, like a soldier."

"Won't there be enemy aeroplanes? What will you do if you meet one of those?"

"Tip my hat and fly off." He lifted her chin and kissed her. "You know the government has called for volunteers. We all need to do our bit to show the Kaiser he can't just trample over the rights and freedom of other nations. This is just the sort of thing that I need to do. I'll miss you dreadfully, Ria. But when I get back, I *will* take you and Josephine up in my flying machine."

She tried not to cry. She had done too much of that already, and she should be supporting him in what he wanted to do. He would hate it if she became so obsessive that he wasn't allowed to do anything without her.

He lowered her onto the blanket, his body pressed against hers. They kissed as if they would never have the opportunity again. When he rolled on top of her, she could feel his need and strained against him. His hand caressed her breast, and then he suddenly stopped and moved away from her.

"Don't stop," she pleaded.

"We're getting into dangerous territory," he said, sitting up.

"I thought you liked danger." Victoria rolled onto her side, propping her head up on her hand. She tickled her fingers along his arm.

"I'm actually very circumspect. It comes with my great age."

"You're only four years older!"

"And you're not even four years older than Fliss." He grabbed her hand and kissed her fingers. "And here you are, trying to seduce me."

"And not doing a very good job."

"Mmm. I wouldn't say that." He lay down beside her, propping his head up and gazing into her eyes. "I love you more than you can know," he said simply. "Can you live with that until I come back?"

"Yes... But can't I come with you? I could stay with Cousin Beatrice and you could visit us when you're not flying. I expect it will take you months to learn." And the war could be over by then, she thought, feeling cheerful again. And Chas would have learned how to fly, which he so much wanted to do. Perhaps it wasn't so bad after all. "And we could make wild and passionate love in the garden or the guest room."

He laughed. "Tempting as that sounds, I'd feel better if you were safely here."

"I'm at least as fearless and undaunted as the Countess."

"I have no doubt. So you must be brave while I'm gone."

"Oh, Chas, you must promise me you'll be careful. If anything happened..."

He cut her statement short by rolling her onto her back and kissing her again. "If ever a man had an incentive to come back, it's me," he reassured her.

.     .     .

Augusta had never been late for lunch without informing them. The rest of the family were already at the table. James rang for the servants.

"Ah, Grayson. Could you ascertain why Mrs. Wyndham is delayed? It's so unlike Mother," he said to the others when Grayson had left.

"I haven't seen her since she went off for her walk," Albert said.

"She seemed terribly upset about the war," Beatrice added. Today's headline in the *Toronto Star* had blared 'WAR'. Britain and Canada were now involved.

"I was in the library until Helena arrived to discuss wedding plans, and Mother hadn't come back by then," James said.

Grayson returned looking concerned. "Mrs. Wyndham doesn't appear to be in the house, and Bayley hasn't seen her since she left for her walk."

"Dear God, something must have happened to her!" Albert said. "She may have twisted her ankle and be sitting somewhere, waiting for help."

They all got up from the table, and James said, "Let's do this in an organized fashion. Richard and I will take the east path. Albert, you and Henry take the west route. The rest of you stay and have lunch. It won't take us long to find her, and then you ladies can take her in hand. Max, you alert Toby that we may have to send for the doctor."

No one was too worried, thinking that Albert's explanation may well be right. With twisted roots of trees and jutting rocks, the path was not easy going. For someone of Augusta's increasing frailty, it may just have become too much for her. But wasn't that just like Grandmother, Victoria thought, not to admit defeat!

The four men met in the middle of the island, having seen no sign of Augusta.

"You don't think she would have taken the long path around the rest of the island?" Richard said, puzzled and worried. "She hasn't done that in years. It's much too far for her."

"Henry, you take the path on the west side," James said. "Richard, you take the east side. Albert, why don't you try the Dragon's Back? I'll go and round up some more help, and send Toby and Will out in the boat to go around the island and meet you at the north end, if you don't find her en route. This is most disturbing!"

It was when James was going back along the Dragon's Claw that he happened, instinctively, to glance down the cliff side. And saw something that made his blood run cold.

He hurried back to the point, feeling that his heart was about the explode with the exertion and the shock. He sent Toby to get the doctor and Will to start up the other boat. Then he fetched Max and Jack, saying nothing yet to the others. Perhaps he had been wrong. Perhaps it had been just a bundle of discarded clothes lying there, half submerged on the rocks.

"Uncle James, what's wrong?" Max asked. "You're quite pale."

"Brace yourselves, lads. I fear that we are about to make a gruesome discovery." He directed Will to drive along the west shore first, where they encountered Albert. "Go back to the house," James shouted to him. "I think we've found her."

Albert waved and walked on. They met Henry at the north-west corner of the island and managed to find a spot where they could pull up so that he could get aboard. They collected Richard at The Shimmering Sands. "What's going on?" he asked.

"I think she's fallen. Off the cliff."

They were stunned, disbelieving. It meant that she was dead.

The wake that washed alongside the boat when they stopped at the base of the cliff made the dark material of her dress sway in the water as if the body were moving.

"Oh my God!" Max cried.

She was lying face down on the jagged boulders that were only a few inches below the surface.

Will edged the boat up as close as he could. Jack climbed out into the knee deep water with Richard right behind him. They clambered carefully over the slippery rocks to the shallower water. They rolled her over, knowing she was beyond help. Richard gasped when he saw her. "Oh, Mother," he said on a sob.

Her face was smashed, her chest, caved in.

As if it made a difference, they tired to lift her gently into the boat. Max angrily wiped away tears. Chalk-faced and shaken, Will produced a blanket which they placed over her, covering her face.

The others, having been alerted by Albert, were waiting on the front dock. "Dear, God, what's happened?" Olivia asked when she saw them.

Richard jumped out of the boat and took her into his arms, hugging her tightly. "I'm afraid Mother's dead. She fell off the cliff at the Dragon's Claw."

"No! Oh no!" Victoria cried. "Grandmother! No! She can't be dead!" She tired to get into the boat. Already on the dock, Jack held her back. She turned on him, trying to squirm out of his grasp, pummelling her fists against his chest, shouting, "Let me go! I have to see her! Grandmother!"

He grabbed her wrists and held her firmly. "Victoria! There's nothing you can do for her," he said gently. He was moved by the anguish of her wail as she stopped struggling. He had been dismayed by the old lady's violent death. But he was also elated, for here was an opportunity for him. Hadn't Molly overhead Augusta telling Zoë that she had left enough money for her grandchildren to be independent? Unless she had changed her will when Ethan Nash had been here.

Victoria collapsed against Jack, sobbing. Olivia had the two youngest children in each arm, pressed tearfully against her skirt. Zoë was comforting Esme. So Beatrice went over and took Victoria out of Jack's arms into hers, saying, "There now, dear. Augusta would want you to be strong." She herself was pale and shocked.

Phoebe was giggling hysterically. Edgar whispered to her to stop.

"Don't you see?" she said gaily. "God told me that he wanted her. Now they're both happy. I'm so happy!"

"That's enough of that nonsense!" Albert said, unusually sternly.

"It's not nonsense!" Phoebe said indignantly. "He *told* me!"

"Hush now," Phyllis said, putting her arm about Phoebe, and trying to draw her away. But Phoebe refused to budge. She seemed fascinated by the blanket-draped body. "I know this is shocking," Phyllis said. "Yes, God is looking after Grandmother now, but we're sad that she's left us."

"I'm not."

"Hush, Beebee! It's unseemly to talk like that when someone has just died."

"I don't understand. If God asked her to come to Heaven, and Grandmother is with Grandfather *and* God, she should be happy, too. Why shouldn't we be happy for her?"

"Because we'll miss her."

"I won't. She wasn't very nice. And she smelled mouldy."

"Shut up, Phoebe!" Victoria cried. "You're mad! Bloody, flipping crazy!"

"How *dare* you!" Phyllis roared. "You inconsiderate, foul-mouthed, wayward..."

"That's enough from everyone!" James ordered. "Show some respect!"

Quivering with anger – at God for his cruelty, at Grandmother for her stubbornness, at Phyllis for her lifelong animosity, at Phoebe for her stupid words – Victoria pulled away from Beatrice and ran, as if she could escape the emotions that threatened to choke her. She ran until she reached the Dragon's Claw.

She leaned against the cliff, gasping for breath, her face wet with tears. How could grandmother have fallen? She had done this walk thousands of times.

Victoria noticed that there was loose gravel on the path. Toby always kept it cleanly swept here, and it hadn't rained, so it couldn't have washed down from the top of the cliff overnight. There must have been an animal at the top which had dislodged the stones. Even so, had Grandmother been so distracted and upset by the war news that she had been careless? Had her cane slipped off a stone and unbalanced her? Had she had a dizzy spell? Had she been startled by something, like a squirrel?

Had someone pushed her? Phoebe had said that God had told her he wanted Grandmother. Surely Phoebe hadn't taken that as an order from these bizarre voices she heard? No, Phoebe would never come along here. It would be more likely that she would be the one to fall. Or decided she could fly.

Victoria sat down on the path, her back against the cliff face, her feet dangling over the edge. Much as she and Augusta had sparred and had their differences, her grandmother had always been there for her. Although not demonstrative, Augusta had still been her main source of affection, except when Olivia and her family were about. Victoria thought how lonely Wyndholme would be without Grandmother. And who would be on her side against James and Helena? Now she wasn't even able to escape to Europe for a year.

"Come away from there Ria," Zoë said quietly. "You're making me nervous."

"I can't believe that she's gone, Zoë. I expect when I go into the cottage that I'll be chided for getting my skirt dirty."

"Whether she's there or not, you'll always know what Grandmother would be saying. She'll still be with you, with us. Come back to the house with me, Ria."

"I'm not sure I can face Phyllis without wanting to spit at her."

"Everyone is distraught, and saying things they don't really mean."

"I think you're completely wrong there. I think when people are upset they say exactly what they mean. But I suppose there has never been any love lost between us anyway. Phoebe worries me."

"Yes. But there's not much we can do except be understanding of her problem, and not judge her too harshly."

Victoria couldn't voice her thought about Phoebe giving God a hand, even to Zoë. "You go, Zoë, and don't worry about me. I'll be along soon. I just need to say goodbye to Grandmother in my own way."

Zoë left reluctantly.

Victoria sat for a long time thinking about Augusta, recalling how her grandmother had seemed proud of her, even as she had chastised Victoria for being audacious or headstrong or rebellious. Hadn't Grandmother laughed at her recalcitrant behaviour that day that Jack had first visited Wyndwood, and she had almost fallen off the roof?

She felt infinitely sad to think that Augusta would now never know how much she and Chas were in love. Surely she would have been pleased, since she liked the Thorntons so much.

A large green dragonfly landed on her knee, gently fanning its wings. For an absurd moment Victoria wondered if it was Augusta's soul. But even if souls were reincarnated, Augusta's wouldn't have had a chance yet. But she took a small measure of comfort from its presence. To share a moment with another creature, no matter how fleeting, made her feel connected to the world.

Victoria noticed a canoe skimming along below. It was Chas. She shouted at him and waved. He looked up, startled. "Good God, what are you doing there? Not thinking of practicing your diving, I hope."

"Oh, Chas! Something terrible has happened!" Shooing away her friend, she got carefully to her feet, feeling for the first time a terrible sense of vertigo as she looked down. She edged away and ran along the widening path to the back bay, arriving as Chas pulled the canoe onto the beach. She threw herself into his arms. "Grandmother is dead! It's horrible, Chas! She fell from the cliff!"

"Good God! You mean where you were just sitting?"

"Yes."

"I'm so sorry, my darling." He kissed her cheek, heedless of anyone watching. "Your grandmother was a feisty old lady. I liked her."

Yes, she was. And Victoria would take a lesson from her book. She would pull herself together, be dignified and strong. She would make Augusta proud of her.

.　　.　　.

But the next few days were an ordeal. James and Albert went to the city with the body that same day. In this heat, a quick burial was important. The rest of the them went to Toronto the next day. All their friends came down for the funeral, having already expressed their condolences at the cottage. The servants from the three households worked furiously to prepare a funeral feast. Hundreds of people attended the service, and many stopped at Wyndholme afterwards to partake of the Wyndham hospitality that Grayson proudly supervised. Victoria cared only that Chas was always at her side.

Once, when they walked hand in hand and Chas gave her a reassuring kiss on the cheek, James was about to intervene, but Beatrice held him back, saying, "Leave them be, James. She needs him." No one else but Helena had seen them.

She said to James later, "I think that those two are in love. Isn't that wonderful, James? Such an excellent match, and one less thing for you to worry about. And when they get married, you and I will have more privacy," she said with a promise in her voice.

Helena was absolutely enchanted by Wyndholme. It was even more fabulous than she had expected. And soon it would be hers. She could hardly contain her joy. And she had not had to confess anything to James. Wasn't everything just perfect?

She, her father, Oswald, and Letitia – the children being left at the cottage with their nanny – were staying at Wyndholme. Already it felt like home. Letitia thought it delightful, and the two of them discussed how Helena would redecorate, for it was hopelessly Victorian. After a suitable period of mourning, of course.

So Augusta's will came as a shock to many. James, Albert, and Richard still divided among them the bulk of the four million dollar estate that remained after Augusta's bequests, although most of that was tied up in the business and investments.

James couldn't forgive Augusta for leaving the house and the cottage to Victoria. Of course this was her revenge for his marrying Helena against her wishes. But he had the money to build another house and cottage for his new bride, as he refused to live in his daughter's, despite Victoria's insistence that the entire family was welcome to carry on as usual at Wyndwood. So all his mother had succeeded in doing was to leave him hating her just a little, and being even more at odds with Victoria.

Helena fumed, but tried not to show it. She doubted that James would build something as grand as this veritable castle. Still, she wouldn't have to live with Victoria. And James was extremely wealthy. No problems this time.

Ethan Nash thought it politic not to tell James the results of his investigations, as instigated by Augusta. It was not his place to offer unsolicited information, especially to one of his best clients, who would not thank him for it. He would file that information away, should it ever be required.

Jack was both happy and disappointed. He wished Augusta had left him the money in one sum, like the others. Twenty-five thousand dollars was a fortune! But she must have seen through his scheme to marry Victoria, clever old bat! So it had been partly his fault that she had stretched out the payment of his inheritance for ten years. She would figure that he wouldn't wait that long to marry Victoria. And yet, she was a substantial heiress after all – the two properties were worth at least another $130,000 – and she could marry him in seven years, when she was twenty-five, if she chose. There wouldn't be that much of his inheritance left to lose, and look what he would gain. But now there was Chas.

Jack decided he would invest most of the initial five thousand in land and stocks. And two thousand dollars per year meant he could live very comfortably, without going into the lumbering business. Already James had said that it was time for Jack to start his apprenticeship at the mill. Now that Augusta was not around, James and Albert, at least, seemed only too glad to be rid of him.

But he was annoyed that his sisters had not received as much as the others. Augusta really was a vindictive old bitch!

Chas said to Victoria, "I suppose I shall now be accused of being after your fortune."

"Surely not! You undoubtedly have more."

"With the way the stocks just dropped, I'm probably only half as rich this week as last," Chas said, unconcerned.

"That's what Ethan Nash said about Grandmother's estate as well. But he said it would bounce back soon, and probably go much higher once the war economy kicked in." So Nash had not bothered to recalculate the estate's worth after the panicked dumping of stocks last week. "Does that mean we'll make lots of money out of the war?"

"I expect so."

"Doesn't that seem morally wrong? To profit from death and misery?"

"Our money will help to finance the factories that build armaments and aeroplanes, and turn out uniforms and tinned beef. That's to ensure a quick victory so that we don't have too much death and misery. The war will likely put an end to the depression, give unemployed people jobs, and probably employ women who wouldn't normally work, to fill in for the men who go off to fight. So everyone will be making more money."

"Should I get a job while you're gone?" Victoria said with a grin.

"If you're filling in for me, all you have to do is play tennis, and take up fencing and cricket."

"Perhaps I should become a nurse. Then I could come over to the war as well."

"You'd be a terrible nurse. You'd just end up breaking lots of hearts instead of mending them."

She laughed. They were strolling in the garden. She sat on the stone wall that separated it from the ravine. "Oh, Chas, I wish you weren't going away! Father has already said he's buying a house for Helena. What shall I do here all alone?"

"You'll have Josephine," he said, perching beside her.

"Of course! That will help."

"And you can write long and passionate letters to me every day. I'll think of you as the princess in her tower."

"The sleeping princess, who won't be alive again until her prince comes to kiss her."

He kissed her now.

Beatrice said, "I'll look the other way sometimes, but not if you get so amorous that you make us old people wish for younger days."

They jumped apart. "We didn't see you," Victoria said.

"Obviously. I'm very happy that you two are in love, and also that it's not up to me to keep you apart all through Europe. A pity that," she added with a grin.

"Cousin Bea..." Chas said.

"I'm already your cousin, am I?"

"Lady Kirkland sounds too formal. Especially as I have a favour to ask."

Beatrice sat down beside Victoria.

"I'm going to England. Rafe has decided not to return to Oxford, but I'm going to join the RFC. Since Ria and Zoë aren't going with you now, may I come instead? You're sailing out of New York on the *Lusitania* in September, aren't you?"

Beatrice was surprised, and instantly felt sorry for Victoria, who was soon to be deserted by both of them. "I'd be delighted to have your company."

"I thought I might ask Jack if he wanted to join the RFC as well. He seems to be keen on flying. And as he was actually born in England, he shouldn't have any problem signing on."

Jack thought it a perfect solution, especially as Chas had offered to pay his passage and expenses until his inheritance came through. He would become a daring aviator, a hero perhaps. It was an honourable way of staying out of the mill. The thousands of bright and adventurous young men who were flocking to sign up were already considered champions by an adoring public fuelled by patriotic fervour. And when Jack returned, he would surely be working for J.D.

Before they returned to Muskoka, Jack mailed a letter to Molly, summoning her to be by her ailing mother's side. She could do nothing more at Wyndwood. It was time for Molly to die.

.        .        .

Victoria read the letter in the tower room, where she liked to sit in the window seat and gaze out over the burgeoning city.

*My dearest Victoria,*

*You have been like a daughter to me. I know that I tried to curb your stubborn, wilful nature, but I am glad for it after all, as it will help you to succeed. I named you for two strong queens, and you have lived up to your namesakes. Now you must take care to choose wisely where to apply your strengths. I hope to help you, even from beyond the grave.*

*I do not trust your father to do right by you, especially if he has remarried. I know that is a sad admission for a mother to have to make about her firstborn, but he suffered greatly because of your mother's death, which is no excuse for his neglect of you, but is an unfortunate reason. So I have arranged my will, as you shall see, to allow you independence. Once again, I urge you to use both the money and freedom wisely. Remember that you promised to make me proud. I shall be watching, never fear!*

*And Wyndholme shall never be allowed to reject you.*

*Don't trust Helena. She is a manipulative gold-digger and has told us a pack of lies. She is not worthy of bearing the Wyndham name.*

*Be wary of your cousin Jack. I know he is a handsome charmer and that he's ignited some spark in you, but I don't trust him. He is too hungry. Money will always be his first love, and I think he will do anything and use everyone to get ahead. I don't want you to get hurt.*

*I would also urge you to seriously consider marriage to Justin Carrington. I know that you are friends who share similar tastes and interests. I hope that you also love him, at least a little, for I believe that he does you. Take a lesson from Alexander that passion does not necessarily bring happiness. A good marriage is one that involves mutual respect, affection, and sufficient funds to enjoy the finer things in life. A deep, quiet, and abiding love is better than a blazing, demanding one that can too easily burn itself out or become destructive. Justin is a good man, strong, reliable, compassionate, and he will give you handsome children. Consider it my dying wish. I want only to know that you will be happy, cherished, and cared for, my darling child.*

*Your loving grandmother"*

Victoria wiped away tears. It seemed so odd to have Augusta still telling her what to do. She had thought it strange that the will had stipulated she should have her money immediately, were she to marry Justin. Why had Grandmother settled on him? Hadn't she noticed how well she and Chas got along, even if they had hidden their love from her?

She had also thought it curious that Augusta had stipulated that Jack was not allowed to marry her or her cousins. Was Grandmother right in thinking that he was only interested in her for her money? Surely there had been a genuine spark between them, as even Augusta had noticed.

Jack had been trying to seduce her, but seemed to have given up when he realized that she and Chas were in love. That was hardly the tactic of a man ruthlessly plotting to marry her.

But had he done something else instead? Had he known that Augusta would leave him a substantial amount of money, and somehow caused her death? Victoria immediately chided herself for that terrible and uncharitable thought. Jack might be ambitious, but he would never resort to murder to get ahead, despite Grandmother's misgivings about him.

She would trust her own instincts. And she liked Jack.

# Chapter 18

It had just seemed natural for Jack to return to the island with them, and Victoria had told him he was welcome to stay until he left with Chas.

Jack was painting a picture of Silver Bay for Olivia and Richard. It was early morning, and Molly knew where to find him.

She sat down on a rock and smoked the cigarette he gave her. "I got the letter. I've told them, so I'm leaving today. What's the news?"

He told her the contents of the will.

"*You* did alright! And Queenie's a frigging heiress! But that nasty old bitch only left us half of what you and the others got?" Her Irish accent had disappeared.

"It's still twelve thousand."

"Over ten years, once we're twenty-one."

"It's more per year than most men make. You won't be hungry or have to work. I'll invest the money for you and you'll have lots more. It's a start, Lizzie! That's all we need. I can make us rich and we won't have to kiss ass with James and the others to do it. And you can choose yourself a wealthy husband. It'll work out, you'll see." He gave his eldest sister a warm smile.

She grinned. "It has worked out, hasn't it, Jack? Your plan. Even the old lady dying like she did. Convenient, wasn't it?"

"Luck has to be on our side sometimes," he replied. "But don't take any chances. Send the letter from Molly's brother, informing them about her death, in a couple of weeks." Molly Jones had worked with Lizzie once, but had died of influenza. So Lizzie had stolen her identity for a while. "And transform yourself. It was as much as I could do to keep Zoë from rushing over to visit our family when we were in the city. She's the one I'm really worried about. She's smart and observant."

"Don't worry. I'll be my old self. Brash and mouthy. No longer the meek little maid with a heavy Irish brogue. You have to admit I'd make a great actress."

"Yes, indeed." And Jack knew how beautiful she looked when she didn't scrape her luxuriant, auburn hair, now tinted black, so viciously from her face. It wasn't likely that anyone would recognize her. People didn't pay close attention to servants. "So which rich fellow do you have in your sights?"

"Unfortunately Chas is taken. Rafe perhaps. The others are all rather boringly nice."

Jack laughed. "I'll make introductions soon." But when he told her about going overseas with Chas, she frowned.

"Do you have to? It'll be dangerous."

"I'm a survivor, sweetheart. And it's important for me to stay close friends with Chas. He and his family are our ticket to success. Can you think of a more ideal way for me to form a strong bond with Chas than to go off to war with him?"

"Probably not. Christ! So we'll have no one to run interference when the tiresome Zoë comes to do her good deeds, making amends for the family rift and all that crap!"

"Be nice, Lizzie. She means well."

She sucked on the cigarette one last time and tossed the butt into the lake. "Not in my character. But I'll become the affectionate cousin, grateful for the well-meaning crumbs that are tossed in my direction. *Oh, how kind! How considerate! How generous!* Bugger it!"

"Make sure you curb that cussing tongue of yours. You're going to be a lady now."

"Don't worry. I've been watching them. I'm a quick study."

"I'm coming down next week to help you move into the house. You and Maman should start buying furniture, so it can be delivered as soon as we have possession. We have the money from Richard, and I got a few hundred dollars advance on my inheritance, and left some of it with Maman. So you and the girls should splurge and make yourselves special evening gowns, because I expect that you'll soon be invited to visit."

"Oh, crap! I hate it here! I can hardly wait to get back to the city."

"It's different here when you're just enjoying yourself. Now you'd better get back, Molly Jones. Sure, won't I be missing your blessed little self," he added in a convincing Irish accent.

"Ah, get away with you then!" she countered, bestowing a kiss on his cheek. "I suppose I *am* a bit of an heiress, too." She swayed her hips as she sauntered away.

.   .   .

Victoria no longer had any reservations about meeting Chas at The Shimmering Sands in the early mornings. She didn't care if they were discovered. It was really only for Augusta's sake that she had wanted to remain respectable.

"Will you make love to me, Chas?" she asked on the first morning that they were back. As usual, he had stopped kissing her when things became too heated.

"It's not a good idea, my darling."

"But why? Don't you love me?"

"Of course I do, Ria. I just don't want you to get hurt."

"I can't be hurt more than I am now, thinking that you don't care enough about me, even as you go off on some dangerous adventure."

He nuzzled her hair as he said, "I care too much."

"Don't leave me like this, Chas! I want to know what it's like to be loved. I want you to be the one who shows me. I'll be in agony until you return, but at least I'll have memories to help me through the days."

"Oh, my darling girl. Do you really know what you're asking?"

"Yes. I'll be a fallen woman," she quipped, trying to lighten the mood.

"Then let me show you how to fall deliciously and irrevocably in love."

His lovemaking was tender, almost worshipful. When she gasped at the pain of his entry, he murmured against her cheek, "I'm sorry, my darling. It'll be better now."

It was ecstasy. Victoria had never thought she could feel such exquisite fulfilment and yet longing at the same time.

"Now we truly belong to each other. How can I ever let you go?" she asked, as she lay naked in his arms. "Can anyone ever have felt such bliss? For if they did, how could they ever do anything else?"

He kissed her softly and said, "When we're married we'll do this every night. And in the mornings, and the afternoons between tennis and tea." When she looked at him in astonishment, he said, "You will marry me when I come back, won't you my darling?"

"Oh yes!" She kissed him fervently.

"Now I should find out if your father will actually allow me to marry you."

"You need to ask Albert and Richard. And if they can't agree, your father gets to decide," she told him with a laugh, and explained those terms of Augusta's will, leaving out the bit about Justin.

"But I suppose your father is still your legal guardian until you're twenty-one. So I shall have to ask all of them! Good God! Do I have to slay dragons as well?"

He stopped her laugh with another kiss.

They swam and made love again.

When they met the next morning, Chas came prepared. They could hardly keep their hands off each other, but he interrupted their lovemaking.

"What is that?" Victoria asked.

"It's a French letter. So that you don't get pregnant."

"I like it better without ...that thing," she told him afterwards. "I like to feel your skin against mine, your warmth, and, well..." She blushed.

"Seed," he supplied. "Which is precisely why we have this thing."

"Would that be so bad? If I had your child?"

"Considering that we're not married yet and that I'm about to go far away, it's not ideal."

"We could get married now. You could take me along to the war for our honeymoon."

Chas laughed and ran a finger along her soft cheek. "We'll get married as soon as I can be always by your side. If something should happen to me..."

"Chas! Stop!"

"Please listen, my darling. You're going to be very wealthy once we're married. If something were to happen to me, you would be an even wealthier widow. And a target for unscrupulous men, especially as you'd no longer be under the protection of your trustees. The fortune hunters would be more likely to leave you alone if you don't come into your money until you're twenty-five. You'll be more gown up, and less vulnerable."

"Chas, if anything happened to you, I would die anyway. What difference would money make then?"

"You mustn't talk like that! We have good Karma, remember? I'm coming back to you, and I very selfishly want to spend lots and lots of time alone with you before I have to share you with our children. And for now...."

That was one of the ways they managed to keep the war at bay for a while at least. Victoria ignored the newspapers. She didn't want to spoil any more of the summer.

Both their families gave their blessings to the match. Because they were in mourning, the Wyndhams kept their activities sedate, avoiding dances and balls. But Marjorie Thornton insisted on hosting a small engagement party, just for the island friends. After all, James's wedding was going ahead this month.

Chas disappeared to the city for a couple of days on important business, he claimed, leaving Victoria feeling restless, and wondering how she would survive without him for months. They had only a few precious weeks until he left. How she hated this war already!

Although it was mid-August, the heat was still interminable. Victoria swam at the back bay with the others, but then decided she would do a painting of the Shimmering Sands for Chas to take with him.

When she returned, she was surprised to find him on the veranda with the ladies. The men were in deep discussions in the library with a business associate who was staying for a night – which wasn't unusual. Her cousins were back at the beach, having had their tea.

Just the sight of Chas's smiling face and that tender look in his eyes that seemed reserved for her alone made her happy, and long for his touch. "You're back early!" She had thought she wouldn't see him until the party tomorrow evening.

"Business successfully concluded. And I come bearing an invitation. Aunt Olivia has given her permission..."

Olivia laughed. "We certainly do welcome you to the family, dear nephew-to-be."

"And I'm certain Cousin Bea and Aunt Phyllis concur..." Beatrice smiled and Phyllis harrumphed, but even she couldn't resist Chas's charm. "So you're to join me for a mystery dinner this evening. I shall pick you up at seven."

As they walked hand-in-hand to the dock, he whispered to her, "I've missed you, my darling. I can hardly wait to touch you, to kiss you, to ravish you."

She laughed. "Me too!"

"I'll try to contain myself, at least until tonight."

"Did he say what that's all about?" Victoria asked the others when she rejoined them on the veranda.

"You'll have to wait to find out," Olivia said, beaming at her. "But I think it's wonderfully romantic."

Phyllis said. "I don't approve of how modern young people are doing things these days. It would have been scandalous in my day."

"Fortunately, the world moves on," Beatrice said.

"Let's go and dangle our feet in the lake," Olivia said to Victoria."

"Ah, this is heavenly," Olivia said, splashing her feet about. With no one to see them, they hitched their skirts up to their knees. "I am delighted for you, Victoria. Chas seems very much in love with you, and I can see that you are with him. You're fortunate, as was I. I can only wish you the kind of happiness that I have enjoyed with Richard. We'll talk about wifely obligations and such before your marriage, but if there's anything you'd like to know now...?"

Victoria shook her head. "Only how I'm to get through the empty days and months ahead without him," she said despondently.

"You must spend as much time with us as you like. You're like a daughter to us, you know that." Olivia patted Victoria's hand, incensed that James planned to abandon Victoria at Wyndholme, to set up house with his bride in a new home. He had invited Victoria to join them, but it had been a formality only. At Olivia's criticism of his callous treatment of his daughter, James had replied that he and Helena would check on her regularly and ensure that the household ran smoothly. Olivia had told him scathingly not to bother as she and Richard would be more than happy to do so. James had seemed relieved rather than insulted.

"Thank you, Aunt Olivia." Victoria squeezed her hand in gratitude.

What a lonely child, Olivia thought. She feared desperately for Chas's safety, but wouldn't allow herself to think that he might not return. That would devastate Victoria. They talked for a while and then Olivia said, "Now you should go and prepare for your evening. Don't hold back."

"You look absolutely beautiful, my darling" Chas said, when he escorted Victoria to the boat. "I see I shall have my hands full, beating off bewitched men wherever we go. And dragonflies." He laughed as one landed on her shoulder. "They really do have an affinity for you."

She was dressed in a stunning gown of lavender satin overlaid with matching lavender chiffon elaborately decorated with clear crystal beading and dripping with a beaded fringe. It was what she had brought back from her wardrobe in the city to wear to the wedding.

They boarded the Thorntons' sixty foot motor yacht, driven by the head boatman. A maid stood in attendance.

Zoë took a photograph of them in the stern of the boat, their arms entwined, Victoria leaning her head toward Chas as she laughed at something he said, Chas looking affectionately down at her.

An ice bucket containing a champagne bottle awaited them. He popped the cork as they pulled away from the dock, and poured them each a glass.

"To us," he said, clinking his glass to hers. He handed her a single red rose and a velvet box. "To make our engagement official. Just so the princess isn't tempted to run off with the knave of hearts while I'm gone."

It was a flawless blue star sapphire ring surrounded by a starburst of diamonds. "Oh, Chas! It's exquisite!" It fit her perfectly.

"It's quite a rare stone, so they tell me, and is considered to have special powers. I thought that described you perfectly."

She kissed him, momentarily oblivious of the servants.

"Don't worry," Chas said when she suddenly pulled away. "They've been well bribed, despite what your aunts may think."

As the boat trolled leisurely around the lake, they lingered over a splendid meal in the glass enclosed cabin. By the time the sun melted into the lake, Victoria was nestled in his arms on the leather bench in the stern. She had kicked off her shoes and tucked her legs under her as she leaned against him. "This is heavenly," she said.

And as the stars began to populate the endless sky, they danced to their tunes on the gramophone, each song reminding them of special times.

"*Come Josephine in my flying machine*," Chas sang to her.

"I wish I could!" Victoria said, trying to keep the anguish from her voice.

"You will. We shall buy an aeroplane and I'll teach you how to fly. You'll be an aviatrix – isn't that a delightful word? – and you and I will fly around the world."

They clung to each other as they danced. They kissed as they swayed to the music by the light of the waning moon.

By the time Chas left her in the sitting room at the cottage, with a promise to meet at the Shimmering Sands in the morning, she was even more desperately in love with him.

•    •    •

At tea time on Saturday, Henry announced to them all, "I'm going to the city tomorrow to join up."

"Join what, dear?" Phyllis asked.

"Don't be a fool, Henry!" Albert bellowed. "What do you know about fighting? You wouldn't even be an officer, just a common soldier."

Phyllis shrieked. "What's he talking about? Albert?"

"I'm going to enlist in the army, Mother. I want to do my bit."

Phyllis clutched at her ample bosom and cried, "Henry, you can't! Albert, you mustn't allow it!"

"All kinds of chaps are going off. Look at Chas and Jack. And Archie Spencer was talking about it. I'm sorry Mother, but I've made up my mind."

"What about your work?" Albert demanded.

"You don't need me at the moment. This is a chance for me to do something different, perhaps make a difference."

"I think it's very noble of you, Henry," James said. "There certainly seems to be a lot of excitement and optimism among the young men, going off to show the Kaiser just  what we loyal Colonials are made of."

At his words, Phyllis started to calm down.

"I'll go too, as soon as this blasted leg heals," Edgar said. He'd had his cast removed when they were in the city last week, but his ankle was stiff and swollen and he needed to rest and elevate it. He was at least able to go into the water now, which felt good. But he couldn't put much pressure on his ankle yet.

"Don't curse, Edgar," Phyllis said.

"But I'm getting left out of everything this summer! Henry and Jack and Chas are going to be heroes, while I get to sit around and read about their exploits."

Jack walked up to Henry and put out his hand, saying, "Good luck, old chap."

The two of them had avoided each other since the night that Henry had punched Jack. Everyone waited in anticipation as Henry hesitated and then shook Jack's hand.

Victoria threw her arms about Henry and said, "You're just as crazy as Chas and Jack! And I'm proud of you all!"

"Don't even think about it," Olivia warned Max, who looked as if he wanted to say something. "You have studies to attend to."

Max seemed relieved, and confided to Zoë and Victoria later, "I don't believe in killing people, but if it's somehow necessary to save our country, I suppose I could do it. But I'm not sure what we'd actually be saving it from. I think we need to apply our brains rather than our brawn to solve problems with other nations."

"Good! Then plan to be a diplomat, rather than a soldier," Zoë said, afraid for beloved friends leaving on such a dangerous mission. She would be especially appalled if Max and Blake went to war.

The engagement party at Thorncliff that evening was not unmarred by the war. Archie Spencer declared he was joining up. He had done the officer's training while at the university, since it had seemed a good skill to have.

After dinner, the young people went to look at the kittens. Olivia had agreed that Zoë and Max could have one, so they chose the black one with white paws. "Spats, we'll call him," Zoë said.

Lydia was determined to have one as well.

Vivian pulled Victoria aside in the hallway and confided that Peter had joined the Veterinary Corps. She hugged Victoria fiercely and whispered, "I know how you'll feel when Chas leaves. I don't know how I'm going to survive without Peter! I'd still hoped my parents would let me go to Toronto and that we could be together. I've waited a year, and now I won't even see him before he leaves!"

Eleanor joined them, saying, "I sense something dire."

Vivian tried to regain her composure. "I'm just consoling Ria about Chas leaving for the war."

"But you're more upset than she is, so let's hear the real reason. Is your lover going off as well?" Eleanor asked.

"He's not my lover... That is... Oh, damnation! Yes, he *is* going off and I wish he *were* my lover!"

Chas joined them then, putting his arm possessively about Victoria, and said, "Did I hear mention of love?"

"You two are the perfect advertisement for it," Eleanor said. "And I'm jealous as hell, so kindly don't flaunt it, Chas. I'm mad at you for not picking me."

"I'm sorry, Ellie. There's only room for one girl in my heart now."

"I hope so, or you really will be sorry. I won't have my friend trifled with."

"I've committed to not trifling any more. Vivian, you look rather sad." Chas looked at her questioningly.

"I'm just upset by the war. Don't mind me."

Justin was the other one who had to hide his feelings that evening. After the enticing thought that Augusta had chosen him for Victoria, he was shocked to hear about the engagement. But Victoria was so obviously in love with Chas that he knew he would never have had a chance, even if he had made his intentions clear sooner.

"We seem to be the wet blankets tonight," he said to Vivian when the group had moved to the ballroom. "What's wrong, Sis?"

"All these changes, the uncertainty. I hate to think of Chas going off and leaving Ria. What if he doesn't come back? I can't bear to think of it!" She hugged herself.

"Is Peter going then? Is that what this is really all about?"

"How did you know?"

"That you loved Peter? Not hard to guess, since Papa dismissed him for no good reason, packed you off to Europe, and you've been pining ever since. I liked him, by the way."

"He's studying to be a veterinarian. But he's only done one year, so I don't know why he's abandoning it all now. He says the experience will be helpful, and that he needs the money, although I gave him as much of my dress allowance as I could. And, of course, he's trying to do his bit, which is really noble of him, and one of the reasons I love him. He's such a good person, Justin. If only Papa would realize that, instead of rejecting him for his lack of social status and wealth. It's so unfair!"

He gripped her shoulder. "I know. I wish I could help. Come and let's dance."

Their hearts weren't in it, but they tried to maintain a cheerful façade. Vivian said to him, "I hope you're not too much in love with Ria."

"I'd had hopes," Justin said.

"I'm sorry."

"I suppose we can't help who we fall in love with. Chas actually does seem to be in love with her, which rather surprised me. He's not usually serious about anything except winning at games. I hope he'll be good to her." And he hoped that Augusta was wrong in thinking that that marriage would be a disaster. He really wanted Victoria to be happy. And he would honour his commitment to Augusta to look after her.

Jack, meanwhile, was dancing with Eleanor. He had decided that he needed some diversion. Without jeopardizing Felicity's infatuation with him, he would take pleasure where he could find it. He figured that Eleanor was the only girl in this circle of friends who he might be able to shag, especially since she had always eyed him with interest. He said, "I guess we're both disappointed, now that Chas and Victoria are engaged."

"I thought you were rather smitten with her."

"Being just a cousin, I didn't really hold out much hope. But I'm sorry I've ignored the other beauties around me."

"Hell's bells! You're not going to try to flatter me now, are you?"

"I thought we could console each other."

Eleanor chuckled and said, "I'm not averse to a bit of consolation."

"I'm going out for a smoke after this dance. I might stroll down to the pavilion."

Eleanor arrived shortly after Jack did. He kissed her hungrily.

"You don't waste time, do you?" she said, when they stopped for a breath.

"We've wasted enough time already. I'm leaving in a few weeks."

"Then it's heartless of you to toy with my feelings, perhaps make me fall in love with you."

He kissed her between each sentence. "Would that be such a bad thing?"

"Not if you meant it."

"I thought you were hot stuff from the moment I first saw you."

She laughed. "That's just my red hair."

"God, you are a temptress," he said after another scorching kiss, surprised at how aroused he was.

"I think you could make me stop pining for Chas."

"I wish I weren't going away tomorrow."

"You'll just have to hurry back. And now we'd better return to the party."

.    .    .

Before Jack went off to the city, Zoë said, "You should bring your sisters with you for a holiday when you return. Oh, goodness! Is that alright, Ria?" She had forgotten that Victoria now owned the cottage. A bizarre notion, actually.

"Yes, of course. We're looking forward to meeting the rest of our cousins," Victoria said.

Phyllis grunted, but Victoria shot her a look that brought bright spots to Phyllis's cheeks. There was a great deal of satisfaction in being in charge, Victoria thought.

Jack was away for four days. His family was ecstatic about their new house. The girls went racing through the rooms, declaring it a castle. Even Maman was pleased, particularly with the sunroom off her private bedroom.

"This is more than I ever hoped for with your father," she said sadly. "I never wanted a grand house, like Wyndholme. Oh, yes, he showed me one day. We walked past. C'est magnifique! But this... this would have been heaven!" She touched his arm. "You've done well, Jacques. But now we have a chance to be happy and settled, and you have to go off to a stupid war, and worry me with something else! Why are you going? You have money now – a fortune! – maybe a job with the family."

"I'm going with my friend, Maman. There will be a much better job for me when we get back. It's exactly what I want." The Toronto Stock Exchange still hadn't reopened, so any chance of working for J.D. seemed unlikely for a while. Jack would leave instructions with J.D. and the lawyer, Ethan Nash, about where to invest his $5000 once the funds were paid out by the estate.

Jack helped them arrange furniture, put up draperies, and put an ad in the newspapers for lodgers. He took the girls to Eaton's to shop for clothes and sundries so that they could enjoy their week at the cottage. On the last night before returning to Wyndwood, they had a delicious meal in their elegant new dining room, with fine wine and much excitement and laughter. Jack told the girls about the people they would meet, and more stories about the summer on the lake.

"With you all gone, " Marie said, "This place will seem too big and lonely. I never thought I would ever say that."

"You could come as well, Maman," Jack assured her.

"Never! But I want you girls to enjoy yourselves. Jacque is obviously in love with the place or he would now stay here with his poor Maman."

"Maman! You know it's where I need to be to get ahead. Having connections is the only way. Just think of the people I already know, with whom I socialize. Chas Thornton is my good friend, and soon he will be our cousin by marriage."

Later, when fifteen-year-old Emily and thirteen-year-old Claire had gone to bed, and Marie was soaking in the tub, Jack and Lizzie sat on the small balcony off her third-floor bedroom, smoking cigarettes and finishing the wine. Because of the heat, the girls were actually sleeping in the main bedrooms on the second floor, Emily and Claire sharing the large front room. But Lizzie loved sitting on her balcony and watching the activity on the street. And because of the heat, many people were still lolling on front porches or strolling about. They had already met many of their neighbours. The Wyndham name was certainly recognized.

"So Queenie and yummy Chas are really getting hitched," Lizzie said. "Too bad for both of us."

"I have my sights set elsewhere. I'm grooming Felicity Thornton."

"Christ! Cradle-snatching now, are you?"

"Don't worry, I'm not touching her. Yet. She's smitten by my dashing good looks and immense charm."

"Poor little bitch! So you're going to play up to her romantic, girlish ideals, and go in for the kill when she's a few years older, and still besotted with you, you hope."

"You make it sound so heartless. Chas is my friend, and I wouldn't treat her badly. She's a nice kid."

"And she'll be even more attractive when she's wrapped in her daddy's millions."

"Oh yes. But in the meantime, I'm enjoying the delights of Eleanor Carlyle."

"The redhead who's studying to be a doctor?"

"That's right. Nice bit of skirt, actually." He was surprised that he found her so sexually appealing that she hadn't been out of his thoughts since the night of the engagement party. She wasn't beautiful like Victoria or Vivian, but with her copper-coloured hair and green eyes, she was certainly attractive. And yet there was something more, something he'd noticed about her the first time they'd met, that made her alluring and irresistible.

"Are you playing dangerous games?"

"I'll be careful. I won't do anything to alienate Felicity's affections."

"But you're not content to enjoy what you've already got? Live here? This is a decent place. We would have thought ourselves in paradise once."

"Are you content, having seen how our cousins live? What the possibilities are?"

"I want to be on the other side of the serving dish for once!" Lizzie said with determination.

"So have you been practicing your manners? Your hair looks good, by the way." It was a bit lighter than her natural colour, a more golden auburn, but at least she no longer looked like Molly Jones.

"It should. It took several applications of peroxide to take out the black dye. Maman was suspicious, but I convinced her I had died my hair in a fit of madness. And yes, I promise I will behave. At least socially. I may practice my vampish charms on some of the men."

"Are you nervous at all?"

"Only in case I do something stupid, like let on I know something or even where to find something when I really shouldn't. That's not easy, since I cleaned every inch of that frigging cottage. But I can't be too ignorant, because you've obviously told us some things. Help me if you see me about to put my foot in it. I expect I'll be confident and haughty enough to fool the servants, even if any of them think they see a physical resemblance to Molly."

"I'm sure of it. People's expectations really do influence their perceptions. Dress and act like a lady, and you are one."

But Lizzie did feel nervous when they arrived at the front dock the next day. Emily and Claire were already awed by the beautiful lakes, the picturesque trip on the *Sagamo*, the largest steamer in the Muskoka fleet, and now the sight of the massive summer home. She would take her clues from them, acting wide-eyed and apprehensive.

"How wonderful that you've finally arrived," Olivia said, coming down the path to meet them. She greeted them with a warm smile and sincere hugs.

Jack introduced them, and Olivia said, "We've been so looking forward to your visit. Now let me show you your room – we've put the three of you together – and then you might want to have a swim before we have tea. You'll find the lake is lovely and warm, since we've had such a hot summer."

Jack helped Grayson carry their bags up to the guest room on the east side, while Richard and Beatrice greeted the girls. Olivia took them to their room, pointing out the bathroom en route, and said, "Take whatever time you want to unpack and then come down to the veranda. We'll have some lemonade waiting for you, and then we'll go for a swim, if you'd like."

"Oh, yes!" Claire said. "Thank you, Aunt Olivia."

"It's a lovely room," Lizzie dared to say, and was relieved that there was no sign of recognition on Olivia's face.

"Do let me know if there is anything you need or have forgotten to bring," Olivia said. "I'll see you downstairs."

When she had shut the door, Emily exclaimed, "We have a balcony! Just look at the view! It's no wonder Papa talked about the island so much." Through the scattering of pines and maples they glimpsed the densely-treed shoreline of Mortimer's Island, broken up by clusters of smaller, shaggy islands and granite boulders floating on a liquid sky. To their right were the Stepping Stones, and fragments of the Silly Isles. Tatters of white clouds, like torn lace, drifted across the intensely blue sky, but cast no shadows or reflections.

Lizzie wondered if she would like it any better here now that she had a large, airy bedroom, access to a bathroom, and others waiting on her. It would be odd to order the butler about and have Libby serving her. Poor old Grayson was still here, so Mrs. Grayson obviously hadn't found someone to replace Tom yet. She wondered how Grayson liked sleeping above the washhouse instead of in his cozy suite of rooms at Wyndholme. Being a servant really was a bitch.

They didn't have much to unpack, and the younger girls were eager to go for a swim. They met Albert, Phyllis, and Phoebe on the veranda.

Lizzie wasn't surprised that "Aunt" Phyllis was not very friendly, but the old bag  tried to be civil, since she was also a guest here now. Imagine Queenie owning all this and frigging Wyndholme and a sodding fortune! It really was too bad that Jack hadn't seduced her before Chas did. Speak of the devil, here they were pulling up to the dock in Chas's boat. With tiresome Zoë. And Max, who reminded her of an eager puppy dog.

Introductions were made and Victoria said, "I'm so glad that you could come! We've just been visiting our kittens, which are still too young to come home with us. Perhaps you'd like to see them with us tomorrow? We go over every day." And she and Chas would sneak off for a few stolen kisses, which Zoë and Max were now used to. Even though they still met every morning at the Shimmering Sands, they couldn't get enough of each other. It was heavenly.

"We'd enjoy that," Lizzie said. "Jack has told us so much about his summer here, but we really can't believe he's as good a tennis player as he claims, so we'd like him to prove it." Shit, shit, shit! No one had mentioned that the kittens were at Thorncliff, although Jack would have told them about the tournament. But no one seemed to notice.

Chas laughed. "Sisters are always skeptical, aren't they?" he said to Jack. "Ria and I will allow you and Fliss to play a rematch.

Let's make it tomorrow. Well, I should be off. We're all going to
Oaktree tonight for a concert, Jack. I'm picking up a group of you
at half past eight.. I hope your lovely sisters will feel up to joining
us."

"It sounds delightful," Lizzie said, giving him a coy smile.

Esme and the boys immediately took to their new cousins.
Edgar eyed Lizzie with interest during dinner. Zoë was less
gushing than Lizzie had anticipated, but seemed intent upon
making them welcome and their stay, pleasant.

Lizzie found it hard not to burst into laughter at finding
herself being served at table by Grayson and Libby. She, of course,
knew just how to treat servants, mostly by pretending they weren't
there.

And she was thrilled with the evening gown Maman and
Emily had made for her. The amber silk taffeta trimmed with jet
beads accented her hair and complimented her large hazel eyes.
Jack told her she looked like a burnished goddess. It was amazing
how sophisticated she felt, and ready to do social battle.

And her first conquest appeared to be Rafe Thornton. As soon
as she stepped into Chas's boat, she felt Rafe's eyes on her.

After introductions had been made at Oaktree, Lionel
Camford said to Lizzie, "I say, I haven't seen you on the lake
before. I say, Jack, why have you been hiding your sisters away?"

"To keep them out of your clutches, of course, Lionel," Chas
quipped.

Lizzie was thrilled to think that a millionaire like Lionel was
attracted to her, and practiced her charms on him, although she
suspected nothing could ever come of it. Not that she liked him in
any case. But what a sense of power to have him almost grovelling
at her feet. She glowed with joy.

"Your sisters are quite beautiful young women," Chas said to
Jack. "But I shouldn't be surprised, since they are Wyndhams.
Claire looks somewhat like Ria, only with dark hair. I expect you'll
have your hands full with them."

Claire and Jack had both inherited their father's blue eyes,
while Lizzie and Emily resembled their mother. Both looked older
than their years, and were certainly drawing a lot of attention.

Jack decided he needed to look after Emily in particular.
Lizzie was street-wise, but Emily was a bit of a dreamer. She
wasn't aware of how attractive she was, especially dressed in sage
green moiré silk, which made her hazel eyes look even larger than
usual.

The Oakleys had a friend visiting from New York who had brought with him the up-and-coming songwriter, Hugo Garrick, whose catchy tunes, some of which had been featured in the Ziegfeld Follies, were particularly popular with the young crowd. Also visiting was Garrick's glamorous "leading lady", Sadie Burke, who had performed with the Follies and was an emerging star in musical theatre. Hugo and Sadie had agreed to perform for Oswald's friends, Hugo at the piano. Sadie shimmered in a red and black sequined gown and headdress that completely covered her hair and sprouted enormous black feathers. Her voice was just as mesmerizing.

Emily, in particular, was spellbound. When the formal concert was over, people drifted off to other rooms – the men to smoke or play billiards, the women to the sitting room for coffee. The young people crowded around Hugo and Sadie at the piano, encouraging them to keep performing. Sadie sang one more song, and then excused herself. Hugo played absently on the piano as people asked him questions.

And Emily couldn't resist singing. She had wandered onto the terrace and didn't think anyone was paying her any attention. The music was just so wonderful and she loved to sing. She strolled alongside the reflecting pool, so overwhelmed by the opulence of this place and the beauty of the night-time lake, that she hadn't noticed the music had changed to a gramophone record.

"You have a remarkable voice," Hugo said, startling her. He lit a cigarette. "Sing some more for me."

"Oh... I couldn't!" She was shocked that anyone had heard her, but especially this handsome young songwriter from New York.

"You wouldn't like to sing on stage, like Sadie does?"

"Oh, but I would!"

"Then sing for me. If you can't do that, how can you face an audience of hundreds?"

Emily had loved singing since she was a child, and had dreamed about being a star ever since Maman had mentioned her own short career. Years of hardship and hopelessness had toughened her. Her dreams might be answered now if she could pull herself together. She looked into his dark eyes and began to sing one of his songs. And once she'd started, it was easy, because the music always possessed her. Singing to herself was how she got through long, tedious days of making dresses for people like these. The other girls in the sweatshop had liked listening to her, when she could get away with it. The boss had considered her singing a distraction.

A few young lovers who roamed about outside, including Victoria and Chas, heard Emily and were astonished. Her voice was seductive, alluring, and yet pure. "You have talented cousins," Chas said to Victoria.

"So it seems." They wandered up to Emily.

"You have an amazing voice," Victoria said when Emily had finished.

"She does indeed," Hugo agreed. "But it could do with some formal training. You've never had any, have you?"

"No."

"What's your name?"

"Emily Wyndham."

"Winsome Emily Wyndham. Nice. You won't even have to change that for the stage. Sadie's was Burkowitz, but that wouldn't have gotten her anywhere. Yours has a good Anglo-Saxon ring to it. How old are you?"

"Fifteen."

Hugo seemed surprised and disappointed. He took a calling card from his pocket. "Get some training and local stage experience, and come to see me in a couple of years. I think I can help you." He smiled warmly at her.

"Oh, thank you, sir!"

"It's Hugo." He winked at her and walked off.

"It seems you've made a conquest, Emily," Victoria said. "Do you want to pursue a stage career?"

"Oh, yes!" She could hardly believe her luck. She wanted to shout with happiness.

"Then you should get acting and dancing lessons as well. I'll help you arrange those, if you like," Victoria said.

"Would you?"

"Of course. Grandmother wouldn't have approved. But actresses are much more acceptable now, with movies and Hollywood and such. You might become a screen star, like Mary Pickford. She's from Toronto, you know. Oh, this is fun, having more cousins! Come along, Emily, and join us in a glass of champagne to celebrate the beginning of your musical career." Victoria, holding onto Chas with one arm, now hooked her other around Emily's and the three of them returned to the ballroom.

Victoria had no idea how much she had endeared herself to Emily in that brief but heartfelt moment.

Jack and Eleanor, meanwhile, had wandered far enough around the island to escape the others.

"I've missed you," he said. Once again their conversation was punctuated by kisses.

"Good! I wouldn't like to think that I was just some bit of skirt that took your mind off Ria for a few minutes."

"Hardly. I've been thinking about you all week. You've bewitched me somehow."

"In the old days they burned women who practiced medicine as witches."

"Good thing you didn't live in those days."

"Edelina might say that I had, in a previous life."

"And you're still smouldering."

She laughed delightedly. "You really are beginning to give Chas some competition."

"I like to win."

"But I'm only the consolation prize."

"I wouldn't say that."

In the ballroom, Lizzie was dancing with Rafe, who was still relatively sober. He said, "Well, Miss Wyndham, this must be a rather novel experience for you. I understand you didn't actually grow up in this environment." He was goading her.

"My father often talked about Wyndwood, so I feel well acquainted with it. So far it hasn't been a disappointment, since I knew it would be somewhat rustic," she said nonchalantly.

He laughed.

She smiled. "Jack pointed out to me that our aristocratic ancestors were not always flush with ready cash. But breeding is what's important in the end, don't you think, Mr. Thornton?"

"I think you can convince me."

Which is what Lizzie set out to do that week.

The next morning the girls had canoeing lessons from their cousins, Victoria teaching Emily, Zoë with Lizzie, and Esme with Claire. The two of them had been delighted to find someone of their own age, and were already fast friends. The girls caught on quickly and enjoyed themselves, even Lizzie.

After lunch, they took *Dragonfly* over to Thorncliff. Victoria was driving, as the boat was now hers, much to Edgar's chagrin, and she needed more practice. James had cancelled the order for the new family yacht after Augusta's death, as it was decided that each family should now have their own runabout. After all, they were building their own cottages and boathouses, including James, who had selected a site close to the gazebo, about halfway up the west side of the island.

Victoria had been dismayed that everyone was deserting her, but now that she and Chas were getting married, she would enjoy sharing the solitude with him. After all, he would be back by next summer, and she would be planning a wedding at Wyndwood.

Victoria and Chas were beating Felicity and Jack on the court, but Lizzie was impressed with her brother's skill. Jack had explained the rules to his sisters earlier that day when they had visited his impressive room, and Lizzie was grateful not to be ignorant of the game as Rafe joined her.

"Do you play as well as your siblings?" she asked him.

"Almost."

"I didn't know her, but I'll never forgive my grandmother for not *wanting* to know us, and for depriving us of all this. Our birthright, I think. This morning we learned how to canoe. What fun that was!" Of course, she hated the old bitch for much more than that, but she needed to remind Rafe that she was a Wyndham, no matter that she had grown up destitute. She tried to look wistful.

"I can teach you tennis, if you like."

"Would you? I'd enjoy that. But I doubt I could ever be as good as your sister." She was actually terrified of having to learn, because it certainly didn't look easy. But anything that threw her together with Rafe was worth trying.

So when the match had finished, with Victoria and Chas once more triumphant, Rafe dragged Lizzie onto the court while the others had refreshments.

"I'm not even dressed properly," she laughed.

"It doesn't matter. I'll just show you some of the basic moves and strokes for now," he said suggestively, standing close behind her and holding her hand as he demonstrated the forehand.

To show that she was a good sport, she laughed when she missed balls or shot them wildly out of bounds, even into the lake. But then she started to get the feel for it, and Rafe said, "You don't give up easily, do you?"

"Not when it's something I really want. Thanks for the lesson, Mr. Thornton. I'd like to learn more."

"It's Rafe. And I'll call you Lizzie, if I may."

"Of course." She smiled.

"How about another lesson tomorrow? I can always pick you up if the others are doing something else."

She looked directly into his eyes. "I'd like that."

But Chas arranged an impromptu dance for the young people that evening at Thorncliff, so Lizzie had plenty of opportunity to be with Rafe.

When she danced with Jack, Victoria said, "I wish Grandmother hadn't been so stubborn, and had had a chance to meet your sisters. She would have loved them. Of course, what I really wish is that your family hadn't been disowned at all. You should have been here with us every summer! Will you and the girls come and stay with Chas and me next summer? And your mother, of course. We'll have lots of room, with everyone else moving out."

"We'd all like to spend time here. Not Maman, perhaps. But thank you, Ria. I think it will be especially good for the girls, having a chance to be part of the larger family, having some fun instead of always working."

"Good! I'm looking forward to getting to know them better. It's rather odd, but I feel as if I know Lizzie from somewhere."

Jack chuckled to hide his consternation. "It's not likely that you two would ever have crossed paths."

"I know, and yet there's something about how she moves that's familiar."

"Perhaps it's like one of our cousins. Some sort of family trait."

"I expect so. She seems to be hitting it off with Rafe, but do keep an eye on her, Jack. Rafe can be a bit of a pill, especially when he's squiffed."

"I will, although Lizzie can take of herself." He was thankful that Victoria had dropped the topic of recognizing Lizzie.

Claire had been happily left at Wyndwood in the care of Esme, but Emily had been allowed to come. Chas asked her quietly if she'd treat them to a tune. She blushed but agreed. Max offered to play for her, and she entertained them to several songs, much to everyone's delight, including hers.

Felicity liked Jack's sisters, especially Emily, who wasn't much older than she, so the two of them spent time talking. Jack had primed his sisters well on the train trip up here about how much to say about their past.

No one dressed formally, so Lizzie was wearing one of the lacy tea gowns that Jack had bought her at Eaton's. It made her look rather demure and innocent. She knew exactly how she wanted to play Rafe, with a hint of naughtiness, but still a virtuous girl who would expect him to do the right thing by her when she finally allowed him to seduce her. So when she stepped onto the veranda with him, she allowed him one kiss and then put her finger to his lips and said, "That was nice, but I hardly know you." She leaned rather provocatively against a stone pillar as she said, "Jack tells me you're an expert on horses."

It was easy to keep him talking, and she allowed him another kiss, one filled with promise, before suggesting they rejoin the others.

Jack, meanwhile, had gone off to the pavilion with Eleanor. After a feverish session of kissing, he said, "I don't know how much more of this I can stand without making love to you."

"Why don't you?"

"Because I can't make you any promises. You've captivated me. I can't stop thinking about you, Ellie. But I don't know if that's love. And I can't go away leaving you wondering what there is between us." He was surprised at his own honesty, but he really didn't want to hurt her, and he sure as hell didn't want any sense of commitment between them.

"I don't need guarantees. I'm not looking to get married, not yet anyway. I have a career to consider. But I like you, Jack. I'd like us to be more than friends."

He could hardly believe it. "You're an amazing girl, Ellie." They arranged that she would canoe over to Wyndwood early in the morning, meeting him at Silver Bay.

"Come prepared," she told him. "I don't want to risk getting pregnant."

With her untamed wavy mane loose about her shoulders, Eleanor looked like she had stepped out of a Rossetti painting the following morning. When Jack told her, she laughed. "So now I'm a pre-Raphaelite beauty am I?"

"Definitely! Will you let me paint you? It'll also give me an excuse to see you."

"Yes, alright. I'll be interested in just how you *do* see me."

They walked hand in hand to the top of the Dragon's Back, Jack carrying a blanket.

"What a splendid view!" she said.

"And far enough from Ouhu that I won't feel your parents are watching us."

Now that they had come to the point of consummating their relationship, they took things slowly. Eleanor made sure that Jack had a condom. They were both more than ready when he finally took her.

"Christ, Ellie, you didn't tell me you were a virgin," he said to her as she lay in his arms afterwards. He didn't know why it bothered him, except that she might now feel he had some responsibility or obligations toward her.

"Does it matter? Aren't you pleased to be the first one? The one who's shown me how wonderful sex can be? It was bloody marvellous, by the way. And why did you think that I was experienced?"

"Because you exude an aura of sensuality. And you seem so comfortable with it."

"I never intended to be a repressed virgin. I was just waiting for the right man to come along. The problem is that I'm left wanting more of the same, and you'll soon be gone."

"You mean you won't wait for me to come back? You'll take another lover?"

"And you won't?"

"Touché. But she won't be like you. You really are special."

"Good. I don't want to be ordinary. And I don't want you to forget me." She kissed him, arousing him again.

"You really are a witch," he said. "You can wake the dead."

"What I really want is to paint you in the nude, so I can keep your tantalizing vision with me always," Jack whispered to her later that day when he arrived at Ouhu with his painting gear.

"I'm sure we can arrange that as well," she replied. "Tomorrow morning? After the main event?"

But Sunday morning brought a violent thunderstorm, so the Wyndhams didn't even go to church, but had family prayers in the sitting room, with James presiding. The rain had moved out by early afternoon, and the friends met at Thorncliff for tennis and dancing. With Augusta no longer keeping reigns on Sunday activities, the young people were given more freedom.

Jack managed to start his nude painting on Monday morning, finishing the other in the afternoon.

"Is that really how you see me?" Eleanor asked, examining the formal portrait which he gave her. He did another, smaller one, for himself..

"It's how the world sees you," Jack said.

"Surely only you. That's much too beautiful to be me."

"Strong, sensitive, sexy. That's definitely you, Ellie."

"Now I really am in danger of falling in love with you."

Having examined her intimately to paint her, Jack had to admit that he, too, was in danger of falling for her. She had a perfect body, well-proportioned, her pale skin flawless, save for a few freckles. He wondered how he could ever have thought her only mildly attractive. And sex with her was all-consuming.

When he had finished the nude, he said to her, "If ever I become a famous artist, people will look at this and wonder who this goddess is. And someone will discover that it's their doctor and be scandalized."

She laughed. "Then let's hope you never become a famous artist! By the way, Blake is wondering why I go canoeing so early every morning. I've told him I'm connecting with my inner self."

Jack laughed. "So now allow *me* to connect with your inner self." He was surprised at how much he enjoyed being with her. If only she were rich, he could happily spend his life with her. Unlike Chas, he found her sharp intelligence and crusading spirit stimulating rather than intimidating.

Lizzie, meanwhile, was keeping Rafe interested but not allowing him too many liberties. She would not be an easy conquest, she'd decided. He had been teaching her tennis with patience and humour, prompting Victoria to say to Chas, "Rafe seems in unusually good spirits these days."

"I think he's fallen for your cousin. He didn't even want to go off to the city with Pater this week."

"Maybe Lizzie will be good for him."

"You mean curb some of his vices? Let's hope so. Will you keep an eye on them while I'm gone? Make sure that Rafe doesn't take advantage of her?"

"You mean like his big brother did me?"

Chas laughed. "But I'm doing the honourable thing."

"Is that the only reason you're marrying me?"

"Of course not, muggins. It's because I can't keep my hands off you. And because I've always fancied Wyndholme."

"You're incorrigible!" Victoria laughed as Chas took her into his arms and kissed her tenderly.

"And most of all because I'm madly, completely, deeply in love with you." He kissed her again.

"Stop flaunting it, you two," Eleanor said as she and Jack came upon them.

"And what's your excuse for being here?" Victoria asked. They had wandered away from the tennis court to the diving cove.

"We thought it would be fun to have another swimming party here. Jack's sisters haven't done that yet."

"So you had to come and check, what exactly? The water temperature?" Chas asked wryly.

"Looking for our host. After all, we'll expect some food and drinks," Eleanor said. Jack was impressed with how easily she had improvised an excuse.

"Yes, why not," Chas said. "We may not have many more hot days this summer." The nights were cooler now and the days, less humid. Still, August had been hotter than usual as well.

So they all went home to fetch their swim suits. They scouted out the water for deadheads before anyone was allowed to jump or dive. This time Edgar was able to go into the lake. Eleanor and Blake, not happy with the way his ankle was healing, suggested he sit in the shallow water and just rest his foot. "Hydrotherapy," Eleanor said.

Rafe persuaded Lizzie to jump from the cliff. He offered to hold her hand and they jumped together. It was thrilling. She didn't object when Rafe pulled her close after one of their jumps. Emily and Claire were allowed to jump from a lower ledge, much to their delight. Victoria practiced her dives, graduating to the next scary level. Jack and Eleanor managed to escape around the bluff for a few passionate kisses.

They had a steak cookout at Sunset Point, but just for the young crowd this time. And afterwards, they danced to gramophone records in the pavilion. Jack made sure to pay some attention to Felicity, to keep her happy, but she noticed that he was spending more time than usual with Eleanor. But that wasn't a problem, as Eleanor was going to be a doctor, and wouldn't have time to be married. Married women were always at home looking beautiful and planning social events.

By the time Jack's sisters were supposed to return to the city, they had experienced a heady whirlwind of activities, including dinner and dancing at The Grand. Even Lizzie had thoroughly enjoyed herself and was reluctant to go back. Jack had been right in saying that it was completely different here as a guest. This life was so easy to get used to that she could understand his passion never again to settle for anything less. And neither would she.

"Must they go, Mama?" Esme asked Olivia. "They've hardly been here at all!" They'd just had a last swim at the back bay.

"Why do they have to go back so soon?" Olivia asked Jack.

He didn't really have a good explanation. He hadn't been sure how they would fit in or how desperate Lizzie would be to get back to the city, so he had thought that a week would be long enough. "They're supposed to help Maman prepare for boarders. And the wedding is on Saturday, and since they weren't invited..."

"Leave that to me. Oh, do let them stay! At least until after Labour Day," Olivia pleaded. That was the first Monday in September, which was the 7th this year, as late as it could get, and still eleven days away. Most summer people stayed at least that long, although many, like the Wyndhams, stayed well into September.

"I expect Maman could manage a few more days without them. What do you think, girls?"

Claire shrieked with joy as she and Esme hugged each other. "Could we really stay, Aunt Olivia?" Emily asked. "I've never been so happy!"

Lizzie said, "You are all so thoughtful and kind. This has been so much fun. It would be wonderful to stay longer."

Jack was proud of them all. He knew that Claire and Emily spoke from the heart, but Lizzie was also exhibiting proper social graces.

"I'll send Maman a telegram then," he said.

Helena agreed that three more young guests were welcome to the wedding. They were family, after all, she said.

Phyllis was not thrilled that they were staying, and Phoebe said, "I don't know why Molly thinks she's Jack's sister and can stay here. Just because she made her hair lighter."

"What are you on about, Phoebe?" Victoria asked. They were just getting ready for bed.

"Molly, our maid. She's calling herself Lizzie and sleeping in a guest room."

Victoria and Zoë looked at each other in puzzlement. "What makes you think that Lizzie is Molly?" Zoë asked.

"Because she looks like her. Except for the hair. Their eyes are the same."

"Lots of people have hazel eyes," Victoria said. "Emily does too."

"Resentful eyes. I notice eyes. They speak to me." They were like windows into the mind, to see the voices inside.

"Molly is shorter, with black hair, and she's Irish. And she's gone home to nurse her mother," Zoë said patiently.

"You two don't really know anything, do you?" Maryanne, the doll, turned one face to them and then the other.

# Chapter 19

The day before James and Helena's wedding was so stormy that the friends didn't even have a chance to see each other. Victoria thought she would go mad with longing. Tomorrow there would be no time to see Chas in the morning, because everyone would be up early to prepare for the wedding, and it would be hard for her to sneak away.

Being confined in the cottage with aunts and cousins, playing games, reading books, and listening to them playing piano and singing, Lizzie had second thoughts about staying. If this dragged on, she would soon be desperate to leave.

The wind sucked and blew as if determined to relocate the cottage. The walls shook, the windows rattled, smoke blew back down the chimney at times, for they had both fireplaces lit. And the thunder, when it came, tried to shatter the house with its pummelling noise. A barrage of lightning flashed almost continually. Even those not normally afraid were nervous.

Phoebe, of course, was under the piano, shrieking, which added yet another dimension of disquiet.

But when the storm receded, Phoebe gave another shrill scream and yelled, "Make her go away! Make her stop looking at me!" She was staring, petrified, at the empty wing chair that had been Augusta's favourite.

Augusta sat glaring at Phoebe, her eyes blazing like red hot coals, growing bigger until they threatened to obliterate her face. Phoebe screamed. "I'll be good! Don't let her get me. Make her go away!"

"Beebee dear!" Phyllis cried. "Whatever is the matter?" She got down on her knees beside the piano with difficulty.

"Oh, Mama! It's Grandmother! She's being mean and ugly and I can't help being scared by the storm, but she's staring so hard at me that her eyes are melting her face. Oh, Mama, make her go away! She's supposed to be in heaven, but she looks like she's crawled out of hell!"

Everyone looked over at Augusta's chair, although they knew it was empty. But Victoria sometimes wondered if mad people – for surely Phoebe was mad – were actually those who saw things through some sixth sense that others couldn't. It was an unsettling thought. Whatever Phoebe saw or thought she did was obviously horrific, and Victoria felt sorry for her. It was easy to dismiss her ramblings as nonsense, but she must be terribly frightened.

Victoria went deliberately to the armchair and sat down. She smiled at Phoebe and said, "I've told her to go away. It's my house now, and she's not to come back unless we invite her. Alright, Phoebe?"

Augusta had disappeared.

Phoebe scrambled out from under the piano and into her mother's arms, where she began sobbing.

Lizzie, who had seen some of this behaviour before, was not as shocked by it as her sisters.

"That poor child needs help," Olivia said. "How can you let her suffer like that?"

"I think it's high time that we have our own place," Phyllis said icily, "so we won't have to listen to your unwanted, ignorant opinions any longer! You think that your children are so perfect? Well, I would worry about them being corrupted if I were you, since they like to associate with Bohemians and other morally inferior people."

"I think you've said quite enough, Aunt Phyllis. We must be mindful of the other guests," Victoria said pointedly.

"Yes, and Augusta would be turning in her grave if she knew *they* were here. And as for *you*, Miss! You will *not* speak to me in that impertinent tone. Just because Augusta lost her senses and left you ten times more than your cousins, doesn't mean that a brazen troublemaker like you can tell *me* what to do! I am still your aunt, God help me!"

"That really is enough now, Phyllis," Richard said firmly, looking at Albert to curb his wife's venom. Albert looked away.

"Yes, I've put up with more than enough all these years. Come along, Beebee," Phyllis said. "We're going to summon Bayley to help us pack. We'll return to the city after the wedding. Things have changed too much around here for my liking. Come along Albert. Grayson can help you, Edgar."

"Mama, really! The summer's not over yet."

"It is for us."

"I've hardly had any because of this blasted foot!"

"You heard me!"

"Bloody hell!"

"And that's enough of *that* kind of language."

"If it weren't for this *bloody* leg, I'd *bloody* well go to war with the others!"

"Do as your mother says!" Albert ordered.

"Bloody hell!" Edgar swore as he stomped off with his cane.

"Oh dear," Beatrice said when they had left the room. "It does seem that relationships change within families when someone dies. It really will be good for all of you not to be living in each others' pockets all summer."

James came out of the study, and seeing the solemn faces, asked, "Have I missed something?"

The disintegration of a family, Victoria thought.

.    .    .

The day of the wedding dawned bright and clear, if somewhat cool. Oaktree was once more garlanded with flowers, but more sedately this time, in pink and white. As Helena had wanted to keep it simple, and had no family or friends from home to attend, there were fewer than a hundred guests.

The Grecian pillars alongside the terrace were draped in satin ribbons, beaded tulle, and masses of white roses. This was where the minister set up the altar.

Victoria had to admit that the bride looked lovely in ecru trained satin overlaid with cascading delicate white lace trimmed with embroidered gold flowers. Letitia had summoned her dressmaker from Pittsburgh to create the gown. Helena carried a bouquet of red roses and white lilies.

James could hardly believe how beautiful she looked. He had spent the past two weeks finding a house for them in Toronto, and thought that she would be pleased to be living in a fashionable enclave of newer houses close to the Eatons, Mackenzies, and Sir Henry Pellatt's Casa Loma, on the bluff overlooking the city. It was also quite a distance from Wyndholme.

Helena was delighted with how everything had turned out, even the weather finally co-operating, although the servants had had to start decorating before dawn, since they could do nothing yesterday. She had been genuinely touched and suitably grateful for Victoria's present, which the girl had delivered a few days ago. And hopeful that she would be able to get along tolerably well with her step-daughter. Even the new eight-bedroom house sounded wonderful, although it certainly wasn't on par with Wyndholme or their illustrious neighbours, from what she could gather. Still, it was a beginning. Tonight they would stay here. Tomorrow they would overnight at Wyndholme for the last time, and then go off to

New York for a month-long honeymoon. The new house would be theirs by the time they returned.

After the ceremony on the terrace, guests gathered around the bride and groom to offer congratulations and chat. An early dinner would be served in the ballroom later, followed by dancing, but for now, drinks and hors d'oeuvres were being passed around. An orchestra was starting up.

Letitia said brightly, "Oswald is so sorry that he couldn't be here today." He had returned to Pittsburgh shortly after war had been declared by Britain, to re-tool one of his factories. "He's been so busy setting up to produce armaments. He says one of the good things about being a neutral nation, other than not sending our young men off to war, of course, is that we have twice the market for our goods." She laughed delightedly.

"You mean he'll sell to Germany?" Victoria was appalled and outraged. "So they can use Oakley bullets and shells to try to kill Chas and Jack and Henry and Archie?"

"That's enough, Victoria!" James commanded. "That's business. You don't know what you're talking about."

"Leave it, Ria," Chas cautioned quietly, trying to draw her away. But she shook him off.

"Business? It's morally reprehensible! How can you live with the thought that your enormous profits are bought with the blood of your friends, Letitia?"

"It's your behaviour that's reprehensible!" James was livid. Helena put her hand on his arm as if to restrain his temper, but it made no difference. "How *dare* you try to spoil this day, insult our friends, embarrass our guests with your typically inconsiderate behaviour? You owe us all an apology!"

"I don't owe *you* anything! Letitia, I'm sorry for speaking my mind at such an inopportune time. Excuse me!"

As she ran away, Victoria heard Letitia say, "Oh dear, she is rather young still, isn't she."

Chas caught up to her near the dock. She tried to shrug him off but he held her firmly by the shoulders. "Ria, darling..."

She was fuming. "You all think this war is a game! Where the winner is the one who can make the most money or kill the most people!"

"Calm down, darling."

"How can I when everything is going to hell? You'd rather risk your life than stay with me!"

"That's not true. I don't want to leave you."

"Then why are you going? What are we really fighting for?"

"To stop oppression. We all have to do our bit."

"They don't need you, Chas. I do."

"If everybody believed that one person can't make a difference, then no one would go. I need to do this, Ria."

She turned away from him and said coldly, "Would you take me home, please?" When he hesitated, she said, "I'll bloody well swim if I have to!"

She didn't sit beside him, but at the back of his boat, hugging herself, afraid she might fly apart, explode with anger. Chas didn't take her home, but to Thorncliff.

She stayed in the boat. "I want to go home, Chas. I'm not good company right now. I might say something that I *will* actually regret."

"Like what? That you love me so much that you're terribly hurt to think I'm deserting you, just like your grandmother and father have?"

She burst into tears then, doubled over in her grief. Chas crouched down in front of her and took her hands in his.

"I'll be back soon, my darling. And one day, many years from now, you may think, *who is that tedious old codger who's forever by my side?*"

She laughed through her tears. "I hope you will be there! Oh, Chas, I'm so scared!" She was in his arms then, weeping against his shoulder.

He held her and soothed her until her tears were spent. Then he took her into the house. To the footman who greeted them, he said, "Bring a bottle of champagne to the morning room, Leonard, and ask chef to prepare a dinner for two to be served in the pavilion at half-past seven. And then you and the rest of the staff may have the time off until dinner."

"Yes, Mr. Chas."

After Leonard had delivered and poured the wine, Chas said, "Bring your glass, my darling, and follow me." He brought the bottle and led her upstairs.

She knew it was his room as soon as they entered. There were more trophies, and photos of teams – rowing, cricket – and just Chas, triumphant on the court, in his fencing gear, in his university gown.

"What are we doing here?' she asked hesitantly.

"We, my darling girl, are going to have an early honeymoon. Come here."

"Aren't you worried we'll be caught?"

"We won't be. The staff have been told not to bother us, and everyone else is at the wedding and will be until at least midnight."

Chas pulled the pins from her hair as he sang,

*Come to me, my melancholy baby*
*Cuddle up and don't be blue*
*All your fears are foolish fancies, maybe*
*You know, darling, I'm in love with you*
*Every cloud must have a silver lining*
*Just wait until the sun shines through*
*Smile, my darling Ria, while I kiss away each tear*
*Or else I shall be melancholy too.*

She laughed at the modified lyrics which made him pronounce "tear" with a strong British accent in order to rhyme with her name.

"That's better," he said.

Slowly he undressed her, kissing and caressing her as he went along.

"You're driving me mad," she said breathlessly.

"We have hours yet," he said.

This time she wouldn't let him use the French letter, and he hesitated only a moment before complying. It was more enjoyable for them both.

As she lay in his arms, she said, "Now I'll be able to picture you when I'm thinking about you in bed at night." The room had a splendid view of the lake, right from the bed.

"I was going to say that this is where we'll be every day next summer, but then I realized that we'll actually be at Wyndwood, won't we?"

"Just the two of us. And Josephine. And the servants. And maybe some guests. I've told Jack that he should bring his sisters up again. I feel sad that they've missed out on so much all these years."

"We've been lucky to grow up here."

"Yes, and to have so many good friends. I wonder why it took us so long to fall in love."

"I think I've always loved you, even when you were still in nappies."

She laughed. "You would hardly have been out of them yourself."

"It's taken me all these years to get beyond that image of you and realize you're a caring, intelligent, generous, courageous young woman who lights up my life."

She kissed him gratefully, and then said, "I'm glad you think so, since I seem to have alienated half my family and probably some friends." She told him what had transpired yesterday.

"Tempers will cool."

"I am sorry that I argued with Father on his wedding day. But I'm not sorry for speaking my mind. Letitia was positively glowing with pride and avarice. She was amused by it! Doesn't she realize that she's boasting about helping our enemy?"

"Germany is *our* enemy, though. Not theirs. The Americans see this war completely differently from how we do."

"And you think I should have kept my mouth shut."

"I think you were magnificent. You were just saying what many of us were thinking. I might have chosen a better time. But I think your apology covered that. Let me show you just how magnificent you are."

Much later they decided they had better get dressed and prepare for dinner. "It took Bayley ages to do my hair this morning," Victoria said, struggling to pin her curls into something not resembling a rat's nest. She had been reluctant to dismiss Bayley, Augusta's lady's maid, who had always helped the rest of them with gowns and hair anyway. "Now I shall look as if I've spent a naughty afternoon making love."

Chas laughed. "You look radiant. And you're tempting me all over again. Here, let me help."

At the pavilion they found an ice-bucket with more champagne awaiting them. "I thought this would be more intimate than the dining or morning room," Chas said, pouring her a glass.

"It's a lovely spot. You have a romantic soul, Chas."

He clinked glasses with her. "You inspire me."

The dinner was delectable, as usual. Then they danced long into the night. When Chas took her back to Wyndwood just before midnight, he stopped the boat so they could watch a brilliant display of northern lights.

"Do you think life will ever be like this again?" Victoria asked wistfully, watching the heavens undulate with green and then multi-coloured lights.

"It wouldn't be the same, even if there weren't a war."

"When I think of past summers, they seem more or less the same. Idyllic. I knew the moment that Jack whispered to Grandmother at The Grand, that this one would be different. But I know it's silly to blame him for all these changes. And how can I lament, when loving you is the most wonderful thing to ever have happened! Thank you, Chas, for being my friend as well as my lover, for making me feel cherished and needed, for taking such good care of me."

"I've made it my mission in life," he said, giving her a kiss, "so you can tell Zoë that I finally have a worthy calling."

She laughed.

Victoria was glad that the others hadn't yet returned as she prepared for bed. She didn't really feel like explaining herself. But when Zoë came into the bedroom a short while later, she knew that Victoria wasn't asleep. She sat down on Phoebe's empty bed – Phyllis had moved her into their room yesterday, and it had been odd not to have Phoebe and Maryanne beside her. Esme and Claire, who were getting along famously, had been allowed to move into the other guest room so that they could chatter without disturbing everyone else. So only Zoë and Victoria now shared this room.

"You were right," Zoë told her. "You said what the rest of us were too cowardly to."

"You mean too polite to."

"Ellie thought you were superb. She doesn't much like Letitia anyway – thinks she's a bit of an empty-headed fashion plate. But it's sometimes hard to balance social obligations with personal convictions."

"You were all too nice to walk out and abandon Father on his wedding day. But his hot-headed, irresponsible daughter wasn't, of course."

"At least you don't feel like a hypocrite. Papa says if we examined business practices too closely, we'd all be a lot poorer. That we shouldn't malign Oswald or think that he is trying to undermine our side in this war."

"It's just business," Victoria said snidely. "I was wrong to ever think that I could be involved in business then! Chas said that our investments in Flavelle's pork packing business will be hugely profitable. That we'll be benefiting through dozens of other investments that we've made. But at least we're providing supplies for our troops."

"But if we took the moral high ground, we probably wouldn't have many investments. I think Papa is right."

"Well, I wouldn't want to be poor, to give up all this. So I'm a hypocrite after all."

"No, just a realist. But we need to do whatever good we can with the bounty we do have available to us."

"And so I shall!"

"So what did you do all day?"

"I was with Chas at Thorncliff. We had a wonderfully romantic evening. He says I'm to tell you that his mission in life is to look after me."

Zoë laughed. "Well, that's certainly a step in the right direction. I am glad that you have him, Ria."

"I wish he weren't going away so soon."

When, a few days after the wedding, they couldn't make love because Victoria had her courses, Chas was mightily relieved, which puzzled her until he told her it meant that she wasn't pregnant. How ignorant she was of such things!

But how difficult those five days were when she knew how little time they had left. They still met at the Shimmering Sands, but Chas now brought two blankets, as the mornings were chilly. Sandwiched between them, they lay in each others' arms, talking and kissing and planning their future.

During the last week of summer, the builders started on Richard's cottage at Silver Bay, so Jack and Eleanor met at one of the Silly Isles for their morning rendezvous. Jack's sisters were taken on excursions and picnics, improved their canoeing skills, and Lizzie began to enjoy tennis. She was also quite sure that she had Rafe interested. She had managed to keep him from pawing her too much, but had allowed him a few searing kisses so that he was now constantly at her side. She felt immensely powerful.

But the summer was drawing to a close. Because of the war and so many heads of households having already gone home to ramp up war production, there was no Labour Day ball. The Fremonts would have hosted it this year. Instead, there was a small gathering at Thorncliff for the island friends, and even among them the numbers had dwindled.

Letitia sent her regrets, saying that she was packing to go home. They wondered if she felt awkward among her Canadian neighbours just now. Eleanor didn't give her that much credit for sensibility or sensitivity. But they all wondered if Letitia had ever done anything as mundane as pack anything herself.

Edward and Simon Carrington had come back only for the wedding, having left soon after war had been declared, to secure government contracts and re-engineer their mills. No one really needed carpets when the troops required blankets and uniforms.

Senator Spencer had hurried to Ottawa in early August. Archie and Henry were in the camp at Valcartier, in Quebec, with the tens of thousands of other volunteers.

Albert and his family were back in Toronto. J.D. managed to return to Thorncliff for the long weekend.

Richard, Olivia, and the children were now among the few who were actually staying beyond the weekend, unlike other summers when most of them stayed until late September. They were eager to oversee the building of their new cottage. Their own servants would be up for the duration, while the Wyndholme staff returned to the city. Freddie Spencer would stay with them as well, to supervise the first few weeks of construction, as his mother was closing the cottage early.

Zoë heard that she had been accepted at the university, having applied after it was evident there would be no European trip. She was thrilled. Her parents were allowing her to live in the university women's residence, since it was too far to travel daily to home. She could hardly wait! Max would be living on campus, of course, as well as Freddie and Justin, while Eleanor and Blake lived nearby. It was too exciting!

Jack and his sisters left on the Tuesday, along with the Carlyles, as the Professor had to return to work. University classes didn't actually commence until the end of the month, which gave the students another few weeks of freedom. Justin was helping his mother and sisters close the cottage.

Chas said that he had to pack and put his affairs in order, so he planned to leave on Thursday. Victoria and Beatrice decided to go with him. She and the boys were due to leave for New York on the following Monday, to set sail for Liverpool on the Thursday. Marjorie Thornton decided to close the cottage early as well.

So on Wednesday, Chas and Victoria went to visit Edelina. They had last been to The Colony to tell her about their engagement. She had been genuinely pleased for them.

Now there were only Father Paul, Frieda, and Gil, the scarred handyman, left. Anton was trying to make his way back to Russia. Laszlo had gone to the States, where Hungarians were not the enemy. No one else was staying.

"Which is unfortunate," Edelina said, "because the autumn is the most beautiful time here." Already the maples were changing to crimson, orange, and gold.

"Is it because of the war?" Chas asked.

"Not because they've volunteered to go," Edelina replied with a laugh. "Some of them just don't want to be associated with the enemy."

"You're not the enemy!" Victoria said indignantly. "You were born here. You're more Canadian than some of them, I'm sure."

Edelina smiled sadly. "Oh, I don't think they bear me any ill-will or hostility or think me a potential spy. But people have reputations to maintain, especially if they are just starting out. It might not be politic to hang about with someone with such an obvious German name as mine, and a German servant who can barely speak English. An enemy alien, Frieda's called."

"I can't believe people can be so small-minded," Victoria said. "Especially as we like to think that artists and poets are free thinkers."

"Who still have to make a living. They haven't all abandoned me, of course. Not my real friends. Quite frankly, some of the others are merely dilettantes who have no serious conviction to art or to anything other than self-important posturing. I'm happy I no longer have to feed them!"

"Well, I hope that no one causes you any problems, Edelina," Victoria said. "You will let me know if I can help? When are you going back to the city?"

"The end of October. Then Paul and I are off to India until March – as long as we don't have any problems getting there. Gil and Frieda will look after each other while we're gone."

Before they left, Edelina gave them each a warm hug. To Chas she said, "Please take care of yourself, my friend."

"And you."

Judging by the meaningful look that passed between them, Victoria was convinced they had been lovers. She was irrationally jealous, considering Chas had committed himself to her. Anything that had happened between him and Edelina had been before he and Victoria had acknowledged their love. But she hated to think that Chas had treated any other woman like he did her. Yet she had also been aware that he was an experienced lover. It was probably best never to know about his previous affairs.

When they met at the Shimmering Sands the next morning, their lovemaking was bittersweet.

"God, I'm going to miss you!" Chas said. "I must be mad to leave you."

"I think so." But she knew there was no use in trying to persuade him to change his mind. They'd been through that too many times before. "I made this for you, so that you don't forget," she said, handing him the painting of the Shimmering Sands. "I didn't make it too big, so that you could take it along easily."

"It's beautiful, my darling. You're getting very good. Thank you. Although I could never forget. Any of this."

Because of the hot summer, the lake was still relatively warm. They had their last swim as the early morning mist danced across the still water.

That evening, Victoria, Beatrice, and a playful Josephine were ensconced in the large emptiness of Wyndholme.

Victoria planned a going-away dinner party for Chas, Jack, and Beatrice on Saturday evening. All the Thorntons would be able to attend, as well as the Carlyles, and Jack and his sisters. And a grateful Edgar – Victoria didn't invite the rest of his family.

On Friday, Victoria and Beatrice dined at Thornridge. The estate was in the countryside north of Rosedale, but easily accessible by automobile. It was an impressive, rambling stone house with thirty-five rooms, seventeen fireplaces, and an elevator. Formal gardens, a tennis court, a private nine hole golf course, and extensive stables and paddocks were scattered among the thousand acres of grounds. Bridle paths led through the rolling woodlands and down into and through the Don Valley ravine.

Chas showed them his awesome collection of paintings, which he had brought back from Europe. Monet, Renoir, Cezanne, Van Gogh, Sisley, Klimt, Picasso. "I'll hang yours next to them," he said to Victoria. "So keep painting."

Beatrice was interested in the stables, where Kate was happy to give her a tour. Chas took Victoria for a stroll through the terraced rock garden that dropped two hundred feet to the river, where the Thorntons had a boathouse and a small summerhouse. As soon as they were inside, they kissed frantically.

"Damn this war!" Chas said. "Rowing on the river this morning I was thinking I would much rather have been making love to you on the beach."

"Can we spend tomorrow and Sunday together?"

"Every minute. Let's go riding tomorrow. Cousin Bea will like that as well. And you and I will go for a row. And Sunday we can play golf and tennis, and you can join us for dinner again."

And Monday he would leave. Victoria couldn't bear to think that it would be many long and lonely months before she'd be in his arms again. She viciously pushed away thoughts that she might never be.

To keep from breaking down, to not destroy their last precious days together by being melancholy, Victoria made a supreme effort to regain the light-hearted, flirtatious mood they had so long enjoyed in their relationship.

With forced gaiety she said, "So you're going to take me for a row, row, row, way up the river, are you?" Referring to the suggestive lyrics of the song.

Chas laughed, and started to sing, as he twirled her about.

*And then he'd row, row, row, way up the river*
*He would row, row, row. A hug he'd give her,*
*Then he'd kiss her now and then, she would tell him when,*
*He'd fool around and fool around, and then they'd kiss again,*
*And then he'd row, row, row, a little further*
*He would row, oh, oh, oh, oh.*
*Then he'd drop both his oars, take a few more encores,*
*And then he'd row, row, row.*

"How can you remember all the lyrics to the songs?" Victoria asked with amusement as he dipped her and brought her back into a seductive hug.

"I have little else to fill my empty head."

"Stop! I won't have anyone, not even you, insulting my fiancé like that."

Chas laughed. This time their kiss was less anguished.

Beatrice wholeheartedly approved of their plans for the next two days. She was an accomplished equestrian, and had been impressed by the Thornton's horses, as well as by Rafe's passion for them and knowledge of breeding.

But Victoria was astonished when Chas presented her with her mount after their ride the next day. He was a splendid chestnut, well-tempered, but lively.

"I've bought him from Rafe. You can keep him here if you like. But he's yours, my darling. You and Fliss can go for rides. His name is Calypso."

"Like our dear old boat! He's beautiful! Oh, thank you, Chas!" She threw her arms around him, despite their audience.

"An expensive beast, I'd say," Beatrice remarked astutely.

"Rafe knows what he's doing. Unfortunately, he's not such a good judge of horseflesh when it comes to the races," Chas said.

Felicity, who had gone with them, said, "*Will* you come riding with me, Ria?"

"Of course! I'm looking forward to it. Your wonderful but sly brother is trying to make amends for not being here himself." She looked at Chas askance. "But even though this lovely horse is not a particularly good substitute for him, I will enjoy his company as much as I can. And yours, of course."

"I'm so excited that you're going to be my sister!" Felicity exclaimed.

"So am I!" Victoria replied, suddenly realizing that. "I've always wanted a sister. This *is* a bonus." She took Felicity's arm in hers as they strolled back to the house and said, "We should do lots of things together this winter, so we don't miss Chas too much."

When she and Chas went for their row, he said, "Thank you for being so attentive to Fliss."

"You don't have to thank me, Chas. I like her enormously, and I'm truly thrilled that she's going to be my sister."

"She doesn't have a lot of friends. Mumsy is somewhat vague, and certainly not good company for a child. Rafe will be here this year, but is too busy with his own pursuits. Pater is rarely around."

"Then I can sympathize. If it were up to me, she could move into Wyndholme."

"Now that she's growing up, she needs some compassionate guidance."

"I shall look after her with great pleasure, have no fear. And you *are* sly. Trying to find ways to keep me occupied."

"I want to be sure that you don't have time for a romantic dalliance."

"Even the Prince of Wales wouldn't interest me. And I understand he's quite a charmer."

"I knew him at Oxford. He was in Magdalen College too, but behind me in years."

"Did you?"

"Yes, my darling girl. And he's interested in aeroplanes as well. But I don't suppose the King will allow him to join the Royal Flying Corps."

The party at Wyndholme that evening was a cheerful affair, despite its purpose – to say goodbye.

Victoria sent the Rolls to pick up Jack and the girls, and they were the first to arrive. When she gave them a tour of the house, Lizzie made sure she was as amazed and awed by it as her sisters. She also made sure she was at her most charming, knowing she needed to impress Rafe's parents as well as him.

Edgar still hobbled and complained about his ankle, so he was treated to a medical consultation.

Blake said, "There's probably some calcification of the ankle joint."

"And what does that mean?"

"That you won't be going to war," Eleanor said.

"You mean I'm a cripple?" Edgar was aghast.

"The joint will loosen up a bit," Blake said. "You have to exercise it. Perhaps try some of that new physiotherapy. But I suspect you'll always have some problems with it."

"Terrific!" Edgar said sarcastically. "Now I don't even have an excuse to get away from home."

"You can come and keep me company sometimes," Victoria said. "It's going to be very quiet here." And Zoë wouldn't be just around the corner anymore.

"Yes, alright. But bloody hell, I wanted to join the RFC as well!"

"You'll have to stick to boat racing," Chas said.

"I'm having one built, did I tell you? Twenty-eight feet with a 6 cylinder, 135 horsepower Niagara engine."

"135 horsepower! Good God."

"Fat chance you'll have of beating me in the Regatta next year. I'll likely get her up to thirty miles an hour."

"Won't that be a little fast for Aunt Phyllis?" Victoria asked with amusement.

"Papa's ordered a launch for the family. This beauty is all mine. *Firefly*, I'm calling her."

"Why is it that boats are female?" Eleanor wanted to know.

"Because men are so enamoured of them and devoted to them," Chas said.

"Because men can control them," Edgar said.

"And since they *have* no control over women, the boat becomes a substitute," Eleanor said. "That makes sense."

They all laughed.

"I, on the other hand, have complete control over my new male," Victoria said, and told them about Calypso.

"And here I thought you meant me," Chas said. "And I was going to agree with you." He gave her a warm smile.

"Are you bringing him here?" Rafe asked.

"No, we haven't had horses since Grandmother gave up riding to hounds ten years ago, and I outgrew my pony. We don't even have carriage horses anymore, since we got the Rolls. So will you look after him for me?"

"Yes, of course."

"You must come and see us as often as you like, my dear," Marjorie said to Victoria. "I just can't imagine you here all on your own, you poor child!"

"Chas has promised to be back soon. And perhaps Fliss will come and stay with me sometimes."

"I'm sure she'd like that. Where is she?"

"I think she and Emily and Claire are in the tower," Victoria said, for the girls had asked permission to go up. "They all seem fascinated by it."

Mrs. Hadley had outdone herself with a splendid dinner. Grayson seemed happy to be back, and ensured that everything went smoothly, as usual.

Earlier that day, he had said to Victoria, "Mrs. Grayson and I are tremendously grateful for Mrs. Wyndham's generous bequest to us." She had left them each three thousand dollars.

"It is our intention to return to England and buy a small establishment in Cornwall, to run an inn or seaside hostelry." They had come from England specifically to work for the Wyndhams. Augusta had not been happy with the quality of servants here, and had posted an ad in the *London Times*. That had been twenty years ago.

"In the present circumstances, we will not, of course, leave you alone, Miss Victoria. We feel that we are acting *in loco parentis*, so to speak." He'd seemed pleased to use the Latin phrase. "But should circumstances change – once you and Mr. Thornton are married, for instance – we would like you to know that we will tender our resignations, with deep regret."

"Thank you, Grayson. I am grateful that you will be staying with me for the time being. I can't imagine how this house would run without you and Mrs. Grayson. But I certainly appreciate your position, and would be grateful if you were to begin grooming others to replace you. You've had no luck with a new footman?"

"Unfortunately, no one who meets our standards. So many young men are going overseas. But we shall keep trying. Thank you, Miss Victoria."

After dinner, they persuaded Emily to sing, and some of them sang along as Chas played tunes on the piano. Dancing wasn't really appropriate with so few of them, although Victoria wanted nothing more than to be in Chas's arms.

But she suddenly had an idea. She drew Eleanor aside. "I want you to be honest, Ellie. Are you and Jack in love?"

"Why do you want to know?"

"Because time is short, and they're leaving us. I thought we could go to New York to see them off. I'll pay."

"Then I'm coming!"

Chas was delighted when Victoria told him. "You and Ellie will be alright, getting home by yourselves?"

"Of course! We are modern women who can manage to look good *and* follow a train schedule at the same time."

"Very droll. But women who look as good as you two need to be careful."

"Don't worry!"

On Sunday evening, Victoria and Beatrice dined at Thornridge again, this time joined by Jack and Eleanor.

"Hell's bells," Eleanor said when they arrived. Chas had sent his chauffeur to pick them up. "If I'd known Chas had all this, I might have tried harder to get him to fall in love with me!"

"That doesn't sound like you, Ellie," Jack said, stung.

"I'm trying hard not to be materialistic, but hell, this kind of affluence is terribly seductive. I could see running at least half of this estate as a home for orphans or unwed mothers."

Jack laughed. "Have you never been here?"

"No, we don't associate with the Muskoka crowd during the rest of the year. Except for Olivia's family. We're not 'in the swim', as they say. I'm not saying that Chas is a snob – he's been away at Oxford for four years, and at boarding school before that. But our families don't have much in common, do they? Especially not money. I can't even afford to dress properly for these sorts of occasions. I'm lucky if I can manage something off the rack from Eaton's."

"I think you look delectable."

"That's because you don't even see the dress, but are anticipating me being out of it."

He laughed. "I wish I could manage that! There's no more time. I'm going to miss you, Ellie."

"Me or the sex? No, don't even answer. I don't want to hear any lies."

"Sex wouldn't be half as much fun with anyone else."

Jack, too, was impressed by Thornridge, and more determined than ever to keep Felicity infatuated. To that end, he made sure to be solicitous, and told her how happy his sisters had been in her company yesterday.

"I'm so excited that they're going to be my cousins soon!" she said.

Jack also talked to J.D., asking him to buy several hundred acres of the adjacent property for him once his inheritance was available. Jack was convinced that it would be a terrific investment, since the lands weren't far north of the ever-expanding city.

It was an eager group that took the train to New York early on Monday. They stayed at the elegant Waldorf=Astoria hotel on Fifth Avenue. Victoria and Eleanor were next door to Beatrice, while Chas and Jack were across the hall.

They spent a heady, delightful day at Luna Park on Coney Island, awed by the extravagance of its Oriental architecture, with

over 2000 towers and minarets, its Hanging Gardens of Babylon
with tens of thousands of plants, the Japanese Roof Garden,
dozens of buildings and rides. They caroused on carousels and
ferris wheels, on flying swings and roller coasters. They rode
elephants and watched ostriches race against bicycles and horses.
They plummeted down a water chute into a lagoon, and careened
about the Dragons' Gorge. They stopped at the Musical Flower
Garden to admire the blooms, which surprised them by bursting
into song.

Eleanor said, "They remind me of Chas, always breaking into
song." They all laughed as Chas sang along with the flowers.

They dined on hot dogs, Coca Cola, and ice cream cones.

By late afternoon, Beatrice declared that she could no longer
keep up with them, and settled herself into the Parisian Café with
a gin and tonic while the young people had Tango lessons at
Vernon Castle's Summer Dance Hall. They all dined in the Casino
Ballroom, and danced some more as the one and a half million
park lights blazed into the night sky.

On Wednesday they visited the Statue of Liberty, Central
Park, and the Metropolitan Museum of Art. After a fine dinner in
their hotel, they attended a whimsical play, starring Douglas
Fairbanks, on Broadway.

It wasn't yet eleven when they returned to the hotel, and no
one except Beatrice was ready for this last day to end. She agreed
to join them for a drink in the ballroom before retiring. On their
way there they had an unexpected encounter.

"Father! Helena," Victoria said in surprise. "Are you staying
here?" He had never told her, and after the incident at the
wedding, she hadn't asked the rest of the family.

"We are. And what are you doing here?" James asked coldly.

Chas had put his arm about Victoria to lend his support, and
she was grateful, for she felt suddenly nervous. She hadn't
communicated with her father at all since running away from the
wedding. "Eleanor and I are seeing Chas and Jack and Cousin
Beatrice off. They're leaving tomorrow."

"I wish you luck, chaps," James said, shaking their hands.
"Knowing you, Chas, I expect you'll do yourself proud and come
home with a chestful of medals. And Beatrice, we hope you'll come
to visit us again."

"Oh yes, do!" Helena added. It was always good to have
aristocratic relatives to flaunt.

Victoria noticed how elegant Helena looked. She was wearing
a stunning velvet opera cloak, heavily beaded and trimmed in fur.

"I should like that, but I hope my next visit won't be quite as eventful," Beatrice said. "I trust you've had a good stay in New York?"

"It's been heavenly!" Helena said, smiling fondly at James. He had taken her shopping for jewellery, furs, and an expensive new wardrobe. They dined in the finest restaurants, saw shows on Broadway, and took rides through Central Park. James was an ardent if not considerate lover. He seemed determined to create a son.

Chas said, "Will you join us for a drink?"

"Thank you, no," James said. "I think we're ready to retire. Safe journey. Good night."

Victoria sagged against Chas, hurt that her father hadn't even asked about her plans, or suggested they get together the following day. Of course she shouldn't have expected it, for he was obviously still angry with her.

Into the awkward silence of their departure, Beatrice said, "I hope that marriage mellows James. Before it's too late, I hope that he realizes how lucky he is to have you as a daughter, Victoria."

She forced back tears at the kind words, clinging to Chas's arm as they went into the ballroom.

Helena meanwhile, was pleased that there was no reconciliation between father and daughter, even though she felt that James was a bastard for treating Victoria so harshly. But Helena didn't want her children to have to share any of James's fortune with Victoria. So she would make sure that that rift never healed completely. And also that James had children, even if it was necessary for someone else to father them.

In the ballroom, Chas ordered a magnum of Moët champagne.

Jack realized that the wine cost as much as most men earned in a week, and wondered if he would ever spend money so freely, even if he did have the Thorntons' immense wealth.

When Beatrice had finished her glass, she said, "I'm off to my bed. I don't believe in people your age having chaperones. You're old enough to know what you're doing. But I trust you will look after one another. We have an early start, so we'll meet for breakfast at seven."

When they danced, Chas said to Victoria, "I'm sorry your father hasn't forgiven you."

"I shouldn't expect anything else. He will demand an abject apology before condescending to tolerate my presence. But I'm damned if I'm going to give it!"

"I worry about you, my darling. Being all alone."

She told him that Olivia and Richard would be looking out for her, and what Grayson had said.

Chas laughed. "*In loco parentis*! Then I'm mightily relieved, because I believe that Grayson is a man of his word. I'm sorry he wants to return to England. I would have been happy to have him as our butler until he was old enough to be put out to pasture. He wished me luck, did you know, and said that it was men like me who made our empire great. I was touched."

Victoria's senses were heightened by the realization that this would end too soon. She was acutely aware of the long, sensitive fingers that entwined hers, of the gentle smile that reached his expressive eyes. He could seduce her just by looking at her. And she had an idea.

When they sat down to another glass of champagne, she whispered to Eleanor, "Would you do me a tremendous favour and stay here with Jack for a while?"

"Slinking off for a bit of sex, are you?"

"Ellie! Don't think badly of me, but..."

"Jack and I are not averse to a bit of sex ourselves. So I'll go to his room and Chas can come to ours. I suppose we need to be back in our rooms before dawn. Shall we say five o'clock? Don't look so shocked."

"Oh, Ellie! Thank you!"

"Not at all. I can hardly wait!"

They went up together and paired off without being seen. When they were in her room, Chas said, "I don't have any protection."

"Good! I want you all to myself, with nothing between us."

They took things slowly, savouring their last few hours together. Victoria was determined not to miss a moment with Chas, but, when she awoke with a start, she was surprised to find she had drifted off to sleep.

Chas said reassuringly, "It's alright. We still have an hour."

"I didn't mean to fall asleep. But what a luxury to wake up in your arms."

"You're not the witch you warned me you might be."

"That's because you were right. You said I wouldn't be with you beside me." How long ago that flippant conversation at the Midsummer Night's Dream party seemed. Too much had changed since then. "Chas, are you frightened at all? Don't be manly or chivalrous and make light of things to protect me. I want to know what you're truly feeling."

"I'm excited. Terrified. And dreadfully unhappy to be leaving you."

They made love again, desperately this time. Victoria couldn't stop her tears. Chas kissed them away, saying, "You've been terribly brave, my darling."

"Oh, Chas, I love you so much! Please come back to me."

"I will, Ria."

They had agreed that Eleanor would come to their room at five, and then Chas would sneak back to his. He was dressed when she quietly walked in, looking rather dishevelled.

"Don't say anything," she said to him. "It would only make me laugh, and I'm not in the mood. It seems so easy for you men to go off to become heroes in some vague war that none of us really understands. So I'm not about to forgive you at this moment. I need some sleep before I can deal with this."

But she and Victoria didn't sleep.

When Chas had gone, Victoria said, "I didn't realize that you and Jack were so close."

"It came as rather a surprise to me as well."

"Are you...?"

"Engaged? No. Ever going to get married? Perhaps. But probably not. Do I love him? Yes. But not to the exclusion of all else, like my career." She suddenly threw her arms about Victoria and said, "I don't really know what I'm doing!"

"Do any of us?"

They were at Cunard's Pier 54 well before nine, for the ten o'clock sailing, having sent their luggage on ahead.

"Hell's bells! It looks like a large block of New York City broke loose and floated in here," Eleanor said of the massive ship with four tall funnels.

"She's almost 800 feet long," Chas told them. "And was the first liner to make the crossing from New York to Liverpool in under five days."

Taking a tour of the *Lusitania*, they were even more impressed.

"It's a floating palace!" Eleanor exclaimed when they saw the double-tiered, gilt and white first-class dining room in the style of Louis XVI with an ornate domed ceiling and fluted marble columns. A Regency smoking room, panelled in walnut, also had a stained glass dome. An Adam-style writing room and library had walls hung in silk brocade.

Their gilded staterooms were princely, with marble bathrooms, a separate parlour, with a fireplace in Beatrice's rooms, and porthole windows overlooking the Boat Deck. Chas and Jack shared a suite. Jack was astounded by the luxury, and grateful that Chas was paying the enormous sum that was practically a year's salary for him.

It was another wrench for Victoria, thinking that this was supposed to have been her and Zoë's suite. She and Chas should be going to Europe together now.

Beatrice left them alone to say their goodbyes.

"She's beautiful, but is she safe?" Victoria want to know.

"Virtually unsinkable," Chas assured her.

"That's what they said of the *Titanic*," she reminded him.

"The Cunard line has never lost a ship, which definitely can't be said of any of its competitors."

"But what about this talk of German submarines?" A British naval ship had been torpedoed just two weeks earlier.

"They're not after passenger liners. Anyway, the *Lusitania* can outrun anything else on the seas. I'll send you a telegram when we arrive. And you send me one when you get home."

Chas took her into his arms and gave her a lingering kiss.

She clung to him as the "all-ashore" gong sounded.

"I love you, Ria. Always remember that."

She didn't want his last image of her to be of her misery, so she smiled brightly and said, "And you remember that we have to defend our canoeing victory in the Regatta next summer."

"Indeed I will."

The ship's band was playing *It's a Long Way To Tipperary*. She hugged Beatrice and Jack and then she and Eleanor were standing on the busy pier as the *Lusitania* backed into the Hudson River, accompanied by three tremendous blasts of her horn. They waved, along with the hundreds of others on the pier, and now it no longer mattered that tears were streaming down her face.

When they could no longer be seen by those on board, Eleanor put her arms around her and said, "Men are such fools. They don't know when they should be satisfied. They're little boys who constantly need adventures."

"Is that all this is, an adventure?"

"Justified by patriotism and some noble sentiments about defending freedom. Hell, war is just stupid! Come along. We need to keep busy."

Victoria was no longer in the mood for sightseeing, so Eleanor suggested they do some early Christmas shopping. Victoria bought wrist watches for almost everyone at Cartier, the jeweller on Fifth

Avenue. Despite Eleanor's protests, Victoria bought one for her as well, as a souvenir of their trip to New York.

They had an early dinner, and then boarded the overnight train for Toronto. Although they had a sleeper berth, they didn't sleep much, but spent most of the time talking.

Victoria sent Chas a telegram saying, "Home safely, but sadly. All my love, Ria."

And Wyndholme seemed exceptionally empty now, with not even Beatrice visiting.

A telegram arrived for her later that evening. It read simply, "Meet me tonight in dreamland, my darling."

# Chapter 20

My Darling Ria,

It's a gentle day here at Bovington Abbey. I had a long row on the river this morning, imagining you sitting in the boat with me. Instead there was a dragonfly, which Cousin Bea says is not at all common, as on our lake, and most unusual for this time of year. I expect it is one of your fairy folk that you have sent to watch over me. It stayed with me for quite some time, which was strangely comforting.

Let me tell you a bit about Cousin Bea's delightful country estate on the Thames, near Marlow, so you can picture us here. Bovington is a Tudor manor house that was once part of the monastic enclave of the real abbey, which was destroyed after the Dissolution of the Monasteries by naughty old Henry VIII. Jack is astonished by its great age and charmed by its ambiance, as am I. It even has a ghost, whom I have yet to meet. Lovely gardens and park-like lawns slope down to the river, where there's a small boathouse – don't picture our big ones on the lake! – and dock – ditto. There's a grass tennis court which we've already used, and stables with several fine horses. How fortunate we are to have such a generous and amiable cousin to take us in. She says that Bovington Abbey and her London townhouse are open to us anytime we have leave, and she includes any of her new Muskoka friends in that invitation. I believe she mentioned it to Archie, and, of course, Henry, before they left. I wonder when they will arrive with the Canadian Expeditionary Force.

It seems that Cousin Bea has a friend in _very_ high places, who may not be mentioned by name, but who has agreed to put in a word for us with the RFC recruiters. I do have my connection as well, of course, but as there is no reference for Jack, we need other strings to pull. A lot of chaps are trying their luck, and those who are already commissioned officers have the first crack. There aren't enough aeroplanes or instructors to accommodate us all. In the meantime, I've found a civilian flying school nearby, so Jack and I will be getting some training, which must surely give us a leg up.

Your cousin, Lord Cedric Devenish, thinks it's a great lark and wants to join us. Wasn't he surprised when I told him that I was engaged to his Canadian cousin, and brought another along with

*me! The three of us are going to visit him this weekend. Cousin Bea
says its been a while since she's seen the family.*

*I've been trying to picture what you've been doing, and
speculate that you may have gone back to the cottage. I miss you,
my darling. You're never out of my thoughts or dreams. I already
have a list of things I intend to show you, and do with you (other
than the obvious, which I am longing to do!) when we are here
together – perhaps on the first leg of our honeymoon? Take care, my
darling.*

*Love, Chas*

He was right to think that she had gone back to Muskoka for
another week. Richard and his family were there for most of the
time, and then the Graysons brought the staff up to close the
cottage, so she stayed as long as she could. She painted some
autumn scenes, including one of the pavilion at Thorncliff,
surprising the caretaker and his wife, who, like Toby, over-
wintered there in their own small house behind the main cottage.
They brought her tea and admired her painting, which she told
them was a present for Chas. She did another one for the
Thorntons.

She visited Edelina, staying for a simple but companionable
dinner. Frieda sat down with them, which Victoria thought highly
unusual. But she was able to converse with her in German, which
delighted the older woman and impressed Edelina.

"I was good at languages in school," Victoria explained. "I can
speak French quite well, and German and Italian, tolerably. Our
trip was to have given us practice as well as allowing us to explore
the museums and see the sights."

Sensing her profound sadness, Edelina said, "I'm sure that
you will see Chas again. But I know it must be very hard for you."

"I also feel rather lost. I don't know what to do with myself. Of
course, I'll do some war work – raising money for the Patriotic
Fund, that sort of thing. But it doesn't seem like enough. I'm
actually beginning to understand why Chas wanted to go. But I
don't suppose they allow women there, except for nurses, and
that's something I couldn't do, and it takes time to learn anyway."

"I doubt that Chas would let you go," Edelina said. "He'd want
you out of danger."

"I welcome danger at the moment! I feel so restless! So
useless!"

Once she was back in Toronto, Victoria rode with Felicity
frequently. She was a day student at the same private girls' college

that Victoria and Zoë had attended, and where Esme now was. It was only a few blocks from Wyndholme, but Felicity had to be chauffeured to and from school daily, so Victoria sometimes picked her up on the way to Thornridge.

Rafe had decided not to continue his university career, so he was often in the stables, and seemed a different person there. More personable and certainly capable. Victoria warmed to him a little.

One day he said to her, "Calypso really is a splendid horse. I'd like to breed from him. I'll pay you stud fees."

"By all means."

"Do you see much of your cousins? Jack's sisters?"

She had found singing, dancing, and acting classes for Emily, and paid for her to attend them. But all that had been done via letter, since they didn't have a telephone, and Victoria hadn't yet been to visit. "No, but I really should."

"I believe I promised Lizzie that I would teach her to ride. So you might consider bringing her along one of these days."

"I'll certainly ask her. You will be kind to her, Rafe? She's not used to the ways of society, to the flirtations and such. I wouldn't want to see her get hurt."

Rafe laughed heartily. "You and Chas really were meant for one another! He said almost the same thing to me before he left. It seems that neither of you trusts me." He looked at her challengingly.

"I recall occasions when I've had to curtail your, shall we say, ardour?"

"You should be flattered that I find you, shall we say, alluring?" he mocked.

What she saw in his dark eyes for a brief moment was a frustrated boy who lived constantly in the shadow of his charismatic older brother. But if Rafe had any feelings for her, he had chosen an unfortunate way to show them. Perhaps his aggressiveness was a reaction to Chas's gentility.

Although dark-haired, his features more chiselled, he reminded her too vividly of Chas. It was sometimes heartbreaking to be with him.

"*I* would have stayed with you," he said, giving her a rueful smirk before walking away.

The letter that awaited her when she returned to Wyndholme eased some of the pain of those words.

*My Darling Ria,*

*I can fly! I had my first solo flight today and it was exhilarating, unbelievable, magical, mystical! I can't even begin to* describe what it feels like to soar through the air like a bird, to see the roads and trees and houses grow smaller beneath your wings, which have become an extension of yourself. I think you will adore it as well. My instructor says that I'm 'a natural', meaning that I have an affinity for it, I suppose. It certainly feels that way to me. Perhaps I was a bird in a previous life.

Jack and I have had our interviews with the RFC. It seems that being an accomplished horseman who also excels at outdoor sports is what makes a superlative pilot. The fact that I can sail, and also drive boats and automobiles is apparently helpful, as is the fact that my French is impeccable, and my German good enough should I land behind enemy lines. I expect that even my fencing skills may be useful, should I get into a duel with the enemy! Jack had to exaggerate his equestrian and driving accomplishments, but we did both get accepted. The fact that we've already had several weeks of flight training and solo flying probably helped as well.

Devenish also got in, so the three of us are soon off to the Central Flying School in Upavon, near Salisbury. We're going to London to shop for our flying gear, as sheepskin-lined leather coats, gloves, and such are essential. It's jolly cold up there!

I've heard that our Canadians have just arrived, 32,000 strong. Imagine it! I think they are being billeted at Salisbury Plain as well, so we shall see Henry and Archie soon. Odd, don't you think, to be meeting up again here?

Jack had his 21st birthday last week, so we all went up to London to celebrate. After dinner at the Ritz, we went to Covent Garden to see the astonishing ballet, Sheherazade, by the renowned Russian impresario, Diaghilev. The Ballet Russe is all the rage in London, as you will discover.

Cousin Bea has a delightful London townhouse, fully staffed at all times so that she or any of her friends can breeze in and out at leisure. What fun you and I shall have here next year!

I'm so pleased that you and Calypso are seeing a lot of each other. And that you and Fliss are as well, of course. Yes, I think you're right that Rafe is happiest and most pleasant to be around when he's with his beloved horses. Hopefully, racing them as a breeder, he will be less likely to bet recklessly on the gee-gees and get further into debt.

I always expected that Zoë would be in her element at university, and I know she'll do well. Max will persevere. I think that, like me, he doesn't really know why he's there. In my case, I had great fun, and did actually learn a few useful things. It's good *that he's joined the Officer Training Corp at the university, in case this war does drag on. If he has to join us, he'll have more options as an officer. Tell him to learn Morse code as well, especially if he wants to join the RFC.*

*I suppose I should be jealous that Justin takes you to the opera, but he's a good chap and friend, and I trust him not to try to steal my darling girl. I'm also confident enough to believe that there is no room for another in your heart, for which I am profoundly grateful, my darling. So I'm happy that you are not so much alone, but have your friends to look after you.*

*I expect the next time I write it will be from Upavon, where I shall be a 'Probationary Flight Officer'. I can hardly wait to take you up in my flying machine!*

*I love you and miss you, my darling. I want nothing more than to hold you in my arms at this moment. With some kisses as well, of course. And you know where they always lead...*

*Your adoring Chas*


Victoria decided to visit Eleanor, and also Jack's family, that evening. She liked to drive herself in the Rolls, so she wasn't really surprised when George, the chauffeur, asked to speak to her.

"Pardon me, Miss Victoria, but your father has asked me to come and work for him. It seems that I'm not required all that much here anymore."

How dare her father try to take her servants!

But George went on before she could say anything. "But I was thinking to join the army. I expect they can use an experienced mechanic and driver. So I'm sort of giving notice, Miss Victoria, if that's alright with you."

George, who was in his mid-twenties, seemed to know everything there was to know about engines. And he had given Victoria an idea that sent a shiver of excitement down her spine.

"That's very noble of you, George, and I expect you're absolutely right that they need skilled people like you in the army. But I must ask you to do something for me before you leave us. I want you to teach me everything you can about engines, and maintaining the Rolls. So that I can look after it while you're gone. Of course your job will be awaiting you when you return, if you want it." What she didn't say was that with those skills, she, too, might be of some use to the army.

George couldn't hide his surprise. "It's dirty work, Miss."

"I quite understand, but I'm determined to do it in any case."

"Yes, Miss. We can start tomorrow morning, if that suits."

"Splendidly!"

"Hell's bells, Ria!" Eleanor said a little later. "You're going to become an auto mechanic?"

"A driver for the army, I hope. But I know I'll need to be able to fix the car as well as drive it."

Eleanor laughed. "You never did behave conventionally! I admire your spunk."

They told each other of the letters they had received from Chas and Jack, the latter giving a glowing description of the massive ancestral estate that their cousin, Lord Devenish, would inherit.

"Sounds like you're practically royalty," Eleanor said. "Thinking about you mucking about in the black, oily depths of an engine seems doubly absurd. Then again, you aristocrats have always been eccentric."

"Do stop, Ellie!" Victoria laughed. "We women can surely do anything men can. You, of all people, have always maintained that."

"Absolutely right. But I still find it hard to envision someone as refined as you fixing an automobile. And this idea of working for the army – that's not likely to happen."

"Just wait and see!"

"Oh, I look forward to it," Eleanor said with a laugh. "What would I do without friends like you who make life so interesting?"

"I'm off to pay a quick visit to Jack's family. Do you want to come along?"

"I really must get back to my studies."

"I've never met Jack's mother. I'm almost afraid to. Grandmother was so hostile to her that I feel as if I have to somehow make amends."

"She seems wary and somewhat suspicious, which may come across as unfriendliness. I think she – they've – had a hard life, much harder than Jack has ever let on to me. So I expect there's bitterness as well, especially against your grandmother. But she must be a good person, as Jack is a dutiful and caring son, and the children are all so likeable. For someone who's ready to take up the call to do battle against the enemy, you shouldn't be afraid of Jack's mother!" Eleanor laughed.

"No, of course not." But Victoria still felt some trepidation as she knocked on the door. They lived just around the corner from the Carlyles, so Victoria had left the car there. Zoë had told her that her parents had bought this house for Jack and his family, and that they had only recently moved in. Victoria was impressed with the house and Uncle Richard's generosity.

She was grateful that Emily answered the door. "Victoria! How wonderful!" She threw her arms about her. "Come in! Lizzie! Claire! It's Victoria! Maman, come and meet our cousin. Your niece, I guess she is."

"Mrs. Wyndham – Aunt Marie – it's a great pleasure to meet you at last. We've been so fortunate to get to know your delightful family this summer."

"Pretty words," Marie said snidely.

"Maman, Victoria was so kind to us at the cottage, and has invited us all back next summer," Lizzie said quickly to cover up her mother's enmity, and warn her to be hospitable. She knew that Maman saw Victoria as a representative of the family that had so cruelly rejected her and Alex, and plunged them into poverty. It was, after all, how Lizzie also felt. Unlike her sisters, she could never forgive Victoria for having always had an easy and luxurious life while they had had to work like slaves to keep from starving. She also resented the fact that Victoria had been left a fortune, while she and her sisters had received a pittance in comparison. But she also knew that they needed to keep up an amiable relationship with Victoria and the others if they were to reap any more benefits from the family and their connections. "Can we offer you some refreshment?"

"Tea would be lovely, if it's no trouble."

"Not at all. Come into our sitting room." Lizzie was proud with what they had done with the house so far, although it couldn't compare to Wyndholme or even the cottage, of course.

Victoria said, "I've brought something for you all. Some of your father's things. I thought you should have them." Now that Augusta no longer needed them. There were several photographs of Alex throughout his childhood – one on his pony, another in his school uniform, one of him flourishing the Stepping Stone Cup, one of him in a canoe – a few books with his name and age inscribed inside, and paintings he had done of the island. Victoria had kept several for herself, since some were quite similar. He probably kept painting certain scenes to perfect his technique. But he hadn't been as good as Jack.

"This is so wonderful!" Emily said, tears springing to her eyes. "Oh, Victoria, thank you!"

Even Lizzie was moved by these relics of her father's previous life. Marie said, "I will make tea."

"I think Maman is rather overcome," Lizzie said. "This is very kind of you, Victoria."

"It's where they rightly belong... So, have you managed to find boarders?"

"Yes. We have two university students sharing the large front room, a lady type writer, who works in an office, and a young graduate who has just started a job as a pharmacist. It's working out well so far. They certainly enjoy Maman's cuisine."

"Jack told me she was a good cook. How are the lessons going, Emily?"

"Smashing! It's like a dream come true! I don't know how to thank you, Victoria."

"Not at all! I'm happy I could help. You don't know how sorry I am that it's taken so long for us to meet you. We didn't even know you existed until Jack showed up this summer. Much as I loved my grandmother, I can't forgive her for her treatment of you. But since we can't change what's past, we must do what we can now. So, I have a couple of invitations. First of all, Lizzie – Rafe wants to know if you still want to learn to ride?"

"Oh, yes!"

"Then come with me to Thornridge tomorrow after lunch. I'll pick you up. And secondly, why don't you all plan to come to Wyndholme for a weekend? I get rather lonely, so I thought I would ask Esme and Felicity to stay as well, and invite some of our friends to come for a party one evening." The idea had just that moment occurred to her. "Shall we try for next weekend? That's Halloween. We have some costumes in the attic. That could be great fun."

Claire's eyes glowed with excitement. "Could we?"

"Yes indeed. Come on Friday in time for dinner. I'll send George to pick you up at five."

"What do I wear for riding?" Lizzie asked before Victoria left.

"I have an extra riding habit. You're about my size, so it should fit."

Although Lizzie was bigger in the bust, it fit quite well.

Rafe seemed pleased to see her, Lizzie thought. She was terrified of horses, which he must have sensed, for he introduced her to them with such affection for the animals and consideration for her that she soon felt able to touch them and appreciate their beauty. When Victoria set out for her ride, Rafe had Lizzie mounted and walking about the paddock. By the time Victoria returned, Lizzie felt quite comfortable, and was learning how to use her knees to control the animal. Like Victoria, she sat astride, wearing breeches covered with a split skirt.

So Lizzie went to Thornridge every day after that, Rafe picking her up if Victoria wasn't going. Lizzie had decided that she would do anything to get Rafe to marry her, to be forever a part of this extravagant, exciting, hedonistic lifestyle. She laughed to herself to think that Jack also had his eye on this amazing place, through Felicity. But she had to admit that Rafe was intriguing and decidedly handsome. If he was a bit dissipated, as Jack had led her to believe, then perhaps she could take him in hand and control him through his vices.

Besides her daily, messy lessons in auto mechanics, Victoria had a few other considerations to distract her. Some good ones – Chas sent her sporadic telegrams like "This time next year we will be in Paris together. Forever yours, my love.'"

And she had a surprising letter from Henry.

*Dear Victoria,*

*I know now what I wish – nay, need – to do with my life. I was born into the wrong place, for as soon as I landed here in England I knew I was home. The smells, the sights, the tastes are all so familiar to me. I feel happy here as I never have at home. You will think this sacrilegious, for I know how much you love Wyndwood, but I would trade it easily for a life here. My soul has trodden these lanes before. I wouldn't be surprised if I had been one of the monks who once inhabited Cousin Beatrice's delightful Abbey.*

*If I survive this war, I will stay in England to study history, in particular, the mediaeval times. I wish to become a fusty, dusty old Oxford professor, and you will visit me and marvel at the glorious architecture and ancient culture that surround me.*

*And now that you have recovered from riotous laughter or utter shock, you will think your staid cousin has gone quite mad. But truly, Victoria, I have just come alive! Thank you for giving me the courage and impetus to take a chance, to make a change, to break away from everyone's expectations and demands of me.*

*If I die tomorrow, I will die happy.*

*To show you just how odd this new world of mine is at the moment, I'm in the same regiment as Grandmother's former footman, Tom, who was dismissed this summer for unseemly behaviour. Because we are the same rank – which is just a private – he treats me with great contempt, as if to make up for all those years of subservience. He's a vulgar, nasty, and belligerent fellow, in truth, but of course we never saw that side of him. I find it somewhat disturbing to discover such duplicity in a person. In any case, I shall stay well upwind of his bullets!*

    *Affectionately, your cousin, Henry*

One day, Helena showed up, unannounced, for tea.

Victoria had seen her and James only briefly after their honeymoon, when he had come to collect his things, and Helena had said that Victoria should come to dinner when they'd settled in. But she had heard nothing from them since then. If she'd been a bit disappointed, she hadn't been surprised, since they were just awkward in one another's company.

She was lucky to have family and friends who did care for her. Edgar joined her for dinner once a week, and Aunt Olivia had her to dinner at least twice a week. Sometimes Zoë, Max, and Freddie dropped in to see her, Justin came by or took her out once a week, and Vivian wrote often.

"I'm so sorry we haven't had a chance to see you, Victoria," Helena said once she was seated in the conservatory. She seemed even more poised than she had in the summer, making Victoria think that it didn't take long to develop airs when one was sure of one's situation. "Your father is so tied up in his work, what with the war and all, that our entertaining has somehow been related to business. I just wanted you to know that we haven't forgotten you."

"Indeed." Victoria had no interest in mealy-mouthed platitudes, or crumbs thrown in her direction. "I've been busy myself. I've just learned how to take apart and reassemble an automobile engine," she said with malicious pleasure.

"You're serious?" Helena said in surprise.

"Of course." She showed her grease-encrusted hands proudly. She had tried soaking them in lemon juice, olive oil, and various soaps, but it took days to get rid of the grease. As she had just finished another lesson, she was particularly black.

"Heavens! Your father will be amused."

"Particularly since he couldn't steal George from me."

Helena was pleased with the way the conversation was going, since James wouldn't be once he heard. "He needed a chauffeur, and you obviously don't."

"Don't tell me that he's taking the streetcar now?"

"He has found a capable young man."

"As they all seem to be going off to war, it might be a good idea for Father to learn to drive himself. It can't be that difficult, since I can do it." Helena didn't seem to catch the sarcasm.

"I'll tell him, shall I? I've decided to invite the entire family to dinner next Saturday, so I hope that you can join us."

"I'm afraid I have friends coming over. Some other time perhaps." The fact that Richard, Olivia, their children, and Edgar were coming to her party, meant that Helena would only have Phyllis and Albert, and poor Phoebe, who wasn't allowed to come to Wyndholme.

"Yes, of course. Well, I must be off. I'm collecting for the Patriotic Fund. This war is keeping us all busy."

"Isn't it just?"

How glad Victoria was that her father had decided not to live at Wyndholme after all. She couldn't imagine having to put up with Helena every day. Nor be reminded of her father's animosity.

Her friends were eager to attend the Halloween weekend. Vivian and Lydia came to stay. Simon was recently engaged to a Guelph girl, and spent every free moment with her, so he didn't come. But the rest of her friends, who were in town anyway, would be at the party on Saturday night.

Felicity was thrilled to be invited to stay. She, Esme, and Claire shared a room. Lizzie and Emily shared another. Friday evening they had a delightfully spooky time playing with a Ouija Board. It had become a popular parlour game during the last decade for divinations and supposedly communicating with the other world. Superstitiously, Victoria didn't ask it any questions about Chas or their future together.

On Saturday they carved pumpkins under the guidance of the head gardener, and set their grimacing jack o'lanterns strategically about the house. Victoria and Jack's sisters chose ghoulish costumes to fool the spirits that would wander the earth this night when the veil between the living and the dead was very thin. The others had brought their own.

So it was a frightening assembly of witches, demons, ghosts, grim reapers, the undead, and even a skeleton – Blake – who sat down to dinner that evening. Wyndholme was lit only by candlelight, which played creepy shadows across the walls. The children were thrillingly scared.

After dinner they had a few chilling games of hide and seek. With so many large rooms, dimly lit, the younger ones seemed happy to be caught.

Rafe managed to sneak a few kisses with Lizzie behind drapes and in dark alcoves.

They bobbed for apples, and sat around the fire telling ghost stories. Richard's were particularly believable.

When the younger children had tired, Richard and Olivia went home with the boys, and the girls went to bed, to talk and giggle. The rest of them danced. Even Edgar managed well enough, with his somewhat improved ankle.

When Justin danced with Victoria he asked with amusement, "So have you really become an auto mechanic?"

"Do you doubt it?" She showed him her fingernails. "These are not just part of my witch costume. I can't get the grease out!"

He laughed. "You never cease to amaze me, Ria."

"Good! I don't like being predictable."

"Will you come to a concert at Massey Hall on Friday?"

"Yes, of course. Thank you, Justin. Although I don't know why you're so generous with your time. I'm sure there are more deserving girls you should be taking."

"I doubt that."

There was something in his warm and gentle eyes, in his indulgent smile that made her realize, with intense regret, that he was in love with her. Knowing him and recalling what Augusta had written, she thought that he may well be fulfilling some obligation to her grandmother. How typically honourable of him.

"Justin, it may be presumptuous of me to say this, but if Grandmother extracted any promises from you to look after me, please don't feel obligated. I'm quite capable of looking after myself. Although I do value your friendship and enjoy spending time with you, I also feel it's unfair to you."

"I'm not doing anything that I wouldn't gladly do. Yes, your grandmother was concerned about you, but now that you have Chas, I know that you will be well looked after. So I really would like to take you to the concert, as a friend."

"Then I am indeed blessed."

Her smile was a wrench for him. She was wrong to think that he was sacrificing himself to spend time with her. There wasn't anyone else who remotely interested him. Perhaps one day he would find the kind of all-consuming love that he realized Chas and Victoria shared. In the meantime, he was grateful just to be with her.

She said, "I think it's super that Vivian is training for the VAD." The Voluntary Aid Detachment was a group of volunteers trained by St. John Ambulance to help with nursing and other duties. Victoria had decided that she, too, would take the training, since that would make her eligible to drive ambulances, so she was disappointed to discover that she had to be at least twenty-one to qualify.

"She's plotting to get sent overseas, at least to England, so that she can be near Peter – I realize you know about him, so I'm not breaking any confidences. But I think that's unlikely. Good lord! It just occurred to me why you've taken up fixing automobiles. You're planning to get a job as a driver. Hoping to get sent to the Front, no doubt."

She laughed. "You do know me well, Justin."

"And well enough to know that I haven't a hope of persuading you of the folly and danger of your ambitions. In any case, Chas wouldn't let you."

"Hell's bells! Everyone seems to think it's up to him to decide what I can do!"

"Even if you got to the Front, you'd be unlikely to meet up with Chas. He'd be worried about you and that would impact his ability to fly, which could cause him to crash, so he would be invalided home and you would be stuck in France."

Despite the sudden vision of Chas crashing – but *not* surviving – Victoria was amused by this argument. "You will make a good lawyer, Justin. You've almost convinced me."

"Almost doesn't win a case." And he hoped he was right that she didn't have a chance of getting overseas.

When she had a moment, Victoria took Eleanor aside and confided something that had been bothering her all week. "Ellie, I think I'm with child." She had missed her last two courses.

Eleanor looked at her with a mixture of surprise and pity. "You didn't take precautions?"

"Not always. Not that last night in New York."

"Bloody hell!" Seeing the anguished look on Victoria's face, she said, "It doesn't matter. You and Chas are getting married anyway."

"But not yet! And he really didn't want children so soon. Swear to me you won't tell him, Ellie. Please!"

With great reluctance, Eleanor said, "If you insist. But I really think that *you* should tell him. He needs to know."

"Why? He can't come home now. I don't want him upset or worried. He doesn't need distractions."

"You're not thinking of terminating it?"

"Of course not! How could I? It's a part of me and Chas. I cherish it! Oh, bloody hell, Ellie! I hope he comes home before summer!"

"Early June it'll be due. I'll work out the date for you."

"Please don't tell anyone else. Somehow I have to keep this a secret."

"Until you're as big as a house, and then you won't be able to persuade anyone that you've just been overeating."

Victoria looked worried, so Eleanor hugged her and said, "I'll look after you. Don't worry. It's still possible that your period is just late. Anxiety can do that. I'll check you out in a couple of weeks, to be sure."

But Victoria was sure even before Eleanor confirmed it. There were subtle changes in her body, and an odd sensation that she was nurturing a new life within her.

Eleanor figured the baby was due June 9th, which was Chas's twenty-third birthday. Victoria would turn nineteen just four days before that.

Her delight at carrying Chas's child was tempered by the fact that he had several times stated that he didn't want to have children yet. But she was certain that when he came home to find her pregnant, he would soon get used to the idea, and be pleased. He was, after all, good with children and surely wanted his own.

She wondered how long she could pretend that everything was normal. Already she'd had to tell Mrs. Hadley that there were certain foods – like pork – that she was not interested in, her excuse being that it was needed for the troops. In truth, the smell and taste nauseated her. But for now, no one could tell she was pregnant, so she didn't curb her social engagements or stop riding. At least not until the snows came. But she had to abandon her idea of going overseas.

.        .        .

*My Darling Ria,*

*Forgive me for taking so long to write this time. I couldn't find the words. I had so wanted you to meet your cousin, Cedric, and after all that I had told him about you, he was eager to meet you as well. He was enchanted by Zoë's photo of you in the canoe, and had pretty well booked himself into Thorncliff for a least a month next summer, as he was determined to come to our wedding.*

*I deeply regret to say that he died several days ago. We could hear that he had engine trouble shortly after his take-off, and he should have put the aeroplane down in a nearby field. But he turned down wind, trying to come back to the aerodrome. At such a low altitude, he lost his flying speed, stalled the engine, and crashed. It has shaken us all.*

His family doesn't even have the consolation of thinking his death somehow heroic.

Jack and I are thankful that we had plenty of preliminary training, as we feel much better prepared than the other recruits, and wouldn't have made that mistake. But they are scrambling to train us as quickly as possible on old aeroplanes, and Cedric hasn't been the only casualty.

But I don't want you to worry about me, my darling. You may laugh to hear that I am known for being careful and precise. I always check the aeroplane rigging myself, and do feel some instinctive understanding of aerodynamics when flying. Maybe it's all those years of being buffeted in the sailboat by Muskoka winds.

And now I have my special talisman to protect me! Thank you, my darling, for your thoughtful and beautiful gift. You are right that your fairy folk will bring me good luck. I shall never take it off.

Victoria had had a golden dragonfly pendant made for him, on a thin gold chain.

Some chaps have St. Christopher's medals or a sweetheart's garter or a teddy bear for luck. Mine is by far the best!

We spent a delightful weekend in London with Henry and Archie, who were thankful to get out of the ubiquitous mud of Salisbury Plain. It's been an unusually wet autumn, and our troops are not enjoying their sojourn in England. They say they can never get dry! Henry seems a bit friendlier to Jack these days, and happier within himself. Cedric had still been with us, and was overwhelmed by all these cousins popping up.

Fliss wrote to me about the Halloween party as well. She was so excited, and thinks you are the best soon-to-be-sister in the world. She's also impressed with your mechanical skills! Why didn't you tell me that you had taken up automobile repair? I expect you're doing your bit for the war (how exactly?) , but I also wonder what you're up to? I never take anything for granted with you, my surprising darling...

What Chas couldn't tell Victoria, Jack wrote to Eleanor.

...We all ran up to the wreckage, and could see that Cedric was injured, but still alive. But we couldn't get him out before the petrol tank burst, and flames shot up, engulfing him. We couldn't extinguish the fire. The poor beggar was burnt alive. Christ, Ellie, I've never seen anything so gruesome! If we have to die in this bloody war, dear God, don't let it be so cruelly. We're all haunted and terrified by the spectre of fire now, of becoming a "flamer". Most of us carry our pistols with us, just in case.

*Chas has taken it very hard, feeling responsible for enticing Lord Devenish into joining up. That's foolish, of course, as Cedric needed no encouragement. He thought it a jolly great adventure. In fact, it was probably this flippancy that made him treat things too lightly. We're constantly being told or otherwise being made aware that flying is a dangerous thing to do. It takes skill and concentration and quick thinking and a lot of bloody nerve. It isn't a game.*

*Chas doesn't want Victoria to know how horribly Cedric died, so please don't pass this along. As a doctor you have seen or will undoubtedly see worse things. I admire you tremendously for your courage to deal with such things, Ellie. What a woman you are! And one whom I wish I were holding right now, running my hands along your perfect...*

*. . .*

*My beloved Chas,*

*I am deeply saddened and sorry to hear about Cousin Cedric. How tragic that an energetic young life can be so quickly extinguished. Daily we read about the battles and casualties, but they become somewhat meaningless until it's someone you know, and our troops aren't even in France yet. Of course I only knew about Cedric from what you have told me, but I feel his loss keenly. I keep thinking that we should all be at the French Riviera by now, on our Grand Tour. How naïve and carefree we once were!*

*I worry about you more than ever, but you must promise me to hold nothing back when you write to me. Don't spare me the frightening details of your life or how you feel about what you experience, which I know you will want to do. I want to share everything with you, to live every moment with you no matter how dangerous. To know that you have managed to get yourself out of difficulty will actually give me some peace of mind. Please don't cut me out of such a large part of your life.*

*My life, on the other hand, is quite uneventful. I, along with the rest of the family, was invited to dine at Father's new house. It's very modern and quite spacious — nothing like Wyndholme, of course, which I think irks Helena. But I found it delightful. It's not far from Sir Henry's Casa Loma. Which reminds me. Grandmother's lady's maid, Bayley, has gotten herself taken on there as maid to Lady Pellatt. Bayley, quite rightly, didn't think I really needed her.*

Being practical, I had George, our chauffeur, teach me everything he could about looking after the Rolls before joining up, hence my newly acquired mechanical skills. Will, one of our under-gardeners, who was at Wyndwood all summer, has also left. Our maid, Molly, whom you may have seen at the cottage this summer, has died. She went home in August to nurse her mother, and fell ill herself. Poor girl. She can't have been very old. Another of the parlour maids and the kitchen maid are going to work in a munitions factory, where the pay is much better. But I do worry about their safety. If any more leave, I may have to close Wyndholme for the duration of the war, and find myself and Josephine a few rooms somewhere. What I would like best of all would be to come to England and be able to see you when you are on leave. And if this war drags on past the spring, then be assured that I will!

Rafe – with surprising patience – has been teaching Lizzie to ride. From someone who was terrified of horses, she has become comfortable, knowledgeable, and quite skilled. Wyndham stubbornness? She is very much Jack's sister. She and Rafe seem to be getting on rather well, and, yes, he is gentlemanly towards her – at least in my presence. I think I may have underestimated him, for which I feel rather ashamed. He is your brother, after all!

Fliss feels quite grown up now that she is fifteen. I had a small party for her, and most of our Muskoka friends were able to attend. Of course your family also had a celebration, with a large number of guests.

She really misses you, and sometimes gets worried and melancholy, saying it was quite different when she knew exactly on which day you'd be home again from Oxford. Rafe is trying to spend time with her, but he doesn't have the easy, bantering relationship that you and she share.

Father and Helena are going to visit the Oakleys in Pittsburgh for Christmas. Thankfully, but not surprisingly, I wasn't invited. I've asked the rest of the family to celebrations here, as usual. I will also have our friends come for dinners, and, hopefully, Vivian and Lydia will be able to stay again. Zoë will move in with me for a while during her holidays, and I will also ask Ellie and Fliss. So I hope to have a houseful of people, and you are not to worry about me.

You are forever in my thoughts, and I ache for you. But I am trying to be brave. So you must fulfil your promise to take care and come back to me.

All my love, always, Ria

*My Darling Ria,*

*How unrealistic it was for us to think we'd be home by Christmas! We haven't even reached the Front yet.*

*But I expect that Jack and I will be sent to France early in the new year. For now, we were able to get a few days leave over Christmas, and will be staying with Cousin Bea at Bovington Abbey, along with Henry and Archie. Quite a merry Canadian party we shall be.*

*I've sent a parcel for you in the care of Fliss, who has strict instructions not to give it to you until Christmas Eve. I am glad that you won't be alone over Christmas, for I expect you may feel the absence of your grandmother most keenly then. I wish I were there with you.*

*Jack and I have both received your Christmas boxes and will save them, as instructed, until Christmas morning...*

Victoria had sent Chas a small version of the painting she had done for him of Thorncliff, so that he could carry it with him easily, along with a photo of a painting she had bought for his collection. It was an autumn scene in Algonquin Park by Edelina's friend, Tom Thomson, whom they had met this summer. She also sent him *Flint and Feather*, a collection of poems by Pauline Johnson, a part Mohawk Canadian poet who had died the previous year. In that volume were poems about Muskoka. For Jack, there was an engraved silver cigarette case. She had also included some of Mrs. Hadley's rum-soaked Christmas cake for them both.

On Christmas Eve, Victoria was invited to dine with the Thorntons as their only guest. They were delighted with her presents – a watercolour of Thorncliff for J.D. and Marjorie, a stylish Cartier wristwatch for Fliss, and a painting of Calypso for Rafe, which had been a real challenge for her. He seemed truly pleased with her effort. From Fliss and Rafe she received an expensive new saddle, and from her soon-to-be parents-in-law, a beautiful Tiffany stained glass panel depicting a brilliant sunset lake scene, which J.D. had commissioned for her from the famous American artist. She was deeply touched by their thoughtfulness, and realized that they were her new family, which cheered her immensely.

When she arrived home to a dark and silent house, there was a telegram awaiting her. "I'm there with you, my darling. Can you feel me? I will always be wherever you are. My love has no boundaries. It should flow to you like night-time whispers across a summer lake."

She broke down then. When she had finished crying, she asked Grayson for a bottle of champagne, and told him that the staff should enjoy some as well. She sat in the window seat of the chilly tower, looking over the snow-bright city night, and raised her glass. "To us, Chas," she said into the darkness. "The three of us."

She kept the present he had sent her beside her bed that night and opened it in the morning. Within a distinctive blue box was a an exquisite dragonfly brooch made of platinum, the wings lacy and delicate, and edged with tiny diamond chips which shot light in all directions. The body was studded with bright blue sapphires; the eyes were sizable diamonds. The note read, "It seems we think alike! I had this designed for you at Tiffany's in London before I received your beautiful good luck charm. May this be equally lucky for you, my darling."

Jack had sent her a marvellous sketch of Chas, and they had included photos of themselves in front of flimsy biplanes, looking elated. And oh so young. For a moment, Victoria felt infinitely older.

The present that Helena had dropped off for her before leaving for Pittsburgh was a mink cape. No one could say that James and his new wife were niggardly to his daughter.

The rest of the family arrived in the afternoon. More presents were opened and exclaimed over, and they enjoyed their usual fine Christmas feast. Zoë stayed, and the next day, she and Victoria went to visit Jack's family, who had declined the invitation to join them the previous day. The girls were overwhelmed by the expensive Cartier watches Victoria had bought them. For Marie there was a lovely Art Nouveau lamp for her new house.

Vivian and Lydia arrived that evening for a week's stay. They brought Victoria a present from Justin. It was a first edition of Thomas Hardy's *Far From the Madding Crowd,* "Which I know you enjoy," he had written.

Eleanor joined them for a few days, and later, so did Felicity. And all during that delightful week she said nothing to any of the others about the baby. She couldn't even tell Zoë.

They heard echoes of sanity from the war front. Soldiers in the trenches from both sides called a Christmas truce, sang songs with one another, exchanged presents, played impromptu games of soccer in no-man's-land, laughed together. Surely that was a sign that the ordinary men from both sides detested what they were required to do, and recognized the humanity of their "enemy". Unfortunately, it didn't last.

* * *

*My Darling Ria,*

*We have our wings! And we're departing imminently for France – as soon as this weather lifts. Jack and I and a few others are flying some aeroplanes over. There was a devastating storm in France a few days ago which apparently destroyed a large number of aircraft. It seems Jack and I will be joining the 2nd Squadron, and are pleased that so far, we are still together. Even though I've only known Jack for a few months, we have shared memories of last summer. That gives us some connection with home.*

*Which your beautiful paintings do as well, my darling! And those poems, especially the ones that mention* our *lake and the Shadow River, where we've had so many picnics, are so evocative that I can instantly picture our summers, not without some poignancy. I do hope that we shall return before summer comes again. So thank you, my darling, for your thoughtful, wonderful presents. Tell Mrs. Hadley that her cake was so much appreciated by all that we had to fight to keep some for ourselves.*

*We had a delightful time at Bovington, and met some of Cousin Bea's friends. I also met up with a few old Oxford chums, many of whom are volunteering. Having heard what happened to Cedric, and one, having already lost a brother, none of them see it as a lark anymore, but do believe that it is their duty. From a group of easy-going optimists we have become a rather grim lot. I know you also feel that our generation is being abruptly, even brutally, thrust into adulthood. I hope that we shall be allowed to grow old. I'm sure that you and I will.*

*Lovingly yours, Lieutenant (!) Chas*

* * *

*Dearest Lieutenant Chas,*

*How dashing you look in your uniform! Thank you for sending the photos. But it appears to me as if your cherished aeroplane is constructed of matchsticks and paper! May it be as nimble and* 'aerodynamic' as the dragonfly, which also seems delicate, but is surely a master of the air.

The brooch is exquisite. I wear it every day. I can't imagine anything more appropriate for me. Thank you, my love.

I don't think it's adulthood we've been suddenly thrust into, but some sort of nightmare that most people never have to live through. I'd rather we weren't a part of an era that history might reflect upon as having been a major turning point because of its violence or sacrifices. I hope it all ends soon.

In the meantime, I'm back to doing Red Cross work. All very useful, I know, but it doesn't seem enough when compared to what you're doing...

In truth, Victoria was beginning to experience inertia. She had felt the baby kick for the first time, and realized how miraculous it was to have this life growing within her. All she really wanted was to set up a home with Chas, to have the opportunity that the previous generations had had – marriage, children, safety, happiness.

Even though her pregnancy wasn't detectable yet, she scaled down her social life, although she still went out with Justin. He would be suspicious if she suddenly stopped without good reason.

So the winter weeks were both tedious and worrisome, brightened only by Chas's letters.

My Darling Ria,

I had my first crash landing today. Don't be upset! My observer and I walked away from it unharmed. All the chaps have crashed at least once. It can be because of engine failure, running out of petrol, or damage to the aeroplane from "Archie" – that's what we call anti-aircraft fire from the ground.

In my case it was Archie that got my poor aeroplane, but I was able to bring her in for a landing, although a bit rough, in a field not far from our aerodrome. She can be repaired, and I needed only to steady my nerves with a bottle of champagne afterwards.

The first time I went up in France, I met with a German aeroplane above our lines. We waved to one another, neither of us being equipped with, in my case, anything more than a side-arm. As we are already doing something risky, we like to acknowledge the other brave chap. I don't like the idea of having to kill someone – a little late perhaps to think that way.

So I'm glad that my job is doing reconnaissance, for which I fly a BE2c, two-seater biplane. I have a trained observer with me, who takes photographs and can send information via Morse code *(which I can also do, in a pinch). My observer, Colin Loftus, is a good chap, about nineteen and hoping to become a pilot eventually. Observers can apply for pilot training after three months on active duty. I'll be sorry to lose him, as we make a good team.*

*We all have nicknames, and his is Lofty, partly because of his name, of course, but also because he is very tall, and he always says to me "Prepare to go aloft, Chase!" as we get ready for take-off. He was at Cambridge and joined up at the outbreak of the war, spending a few months in the trenches, which horrified him, so he asked for a transfer to the RFC. He's much happier here.*

*My nickname is Chase, because the other chaps think I'm hard to catch in the air. Jack is Bouncer, because of how he lands his aeroplane, his first touchdown always a bit tentative, as if he can't believe he's back on the ground.*

*In any case, for reconnaissance I have to fly quite low and level over enemy territory. We're sometimes up for four hours at a time. How strange to fly over a rabbit warren of trenches, and how awful to see the explosions from artillery firing on our troops. And scary to see some of those hurtling in our direction. But I'm quickly learning acrobatic flying, which was discouraged in training, but is necessary for survival here. We really do learn as we go along.*

*I've told you all this precisely so that you <u>don't</u> worry about me! Dragonfly – the name of my aeroplane – and I are as one. Jack has painted a dragonfly on the side of my machine....*

Victoria  thought she wouldn't be so terrified if she were actually there with him. She had this superstitious feeling that he would be protected just by her presence.

.    .    .

*My Darling Ria,*

*God, this war is hell! We lost Lofty today. I wonder what I could have done to save him.*

*We were doing our reconnaissance well behind enemy lines, and were heavily fired at by Archie, but I managed to avoid it. What I hadn't anticipated was a German aeroplane coming out of the sun and firing at us with a machine gun. I dodged as best I could, but the BE2 is not sprightly. I could see that Lofty was hit, and turned immediately back to base. But it was more than an hour away. As usual, we had a strong head wind going back, so I got us over our lines and put down as soon as possible. Didn't even try to get back to our aerodrome. He was barely alive when we landed, and we were told that he died in the ambulance on the way to the field hospital.*

*What a bloody waste!*

*Of course we try to keep the other side from spying on our troops, but this seems to be an indication of where we might be heading – towards aerial combat. I hadn't anticipated that we would be trying to shoot each other out of the sky!*

*I'm sorry, my darling, for being so angry and disillusioned. I wanted to spare you all this. But you wanted to know. And I should do the right thing and pretend that all is well and we are having a jolly old time here. But I'm finding it increasingly hard to  believe that the sacrifice of fine young men who should be the future of their nations is justified.*

*I understand that our Canadians are now in the trenches, God help them.*

*And so, my darling, I am physically well, but diminished by the premature death of yet another friend. I long to be with you. You must be strong, to exemplify all that we are fighting for. We want only to come home, and, hopefully, to a world not radically altered. How right you were to question our generation's future.*

*Love, Chas*

---

Victoria had additional worries. By late March, she was finding it difficult to hide the bulge of her pregnancy. So she stopped going out. When family and friends came by, which they often did, she made sure to wear an enveloping shawl, which not only hid her condition, but made her seem ill. Olivia wanted her to move into Rosemullion so she could be looked after, but Victoria insisted she was fine and just needed rest.

She felt panicked sometimes, realizing that she was soon to create a terrible scandal, that would reflect badly upon the rest of the family. Her father would undoubtedly disown her, but that was of little consequence, since he had virtually done so already. She had been invited only once more to his home.

It was the others and the Thorntons she was most concerned about. But she felt unusually powerless to act. She dreaded telling Chas. He had too many worries already.

But things were taken out of her hands.

Justin confronted Eleanor at the university one day. "Ellie, there's something wrong with Ria, and I'm sure you know what it is."

"I do. But I can't tell you, Justin." She looked him directly in the eye. "I'm sworn to secrecy."

"Good Lord!" He understood immediately. "Does Chas know?"

"No. She doesn't want him upset. It was fine when we thought he was coming back in a few months. But that's no longer realistic. Things aren't going to be pleasant for her once people realize."

He was well aware of that, and felt angry with Chas for having left Victoria after compromising her. He should have married her right away. If he were killed now, she would be in a difficult situation. He had to admit that this obvious indication of their having consummated their love was like salt in his wound.

But what he did next was something he would forever regret.

. . .

Victoria had a telephone call from Vivian. "Are you alright, Ria? Justin says you've been ill for weeks now. May I come and help? Practice my nursing skills, which I haven't had a chance to do?"

"I'm just a bit under the weather. And melancholy too. I miss Chas. You really mustn't trouble yourself about me, Vivian."

"But may I selfishly ask to come and stay? I'm going crazy here."

Victoria hesitated. "Vivian, I don't want to be inhospitable, but I don't think I'm up to company just at the moment."

"Ria, there's something wrong. I can sense it. Please let me help."

Victoria thought that she couldn't keep this secret much longer, and certainly needed understanding friends.

"Yes, alright."

Justin had told Vivian, of course. When she arrived the following day, she hugged Victoria fiercely. "Oh, Ria! You shouldn't have been keeping this to yourself!"

"I didn't want everyone to despise me."

"Some of us are understanding. You *are* getting married after all. And at least you know what it's like to make love. I wish I did!"

"Perhaps it's better not to. It's too hard to stop once you know how divinely wonderful it is."

"Have you not told Chas? Somehow I would have expected him to come and whisk you away."

"I couldn't burden him with this. You must promise me not to tell him, Vivian!"

"Oh, Ria. He should know! You should go over and be with him."

"How can I when he's in France?"

"You can stay with your cousin in England. He must get leave, and you can get married before the baby is born. Not the wedding at Wyndwood that you had planned, but the war has changed everything anyway. And I will come with you! I've decided that I'm not going to get anywhere with the VAD here. I'll try to get taken on in England, work in a hospital there. That way I can see Peter when he has leave. So we should start planning! First of all, you need some comfortable clothes, because you are going to be getting bigger. How far along are you?"

"Six months."

"So the sooner we go, the better!"

"Vivian, did Justin put you up to this?"

"Only to ask me to come here. He guessed. He doesn't know that I'm taking you to England. Now we need to think about closing the house."

Vivian stayed for a week, and then decided to go home and put her own affairs in order. And convince her family that she needed to go and do her bit for the war.

•  •  •

*My darling Ria,*

*You muggins! Why didn't you tell me you were with child? Never mind who told me. Our friends are concerned about you.*

*Yes, I know you recall my saying last summer that I didn't want children underfoot yet. Believe me, I have aged decades since then. I've seen too many men die, and I know that there is nothing so precious as a life. A new one will bring a ray of hope and sunshine into this miserable and crazy world. I'm ecstatic! You know how much I love you. Of course we must marry right away, while you can still travel. I can hardly wait to see you, to touch you, to make wild and passionate love to you.*

*Take the Lusitania if at all possible. She is the fastest and safest ship on the seas and can easily outrun the German submarines. She's also a delightful ship, as you know. Let me know*

*your arrangements so that I can wrangle leave. Hurry, my darling!*
*I can hardly wait to hold you in my arms!*
*Your impatient and devoted Chas*

Victoria booked a passage on the *Lusitania* for the May 1st
sailing. The ship was only departing from New York once a month
now, and they'd just missed the April crossing. In any case, there
was still too much to do. But once they arrived in England,
Victoria would still have a month until the baby was due, and
Chas had a good chance of getting leave by then.

Telegrams back and forth to Beatrice assured her that she
and the baby were most welcome, Beatrice saying wryly, "I see I
didn't perform my duties as chaperone adequately, so let me now
be a welcoming host. I shall be delighted to see you and Vivian
again."

Victoria decided that Wyndholme should be put to good use,
perhaps as a convalescent hospital. Now that the Canadian troops
were engaged in battles on the Western Front, there would
undoubtedly be casualties coming back soon. She broached the
subject with Olivia. First telling her about her condition.

Olivia took her into her comforting arms. "You should have
told me sooner! Did you think I wouldn't understand?" She had to
admit that she was shocked, and surprised at Chas for taking
advantage of Victoria. "I saw how much you and Chas are in love.
It's this blasted war that's thrown everything into turmoil! So I'm
glad you're going to stay with Beatrice, and be with Chas when
he's on leave. But I am sorry we'll miss the wedding. Now tell me
what I can do to help."

Olivia thought it a wonderful idea to make use of Wyndholme
as a hospital, and agreed that she would oversee the running of it,
and raise funds to keep it going. It gave her something important
to do for the war effort. Victoria stipulated that the staff should be
kept on – those who chose to stay – at her expense.

Josephine would move into Rosemullion where she could play
with her brother, Spats.

Before Olivia left, she agreed that no one except Richard and
Zoë, and perhaps Max, should know about Victoria's condition. The
others would learn about it once the baby was born.

Rafe came by one afternoon and delivered a small box, saying,
"Chas asked me to bring this around. He says you're to wear it.
Propriety and all that. Bloody hell, Ria, you and Chas are such
hypocrites! Telling *me* not to take advantage of Lizzie! But it's
alright for Chas to fuck you."

"Stop it!" She was always slightly shocked by the word 'fuck', not only because she rarely heard it, but also because it was such a harsh, vulgar, vicious word that had nothing to do with the beauty and joy of making love. "We were engaged."

"He should have bloody well married you before going off to pursue heroics!"

She felt unusually emotional these days, and couldn't stop some tears from escaping.

Rafe stroked her arm with surprising tenderness. "I'm sorry, Ria. I'll look after Calypso for you."

She nodded.

The box contained a wedding band to match her engagement ring.

When Justin came to see her, she asked, "Did *you* inform Chas?"

"Someone had to. So you can be angry with me if you like, but..."

"I'm not angry, Justin. I should have told him myself right away, and gone to England. I've wasted all these months. And I'm scared! I'm so afraid that now that I'm on my way to be with him, something will happen to prevent our being together."

"You mustn't think like that, Ria. I wish I were coming with you. I've seriously considered it."

"But your exams start in May, and I can't wait any longer to go. You can't throw away the entire year. You'll be finished law school soon. Vivian and I will be fine on our own."

Grayson spoke to Victoria. He and Mrs. Grayson had already decided this would be a good time for them to leave her employment. "Mrs. Grayson and I are going to be travelling to England on the *Lusitania* as well, Miss Victoria. We decided it may as well be that ship as another, and this way we may be able to offer you some assistance, especially in the present circumstances."

Victoria didn't fail to get his meaning. She blushed. "Thank you for your loyalty, Grayson, despite the scandalous circumstances."

"Miss Victoria, we are devoted to this family. We've known you since you were a baby. As we haven't been blessed with any of our own, we look upon you as our child, presumptuous as that may sound."

"Not at all! I'm touched, and pleased." So much that she was almost moved to tears.

"So we're not about to judge you. We know that you were already affianced, and Mr. Chas is an honourable and good man – none better. We're delighted that you are to be married."

"Thank you, Grayson. I shall be grateful for your company. And you and Mrs. Grayson must come to our wedding! But please allow me to pay your passage and travel expenses."

"That's not necessary, Miss Victoria. I've already booked us into cabin class."

"I must insist, Grayson. Let it be my contribution to your new venture. And you must stay at the Waldorf=Astoria in New York with us."

"Thank you, Miss Victoria. And we would be delighted to attend the wedding."

"I shall miss you both. Very much." Without overstepping the boundaries of their relationship, the Graysons had been more than supportive these last months. They had helped Victoria learn whatever she didn't already know about running a household, including verifying the accounts. Unobtrusively, they had always been nearby, anticipating her needs and not allowing her to feel abandoned.

"Perhaps you and Mr. Thornton will come and stay at our inn?"

"Oh, yes! You must let us know all about it."

Felicity, who didn't know about the baby, was terribly sad to be missing the wedding. "Couldn't I come? School is stupid and boring anyway! I'm going to miss you, Ria."

"We'll have a proper wedding when Chas and I return, and you can be a bridesmaid."

"Can you do that? Have two weddings?"

"I don't see why not. Our wedding in England will be simple."

"Why don't you just wait until Chas gets back?"

"Because I miss him too much. And he gets lonely, too. So I'm going over to look after him. I'll write every week, and tell you all about England."

If the Thorntons suspected anything, Victoria wasn't aware of it. J.D. set up an account for her with a bank in England, starting her out with $50,000, and told her to buy a house, if she and Chas preferred to have their own place, rather than stay with Beatrice.

Marjorie said, "I am delighted that you and Chas will be together, my dear. I think having you nearby will give him strength. I do worry so! His letters are always cheerful, but he's a sensitive boy and all this killing... Well, let's hope it doesn't go on much longer. I'll be happy when you're both home again."

Jack wrote to Eleanor,

*It's good that Ria is coming, and the baby has cheered Chas up immensely. I was getting worried about him, as his friends' deaths have really rattled him. I don't mean that he's lost his nerve – some chaps do – but that he was becoming fatalistic, thinking he would be the next to go. Now it's as if that seemingly inevitable course has been averted...*

Olivia decided that there should be a family dinner to bid farewell to Victoria. They had transformed Wyndholme, putting things into storage in the attics to prepare for the hospital, so the dinner was at Rosemullion.

Victoria had had a new wardrobe made, including a wedding gown, and managed, with the clever help of tunics, to hide her increasing bulge fairly well.

Olivia helped with the concealment by having the lights very low, and seating Victoria so that she wasn't close to the scrutiny of Helena or Phyllis. The men were less likely to notice. She hadn't counted on Phoebe, who said, "Are you like Alice, Victoria, growing all different sizes? You look bigger today."

Helena's eyes took on a knowing look, as Victoria countered, "It must be because the world is going mad, like in Wonderland."

"'Oh, you can't help that,' said the Cat: 'we're all mad here. I'm mad. You're mad,'" Phoebe quoted. "'How do you know I'm mad?' said Alice. 'You must be,' said the Cat, 'or you wouldn't have come here.'"

"That's enough of that Phoebe," Albert said firmly.

Edgar looked concerned for his sister, and tried to change the subject by saying, "I don't see why you're so impatient to see Chas, Ria. It seems a bit risky to be going overseas, what with all the submarine activity, and Zeppelins bombing England."

"There's only been one bombing. Anyway, I can be more useful in England than sitting about Wyndholme, waiting for Chas to return. Since I can drive a car and fix it, I expect I can drive ambulances for the Red Cross."

James snorted. "You never have been conventional. I expect Chas will have his hands full with you."

"Oh I do hope so," she countered, looking defiantly at her father.

Edgar diffused the situation by saying, "You make me feel even more useless! A girl going off to the war, and all I can do is hobble to the office and make sure the profits keep rolling in."

"Is the ankle no better then?" Victoria asked.

"Some days it's not too bad, and others, I can barely stand."

"I'm glad that you can't go to war," Phyllis said. "I'm distraught enough with worry about Henry."

"I hope no one else has to go," Zoë said. Later, she told Victoria that she was uneasy. "I know it's silly, but I had a dream and...," She couldn't tell Victoria. It was too horrible, and might distress her. "Well, I don't believe in premonitions, but I'm suddenly afraid. I detest this war! Do take care, Ria! I should be going with you."

"Don't be silly! You can't miss your exams and fail your year. Vivian and I will be fine. After all, we have Grayson to look after us."

Zoë chuckled. "Who would have thought him such a father hen? I am glad he and Mrs. Grayson will be close by." She gave Victoria a hug, "I wish I could be at the wedding."

"You were supposed to be my Maid of Honour. But things haven't worked out at all like we had planned. We should be in Switzerland now, perfecting our languages and posture."

"Not with you in that condition!"

"That's true. I expect we would have gotten married in Antibes or Paris or..."

"Bovington Abbey, just like you will be. I'll miss you dreadfully, Ria! And summer just won't be the same without you at Wyndwood."

"That will be very strange, not spending summer at the cottage. But we might be back before it's over."

But Helena called on Victoria a few days later. "You should have told us you're with child," she said without preliminaries.

"As I'm about to leave, there shouldn't be any scandal. Unless you make one."

"Don't be childish! It's not in anyone's best interest that society be aware of your indiscretions."

"Helena, what do you want?" Victoria asked wearily, not interested in arguing with her.

"Your father is incensed, so I thought it best to come alone."

"Why? Because he's going to be a grandfather before becoming a father himself?" She could see that the barb hit home. "Why did you tell him?"

"Because he *is* your father. And we have to preserve the family's reputation. So your father thinks that it would be best if you and Chas stayed in England for several years, before returning with the baby. People may tend to forget when you actually left and married. If they were to discover that the baby was born this summer, it doesn't matter that you can claim you were already married, because they'll know the timing doesn't work out."

"So we're to be banished? Doesn't it worry you even a little, Helena, to want to bear children for someone who has so little affection or kindness for his own daughter?"

"He'll be different with our children." Helena stared at her with a mixture of triumph and pity.

"Can he be sure they *are* his children?"

The slap was a surprise, but not very painful.

"You are a nasty little bitch! It's no wonder your father dislikes you. I have tried to be tolerant and understanding, but you're not willing to reciprocate."

"So you're both going to disown me. What a surprise. I'm sure you can find your way out, Helena."

.      .      .

A few days before they left for New York, Victoria and Vivian heard that Archie Spencer had been killed in the Second Battle of Ypres, one of the many to die a horrible death, choking, drowning as his lungs were liquefied by chlorine gas. The Germans had launched a terrible new weapon.

The world really had gone mad.

# Chapter 21

Victoria and Vivian didn't see the warning issued by the German Embassy in the morning papers, but it was the buzz at the Cunard pier as reporters swarmed about, one of them ghoulishly announcing he had just taken a photograph of the *Lusitania's* last voyage.

"What are they talking about?" Vivian said with concern, as the press overran the Promenade Deck of the ship, looking for celebrities to interview.

Having overhead them, a rather striking young gentleman raised his wide-brimmed Stetson hat to them as he said, "Please don't distress yourselves, ladies. The Kaiser is trying to frighten us by telling us what we already know – that Germany is at war with Great Britain, and that we are about to sail into a war zone. I don't intend to be intimidated or dissuaded. Oliver Dalvay at your service, ladies." He bowed to them. With his long hair, silk cravat tied in a loose bow at his neck, and flowing, ankle length coat, he looked ruggedly foppish.

"Mrs. Thornton and Miss Carrington," Victoria said, hoping that no one wanted to see her passport, but knowing that she couldn't be Miss Wyndham and so obviously pregnant. "My husband insisted that we sail on the *Lusitania* because of her speed."

"Yes indeed, Madam. She can outrun any Hun submarine. Idle threats, trying to unnerve us, that's all this is. I could have sailed on an American ship, but I like the old *Lusy*. The best of the ocean greyhounds, to my reckoning. So we won't let crazy Billy terrorize us. Do look, here comes Alfred Vanderbilt. Did you know that he was booked to sail on the *Titanic*, but changed his mind a few days before? I'd say he has good instincts or good luck."

Alfred Vanderbilt, tall and dapper in a grey pinstripe suit, sporting a pink carnation in his buttonhole, caused a stir among the reporters as he embarked. He was obviously unconcerned about the threat.

"And there's the renowned impresario, Charles Frohman with the actresses, Rita Jolivet and Josephine Brandell."

"There's Sadie Burke. Remember she sang at the Oakley's musicale last summer?" Victoria said to Vivian.

"She's becoming quite famous," Oliver Dalvay said.

"We seem to be in illustrious company," Vivian commented.

"One usually is on the *Lusy*."

"Your name is familiar, Mr. Dalvay," Victoria said.

"You're too kind, Madam. I am but a mere scribe."

"You write for *Life* magazine and have published novels," Victoria said in recognition. *Life* was a weekly American humour publication that included cultural reviews. "A young Mark Twain, I've heard you called."

"A most flattering accolade, to which I sincerely hope to aspire."

"Are you travelling to Britain on business, Mr. Dalvay?" Vivian inquired.

"My business is also my pleasure, I'm happy to say. I'm writing a satire on the stupidity of war. This warning is exactly the spice I need. And what brings you lovely young ladies into the arena of war?"

"My husband is with the Royal Flying Corps," Victoria explained rather proudly. "I'm going to join him in England. Miss Carrington is planning to volunteer for the medical services, as she has already been trained in Canada, but would prefer to be closer to the front lines and her fiancé."

"Very noble of you all! Do let us get together later as I am most interested to hear news from the people actually in the action, not just the politicians and press. I'll bid you good day for now." He tipped his hat and walked off, jauntily swinging his cane.

Victoria had requested the same suite that Chas had had, so she felt close to him there. She didn't know how he had managed it, but a dozen red roses awaited her. The note read, "Safe voyage. I'll be holding you in my arms before the roses fade, my love."

Grayson had made certain that the proper luggage had been brought to her stateroom, some of it not being wanted on the voyage, and Mrs. Grayson unpacked her things. The Graysons were very pleased with their second class accommodation, which was, apparently, as good as first class accommodations on some other ships.

Vivian was delighted, and said this was far superior to the *Empress of Ireland* which had taken them to and from Europe last year, just before her last, fatal voyage.

They went back on deck to watch as the ship left port. How odd to think that only eight months ago she had stood on the pier weeping as Chas had sailed away from her.

"Hell's bells!" Victoria said. "Isn't that Lady Dunston?"

"Is it?" Vivian replied. "Oh, yes, the Dunstons visited the Thorntons two summers ago, didn't they?"

"Yes. We do business with Sir Montague Dunston – he owns the Transatlantic Steamship Line, and we ship our lumber through him. Grandmother and I went to Montreal with Father once, and we dined at their home. Oh, hell! She's very much a social creature who stands on ceremony and takes her position as the wife of a knight very seriously. Her son, Percy, who was at Oxford with Chas, has married some aristocrat's daughter. He graduated a year earlier than Chas, and stayed in England to manage some of the family business from there. I expect Lady Dunstan is taking her two youngest daughters off to England to find them suitable blue-bloods as well. Remember how the girls constantly flirted with Chas that summer? He'd canoe over to Wyndwood to escape them for a while. They've probably heard of our engagement, but no wedding. Bloody hell!"

Any hope of avoiding Lady Dunston and her two nubile daughters was out of the question, as there were only a couple hundred first class passengers. But Victoria hadn't expected to encounter them at the Captain's table on the first evening. She was introduced as Mrs. Thornton, but Lady Dunston said, with obvious disdain, "I was sorry to hear about your grandmother, *Miss* Wyndham."

"Thank you. Yes, her death was very tragic. And it's *Mrs. Thornton*, actually. I married Chas in September, just before he went to England to join the RFC."

The Dunston girls looked shocked. "We heard about your engagement, but not your marriage," Lady Dunston said pointedly.

"In deference to my grandmother, we had a simple ceremony and a brief honeymoon in New York before Chas left. Of course we had all expected the war to be over by Christmas, but since it now seems to be dragging on, I've decided to go to England to be with him whenever he's on leave. I'm staying with my cousin, The Countess of Kirkland, but my father-in-law suggested we might want to buy our own house. I certainly hope the war doesn't drag on so long that that becomes necessary!"

Lady Dunston would eventually find out that Victoria had lied to her. But it was important for now not to be ostracized in this elite society. She made sure that her rings were on display, and noticed that nineteen-year-old Gwendolyn Dunston had taken a keen interest.

With obvious envy and disappointment, Gwendolyn said, "Chas and Rafe stayed with us on their way back from Oxford last spring. We had no idea that you and he were so… involved."

Victoria said lightly, "We've known each other forever, but there was something magical about last summer that made us realize we were in love. Aren't we lucky?"

Lady Dunston eyed Victoria suspiciously, but turned away, addressing her neighbour, Sir Ian McTavish. "Sir Ian, I understand you're the laird of a Scottish island. How romantic! My ancestors are Scottish, as are my husband's."

The other people at the table were Commander Stackhouse, an explorer who was planning to survey the Antarctic coastline, Sir Hugh Lane, art expert and director of the National Gallery of Ireland, David Rhys Griffiths, Welsh coal magnate and former member of the British Parliament and his daughter, Lady Meredith Powell, an active suffragette, Theadora Prescott, the outspoken American journalist, feminist, and heiress, Oliver Dalvay, and Alfred Vanderbilt.

The fabulously wealthy Alfred, who was renowned as a womanizer with one divorce and several scandalous liaisons behind him, was not only dashing, but most charming and pleasant to all.

They met Captain Turner briefly, but he was rather taciturn and seemed happy to leave the socializing to the personable Staff Captain John Anderson.

"What do you think of this German warning?" Oliver Dalvay said.

"A bluff," Sir Ian McTavish said. "No civilized nation would attack a ship carrying women and children. It's completely against the maritime code of ethics."

"We've been assured a British armed escort once we're close to England, haven't we?" Lady Dunston asked the Staff Captain.

"Indeed, Lady Dunston. And there isn't a German submarine that could catch us in any case."

"I understand you've found some stowaways on board," Commander Stackhouse said to Captain Anderson. "Three Germans."

There were gasps around the table. "Good Lord!" Oliver Dalvay said. "This is turning out to be an interesting journey."

"We have them well secured in comfortable cells," Captain Anderson said.

"Spies, do you think?" Theadora Prescott asked with enthusiasm. "Or saboteurs?"

"They'll be properly interrogated in Liverpool," the Staff Captain said. "In the meantime, they pose no threat."

By the end of the meal, Victoria and Vivian had fallen into an easy friendship with Theadora Prescott, Lady Meredith Powell, and Oliver Dalvay, all of whom were in their late twenties. Instead of staying for the dance, the group took a walk about the Boat Deck and then sat in the verdant, glass-roofed Verandah Café to chat and sip wine.

Theadora was fascinated by Lady Meredith's account of her own sabotage as a member of Emmeline Pankhurst's Women's Social and Political Union – trying to set a letterbox on fire, for which she was promptly arrested. "My husband, Sir Humphrey, was not at all pleased with me. He wanted to pay the fine, but I needed to make a point. After all, arson is not in my nature, nor is any type of violence. The prison cell was an abomination." She shuddered. "It reeked of human effluences. Like other imprisoned suffragettes, I went on a hunger strike. I'd heard how some of the others had been force-fed. It was so barbaric and revolting that it took all my willpower to stop eating and face the same fate. But they released me after five days, much to my relief, I'm rather ashamed to say. One does like to be able to stand up for one's beliefs, and I shall certainly never stop fighting for women's suffrage."

"I'd say you were darn brave, Madam!" Oliver opined.

"I expect this war will actually help our cause," Lady Meredith said wryly. "Already women are taking over men's jobs as they head off to the Front. When we prove ourselves equal to men in what has traditionally been their spheres, they surely can no longer deny us the vote. I'm helping my father run the business already. You yourself, Miss Prescott, are venturing into men's territory."

Meredith and Theadora were both handsome women, the latter being more elegantly turned out.

Theadora smiled and said, "Yes, they like to keep me reporting on society and women's issues. Wouldn't they just love me to tell them what Alfred Vanderbilt wore tonight, what witty remarks he made, and which ladies took his fancy? But as a citizen of a neutral country, I plan to get into the war zone and try to report real news from both sides. Fortunately, I have the means to be freelance, and can do stories on whatever I choose. I expect I shall find interested newspapers. And do all call me Theadora. Do you mind if I smoke?"

They agreed to be on a first name basis, and all accepted cigarettes. Victoria knew they were risking censure by smoking in public, but she didn't care. The war was changing a lot of things.

"You ladies make me feel quite lackadaisical, as I have done nothing more challenging than stand up to a heavy-handed editor," Oliver said. "Are you really going to go behind the frontlines, Theadora? The enemy lines?"

"Wouldn't you like eyewitness accounts of Victoria's husband's aeronautical exploits and Vivian's work with the wounded? And the Germans aren't our enemies, Oliver. Not yet, at any rate. How about seeing the war from their perspective, to balance out the Allied propaganda we hear?"

"You have more integrity than I, Theadora, if you can report impartially on this war," Oliver said. "Perhaps I'm a bit of an anglophile, but I am certainly on the side of the Allies. This poison gas the Germans just began using at Ypres... well, it's just not civilized!"

Lady Meredith chortled. "War isn't civilized."

"No, of course, but it seemed to have some unspoken rules, some parameters of decency in which to fight."

"I think this war has blown away any chivalrous conduct in warfare that may have existed," Theadora said.

"You'll have me volunteering soon," Oliver said.

Theadora was amused by his worried expression. "You'll achieve more with the pen than the sword, in my opinion, Oliver. I've read your work."

"I'm not sure whether to be flattered that you approve of my scribbles, or unmanned that you think me an incompetent warrior," he said with a grin.

"Please do be flattered," Theadora said with a tinkling laugh.

The new-found friends met daily, sharing their meals and discussing ideas and concerns. Otherwise, Victoria restricted her activities, in part because she was feeling the weight of her eight month pregnancy, and also because she wanted to avoid unwelcome attention as much as possible. Besides, obviously pregnant women weren't supposed to flaunt themselves in public. She was happy to sit and read a book in her suite, take a stroll, do a sketch, or recline in one of the deck chairs with the warm sun on her face.

Timothy Eaton's daughter, Josephine Burnside, and her twenty-year-old daughter, Iris, were also on board, and knew Victoria and Vivian. Their family cottage in Muskoka was at Windermere, not that far from Wyndwood. Victoria avoided them as much as possible, maintaining her myth of having married Chas in a small and quiet ceremony.

The Graysons came by daily to check on her, and she told them of her little subterfuge. They agreed it was sometimes necessary to dissemble.

But Lady Dunston visited Victoria in her stateroom just a few days into the voyage. She refused to sit down.

"I've had a telegram from Sir Dunston. You're not a very clever liar, *Miss* Wyndham."

Bloody hell! "I try not to lie at all, Lady Dunston. But sometimes one must prevaricate to protect others."

"Your own reputation, you mean."

"I don't care much for my reputation, Lady Dunston. Chas and I are going to be married next week. We will be happy, and not give a toss what others think about us. I'm concerned for the Thorntons and my own family. They don't even know."

"You should have thought of that before you behaved so wantonly. You're not morally sound to be accepted in society, and I shall be sure that everyone knows it."

As she turned to go, Victoria said, "I think you should be careful, Lady Dunston. If you scratch the veneer of society you'll discover that men tend to have mistresses, and I daresay, some bored wives take lovers. The hypocrisy of society is that only those who are caught are shunned, even though we all know it goes on." She looked hard at Lady Dunston. "Rather a shallow view of morality, don't you think? And considering that Chas and I were already engaged to be married and are deeply in love, our showing that love for each other prematurely is nothing like as reprehensible as adulterous behaviour."

"Are you implying something, Miss Wyndham?" She seemed slightly uncertain, as if wondering if Victoria knew something to her detriment. And Victoria wondered if she had hit a nerve. After all, if J.D. had a mistress, wasn't it likely that Sir Dunston might as well? Bless Chas for telling her that!

"Of course not, Lady Dunston. I just think that we are all vulnerable, and should be careful whom we criticize. I don't expect you really wish to harm or upset your friends and business associates." She emphasized the last, in case nothing else would change Lady Dunston's mind.

"It's a pity that Chas had to settle for a scheming young woman like you, Miss Wyndham, when he had his pick of decent girls. But I wouldn't have expected anything less from him than to do the honourable thing and marry you. You will avoid my company and that of the other respectable people on board, or I shall be forced to expose you. Good day."

Victoria was fuming when Lady Dunston swept regally from the suite. She'd had to bite her tongue to avoid a retort, which she knew might only make things worse. At least the old biddy would keep her secret for the moment. But what a nerve to suggest that she had tricked Chas into marrying her! He would be amused, so she allowed the anger to pass.

She took a book and went out to lounge in a chair on the deck. A steward brought her a blanket and a cup of tea. The ship's doctor stopped by to ask her how she was feeling.

"Quite well, thank you, Dr. McDermott. A bit tired perhaps."

"What better way to rest up for your confinement than to take the sea air?" he said convivially.

"You must think it odd that I should travel so late."

He chuckled. "Not at all. In fact, we have expectant mothers booking trips just in time to have their children born at sea. We have an excellent twenty-four bed hospital facility here, and all the medical services are included in the fare."

She smiled. "I shall try not to burden you."

"Not in the least! With this smooth crossing, I've had hardly anything to do. You will let me know if you have any concerns whatsoever?"

"Indeed, I will. Thank you, doctor."

While they had been speaking, a young girl of about thirteen had sat down beside Victoria. She was a pretty, toffee-haired child with a sailor-style dress and huge bow in her hair. "Were you seasick at all?" the girl asked Victoria after the doctor had left.

"Surprisingly, no. I suppose that's because I'm used to being on the water all summer. Were you seasick?"

"Oh yes. Frightfully, for two days, but I feel better now. Nanny said I could wander about. I'm Alice Lambton."

"Victoria Thornton. I haven't met your parents."

"Oh, they're not here. Mummy died last year. She was going to England because my grandmother was sick. She was on the *Empress of Ireland*."

The sinking of the *Empress* last May in the foggy, night time waters of the St. Lawrence River had been in the news for months. The inquiry had established that the Norwegian freighter that had collided with the *Empress* had been at fault. Over a thousand people had died in that tragedy. "I'm so sorry, Alice! That's terribly sad."

Alice nodded as she looked down at her fiercely entwined fingers.

"Are you going to visit your grandparents?"

"I'm going to live with them. Daddy thinks that I'll get a better education in England." She frowned. "But I think that he just wants to spend more time with his new wife and not bother with me."

Said so matter-of-factly, the words were robbed of self-pity and were therefore all the more poignant. Victoria understood completely. "So you're travelling alone?"

"With Nanny Smith. But she's boring. She just wants to play cards with other people down on our deck, and go dancing in the evenings."

Victoria felt deeply sorry for the lonely child. "Would you like to come for an ice cream with me?"

"Oh yes please!"

They went to the Verandah Café where Victoria ordered two chocolate sundaes.

"It looks like a summer garden here," Alice said with approval. There were plants and flowers everywhere among the deep wicker chairs and tables, and dangling from the glass ceiling. "Daddy owns a dairy and we have the best ice cream in Ottawa. But this is good, too. I like your dragonfly."

Victoria was never without her brooch. "My husband gave it to me for Christmas. Dragonflies and I seem to get on well."

"Why did you say that you're on the water all summer? Do you travel back and forth on the ship?"

"This is the first time I've been on such a large ship. But we have a cottage on an island in Muskoka – that's an area of beautiful lakes north of Toronto – and so we're always out canoeing and sailing or on small boats."

"That sounds like fun! Do you own the island?"

"My family does. I own a part of it and the cottage where all my cousins and aunts and uncles stay with me all summer."

"You are lucky! I don't have any cousins in Ottawa. But I do in England. Do you swim?"

"Oh yes. We even have swimming races."

"I can't swim. Mummy couldn't swim either. But Daddy said it wouldn't have made any difference. Do you think we're going to sink?"

"Heavens, no! If I'd thought that, I wouldn't have come. Are you worried?"

Alice shrugged. "I've heard people talking about how submarines might try to sink us."

"We're faster than any submarines. But if ever you're scared or if we did see a submarine, would you come and tell me and we could look after each other?"

Alice's large, tawny eyes brightened. "Oh, could I? Really?"

"Of course. We're friends, aren't we?"

Alice had a lovely smile. "This ice cream is even better than Daddy's! Is your husband with you?"

"No, he's at the war, but we're meeting up in England. I'm travelling with one of my cottage friends."

"Do you have a picture of him?"

"As a matter of fact I do." Victoria took it out of her pocket. It was the one that Zoë had snapped the evening Chas had taken her out on the lake to officially propose. How long ago that seemed now! And how the memory of it could still make her weak with joy and longing. "It was taken on his boat. He has an island, too."

"He looks nice. So does your lake."

"Do let us see," Theadora said as she and the others descended upon them. "What a telling photograph! Young love. You do make a handsome couple."

Victoria introduced Alice, and the girl was offered another ice or a soda or cake by the others, all of which she declined. Tactfully, Victoria told them about Alice's situation, so when they had finished their coffees, Theadora and Oliver asked Alice if she'd like to join them for the egg-and-spoon race. She went off happily with them.

Lady Meredith commented, "I think we have a romance blossoming."

"Theadora and Oliver?" Victoria asked.

"They do seem to get along well," Vivian said.

"I'm envious of you all," Meredith confessed. "I don't know what it's like to be in love, but it seems to be wonderful. I married because my father wanted me to, and I had no better options or offers. Humphrey was a friend and neighbour, but he's twenty years older, and we have quite different interests. He's a good sort, mind you. Stood behind me even while he disparaged my involvement with the Pankhursts. But there's something missing."

"Children?" Victoria suggested.

"Yes. But I would like to experience some real, thundering passion sometime."

"Passion can be painful," Vivian said, and told Meredith about her love for Peter and how her parents were determined to keep them apart.

"I wish you well, both of you," Meredith said. "It must be frightening for you, knowing that your men are in constant danger. Oh dear, I shall be worried about them for your sakes! We must keep in touch once we're in England. Now tell me about Alice."

When Victoria had told them what little she knew, Meredith said, "I was eleven when my mother died. But that brought my father and me even closer together. He started teaching me all about the business when I was only twelve, agreed that I should attend Oxford, even though they don't actually grant degrees to women – yet! – and never told me that I couldn't do something because I'm just a woman. Quite the contrary. Being his daughter, I'm expected to be able to do anything!" She chuckled.

"You're very lucky," Victoria said.

"Yes, I do know that. I suppose that's why I had no objections to marrying Humphrey when my father suggested it. I knew that he had only my best interests at heart."

Alice came bounding back, proudly showing them her prize as runner-up – a *Lusitania* badge.

So the group of friends adopted Alice. She spent some time every day talking to Victoria either on deck or in her suite, wanting to hear all about Victoria's family and her summer life in Muskoka, and then went off for more energetic pursuits with the others.

She was also with them when they attended Sir Ian McTavish's demonstration of how to put on their life jackets properly. He had not been happy with what he considered lax preparations for their entering the war zone. Life boat drills had been for the crew only. There seemed to be no sort of plan in place should evacuating the ship become necessary. At least the passengers should know where to find their life vests and how to use them. Captain Turner was not best pleased with this demonstration, since he didn't want any panic among the passengers.

Although Victoria didn't usually attend the evening dances or concerts with her friends, she did go along to the traditional passengers' talent contest which raised funds for the Seamen's Charities, and which was the last important social event of the voyage. It was held in the Georgian style first-class lounge, which was beautifully appointed with mahogany panelling and wood-burning fireplaces, plush settees and easy chairs, and a splendid stained glass ceiling.

Vivian played a short but brilliant piece on her cello. Oliver Dalvay recited a humorous poem he had written about this voyage, which included many of the passengers, much to everyone's delight. The Welsh choir, on their way home from touring Canada and the United States, enchanted them. Sadie Burke sang smoulderingly. There were magic tricks, piano performances, and more singers.

Captain Turner addressed the audience during intermission. "Ladies and gentlemen, we've had a warning from the Admiralty of submarine activity off the Irish coast. On entering the war zone tomorrow we shall be securely in the care of the Royal Navy, so, of course there is no need for alarm. Tomorrow we'll be steaming full speed for Liverpool, and should arrive in good time. Might I ask you all to refrain from lighting cigarettes on deck? Thank you. Do enjoy the rest of the entertainment."

Although the talent show continued, it was a subdued and unsettled audience. The friends left to go to the Verandah Café.

"We haven't been making good speed," Lady Meredith said. "My father discovered that one of the boilers has been shut down to conserve fuel. One of the advantages of this ship is that it can outrun submarines, but we're barely above their speed now."

Victoria felt the baby kick, and absently stroked her stomach.

"I've heard that Commander Stackhouse is a British agent on a secret mission," Oliver said. "And that we're carrying tons of munitions. Which makes us a legitimate target for the Germans."

Victoria wondered wryly if any of them were Oswald Oakley's armaments.

"I'll be relieved when this journey is over!" Vivian said. Victoria had never seen her so agitated. "It's all been too perfect — the weather, the smooth seas. But it's like the calm before the storm. I feel so uneasy."

Early that morning, the crew had loosened the twenty-two wooden lifeboats and swung them clear of the railings. At sunset, they had extinguished all outboard lights, placed covers over cabin skylights and portholes, and drawn curtains in the salons.

"If anything happens, let's agree to meet outside here," Theadora said. "The lifeboats are close by."

"And let's be sure to look out for Alice. I don't trust that nanny of hers," Victoria said. Alice was in second class, but Victoria knew the number of her cabin.

Many passengers paced the deck that evening. Some were too nervous to go to their cabins, and decided to sleep in the lounges. Victoria and Vivian talked late into the night, making promises to each other of what to tell family and friends should something happen to them. Having worked themselves into an emotional state, they slept fitfully for only a few hours.

They woke to a dense fog and the eerie blast of the ship's foghorn every minute.

"If the Germans didn't know where we were, they do now!" Victoria said, scrunching her pillow over her ears.

By noon, the fog had burned off under a bright sun, the sea was a glassy sapphire blue, and the Irish coast was a welcome sight. But two things puzzled the passengers. The slow speed of the ship and the fact that there was no naval escort.

All having slept badly, the friends had a late lunch. By then some of the excitement of nearing port was animating everyone. On such a clear and calm sea, surely the lookouts would see a periscope in good time, so there was no immediate danger of submarines.

The orchestra began playing "The Blue Danube" as they left the dining room. When they reached the Boat Deck for a stroll, Oliver looked over the starboard side of the ship and said in quiet awe, "Oh my dear God! Is that a torpedo?"

It looked like the frothy wake of a small boat, Victoria thought, the instant before it hit.

They felt the shuddering impact, and a moment later there was a tremendous explosion that sent a huge geyser of water and wood and iron and cinders shooting into the air and raining down on the deck. As they were at the stern, no one was hit by debris, only sooty water, but they were thrown hard against the rails. Theadora lost her footing, but Oliver grabbed her as the boat listed to starboard. People began appearing on deck, looking dazed and frightened. The few officers were trying to stave off panic.

"We have to fetch our life jackets. I'll get yours," Vivian said to Victoria.

"No! We'll go together. We'll meet up near the Café," Victoria said to the others. "Look for Alice!"

"I'm going to find my father!" Meredith said.

They fought to keep their footing against the tilting of the boat to reach their stateroom, which, fortunately, was on this deck. Oliver and Meredith were one deck lower.

But the ship lost power as Victoria and Vivian were rushing down the corridor, which suddenly went black, and they tried not to panic. They stumbled against others frantically trying to get to their cabins or onto the deck. In their stateroom, they ripped the coverings off the portholes to let in the light.

"We should take off our skirts and shoes, to reduce the weight," Vivian said. How well they knew from summers on the lake that heavy wet clothing could drag you down.

As Victoria had a loose-fitting wool gown on, she stripped it off completely while Vivian dispensed with her skirt. "Rather risqué, but who the hell cares?" Victoria said, re-pinning her dragonfly to her chemise. She had already decided that morning to wear Augusta's pearl and sapphire necklace and matching earrings in case anything should happen, so she presented a strange picture now in her undergarments, with her bulging stomach and elegant jewellery.

"I'm so sorry I dragged you into this, Vivian!" Victoria said, hugging her tightly. "You should be safely in Guelph."

"Don't be silly! I chose to come, to be with Peter. Don't ever fool guilty! We'll get through this, Ria. Now let me help you on with your life jacket."

They groped their way back through the sloping, dark hallway to pandemonium on the port deck. People were scrambling for life jackets, screaming for their children, jostling to get to lifeboats, and clinging desperately to the railings. There was no sign of their friends or Alice or the Graysons.

Victoria tried to go down the stairs to find the girl, but couldn't push through the tide of panic-stricken people struggling to come up. Vivian pulled her back and said, "She knows where to find us."

Captain Turner appeared on the bridge and shouted, "Don't lower the boats! The ship can't sink. Will the gentlemen kindly assist me in getting the women and children out of the boats?"

The ship, her engines dead, was still plowing swiftly and uncontrollably through the water. Some of the lifeboats that had been lowered just capsized on hitting the water at such a speed.

But as water began lapping over the bow, people ignored the Captain's commands and fought to get into the lifeboats and launch them. Because of the list to starboard, the port side boats were swinging inward. Crew and passengers tried to push the heavy and heavily laden boats outward but some crashed hard against the ship, crushing people on the deck who were in the way. Another plummeted onto the sloping deck and slid down the blood-splattered promenade, as people tried, too often in vain, to jump out of the way. Boats that managed to get lowered down the side of the ship caught on the protruding rivets, and dumped people out. With others, the tackle slipped so that the boats tipped, spilling people into the water far below. One boat crashed on top of another, crushing everyone beneath. People tumbled down the deck into the sea. Some stripped and dove in.

Victoria and Vivian were horrified by the carnage. "Better to swim for it," Victoria said.

They fought their way uphill to the stern of the starboard side of the ship, where things were little better. Here the lifeboats were swinging outward, with a six or seven foot gap between them and the ship. People were throwing their babies and small children to others who had been able to jump or crawl across a bridge of oars into the boats. A man grabbed Victoria to toss her into a boat, but she fought him. "Let go of me!" she shouted.

And found herself pulled away by Oliver. Theadora had also appeared, and a moment later they heard Alice call, "Victoria! I'm here, like I promised." She slid down the deck toward them, but Oliver caught her.

Victoria pulled the child into her arms for a thankful hug. "Where's your life jacket?"

"Here you are, young lady," Alfred Vanderbilt said, strapping her into one. He and his valet had been helping as many women and children as possible to find and secure life vests, and hand them into boats. He himself was not wearing one.

"Where's your nanny?" Victoria asked Alice.

"I don't know. I haven't seen her since this morning."

Victoria noticed Lady Dunston sitting rigidly in one of the lifeboats, her face vacant and bleeding. There was no sign of her daughters.

She just caught a glimpse of the Graysons, fortunately wearing life jackets, further down the deck, and gave them a sad smile as she and Vivian took Alice firmly in hand between them. "Get ready to jump. We'll see you in Ireland," Victoria said to the others.

"I can't swim," Theadora admitted, gripping Oliver's hand tightly. She gave him a swift kiss and promised, "There'll be more for you later," much to his delight.

"Kick your feet and move your hands like a dog paddling," Victoria advised the non-swimmers, as a wall of icy green water rushed up the deck and pulled them into the sea before they even had a chance to jump. Alice's hand was torn from her grasp as they were sucked under.

It had been less than eighteen minutes since the torpedo had struck. Only six lifeboats had been successfully launched.

Victoria felt herself tumbling into the black depths, debris smashing against her, a rope trying to ensnare her, a sharp Marconi aerial grazing her leg. She struck out, trying to right herself. Just as she felt her lungs would burst, she surfaced. The ship had gone, but in its place was a sea of thrashing humanity amid a thick blanket of debris.

Suddenly there was a violent underwater explosion that sent up clouds of steam and a tidal wave of churning water that smashed swimmers, bodies, and wreckage into each other. Victoria, rammed into by a chair and a bloody corpse, was forced under again, and struggled to find a place to surface amid a dense mass of floating deck chairs, hencoops, oars, doors, people, and another corpse with half his face and one arm gone. She didn't see Vivian or Alice or the others, and shouted their names. But hers was only another tiny voice amid the screams for missing family and friends, howls of pain, and cries for help and mercy.

A man with no life jacket grabbed hold of her in a panic, and she sank again, but managed to kick free of him and swim away underwater. When she came up, he was nowhere to be seen. She saw others flailing their arms feebly as they drowned. Some clung to lifeless bodies kept afloat by life jackets. Others tried to right capsized boats, and failing that, to clamber onto the keel. Absurdly, some people were floating upside down, having put on their life vests incorrectly. The bodies of babies and children drifted by like water lilies.

Victoria began swimming toward distant lifeboats that were hauling in survivors. Some of the collapsible boats, which had never been launched, had nonetheless been torn free, and people climbed onto those rafts, even though the canvas tops hadn't been removed.

But the debris was thick and the current, strong, so she couldn't seem to get any closer to them. The water was numbingly cold, and her limbs would no longer obey. She found it painful to breathe and her body ached and burned in places. She had to find something to cling to.

There were boxes and wardrobes and barrels bobbing about. Frantic people were scrabbling to hold onto to some wreckage, even fighting over it, often tumbling off it again and again.

Victoria managed to crawl into a wicker chair from the Verandah Café, and almost laughed at the absurdity of lying in it as she gazed up at a perfectly blue and sunny sky. It was almost like an innocent summer sky in Muskoka. She was not completely out of the water, but it was better than being totally immersed. Still, she was shivering violently, despite the strong sunshine. She noticed a long gash on her leg that was bleeding, but not stinging so much now that it was mostly out of the salty water. Something warm trickled down her face. She put her hands across the bulge of her stomach as she said reassuringly, "We'll get through this, little nipper. Daddy will come and get us in his aeroplane."

She thought that Chas was not really that far away, that he was probably seeing the same brilliant sky. As the sea seemed to grow quiet, someone in a thin voice was singing "Abide With Me" but she liked *their* song better.

Chas began singing to her *"Come Josephine in My Flying Machine"*. She felt intoxicated, joyful as he whirled her about in their special dance. *Up, up, A little bit higher. Oh! My! The moon is on fire...* She lost consciousness with a smile on her face.

. . .

In the blue skies over France, Chas had a sudden and sharp feeling of dread. He lost his concentration for a moment, but as there was no enemy action, it wasn't critical. So he couldn't understand his lingering unease. If it wasn't for himself, this presentiment of danger, was it for Ria? *Oh my darling girl, be safe.*

It wasn't until late that evening that he heard about the *Lusitania*.

. . .

It was more than three hours later when someone on one of the rescue vessels, the trawler, *Bluebell*, saw flashes of light amid the wreckage and corpses floating around them. But when they arrived at the source of the light it was to find yet another body, that of a very pregnant young woman. The flashes had come from the late afternoon sunlight reflected from a splendid sapphire and diamond ring on the hand that rested on her swollen belly.

But they fished her out of her wicker chair and laid her on the deck, on top of the other bodies.

Alice Lambton, stripped of her wet clothes and wearing a large fisherman's wool jumper that came below her knees, thick socks, and a blanket about her shoulders, recognized Victoria. She shrieked and ran to her, throwing her blanket over Victoria's lifeless body and hugging her fiercely.

One of the fishermen tried to pull her away, but Alice cried, "She's not dead! I know she's not dead! Please take her somewhere warm. She'll be alright."

They had already had someone awaken from seeming death, so the burly fisherman picked Victoria up in the blanket and carried her down to the mess room, laying her on the floor by the stove. He stripped off her wet clothes, wrapped her in a couple of blankets, and placed warm bricks at her feet. Alice lay down beside her, between the blankets, and held onto her saying, "Please come back, Victoria. Please don't be dead." She rubbed Victoria's arm as if she could force her back to life.

Victoria regained her senses, wondering why her bed was so hard and she, so cold. She started shivering again.

Alice squealed with happiness. "Oh do give her something hot to drink," she begged one of the sailors. He took a cup of tea, propped Victoria's head up, and trickled some of the warm liquid between her chattering teeth.

"Sure, that do be a miracle," the fellow said.

"Oh, Victoria, I knew you'd make it!" Alice said.

Victoria smiled weakly at her, but didn't have the power to respond. The fisherman patiently fed her the tea, and the shaking became less violent. He carried her to the captain's bunk and put more warm bricks around her. Alice never left her side. She cuddled up against her as Victoria drifted into sleep, listening to a bereaved mother berating Captain Turner, who was also on board the *Bluebell*, for the lack of organization and discipline on the *Lusitania* which had caused so much unnecessary death.

By the time they arrived in Queenstown on Ireland's southeast coast, Victoria was awake, and managed to whisper, "I'm so glad to see you, Alice. Stay with me."

"I will!" Alice promised, tears trickling down her cheeks. "I haven't seen the others."

Still wrapped only in her blankets, Victoria was carried ashore by the burly fisherman. She and Alice were billeted in a large private house with a few other ravaged souls. They were given brandy-laced tea, and food that Victoria couldn't choke down. She was told that a doctor would come eventually to tend to her wounds, although someone gently cleaned them. She was hardly aware of them, only of the pain in her ribs when she breathed.

They asked her who should be sent a telegram to reassure her family. She hadn't even thought about that, but didn't know if a message to Chas would get through quickly, so she gave them Beatrice's address. She would inform the others. She told Alice to inform her family that she was with a friend and would be looked after.

Victoria lay gratefully in a soft and delicately scented bed with thick down covers, clad now in a cotton nightgown. She had her dragonfly brooch clasped in her hand. "What happened to you?" she asked Alice, who climbed in beside her.

"I think I went to the bottom of the sea, but it didn't want me, so it spit me back up. I couldn't find you! But I found an oar and lay on it and did what you said. I paddled like a dog. I came to a lifeboat and they took me in. We found lots of people, but not... And then the fishermen finally came."

Victoria hardly slept again before she felt the searing pains. The baby was coming. Barely able to gasp for breath, she doubled over, clutching her belly. Alice woke immediately. She didn't even ask what was wrong, but ran for help.

The next hours were a blur of hell for Victoria. At times she felt sure that she had entered Dante's inferno, the ship's sinking being the portal. Each contraction sent a dagger of pain through her ribs as well as her abdomen. When he finally arrived, the baby was stillborn.

When the overworked doctor turned up, he stitched the gashes on her forehead and leg, and told her that she had three broken ribs and was lucky to be alive.

Alice kept her from plummeting into despair.

.     .     .

It was late afternoon when Victoria woke again. She didn't know where she was at first, but just enjoyed the softness and warmth of the bed and the bright sunshine streaming in the window. And then the horror of yesterday flooded back to her. She touched her empty and aching belly and began to weep, but that was so painful because of her ribs that she thought she would go mad with the agony and the grief.

Looking frightened and worried, Alice came and sat on the edge of the bed, reaching for Victoria's hand. Victoria took it and held on tightly. She tried to stop crying, telling herself that Chas had not wanted children yet anyway, that she and Chas now had a chance to be selfishly devoted only to each other. And that helped. If she had had to choose between Chas and the baby, of course it was Chas's survival she was most concerned with. Perhaps this was the choice that had been made for her on some sort of celestial balance scale.

But the baby had seemed so real to her. She had talked to him through all those miserable, lonely months at Wyndholme. He had been her companion, as well as a part of her and Chas. But surely it was even worse for those parents who had known and nurtured their children for years, and had been called Mummy.

She suddenly remembered Vivian. Dear, God, where was she? And what about the others?

She tried to sit up, but was too weak.

"Can you take some tea and food now, Victoria?" Alice asked.

"Water," she croaked.

Alice piled pillows beneath her head and helped her to drink from a glass that had been standing nearby.

"Have you heard about Vivian? The others?" Victoria asked.

"No," Alice said, hastily brushing away a tear. "I'm so glad you're going to be alright, Victoria. You must be very sad."

Trying to push away despair, Victoria said, "Your pretty hair looks like it's been dunked in oil."

"Yours is black, too," Alice replied with a grin. "Mrs. O'Rourke – she's the lady who lives here – she wanted me to have a bath, but I said I wouldn't leave you until you were better."

"Oh, dear, so we're fouling the lovely white sheets. We must be terrible guests."

"Not in the least," an energetic lady said, bustling into the room. "The bedding can be replaced. I'm delighted to see you looking marginally better, Mrs. Thornton. I'm Kathleen O'Rourke. We met last night, but you weren't in a fit state to take note of anything. I've had a telegram from your cousin, Lady Kirkland, who says, 'Thank God. I'm on my way.' I expect she'll arrive tonight, and is most welcome to stay with us. And you must feel that you and Alice can stay as long as you like. You've been through a terrible ordeal, and need some time to heal. I know that emotionally it will take much longer. Now please do try to take some broth."

She helped Victoria to sit up, careful of her fractured ribs.

"Will you call me Victoria?" she said to her hostess.

Mrs. O'Rourke said, "A pleasure, my dear, if you call me Kathleen. The doctor left a draught for you if the pain gets too bad. Alice, shut your ears for a moment. Victoria, you should know that your breasts are going to be tender and leaking for a while, but that's quite normal. I'll bring you some warm compresses that will help the discomfort."

"Leaking?" Alice asked.

"Milk. That's how babies are fed. You were supposed to have your ears closed," Mrs. O'Rourke said with a grin.

Alice giggled. Victoria was grateful to their benefactress for making the child smile. She had seen too much atrocity this last day.

Kathleen O'Rourke left, but came rushing back a short while later, saying, "You have visitors! I've taken the liberty of bringing them up."

Theadora and Meredith came in to delighted shrieks from Alice. They gave her tremendous hugs, and kissed Victoria's cheek, Theadora saying, "I'm afraid to touch you. You poor, poor girl! My heart breaks for you. But I'm damned glad to see you! We've been looking all over for you. Oh, hell, I'll hug you anyway, so just shout if it hurts."

"How did you manage?" Victoria asked, thinking how well, even elegant, she looked, despite her obvious bruises.

"Well, I could write a book about it," Theadora said. "In, fact, I think I will. In the meantime, I've already filed a story with the *New York Times*, the *London Times*, and a few others. I couldn't sleep anyway last night."

"She's no slouch, our Theadora," Meredith said. "If you'd seen the state of her yesterday!"

"Do tell."

"Well, my dears, you'll never believe this. I hardly can myself! But when the ship went down, just after we got swept into the sea, I was sucked into one the of the sinking smoke stacks. I thought I was done for, but wasn't I amazed to find myself blown out of it again! Most of my clothes were ripped off, but fortunately, not my life jacket. Bless Sir Ian McTavish for showing us how to put them on properly. He's fine, by the way. He's at our hotel. So I floundered in the water for a while, perching on a board, but then I was picked up by none other than Meredith, who didn't even recognize me. I was completely covered in oily, black soot. Worse than a coal miner, Meredith said when I said hello to her. It took me hours to scrub myself clean, but it's still in my pores. And my hair's coming out in handfuls. Shock, they tell me. Meredith, by the way, should be given a medal. She saved at least fifty people. If it hadn't been for her gutsy insistence and wonderful high-handedness, those cowardly men in her boat would have left us all to die!" Theadora's hand shook slightly as she touched a knuckle to the corner of her eye.

Meredith took up the story. "I was swept into the water as well, but came up not far from a half-submerged lifeboat. Several men managed to bale it out with boxes and tins that they picked up from the floating rubble. And I was right there, demanding to be taken onboard. They pulled in a few of us, but then got worried as so many scrambled to get aboard. The boat rocked dangerously at times, and I thought we would all be dumped back into the sea. The men actually began rapping people's knuckles, to make them let go of the boat. They were anxious and said we had to get away to save ourselves, that we couldn't save everyone. Well, that just didn't do! So I took charge. I said we would be fine if we were organized and worked together. Some people just need a firm hand. One fellow looked like he wanted to throw me back in, but I drew myself up and stared him down. He became quite meek and helpful. And once we had a few more on board, it became our mission to save as many as possible."

"Isn't she magnificent!" Theadora said.

"What about... the others?" Victoria asked.

"I found my father," Meredith said. "He was already at the hotel when we arrived. He'd been lucky to get into a lifeboat at the last minute, one that was successfully launched. We haven't seen Vivian or Oliver. Some people were taken to Kinsale, so survivors are still drifting in and they're lodged all over the place and in hospitals. It will take time to locate people. They're not in the morgues. We've checked," Meredith said grimly. "So don't give up hope."

But Theadora once again wiped her eye, and Victoria realized she was keeping up a cheerful front for their sake.

Kathleen O'Rourke came in with a tea tray that included thick, raisin-studded Irish scone bread, but Victoria had no appetite and only managed to sip some tea with trembling hands. Her head ached and she felt deeply chilled again.

"Tell us what happened to you," Meredith said.

When Victoria finished her tale, she added, "The fishermen told me that it was my ring that attracted their attention. They were looking for survivors first, before collecting the dead. And if it hadn't been for Alice's insistence that I *was* still alive..."

"It doesn't bear thinking about," Theadora said. Trying to brighten the mood, she added, "Well, you two have really been lucky with your digs. We're in a rather third-rate hotel. Not that I'm complaining, mind you. The people are generosity itself. But this is luxurious in comparison. Now! We need to find you two some clothes. I stuffed some money into my bodice, and that garment, fortunately, I was still wearing. So I've already been shopping, as you can see. Not the height of fashion, but it's warm," she said of her tweed suit. "Yesterday, I thought I would never be warm again, but at least I didn't spend over three hours in the water like you did."

"Will your husband be able to be with you soon?" Meredith asked Victoria. "Does he have leave due?"

"Yes. We're getting married next week," Victoria said, too tired to think straight. Realizing her mistake she added, "Oh, dear. You'll think badly of me now, but Chas and I *were* engaged when he left last September."

Theadora said wryly, "Quite honestly, Victoria, I didn't really think you were married. I would have considered it foolish to travel in your condition in such uncertain times. I would have come over earlier or waited until the baby was a few months old at least. So, no, I'm neither shocked nor scandalized. Nor do I believe that love is the sole prerogative of the married state."

"Will you all come to the wedding?" She looked at them hopefully.

"I'd be delighted!" Meredith said. "Women need to be liberated from the idea that they are solely to blame for the consequences of shared passion. Besides, you two are so obviously in love that a piece of paper doesn't make a whit of difference."

"I'm looking forward to meeting this handsome Chas of yours," Theadora said.

"I need a flower girl," Victoria said, looking at Alice.

"Oh, could I? I love weddings! Oh, I am so glad you're not already married! It'll be such fun!"

"But please keep my secret. Most people are not as understanding as you."

"Of course, Mrs. Thornton," Theadora said. "Now we should let you rest. We'll take Alice shopping. I see she's wearing some older Miss O'Rourke's rather larger clothes. We'll bring some things for you as well."

When they had gone, Alice promising she wouldn't be long, Victoria allowed herself to weep, despite the pain. She hadn't even named the baby. What had they done with him?

She awoke in the throes of a nightmare, feeling the ship drop away beneath her, icy water rush into her lungs, surfacing amidst a bloody sea of broken bodies, of dead children bobbing like grotesque dolls in the swell, her own tiny baby among them, always just beyond her desperate reach. And Vivian was there, smiling as she floated by on her back, her beautiful, long, dark hair spread out around her like a halo, her deep blue eyes staring up at a deceptive summer sky. Victoria was sweating and groaning, doubled over in pain both emotional and physical.

Beatrice said, "There now, my dear. It's all over." She touched Victoria's forehead. "Good Lord, you're burning up!"

"Cousin Beatrice, I hurt so much." There was a never-ending contraction in her womb. Beatrice gave her some of the opiate the doctor had left for her.

Victoria was aware of only snatches of events after that. Beatrice trying to get her to drink some sweet and tangy tea, the doctor examining her, people murmuring amongst themselves, Alice begging her to please be alright, more liquid trickled down her throat.

The dream came again and again, and when she finally awoke she felt like she had that morning at Thorncliff, when her head and bladder had been about to burst, her throat had been raw and dry, and she had been light headed. But Chas had been looking after her then. If only she could go back to that perfect summer day! If only the disaster were a hideous dream.

Someone stroked her cheek gently. She opened her eyes. She must still be dreaming, because Chas was lying beside her, propped up on his elbow, looking lovingly down at her. "You're a dream," she whispered.

"I sincerely hope not. I've just had the pleasure of gazing into the most beautiful turquoise eyes, which I've been longing to see again."

"You really are here! Oh, Chas!"

He hugged her carefully, and murmured, "Thank God! I thought I'd lost you." He kissed her face gently, and wiped away the tears that trickled onto her pillow.

"I lost our baby."

"I'm so sorry, my darling. I can't forgive myself for putting you through all this. You were right. I should have married you last summer and taken you with me. Can you ever forgive me?"

"I just want to be with you, Chas. Forever and ever. But I also need to go to the bathroom right away," she said, feeling desperate to relieve herself.

He laughed then, joyfully, like someone who had been given a reprieve. "Allow me to carry you, my darling." He picked her up, careful of her ribs, but she winced and he cursed himself for his clumsiness.

"It's not your fault. I hurt everywhere," she said.

"I'm not surprised. You took quite a battering. You have bruises and scrapes all over."

"You've examined me, have you?"

"Intimately."

She was so weak and unsteady that he refused to leave her alone. "We're going to be married soon, so let's not be modest. I already know and love every inch of you. I've also watched you throw up, remember?"

"You still want to marry me?"

"Of course, you muggins. More than ever."

"What about those ruthless men who might be after my money?" she managed to quip.

"What a presumptuous ass I was, thinking that you couldn't look after yourself! When time seemed to be endless and I was caught up in the excitement of the war, and thinking I'd be with you by Christmas, there didn't seem to be any hurry to get married. But now I want to spend every precious moment with you. Facing your own mortality daily makes you mature rather quickly."

Victoria felt awkward dealing with her blood-soaked pad, but Chas simply said, "We men don't know how lucky we are. And I can't even imagine what you've been through, with the baby and the shipwreck. You've had a harder war than I." He ran his hands agitatedly through his fair hair. "I knew you were in trouble. I could feel it that very moment, while I was flying. But I never imagined how horrible it was. Your friends have been filling me in on the details. By the way, you have quite an entourage who can hardly wait for you to recover." He told her that Alice was sharing a room with Beatrice, and that Theadora and Meredith, unwilling to leave Queenstown until Victoria was out of danger, had been invited by Kathleen O'Rourke to stay when the other survivors had left her house.

"How did you get here so quickly?" she asked him as he carried her back to bed. He propped her up on pillows, and gave her a glass of water, which she hadn't even realized she craved.

"As soon as I heard about the ship being torpedoed, I threatened to fly my aeroplane to Ireland. They threatened to shoot me for desertion, and then decided that I was no use to them either dead or alive, in the present circumstances, so the CO took pity on me and gave me compassionate leave. By the time I arrived at Cousin Bea's she had gone, but left instructions. She had sent me word after receiving your telegram, but I was already underway, so I didn't know that you had survived until I arrived at Bovington. I think I would have killed anyone who tried to stop me from finding you. So I've been here for two days already."

"Two days!"

"You were deathly ill, my darling. You had an infection of the womb, which is very dangerous. With everything that you had endured, we weren't sure you were going to pull through." He settled down beside her and gently touched the bruised skin around the stitches on her forehead. "I didn't realize how deeply I loved you until I almost lost you."

Victoria laid her head against his shoulder, happy, despite her underlying sorrow. Nothing else was as important as being with him. And they would have more children.

Chas said, "What an ass I used to be, talking flippantly about being in love with every woman, as if I knew what love was, as if it was just a frivolous game and not an all-consuming passion, and the willingness to sacrifice one's very life and soul for someone else. I don't know how you put up with me."

"Because I saw through your shallow façade. And I love you. Oh! We're supposed to be married in a few days!" Victoria suddenly realized.

"We'll do it next week, or whenever you're well enough. I have a month to spend with you. I've sent word to Jack to try to postpone his leave if possible."

There was a knock on the door and Alice came in. Her face lit with a huge smile when she saw that Victoria was awake. She rushed to her side, but was mindful of Victoria's ribs as she threw her arms about her. "Are you better? Really and truly this time? Is she, Chas?"

"On the mend," Chas said. "We need to ply her with lots of liquids – champagne is out for the moment, I'm afraid. And maybe wash her hair, so she's back to the golden haired girl I knew last summer. I really don't think that oily black is that becoming on her, do you?"

Alice laughed gleefully.

"So young Alice, could you inform the household that Sleeping Beauty is awake and in need of fattening up?"

Alice giggled and said, "I do like your husband, Ria. I want to have one just like him when I'm older."

It was Chas's turn to laugh. "I'm flattered. Now I expect my head will balloon to twice its size."

Alice ran off giggling.

"She's a sweet girl. Thank God you took her under your wing, not only because you probably saved her life, but because she then saved yours. But what a horrific experience for a child. For all of you. I've heard some of the hardened sailors who were there at the rescue say that they could never have imagined such carnage. And from what I've seen..." He stopped, frowning bleakly.

"You've been to the morgues? But you haven't found Vivian." Somehow she knew.

"Neither there nor anywhere else. I'm sorry, my darling. I can't believe that we'll never see her again. And we've lost Archie as well. I think back to our summers in Muskoka, and they seem so far away, in an age of innocence and ignorance that I can hardly believe ever existed. I feel as if every moment we have now is a gift. We were so careless with time before."

"I'll have to write to Peter," Victoria said, brushing away her tears. She wondered that she had any left. "And Oliver?"

"Thea says that someone saw him in the water, looking battered and in distress, but no, they haven't found him either."

"The Graysons?"

"No, my darling."

Alerted by Alice, the others flocked into the room. "Now you really must stop scaring us, Ria – by the way, I think that name suits you better," Theodora said. "And I approve of your *husband*."

Beatrice kissed her and said, "You have your grandmother's spunk. Thank God! Now here, you must drink this. It's Kathleen's special potion for female disorders. I have no doubt that it helped, for that fool of a doctor had nothing to offer." Except to tell them that Victoria would likely die. Chas's joy at finding Victoria alive had quickly turned to despair when he realized how ill she was. But if anyone had ever kept someone alive by sheer willpower, it was he. The poor boy must be completely exhausted, for he had hardly slept on his journey from France, or since.

Victoria recognized the taste. It had been the strange seawater in her dreams. But it was quite pleasant. "What is it?"

"Raspberry leaves, peppermint, and Shepherd's purse. Oh, and catnip, I think."

"Chas has been patiently dripping it into you for two days," Theodora said. "If he weren't such a dashing aviator, he would make a good nurse. He's barely left your side since he arrived."

"Now that you're out of danger, Victoria, we will head off to Wales tomorrow," Meredith said. "Theodora will stay with us in Cardiff, and you can let us know when the *event* is going to take place. We shall look forward to that! It will do us all a world of good."

"Is there nothing more we can do here?" Victoria asked.

"I'm afraid not," Meredith said grimly. "There are no more survivors. Bodies are still floating onto beaches, but we haven't found... our friends."

"Who have you found?"

"Lady Dunston is alive, but both her daughters are missing. Your Muskoka acquaintance, Mrs. Burnside survived, but not her daughter. The actresses, Rita Jolivet and Josephine Brandell, are alright, but Charles Frohman didn't make it. In the morgue we saw Commander Stackhouse, Sir Hugh Lane, Dr. McDermott, Staff Captain Anderson." Meredith mentioned several more. "And Alfred Vanderbilt is still missing, although there's a hefty reward for anyone who finds his body."

Victoria was shocked by all the dead. "How many survived?"

"Seven hundred and sixty-one," Theadora said. "Leaving 1198 dead or missing. Oh, and the three German stowaways. Everybody's forgotten about them. And your baby, Ria. He's also a victim of this atrocity."

"Theadora has been interviewing people and writing accounts for the newspapers." Meredith said. "She has more courage than I to hear those ghastly stories. Some people lost all their children. Entire families perished, some found in each others' arms. Only 4 of the 39 babies onboard survived." Meredith shook her head.

"Most of the survivors have left," Theadora said. "Some are still in hospitals, of course. But anyone well enough to stagger away has gone. There's too much horror lingering here. Even the officials, sickened by what they have seen and trying to help survivors, identify bodies, and inform relatives, are feeling the strain. The townspeople have been compassionate, and they, too, have witnessed more gruesome sights than anyone should ever have to deal with. After this, I'm not sure I'll have the courage to go to the front lines. Oliver was probably right." She broke down then, and hurried from the room.

"I'll see to her," Meredith said. "She has a tough shell, but it's beginning to crack. That's why we need to get away."

"Alice and I will probably leave tomorrow as well," Beatrice said. "We're going to stay with her grandparents in Oxford for a few days, and then she's coming to Bovington Abbey with me. Her family is anxious to see her, and we do have to make preparations for our *event*. Including outfitting Alice with a new wardrobe, and a special dress. So we may be in London for a few days as well."

Beatrice was enjoying the child's company. Alice was so devoted to Victoria, that she had been desperately unhappy these last three days that Victoria had hovered on the brink of death. The poor child had suffered so much this past year that Beatrice would do whatever she could to brighten her life. She laughed at herself for a moment, thinking that it had taken almost fifty years for her maternal instincts to surface.

Alice, who had plunked herself on the edge of the bed beside Victoria, a leg tucked underneath her, said, "Will you be alright without me, Ria? I know you have Chas to look after you, and he's doing a pretty good job. But every time I go away, you seem to get worse."

Victoria smiled at her and stroked her head. "I'll be fine now. Thank you, my dear friend. We'll come as soon as I can walk. And hopefully your family will let you stay with us as long as you like, or until you have to go to school."

Alice smiled happily. "Oh, Cousin Bea, we have to find a special dress for Ria!"

"Theadora and Meredith bought you some clothes, so you'll at least be able to get to England," Beatrice said to Victoria.

Kathleen O'Rourke came in bearing a tray. "Victoria, we are so delighted to see you on the mend! Here's some beef broth with Guinness – nothing like it to strengthen the blood – and some freshly baked bread. And more of my special tea. For dinner, we'll bring you more soup and an egg on toast. Tomorrow you can probably handle a stew. We'll have you on your feet in no time at all. Chas, there's tea and scones here for you."

"You've been so kind to us, Kathleen," Victoria said.

"It's the least we can do. And Chas, there really was no need, but thank you for that wonderful basket from Fortnum and Mason's that arrived this afternoon! We don't get such delicacies around here."

"That's the least that *we* can do, since you won't accept any payment," Chas said.

"I'd say that having new friends is payment enough."

Victoria was almost too tired to eat, but Chas forced her, and she felt somewhat better afterwards. A maid delivered two large bowls of warm water, one soapy, the other scented with lavender.

"Now my darling girl," Chas said when the maid had gone. "I'm going to give you a sponge bath, which will refresh you. Kathleen told me how to do it, but you'll have to bear with me."

He put a rubber sheet on top of the bed, covered it with thick towels, and then laid her on top after stripping off her nightgown.

He covered her with more towels and uncovered one part of her at a time, ran a wet, soapy cloth over her, scrubbing where necessary, rinsed and dried her, and moved on.

"That feels lovely," Victoria said when he had finished with her right arm.

Chas kissed her hand. "You don't taste so salty now. But I'm hard put to decide what's a bruise and what's oil and soot. So shout if I'm scrubbing too hard on the wrong spot. I sponged you once before to bring your fever down, but didn't try to clean you up."

"Oh, dear, I must look like a chimney sweep."

"The most beautiful one I've ever seen." He grimaced when he looked at the large bruise that wrapped around to her back from beneath her right breast, and didn't touch her there. "Will you tell me what happened? Every detail that you can remember. I need to know, and it might help you to talk."

She didn't want to relive it, but she couldn't escape from it anyway. Grisly images randomly flashed into her mind. She was weeping when she finished, but not for herself. "Seeing the dead and dying children was the worst," she sniffed. "Dear God, I hope that Vivian didn't suffer!"

Chas looked pale and grim. He cleaned carefully around the stitches on her leg, which went almost from knee to ankle, the wound red and swollen. "I don't think she could have suffered more than you. How are your ribs? Can you breathe?"

"Not easily."

"Tomorrow I'm wrapping you up and taking you outside for some fresh air and sunshine. The O'Rourkes have a pleasant patio overlooking the sea. If you can bear to. But the doctor says you might get pneumonia if you don't breath deeply enough. Alice and I couldn't survive your getting sick again."

When he had finished washing every part of her but her hair, he helped her into a new lacy nightgown that Theadora and Meredith had bought. "I feel much better now," Victoria said. "Thank you, Chas. You are the most wonderful husband... and nurse."

He lay down beside her and kissed her tenderly. In an anguished voice he said "I wish I had spared you all this!"

"Chas, what happened to our baby?"

"We buried him yesterday. We couldn't wait for you to recover. I named him Reggie, after your grandfather. Reggie Wyndham Thornton – I wanted to be part of him too. Reginald seemed too big a name for him." Chas broke down then and wept, holding onto Victoria as tightly as he dared.

Beatrice, Alice, and Kathleen O'Rourke knocked on their door later that evening, planning to bring in some supper, but there was no answer. They peeked in quietly to find both Victoria and Chas sleeping deeply, she, still lying in his arms.

"The poor wee dears," Kathleen said, closing the door carefully. "I'll not trouble them with supper. We'll leave a tray of cheese and bread later on, in case they wake up hungry in the night."

"Yes, sleep is what they both need," Beatrice said.

"It's so sad to think they may never have children now," Kathleen said as they walked away.

"We won't tell Victoria just yet. Chas will when the time is right." Beatrice hoped that the doctor was wrong in his prognosis that the infection would probably leave Victoria infertile.

The grey light of dawn was just seeping into the room when Victoria awoke. Chas was still sleeping. She looked at him, amazed and grateful to think that she would always have him beside her, in the night, in the mornings. She wouldn't think of him returning to the war just yet.

When he opened his eyes, she said, "Do you know the next best thing to making love with you? It's to wake up beside you."

He smiled and stroked her brow. "Another good reason to get married then," he said. "How are you feeling this morning?"

"Hungry. Very much in love."

"That's the best thing I've heard in days."

Later that morning Mrs. O'Rourke came and said with a smile, "Another visitor for you."

Grayson shuffled in. He looked haggard, uncharacteristically slumped, with one arm in a cast and a sling, and stitches down one side of his face. And he was alone. But his face lit with a smile as he said, "Thank God! I am so sorry about the baby, Miss Victoria. But delighted to see you. And Mr. Chas."

"Oh, Grayson, I'm so thankful to see you as well!" She held out her hands to him, wanting to embrace him, but knowing that would just embarrass him. He took her hands in his uninjured one in a strong grip. "Mrs. Grayson?"

He shook his head sadly. "I haven't found her. And I heard about Miss Vivian. Dear God, this is a terrible tragedy!"

Chas pulled up a chair and urged Grayson to sit down. "We were looking for you, Grayson," Chas said. "I checked all the hotels and hospitals."

"I was in Kinsale. Out for days they tell me. I arrived here yesterday and have been asking around."

"Will you come to Bovington Abbey with us?" Victoria asked. "You need to recuperate as well."

"Might I be taken back into your service, Miss Victoria? It was never really my dream to leave and start an inn in England, and now that Ida – Mrs. Grayson – is no longer with us, I have no heart to do something like that on my own."

"Of course, Grayson," she said. "You're like family to me. And Chas was saying how much he wished you were staying with us."

Grayson seemed about to break down, but pulled himself up and said, "I'm staying at the Queen's Hotel when you need me."

"Oh no you're not, Mr. Grayson," Mrs. O'Rourke said as she bustled in with tea. "I have plenty of beds now that my other guests have gone. Please come and stay with us."

He smiled gratefully. "That would be a treat. Thank you, Madam."

Victoria improved rapidly over the next few days. Chas kept her laughing and made her walk a bit further every day to keep her lungs functioning well, although breathing was obviously painful for her. They both fell into exhausted sleep every night. But the nightmares came, and Chas held her until she slept again.

A week after the disaster, they went to the graveyard. Chas said, "I've ordered a headstone. Red granite, like our Muskoka stone. The inscription will read 'Reggie Wyndham Thornton, beloved infant son of Victoria and Chas. Innocent victim of the *Lusitania.*'"

Victoria wept in Chas's arms. They stood like that for a long time in the hillside churchyard overlooking the sea.

*By the sea, by the sea, by the beautiful sea,*
  *You and I you and I, oh! How happy we'll be...*

Alfred Vanderbilt, Sadie Burke, Ida Grayson, Oliver Dalvay, and Vivian Carrington were among the nine hundred whose bodies were never recovered.

# Chapter 22

Bovington Abbey was a splendid two storey Tudor house of limestone rubble with two transverse wings that sheltered a stone-flagged loggia and courtyard. Built in the 14th century, the house had undergone several renovations over the centuries to accommodate gentrified living. So it now had marble bathrooms and a large conservatory where, Beatrice confessed, she spent much of her time.

Victoria thought it enchanting.

"It even has a ghost!" Alice told her gaily. "But I haven't seen her yet."

They were taking tea in the conservatory amidst potted palms. "Do tell us the story," Victoria urged.

"She was a daughter of the house, back in Elizabethan times," Beatrice said. "And in love with the stable boy, which, of course, was inappropriate in her position. The young lovers planned to elope and were just getting into a boat when they were discovered. He was whipped and dismissed, and she was locked into her bedroom in the east wing. When it was discovered that she was with child, her parents decided she must be married straight away. They chose a rather disagreeable, middle-aged landowner whose sickly wife and heir had died, and who was looking for a strong young woman to supply him with offspring. They hoped to fool him into thinking the child was his. But on the day of the wedding, the distraught girl jumped to her death from her bedroom window. I would have though she might break a leg or two, because it's not such a height as to kill someone. Still, I suppose it depends on how she fell. In any case, she's been seen in her wedding finery, wandering the east wing. I've put you in the west wing," Beatrice added with a grin.

"I trust you're not afraid of a ghost, young Alice," Chas said.

"Oh no. She sounds so sad and I'm sure she doesn't want to hurt anybody. She's probably searching for her lover."

He suppressed a laugh. "I expect you're quite right. I certainly haven't seen her when I've stayed before, so I don't suppose she fancies me."

Because there wouldn't be anything for Grayson to do at Wyndholme until it was no longer needed as a hospital, it was decided that he would stay in England as long as Victoria was there. He wanted to keep busy, so Beatrice offered him the position of butler in her London house, where she had only a footman doing those duties at the moment, once Grayson had had a chance to recuperate at Bovington. He was well pleased.

Chas took Victoria to London so she could replace her wardrobe, as she had, of course, lost everything. She was glad that she had left the bulk of Augusta's jewellery with Olivia. She had only wanted something of her grandmother's to wear for the wedding, and thus had brought the pearl and sapphire necklace and earrings, which she still had.

Beatrice's London abode was a delightful Victorian terraced townhouse on Lancaster Gate in the fashionable Bayswater district. This was an open-sided square facing Kensington Gardens and Hyde Park, so they strolled about there daily as Victoria regained strength.

Beatrice had told her that she and Chas must stay in London or Bovington, as they chose, and not feel obliged to keep her company.

On fine days, they took tea on the balcony over the Doric portico, which overlooked the Gardens through the plane trees on the square. They dined at home every evening like any long-married couple, and every night she lay blissfully in his arms. He soothed her when the nightmares terrorized her, or when the horror of it all flooded back suddenly and sharply, bringing her to tears.

Jack had managed to postpone his leave for two weeks, and met up with them in London, just before they returned to Bovington Abbey.

"I've never been so glad to see anyone!" he said, hugging Victoria carefully, grateful to hold her in his arms again. He had been appalled by what she had been through, and realized to his own surprise that he truly loved and cared about her. But it was still Eleanor he dreamed about and craved. She had really gotten under his skin. "I'm so sorry about the baby. And Vivian."

She cried a little, and he let Chas take her into his arms, although he wanted to comfort her himself. He was even more shocked by the details of her brush with death, which Chas told him about when Victoria was resting. Her ribs still pained her and her leg had not yet healed, and since she slept badly, Chas insisted she nap in the afternoons.

"I can't stand the thought of having to leave her again so soon," Chas said, running his hands through his hair in agitation. "She's still so fragile. What she's been through would have broken most people. You should have seen her when I first found her in Ireland. She was barely alive." He shook his head in disbelief. "She was so terribly wounded, and then giving birth in her condition, losing the baby after all that, and getting the infection! And now she may never be able to have children, when she wanted them so much. Hell, I shouldn't have told you that! You must promise never to let her know. The doctor may be wrong."

Jack said, "Of course I won't tell her. Aren't you concerned about not being able to have children?"

"I expect we would have had beautiful children, and yes, I think it's sad that we may not. But I love her, and nothing else is as important. I suppose that's one of the sacrifices the war has already demanded of us.

"I didn't go into this war thinking about killing. Very naïve of me, I know. But now I could gladly kill every German soldier. Isn't that one of the worst things about this war? That we lose our humanity? I expect that the men in the submarine that torpedoed the *Lusitania* have wives, sweethearts, sisters, or children of their own. Did they realize what they were doing? We carry out our orders, whether we agree with them or not. That's war. That's insanity."

"They had me dropping bombs last week," Jack said. "I don't think I did any real damage. It seems so impersonal doing that. You don't actually see the people you might be killing. Did you know that Moorhouse is being awarded the Victoria Cross posthumously?" One of their colleagues in the 2$^{nd}$ Squadron, William Rhodes-Moorhouse, had died last month as a result of the wounds he received from enemy fire after dropping bombs on the rail junction at Courtrai. "He's the first pilot to receive the VC."

"I don't have the heart to go back now," Chas said despondently.

"Try to get some more compassionate leave," Jack suggested. "It would be good for both of you. This whole *Lusitania* issue is helping propaganda. Surely the survivors deserve some recognition and support for having endured the horrors that the government now capitalizes on."

Chas telephoned Beatrice to ask if she could use her connections yet again to get him extended leave, explaining his reluctance to abandon Victoria just yet.

"Of course. And you're quite right. Leave it with me, Chas," she said.

When Victoria rejoined them, they went for tea in the sumptuous Palm Court at the Ritz. 'Tea at the Ritz' had become quite a social event, so the tables were filled with fashionable people, many in uniform. She said, "I'm the envy of every woman here, being with two such handsome aviators. You do look dashing in your uniforms!"

Theirs had been tailored especially for them in London, as the military gave each recruit only one. For people like Chas it was nothing to pay £50 for a custom-made uniform, more than the yearly salary of a servant, and Jack was grateful that Chas had also paid for his, as well as the requisite leather coats, boots, helmets, and fur-lined winter gear.

"And the men are all wondering who the beautiful young lady is who commands such attention," Chas said with a grin.

"They're more likely marvelling at my stylish scar," she quipped, her hands shaking as a burst of memory gripped her. She fought hard to keep back tears. Chas squeezed her hand reassuringly.

"Chas Thornton!" an elegant young woman said, coming up behind him. "How absolutely delightful to see you again. Quentin told me you were over, and I'm desolated that you haven't come to see me yet!"

"Sid!" Chas exclaimed in surprise as he rose to his feet to give her a quick embrace. To Victoria he said, "Darling, this is Lady Sidonie... Dunston, I suppose it is now. Percy's wife." Percival Dunston was the eldest son of Sir Montague and Lady Dunston of Montreal. "Sid, I'd like you to meet my... wife, Victoria, and my friend, Jack Wyndham. They are Cedric's Canadian cousins."

"How astonishing!" Sidonie said, and Victoria wasn't sure whether the surprise was that she was Chas's wife or that she and Jack were related to someone Sidonie obviously knew well.

Chas seemed to sense Victoria's bewilderment that he and Lady Sidonie appeared to be such good friends, for he explained, "Sid is the youngest sister of an Oxford friend of mine, Quentin, Viscount Grenville, eldest son of the Earl of Bisham. Have I got it right, Sid?"

"Precisely," she assured him with a smile.

"Will you join us?" Chas asked, drawing out the fourth chair at their table for her.

"Just for a moment. I'm with a party." She nodded toward a group of officers and ladies in a far corner, and motioned away the waiter who was dutifully approaching.

"Percy's not here?"

"No. He's at the Front. I'm entertaining some of his friends. I didn't realize that there were so many people in Montreal," she said dryly

Chas laughed, saying, "You haven't changed a bit, Sid."

"Good Lord, I hope not!"

They exchanged family news, Sidonie assuring Chas that both Quentin and Percy were surviving at the Front and due home on leave soon, so of course, they would all have to get together if Chas was still here.

"I do approve of the uniform. I should have known you'd be nothing less than a daring aviator. Percy says you're crazy to want to fly, but isn't surprised. He's putting in a few months at the Front to demonstrate his bravery, and then he's going to wrangle a nice, safe desk job at HQ for the duration." Sidonie seemed slightly contemptuous of her husband. "Lady Dunston is doing her utmost to ensure that."

With a wry grin, she said to Victoria, "I have to tell you that my mother-in-law has warned me about you. You *have* been a naughty boy, Chas! Isn't it good that I enjoy flouting my mother-in-law's rather plebeian edicts? I have no intention of depriving myself of your company, Mrs. Thornton." Then she added, with a wink to Victoria, "I do think I should have chosen you, Chas, instead of Percy. One tends to forget that one marries the family as well as the man."

Sidonie was a beautiful woman with remarkable green eyes, flawless ivory skin, and raven-black hair. Victoria recalled that Percival Dunston was a likeable enough fellow, but not one to set many hearts aflutter – except through his immense wealth. If Sidonie had truly had a choice between Chas and Percy, Victoria had no doubt that Chas would easily have won. Obviously he hadn't cared enough for her. So she didn't take offence at Sidonie's flippant remark, but did wonder if she and Chas had been lovers. And was very much afraid that they had. There was something in the way they looked at one another that hinted at a closeness and understanding beyond that of casual friends. Victoria knew she mustn't allow jealousy to creep into her relationship with Chas. He had chosen to marry her, and she had known that there had been other women in his life. But it was still a shock to meet them.

Victoria had already told Chas about her encounter with Lady Dunston on the *Lusitania*, so he said to Sidonie, "I don't envy you your mother-in-law. She was determined to land me for one of her daughters. Poor souls." he added, as the two youngest had died on the *Lusitania*. "If she's going to start flinging mud, then she had best be armoured. I expect she wouldn't be too pleased to have Sir Dunston's indiscretions spread about."

"Shall I blackmail her then?" Sidonie asked impishly.

"Only as a last resort," Chas replied with a grin.

"It's *so* wonderful to have you back, Chas," Sidonie said with a warm gleam in her eyes as she laid her beautifully slender hand on his. "What fun we used to have at Blackthorn Park when you and Rafe and Cedric and Hugh came to stay!"

"Blackthorn is Sid's family estate in Berkshire," Chas explained to Victoria and Jack.

"Be fair. It's a crumbling Elizabethan pile – which, by the way, I adore – and which has benefited tremendously from an influx of Dunston money," she said carelessly. "You'd hardly recognize it, Chas. But Quentin will still have to marry an American heiress if he wants to keep it going." To Victoria and Jack she said, with self-deprecating amusement, "My grandfather was rather too fond of slow horses and fast women, so he almost bankrupted the estate. My father, fortunately, has managed to redeem the family honour somewhat."

Victoria was surprised at her candid confidences. But then decided that Lady Sidonie probably enjoyed being slightly outrageous and definitely unconventional.

"He'd do even better if he got rid of the insatiable ancestral pile," Chas said.

"Never! Queen Elizabeth stayed there. We couldn't possibly let anyone else sleep in her room," Sidonie said with a smirk.

"One Christmas, when we all stayed at Blackthorn," Chas related, "Sid dressed up as Queen Bess and pretended to be a ghost, drifting down the corridor in the dead of night, making sure we heard her. Of course, none of us was fooled, but she got a fright when she wafted into the 'Royal suite' and saw a shape under the blankets suddenly rise up. It was Quentin, who was trying to teach her a lesson, since she had done this before to guests." He smiled at her while she laughed. "Sid seems to have a penchant for dressing up. She was determined to come to visit us in Oxford, but girls weren't allowed in our rooms. So she borrowed her younger brother's clothes and identity, and came to stay with Quentin for an entire weekend, with no one, except Quentin's friends, of course, any the wiser."

Had she slept with Chas then, Victoria wondered. Surely they would have thought it a great lark. Victoria began imagining the scene, the two of them laughing together under the sheets as they defied the dusty rules. Victoria chided herself for having too vivid an imagination. But it was the sort of thing she herself would have delighted in doing, and felt somehow certain that Sidonie was not unlike her in spirit and temperament.

Sidonie gave Chas a swift kiss on the cheek, and said, "Alas, I must go and do my duty. It's been a great pleasure to meet you both," she said to Victoria and Jack. Turning back to Chas and pressing a card into his hand, she said, "I really do hope that you will all come to visit. We have a townhouse in Grosvenor Square, as well as a place in Bucks. How's the baby, by the way?" she asked Victoria with a conspiratorial smile.

"I lost him."

Sidonie appeared truly shocked. "Oh, I *am* sorry! How tragic. You *have* had a bad go of it. Don't worry about Lady Dunston," she added. "I won't allow her to ostracize you from society. She's only an unsophisticated Colonial, after all."

Once again there was silent communication between Chas and Sidonie.

Despite the reassurance, Victoria didn't feel inclined to be part of a social circle where she was bound to run into the censorious Lady Dunston. And at the moment, she wanted only to spend quiet and intimate times with Chas.

Although the baby was never far from her thoughts, to be reminded by a stranger that the child should be with her still, growing inside her, sent a shaft of pain through her. And in an instant, the room became liquid, dissolving into the blood-soaked Irish Sea, the people around her bobbing amid the wreckage of chairs and tables. Victoria closed her eyes to expunge the grisly scene, but when she opened them she was no longer in the elegant Palm Court of the Ritz, but in the dining room of the *Lusitania*.

She suddenly went very pale. Her heart was pounding, racing; she felt as if she couldn't breathe. Trembling, nauseated, she struggled against suffocating fear to rise, saying, "I can't..." and ran from the room out into the street. Chas was right behind her. She was clinging to one of the pillars, gasping for breath. The concerned doorman was going over to her when Chas said, "I'll see to her."

She collapsed into his arms, her ribs stabbing her as she panted. She was dizzy and felt she couldn't get any air. Chas stroked her and said, "Try to slow down your breathing, Ria." To the doorman he said, "Kindly fetch a chair and a glass of water."

Jack joined them, but stood helplessly by. Chas was right to think that she needed him just now. "It's like shell-shock," Jack said, talking about the newly-recognized phenomenon that was coming out of the trenches with battle-fatigued soldiers. Most of them were only given some rest and sent back.

"I think you're right," Chas said. "Breathe gently, my darling." She was wheezing and still hyperventilating.

A concerned manager came out with the doorman. Chas lowered Victoria onto the chair and told her to put her head between her knees. He kept rubbing her back.

"Shall I send for a doctor?" the manager asked. "Wouldn't the young lady be more comfortable inside? I can arrange a room for her to lie down in."

"I'm afraid that your hotel reminds her of the *Lusitania*," Chas said astutely.

"Oh, dear me. You mean... she was on board?"

"Unfortunately."

"Oh, dear God! Is there anything we can do?"

"Perhaps just bring me the bill and hail us a cab."

"Please don't worry about the bill, Lieutenant. I do hope the young lady will be alright."

"Thank you."

She was breathing normally by the time they arrived back at the house, but still quivering. "I'm afraid I'm not ready for that sort of thing yet. I'm sorry to have spoiled the afternoon."

"Nonsense!" Chas said. "I should have realized that the ambiance might remind you. Come and lie down for a while." Chas took her up to their room and lay on the bed beside her.

"Memories suddenly ambush me," she tried to explain. "And I feel a panic that I can't seem to control." Tears rolled down her cheeks.

"It will take time, my darling. You've been through a terrible ordeal. No one expects you to be able to forget that and just carry on as usual. I'm going to stay with you as long as I can. Cousin Bea will try to work her magic with her friends in high places. I sometimes wonder if one of them isn't Winston Churchill – he's the First Lord of the Admiralty – since she does know him, but she's not forthcoming."

"I'd be so happy if you could stay with me, Chas!"

He kissed her. "Me too."

The three of them had a convivial dinner. Chas and Jack regaled her with whatever benign escapades and amusing tidbits of their new lives that they could dredge up, of course avoiding any of the atrocities that they had witnessed.

The next day they returned to Bovington Abbey. The wedding would be in a week.

And it was a delightful week, not only because of the weather. Chas took her, and sometimes Alice, boating on the river. One day, a dozen or so dragonflies hovered about them, some landing on Victoria. Alice squealed and said, "They look like your brooch has come to life!"

Chas and Jack taught Alice to play tennis, with Victoria cheering from the sidelines. She and Jack did paintings of willows dipping tendrils into the Thames, and portraits of Chas and Alice and Bovington Abbey.

Chas was summoned to report to the War Office in London. When he returned he said cheerfully, "They've given me two more weeks of leave."

Victoria had fewer panic attacks.

And letters began to arrive from home.

*Dearest Ria,*

*So much sorrow. I don't even know where to begin. Except to say that I – we – are overjoyed to hear that you have survived, despite everything you've been through. Zoë filled us in on the horrific details. I'm truly sorry about the baby. How I wish you could have been spared all that. I shouldn't have interfered.*

*It's hard to believe that Vivian is gone. We were very close, and I know you were good friends. Please don't feel responsible, as I expect you will, knowing you. She knew what she was doing, and that there was some measure of danger. God, this war is barbaric!*

*The death of so many innocent souls, especially the children, has fuelled the propaganda war here and in Britain, so I understand. Hard to think that you and Vivian and your tiny baby were pawns in this war.*

*I shall join up, for I can no longer sit here complacently reading the stories of places I have never heard of where so many young lives are being blown apart.*

*So, my dearest friend, I expect we shall soon meet in England. Take heart. Be well. Best to Chas, Lady Beatrice, and Jack.*

*Affectionately, Justin*

*Dear Victoria,*

*I'm thankful that you've survived such a terrible ordeal. From what Beatrice has told us, you are lucky to be alive. How tragic about Vivian. I know her family is devastated. Sorry to hear about Mrs. Grayson as well. Please pass along our condolences to Grayson.*

*We've heard that the young Dunston girls and Iris Burnside are also missing. What a shocking war this has become!*

*Some good news is that Helena is expecting. Our child will be here for Christmas. I hope that you will be, too.*

*We'll be using the cottage this summer, as it's been hard to find men to build our new one. Richard's is now finished, and when Albert's is done, we should be able to get started on ours.*

*We wish you and Chas every happiness, and pray that this war doesn't claim any more of our friends and family.*

*Affectionately, your father*

*Dear Ria,*

*You must have good Karma, but I can't imagine the horrors you have survived. You poor brave and wounded soul! I know you will never fully recover from such an ordeal. It has scarred you more than physically. Is there is anything at all that I can do to help? Blake wonders if you suffer nightmares and melancholia. He wants to help as well.*

*He is devastated by Vivian's death, and has decided to chuck in his psychiatric studies and enlist in the medical corp. I worry, as I think he has a Freudian death wish just now. What hell this war has become!*

*Edelina will write, but is currently suffering from the anti-German sentiment in the city. Of course she doesn't even consider herself German, but her name is, and poor Frieda obviously is. One unfortunate German shopkeeper in Toronto was tarred and feathered! A practice that I thought had disappeared with the civilization of our backwoods culture. But the world isn't at all civilized just now, so why should I be surprised?*

*Be strong, be happy.*

*Love to Chas and LadyBeatrice, and you, of course. I miss you, dear friend. Please take care! Ellie*

*Dearest Ria,*

*You can't imagine how terrified we were when we heard about the Lusitania's sinking, and how deliriously happy we were to receive Cousin Beatrice's telegram telling us that you were safe! But when we heard the full story from Chas, we were horrified by what you had been through. Mama cried and cried. Ellie says it's a miracle you survived. How thankful I am that Chas was there to look after you! But the poor, poor baby! How can I even express how sorry we are?*

We're also in shock and disbelief about Vivian! I wish she had known – and appreciated – how much Blake loved her. He's off to do his bit now, one of the many who thinks that warfare against women and children is barbaric. But the men suffer, too, and I know that dear Archie didn't have a gentle death. So now more are going willingly to their slaughter. Where did all this madness come from? Were we too happy, too complacent, too ignorant of what was really going on in the world? Living in some fool's paradise? Is this some sort of punishment for our hubris?

Max, who I think is a pacifist at heart, is looking grim and wrestling with his conscience about joining up. So far we've persuaded him not to.

I'm terrified. My premonition did come true, which is frightening in itself. I dreamt of a ship exploding and sinking, of you and Vivian floundering in the sea. Perhaps if I had told you, you wouldn't have gone. But I also believe that nothing would have stopped you. You must think me quite batty!

How much our world has changed since this time last year! How unfair!

Sorry to be so glum. I should be trying to cheer you up. But I know that you are forever changed by the hell you have endured, and would not be helped by empty platitudes.

I hope that you and Chas can find peace and happiness, and take strength from one another.

Please give our warmest regards to Grayson, as well as our sympathies. I feel strangely happy that he is there to look after you in some measure.

We all send our deepest love and best wishes to you and Chas.

I miss you dreadfully, my dearest friend and cousin!

Love, Zoë

Dear Ria,

Chas said you almost died and I was sooo glad to hear that you are alright! I was so excited about the idea of your being my sister, and would have been crushed if anything had happened to you.

How dreadful about Vivian. She was so beautiful!

Rafe says to say that Calypso is fine. Mummy is really worried about Chas after what happened to Archie.

Chas says you have a new friend, Alice. Of course I'm sorry she doesn't have a mother, and was on the Lusitania, but I wish I could be her and be with you both now!

*Even better, I wish you could both come home and that summer would be like always in Muskoka!*
   *Love, Felicity*

.   .   .

Beatrice had invited Theodora and Meredith to stay for the weekend of the wedding, so they arrived on Friday. Like old friends, they were all delighted to see each other, and Victoria realized that the tragedy had forged a bond between them that might have taken years otherwise. For Alice it was like having an entire new family.

Theodora said, "Your cousin, Jack, is quite a charmer as well. I may just have to go to your Muskoka some time and see what other treasures you have hiding there." They were finishing tea in the garden. Jack and Chas had just gone back onto the tennis court with Alice.

"Oh, I wish we could all go to Muskoka! Promise me you will come one day, both of you," Victoria urged.

"I should like that," Meredith said.

"Oh, yes," Theodora agreed. "In the meantime, I have to tell you that I've been writing an account of the *Lusitania*, for publication as a book. I already have a London publisher interested. I'm telling your story as well, but I won't use your name. I hope you don't mind, but I do think that people need to hear how horrific it was, and the amazing stories of the survivors. And I expect that you don't like to talk about it."

"You're right. I try *not* to remember, but I get these waves of panic sometimes."

"Yes, I know what you mean. Meredith is handling it better than I am. I'm thankful she's been looking after me," Theodora said, giving her friend a warm smile.

"And you have the added burden of mourning your child and your friend," Meredith said to Victoria. "My father, who didn't even go into the ocean like we all did, has nightmares about the sinking, and says he's afraid to travel across the Atlantic again."

"Maybe it is better to talk about the tragedy, rather than repress it," Theodora suggested.

"Is that Freud talking?" Victoria asked.

Theodora laughed. "I don't know enough about him, but perhaps we think alike."

Something else arrived that afternoon – a new Rolls-Royce Silver Ghost. Chas said, "It's yours, my darling."

"How wonderful! How beautiful! Thank you, Chas."

"Give yourself time to get used to it, because everything is backwards."

"But not in the engine, I hope, since I've come to know it intimately." She laughed.

After dinner that evening Chas played the piano, and the others sang along for some of the songs. How they reminded Victoria of last summer! Chas said, "When Ria's feeling better, we'll have to show you our special dance that we do to this one," and began playing *Come Josephine in My Flying Machine*.

And in an instant she was plunged back into the frigid Irish Sea, looking up at a placid sky and hearing Chas singing to her. She couldn't suppress an anguished cry as she ran outside. Tears were streaming down her face when Chas took her into his arms. "You sang that to me when I was in the water. I told Reggie that you were coming for us in your aeroplane. But I don't want to remember that when I hear that song. I want to remember last summer."

She didn't see the anguished look on his face as he murmured into her hair, "I should have been there for you."

Then he started waltzing her slowly about the flagstone patio and said, "Pretend we're on the tennis court at Thorncliff. Smell the pines. Remember Rafe playing the song over and over as we all laughed and danced. Remember how happy we were." He sang softly, "*Oh! Say, let us fly dear. Where, kid? To the sky dear... Come Josephine in my flying machine, Going up, she goes! Up, she goes!*" Mindful of her injuries he whirled her about. "It's still our song, Ria. And we'll dance wildly around the tennis court again sometime."

"There's nothing I want more in the world than that," she said.

He kissed her tenderly and said, "I think I need to put the bride to bed."

"Some bride I am when I can't even make love to you!"

"That will come. I'm just thankful to be with you."

"Are you sure you still want to marry me, Chas? Now that there's no baby..."

"I seem to recall asking you to marry me well before it became necessary. I love you more than ever, Ria. Having almost lost you, I realize that I don't want to live without you. You mean more to me than life itself."

"It was your love that saved me. The ring that you gave me as a token of your love. Your determination to get me through the infection." She clung to him. "You're a part of me, Chas. You make me feel whole. Without you, I'm a lost soul. Please don't ever leave me."

"Never willingly, my darling."

The words they spoke at the wedding ceremony the following morning could not have bound them more closely than those they had spoken the night before.

Victoria was radiant in a lilac silk gown and a hip-length white lace jacket. In deference to her mourning, she didn't want to wear traditional white, nor have an elaborate wedding gown. White roses were scattered through her hair, and, for a few moments, two dragonflies as well.

Chas laughed and said, "I really am marrying a fairy princess."

"Do you know what I've decided? That I'm going to be Ria Thornton. Victoria Wyndham belongs to another time. I want to start a new life with you, Chas."

He kissed her with obvious delight. She seemed to be regaining her spirit.

The ceremony was held at All Saints Church in Marlow, which sat on the riverbank alongside its cemetery. Alice was thrilled with her lacy white dress with a lilac satin waistband and hair band. She and Ria carried bouquets of white roses and blue forget-me-nots. Meredith took photographs, Beatrice gave the bride away, and Theadora had agreed to be the Maid of Honour. Jack, the Best Man, found her interesting. But only as a diversion. He really wished that Ellie were here.

Chas had invited a couple of Oxford friends – but, fortunately, not Lady Sidonie and her family – and Beatrice had invited their relatives, so Ria had a chance to meet Cedric's family. They had a splendid luncheon at Bovington Abbey.

When the guests had left, Chas said to Ria, "Now I want you to get into your riding gear. I'm about to give you your wedding present."

Puzzled, delighted, and feeling better than she had in weeks, Ria was immensely curious. The others, obviously aware of what was happening, waved them off happily as Chas drove away in the Rolls.

Before long, they pulled into a small aerodrome. Chas handed her the new fur coat he had bought for her and said. "You're going to need this." He put on his leather coat. "And these," he said, giving her a leather helmet, goggles, and gloves. He kissed her as she looked at him in astonishment. "I'm taking you up in my flying machine, Mrs. Thornton. Are you ready for this?"

"Oh, yes!"

For two hours they flew like birds – or dragonflies – over the countryside, along the Thames, over patchwork fields and city spires. Ria was enthralled. She could understand Chas's fascination with flying, and was so impressed by his skill.

"That was exhilarating!" she said when they had landed. "You couldn't have given me a better wedding present. Now I know something of what you experience, and I do see why you want to fly. Thank you, my love."

He kissed her, saying, "I'll teach you to fly one day."

She twined her arm about his and said happily, "I'll hold you to that. Is this where you learned?"

"In that very biplane, an Avro 504. And there's my instructor. Let me introduce you."

Dressed in men's riding breeches and a leather coat, the instructor was a tall, middle-aged woman with bobbed hair. "Ria this is Peggy Kendal. She and her husband, Sebastian, own the aerodrome, but he was recruited by the RFC early on to teach at Upavon, so Peggy's been keeping the place going on her own. Her students are eager to get into the RFC and not willing to wait for training spaces to open up."

"And can afford it," Peggy added.

"Perhaps she could teach me to fly then." Ria looked hopefully at Chas. When he hesitated, she said, "Don't tell me it's too dangerous or I won't let you go back to France!"

He looked quizzically at Peggy.

Ria said quickly, "I can take apart a Rolls-Royce engine, *and* put it back together again."

Peggy chortled. "Brilliant! You've got the right attitude. Flying isn't a pastime for prissy misses. I can fit you in. Can you be here early in the mornings?"

"As early as you like!" Ria was thrilled.

"But not until after our honeymoon," Chas said. "Thanks, Peggy. You're a better teacher than most of the ones I met at Upavon."

"That's what Sebastian tells me as well. The lads that we send them, like you, are already better than some of the instructors," she said with a chuckle.

"Oh, thank you, Chas," Ria said gleefully. "That really is the best present!"

"I hope so," he said. "It is risky. And I'm concerned about your panic attacks."

"They're not coming as often. Maybe this will help me to forget. Don't look so worried, Chas. At least I won't be encountering any enemy aircraft."

"I sincerely hope not!" he laughed.

"Besides, you said you were going to teach me anyway."

"But then I'd be with you, and would make sure nothing happened to you."

"My guardian angel."

"Precisely. But I do trust Peggy to look after you."

When the others heard, Beatrice said, "You never cease to amaze me, Ria. First a car mechanic and now a pilot." With a smile she added, "I have to admit that if I were younger, I'd be tempted to do the same."

Meredith said, "That's the spirit, Ria!"

Alice said eagerly, "Will you take me flying?"

"When she's had at least a hundred hours of solo flying," Chas said.

"So many? What have you done so far?" Ria asked.

"About two hundred."

The next day, while the others headed off to London, Meredith having a house there as well, Chas and Ria boarded a train for the Lake District. Chas had told her only to pack for a week in the country.

"Windermere!" Ria exclaimed when they arrived at the station. "Like our Windermere?"

"I expect someone thought so when they named that hamlet on our lake. Or was the hotel there first?" he wondered, referring to Windermere House on their Muskoka lake.

They were met by a driver with a horse and cart. When the long, narrow lake came into view, Ria was thrilled. "What beautiful hills!"

They were taken to a substantial Victorian house on the lakeside, with extensive grounds. "It's Hugh Paynter's family's shooting box." Hugh was one of Chas's Oxford friends who had been at the wedding yesterday. "An indulgent week here is his wedding present to us."

"It's glorious! Oh, Chas, how lovely to be by a lake again. I'm going to miss Muskoka terribly, but this is delightful."

Built of sombre grey stone, the house was rich with warm wood interiors, and commanded stunning views of the lake. A balustraded stone patio overlooked the terraced gardens and lake below.

A delectable dinner awaited them. Every amenity had been prepared for them, including expensive wines.

Chas raised his champagne glass to her and said, "To us, Mrs. Thornton. How wonderful to call you that."

It was a heavenly week. They sailed, took a tour of the ten-mile-long lake on a steamer, and walked the fells. They had no interest in seeing other people or finding out what was going on in the rest of the world. One rainy day, they stayed in bed, reading Wordsworth's poetry to each other, as he had been passionate about the Lake District, and had lived nearby.

Ria said seductively, "I think I'm ready to be a real wife now."

"Are you sure, my darling?"

"Oh, yes."

They managed to get dressed for dinner.

Ria would have forgotten about her nineteenth birthday had Chas not presented her with a gift – dragonfly earrings to match her brooch. "How beautiful!"

"I also have a canoe on order for you. It should have arrived by the time we get back."

"That's marvellous! Thank you. You spoil me, Chas. Especially as I already have everything I want. You."

"Ah, but one day, when you're tired of my snoring and my pompous prognostications on the state of the universe, you'll be happy you have your trinkets."

She laughed. "Of course I love them. But they'll never replace you."

"Good! Come here, you temptress. I can't seem to keep my hands off you."

The week was over far too soon. And they were shocked to find that London had been bombed by German Zeppelins and seven people had been killed on the previous Monday, and that enemy aircraft had been bombing southeast coastal towns the past few days.

Jack had already left for France. Alice's family wanted her to come home for a while, so Chas and Ria took her to Oxford. They had a leisurely drive through the pretty countryside, stopping for a long lunch in a quaint pub. Ria was entranced with the park-like woodlands, the tidy hedged fields, the rolling hills, the shallow streams, the ancient villages. It was all so civilized compared to the wilderness that they knew and loved. But history was in the very air here, and Ria could understand Henry's fascination with it. He would be particularly enchanted by Oxford.

Alice's grandparents, Peregrine and Phyllida Milford, were a rather antiquated couple who seemed to fit right into their venerable surroundings. Peregrine had been a professor of medieval history, but was now retired, at least from teaching. It was evident by the unabashed scattering of books and papers everywhere about the modest sitting room that he was still very much a scholar.

The Milfords had three sons and two daughters still living, all with families of their own, so Alice was going to be meeting her cousins. As the grandparents were kindly, but rather vague, Ria was glad that Alice would have younger people about. But when she offered to have Alice back with her at Bovington until school started, the Milfords were pleased to accept, as they were obviously not equipped to entertain or otherwise look after a young girl. Alice was delighted.

The Milfords offered Ria and Chas a room, but Chas had already booked them into the Randolph Hotel, not far away, and the old couple seemed relieved. But the newlyweds did stay to dinner.

The fact that Chas was an Oxford graduate seemed to please the Professor and give the Thorntons greater credibility as chaperones for Alice. Ria said, "My cousin, Henry, is hoping to study history at Oxford. When the war is over. He's on the front lines right now."

"I thank God that my sons are too old to go to war, and my grandchildren, too young," Phyllida said.

"Oscar is seventeen, dear," Peregrine pointed out. "So if this war drags on..."

"We shall pray to God it doesn't."

"Your cousin must be sure to look us up when he comes to Oxford," the professor said to Ria. "Now I must ask you, Lieutenant Thornton, if you've seen any great destruction of historic buildings in Europe. It worries me that irreplaceable architecture is also a victim of this war."

"I'm afraid that there are towns and villages that are being reduced to rubble," Chas said. "In Ypres, for instance, I saw remnants of what must have been a magnificent medieval building, the Cloth Hall, and a cathedral beside it. The city's under constant bombardment, so there won't be much of it left to salvage."

The professor shook his head in consternation.

"And now the Germans are bombing us!" Phyllida exclaimed. "What's to safeguard Westminster Abbey, and Buckingham Palace, and even Windsor Castle?"

"Or, indeed, Oxford itself?" the professor added.

"We do have the Home Defence squadrons," Chas assured them.

Later, when she and Chas walked to their hotel, Ria said hopefully, "Can you get posted to Home Defence?"

"Eventually. It's where they send us for a respite. I expect I have to put in a few more months at the Front. Or lose my nerve. Some chaps don't last long on the front lines."

"Then I wish you weren't so heroic!" she said, hugging his arm close to her.

"We have to win this war, Ria. But I promise that as soon as I can, I'll come back. I won't be more heroic than absolutely necessary," he said, kissing her brow.

Ria was delighted by Oxford – the city and the university. Chas took her on a tour of his old college, Magdalen. She was enchanted by the centuries-old buildings, the peaceful cloistered quadrangle, and the riverside walks. And he took her punting on the Cherwell.

She said, "If I'd known that this is what university life entailed, I would have been more interested in attending. No wonder Zoë wanted to come here. But, alas, I am no intellectual."

"Don't underestimate yourself, my darling. You have a hungry mind and adventuresome spirit."

"But no passion for anything in particular. Except you," she added with a grin.

"Then let me see how I can exploit that," Chas said suggestively.

They browsed in Blackwell's book shop, and wandered through the Ashmolean museum, across the street from their hotel.

On Chas's twenty-third birthday, Ria tried not to think about the fact that the baby had been due that day. She presented Chas with a first edition of Rupert Brooke's newly published poems, *1914*. The handsome, energetic young poet had died in April from the complications of an infected mosquito bite on his way to fight at Gallipoli. Ironically, one of the poems in his collection began, *If I should die, think only this of me: That there's some corner of a foreign field   That is forever England.* He was buried on the Aegean island of Skyros. Ria prayed that something similar would never be Chas's epitaph.

She also gave him a white silk scarf monogrammed with their entwined initials. "Jack said that you pilots need something smooth and soft around your necks, as you're always craning about, watching for the enemy. I expect you already have one, but I hope that this one brings you luck as well as keeps you from being chafed."

"Thank you, my darling. I shall wear it like the knights of old wore their lady's colours."

They chose a sunny day for their return journey, and Chas suggested that Ria drive, so that she become acquainted with driving on the left side of the road. It was a bit tricky at first, especially shifting gears with her left hand, but she soon caught on. She did find the narrow roads somewhat disconcerting, especially when meeting up with another car or horse and cart. One of them would often have to pull over to allow the other to pass, not always easy when the road was bordered by hedgerows or stone walls. Once she had to brake abruptly as they came upon a flock of sheep being driven down the highway.

But she did enjoy the drive, saying, "I can understand Toad's craving for the open road."

"Toad?"

"From Toad Hall. Don't tell me you haven't read *The Wind in the Willows*?"

"I must be a philistine, but, no, I haven't."

"You've had a deprived childhood. Or were too old when it was first published," she added with a grin.

"Quite possibly, my child bride," he quipped.

"It's a super story, and it's been brought so much to life for me during this trip and at Bovington Abbey, which I imagine as Toad Hall. I'll read you the book. In bed."

"I shall look forward to that."

Like carefree children, they delighted in the adventures of Toad and Mole and Ratty and Badger, Chas agreeing that Bovington was an ideal setting for the story.

"When we have children," Ria said, "let's bring them here to read the story. It'll be so much more fun."

"Indeed it will," he said, kissing her.

During his last week of leave, Chas took Ria to Stonehenge, which she had wanted to see ever since reading Thomas Hardy's *Tess of the D'Urbervilles*.

The war was so much more a reality there because of all the military encampments on Salisbury Plain, and troops everywhere. The Central Flying School at Upavon was also nearby.

So it was an odd juxtaposition to see the mammoth prehistoric stones rising out of the plain, while aeroplanes careened overhead. And yet, when they wandered among the stones, Ria felt an overpowering sense of pagan antiquity not diminished by the buzz and drone of these new man-made wonders. They marvelled at the construction of the megalithic monument, but could be equally amazed at the idea that men could build machines that carried them up into the clouds.

They stayed in Salisbury for a couple of nights, taking in the awe-inspiring cathedral. Almost eight hundred years old, it was another marvellous feat of human ingenuity and craftsmanship.

"I feel dwarfed by all this accomplishment and history," Ria admitted.

"It is rather humbling, isn't it."

"What is our generation going to leave behind, do you think? Just a lot of destruction?"

"I sincerely hope not. Surely all our innovations for killing each other more effectively will lead to some good. They're continually improving our aeroplanes."

"You mean by adding machine guns?"

"By making them faster, and more manoeuvrable."

"And safer and more reliable, I hope," Ria said, for Chas and Jack had told her about all the malfunctions in the aircraft that had brought them and their colleagues down numerous times, fortunately, unharmed for the most part. "And I don't understand why you can't have parachutes. You said that the fellows in the observation balloons have them."

"They can't get out of the way when the enemy attacks them, so they need to abandon ship. But we're not suppose to abandon our aeroplanes when they get into difficulty, but try to bring them down safely. We often manage to fix our machines after we crash them."

Chas was to leave soon, picking up a new aeroplane from Farnboro and flying it to the RFC Headquarters at St. Omer in France.

Ria tried not to dwell on his departure. They spent the last few days of his leave in London, where they met up with Lady Meredith and Theadora. Chas had asked Beatrice to join them, so that Ria wouldn't suddenly be alone.

During dinner at the Savoy, Meredith announced, "As there doesn't seem to be a foreseeable end to this war, I've decided that there are plenty of things to be done. So I want to enlist your help, Ria. I've already got Theadora writing and editing a magazine that

I'm launching. It will be called *Home Fires*, after Ivor Novello's song." She was referring to *Keep the Home Fires Burning,* a sentimental tune that was especially popular.

"We're going to report from the home front to let people know what's going on with the war effort. I'll charge the public to help defray costs, but distribute them free to the chaps at the Front. We want to give them something uplifting, and things to look forward to when they're on leave, like the shows that are popular in London. But we also want them and others to be aware of how non-military people are caught up in the perils of this war. So the first issue will talk about the *Lusitania* and the Zeppelin bombings. It'll remind our chaps what they're actually fighting for."

Theadora said, "We've been visiting hospitals, trying to cheer up the wounded men, writing letters for them, bringing them cigarettes and chocolate, that sort of thing. And we've heard too many terrible stories about the conditions in the trenches – the mud, the rats, the deafening noise, the rotting mutilated bodies of men and horses, the pervasive stench of death and decay. We're going to make sure that people at home have some idea of what it's like on the front lines, although we'll have to abide by the censorship laws, of course. I expect that if people really knew all the horrors, they would refuse to keep sending their sons to the slaughter. That applies to both sides, so might that not bring a quick end to the war?"

"If only it were that simple! And if it were up to women, I daresay that would work," Meredith said. "Still, we will do what we can. Rudyard Kipling has agreed to contribute to the first issue as well."

"You know Kipling?" Ria asked.

"He's an old friend of my father's. And we happened to meet up with him at The Duchess of Connaught's Hospital at Cliveden – which is the estate of my friends, Lord and Lady Astor. It's under the auspices of the Canadian Army Medical Corps." H.R.H. the Duke of Connaught was Canada's Governor General. "Rudyard's been visiting the wounded regularly, and he suggested that something should be done for the overseas men upon their discharge from hospital or when they're on leave. There's nothing more disheartening than to be thousands of miles from family and 'home fires' and find oneself alone on leave. And many of the lads are country boys and aren't used to cities, so London can be rather intimidating. I've decided to start a residential club for the Canadian boys, someplace they can go for a nourishing meal, a real bed, a hot bath, some companionship from 'back home'. A comfortable, homey environment where they can write letters, play pool, talk to the other fellows."

"That's a splendid idea, Meredith," Chas said. "We're lucky to have Cousin Bea, but most chaps don't have anyone on this side of the pond."

Beatrice said, "I noticed that the Canadian Red Cross is looking for country homes where convalescent officers will be welcome for a few weeks of rest before being shipped back to the front lines. And I've decided that Bovington Abbey can easily handle at least two at a time, even allowing extra rooms for friends who may show up."

"Super idea," Ria said. "As is yours, Meredith. I know a few girls in Canada, like my cousin Zoë, who could contribute articles from the Canadian home front for your magazine, and I know that Zoë would raise funds for your club."

"Excellent!"

"What do you want me to do?"

"Well, I've also decided that some of the men may want a quieter environment for relaxation, so I've found a suitable estate on the Thames between Marlow and Henley, with a tennis court, some boats, and a golf course nearby. It's not far from the convalescent hospital at Cliveden, so it's another place that the men could go when they're discharged from there. I was wondering if you would care to organize and run it?"

"Meredith, how smashing! Of course I would!"

"I thought I could count on you. Your experience running your own household will be helpful, and I will introduce you to bookkeeping. Mrs. Kipling has agreed to be the Chairman of the executive committee, and Rudyard, Earl Grey, and Lord Milner are going to be patrons. We're calling them the Maple Leaf Clubs."

"Which house is it?" Beatrice wanted to know.

"Thameshill Park. Not far from you, actually."

"Indeed it isn't."

"The Astors put me on to the owner because she's finding the house too large at the moment. Her daughter is a VAD and posted at the Royal Victoria Hospital down in Southampton. Her son is an engineer working at the Royal Aircraft Factory, designing new aeroplanes. And her husband..."

Chas interrupted, "...is training pilots at Upavon. It's Peggy Kendal, isn't it?"

"Yes, it is. Of course! She owns the aerodrome where Ria's going to take lessons, doesn't she?"

"Yes."

"She's going to rent a cottage outside of Henley for the duration of the war."

"Well done, Meredith," Beatrice said. "Thameshill is quite an estate." To the others she said, "It's something of a Victorian castle. You'll have your work cut out for you, Ria."

"I can see you'll be keeping my wife busy," Chas said with a grateful smile to Meredith.

"We must all put our talents to work," she replied. "And I think that Ria has yet to discover all of hers. I find that some gently reared ladies are dynamic organizers, and that if their resourcefulness and skills were allowed to blossom in spheres outside the domestic, they would give men worthy competition."

"That's exactly what we men are afraid of," Chas said with a chuckle. "We might be ousted from our lofty positions and become mere drones."

Theadora said. "I think you should be Prime Minister, Meredith."

"Perhaps I shall," she laughed. "My father's been made Viscount Glamorgan, with a special remainder to me so that I can inherit the title if he has no son. I think this was in appreciation for our having survived the *Lusitania*. Father was on war business for the government, securing munitions contracts in Canada and the United States. Of course he was also doing business of his own in Canada, buying into some mining interests. That's one of the reasons we feel such a connections to our Canadian friends. In any case, he'll be in the House of Lords, and I intend to succeed him when that time comes, hopefully not for many years. In the meantime, we women will show the nation what we're made of!"

They went to Covent Garden to see the opera, *Madame Butterfly*, which they all thought terribly tragic, but beautifully presented. Chas was unusually pensive.

That night in bed he said, "I'm already feeling rather jealous of all the young men who are going to come under your wing, and those officers who will be ogling you in admiration across the dinner table at Bovington."

She laughed. "They can ogle all they want and say witty and flattering things to me, but I will be completely impervious to their charms and flirtations. There is only one man who can touch my soul," she said, kissing him meaningfully. "And I don't want you to worry about me, Chas. I'm stronger now. The panic attacks are not as frequent. I can cope. You must promise me to look after yourself."

"I will, and you must promise me that you will always remember how much I love you. No matter what happens." He said it almost fiercely as he rolled on top of her, gazing intently into her eyes.

"You're scaring me, Chas." She wondered if his suddenly serious demeanour was a result of a premonition or a sense of doom.

"I'm sorry, my darling. I'm just unhappy to be leaving you again. I should have leave again in three or four months. It'll depend on how active things get, and whether our squadron is at strength."

Meaning whether they were able to replace the dead, Ria knew, although Chas never talked about that.

Neither of them slept much that night. They clung to each other as if they could forever hold onto that moment, and keep the world and the future at bay. Morning came all too soon.

Grayson was now in residence at the London house, his arm still in a cast, but back to his usual efficient, controlled self, if somewhat softened by sorrow. Ria decided that she could use his help at Thameshill Park. She told him about the project and said, "Of course I understand if you would rather stay here. The decision is entirely yours, Grayson."

"Thank you, Mrs. Thornton. This is a most congenial house, to be sure, but I don't think my services are required here. The footman has been doing an admirable job, and as he's not fit for military duty, he won't be leaving to sign up. I should enjoy taking charge of the staff at Thameshill Park." He smiled, looking genuinely pleased. Ria suspected that he felt he would be doing some useful war work there, and also that he was still somewhat *in loco parentis* and wanted to be close to her. She was touched by his paternal attitude, wishing her own father showed as much concern.

"That's super! Thank you, Grayson. I think it will be quite a challenge for me, so I shall appreciate your help."

Just before Chas left for Farnboro that morning, they had word that Henry had been seriously wounded.

•       •       •

They took the remains of his arm off at the main dressing station, where only emergency cases were treated before being sent on. They patched up his facial wounds properly at the casualty clearing station and then sent him to the base hospital on the French coast. When they judged that he was ready to travel, they put him on a hospital ship for England. Ria had already gotten word through that he should be transferred to The Duchess of Connaught's Hospital at Cliveden, which was only about six miles from Bovington Abbey.

When Ria was notified that Henry had arrived, she and Beatrice motored over to see him.

She gave him a desperate hug. The left side of his head and face was wrapped in thick bandages. His left arm was missing below the elbow.

"Good Lord, Henry! What a terrible way to end your war, but I'm so glad to see you!"

He managed a lopsided grimace. "It could have been much worse. Only a lunatic could imagine such a hell as this war. I'm grateful to be out of it. What's an arm when so many have lost their lives? And look at you," he said, referring to her scar. "You weren't even supposed to be involved in this war."

They talked for a long time, smoking cigarettes that Ria had brought. "I'll come as often as I can." She told him about the Maple Leaf Club, and how their preparations were coming along.

Henry said, "I'm glad to see that you've found an admirable outlet for your energy and talent. I've always felt that, as your eldest cousin, I should be guiding you, but you were never amenable to direction. So I'm happy to relinquish that responsibility."

"I never knew you felt that way, Henry. How sweet of you."

"I expect I didn't do much except make you want to rebel. Now I'm glad you have such spunk. I wonder if you or Cousin Beatrice could do something for me? They're planning to send me home soon to convalesce, since they can't patch me up and send me back into the trenches. But I don't want to go back to Canada. I should be well enough by the fall to attend Oxford, if they'll have me."

"Leave it to me," Beatrice said immediately. "I'm sure I can arrange a discharge from the army for you here. And when you've finished your medical treatment, you'll come and stay at Bovington until you head off to Oxford. I'll look into that for you as well."

"And we have friends at Oxford. A professor emeritus of medieval studies – Alice's grandfather." She had already told him a bit about the Lusitania, although she never mentioned the baby.

"Jolly good!" Henry looked happier than Ria had seen him in a long time, despite his disfiguring injuries, which must still be painful. He'd told them that his left ear was missing as well, and that he might be permanently deaf on that side. "Could you write a letter home for me, Victoria? I'll dictate it to you."

"Of course. Do you think you could call me Ria? I'm not Victoria Wyndham anymore."

He didn't question her, but just said, "I'll try to remember, Mrs. Thornton."

While they were doing that, Beatrice went to talk with some of the other wounded men, who were pleased with a visit.

"Do you know what today is?" Henry asked her when they'd finished.

Ria thought for a moment and said, "Hell's bells! July 1st. The Stepping Stone Marathon and Dominion Day Ball." Memories of last summer flooded back to her. It was hard to believe that she and Chas hadn't even fallen in love then, that she had been enamoured of Jack. "I wonder if they're even having them this year. Zoë didn't say."

"That's one race I'll never have to do again," Henry said with a chuckle. "Nor the Regatta."

"Didn't you have fun?"

"What, losing all the time? It's fine and dandy for people like you and Chas, but some of us never measure up."

"I expect your strengths lie elsewhere, dear cousin. Oh, I'm suddenly very homesick for Wyndwood!"

"Are you staying in England then?"

"As long as Chas is here or in France. Nothing else is as important as being with him."

Henry said, "You're lucky to have such a relationship. I don't expect I'll ever know what that's like. I was rather in love with Vivian, although I knew nothing could ever come of that. And I know I wasn't much to look at before, but now I'll be downright repulsive to women." He sighed.

"Oh, Henry, that's not true. I expect you'll find some girl who'll appreciate you."

"I doesn't matter. I'll have books for company."

"Wait until you see Oxford! It almost makes me want to go there." His eyes glowed when she told him about her visit with Chas.

"I expect I can't punt, but otherwise it's going to be the stuff of my dreams. If it's not too much trouble, could you bring me some books on English history when you next come?"

"Even better, I'll ask Professor Milford if you can borrow some from his extensive library. Alice is coming to stay with us for another month or so, now that she's visited all her cousins."

"Thank you, Vic...Ria."

"I'm so glad you've come back to us, Henry. Were you with Archie when...?"

"Archie, the poor sod, was an officer – he'd done the OTC training at university. They don't last long in the front lines." When he saw Ria blanch, he said, "Of course it's different in the RFC." He didn't tell her that it was known as the 'suicide club' among the infantry.

Ria sent a telegram to Zoë that read, "Henry maimed but will be OK and out of war. In good spirits. At Canadian hospital near Bovington. Happy Dominion Day! Wish we were there. Miss you all. Love, Ria."

# Chapter 23

Helena looked out at the steady rain, intensely annoyed. It was a grey, heavy day, the suffocating kind that didn't show any signs of releasing its grip. It was as if her first event at the cottage was jinxed. They wouldn't be able to hold the Stepping Stone Marathon – the first time in over twenty years that it had been rained out. It was stifling hot and the swimmers probably wouldn't mind, since they would be wet anyway, but the accompanying boats and spectators would be loathe to be out in this unrelenting downpour.

At least the ball could continue, since they had the roofed pavilion and had already set up a marquis to expand the space. She knew she would be judged against the successful balls of previous years, but without the old staff – people like the Graysons who made everything run efficiently and effortlessly, and Mrs. Hadley with her years of experience catering to large numbers – Helena was concerned. It was difficult to get good help these days. Young men and women were enlisting or doing more lucrative war work.

Helena had declined Olivia's offer of help, as she'd wanted to take all the credit herself. Now she wondered if she hadn't been a bit foolish. It was always good to have someone else to blame if things went wrong. At least she had accepted the offer of Olivia's staff for the evening.

In any case, she intended to shine tonight. She enjoyed being in charge of Wyndwood – they'd started calling it the "big cottage" now that Richard had his smaller one at Silver Bay. But she was looking forward to the modern and even bigger cottage that she had persuaded James to build. She wanted it at least to compare with the Oakleys or the Thorntons, and have an indoor ballroom and billiard room.

In the meantime, she had insisted that she and James take over Augusta's old bedroom, although James had been reluctant. But Helena had been adamant that they should have the largest and best room, with their own private screened balcony, since they were in charge. Albert and his family were still in residence, since their cottage probably wouldn't be completed until late summer. And just now, she and James had several friends to stay, including her father.

He had done extremely well with his investments, made at the suggestion of James and Oswald, and using money borrowed from them. His debts squared, he now lived well in the posh Vanderbilt residence Hotel in New York, built by Alfred Vanderbilt, who had occupied the top two floors of the twenty-two storey building.

Helena had told all her friends how her step-daughter had dined and partied with Alfred aboard the *Lusitania*, and been saved by the lifebelt that he had given her, thereby losing his own life. When James had tried to correct her, she had merely said, "But surely Victoria would have given her life jacket to the child, so Alfred, in essence, saved Victoria's life by giving up his to the little girl. It all comes to the same thing in the end."

If James was at all concerned by his wife's sophistry, he didn't show it.

How pleased Helena was that Victoria was staying in England. She was also relieved that she had lost the baby, since Helena didn't fancy being a step-grandmother. That made her seem much too old. And of course, there would be no scandal now, as not even Albert's family or the Thorntons knew about the stillborn child. Recalling Victoria's rudeness and arrogance the last time they had met, Helena thought the girl had deserved her misfortune. She had needed bringing down a peg or two.

Helena was thrilled with her own pregnancy. James, of course, was overjoyed, and treated her with reverence and great care. She used his fears for her safety to good advantage, getting everything she wished for just by casually mentioning something. She already had quite a collection of jewellery, and surely the best wardrobe in Toronto. Their house had become a showpiece, and Helena was gaining a reputation as a society hostess.

So now she would try to rival Letitia's reputation as premier hostess on the lake. After all, hadn't it been her idea last year to decorate Oaktree with tens of thousands of white flowers? This year's Summer Solstice Picnic had been merely that – a lavish picnic on some dreadful, empty little island.

Of course Helena was sensible to the fact that everything needed to be scaled down because of the war. Excess in anything frivolous would be considered unpatriotic as well as crass. But being creative using few resources would surely earn her accolades.

So she had decided to create a desert oasis. The pavilion and marquis were draped with pink chiffon tied back with gold braid, to suggest exotic tents. She'd had Toby and his fourteen-year-old helper, Tim, from Port Carling, spend days digging up wheelbarrow loads of sand and encircling the pavilion with it. Olivia's children had, fortunately, pitched in to help. Dozens of potted palms were grouped about the sand dunes. By offering generous payment, she'd convinced one of the carpenters working on Albert's cottage to take some time out to construct an eight foot tall pyramid of balsa wood, which he'd painted beige and coated in sand while still wet, giving it a realistic rough texture like stone. She'd had Toby chop down several trees to the east of the pavilion so that the pyramid could sprawl there surrounded by sand and torches. Crossed palm fronds decorated the doorways to the house, while more palms sat about the veranda, where the posts were also draped with chiffon.

And she would be the queen of the desert in her rich gold and white Cleopatra costume. She'd even had a gold band made, like a snake slithering up her arm, and a broad, gold neck collar. She had an elaborate, beaded and braided black wig that fell straight to her shoulders. Across her forehead was a gold band with a ruby-eyed cobra head jutting out at the centre.

"You look stunning, my dear," James said that evening, truly impressed and proud, although he did wonder at the expensive looking jewellery. Their costumes had always been fairly simple and sometimes cobbled together. But Letitia and Helena were taking the fancy dress ball into new realms.

"Thank you, dear James. I have to admit that I do feel somewhat nervous that everything will go smoothly. At least it's finally stopped raining."

"I'm sure everything will be splendid, my dear. You are a master at organization," he said, giving her a peck on the cheek. "I'm such a lucky man."

Olivia, meanwhile, was also glad that it had stopped raining, since they had to walk over from Silver Bay. She was absolutely delighted with the new cottage, which was spacious enough for her family and guests, and hers to do with as she pleased. Her parents and sister, Marguerite Kendall, and her family were visiting, and Jack's three sisters would stay for several weeks. Olivia had decided that with all her responsibilities, raising funds for the Wyndham Convalescent Hospital and being Chairman of the Board that ran the facility, she really couldn't take more than six weeks of holidays. Zoë, too, helped out, as did Eleanor and Hannah Carlyle, so many of them were not staying long in Muskoka this summer.

The Carringtons had not even opened their cottage, since Justin was already at the army camp at Niagara-on-the-Lake, and Simon was too busy with work and preparing for his wedding in August, to which they were all invited. So Zoë had invited Lydia to stay at Silver Bay as well, for as long as she liked. The poor child was devastated by her sister's death, and no longer the cheerful, light-hearted girl she had always been. Max was very attentive to her, and it seemed to Olivia that a romance might be blossoming there.

Zoë had found herself an old medieval dress in the costume trunk at the big cottage, but Jack's sisters had been busy with their needles and came prepared. Lizzie was resplendent as Cleopatra. She hoped that Rafe would be at the ball.

She had become a proficient rider under his tutelage, but hadn't seen him for months or been invited to ride to hounds with him, as he'd promised. It was because she hadn't allowed him to fuck her, she knew. But she also knew that once she did, he would feel justified in thinking her lower class, and just some tart that he could use and discard at will. Jack had always told her that her virginity was a commodity, and she had hung onto it, despite great temptations at times. Things had become pretty hot between her and Rafe.

It might take time, but she was sure that he could be won over. She was convinced that she was more beautiful and audacious and sexy than any society girl he knew. At least now that Queenie and Vivian were out of the picture.

Helena was shocked and furious when she saw Lizzie, who looked more alluring as Cleopatra, despite her simpler costume. She had the advantage of youth, height, and beauty, and didn't need expensive gold jewellery to create an impression. Her mother was a skilled seamstress who knew how to accentuate her daughter's figure, and, having been in the theatre, had used inexpensive decorations to good effect.

Letitia came dressed as a flower, with cascading layers of pink chiffon petals and green leaves. Helena thought her slightly ridiculous, for now that she was nearing forty, Letitia was no longer the ingénue she liked to pretend she still was. But Letitia was an important friend. "How dazzling you look, Letitia. As always! And how wise to have something a bit unconventional. I feel quite upstaged by that little Wyndham girl."

"How can you say that, Helena? Yours is by the far the more authentic and beautiful costume. What exquisite jewellery you have! And how lovely you've made all this. I'm so glad that everything isn't cancelled because of this silly war. Oswald has determined that the Regatta shall go on as usual, especially as we now have the Country Club." The Summer Residents' Association Golf and Country Club had opened two weeks ago with a ball, but not many summer residents had been in Muskoka yet.

When Lizzie danced with Rafe, he said, "Lionel Camford seems rather stuck on you tonight."

"Yes, he does. But the feeling is not mutual. I find him a bit of an ass."

Rafe chuckled. "His millions don't compensate for that?"

"Do you think me mercenary, Rafe?"

"Completely. You may have noble lineage, but doesn't make up for an impoverished childhood."

"Jack's investments have already paid off handsomely, and I'll be quite independent once I'm twenty-one. It may not be the fortune that you're accustomed to, but it means that I don't have to rely on a man to survive. I can choose where to give my affections. Certainly not to a buffoon like Lionel."

Rafe laughed. "I do admire your spirit, Lizzie. And your luscious body as well, as you know."

"And I'm still off-limits, Rafe. Unless you marry me." She looked at him wryly.

"You're a cock-teaser, Lizzie. And you're not the only girl around."

"So why are you wasting your time with me?" She started to pull away from him, but he held her close.

"Come and play tennis with me tomorrow."

"I'll think about it."

Edgar managed to shuffle about with Eleanor, although the sand dunes were beginning to encroach on the dance floor, making it unpleasantly gritty underfoot. "Damn fool idea to spread sand everywhere," he complained. "And tomorrow it all has to be carted back down to the beach."

"Ria will be amused," Eleanor said.

"Not by the fact that Helena had some of her trees cut down, without even asking. This point is all Ria's property. I can already imagine her magnificent fury when she confronts Helena with that. Not something I want to miss."

"I don't expect that will ever be an easy relationship."

"Speaking of relationships, you might as well give in and marry me, Ellie. There aren't any other men left but me," he said with a grin.

"I doubt that you would enjoy being married to a working woman. I wouldn't be at your beck and call all day, telling you how wonderful you are and making sure that your bath was hot and your cocktail, suitably cold."

"If you married me you wouldn't have to work, Ellie. And I would bestow presents and dozens of children on you to keep you happy and busy."

She laughed. "As appealing as that sounds, I must thank you for the honour, but decline. Beside, Jack has already claimed my heart."

"Damn him for stealing my girl! I knew he'd be trouble the moment I set eyes on him."

"I've never been 'your girl', Edgar, just your friend, which I shall always be. And I doubt that anything will come of my relationship with Jack. I have my career to consider."

"And he'll marry for money and status, just wait and see. Then you'll be happy you have me, doggedly devoted to you, waiting to put your broken heart back together."

"I shall remember that!" she said with amusement. "Have you heard anything more about Henry?"

"Ria sent a telegram to Zoë today. She's seen him and says he'll be alright, thank God! I expect we'll hear more about his injuries soon."

"You see, you are lucky to have that stiff ankle. It'll keep you safe."

"It's more than stiff. It's bloody painful at times. And I didn't' want to stay safe here and be branded a coward. Some blasted woman gave me a white feather in the street a few weeks ago in Toronto. So now I'm taking my cane wherever I go, whether I need it or not."

Zoë was pleased to see Lydia smile as Max danced with her. She, too, thought that something serious was brewing between them, and was glad of it. How she wished that she and Blake could have such a relationship. They had met often at the university this winter, and had interesting and stimulating discussions. She had begun to think that perhaps he was warming to her.

But when they had finished dancing, he said, "Come and walk with me." When they were down at the back bay, he said, "I'm leaving tomorrow, Zoë. I'm being posted overseas soon. Maybe not to France at first, because I'm still quite inexperienced. But I hope to get there eventually, to feel that I can make a real difference where it matters – at the front lines. I can't leave with you thinking that there could ever be anything more than friendship between us. It's not fair to you." Seeing the shocked expression on her face he added quickly, "No, Ellie didn't tell me anything. I'm not blind or insensitive," he said gently. "I know how painful and unfair it seems when you love someone who can't feel the same for you. The last thing I want to do is to hurt you, my friend. So you must try to let go of me, to find happiness elsewhere."

Zoë thought her heart would break, especially as he looked at her with tenderness and affection that seemed to belie his words. "You might feel differently in time," she said desperately.

"You are a very special and wonderful person, Zoë. You deserve better – a devoted lover, not just a friend."

She bit back her tears. "Will you kiss me, Blake?"

"Zoë..."

"Please! I can't bear to think that you didn't even give us a chance."

His kiss was sweet and lingering. "Don't harbour illusions, Zoë. Don't cling to a fantasy."

"Isn't that what you're doing, Blake? Why can't you open your heart to new possibilities?"

"Because I'm going away, and I don't know what this war will have in store for me, for us."

"We all have to take chances, be prepared to be hurt. Do you think I can stop loving you just because you tell me I should? We've had such wonderful times together, especially this past year. We think alike. Do you really believe that you couldn't fall in love with me in time?"

"We don't have time," he said, running his fingers along her cheek.

"I can wait."

"Oh, Zoë, I can't promise you anything."

"I don't need promises. I just don't want doors closed."

She melted into his arms when he kissed her this time. "Please don't shut me out of your heart, Blake."

"It doesn't seem right to leave you with hope," he said, stroking her hair.

"Why not? Hope is what keeps us going. If you meet someone else and fall in love, then I'll have to live with that. But if you realized that you loved me, I'll be here waiting for you."

He kissed her more passionately this time. "I don't deserve you, Zoë."

She was ecstatic.

They spent the rest of that long night dancing mostly with each other, taking breaks to sit and talk. Because it was such a hot night, they went down to the boathouse dock, pulled off their shoes and stockings, and dangled their feet in the midnight black water.

Zoë told Blake about Ria's friends in England, and their war projects. "I'm going to write for *Home Fires* , and I've talked Emma into contributing, which wasn't difficult." Emma Spencer was going off to university in the fall. It was no surprise that she was planning to major in English, for she'd been writing clever plays for their entertainments over the years. And now that she had lost her brother Archie, she had an intense interest in the war. "Ellie just agreed to do a report on the convalescent hospitals here, and Lydia is helping me with fundraising for the Maple Leaf Clubs."

"I think you're going to do great things, Zoë." He said it as if he were divining her future, of which he would have no part.

Lightly she said, "I feel quite a sloth compared to Ria. Imagine, she's going to run a Club for our boys in some massive estate."

"I'm glad. It might help her. Chas wrote to me because he was concerned about her. She's been severely traumatized by her experiences." He looked down, becoming suddenly quiet, and Zoë knew he was thinking about Vivian. It was hell to feel jealous of a dead friend! She put her hand over his. Blake looked up at her in the moonlight, and she couldn't fail to see the anguish in his eyes.

"We'll help each other get through this," she said to him. "All of us. I will count my blessings every day that I still have my friends."

He took her hand in both of his. "You're absolutely right. And I am truly thankful for you, my dearest friend. Just don't expect too much of me."

# Chapter 24

Ria and Alice finished their tennis game, and went to get glasses of lemonade that awaited them on the patio. She was surprised to see Blake Carlyle talking to Beatrice. His face lit up when he saw her. Without speaking, he took her into his arms. Beatrice ushered Alice into the house.

"It's wonderful to see you!" he said. "Thank God you're alright."

"I know how you felt about Vivian. I'm so sorry..."

"I still can't believe it. I expect that the next time I'm at the cottage, she'll just be there, like she always has been." They clung tightly to one another.

Then he looked at her assessingly. "I like the hair. Very chic and daring." Ria had bobbed her hair to chin length to make it more practical for flying. "It makes you look... I don't know. Formidable, perhaps."

She laughed. "I wonder if Chas will think that. He doesn't know yet."

"And that's a very becoming battle scar, honourably earned. Soldiers get medals for much less. How are you holding up?"

Ria knew that she could tell him everything. And she did.

"And these attacks of uncontrollable panic are lessening?"

"Yes. They come mostly at night now, waking me out of a sound sleep. It's harder without Chas here. But the nightmares don't want to leave me. Each time it feels as if it's real and new. Sheer horror."

"It's understandable. Talking might help. Will you tell me everything about that day?"

Beatrice had sent out a bottle of wine, and Ria downed a glass before saying reluctantly, "Yes, alright."

Blake was even more pale than usual when she had finished. He said, "I expect Vivian had a merciful death. Whereas you, my dear friend, have been through hell. You're very strong, Ria."

"I don't often feel that way."

"I expect that all this work on the Club is helping. You should see what Zoë has sent along! Crates of blueberry jam and maple syrup..."

"Real maple syrup? How divine!"

"A thousand wool blankets donated by the Carringtons."

"Super! That should be more than enough for both locations."

"An impressive collection of Canadian art from Edelina and her friends from the Algonquin Group. You remember Tom Thomson?"

"Yes, of course. I bought one of his paintings for Chas. Those should remind the boys of home."

"Zoë says to tell you that she's found some organizations, like the Men's Canadian Clubs and the Imperial Order of Daughters of the Empire, to help sponsor you, so they're collecting funds. And imagine this – she managed to get $5,000 out of Oswald Oakley."

"Ah, blood money. Good for her!"

"Another five out of the Camfords, who couldn't be seen to be less charitable. Zoë cleverly told them all that their generosity would be mentioned in the first edition of *Home Fires*. So she managed to shame your father and Helena into giving the same. She approached other business associates of your family, like Mackenzie and Flavelle. In all, I've brought a cheque for $50,000."

"Zoë is magnificent!"

"Yes, I've begun to realize that."

Ria looked at him quizzically, and Blake said, "I've taken her for granted much too long. I think I was rather dazzled."

"Are you ready to move on yet?"

He shook his head in consternation. "I know that Vivian was coming over to be with her fiancé. Justin told me. But I never wanted to believe that I had no place in her life. I think I've been a fool."

"You're only a fool if you don't accept things you can't change, and don't take advantage of what you do have."

"How wise," he said with a smile. "Perhaps you should be the psychiatrist."

She laughed. "Oh, it's so good to have you here! You seem to have brought a little bit of Muskoka with you. How I miss it! How long can you stay?"

"Only a few days, I'm afraid."

"Where will you be posted?"

"At the military hospital at Shorncliffe, fortunately. What I didn't want was one of the specialist ones, like the venereal disease, or tubercular, or typhoid hospitals. Not that those aren't important, but they'd seem so far removed from the battles."

"That's important for you? To feel closer to the action?"

"Yes. I'm going to try to get posted to France. I know I'm not an experienced enough surgeon to get close to the front lines yet, but even at the base hospitals I'd feel more useful."

"Shall we go and visit Henry? He'll be so pleased to see you."

He was delighted.

"Soon, more of us are going to be over here than back home," Blake said.

"I really hate to think of any of my friends having to go into the trenches," Henry said. "And I don't *really* mind all this, you know," he said, indicating his arm. "I might have shot it off myself if I'd thought of it, just to get away."

"It's that bad?" Blake asked.

"Worse." Henry looked at Ria and then back at Blake.

"You can tell us, Henry. I know it's not pleasant, but I've seen some pretty gruesome things myself," Ria said.

"And so you have enough to frighten you. I refuse to add to your store of horrible images. And now I want to hear about the Dominion Day Ball."

When Blake had finished, Ria said, "The bloody nerve of that woman, cutting down my trees!"

"Edgar says he can hardly wait to see you lambaste her for it," Blake said. "I think Ellie intends to sells tickets."

She laughed.

Henry said, "Why don't you go and brighten the day for the other chaps, Ria? They're all in love with you, and so envious of me."

"I know when I'm not wanted," she replied with a grin, although she always brought chocolates and cigarettes for the other fellows in Henry's ward, and spent a few minutes talking to them.

When they drove back to Bovington, Ria asked, "Is Henry's story so bad that I can't hear it?"

"I don't think anyone should have to hear those sorts of stories, let alone have lived them," Blake said grimly. "But Henry seems to be coping well. And you really seem to have settled in here, Ria. I'm in awe of anyone who can drive on either side of the road and you can do both."

"I'll take you up in an aeroplane tomorrow, if you like." She laughed at his stunned expression. She had told no one at home yet about her flying lessons.

"You *are* serious, aren't you?"

"Oh, yes. I've already logged ten hours of solo time. They send fellows to France with only fifteen hours." Ria loved flying. Of course it had been nerve wracking at first, but Chas was right to say that Peggy was an excellent teacher, very receptive to her pupils' abilities and concerns, never pushing them beyond what they could comfortably do. So Ria didn't do her first solo flight until both she and Peggy knew she was ready. Unlike the rushed RFC training, according to Sebastian, where novices were sometimes sent up alone after only two hours of dual control training with an instructor. They lost new recruits daily to accidents, the number of fatalities higher than those from enemy action.

But Peggy had told Ria that she was a quick study, and better than most men she had taught, except for Chas. He was her star pupil. It was comforting to know that.

"Good God, Ria. I'm humbled by your courage and abilities."

She laughed. "Perhaps you should reserve judgement until you've seen me fly."

"I think that anyone who even wants to fly is either brave or crazy. And I must be crazy because I will put my life into your hands. Whether I'll be able to sleep tonight or not is another matter," he added with a grin.

"We'd better be sure to give the doomed man a good dinner then."

"You don't have any panic attacks when you're flying?"

"Chas was concerned about that, too, so he had Peggy keep a close eye on me when she took me up. I suppose I'm so concentrated on flying, and so exhilarated by it, that everything else falls away."

"That's good to hear."

"Especially for you," she teased.

When they arrived at Bovington, the two convalescent officers who were guests had just returned from golfing. Blake was surprised to see Lieutenant Philip Pottinger.

"Good God, Philpot! What are you doing here?" Blake asked.

"You two know each other?" Ria asked in astonishment.

"We were in high school together," Blake answered.

"Jolly good to see you again, Carlyle. Can't believe all the fellows from home I've run into over here."

They caught up on their lives, and then Blake said, "So what are you recovering from?"

"Got gassed a bit at Wipers – that's Ypres to you civilians – and developed bronchitis. But they tell me I'm just about ready to go back."

Ria thought that the young man was hardly ready in spirit. He looked frightened, but tried to put on a brave front.

The other young officer, Captain Robert Armitage, was recovering from an attack of nerves, which was becoming known as shell-shock. Ria had noticed that he seemed to be holding onto himself tightly, trying not to let his hands shake, as they were wont to do.

Blake seemed most interested from a psychological perspective. After dinner he said to Ria, "I'm going to ask you to do something really difficult. I want you to tell Captain Armitage about your experience on the *Lusitania*. You don't have to talk about the baby if you don't want to." When he saw her panicked look he said, "It might help him to open up. I think he's in a very fragile mental state. If they send him back like that, it will likely push him over the edge."

He asked Beatrice to keep Alice occupied elsewhere, and then, over coffee in the drawing room, said, "I don't suppose you fellows know that Mrs. Thornton was on the *Lusitania*."

"Good Lord! Were you really?" Lieutenant Pottinger asked. "Is that where you got that scar?"

Hesitantly Ria began talking. When she had finished, she realized that the exercise had been as much for her benefit as Captain Armitage's, for she felt somewhat lighter. She gave Blake a wry look, and he winked at her.

"Mrs. Thornton is suffering from neurasthenia, now also called shell-shock, which is quite understandable. Our minds and bodies can only stand so much stress. It's hardly surprising that she has recurring nightmares and sudden waves of panic."

"Bloody right!" Lieutenant Pottinger said. "I keep seeing that green cloud coming at me, and if someone hadn't told me to piss on my handkerchief – sorry, M'am – and breathe through it, I'd have been done for. Gives me the shakes just to think about that."

Without looking at them, Captain Armitage said quietly, as if talking to himself, "My men were blown up all around me. I don't know how I survived with only a few minor wounds when I had bits of my friends all over me. All that blood and gore. And the stench. It never leaves my nostrils. I can barely eat at times, especially when I smell raw meat. I lay in a muddy, bloody crater and couldn't move. I only had parts of people for company. A leg, an arm, a torso. A head that looked like a grotesque soccer ball. I was paralysed. Thought I'd caught a bullet in my spine, but when they finally got me out, two days later, the doctors couldn't find anything wrong with me. I just lost my nerve. I'm a coward." He suddenly burst into tears and shook violently.

Ria went to his side and took his hand in hers. "You can't possibly think that. No one should have to experience such monstrosities!"

"I'm sorry. I don't know what's come over me. This is very embarrassing."

"Not at all. Ria's right," Blake said. "It's not normal or humane for anyone to have to live through something so terrible. No reasonable person could experience that and not be affected. How did they treat you?"

"Electric shock therapy, baths, and massage. I started walking again. And then they told me I needed to buck up and be manly."

"Not much sympathy there," Blake said. "I think you've done your bit, and should be invalided out. It would be cruel to send you back."

"I don't suppose you could put in a word for me, Captain Carlyle?"

"I will try, but I'm not sure my opinion will have much weight. But here's something for you to think about. First of all, you're not alone. From what I've heard, lots of men are suffering terrible anxieties. And little wonder. We're all taught that killing is a sin, and then our country sends us out to do just that, and calls us heroes if we do it well enough. Anyone with an ounce of humanity and empathy for other human beings could only recoil in horror from scenes like you and Ria and Philpot have described. Is it any wonder that your minds want to suppress those images? And if it's any consolation, as a doctor I can tell you that your friends didn't suffer. They died instantly. Don't feel bad for them. Think about helping yourself. Talking, crying, admitting your weaknesses and fears, finding pleasant things to occupy you are all legitimate, healthy ways to look after yourself. There's no shame in any of it. The shame is with people who make you feel less a man or a soldier for having such feelings. So when you're at your medical board, don't downplay your symptoms. Tell them exactly how you're suffering. They might at least give you several more months of leave, even if not a discharge."

Captain Armitage seemed to have visibly brightened. "Thank you, Captain Carlyle."

When Ria and Blake went to find Alice to take her for a row, Ria said, "Dear God, I hope that stories like his are the exception, but I rather doubt it."

"As do I."

"I expect Henry's was equally appalling?"

"Yes."

"You're really good at this, and helpful, Blake. I hate remembering, but every time I'm forced to talk about it, it gets easier."

"Repressing it in your conscious thoughts just makes it all the more powerful in your subconscious, like when you're sleeping. Obviously you're never going to forget it, but you have to come to terms with it, not let it terrorize you."

"You're very wise. With your psychiatric training, shouldn't you be working with people like Captain Armitage?"

"I would enjoy that, but as I'm not experienced, I don't have much say in my appointment. But when I meet casualties like him, I might at least be able to intervene, and be sure they get proper treatment."

"Is there 'proper treatment'?"

"Probably not. It's all so new."

"Then perhaps you can make a significant contribution to the world of medicine by putting forth your own theories."

Blake chuckled. "You'll have me nominated for the Nobel Prize next."

"And why not? I expect great things from you."

He laughed delightedly. "Now what about Alice? Is she suffering nightmares?"

"You need to talk to her as well. Aren't we lucky to have our own psychiatrist to look after us."

Alice was happy to talk to Blake as he rowed them up the river. After she had told her story, he asked, "What haunts you the most about your experience?"

"In my dream I see Mummy under the water. She's like a mermaid and can breathe but I can't and she's smiling at me and waving her hand for me to come to her but I can't go to her even though I want to and I can't go up to the top even though I need to breathe and I get scared because I think she wants me to die so I can be with her and I don't want to die but I do want to be with her." Alice began sobbing.

Ria was close enough to put her arm about the girl. She made sure Alice always wore a life jacket, although she had started teaching her to swim.

Blake pulled the boat over to the shore, under the drooping branches of a willow. Gently, he said, "Your Mummy, like all good Mummies, wants only the best for you. So she doesn't want you to die. She just wants you to know that she is always there to look after you, wherever you are."

"Do you really think so?" Alice gasped between sobs.

"I most certainly do! I know you must miss her dreadfully, but she's watching over you. She'll be proud to see you growing up, having a family of your own one day. She's a big part of you. I expect you have her beautiful eyes and maybe her nose."

"It's what Grandma says. And her chin." Alice managed a smile.

"Your Mummy would never hurt you. I expect she was the one who helped you get back to the surface. You are a very brave girl, Alice. I'm so honoured to know you. And I have to thank you for saving my friend's life."

"She's my best friend, too!"

"Then you be sure to tell her about your nightmares or anything else that's bothering you."

"Thank you, Blake. I do like all your friends, Ria. You're so lucky."

Ria smiled at Blake, "I know."

She always rose at six and was in her aeroplane by seven. Peggy was reluctant to let Ria take a passenger, but Blake charmed her, and was delighted with his hour in the air.

"That was immensely exciting," he said as they drove back to Bovington for breakfast. "I can only imagine what Ellie and Zoë will say when they hear."

"Do let me tell them first that I'm taking lessons. Then you can send a letter describing what an accomplished pilot I am. Or else I'm sure Zoë will disown me for putting your life at risk."

After breakfast, he and Alice accompanied Ria to Thameshill Park, which was only a few miles away on the other side of the Thames, towards Henley. By river, they were only a mile apart, and Ria sometimes canoed over.

"The estate has sixty-five acres – about the same size as Wyndwood. Oh, how I miss it! Anyway, Peggy agreed to let me plow up a few acres of meadow to plant a kitchen garden that can service the Club. We're off to a bit of a late start this year, but should be able to get a decent crop of potatoes, onions, carrots, and such. There's an orchard as well."

"You managed to find workers?"

"Peggy left a lot of her staff here, since she didn't need them all in the much smaller house she's renting, so we have most of the groundsmen. At least the elderly ones. The young ones had all gone off anyway. Alice and I are helping out, and will invite any of the men who will be staying with us to pitch in with the garden if they feel so inclined. I've found local ladies to volunteer to make beds and serve meals and such. And we've hired a couple of cooks, kitchen maids, and charwomen. We're sending the laundry out to some women in Marlow who've volunteered to do it for the cost of the soap. And we have a couple of young women who wanted to be VADs but aren't old enough, so they've volunteered to be secretaries, helping us with the accounts, booking in the men when they arrive, that sort of thing. Meredith has been teaching me about bookkeeping, which is my least favourite part of all this, but at least I'll have some help."

Thameshill was an enormous, fanciful, crenellated, confection of a house, its multitude of leaded windows set in rippling bays. It sat on a hill overlooking the Thames where the river swept around a bend. As they drove through a Gothic archway into a large courtyard, Blake said, "Wow, the aeroplane business must be good."

"Peggy and Sebastian are both from wealthy mercantile families. The aerodrome is just their hobby. Oh, I should tell you that Grayson is now *Mr.* Grayson, as I've made him manager rather than butler. I thought it would give him more clout with the guests, since he will really be running the place. I expect he'll feel he's managing a hotel rather than a household."

Grayson greeted them at the door, saying, "A very great pleasure to see you again, Captain Carlyle."

"Thank you, Mr. Grayson. I'm delighted to see that you're recovering. We were all very sorry to hear about Mrs. Grayson. It's so tragic."

"Thank you, sir."

"This is quite the castle you have in your charge, and a most worthwhile project."

"Indeed it is. Mrs. Thornton has great faith in my abilities, for which I'm grateful. I trust she won't be disappointed."

"Have no fear of that Mr. Grayson," she assured him. "You are a master at organization, and I know I couldn't possibly do this without you. I'm going to show Dr. Carlyle around and then we'll put him to work for a while."

The baronial Great Hall had soaring, two-storey tall windows, a minstrel's gallery, and an engulfing stone fireplace. "We've put the Kendals' antique furniture into storage in the attics. So we've furnished this very practically with a few sofas and lots of easy chairs and side tables."

The gilded, marble-pillared, mile-long dining room, lit by four crystal chandeliers, had twenty round tables with four or six chairs around each. She took him through the billiard room, smoking room, and conservatory, which now had a ping-pong table as its centrepiece. "This was the music room," Ria showed him, "but we've turned it to a dormitory. So we've put twenty beds in here, and converted the cloakroom into a bathroom, with Peggy's blessing, of course. There's a downstairs loo as well, and six bathrooms upstairs. The library is our office, and the morning room beside it is now Grayson's quarters."

There were a dozen bedrooms upstairs with half a dozen beds in each. "We'll have the capacity for ninety-two men, so we've not only had to buy the beds and furniture, but also the bedding, dishes – since we couldn't possibly use the Kendals' china – kitchen equipment, and so forth We'll be charging the men two shillings a day for accommodation and three hearty meals. It won't come anywhere close to covering the costs, especially as food is increasingly expensive, so Zoë's sponsors will be most helpful.

"The Thorntons offered to pay for the furniture in both houses, so I managed to get some good deals, buying in such bulk. Cousin Bea has donated three more skiffs, three dozen fishing rods, tennis racquets, soccer balls, and twenty bicycles. Chas and I are supplying half a dozen canoes, which Edgar is arranging for us, and a motorcar so that men can be picked up from the hospital or the train station in Marlow. I've found an eager young woman to drive it, and encouraged her to get some training in car repair in the garage in Marlow while we wait for everything to be ready. I'll do some chauffeuring as well with my car, but can't rely on always being around. And I've found some Girl Guides to make dressing gowns so each man has one for use during his visit."

"This is truly amazing, Ria. *You* are amazing! What a project."

"It's been keeping me from dwelling on things, like the baby and Chas not being here and wondering if he'll be one of the lucky ones."

Seeing her sudden distress, Blake put his hand on her shoulder as he said, "It must be very hard for you. All the more reason to admire what you've accomplished."

"It's Grayson who does it all. I just come up with ideas and talk to people."

"Don't underestimate yourself. I'm really proud of you."

She smiled gratefully. "It's odd how this war has affected us. Like Chas, I had no goals, except to enjoy myself, see the world, have adventures. And suddenly, we're doing things that actually matter. It feels good to make a difference. I suppose it's made us grow up."

"We don't all easily find our path in life or realize our talents early. I suppose the war has precipitated that for you."

Her light-heartedness regained, she said, "You'll find this amusing. The British are very class conscious, as you probably know. The army doesn't approve of officers fraternizing with the men. But we've decided we're going to be a bit more Canadian and allow *both* officers and men here. So those officers who can't find accommodation at a place like Cousin Bea's can come here. Having said that, we still think it'll work better if they have separate dorms."

"Well done! Now what can I do to help?"

"Put up the paintings that you've brought. You and Alice can decide where they should go. I'll be in the office."

When she'd finished sorting through the paperwork for the day, the pictures were up and Blake and Alice were pulling weeds in the garden, along with Lieutenant Pottinger and Captain Armitage, who had rowed over to help out.

．　　．　　．

*Dearest Zoë,*

*I wish you could have been at the official opening of our Maple Leaf Clubs today! It was held at our London Club in Berkeley Square, with the honours being done by our own Prime Minister. Sir Robert Borden mentioned your astounding contribution by raising so much money for us. You really have worked wonders!*

*We seem to have started a trend, as some other residential clubs for overseas men are also being created. Their Majesties are so impressed by our work that they want to have their names associated with the clubs. So they are now to be called 'The King George and Queen Mary Maple Leaf Clubs'.*

*We had already opened our doors last week, and have been inundated by boys eager for a bit of Canadiana in Britain. (We had informed all the convalescent hospitals about our Clubs.) I wish you could see their faces when they arrive at Thameshill. (I hope you received all the photos I sent of the house and setting.) They are overwhelmed by the luxurious surroundings and the friendly reception they receive, to say nothing of the comforts and delicious meals. One lad from Winnipeg said he thought it was Buckingham Palace or the Ritz, which, of course, he could never afford.*

*A few of the boys have summered on lakes and were delighted to find we have canoes for their use. Others are eager to learn. I think I may have to order some more!*

*Chas said I must be careful not to break too many hearts, as they are all sure to fall in love with me. I think they love me for my Canadian accent. I seem to remind them of the girls back home. Many are so young, and yet have such ancient eyes, undoubtedly from their horrific experiences in the trenches. One of the officers told me we're helping with moral, that the men feel appreciated by those back home, and a boy who's surely not yet eighteen (I expect he lied on his papers) said the Club really helped with his homesickness.*

*If only you could come and see how much good you've done with your work! I'm going to suggest to Emma that she write an article about you and your accomplishments for Home Fires. By the way, the first issue is out, and getting rave reviews. I'll enclose a few copies for you.*

*Lady Sidonie, whom I can't help liking, despite my conviction that she and Chas were lovers, has invited me to a few entertainments at her London residence, in defiance of her mother-in-law, the redoubtable Lady Dunston. I've been fortunate enough not to meet up with that dragon, and sometimes think that Sidonie invites me deliberately to provoke Lady Dunston and discourage her from attending the functions herself. I'm quite happy to help!*

*Sidonie has quite a distinguished social circle, including Sir Max Aitken, an odd little Canadian of great wealth and influence here. He's the official Canadian 'Eyewitness' or war correspondent, head of Canadian War Records, and a friend of Rudyard Kipling, as well as being a British MP. An extremely clever man whom I don't trust for a heartbeat. His forte is propaganda – at the moment – but whatever fits the bill to advance his career, is how I see it. He has a penchant for pretty women, despite being married. Unlike most, I'm not flattered by his attentions, and find him rather bumptious.*

*Sidonie's war work, not surprisingly, is to entertain convalescent Canadian officers. This she does through the Canadian Red Cross 'Drives and Entertainment' section. As you may have heard, the energetic Lady Drummond from Montreal has established an Information Bureau within the CRC to keep Canadian families updated about their men overseas, and also to help look after them, whether wounded, on leave, or as prisoners-of-war. With the Dunstons being friends of the Drummonds, of course, it was only natural that Sidonie should become involved. She says she has a special fondness for the lovely Canadian men, who she swears are taller and handsomer than any Brit! Because she can drive and has a motor, she takes them on outings to concerts in the park, picnics in the country, or for tea at her London home. Sometimes she takes them to the theatre, and those she really likes are invited to weekends at her country estate or the ancestral home, Blackthorn Park. Of course, there are always a dozen other guests as well, although I haven't had time to visit as yet.*

*Henry is now recuperating at Bovington. Cousin Bea managed to get him discharged from the army here, although they were reluctant to do that. Henry had to sign away his right to free transport to Canada, and show evidence that he either had a job or independent means of support. He didn't want to come up to London just yet – he's trying to get used to his new image. I'm afraid half his face is terribly scarred from the shrapnel. The wounds are still quite livid, but will surely fade over time, although his face will look like a battlefield with trenches. He's very stoical, as you'd expect from Henry. I think that Blake helped him deal with things as well.*

*It was so wonderful to see Blake. He certainly seems to have a new appreciation for you, so don't give up hope there....*

When Ria returned from posting her letter to Zoë, there was a telephone call for her. It was Henry. Since he had stayed at Bovington and could entertain Captain Armitage, who had managed to get another month of leave, and a new officer, Beatrice had been able to come to London with Ria and Alice.

As soon as she heard the tone of his voice, her blood froze. "A telegram's come for you."

She knew he meant an official one. Dear God, no! "Will you open it please, Henry?" She thought she would scream. Her mind railed against the thought that Chas could be dead. Surely she would have known somewhere inside herself!

She heard the sigh of relief as Henry said, "He's been wounded. Not severely. I can't tell you what good news this is, silly as that may sound!"

"You're absolutely right, Henry." Thank God, thank God, thank God! She began to cry.

*Dearest Ellie,*

First let me assure you that Chas and I are alright, but I am writing to you from the base hospital, and both of us will soon be sent to England to recuperate.

As to what happened... We were part of an early morning bombing raid on German aerodromes, involving several squadrons. Chas, Lt. Reid, and I from 2nd Sqn went up together, each of us having 6 bombs to drop. We don't take observers on bombing missions, and as such, are unarmed, except for our pistols. My machine wasn't behaving well (hardly news, is it?), and I was the last to drop my load. We scored fairly well, destroying some of their aircraft and making a mess of their aerodrome. But two German pilots from another airfield managed to get aloft in their new Fokker Eindekkers, which is a monoplane, a single-seater fighter that has a synchronized machine gun that fires through the propeller. It's faster and more nimble than our stable, lumbering BE2s, which are good only for reconnaissance. So they took after us, and we had to push our planes to their limit to try to outmanoeuvre the Fokkers. Bloody unnerving when you hear the rattle of the machine gun, and know that you have only your flying skill to defend yourself. Or hope that the Hun machine guns jam as often as ours do!

I saw Reid's aeroplane go into a steep dive, with one of the Fokkers on his tail.

My plane was hit, breaking one of the struts so that I didn't dare do any more acrobatics or I would have put it into a fatal spin. So I just tried to go PDQ back to base, as we were well behind enemy lines, and I was damned if I was going to put down there and become a prisoner. My engine problems got worse, and I soon lost altitude.

Chas could see that I was in difficulty, and being preyed upon by the other Fokker, so he engaged the Hun in an heroic battle – Chas, of course, without any weapon against a faster plane with a machine gun. Not good odds. Chas flew right at him, swerving off at the last second, looping back in an 'Immelman turn' to get above him and try to force him down.

Of course I didn't see much of this as I headed back, wondering if I was even going to make it. The bloody engine eventually quit altogether, so I was coasting back. I was so low by the time I crossed the lines that Archie couldn't even fire at me, but I'm surprised that the machine guns didn't finish me off. Still, I think I startled them by being so low that they didn't even know what to make of me, and were probably afraid that I was trying to strafe them. Anyway I barely missed the trees on our side and crash-landed none too gracefully this time, as I didn't have time to scout out a good landing field.

Some of our troops came running over and dug me out of the wreck. I have to admit I felt a bit panicked, expecting the bloody plane to explode and roast me. You'll be surprised that I have only a few cuts, lots of bruises, a twisted ankle, wrenched shoulder, and sprained wrist.

Chas, on the other hand, was wounded in the arm and thigh by the Fokker's machine gun fire. The brave and reckless ass was already hit and bleeding when he diverted the Fokker from finishing me off. He even managed to drive him down, because it seems that the Hun's machine gun did seize after all. Chas encountered heavy Archie on his way back, which damaged his machine pretty badly. But he managed to get to our aerodrome and do one of his perfect landings, even though he'd lost a lot of blood. He's a bloody brilliant pilot! For his heroism, which probably saved my life, he's going to be awarded a Distinguished Service Order, which is the highest honour in the British forces after the Victoria Cross. I was "mentioned in dispatches" for my bravery in bringing the wretched, traitorous aeroplane back despite all odds, although there wasn't much salvageable, and it wasn't bravery so much as cowardice in not wanting to become a prisoner. But who am I to argue? Anyway, I think we should all be given medals just for flying the damned, treacherous things! We lose more men to equipment malfunctions and accidents than to enemy action.

Chas and I have both been gazetted Captain. I have to admit a great sense of pride in that. This war is a class leveller in some ways, for we officers, especially the RFC, seem to be held in high regard by others. The esteem comes from one's abilities, not wealth or lineage. Even though I can boast those now, I do prefer being judged on merit. It still seems odd to me have a batman – my own personal servant, just because I'm an officer – to look after me and my kit. Sweeting is a cheerful little Yorkshireman with an open and honest face, but as clever as a fox. He contrives to scrounge all kinds of things to add to my comforts. I'll be sorry to lose him if I'm not posted back to 2nd Sqn. Perhaps I can have him transferred to be with me.

Poor Reid, although lucky to be alive, is now a POW. The Germans dropped a note over our lines to tell us that he was not seriously wounded, but was a prisoner. It was signed by the infamous Immelman! I was damned lucky it wasn't me he took after, since he's a crack pilot. Although Chas was doing the

*'Immelman turn' in his evasive manoeuvres, not everyone can manage it, especially not in our old aeroplanes.*

*I have to say that I have great respect for the Germans. They're always coming up with new innovations that put them well ahead of us. These Fokkers are going to be something to reckon with – aeroplanes that are actually designed for fighting, and not just reconnaissance. That's going to change the way this air war will be fought. Until now, we've just been trying to chase off enemy recce, but if we're going to actively engage in aerial combat, then I sure as hell want to do it in a specialized aeroplane like the Fokker.*

*Chas isn't wounded seriously enough to be out of the war, unfortunately, but I expect that he'll be on Home Defence or training pilots for a while after his convalescence. Not that either one of those is particularly safe, but certainly less stressful.*

*I expect I'll be posted to Home Defence for a while as well, and hope that our aircraft designers come up with a decent new fighter plane by the time I have to go back to the Front.*

*So Chas and I are looking forward to some convalescent time at Bovington Abbey. I wish you were there. I can't tell you how much I miss you!*

*Love, Jack*

Chas ruffled Ria's curls as he said, "Now I can run my fingers through your hair any time without worrying about dislodging your coiffure. It must feel rather liberating."

"Wonderfully so," she replied. The way he massaged her scalp was very sensuous. "I'm sure more women will bob their hair when they discover that." Chas had been surprised when he had first seen her at the Cliveden hospital, but had assured her that the new *do* made her seem even more plucky, confident, and alluring than ever.

He and Jack had been released early from the hospital because Ria had assured the doctors that they would be well looked after at Bovington. She drove them back to Cliveden for medical checkups and therapy as needed. Both were limping, Jack using a crutch under his good shoulder, and Chas, a cane. The flesh wound in his arm was healing well. But his time Ria had to be careful of Chas's injuries when they made love.

She was overjoyed to have him back. It would be months before he was fit enough to resume flying. He had already been told that he'd be teaching at Upavon for a while after his recovery, since his skill as a pilot was becoming legendary.

Now she took him up flying, and he was impressed by her abilities. "I take back what I said last summer about girls not being able to fly. You're better than a lot of the men." She was thrilled with his praise, for she knew it was not lightly given.

"I took Sidonie up a few weeks ago and apparently almost gave Lady Dunston an apoplectic fit," Ria told him. "You've just missed Percy. He was home on leave for a fortnight, and Lady Dunston is hoping that grandchildren will soon be forthcoming, so she frets about anything that Sidonie does that may jeopardize her carrying a child." Ria brushed aside her own sudden sadness, as she added, "Lady D was sure that flying would terrify Sidonie or otherwise – through increased gravity, she thinks – precipitate a miscarriage. So I'm even more in Lady D's bad books. The 'D' is for 'Dragon', by the way."

Chas laughed. "You and Sid have been hitting it off then?"

"Oh yes! A woman after my own heart. I don't believe that you couldn't have had her if you'd wanted to." Ria suddenly realized how ambiguous that sounded, and blushed.

Chas seemed amused. "Much as I like her, I had no interest in marrying her, if that's what you mean. So she settled for Percy, who is an amiable chap, unlike his mother, and came with pots of gold."

"You make her sound mercenary."

"Just practical." Chas took her in his arms and said, "There are not many couples who are as lucky as we are. We can be madly in love and practical at the same time."

Ria laughed. "It's so good to have you home!"

Sidonie dropped in for tea at Bovington that afternoon, saying, "I couldn't wait any longer to ensure that you are truly alright."

"Alive, but not kicking anything just yet," Chas replied with a chuckle.

"Just look at the pair of you!" Sidonie declared. "Canes and crutches like old men! How will you dance at my fund-raising Ball next week?"

"We'll just send wads of money," Chas said. "What's it for?"

"Some sort of Belgian orphan relief fund, I think. What *aren't* people collecting for these days? Under duress, I agreed to host the Ball, at enormous expense, I must tell you. I'd rather see that money going into restoring the west wing of Blackthorn, but Lady Dunston insisted. Wouldn't it be so much easier if everyone just sent in their contributions and we could socialize with only those people we truly liked, instead of everyone? And now if you don't come to the Ball, Lady Dunston most definitely will! Damn!"

The others laughed.

"At least dine with me in London some time soon," Sidonie said.

"We'd be delighted to," Chas agreed.

"Quentin is due home in September, so let's make it then. Just the very nicest people we know. A table for twelve, although that might be stretching it."

They laughed again. "We're honoured to be included in that exclusive company," Chas said.

"You think I'm being facetious, but I do find most people extremely tiresome. They're boringly stuffy, exceedingly silly, or sycophantic social climbers. Give me someone dangerous or roguish or just plain honest and fun-loving! That's why I like you."

"And Max Aitken."

"You know Max?"

"I know *of* him, of course. He's in the same line of business as Pater – a rather brilliant bond salesman from what I've heard. But once he got into mergers and acquisitions, he developed a reputation for, shall we say, sharp practices. I remember the outrage when he was knighted a few years ago, since he'd just been accused of pocketing thirteen million dollars by watering the stock in the Canada Cement merger. I expect one of the reasons he left Canada was his growing unpopularity in the business establishment."

"I think he has much larger ambitions than Canada can fulfill. And he's definitely dangerous," Sidonie said sensuously. "And going places. I always thought that pirates and ruthless gnomes were rather exciting."

"You are wicked, Sid," Chas said.

"I know, darling."

.        .        .

Sidonie called the next day to inform them that Percy had been killed by a sniper near Ypres. "A nice clean death, I've been told," she said, choking back tears. "I *was* fond of him, you know."

"Of course, Sid. I'm so terribly sorry," Chas said. "We all liked him. How tragic. What can we do to help?"

"Lady D is frantic to have his body returned, although you know the army won't allow that. I do feel dreadfully sorry for her, having just lost her youngest daughters, whose bodies were never recovered. But she is hysterical and driving me to distraction. I'm going to have a memorial service for Percy on Saturday. Will you all come?"

"Yes, of course."

There was an amazing turnout at St Paul's Cathedral for the service. "Sidonie wasn't exaggerating when she said that Percy had lots of friends," Ria observed.

Sidonie looked fashionably beautiful in her widow's weeds. Tall and proud, she exemplified that admiral British stoicism.

The food originally intended for the Ball now served the hundreds of mourners who came to pay their respects to the family in Sidonie's London townhouse.

"You're holding up remarkably well," Chas said encouragingly to her at one point.

"Thanks to the cocaine," she whispered, shocking Ria and Chas.

Before they could respond, Lady Dunston descended upon them, demanding, "Who invited *you*? How *dare* you show yourself here, you brazen hussy!"

"Lady Dunston, you forget yourself," Chas said amiably. "You are speaking to my wife."

"I'm surprised at *you*, Chas Thornton, settling for an unprincipled and undisciplined hoyden, whose own father doesn't even approve of her."

Chas, who had put his arm protectively around Ria, felt her stiffen. Before she could retort, he gave her a reassuring squeeze and quickly said, "I know you are wracked with grief, Lady Dunston, so we will ignore that unjustified remark. We're here to honour Percy, and hope that you accept our sincerest condolences for your great loss."

"I want nothing from either of you! Except your departure from my house."

"You forget that this is *my* home, Lady Dunston," Sidonie said calmly. "And I will not allow you to insult my friends. Percy would be appalled."

At those words, Lady Dunston broke down, and her younger son, newly arrived in England to study at Oxford, took her up to her suite, much to everyone's relief.

Jack brought Sidonie a glass of champagne, which she took gratefully.

"Oh, God, I hope I'm not pregnant, but Lady D is desperate that I should be. The brood mare. That's what they bought me for, after all, isn't it?" Her hand shook slightly as she raised the glass to her lips. "I'll never be rid of that woman if there's a child."

"Sid..." Chas began solicitously, but she interrupted him.

"Excuse me, please. I just don't think I can take any more at the moment. I truly was fond of him, you know!" She swept away grandly. Ria was sure the tears held off until she was safely in her room.

Recalling what Lady Dunston had said, Ria wondered whether Helena had been spreading rumours about Ria's relationship with her father. But, of course, they weren't unfounded, were they?

.        .        .

They were expecting Blake at Bovington for the first weekend in September, as he had managed to get a few days leave. He called at the last minute to ask if he could bring an old friend.

"Look who I found wandering about Shorncliffe," Blake said as Ria met him at the train station in Marlow.

"Justin!" She threw herself into his arms.

He thought his heart would break as he held her tightly, gratefully. She was more beautiful than ever, despite the scar. But that reminded him of what she had been through, and of Vivian, and he felt responsible for their having been on the *Lusitania*. Would Ria have gone to be with Chas before the baby arrived if he hadn't interfered?

"I miss Vivian so much," she said to him, trying to stop her tears.

"I know. So do I," Justin replied, brushing away a stray tear from her cheek. With forced cheerfulness he said, "I understand there's quite a Muskoka contingent at Lady Beatrice's house."

"Probably more of us than are in Muskoka at the moment," she replied. "Zoë and Lydia and Ellie have been back in Toronto for weeks, working their magic."

"You've worked some magic as well, from what Blake's been telling me." They talked about the Club on the trip to Bovington Abbey.

The others were all delighted to see Justin. He was at the Canadian army training camp, which was now at Shorncliffe, close to the hospital where Blake was posted.

Beatrice said, "A bright side to all this madness of war is that I've never had such an engaging group of young people keeping me company."

Alice declared yet another of Ria's friends as her own. After she went to bed, Justin managed to talk to Ria about the *Lusitania*. He was deeply moved by her account, and surprised at how well she was now handling it, as Blake had told him something of her earlier distress. Although he knew that Chas was looking after her – and doing it well, despite Augusta's misgivings – he still felt protective of her.

Henry had been accepted at Oxford, and would soon be leaving. But that weekend that they were all together was somehow magical. Ria took Justin flying the next morning, which impressed him immensely. Later they all canoed, rowed, or drove to Thameshill where Ria did her work and the others mingled and helped out. That evening was mellow with good food, wine, and companionship. Captain Armitage and the other officer who was billeted with Beatrice at the moment were pleased to be a part.

They talked a lot about Muskoka. "Did you hear that the *Newminko* burned in May?" Justin asked. The *Newminko* was the supply boat that came to the islands several times a week. "She caught fire at the wharf in Port Carling so they pushed her out into the river. She burned to the waterline, but they're rebuilding her."

"Edgar just wrote, and mentioned that Herb Ditchburn's factory burned down, but they're building a better, brick one. Fortunately, all our new boats had already been delivered," Ria said, as each family now had a runabout, and Edgar, his new speedboat. Toby was the only one using her launch, *Dragonfly*.

"I'd better order myself a new one for next summer, so that I can give Edgar a run for his money when we get back," Chas said, winking at Ria.

"Edgar says that John Eaton's just commissioned a 73 foot yacht from Herb, so you'll have to wait, especially as it's 'Sir' John now." John Craig Eaton had just been knighted for his philanthropic and war work.

"Ditchburns are out of our league," Blake said nonchalantly. "But you should see the boat my parents have bought. It's called a 'disappearing propeller' boat. 'Dippy' for short. It's a large skiff so you can either row it, or lower the propeller, which is in the centre of the hull. It only has a 2 horse power motor, but it can go 9 ½ miles per hour, and is the fastest thing we've ever owned. The propeller and shaft automatically raise into the housing if you hit a deadhead or a rock, and you can run it up on a beach. I didn't have much of a chance to try it out, but Ellie says it's great fun."

"I expect they'll be having races for them in the Regatta before long," Chas said.

"Zoë said it was rather different having the Regatta at the new Golf and Country Club this year," Ria said. "We've been so used to it being held at The Grand. It sounds as if they were lucky with the weather again, because Zoë said that the next day there was a fierce wind and rain storm which lasted a day and a half and brought down our water tower and smashed the two thousand gallon tank. It made a big mess, but fortunately no one was near it, and it even missed crushing the change house. Apparently Helena couldn't possibly stay at the cottage until a new tank was installed, so she and my father moved in with the Oakleys, leaving Albert's family to make do without running water. Hardly a hardship for any of us, is it?"

They were all silent for a moment, caught up in a lifetime of summer memories. Ria wondered if they would all be in Muskoka together again one day, and greatly feared the answer. She wanted to scream at the gods for putting them through all this.

Chas regarded her intently across the dining room table, as if divining her thoughts. He smiled ruefully.

Justin said, "I've brought some photos of Simon's wedding, which Lydia sent me."

"Zoë sent me some, too," Ria said. "It looks like it was a lovely wedding. Isn't it a shame that we all missed it. You must tell us about the bride."

"Grace is quite an accomplished horsewoman – that's how she and Simon met. Her father owns some famous stables, as well as a foundry that's now turning out armaments. Simon took her up to the cottage for a three week honeymoon. Lydia said he should have taken her before the wedding, to make sure she passed the test." When they looked at him questioningly, he explained, "To see if she likes cottage life. Can you imagine any of us marrying someone who wouldn't want to spend summers there?"

"I can't imagine anyone who *wouldn't* want to spend every possible moment there," Ria said. Henry looked at her askance. "Except for Henry, of course. He prefers to be around the ancient stones of England, rather than the rocks of Muskoka."

"He's had twenty-some years of luxurious living on the Precambrian shield," Chas said. "He may well enjoy it again after a few years without central heating in winter and endless days of rain most of the year."

"If camping out on Salisbury Plain in the wettest fall and winter in fifty years didn't dissuade me, then I don't think that lack of central heating will make me long for blistering hot summer days and hordes of voracious mosquitoes at night," Henry said. "You are all connected to the lake in a way I've never really understood."

"I think Henry's been a lost soul, as well as a silent intellectual, but he was always expected to join the business," Ria said.

Chas said, "I couldn't step into my father's shoes either. So the war has given some of us new opportunities. Jack, for instance, has already tripled his investments this year, so Pater is anxious to employ him as soon as the war is over."

"I may take a leaf out of Henry's book and study in Vienna after the war is over," Blake said.

"What? Consort with the enemy?" Ria teased.

"I don't consider Freud an enemy."

"What about joining Jung in Switzerland?" Ria asked. She laughed at his apparent astonishment. "Zoë's been telling me about her psychology studies." She wanted to make sure that he didn't forget about Zoë's love for him, and the realization that they were surely meant for each other.

When Ria dropped Justin and Blake at the train station late on Sunday, she hugged Justin fiercely and said, "I hope we see you before you're sent to France. But if not, please take good care of yourself." She recalled what Henry had said about officers getting killed in greater proportion than the men. She couldn't imagine losing him as well.

He was grateful for the concern in her eyes. "I shall. And I look forward to seeing you whenever I'm on leave. It makes army life more bearable to have friends nearby."

She hugged Blake, and was sad to see them board the train. Chas had come with her this time and put his arm reassuringly about her, as if he knew exactly what she was thinking.

When they returned to Bovington Abbey, there was a letter awaiting them from Felicity.

*Dear Chas and Ria,*

*I can't believe you've missed a whole summer at the cottage! It hasn't been at all the same without you! Hardly anyone's around now, and August isn't even over yet. We had such fun last year, with parties every day, and now I can't even find anyone to play tennis with. This stupid war is really a bore! And I don't even see why you have to be involved, since it's all so far away, and really nothing to do with us.*

*Mummy says she's glad you're wounded and hopes that you'll never be able to go back to the war. She's not as nervous now as she's been since you left. So why can't you and Ria come back home now? I really really miss you!*

*Mummy let me invite Jack's sisters up, but they could only come for a week, and they just left, so that was fun. Emily is starring in a musical play! Well, perhaps she's not the star just yet, but I bet she will be. She really does have a beautiful voice. Mummy thinks it's quite risqué to be on stage, but I think it must be thrilling! Having all those people admire you. She had a letter from that composer fellow who was at the Oakleys' last summer. Remember him? Didn't his friend, that singer, Sadie Something, drown on the Lusitania? Well he wants her to come to New York next year to sing! He said he's going to be in Toronto soon and will see how she's getting on.*

*Lizzie and Rafe seem to like each other sometimes, and other times they pick on each other. I know sarcasm when I hear it! Lizzie's become a pretty decent tennis player, so she and Rafe beat me and Emily. We're teaching her and Claire. Claire is catching on fast, but Emily says she's not much for sports. It was really sad not having our annual tennis tournament this year. Mummy said she didn't have the heart for it, with you away and the world gone mad. Even the Regatta wasn't as exciting or busy as usual. Esme and I won the canoe race though, so that was fun.*

*Zoë and Esme and Max came over a few times to play tennis, and Lydia, and some of the Carlyles, but everyone is involved with "war work" and they were going back and forth to the city and haven't been here at all since the Regatta. Even though Zoë's family has a new cottage. It's not big, but it's rather cute. I do think they're coming for the last week of August, thank goodness! Edgar's family's new cottage is almost finished. They had to make it smaller than planned, Daddy said, since it's hard to find builders and Phyllis didn't want to wait forever to move into her new place. Ria's father has scaled down the design for his cottage as well, which I don't think pleased Helena much. It won't be any larger than Ria's cottage now, but they're planning to start building it soon and have it finished by next summer. Of course, they'll have a new baby by then, too. Oh, won't it be fun when you're back and just the two of you are living at Wyndwood so there'll be lots of room for me to come and stay overnight, and Jack and his sisters can stay for the summer, and anyway, you'll be here for tennis every day!*

*Edgar has a fast new boat, so I expect you'll want a faster one when you get home. He zips about the lake all day and scares Phyllis when he talks about becoming a racer. His ankle still bothers him, which is rather sad since you'd think it would be mended by now and he hobbles about sometimes, obviously in pain and not pretending, like Rafe teases him. He seems miffed that he can't go to war – which is silly, I think – and Rafe says that as long as you're doing your bit for the family, he can just stay home and look after the horses. Edgar calls him a shirker and layabout. That's when Rafe calls him either a faker or a pompous cripple. They're not as witty as you, Chas.*

*Phoebe has gone rather strange, I think. She learned to knit and now knits all the time, day and night. Socks for the soldiers. She seems happy doing it, but I would think it a terrific bore after making a few, and she's made hundreds! But I'm trying to do my bit, too. I've learned how to roll bandages and help Mummy collect money for the Patriotic Fund and Ria's hospital. It's very odd to see all those strange soldiers and nurses living in Ria's house now! Some of them are pretty badly wounded, and Mummy doesn't want me to see them. I think some haven't even got their legs or their arms! How grotesque! Henry must look strange now, too. Please don't let anything bad happen to you, Chas! And Jack. I miss you all so much!*

*Please, please, please can you all come home by next summer, if not sooner? Summers are always my favourite time, but I know now that it's because we and all our friends were together most of the time. Of course I love the lake and being at the cottage, but it's just not the same without all of you here. I hope that summers will always be the same as last year, but I already know that they can't be. Vivian and Archie won't ever be with us again, though I still can't believe that. I expect them to show up at the next Stepping Stone Marathon or Regatta, and tell us all about their adventures while they were away. I don't understand why young people have to die for such frivolous reasons. Honour, patriotism. Are they worth dying for? I hate hate hate death! The idea of it. The permanence. The emptiness. The sadness. I want to scream and punch things and tell God he's cruel and hateful. I would die if you never came home again, Chas. I'm SO afraid sometimes! Some of my school chums have lost their brothers. Stupid expression, isn't it? "Lost", as if they'd just misplaced them through carelessness. What can I do so that I NEVER EVER lose you?*

*Do you think I could come and stay at Bovington Abbey and keep Ria company and be able to see you as much as possible?*

*School is such a bore, and I expect I could go to one there – like your friend Alice is doing – if I really MUST still attend. I'm almost sixteen, you know. Mummy nearly stopped breathing when I asked her. She was thinking about Ria and Vivian's ordeal, but I'm not too afraid of crossing the ocean, only a little. I expect I can be at least as brave as Alice. And soldiers are crossing safely all the time. If only I were older I could do something exciting, like become a VAD, and then Mummy wouldn't be able to stop me going over to England or it would seem unpatriotic.*

*The Oakleys will be hosting a party on the Labour Day weekend and going home right afterwards. Oswald has lots of bombs to make, I guess. Mummy didn't want to go all the way to Guelph to Simon's wedding, so only Rafe and Daddy attended. They wouldn't take me, which I thought jolly unfair, but I had to keep Mummy company. She says it's too hot to travel away from the lake in summer. But Simon and Grace are at their cottage now, so we do see them occasionally. Grace is very athletic and a good tennis player. She and Rafe talk horses non-stop, which becomes rather a bore. I think THEY should have gotten married, although I'm not sure that I really like Grace all that much. Mummy says she "gives herself airs", but just seems to me like a very strong person who knows her own mind and doesn't put up with nonsense. But she's nuts about horses and I think she's looking forward to getting home to Guelph, so I don't expect she'll want to spend all that much time at the cottage in the summers, which is really a shame and hard on Simon. So, I'm really glad she's not married to you or Rafe. I can't imagine a better sister than Ria! People are so amazed and impressed when I tell them that she can fly! She's promised to take me up when she gets home. But I just wish I could come to England!!!! I'm not sure who would be good for Rafe.*

*Please, please, please come back safe and sound and soon! Lots of hugs and kisses to you all. Jack too.*

*Your devoted, heartbroken, and loving sister, Fliss*

"Poor, Fliss," Ria said. "I can imagine how hard it is to be left out of things, particularly at an age when you're really quite powerless, especially as a girl."

Chas seemed quite moved by the letter, and said, "I wish we could bring her over, but I think Mumsy really needs her."

"But you see that you have at least three devoted women – including your mother, of course – who you need to come home to."

Beatrice said, "Make that four. I've become inordinately attached to you all, and feel that you are as precious as any children I might have had. I've started a wonderful new phase of my life, having you here with me. Having said that, I've become rather concerned about my villa in Antibes. I thought perhaps you could go down there and make sure everything is alright. And stay for a month or two if you can. The sea air would be good for you all."

"Do you think we could?" Ria asked in amazement. It was hard to believe that they could travel through a war-ravaged country to the south, where things might be little different than usual.

"I've secured warrants for your travel," Beatrice answered with a grin.

Ria threw her arms about her, "Oh, Cousin Bea, you're magnificent!"

Beatrice laughed heartily. "The boys should be well enough to travel in a week or so. Alice has to go to school, as does Henry. I shall be quite bereft, but happy to hear how things are on the Cote d'Azur. And don't you worry about taking time away from the Club," she said to Ria. "Mr. Grayson and I have things well in hand. Enjoy yourselves. Russell and I had many blissful times there. We particularly enjoyed the autumn, for the French don't descend upon the Riviera until winter, so we had it mostly to ourselves."

Their excitement at going away to a place that seemed to have little to do with war and destruction was tempered by their journey. Embarking at Folkestone, they became part of the flood of khaki-clad soldiers departing solemnly for the Front, or returning, broken, bandaged, dispirited. The dead, or course, had been left behind. The channel was busy with large and small craft, mine-sweepers, and destroyers. And there was the constant threat of German submarines. Aeroplanes flew overhead, some in transit, some on guard. The thunderous boom of bombs and artillery fire was already evident and grew louder the closer they came to France. Ria wore her life belt and Chas never left her side. She hadn't realized how tense she was until they landed at Boulogne and she was able to relax. The train took them via St. Omer, the RFC headquarters, to Paris.

The evening eastern horizon was lit with explosives, like massive fireworks. "You fly over that?" Ria asked Chas with trepidation and disbelief.

"Yes. It makes for a very bumpy ride."

She clutched his arm tightly.

They stayed in Paris only one night, Chas saying, "We'll do Paris properly once the war is over." The streets were filled with uniformed soldiers.

But as they travelled south, the tension seemed to leave the land, untouched by violence as yet.

They came to a wondrous landscape of sea and mountains and cobblestoned villages which summer had not yet abandoned. The air shimmered with a brilliance and colours that had captivated Impressionist artists like Monet.

Chas, who had previously enjoyed the Riviera, seemed pleased when Ria exclaimed, "This is glorious!"

"You'll be interested to know that the artist, Renoir, lives not far from here, although I've heard he's crippled with arthritis," Chas said.

"I saw some of his paintings in your collection," Ria said. "I do like his work."

"It'll be a challenge to paint this landscape," Jack said. "The quality of the light is so different."

"Especially from the Front," Chas said wryly. Jack had been capturing accents of beauty amid the devastation – like poppies in the disturbed soil of hastily dug graves. Chas thought Jack's watercolours extremely moving, and had insisted on purchasing some.

Cousin Bea's villa at Cap d'Antibes was an airy, white, two storey mansion with tall rooms that flowed into one another and spilled onto the flower-bedecked terrace and balconies. It was set amid twisted maritime pines, spikey palms, olive and lemon groves, exotic and fragrant vegetation. A path meandered down the cliff to a small private cove with a sliver of beach. There was a magnificent view of the mountains across the bay.

They swam, sailed, played tennis, bicycled to build up their strength, although Chas's deep leg wound troubled him. Ria drove the rented car, and they wandered the narrow, ancient streets of Antibes and medieval hillside villages that seemed carved out of the rock. They strolled the deserted beaches of Juan Les Pins and Cannes. For a lark, they gambled at the Casino in Monte Carlo, not losing any serious money. Sometimes they dined in the exclusive Grand Hotel du Cap, near Bea's villa, or took tea in its Eden-Roc pavilion on the cliff-edge of the sea.

Jack was overwhelmed by the opulence, even in this time of war and deprivation. He hadn't gambled, of course, but marvelled at those who could repeatedly lose the yearly wage of a working man on the turn of a card without a raised eyebrow or flicker of regret. He became more determined than ever to accumulate that kind of wealth, but not to squander it.

Although he was glad he had come along, he found it difficult to be constantly around the devoted lovers. He played the good friend to Chas and devoted cousin to Ria to perfection, but also with little artifice, for he truly enjoyed their company, wishing only that he could have Ria warm his bed at night. With her seductive combination of vulnerability and fortitude, she was immensely desirable.

At the end of September, they had a cable from Lady Meredith, informing them that the Kiplings' eldest son had died in the Battle of Loos. They sent a telegram of condolence. Ria wondered if they would stay on the Board of the Maple Leaf Clubs.

The following day a cable arrived from Sidonie. *Quentin wounded at Loos. Shattered leg so only good for desk job now. Thank God! No child, which is reassuring, yet oddly devastating. Dragon departs soon. Love to all. Sid.*

Although Chas was still in considerable pain, Jack had healed well, so he couldn't stay longer than a month. He was due back in London for his medical board six weeks earlier than Chas.

In any case, Jack was looking forward to at least a week in London, since he felt a powerful need for a woman. Although there were brothels in France exclusively for officers, Jack never had to buy women, unlike most men. "Nice" girls were particularly drawn to dashing young aviators like him.

Wartime London had the frenetic energy of a never-ending party, a kind of desperation to have fun, despite and because of the heavy casualties that continually streamed into the city from the Front. Young women, excited by the war and with new-found freedom, were only too happy to dine and dance with gallant soldiers on leave or convalescing.

But Jack wasn't interested in giggling schoolgirls with romantic notions of landing an officer. There were plenty of young war widows whose reaction to bereavement was to live for pleasure, since life had become so unpredictable. An experienced woman, especially one of means and not necessarily looking for a husband, was much more to his liking. Although it might be too soon for her, he intended to visit the luscious Sidonie.

He also planned to take advantage of her connection to Sir Max Aitken, the shrewd business genius who was only in his mid-thirties, but who had already accumulated a vast fortune. Jack hoped to learn from and emulate him. And if things didn't work out with J.D., perhaps he would have another mentor.

Ria felt somewhat guilty to be relieved at Jack's departure, but she cherished her private moments with Chas. Now they were able to skinny-dip in the sea and have intimate evenings on the terrace or the beach. While she painted, Chas would lie on a blanket beside her and read poetry to her. Pauline Johnson and Rupert Brooke's poems were among their favourites.

"This landscape is wondrously beautiful. But I do miss Muskoka," she said one day as they sat on the edge of the cliff.

Chas held out his hand to her, and she went to cuddle up beside him on the blanket. "What do you miss most?" he asked her.

"Partly the granite. That sparkling pink and black rock that speaks to me of venerable age and permanence. The untamed forests. The islands. They give the lake an intimacy and warmth that the sea can never have. It's so immense. I think of the warships, troop ships, hospital ships, destroyers, submarines – all those vessels of war that are plying the Mediterranean not far from here – and it seems that even the sea is complicit in this war. I realize they're fairly negligible here, but the tides seem to be the sea grasping, reaching to pull us into its deadly depths." Or, as in Ireland, where it mockingly gave back a few of the *Lusitania* dead. "Our lakes fluctuate between serenity and playful exuberance, but they seem innocent, safe, benign. They speak to my soul. The sea has a cruel, deceptive beauty." The water might be warmer here, but it eventually melded with the icy Irish sea.

"You miss the Shimmering Sands," Chas stated, as if he could read her thoughts.

A vision of the crescent of pale sand abutting the granite slab that dipped into the clear and glassy lake made her sharply nostalgic. "It's one of my favourite places. Especially as I now have very fond memories of early mornings with my beloved." She smiled at him.

He drew her down beside him and kissed her. "Remember what I once promised you between tennis and tea?"

"But we haven't played tennis," she said with a chuckle, recalling exactly what he meant.

"Let's pretend we just finished a set."

"And I won."

"I didn't say this was a fantasy," he quipped as he began kissing her.

He had rolled on top of her when a voice behind them said, with a suggestive laugh, "How delicious. May I join you?"

Ria groaned inwardly. It was Dixie Seaton, the bold, bored, and boozy wife of the up-and-coming American writer,

Montgomery "Monty" Seaton. They were renting a nearby villa, where Monty was working feverishly on his second novel, taking time out from his well-paid magazine assignments – reporting the war from Paris and London. His first book had been critically acclaimed, but Ria had to admit that she hadn't read it yet.

She had made the mistake of inviting their very few neighbours to join them for tennis one afternoon before Jack left. She'd actually had little choice, for Dixie was a force to be reckoned with. Having descended upon the neighbourhood, Dixie Seaton had corralled every English-speaking person into her circle of captive friends. There were some wounded British officers from a villa that had been turned into a private convalescent hospital, and the expatriate, middle-aged Irish painter, Liam Sullivan, with French nymphet, Camille, who was obviously more than his model.

Dixie had informed them – several times – that as the daughter of a United States Senator, she had married beneath her, despite the fact that Montgomery Seaton was a Harvard graduate and an exciting new voice in the literary world.

Dixie, the neglected wife, flirted outrageously with all the men, but had Chas particularly in her sights. She had taken to dropping in uninvited at any time of day. She stood over them now, a cocktail glass in one hand, a cigarette in a long holder, in the other. She had a little-girl prettiness that attracted some men, but Ria thought her blowsy and bloated. When she had first seen Ria's cropped hair she had had hers cut as well, so it now fell like a dark curtain about her pudgy face.

"We weren't expecting you, Dixie," Ria said pointedly.

But Dixie chose to ignore the hint. "Isn't that one of the delicious things about life? The unexpected. Shall we all go for a swim? I didn't bring a suit, but Liam said I should show off my delectable body. Have you seen his nude of me?" Ria had, and thought it crude and boxy, which she thought encapsulated Dixie nicely. "By the way, I told him to come by as well, although I expect he'll bring that tiresome child with him. Ria, be a darling and fetch me another martini."

"We were just about to have tea," Ria said with annoyance. Dixie's attempt to get rid of her so she could get her claws into Chas was just too maddening.

"Is that what you Canadians call it? It looked like steamy sex to me."

Chas hid a grin as he winked at Ria and said, "Let's go up to the terrace."

"I've invited all those lovely soldiers as well. I feel like a party!" Dixie danced her way up the path, falling – deliberately, Ria was sure – against Chas, giggling as he put his arm about her to catch and steady her. She rubbed her head against his shoulder and said, "I do like an athletic man. What lovely muscles you have, Chas."

Ria said, "You might want to lay off the martinis for a while, Dixie, since you seem to be unsteady on your pins already."

Dixie gave her a mock pout, "Don't be a bore, darling. Your path is uneven. And darling Chas is only too happy to lend me assistance, aren't you darling Chas?" She drew a varnished fingernail along his chin and blew him a kiss as she turned her head provocatively to the side, as if brushing him off and inviting him to follow her at the same time.

Ria itched to slap those bee-stung lips.

Liam Sullivan had already arrived with a vacant Camille in tow. She had an elfin beauty that made her seem years younger than she was. Ria, in fact, was younger by half a dozen years. Liam had adopted the French double-cheek kiss whenever he greeted them, much to Ria's disgust, for he invariably squeezed her bottom as well. "Camille is on a sleigh-ride, so just ignore her," he told them, referring to her habit of taking cocaine. "Double whiskey with the tiniest splash of soda for me, thanks. Well, fair and wondrous Ria, have you changed your mind about posing for me? You could be my masterpiece. You have a scarred beauty that would make a telling statement about the war." At their first meeting he had asked her, quite blatantly and unabashedly, what she had done to disfigure an otherwise flawless countenance.

"I have an even bigger and uglier scar down my leg," she retorted sarcastically.

"Even better then. The mutilation of soft, white, pulchritudinous perfection." He spoke the words as if he were tasting and savouring her.

"Be careful how you speak about my wife," Chas said lightly as he prepared drinks from the tray that one of the servants had already brought out, but Ria could tell that he was annoyed.

"Ah, but she's the perfect symbol of the sacrifice of young, innocent beauty for questionable honour and the moral high ground. It's the bloody British sticking their noses in again where they don't belong that catapulted you Canadians into this senseless slaughter. I'm glad to see the Americans have had enough sense to stay out of it."

"I'm surprised they weren't spurred into action by the *Lusitania*," Chas said.

"Can you see Monty using anything sharper than his pen to make a point?" Dixie asked with a note of contempt.

"We're British subjects, as are you," Chas said to Liam. "So you might consider joining the army and doing your bit to help win this war."

"Very droll. I would as soon piss on the English as help them fight. But I'm happy to watch them be blown up. Do you really think you're fighting for a just and noble cause?"

"We're fighting to stop oppression..."

"That's rich!" Liam interrupted Chas. "The British, masters of conquest and oppression, a bunch of pole-up-the-arse, piratical islanders who have tried to take over the world, and damn near succeeded! Empire builders who can't stand competition, and use lame excuses of moral superiority and high-mindedness to justify the glorified sacrifice of a generation of their own young men and the sanctified murder of others. Do you really think they went into this war to 'protect' or 'liberate' the poor, bloody Belgians? Hell, no! They went into this to prevent Germany from gaining more seaports and becoming a power that might challenge their world-dominating supremacy."

As the mood was getting ugly, Ria said, "You dishonour Chas and our friends who are risking their lives, and those who have already died. If you were a pacifist, I would forgive you for voicing opinions based upon conscience. But you'll keep your hatred of the British to yourself, or I'll be forced to ask you not to come here again."

Chas regarded her proudly. Dixie guffawed and said to Liam, "Well, I guess she's put you in your place, darling. Although I don't blame you for not wanting to risk your neck, I do find men in uniform, especially the officers, incredibly sexy."

With a twinkle in his eye, Liam said, "You are a magnificent woman, Ria! I will honour your request, and humbly beg pardon for having upset you. But if you knew the long and bloody history of the Irish oppression under British rule, your warm and generous heart would bleed and you'd forgive this poor, wretched and wounded soul in an instant. So, I'll say no more on this vile subject at the moment because of my deep regard and admiration for you."

"You can really lay on the Irish blarney with a trowel, can't you, Liam?" Dixie said.

"Do you doubt my sincerity, Madam?" he asked in mock indignation.

"Absolutely."

Half a dozen British officers shuffled in, one saying tentatively, "We had word that tea was in the offing."

"Or drinks, as you please," Chas said. They seemed to visibly relax, as if they had been unsure of their invitation.

The tension was alleviated as drinks were passed around.

Monty Seaton wandered in, seeming preoccupied. "Double Scotch, please," he muttered. "Just finished another chapter. Brilliant stuff, if I do say so myself. I'm going to call it *The Doomed*." He looked up as if seeing a group of strangers. He seemed to shake himself as he said, "Sorry. Can't get the characters out of my head."

"As long as we're not part of your fantasy," Liam said.

Still lost in thought, Monty roused himself again and said, "You have nothing to fear, Liam." Which didn't seem to please Liam at all.

"Monty maintains that, but beware what you say," Dixie told them as she downed another martini. "I'm not sure Monty has an original idea in his head. He's like a sponge that absorbs everything he sees and hears. Then he shuffles it about and spews it all back onto paper, and makes you think he's a profound writer." She moved provocatively toward Chas as she threw her husband a mocking, challenging look.

"Actually, I need to talk to you about the RFC, Chas" Monty said, completely ignoring his wife. "I've been inspired by new characters and they've taken the story into a brilliant new direction."

"Yes, of course," Chas said.

"Surely not now!" Dixie protested.

"We'll go into the sitting room, if you'll excuse us for a few minutes," Chas said to the others, and then sought approval from Ria.

"By all means," she replied.

But Dixie said peevishly, "In that case, I'm going for a swim. Anyone care to join me?" She started brazenly unbuttoning her shirtwaist. Ria went up to her and said, "Must you leave already?" as she ushered her off the terrace. Then she whispered to Dixie, "If you insist upon stripping, then I suggest you go home and do it there. I'm not about to have my guests embarrassed by your antics."

"What a little prude you are, Ria. I expect you're no fun at all in bed. Poor Chas."

Ria was hard put to keep her temper. "Your husband is obviously inured to your games. My husband has no interest in you, so you might as well stop trying to seduce him. If you're seeking attention, I suggest you try to charm people with some intelligence, rather than cheap sexuality."

Instead of taking offence, Dixie threw back her head and laughed. "You are a naïve child, Ria," she said, patting her on the cheek. "Men aren't interested in smart women. They are slaves to flesh, to sex. They adore sensual women like me. Believe me, darling. I've had my share of lovers."

Camille, roused from her stupor, joined them and said, "I'll swim with you."

Liam said, "I'm in. What about you, fair Ria?" He squeezed her waist.

As she pulled away from him, she said, "Don't count me into any of your activities. Excuse me while I see to my guests."

They chuckled as Ria returned to the patio. Instead of heading back to her place, Dixie went down to the cove, with Camille and Liam in tow.

Ria tried to calm down as she returned to the officers, who seemed rather at a loss.

"I do apologize, gentlemen." She soon had them at ease, drawing them out, telling them just enough about herself and her family, when it seemed appropriate, to give them common ground. By the time Chas and Monty rejoined them, she had discovered that Lieutenant Ponsonby was a university friend of the younger brother of Chas's friend, Hugh Paynter, who had lent them the family shooting box at Windermere for their honeymoon.

Looking at Ria with awe and admiration, Monty said, "Chas tells me you're a crackerjack pilot."

"You can fly aeroplanes?" Lieutenant Ponsonby squeaked.

She laughed at the men's astonishment. "And tinker with the engines," she told them

"No, darling," Chas said with a grin. "*I* tinker. *You* can actually fix them."

"I'll be dashed!" one of the other officers said. "Remarkable!"

"But I don't suppose they'll let me join the RFC," she quipped.

"It seems to me you've already had your share of war," Monty said. "The *Lusitania*'s sinking must have been a horrendous experience."

Although she was reluctant to talk about it to all these men, Monty cleverly drew her out. Seeing her increasing distress, Chas sat next to her and took her tense hand in his, stroking it lovingly, reassuringly. She didn't talk about the baby, which would have added another dimension of tragedy.

But they were shocked by her abbreviated account. "Of course I read about it in the newspapers," one of the officers said solemnly. "But it's even more appalling to hear it from someone who experienced it first hand. It can't be easy to talk about, Mrs. Thornton. You're very brave."

"You all have stories that aren't easy to share and which, I expect, you all want to forget. But none of us ever will," Ria said. "We've all been permanently scarred by the war." She squeezed Chas's hand tightly.

Touching and jostling one another, Dixie, Liam, and Camille staggered up to the terrace, their half-buttoned clothes clinging to their dripping wet bodies.

With a look of disgust, Monty said, "Come along, Dixie. I think we've disturbed our neighbours enough for one day."

Surprisingly, she followed him meekly, saying only, "Good bye, darlings!" and waving at them absently as she staggered away, reaching for her husband's hand. He took it firmly in his and she chuckled.

Liam poured himself another large whiskey. The others finished their drinks and said they must be off.

"I expect you'll want to see me off as well," Liam said and he poured the remainder of his drink down his throat. "Come, my little dope fiend. Time to go home with Papa."

Camille giggled and draped herself about his outstretched hand.

When they were once more alone, Chas said to Ria, "You can probably use this," as he poured them each a glass of champagne. When he turned to hand it to her, he saw that she was weeping. Putting down the glasses, he took her tenderly into his arms. "I know it must still be hard for you to talk about it," he said.

"It's not even that," she sobbed. "But I never mention Reggie. It's as if I'm denying he was ever real, as if I'm ashamed of him." She shook with sorrow.

Chas stroked her hair. "We haven't forgotten him, Ria. How could we? And our close friends know. No one else needs to share him with us. But he's not a secret, so if you ever want to mention him, just do."

"I want so much to have your children, Chas." She wouldn't admit, even to herself, that she was desperate to get pregnant, so afraid not to have anything of Chas to cherish and love should something happen to him. "Why haven't I become pregnant again? It was so easy the first time."

Chas hesitated. "You've been through a terrible ordeal, my darling. Give it time. We'll certainly take every opportunity to make it happen," he added with a smile.

"If we can keep brash neighbours from descending upon us at inopportune times."

"We'll simply instruct the servants to keep the gate locked, unless we're out."

"Dixie might swim over."

"She's not that close, thank God."

"I should be jealous by her brazen attempts to seduce you, but if you really liked Dixie, I would be more concerned about your judgement and taste in women."

"I find her extremely irritating and foolish. And I should be the one who's jealous, since all the men are in love with you. I'm most concerned about the subtle, smouldering looks that that young Lieutenant keeps sending your way when he thinks no one's looking."

"Good Lord! You don't mean young Ponsonby? He's just a boy!"

"He's older than you, inches taller than me, and more than half-way through a brilliant career at Cambridge. And he's a respectable tennis player."

"With the personality of a wet towel."

"Only because he's smitten into blushing speechlessness in your presence. He's a bright, thoughtful, and surprisingly eloquent person – at least around the rest of us. I expect he'll be Prime Minster some day."

Ria was amused at Chas's easy conviction, but then wondered how many of the men she had met would survive to make their mark on the world.

To avoid the predatory Dixie, Ria and Chas set off early in the mornings for excursions – day-long jaunts with picnic hampers strapped to their bicycles, or car journeys to ancient villages, where they dined in sidewalk cafes overlooking the mountains or the sea.

Because they did like the convalescent officers and Monty Seaton, if not his wife, they hosted a few dinner parties at Bea's villa, and went out as a group to dine at the Hotel du Cap. Dixie seemed somewhat mollified, for she had taken offence at the locked gate.

Ria watched the sunrise from the balcony off their bedroom one morning toward the end of their stay. She hadn't realized that Chas was awake until he wrapped his arms about her from behind and nuzzled her hair. "You seem lost in thought."

"Perhaps only lost," she replied, leaning her head against him. "I've realized that we can never recapture our innocence and youth. After all the atrocities we've seen and heard about, how can we expect life ever to be the same? *We're* not the same. I think it's terribly unfair that we've become pawns and victims in this war. I just want to go home with you, Chas. I'm so terribly afraid that that will never happen."

He pulled her tighter and kissed her cheek, saying, "When the war is over, we'll build a villa next to Cousin Bea's, and spend some of the winter here."

"But not Christmas. I really do like snowy Christmases at Wyndholme."

"So be it. We'll spend the summers in Muskoka, of course. And in between times, I want to design and build aeroplanes."

He said it with such nonchalance that Ria laughed.

"You mock my ambitions?" he inquired, raising an eyebrow.

"No, just your confidence that you can design aeroplanes. Don't you need to be an engineer or physicist or something that takes years to learn?"

"I have an instinctive feeling for aerodynamics. Anyway, I'll hire the engineers to actually do the technical details after I give them the concepts. And I'll open an aeroplane factory in Toronto."

"And I'll run an aerodrome and flying school. North of Thornridge."

"And we'll fly up to Muskoka."

"But not once we have children, because there won't be room for them."

"I intend to design aircraft that can carry more than two people."

"Then we'll need one that carries at least eight. Remember that I want to have half a dozen children."

He pulled her around into his arms and smiled lovingly at her. "Shall we get started on that then?"

.      .      .

Sidonie seemed leaner. And hungrier, Jack thought.

"Jack! How delightful!"

"Chas and Ria send their regards," he improvised. "I wondered if you'd care to join me for dinner tonight?"

"Thank you for the offer, but I seem to be booked for weeks in advance." She was dressed in a loose caftan – with not much underneath, he guessed, judging by the flow of the material around her ample breasts. She offered him a cigarette and he lit one for them both as she poured champagne.

"I'm beginning to despise this life," she said, lounging against the sofa. "It's as if we're all trying to stave off death by frantically enjoying ourselves. If you count drinking to excess, taking dope, sleeping with people you wouldn't care to share your breakfast with as having fun." She blew out a long stream of blue smoke.

Then she threw back her head and laughed delightedly. "That's precisely what you were counting on, wasn't it? Seducing the poor widow."

Jack was taken aback.

"Don't deny it!" Sidonie said. "Besides, I like the idea. You Canadians seem to crackle with sexual energy. And I'm never averse to being seduced by an intriguing man."

·   ·   ·

In late October, on the stagnant Ypres Salient, Lieutenant Philip "Philpot" Pottinger, a recent guest at Bovington Abbey and friend of Blake Carlyle, was disembowelled by shrapnel from a shell blast near Ploegsteert. He died two excruciating days later in hospital.

# Chapter 25

*Dear Zoë,*

*My introduction to Buckingham Palace was not quite what we had envisioned last year. Instead of their Majesties receiving blushing debutantes, the King was pinning medals onto wounded young men for 'acts of conspicuous bravery' or 'gallantry'. I was so proud of Chas! And yet so frightened, for the DSO doesn't end his war. They expect him to go back and perform many more 'acts of bravery'.*

*He's still in pain, although he tries hard to conceal it. I'm sure he played it down during his medical board, but they have given him convalescent leave until the new year nonetheless. Thank heavens! I'm grateful for every day that he's safely by my side.*

*I worry that he might also be somewhat shell-shocked, since he suffers from nightmares as well now, and often wakes in a cold sweat. But he won't share them with me. Sometimes I find him lost in thought, looking almost mournful, but he won't open up. I expect he's trying to protect me from gruesome things, but I feel as if he's shutting me out of his life, as if he's creating a wall around himself beyond which no one may go. I do so want to help him, but you know how he is. He responds with a light-hearted quip, a playful smile, and a kiss, and that is the end of the discussion.*

*I know how foolish it is to wish and hope that this war might end soon, as it so obviously promises to drag on for years to come. How is it possible that we have come to this? Does anything good or noble warrant the mutilation and slaughter of so many fine young men? Doesn't that, in itself, negate the goodness? At the Club I see the scared boys who are hiding behind a cocky facade. Like Chas, they've already experienced unimaginable horrors, and are expected to go back to face more terrible ordeals and the very great possibility of an agonizing, messy death.*

*Instead of raising money to help fuel this war, shouldn't we be trying to end it? I know I'm naïve. And probably unpatriotic. And bitter, and terrified, and angry. I no longer believe in God or a 'just war'.*

*Blake managed a weekend leave and hopes to spend Christmas with us. He says that he's learned more in the last few months than he could possibly have imagined. Apparently, he's quite a skilled surgeon, which seemed to surprise him as much as us. He assures us that he hasn't given up on psychiatry, but that it isn't where his skills are generally required at the moment. I quipped that Freud with a scalpel was a bizarre notion. He has actually been involved in neurosurgery, as he calls it. Surely a bold and fascinating occupation, to remove bullets from brains!*

*I did ask him to talk to Chas, so I hoped that helped. Neither of them was forthcoming.*

*I'm amused to hear that you, of all people, lied to get the St. John Ambulance VAD training. Did they really believe that you are twenty-one? Do you know that you have to be twenty-three to get posted overseas from Britain? So don't get any ideas about going to France. In any case, your dear Mama would be horrified after what happened to Nurse Edith Cavell. I think the Germans made a tremendous error in judgement when they executed her for helping Allied soldiers escape from Belgium, as they have horrified the world by murdering a brave woman, and that has fuelled the propaganda machine here, as elsewhere, I imagine. One would have thought that the Germans would have learned something from the Lusitania.*

*And don't give up on your studies just yet. I know how much university has meant to you, even though you now feel it's all different because the world has changed, and so many have gone off to do war work and that you should as well. At least Ellie is still there, and Max and Emma, and isn't Daphne starting next year?*

*I'm sorry to hear that Freddie is thinking of joining up. I don't want any more of my friends going to the front lines. Can't he find something useful there? Surely they need bright young men to run things at home. How about the government? Perhaps that would put an end to this madness!*

*Jack is in a reserve squadron, on Home Defence, and manages to get weekend leaves quite often, and sometimes we join him in London for a bit of night-life. He says that, except for the tricky night-flying, it's an easy assignment compared with France. He wasn't back from Antibes for the devastating Zeppelin bombings of London and area in mid-October. Meredith and Theadora said it was terrifying, and more than seventy people were killed, with many more injured. One of Chas and Jack's fellow officers recently said to them, wouldn't it be ironic to be killed in an air raid in London while on leave. Can you believe that he actually was?! He was hit by shrapnel in his hotel room, while standing at the window watching the bombing. How bizarre!*

*Theadora covered that in the latest edition of "Home Fires", which I will enclose. I think that she has found her niche. As she* and Meredith are fast friends, I have a feeling that Thea will stay in England. Did I tell you that she had met Montgomery Seaton in the States a few years ago? She agrees with me that Dixie is something of a pill. I'll be interested to read Monty's new book when it appears, for I have a terrible suspicion that Chas and I might find ourselves among the pages. I hope he's kind to us. And yes, I will read his first one, since you've recommended it so highly.

I'm glad to hear that Phoebe is more settled, although she works obsessively, as you say, on her knitting. Edgar thinks she's finally growing up. But I also believe that Blake is probably right, so I do worry about her. Is that horrible Maryanne still about?

Isn't it exciting that Emily is doing so well in the theatre? Imagine her luck, being an understudy and suddenly finding herself a star when she had to take over the lead role. But I do think she's rather young for New York, despite the fact that Hugo Garrick feels she's ready for Broadway. Jack is really concerned about her, for she's only sixteen, and quite impressionable. I truly doubt that Hugo's interest is purely as a patron. She is, after all, a beautiful – and innocent – young woman. Jack feels really helpless and frustrated, being so far away, and has asked Lizzie to intervene, although she's only eighteen. Perhaps you or your Mama could persuade Emily that she has lots of time to establish a career, and shouldn't be in too great a hurry to leave home for an uncertain future. Does that seem uncharacteristic of me? I know if I were her, I would jump at the chance! Didn't Hugo mention the Ziegfeld Follies? But I'm trying to be mature and circumspect, as befits the older, wiser cousin.

Cousin Bea and I are already preparing for Christmas. Alice will be able to stay with us for a week, and I'm hoping all the boys can come. And oh, how I wish you could be here!!! I miss you all so very very much!

With love and hugs and kisses from all of us to all of you, and especially from me,

Ria.

P.S. – Do you think Josephine and Calypso have forgotten me? I wish I could hug them as well!

.     .     .

It even snowed on Christmas Eve, so Bovington Abbey looked magical amid the fluffy flakes, it's ancient stones, which had witnessed other wars and catastrophes, giving a sense that civilization endures despite these dark days.

Jack had managed a week's leave, Blake had ten days, Justin had worked hard to get two weeks, and Henry would also spend a fortnight with them. So it was a merry group that walked the two miles to the midnight service at All Saints Church in Marlow in the snow-bright, gentle night. On the homeward journey, Blake scooped up some snow and tossed it at Chas, and before long they were all laughing as they pelted each other with tiny snowballs.

"Foul!" Henry called. "I only have one arm so it's not fair to have two of you attacking me at once."

"I'll save you, Henry! "Ria cried, throwing herself into Chas's arms and stuffing snow down his collar.

"You vixen!" he said, retaliating with a kiss as he crammed snow under her velvet hat.

Their wild exuberance was a reaction to the continuous stress that the war had wrought, so when they arrived at Bovington Abbey they seemed intoxicated with glee.

Beatrice who had, along with her elderly holiday guests, gone to church by car, greeted them at the door. "Good Lord, but you're all dripping wet!"

"And giddy as schoolchildren" Ria replied. "But oh, what fun!" They'd had to grow up too quickly, so it was a relief to be young and carefree again.

Bea settled them in front of the fire with hot toddies and warm towels, the other guests having already gone to bed. Ria thought how different this was to her lonely sojourn in Wyndholme's tower just a year ago.

"We should get to bed or Santa won't be able to fill our stockings," Chas said, making no move to do so.

"I want to catch him in the act," Blake quipped, his feet up on the fender of the fireplace, drying his trouser legs. "All my father's physics could never explain how the old fellow gets down the chimney, especially with a fire going. And I never believed that Einstein's Theory of Relativity explained how he managed it all in one night."

They laughed.

And no one wanted to go to bed. To sit in the crackling glow of the fire, just being together, was somehow too precious to interrupt with sleep. Ria was curled up on the sofa, in Chas's arms, her legs tucked up beneath her.

Justin tried not to dwell on how he envied Chas, how much he ached to hold Ria in his arms and see that devoted look and loving smile light her face just for him.

They talked of good times, past times, and although Jack had not shared those with them, he could relate to the power of those memories and try to make them his own. He longed for Ellie, no longer surprised at his need of her, and any mention of her whetted his appetite.

When they finally crawled into bed in the wee hours, Chas handed Ria a small box and said, "How lucky I am that I can give you this myself this time."

It was a gold and diamond pendant made in the shape of the Royal Flying Corps insignia. "Consider yourself an honorary member of the RFC, my darling aviatrix."

Ria clung to him saying, "It's exquisite! Thank you, Chas. This is the most wonderful Christmas of my life. I'm probably being premature, but I hope and pray that I can give you the most splendid gift I possibly could. I think I might be with child."

He looked at her in astonishment. "That would be marvellous, my darling. But my most cherished gift is to have you beside me. Anything beyond that is a bonus."

It was nearly dawn when they finally went to sleep. For once Ria had no nightmares.

There was much laughter and jollity as they opened their stockings in the morning, but they had all agreed to exchange presents in the evening, so after a late breakfast the young people went to Thameshill Park to help with the celebrations there. Ria had organized Christmas boxes for each of the men and the staff, much to their surprise. They helped to serve the turkey dinner at two o'clock, Jack showing the others how to do it professionally. He actually enjoyed it, now that it was merely a charitable act.

When Ria put a steaming plate in front of one young man he suddenly grabbed her wrist and said, "Well, I'll be buggered! If it isn't the high and mighty Victoria Wyndham serving *me* at table. If that isn't a turn-up for the books! Hey lads, this here was my mistress once," he said suggestively. "Isn't she a corker? I used to go into her bedroom and touch her silk undies. Ever smelled a lady's silk undies, lads? They had good whiskey there, too."

Ria gazed at him in astonishment and distaste as she tried to shake off his fierce grip. But he held onto her painfully tightly while he grinned at her lasciviously. "Don't even recognize me, do you?" he challenged her nastily.

"Tom!"

"Damn right! The one your family chucked out because the fuckin' maid was asking for a poke and I was just trying to oblige her."

Jack was nearby and overheard the bloody little sod. He reached Ria's side in two strides and dug his fingers into Tom's shoulder until he released his grip on her.

"Bloody hell!" Tom swore. "Get your fuckin' hands off me!"

"You're in the presence of a lady, and will remember your manners, private," Jack commanded.

"The hell, I will! She's not my boss now."

"But the army is."

"Pulling rank, are you, *Captain* bloody Jack Wyndham? Who died and made you king?"

Jack was hard put to control his temper.

Having noticed the scene, Chas joined them and put his arm protectively around Ria. "Do we have a problem here, Captain Wyndham? Someone not in the Christmas spirit? Or has he had too much Christmas spirit?" Tom did seem drunk.

"Did all you bleedin', useless nobs pay for your commissions?"

"Did you hear an obnoxious noise just now?" Chas asked Jack as if Tom weren't there. "We don't allow troublemakers here. Only men who appreciate what the Club has to offer. It would be a shame to spoil the celebrations by having to chuck someone out into the cold, with no turkey dinner. But I'm prepared to do it."

"Fuck you!" Tom said.

"No boyo, you're the one who's going to be fucked if we call the MPs," Chas said calmly, referring to the Military Police, and shocking Ria, who had never heard him swear like that. "What do you think we should charge him with, Captain Wyndham? Assaulting a lady, drunk and disorderly, several counts of insubordination for a start. But I'd rather see him go back to the Front than spend a comfortable time in jail."

The others at the table and those within earshot had become increasingly uncomfortable during this confrontation. They obviously respected the officers, especially as Chas and Jack both had wound stripes on their sleeves, and Chas wore his medal. One of the boys kicked Tom under the table and hissed, "Just shut up, Tom."

"You owe my wife an apology, private. And as she runs this place and can kick you out on your ass if you don't abide by the rules, I suggest it had better be a damn good one. Your best drawing room manners, soldier."

Tom seemed rigid with anger, but said, "Yes, sir! I do humbly beg your pardon, Mrs. Thornton. I was out of line."

"And now one for the officers, whose Christmas spirit will only overlook so much insolence."

"Yes, sir! My sincerest apologies, Captain Wyndham, Captain Thornton. Thank you, sirs!"

Although there was a note of mockery in Tom's contrition, Chas ignored it and said to the men at the table, "Merry Christmas, lads. Do enjoy your feast."

"Hell's bells," Ria said to Chas and Jack as they went off to fetch more plates. "It revolts me to think that we had that nasty creature living under our roof. To think that he touched my private things!"

"Did he? He was lucky I didn't hear that part."

Ria decided not to elaborate. "Chas, I've never heard you swear like that."

"Some men don't respect you if you don't get down to their level. I'm not above swearing when the occasion demands it. Like you, my darling," he said with a grin.

After the meal, Chas played the piano while he and Ria sang, encouraging everyone else to join in. After a few Christmas carols, they got a more jubilant response when Chas switched to popular tunes. *Tipperary* had everyone participating.

Ria spent a few quiet minutes with Grayson, in his room. They talked first about Tom. She didn't tell Grayson all that he had said, for Grayson would think it a dereliction of his duty to realize that Tom had fingered her underwear.

"I always had to keep a tight rein on him, but I did think he had potential," Grayson admitted. "Unfortunately, he had an inflated opinion of his abilities and charms, and unreasonable ambitions, but no integrity. Although he's been swanning around ever since he arrived, he hasn't tried anything with me. He knows I'm in control here, and probably didn't know that you were. I'm sorry you had to be subjected to his rudeness."

"Oh, don't worry about me! Aunt Phyllis would have fainted, but I'm made of sterner stuff!" Then more seriously, she said, "I expect this is a particularly difficult time for you, Grayson. I know it is for Justin. I do wish you'd take some time off, and come to Bovington or relax at Cousin's Bea's London house."

"I'd prefer to stay here, Mrs. Thornton. I have no need of a holiday. I'm most pleased when I can keep busy."

"Yes, of course. Then I hope that you can enjoy these when you have some time to yourself." Chas had chosen some fine Cuban cigars and old port, and Ria had painted a picture of Wyndholme from a photograph. Grayson was delighted.

"And may I do this without seeming too presumptuous?" Ria gave him a quick hug. "Thank you, Grayson, for your unfailing support."

For a moment he looked as though he might hug her back, but he knew his place all too well and said warmly, "It's my very great pleasure, Mrs. Thornton."

When they arrived back at Bovington in the late afternoon, they had a surprise awaiting them. Rafe was standing by the fire, whiskey glass in hand. Chas was the only one who wasn't astounded.

After much back slapping and hand shaking, and a welcoming embrace from his new sister-in-law, he told them that he had some investments to look into for his father and thought he might as well come and spend Christmas with them. "I would have been here a few days ago, but we ran into bad weather."

"I wish you could have brought Fliss with you," Ria said.

"She pestered long and hard, but Mumsy wouldn't hear of it. She was terrified enough at my coming, especially after what happened to you." He eyed her assessingly, but said nothing about her scar.

Chas said to her, "Come with me for a minute," as he helped her back into her mink coat. She looked at him, puzzled, and noticed the silent communication between the brothers. Chas led her to the stables. Amongst Beatrice's horses was a new one.

"Calypso! It is, isn't it?" Ria said excitedly.

"Merry Christmas, my darling."

She threw her arms about Chas and then about Calypso's neck. "Did you make Rafe come all this way just to bring Calypso over?"

"It didn't take that much persuading. And Pater does have some business for Rafe to attend to. But he wants me and Jack to go along as well. Between the three of us, we hope to do him proud. Rafe is looking into some stables here as well, to expand the bloodlines of his horses."

"Oh, this truly is the very best Christmas!"

When they returned to the house, a telegram from her father awaited her.

*Cecilia born Dec. 24. Helena doing well despite difficult time. Merry Christmas to all.*

.  .  .

Of course Helena had hoped for a son. Although she was bitterly disappointed, she wouldn't let James see that. She wanted him to be devoted to all their children. So she made a great fuss of the baby. "Isn't she beautiful, James? I do think it's nice for boys to have older sisters watching out for them. Look at Louise."

James couldn't say that he had seen Louise Oakley, who must now be about sixteen, looking after her brothers at all, but surely Helena would know. He was eternally thankful that she had survived, despite a difficult labour, and was already talking about having more children. She really was a remarkable woman.

"I expect Cecilia will steal your heart," Helena said. "Girls so often become their father's pets. Would you like to hold her, James? She's a sweet baby."

He took her reluctantly from the nurse. She was such a tiny scrap that he was afraid he might crush her or drop her. But when he saw her diminutive, perfect fingers reaching toward him and the helpless, trusting look on her face, he fell in love with her. Here was someone who really needed him and relied on him, was a part of him.

Seeing the softening of his features, Helena was well pleased. Cecilia would become Daddy's princess.

.        .        .

There was no Christmas truce on the front lines this year. But those were happy days at Bovington Abbey. Ria was delighted to be reunited with Calypso, so she and Chas and Rafe rode over to Thameshill Park on soft days, leaving Justin to drive the others in the car.

Alice arrived on Boxing Day, having spent the first week of her boarding school holidays with an aunt, where the family Christmas celebrations had been held. But she was much happier being with Ria and the others, to whom she felt so much closer. They showered her with fabulous gifts – a bicycle from Beatrice that would be kept at Bovington for all the holidays she would spend there; a professional tennis racquet from Chas; an evocative sketch of her and Ria in the skiff under the tendrils of a willow, from Jack; *Anne of Green Gables,* which she hadn't yet read, from Justin; the deliciously grown-up book, *Jane Eyre,* from Henry; and a silver locket from Blake. "You can put a picture of your mother into it and then she will always be with you," he told her.

Ria gave her a chic moss-green velvet dress and a sophisticated and extravagant beaded cloak, saying, "A young lady should always be prepared for evenings at the opera or an audience with the King."

Alice giggled delightedly. She was awed by the sheer lavishness and indulgence of the gifts, and immensely grateful to them all for their thoughtfulness and generosity.

Since she knew she couldn't buy them anything, Alice had written stories and poems for each of them in her free time at school. Beatrice's tale brought to life the legend of the Bovington Abbey ghost. For Ria and Chas there was a charming story set at Bovington, about devoted lovers – who resembled them – who were able to overcome great trials and live happily ever after. The poems the others received were astonishingly relevant. Justin was particularly moved by his about Vivian. There was his beautiful, vivacious, warm-hearted, and generous sister as seen through the eyes of an admiring and observant thirteen-year-old. He was not the only one who had to fight tears when the poem related their final moments together.

*Soft but firm she held my hand,*
*One last time she smiled at me,*
*I felt loved, and brave did stand,*
*As we sank into the sea.*

Ria, however, allowed herself to cry as she hugged Alice, saying, "That is so poignant and beautiful. You've paid homage to our dear friend, immortalized her. May we all have a copy of that poem?"

"Of course!"

"I think that young Alice will become a famous writer," Chas said. "What do you think, young Alice?"

"Oh, I should like that very much. Books are great friends when I can't be with you."

"Well, I think you've created a splendid collection of poems already, and I propose we turn them into a book," Blake said. His poem from her was about mothers, which was also heart-rending, but the one about Vivian was powerful in its simplicity and honesty. From the mouths of babes... "Chas will pay."

They all laughed, but Chas said, "Smashing idea! If you have some more poems, we'll put them all into a volume along with your stories, and print... how many? A hundred?"

"Oh, there wouldn't be *that* many people who'd want to read what I've written!" Alice protested.

"On the contrary. We know at least that many people who would. Better make it two hundred. And let's dedicate the book to Vivian."

They all agreed that it would be a super idea. Alice glowed with happiness. Ria smiled gratefully at Chas. In bed that night, she said to him, "You're going to be an extraordinary, incomparably brilliant father."

"Good God, how am I going to live up to that?" he asked her with a grin.

"Just by being you."

Early the following morning, Ria took Rafe for a short flight. He looked at her with awe and said, "You really are an exceptional girl, Ria. I hope my brother appreciates how lucky he is." He touched her scar gently and said, "I truly am sorry about the baby. When I join up, it'll be with the RFC as well."

This admission distracted her from thoughts of Reggie, and she said, "Are you joining up?"

"I expect I'll have to eventually. If the war keeps dragging on. Even if just to prove to Edgar that I can do something that he can't." He chuckled.

"But Chas says you're hopeless with machines. Why wouldn't you join the cavalry?"

"Because they're outdated for a modern, mechanical war like this. In any case, I'd rather break a machine than sacrifice the life of a horse. I don't believe that they should have to suffer because of man's stupidity and barbarity. And after talking to Henry and Justin, I definitely won't be going into the bloody trenches. Chas has a much cleaner and more civilized life in the RFC. They swim in the canal at the foot of the aerodrome, play tennis and billiards and cards in their spare time or on the days they can't fly because of the weather, or wander into town for omelettes and good, cheap wine. They sleep in tents or huts or billets, not with the rats and lice and decomposing bodies in muddy dug-outs a stone's throw from the enemy. They eat in dining rooms, have champagne. When I have to face danger, I want to do it in a clean uniform after a good meal and comfortable night's sleep."

"Like a condemned man," Ria said thoughtfully.

"Anyway, I *can* drive a car now, and the boats. I've even been teaching Fliss. She admires you and wants to be just like you, even though she's terrified of motors, and certainly isn't going to get her hands dirty on one. But I do think she'll draw the line at flying.

Anyway, I figure that if you can fly, so can I," he said with a roguish grin.

"We'll see about that!" she replied with a laugh.

Chas seemed distracted after opening one of his letters at breakfast, and when Ria asked him what was wrong, he hesitated and then said, "It's one of my Oxford chums. His sister's written to tell me that he's been seriously wounded. He could be permanently blinded."

"How tragic!"

Jack looked at Chas quizzically, since he knew this was an old incident. Chas gazed steadily back at him, and Jack suddenly understood. He said, "I'd rather have any sort of injury than be blinded. Imagine never again being able to see sunsets over the lake, or the early morning mist rising off the glassy water."

Rafe snorted. "You've seen a lot of those, have you?"

"Enough to know that I want to see many more," Jack responded. He didn't understand Rafe's hostility.

Ria had hoped that Rafe would have lost his antipathy toward Jack by now, especially since he seemed to be seeing so much of Lizzie. Surely he didn't still think Jack beneath him. Was he jealous of Chas's friendship with Jack or his own father's faith in Jack's business acumen?

Later that day, she came upon Chas and Rafe arguing. If she hadn't been so distracted, she might have taken better note of it.

"You don't understand what it's like over there," Chas was saying, running his hands through his hair.

"You have it all, Chas. Other men admire and envy you. And you're such a fucking ass! You could at least have been careful!"

"What's going on?" Ria asked.

Chas looked at Rafe as if awaiting a death sentence. With a rueful smirk, Rafe said, "Tarnished heroes." Glaring at Chas he added, "Yes, of course I'll do it," before stomping off.

Chas seemed hugely relieved, so Ria said, "What was that all about?"

"Just a business issue. Nothing important, my darling." She burst into tears, and he took her into his arms, looking concerned. "Ria? What's wrong?"

"I'm not pregnant after all. I had so hoped that this time I would be." She collapsed against him.

He stroked her back as he held her tenderly. "It doesn't matter, my darling. Give it time. I'm happy and complete just being with you. Please don't distress yourself."

But Ria was clinging to a vision of herself and Chas at Wyndwood with half a dozen boisterous children of various ages around the dining room table, discussing their activities for the day – tennis with Daddy, swimming with Mummy, canoeing with cousins, picnics with neighbours.

Alice approached them tentatively. "Are you unhappy, Ria? Can I help?"

Ria brushed away her tears hastily. She put out her hand to Alice and drew her close for a hug. "You can promise me that you'll come to visit us in Muskoka. Every summer."

"Oh, yes! I should like that immensely!"

Meredith and Theadora arrived in time for tea that afternoon.

"Are you alright, Thea?" Ria asked. "You're looking rather pale."

"I could use a strong drink, actually. I'm afraid I still turn into a quivering jelly whenever I have to go through the Severn Tunnel. All the horror of the *Lusitania* comes back to me, and snatches my breath as well as my reason."

"Some sort of claustrophobia?" Blake asked. "Fear of enclosed spaces?"

"Particularly drowning in one. I can't help but recall the terror of being sucked into the smoke stack."

"Good God!" Justin said as she gave them a brief account of her ordeal.

"I've told Meredith that I just can't face going to her estate in Cardiff again if we have to take the Tunnel," Theadora said of the four mile long railway tunnel that ran under the Severn Estuary. "I know it's the most practical way to get back and forth to London, but I'll spend an extra day going the long way around if I have to."

"I can see that Blake is itching to take you aside for a talk," Ria said. "And he is actually very helpful."

"Don't sound so surprised," Blake said with a laugh.

So after tea – Theadora's laced with plenty of brandy – she went off willingly with Blake to the study. Ria said to Meredith, "I thought you might be bringing Humphrey with you." They had yet to meet him.

"Humphrey and I lead quite separate lives. We don't share many interests, and he is happiest in our country house, riding to hounds or hunting when he's not attending to business. I prefer to keep busy in less traditional ways. Humphrey really doesn't approve of women doing much beyond serving tea and presiding in the drawing room." She shuddered. "I feel claustrophobic *there*. Even my father realizes now that we're not well matched.

Although we do like each other, I expect it might be best if we dissolved our marriage one of these days."

"I am sorry, Meredith," Ria said.

"Don't be! We'll both be much happier," she replied cheerfully.

They talked for a while about the success of the Clubs and how they needed to expand the London facilities because of an overwhelming demand for beds.

When Theadora and Blake rejoined them, Meredith said to him, "Ria tells me that you are a disciple of Freud. I had a very odd dream the other night, which I'm certain is significant. It was of a beautiful expanse of wheat field, the stalks heavy with grain, under a Wedgwood blue sky. A winding path through the field beckoned one to follow. But a fierce, thunderous black storm suddenly blew through, pummelling the earth, thrashing the wheat. And then the sun reappeared, and the field was just as it had been, serene and beautiful. Only all the seeds had been stripped from the wheat, leaving it barren."

"Is that what you think this war is?" Blake asked her. "A violent storm that will leave society empty, stripped of its goodness, the productive members sucked dry?"

"Or missing altogether. My thoughts precisely! You *are* clever."

"I hate to think that you might be right, Meredith," Theadora said. As did they all.

They spent a couple of days at Bovington while Meredith checked out the Club. She was well pleased with the organization and smooth running of the place. "Although it almost seems sacrilegious to say it, the war has generated some good," Meredith said. "We've never had a closer relationship with our Canadian cousins, and you, Ria, have discovered hidden talents and strengths."

"And you, Meredith, are certainly making good use of yours," Theadora said. She had informed the others earlier that Meredith had been asked by the government to do some work for the Ministry of National Service.

Because Jack had to report back for duty on January 1st, he, Rafe, and Chas had to go up to London to conduct J.D.'s business. So they all decided to go into town and stay on to celebrate the new year there.

With the blackout in effect, streetlamps darkened on top so that there was only a small circle of light directly beneath them, taxies careening about without headlights, and dozens of searchlights sweeping the sky, night-time London was an eerie place. But bustling with soldiers on leave and people trying to lead somewhat normal lives. The friends went out to the theatre, giving Alice a chance to wear her new dress and cloak, and making her feel tremendously grown-up.

Jack was elated that the business transaction went so well, thanks to him, which even Rafe had to acknowledge, for Jack had asked pertinent and insightful questions before hammering out an agreement. Cables back and forth to J.D. confirmed that they had done well, and all three of them earned a sizable commission. Jack was thrilled as much by the feeling of power that the negotiations had given him as by the money. And the telegram that promised him a job after the war was all he could have wished for.

Whenever he could, he snuck off to visit Sidonie. His Home Defence squadron being stationed near London, he'd had ample opportunity to drop in for brief visits this fall.

"How delicious," she said, stretching like a contented cat after their lovemaking. "I do miss you, Jack. Some men just have no appreciation for the needs of women. They take their pleasure and think one should be grateful for a brief introduction to their member." She rolled onto him, her silky mane fanning over him. "I'd marry you if you were able to support me and Blackthorn."

He laughed. "I wish I could," he said, meaning he wished he had that kind of wealth. But he had no interest in marrying her. She was fun to be with and satisfied his immediate needs, but he knew they would never be enough for each other. Besides, it was Ellie he couldn't get out of his thoughts. He nibbled Sidonie's neck.

"Mmm. You're insatiable," she said delightedly.

"Only with you. You're so delectable."

Although Chas invited her, Sidonie had previous commitments and couldn't join the group on New Year's Eve. They dined late at the Carlton, sitting beneath the glass-domed roof.

"At least there's no full moon tonight," Meredith said. "So the Zepps probably won't raid, since they seem to need the light. I think that my legacy from the *Lusitania* is an irrational terror of air raids. So I contrive to be out of London at full moon if at all possible. Silly, I know."

"Not in the least," Blake said. "It's very sensible to have a fear of bombs dropping around you."

"My father, Theadora, and I were giving a dinner party here recently when we heard the heavy drone of the Zeppelins flying low overhead. We could hear our guns, and the explosions of the bombs, which shook the building, but we carried on. I was hard put to seem unperturbed and surely blathered on stupidly, but no one seemed to notice."

"Because we were all terrified," Theadora said. "I can't even recall eating, which must have been a great insult to the famous chef." She was referring to Escoffier.

Meredith said, "Well, I have terrific admiration and awe for you men who have to face the deafening noise and fear of annihilation constantly on the front lines. I wonder how any of you can remain sane."

"I think that will increasingly become a problem," Blake said. "Unfortunately, if soldiers suffer from nervous exhaustion they're as likely to be shot for cowardice as hospitalized for shell-shock."

"I trust you will do your part to see that injustices like that don't happen, " Meredith stated firmly. "Surely you medicos can straighten out the army brass, tell them what's what."

Blake laughed. "I will certainly try."

There were no New Year's fireworks of any kind.

But it was a special night for Alice, who felt privileged to be out so late with all her best friends, even though they were years older. They were glamorous and bright and exciting, full of life and poised to make their mark on the world. She loved them for not condescending to her, but treating her as an equal, and for their honest and open hearts. She knew that she would always remember this night and all the enchanting days of this unusual Christmas.

.     .     .

Bovington became a sadly quiet place after the boys left, and Ria felt particularly bereft when Chas had to resume his duties, even though he was at Upavon, near Salisbury. She had had him all to herself for over four months, and had become used to his presence, to cuddling in bed with him every night, having him soothe her when the nightmares paralysed her with fear, holding him when he was haunted by the demons of war, spending busy days with him and tranquil hours.

Although he managed to get leave every other weekend, she missed him terribly. She organized the Club so that she assumed less and less of the responsibility. Grayson pretty well ran it anyway, and one of the women, Enid Robertson, who was helping in the office, was more than capable, so Ria trained Enid to take over for her. Enid was the middle-aged, spinster daughter of the local widowed vicar. Clever, reliable, and earnest, she was a quick study and had immense drive and energy. Not only did she run the vicarage and church fêtes and jumble sales, but she raised money for the Red Cross and had recently organized a crèche for working mothers. Ria knew that with Grayson and Enid, the Club was in good hands.

So she managed to take three or four days each week to travel to Upavon and stay with Chas. The landlady at his billet was happy to have her, especially as Ria always brought plenty of food and other valuable supplies.

But her days were long there, whiling away time in their small bedroom, or wandering the lanes. She wished she could fly, or ride Calypso, or work at the Club.

Chas was often distracted in the evenings, saying only that he had had a tiring day. Although the Central Flying School at Upavon was for advanced training of pilots who had already received basic flight instruction at other locations, Chas felt that they hadn't been trained well or long enough before arriving at Upavon. Some only had a few hours of solo flying. The RFC was anxious to keep sending men overseas, as the "Fokker Scourge" had taken its toll.

"I'm doing the best I can," he said in frustration. "But it's not enough. We have crashes every day, and we're doing better than the basic flight training schools. They seem to average half a dozen crashes a day, with some fatalities. It's such a bloody waste! And quite honestly, I'd rather face the Huns than some of the students. It's downright dangerous giving over the controls to them! Some just have no sense of aerodynamics, no feel for the aircraft. They make such stupid mistakes. I keep telling the brass that the boys need more ground training before they're even allowed to see an aeroplane."

"You had lots, did you?"

"As much as you," he replied with a grin. "Which is more than these lads get, unfortunately. And anyway, you and I were special."

"ARE special," she corrected him.

"Indeed, my darling aviatrix. You could show them a thing or two."

"Oh, may I?"

"I would say 'yes', but I don't think the CO would approve."

One day, Ria said to Chas, "I really need something to do. If they won't let me fly, couldn't I at least drive a car? Chauffeur a General, or fix an aeroplane engine? Something useful?"

"I'm sorry, my darling. Don't feel that you need to come here, if it's tedious for you."

"I love being with you, Chas! But we have so little time together, really. The days are long and I feel quite useless. There must be some war work I could do. Just imagine how many men could be freed up to fight if they allowed women to do some of the jobs. Why can't I be a dispatch rider or even ferry an aeroplane over from the factory?"

"Why don't you try to persuade them? You're resourceful, and don't give up easily," he said with an indulgent smile.

"Meredith is actually working on some sort of plan in the Ministry to allow women to assume men's duties in the forces. Maybe I'll get to fly an aeroplane after all when they form the Women's Flying Corps."

"God forbid! They might let you wash dishes or type communiqués, but I doubt that you would ever get near an aeroplane."

But it was meeting with a friend of Beatrice's that got Ria thinking. Lady Aldersley's daughter was a FANY, a member of a daring group of women who provided ambulance and other services on the front lines. The First Aid Nursing Yeomanry had started as a cavalry brigade less than a decade earlier, but now drove motor ambulances. They were volunteers, and most were aristocrats, but all were plucky women who were in the dangerous front lines, determined to do their part. Since the British government and Red Cross services had rejected their offer of help, they actually worked under the auspices of the Belgian government. Lady Aldersley had mentioned, laughingly, that any young woman who arrived in Belgium with her own motorcar and a supply of bandages was welcomed by the FANYs.

So Ria decided that she would do first aid training. Perhaps she could get taken on by the Red Cross and ferry the wounded from the boats and trains to British hospitals. She even had her own car, if necessary.

Chas wasn't thrilled with the idea. "Some of the men have dreadful, shocking wounds," he said to her. "You'll have even more nightmares."

"If I use my car, I can only take the walking wounded," she said. "They can't be that frightening. And I've seen quite terrible wounds at Cliveden."

"Don't you have enough work with the Club?"

"Obviously not, or I wouldn't be here at all. I just want to have the skills, in case I ever need them. Perhaps I can run an ambulance service around here."

"Don't make any long-term plans for Upavon. I won't be here much longer."

"Why not? Surely you don't have to go back to France?"

"That's where my skills are put to best use."

"But they need good pilots to teach."

"And better ones for the new squadrons they're forming. I'm sorry, my darling, but I've been asked to join the 60th Squadron, which is being formed at Gosport. We'll be flying scouts." Which she knew were fighters. "I'm being sent for aerial gunnery training soon and then for some practice on the Nieuport 17, which is called the Superbébé, since its so highly manoeuvrable. I'll be much safer in one of those than the old BE2s."

"You'll be a fighter pilot?"

"Yes. HQ has reorganized and is setting up specialized squadrons. 60 is to be an elite fighter unit. We're doing formation flying on the front lines now, so at least three scouts escort each reconnaissance aircraft."

And engage the Germans in aerial combat to protect their recce planes. Angrily, Ria said, "You're not content to do your bit here, where you're relatively safe?"

"The instructors are usually here for just a short while, as a break from the Front. You know that. It's a thankless job, and most of us hate doing it."

"I always come second, don't I?" she challenged. "I've been bored out of my mind being here, just so that I can spend every possible bloody moment with you. And you jump at the chance of going away and back into danger!" She began stuffing her things into her bag.

"What are you doing, my darling?" Chas asked as he put his arms around her from behind and nuzzled her hair.

"I'm going back to Bovington," she snapped, trying to wriggle out of his embrace. "At least I can do something useful there. And maybe I'll consider going overseas, offering my services to the FANYs. Perhaps I can do something more noble and useful than being a mere wife!"

"Ria, stop," Chas said as she squirmed in his arms. "I don't want to leave you. The Germans have gained air superiority with their Fokkers. We need to fight them with our newest tactics and all the best pilots the RFC has. Jack and I are both joining the

60th. We've been given orders. It's not a matter of choice, but duty."

She stopped her struggle. "You couldn't stay if you wanted to?"

"Only if I pretend I'm lame. Then they might let me teach ground school." He turned her around and kissed her, and started singing one of the latest popular and catchy tunes as he gazed into her eyes:

*If you were the only girl in the world,*
*And I were the only boy,*
*Nothing else would matter in the world today,*
*We could go on loving in the same old way.*
*A Garden of Eden just made for two,*
*With nothing to mar our joy.*
*I would say such wonderful things to you,*
*There would be such wonderful things to do.*
*If you were the only girl in the world,*
*And I were the only boy.*

# Chapter 26

Justin had already had his baptism by fire on the Ypres Salient when he and his men had relieved the British troops at St. Eloi in early April. The British had blown up six enormous underground mines, shocking even themselves with the massive destruction. The explosions had been heard in southern England and had changed the landscape so drastically that there was great confusion on both sides.

The Germans had been driven back, but the area had been under constant German shell fire for a week when Justin and his company had arrived under cover of darkness. They hadn't really known what to expect, there being no reliable information about where the enemy was in this new lunar landscape. Justin's troop had been led into the remains of trenches beside one of the huge mine craters. Of course they could smell the death and decay, but as daylight had crept into the crater, they had been horrified to find themselves amidst a sea of bodies jutting out from the mud and the boggy pool in the centre. A leg here, a hand there. A few heads. As if they had dived in, not realizing that the water was confined to the centre, or were trying to come back out, but were stuck fast in the sucking grey mud. A young lieutenant seemed to be reposing happily in the sunrise beside the slimy pond. A stretcher bearer had been killed in the act of bandaging a soldier's leg, the two leaning together as if in conversation. A couple of men, cigarettes still in hand, with no visible wounds, must have died from the heart-stopping concussion of nearby high-explosive shells. There were at least thirty bodies, and surely many more buried completely in the wet clay.

Some of his men vomited. They had all turned pale. And Justin had had to order them to recover and bury the dead. A few of the British were, miraculously, still alive and were quickly evacuated. But all this was done under heavy bombardment from the German artillery and a great loss of his own men.

After their days of duty there, when they had gone to Poperinge west of Ypres for their rest period, Justin had climbed gratefully into a hot soapy tub and scrubbed himself almost raw in an effort to remove the stinking mud and corruption from his pores. It was days before it left his nostrils.

But on the morning of June 2nd , while he and his company were manning the trenches at nearby Sanctuary Wood, the Germans began an unusually violent artillery barrage, literally blowing men and trees into the air, annihilating sections of the trenches, vapourizing some of the soldiers.

Sanctuary Wood, once a quiet place where men could relax behind the lines, was part of a ridge, along with Hill 62 and Mount Sorrel, which was only a couple of miles from Ypres. It had a perfect vantage over the medieval city – or at least what was left of it. It was the only high ground in the Salient that the Germans hadn't yet captured.

After a few hours of heavy bombardment, the Germans exploded four mines under Mount Sorrel, and then began their infantry advance.

Their trenches and defences mostly destroyed, the Canadians fought valiantly. Justin ordered his men to take defensive positions in nearby shell holes while he took over a machine gun post where the gunners had been killed by a shell blast. Thankfully, he'd had gunnery training.

They managed to stop the German advance along that section of the line, although most of the rest of the line at Mount Sorrel and Hill 62 had to fall back. There was much hand-to-hand combat, and many of his men were killed. He noticed his batman, Sanderson, struggling frantically with his Ross rifle as a couple of German soldiers were almost upon him. The Ross was notorious for jamming when there was any dirt in the mechanism or on the ammunition. Justin took careful aim to avoid hitting Sanderson, and killed both the Germans. His startled batman, a boy of barely eighteen, looked around to see his rescuer, and saluted Justin with a big grin on his muddy face. Sensibly, Sanderson then found himself a safer hole, having scavenged a couple of rifles from corpses en route, and picked off advancing Germans. A strapping farm boy experienced at shooting groundhogs and rabbits, Sanderson was an excellent marksman.

By then reserve units were arriving, and helped what was left of the battalion to form a defensive line, using communications trenches and anything else that they could find for safety.

Justin hadn't even noticed that he was wounded. Of course he had felt the impact of the bullet on his left arm, but didn't realize that it had been broken. The pain had been secondary to the terror and excitement of trying to stay alive and keeping the Germans from overrunning their positions.

It had been a clean and simple break in the upper arm, which was now in a special splint until his bullet wound healed. He'd needed stitches on his hand and above his eye as well. But he was finally on his way back to England, relieved to be out of the fighting for a few months at least, terribly saddened when he discovered that almost ninety percent of his unit had become casualties. Sanderson had fortunately escaped without a scratch, but had come to see Justin at the advanced dressing station to thank him for saving his life.

Justin had smiled at him. "I know you'd have done the same for me, Sanderson."

"Damn right I would, sir! I look forward to serving you again, sir."

"I'll be back, and you, meanwhile, look after yourself. What would you think if I recommended you for gunnery training? Perhaps as a sniper?"

"Oh, yes, sir! Of course, I'd miss being with you, sir."

"Perhaps we'll still be in the same battalion. I'd feel reassured having dedicated and brave young men like you by my side."

Sanderson glowed with pride.

Justin was delighted to hear that the Canadians, through careful planning and with some brilliant new leadership, had regained the critical ridge on the Ypres Salient twelve days later. Yet what a cost to hold onto a few yards of mud – over 8400 Canadian casualties.

.    .    .

*My Darling Ria,*

*I wish you could have been flying with me today. It was an absolutely beautiful, perfect day, the sky so clear that I fancied I could see as far as Antibes, but of course, I couldn't. Although, as we were flying patrol about two miles high, I could see the white cliffs of Dover and the Isle of Wight across a silvery ribbon of Channel. I thought that you weren't much farther away, and perhaps flying as well. How I longed to be with you!*

*How incongruous it all seemed to see the war raging on below us. But from our height, even this looked surreal, the deadliness not visible. The trails of white smoke from bursting barrage shells were tinged with late afternoon sunlight. Zigzag trenches surrounded by churned-up earth looked like the masterpiece of some burrowing animal. Water-filled shell-holes glistened like golden ponds. Even* the lethal puffs of Archie fire seemed like little more than dandelion seed heads drifting and dispersing in the still air.

Beyond this relatively narrow strip of death and destruction lie colourful farmers' fields, clusters of villages, bustling cities, and vast stretches of forests. That seems bizarre as well.

I'm glad that on this occasion we didn't encounter any Germans, for it would have spoiled a perfect afternoon's amble in the skies. We'd already had a couple of skirmishes in the morning, and I brought down another Fokker.

When we got back to the aerodrome I went for a ride before dinner. The cavalry has lent us a couple of horses, but I've been thinking of buying my own. I enjoy a good gallop, especially after a hard day. The enclosed violet I found in the woods.

Our aerodrome is set in a beautiful orchard, and there is a farm nearby where some of our lads get up to hi-jinks, trying to kidnap pigs to surprise one another with a snorting, smelly room-mate, and painting the ducks bright colours. The farmer takes it all very philosophically, but the boys have to pay if they inadvertently hurt any of the animals. One lad, who I'm mighty glad isn't a pilot, wondered if the ducks would now lay coloured eggs!

You'll be amused to know that I have been adopted by a couple of stray creatures. We have several dogs attached to our squadron already, some, like the fox terrier that loves to kill rats, are most useful, but some are just bedraggled, needy, or even crippled. One poor mutt has only three legs, but manages remarkably well and has a cheerful disposition. One sad little beagle has taken a shine to me, and wants to sleep only in my hut. I've named him Snoopy, since he loves to nose around everywhere. I maintain he is a German spy, but like him anyway. Don't laugh! The army uses dogs and pigeons to relay communications. Why couldn't the clever Germans have come up with a tiny camera that is somehow imbedded in Snoopy's teeth or fur? Perhaps a bit far-fetched after all. You'd like Snoopy though, since he's a most affectionate dog.

The cat, on the other hand, just decided that my digs are the best and that she can handle Snoopy – which she does with a blow to his nose if he gets too curious – so she just strolled in one day and took over my bed. I've called her Josephine, for she is a pretty calico, like yours. She likes to be petted, but pretends she is indifferent to my company. She never sits on my lap, but does curl up beside me whenever possible.

So you see, my darling, that I am well looked after.

I managed to flame a Hun observation balloon the other day, which is never an easy feat. The "sausages", as we call them, are *heavily protected by ground fire, including "flaming onions", which are balls of fire shot from rocket guns. It's rather unnerving seeing these strings of fire balls hurtling toward you. So it's hard to get close to the sausages, but if you do, they can be hauled down so remarkably quickly by their cables and windlass that they seem to just vanish. But we can now equip our scouts with incendiary missiles which can bring down a balloon, with luck and good tactics. I guess I had both.*

*I was jolly amused the other day by a very strange sight as I crossed the lines over some hot Archie. There was a plane flying upside down! At first I thought there was a problem, but on going to check, I realized it was just our CO thumbing his nose at the German Archie, and perhaps hoping to attract a "head-hunter" – an enemy scout looking for stragglers or loners to attack. He loves a good fight. Since I'm as good an acrobatic flyer as he is, I joined him – upside down. We must have presented a strange sight to the ground troops on both sides. When we pulled up we also gave them an impressive demonstration of our aerial skills, while we dodged their shells, and had a good laugh afterwards over drinks. But please, my darling, don't try this yourself! Very few of us, no matter how experienced, can fly like this, and you do need the right kind of aeroplane.*

*You may have heard that the infamous German ace, Max Immelman, was shot down and killed a few weeks ago by one of our lads. Of course it's what we're supposed to do, but I do have great respect for other talented pilots, no matter their nationality. Immelman didn't try to finish off wounded airmen, just bring them down and take them prisoner. On the day of his funeral, we dropped a wreath over his aerodrome with a message of condolence and admiration for a brave and chivalrous foe. I realize that, despite everything, I don't really hate the Germans, just the war.*

*I'm glad to hear that Justin is recovering well, and keeping you company. Give him my congratulations for his well-earned Military Cross, and for his promotion to Captain. I heard that he and his men hung on despite terrible odds and tremendous casualties, and all the while he was wounded. Stout fellow!*

*Tell Alice I miss her, too, and hope she is still at Bovington when I finally get leave, although I don't expect that that will be until late August or even September. We are very busy these days.*

*How jolly for you, Justin, and Cousin Bea to be invited, along with all those dignitaries and "titles" and the wife of our soon-to-be Governor General, to attend the Dominion Day celebrations and luncheon at Cliveden. I trust you gave my regards to Major and*

*Lady Astor. I expect the lads had fun with the baseball match as well. That was a particularly busy day for us, but I did stop to think about our many Stepping Stone Marathons and Dominion Day Balls at Wyndwood with great fondness, I must say! I have to reclaim my title one of these days. Next year, I hope.*

*I hope the new petrol restrictions coming in August aren't too onerous for you. You may have to ride Calypso or canoe to Thameshill more often. Perhaps you can get some sort of military exemption, since you use the car to ferry men back and forth to the Club. Surely important war work! Talk to Major Astor, since he knows what you do and probably has connections.*

*As always, I miss you, my darling, and long to hold you in my arms. All my love, Chas*

.    .    .

Ria put down the newspaper, stunned at the increasing number of casualties coming out of the Somme offensive after several weeks. And saddened to find two names that she recognized. Hugh Paynter, Chas's Oxford friend who had lent them his family's Windermere estate for their honeymoon, and Lieutenant Ponsonby, the gangly, blushing young officer whom they had met at Antibes, and who Chas had thought would one day be Prime Minister.

What a bloody waste! And those were only two from the endless columns of names. It was unfathomable.

Justin looked at Ria questioningly over his coffee. They were just finishing breakfast.

"Two more acquaintances," she said simply, not wanting to dwell on things for Alice's sake.

But Alice asked, "Dead?"

"I'm afraid so."

"Is it anyone I know?"

"Actually, yes. Do you remember Hugh Paynter who came to our wedding?"

"Of course! He was a cheerful fellow with the brightest, kindest blue eyes. He told me to keep a journal, because I was living in interesting times, so I have. I thought that he was a little like Chas and that I might marry him when I was grown up. But I was only thirteen then, and I know now that that was a silly idea." Alice paused, thinking about the dream that she had never completely abandoned. "How very sad."

"Yes, it is… What I don't understand is the numbers. Look at today's *Times*. 608 casualties among the officers, with 156 dead, and 5,500 of the ranks. But the reports are always positive, about how we're gaining ground here and driving the Germans off there. 'General Haig reports progress'," she quoted. "Yet every day there are thousands of casualties. Is that success at any cost?"

Justin said, "Of course it's propaganda that we're winning at the Somme. They can hardly tell us that we're losing the war or that tens of thousands of brave men are being massacred with little change in the front lines. Not good for morale. *The Times* scoffs at German reports that we've lost 230,000 men in July alone. That's undoubtedly German propaganda. But I expect the truth lies somewhere between."

"These sorts of stories always terrify me. Aeroplanes escorting bombers were attacked by twenty Fokkers, which were driven off. Two enemy machines were seen to crash to earth and were destroyed. But three of our aeroplanes are missing." She felt a shiver of fear.

"You're really worried about Chas, aren't you?" Alice asked. "Is he at the Somme, too?"

"I'm sure of it," Ria replied. "He's never allowed to tell me where he is. But the RFC supports the army and is especially important in offensives like this one. He said he's been particularly busy. They'd be targeting observation balloons, and escorting reconnaissance planes and bombers on dangerous missions." They also had to keep the air "cleared" of enemy recce.

"I expect that he's the one who shot down those Huns. He's a hero, Ria," Alice stated. "I think he'll be just fine! Would you like to play some tennis now? I told Chas in my last letter that the racquet he gave me for Christmas is a magic one, since I can play wonderfully well now. He said that we'd see just how good I was when he came home on leave, so I need to get lots of practice."

She threw Justin a conspiratorial look, and he tried not to laugh. Her attempt to distract Ria fooled no one.

"What a lovely girl," Beatrice said to Justin when Ria and Alice went to change for tennis. "I still cannot get over the callousness of a father who would send his only child overseas on a dangerous journey in the middle of a war. But by God, I'm glad that he did. Better that we should have the benefit of her delightful company than that she should be stuck with an unappreciative father."

"He's not unlike James, is he?" Justin replied. "Perhaps one of the reasons that Ria and Alice get on so well."

"True enough. James didn't even say goodbye to Ria when she left because he was so annoyed with her for being with child and potentially causing a scandal. She needed sympathy and support, not censure. Olivia tells me that James dotes on his new daughter. I'm glad that he's finally behaving like a responsible parent, but I'll never forgive him for how he's treated Ria. Now what about you? When are you going to let go of Ria?"

Justin was startled.

"It's obvious that you're in love with her."

"I've always enjoyed her company. But then…"

"Augusta gave you hope and burdened you with the promise that you have to look after Ria. That was very wrong of her. Ria has Chas. For your own sake, you need to move on."

"I know that you're right, but it's difficult," Justin said dejectedly.

"Yes. She's eminently lovable, but she's not as fragile as she seems. She's stubborn, wilful, impulsive. Forgive me for being blunt, Justin, but I don't believe that you two would have been right for each other in any case. But she does need you as a friend. Don't ruin your relationship by wanting more than that."

They were interrupted by a visitor.

"Peter?" Justin asked in astonishment.

"Mr. Carrington!"

"Cousin Bea, this is Peter Meyer, Vivian's friend. Peter, this is Lady Kirkland."

"I apologize for being so early, but I have little time and I just wanted to thank Mrs. Thornton for sending me a book," the young sergeant said to Beatrice.

"Not at all! I'm so sorry, young man. Vivian was a delightful young woman. We all miss her dreadfully. But you, in particular, must be devastated," Beatrice said.

Peter seemed surprised by this generous admission. "Alice Lambton's poem was so moving. I don't suppose that she is here?"

"Indeed she is! And would love to hear your comments. Come along, Sergeant," Beatrice said, leading him to the tennis court.

Peter spent the rest of the morning with them, Ria offering to drive him to the station in Marlow in time to catch his train.

"It should have been me that died," he said disconsolately over coffee on the patio. "Not her. I know she was coming over to be with me."

"You mustn't reproach yourself. No one would have imagined that the *Lusitania*, of all ships, would become a victim," Justin said. "It seems from reports that there's lots of blame to be apportioned, from the Captain to the Admiralty, despite the results of the inquest. The ship shouldn't have been going so slowly, and should have been better prepared to handle an evacuation. And where was the promised naval escort?"

Alice went to sit beside Peter. She took his hand and said, "She was so happy when she talked about you. And at the end, she held my hand, trying to reassure me. Can I pass that along to you?"

Justin brushed a tear from his eyes, while Peter broke down. "I'm so sorry," he said.

"We all loved her," Ria said. "There's no shame in showing that."

Before Peter left, Justin said, "Stay in touch, won't you? We need a good vet at our stables. And good luck to you, Peter."

When Ria and Peter had driven off, Alice suddenly burst into tears. Justin held her reassuringly, saying, "You're very compassionate and brave."

"I still miss Vivian! I hate, hate, HATE this war! My friends are dying. Please don't go back, Justin! I don't want you to die as well! Or Chas. Or Jack. I'm always scared. At least Blake should be OK at the hospital."

Justin said, "Interesting times aren't the easiest of times, are they? Let's see how well I can play tennis against the up-and-coming Wimbledon champ."

Alice laughed through her tears. She thought that Justin had the kindest hazel eyes she had ever seen. Because his left arm was in a sling and a cast, she replied, "I'd say 'disadvantage, Justin'!"

"Prove it!"

It was only a few days later that Ria had a visitor. Montgomery Seaton strolled into the sitting room. It was a dark and stormy day, and the house seemed gloomy, as Beatrice was trying to conserve precious energy by not burning too many lights.

"Monty!" Ria exclaimed, slightly at a loss, and wondering how he had found her. "How lovely to see you." She introduced him to the others.

"I recall you talking about Bovington Abbey once," he explained, as if reading her mind. "I hope you don't mind the intrusion, but I wanted to personally deliver a copy of my new novel to you."

"How lovely! Thank you."

"I wanted to explain that it really isn't you and Chas in the book. But I was inspired by both of you."

He seemed a bit uncomfortable, so Ria rang for drinks.

"Dixie sends her regrets. She doesn't like to leave London, so I thought I'd just pop down for the day."

"Do stay to lunch then, Mr. Seaton," Beatrice said.

"Thank you, Lady Kirkland. How delightful."

Over lunch Alice said, "Chas thinks I should be a writer. I'd like that enormously. Is it very difficult, Mr. Seaton?"

"You already have a book published, so you're off to a good start," Monty said kindly. "But generally, yes. Be sure to have lots of writing assignments to support any novel habits you might have – magazines are quite lucrative. But I'm hopeful that this new book will make a big splash. Let me know what you think, Ria."

She started to read it as soon as he left. By three in the morning, in her lonely bed, she found herself both moved and disturbed.

It was the story of an American journalist who, during a Zeppelin raid in London, protects an attractive young Canadian woman who survived the *Lusitania*, and whose ordeal was chillingly familiar. She's married to a gallant RFC pilot. The journalist's wife is an outrageous and beautiful flapper who drinks too much and plans to dance her way through the war with every handsome young officer she meets, including the RFC pilot, who is recuperating from minor wounds. The journalist is never quite sure how serious her flirtations are, and wonders if she's having an affair with the pilot. So he is drawn to the strong, innocent Canadian wife, who seems to be ignorant of her husband's involvement with the flapper, and who is determined to do her part in the war by driving ambulances. When she gets posted overseas, the journalist follows her, but she rebuffs his advances, claiming she's love with her husband. The journalist decides to join the RFC to prove he's a better man than her husband, who ends up being killed in a glorious battle that earns him a posthumous Victoria Cross. The journalist-turned-pilot is torn between his addiction to his wife and love for the Canadian. When the journalist is seriously wounded, the Canadian visits him in the base hospital in France. She realizes that she has long been attracted to him, and that her marriage had been a sham. He realizes that his wife is shallow and unfaithful. But their happy ending is obliterated when the plucky Canadian gets killed by a shell that hits her ambulance. The maimed journalist-pilot eventually reconciles with his wayward and needy wife, but feels doomed.

Monty had cleverly crafted the story to depict not only a generation, but also a society blighted by the war.

Feeling somewhat superstitious, Ria hoped that this wasn't her and Chas's scripted future. Of course Chas had no interest in Dixie. And she definitely had none in Monty, other than intellectually. Still, it was eerie and unsettling reading about people who so closely resembled her and Chas and others she seemed to know. An officer reminiscent of poor Lieutenant Ponsonby was a victim of the insatiable wife, who could be none other than Dixie. Even Liam Sullivan had made it into the book, although he definitely wouldn't be pleased with his character.

She expected that Chas would be amused, particularly at the scene where his character pulls the drunken Dixie character out of a fountain at Trafalgar Square, after she strips naked and jumps in. Throwing his uniform jacket around her shoulders to cover her nakedness, he whisks her away before she can be arrested by the police. Ria wouldn't have been surprised if Dixie had pulled a stunt like that somewhere. Although it was left to the reader's imagination what the handsome pilot and naked flapper did then, it bothered Ria to envision an affair between Chas and Dixie.

And she couldn't help being angry with Monty for appropriating their lives.

.     .     .

*Dear Jack,*

*It scares the hell out of me that you are involved in the Somme offensive. I know you can't tell me, but I'm sure you are. I expect it is no less dangerous in the air, although, as you say, you at least have some control of your actions there, and are not so much at the mercy of ambitious, inept generals. It seems you are more in danger from faulty engines and jammed machine guns leaving you vulnerable. I marvel at your skill and courage, and am awfully proud of you! I wish I could see you receiving your Military Cross from the King. Damn it! I wish I could hold you in my arms and give you a never-ending kiss! Do you realize it's been almost two years since we touched?*

*I miss you more than I can say, especially as I haven't found anyone who could replace you. I won't ask what you've been up to in that regard, since I don't want to know.*

*I'm frustrated because I still have a year of school left, or I would enlist in the Medical Corps right now. They take nurses for overseas service, so why not women doctors? If not, I'll offer my services to one of the independent women's hospitals, which means I could actually end up in France. Even if I only get to work in England, I'll at least be able to see you, and we can pick up where we left off. Delicious! So if this war is still on next year – God forbid! – you can expect to see me over there.*

*Blake is happy to finally be in France, even if only at a base hospital on the coast. He wants to have the experience of a field ambulance or advanced dressing station some time, although I don't understand this obsession that you men have for needing to be right in the thick of danger. Tell Chas I'm miffed with him for getting you both sent back to France in time for the bloody Somme!*

*It's even more frustrating being here when Zoë and Max and Freddie are all going over. Freddie has joined the engineers, of course, and Max, the artillery, which is supposed to be the safest job on the front lines, although I don't see how, as they must surely be obvious targets. Apparently some of his university friends persuaded him to join them. So Max and Freddie are now at training camps.*

*It's been a blistering hot summer, and hell in the city, as you can imagine. Because Zoë and I work at the Wyndham Convalescent Hospital, we managed to get to the lake for only two weeks in July, and took last week off since it's still over 100 degrees in the shade! It's so different at the cottage with all of you gone, and more friends leaving all the time. But lots of tourists have been enjoying Muskoka, especially Americans, as they can't travel to Europe just now. James had to chase off some campers from Wyndwood, who didn't realize that the island was private property. The Regatta went on as usual, although we missed it, and Helena held the Dominion Day Ball at the big cottage, because of the pavilion. Her new cottage is quite grand, but minus the ballroom she wanted, although I think she is pressuring James for an addition already.*

*It is very odd that the big cottage is now empty, awaiting everyone's return. Of course it was cleaned up for the Ball, but nothing's been done to it since. Toby still looks after things there, like keeping the place aired and the mice from taking over. But Zoë and I went through it the other day, just to check, and it seemed almost spooky to me – and you know that I am not very fanciful. It was as if I could hear the ghostly echoes of old music and cheerful voices and children's laughter. The rooms were dark, the lustre had* gone from the furniture, the silver trophies were aged with tarnish, there was a grey layer of dust on the closed piano. The cottage had the peculiar sour smell of long-ago fires, ancient leather books, and musty fabrics. It drove home to me, more profoundly even than the casualty lists, that our lives have forever changed. I was immensely saddened. But I hope that one day Ria and Chas will be able to fill it with children, for a place like that thrives on life and activity.

I think that Claire has been enjoying herself at Thorncliff, and am so glad that she's had the chance to spend most of the summer between it and Silver Bay, with Esme, who is a great friend of hers. But Claire and Fliss also seem to get along remarkably well. I say that with some surprise, since Claire is academically ambitious, and Fliss isn't. Claire, although a year younger, certainly seems more mature than Fliss, who is trying to become an ideal Edwardian girl – frivolous, pampered, with no goals other than to marry well and be a successful, admired society hostess. Perhaps I'm being a bit harsh, but I hate to think of young women today not wanting to take a more important role in this world when there are so many new opportunities. Of course I know that most girls are like Fliss, and that I am the odd one out! And yes, the rich have been raised to think that work is only for the lower classes! So I should be sorry for her instead of slightly contemptuous.

Your poor Maman must feel quite bereft now that Lizzie and Emily have gone to New York. How adventuresome of them, and how adult of Lizzie to take care of Emily, who I agree with you, is still too young and impressionable to be on her own, especially in New York. I'm certain that Lizzie will keep her safe from dishonourable men, and ensure that her talents are well rewarded. Lizzie is wise beyond her years, and wonderfully feisty. Reminds me of Augusta! Too bad the old lady didn't get to know her granddaughters. She would have been proud and impressed, and realized that they were indeed part of her legacy.

Rafe seems both miffed and amazed at Lizzie going off to New York to look after Emily and her career. I still can't figure out if they are in love, or just enjoy teasing and tormenting each other. Rafe is now talking about joining up, partly to prove to Lizzie and others that he's as much a hero as you and Chas, and partly because of the pressure put on young, able men to do their bit for country and Empire.

Speaking of heroes, it's very odd for me to see you and Chas mentioned in the Toronto newspapers for your daring aerial exploits! Imagine Chas being Canada's top Ace! I always knew he had the ability to be more than a dilettante and hedonist. He's become quite the darling of Canada – it doesn't hurt that he is so handsome, especially in his uniform. There's quite a good photo, which The Star keeps using, of him in front of his aeroplane. Your photo is most flattering at well. Don't shoot down too many more Germans, since I don't want you to become even more of a celebrity and the dream of every romantic young woman! I want you all to myself.

Although there's talk of RFC pilot training starting in Canada soon, Rafe says he won't wait, and will do what other Canadians (of means!) have done. He's going to San Antonio, Texas to get private training from the Stinson sisters. I'm more surprised that he's willing to take instruction from women than by his determination to get into the RFC by this route. Chas has told us all, hasn't he, that the RFC's pilot training is inadequate. I have to admit to being shocked that ambulances are always at the ready at the aerodromes for the numerous daily crashes. Good God, but what a dangerous thing you do! And I still can't believe that Ria can fly, although I really shouldn't be astonished by anything she does.

Simon and his bride were at Red Rock for a few weeks. They are still lovey-dovey, but I think that Grace is very much in control. She has refused to let Simon sign up, even though the government rescinded the stipulation that wives must give their husbands written permission to enlist, and Simon didn't go against her wishes. I don't blame her for wanting to keep him at home, for she is heavily pregnant at the moment. But she also didn't want to stay at the cottage long, since she missed her beloved horses so much – not that she can even ride in her condition.

Lydia is pleased that Grace has put her foot down about Simon, but dreadfully unhappy that Max is going. I know that he would much rather stay here, but feels it is his duty to enlist. John McCrae's poem, "In Flanders Fields", has stirred up a lot of patriotic sentiment here. Isn't it amazing that he's from Guelph and that the Carringtons know his family?

In any case, I hope that Max ends up with some sort of desk job, because he's a pacifist at heart. I can't see him happily blasting off shells and other explosives that rip people to shreds. Nor could I see him in the infantry, willingly leading his men to slaughter, like the Somme offensive seems to be playing out. I wouldn't be surprised if Max and Lydia became betrothed before he leaves. I think that they will make a happy little family, if they ever get the chance. God, they both seem so young and innocent. It makes me furious to think of all the havoc that this war is wreaking!

Zoë cleverly managed to get into the first contingent of VADs sent over to Britain by talking to Sir Henry Pellatt, who's the head of St. John Ambulance in Canada. Aren't connections useful? I think he was happy to send her overseas so she that stops badgering him for money for various charitable enterprises, like the Wyndham Convalescent Hospital and the Maple Leaf Clubs. She and Max both leave in September, and Olivia is most anxious, but stoical, as you would expect. She throws herself into even more work at the hospital. Olivia is an adept administrator, and may well find herself at loose ends when the war is over.

Come to think of it, if we had women like her organizing the battles, there would undoubtedly be far fewer lives lost! Is it really possible that the British forces had nearly 60,000 casualties on the first day of the Somme, as we've now been hearing? It's staggering to think of so many young lives annihilated or damaged in just one day. While we were celebrating with a fancy dress ball on a perfect summer day in Muskoka. Ria says she can sometimes hear the thunder of the guns in France when she's in London. We're too far from the war here.

The power outages we've had this summer have made things difficult at times, especially at the hospital, but we really mustn't complain when we compare our still-privileged lives with yours and with those in England. At least we don't have Zeppelins trying to bomb us!

Thank God that Justin is well out of the fighting for now, although I know that our Canadians aren't involved in the Somme – as yet. I hope that he can stay safe a while longer at least. Too bad his wounds weren't just a little more severe so that his war would be over. I try not to think about how much danger you and the others are in, for it makes me shake with fear. I know from our convalescent men how horrific some of the injuries can be – and here we see only those who have survived. Please take care of yourself, Jack.

Of course I won't say anything about what you mentioned in your last letter. But I think that secrets never remain so, and can incubate into monsters if left too long in the dark. When they're finally exposed, they are more destructive than they would have been earlier. I fear that this one will be devastating, and am already extremely saddened by that.

Thank you for sharing your thoughts and your misgivings and your daily life with me. It makes me realize that you love me at least a little. Be careful as well as brave. We have much, much more to share! That's a promise.   Love, Ellie

. . .

"I'm so glad to see you!" Ria said, hugging Jack before they sat down to tea with Beatrice and Justin. Alice had already gone back to Oxford to be with her family for a week before school resumed. "I've been following the Somme but I expect we're not allowed to hear the truth. I worry so much about you and Chas. I wish he could have come home with you!"

"It's a great honour for him to be acting CO," Jack said. Their Commanding Officer had been slightly wounded and would be off for about a month, so Chas wouldn't get leave until at least the end of September. "I expect he'll be CO of his own squadron some time soon. He's a great leader and really is a brilliant pilot, Ria. He's not only fearless and has an astonishing sense of what's going on around him – which can get really tricky in a dogfight with the enemy – but he's also a clever tactician."

Chas and Jack were both Flight Commanders meaning that they each had six other pilots under their command, devised the group's tactics, and led the formation flying. "Chas makes sure that his men understand his strategies for aerial combat, so that they know what to expect and have some sort of course of action to follow in different situations. He's lost fewer pilots than any of us, although all the squadrons have been haemorrhaging pilots at the Somme. But Trenchard's aggressive policy is paying off, and we've finally gained air supremacy over the Germans again. He thinks that we can only win the air war if we keep it above German territory." Major-General Hugh "Boom" Trenchard was in charge of the RFC in France.

"Of course I'm terribly proud of Chas! And you as well," Ria said. They had both recently won a Military Cross for 'conspicuous gallantry and skill', and Chas had received an additional DSO Bar for his bravery in another action that had brought down three enemy aircraft when he had been alone and outnumbered by German Fokkers. He now had nineteen victories, making him one of the RFC's leading aces. Jack was also an ace, having downed six German aeroplanes. "I cut out the citations from the *London Gazette*, but I want to hear all the details from you!"

"First of all, you should see our Nieuport Scouts. You'd appreciate them, Ria. They're beautiful machines, fast, and elegant as well. The cock-pit is finished in hardwood. The French really know how to build aeroplanes. They manoeuvre effortlessly, so Chas can do even more amazing stunts with his plane – which by

the way, he calls *Dragonfly*. I painted one on it. The machine guns
are fixed, so you have to actually aim the aeroplane where you
want it to fire. That takes a bit of getting used to. There's a lever
on the joy stick which you press with your thumb to shoot."

"Wasn't it better when you had an observer manning a gun
that could fire in any direction?" Ria asked.

"The speed and responsiveness of our single-seaters more
than make up for that. Besides, we all cover for each other. There's
a code of ethics. Our first priority is to help each other when in
trouble. That's partly how Chas got his MC.

"His patrol was escorting recce planes taking important
photos deep behind enemy lines. They were accosted by eight
Fokkers, and there was a vicious skirmish. You have to realize how
hard it is to fight when more than a dozen machines are flying
helter skelter firing at one another. It's difficult just avoiding
crashing into each other. And we rarely land any deadly blows in
such an encounter. But Chas saw one of his novice pilots in
difficulty with a Hun right on his tail and sure to shoot him down.
So Chas surprised the Fokker by coming up under and behind him,
and firing a fatal shot. We can actually watch the smoking path of
our tracer bullets, and Chas could see it hit the pilot. The plane
went into a deadly spin."

Ria shuddered, thinking that Chas could just as easily be a
victim.

"But his objectives were to protect the slower recce planes, so
Chas suspected that these Huns were trying to keep the escort
busy, and that a few more were lurking in the clouds, ready to
ambush the BE2s. Knowing his men could handle the dogfight,
even though they were outnumbered, he climbed another thousand
feet, and sure enough, found four Fokkers ready to swoop down on
the recce planes. He surprised the first one and downed it easily,
but the other three then took after him. Chas flies instinctively,
and outmanoeuvred them, flaming one and driving another one
down, perhaps not fatally, so it doesn't count as a kill. Sometimes
they fake a death spin, but then level out in the last few thousand
feet, and get safely away. The third one finally took off, with the
rest of the Huns close behind. Chas is becoming legendary, Ria.
Albert Ball is the leading ace, but Chas is close behind him."

Ria was still assimilating the idea of the "kill". Of course
when Chas shot down an aeroplane it usually meant that the pilot
was killed and, in a two-seater, the observer as well. That was war.

"Not that he's out for glory," Jack said, although he himself
would be if he had Chas's skill and nerve. "He's generous with his

victories, and sometimes attributes them to a member of his patrol, if there's any doubt." Chas was so supremely confident, as if flying and fighting were his destiny. "There are some chaps who go out of their way to try to get victories so that their totals increase, some even flying alone on their days off, looking for trouble. Albert Ball was recently transferred to our Squadron, and he's obsessive about killing Germans, thinking it's God's will. But Chas isn't reckless or bloodthirsty. He just does his job well."

He didn't tell them how many planes and pilots the RFC had lost so far just in the first couple of months at the Somme – one hundred percent. He and Chas had been lucky perhaps, but it was more because of their experience and skill that they had survived unscathed in this offensive. Many of the novices lasted only days before becoming casualties. The turnover was shocking, but not surprising, since the boys were sent over barely able to fly, with no training at all in aerial manoeuvres that were so critical to fighting and staying alive.

"I do think it's lucky that you two have managed to stay together in the same squadrons all this time," Beatrice said.

"That's only because Chas volunteered my services as well," Jack said with a chuckle.

"What do you mean?" Ria was suddenly wary.

"Didn't Chas tell you? When Boom Trenchard visited Upavon back in March, he happened to see Chas demonstrating some aerial gymnastics, and congratulated him on his superb skills. That's when Chas mentioned that he was looking forward to getting back to the front lines where he felt he would be more useful, and that he had a friend in the Home Guard who was equally skilled. So a few days later we got our marching, or rather, flying orders."

So Chas had lied to her – or at least prevaricated, which amounted to the same thing. Ria was stunned and hurt. He had wanted to go back.

# Chapter 27

My Darling Ria,

As you're reading this, the inevitable must have happened. From the time I set foot in France, I had a sense that I would not survive this war. I wish I had spared you so much. If I hadn't succumbed to your considerable charms, I wouldn't have left you with the hope that we had any sort of future together. You would be safely in Canada, never having gone through the hell of the Lusitania and its aftermath, and only briefly saddened at the thought of yet another old friend who would never again dance with you at our summer balls, but not profoundly affected by my passing.

Yet how can I wish that the most wonderful, precious days of my life had never happened?

I expect that at this moment you're angry and hurt as well as sorrowful. I never meant to hurt you, my darling. And yet I have, in so many ways, haven't I?

Let me try to explain about Madeline. I was in a state of deep despair, having just lost Lofty, my friend and colleague, and still mourning Cedric, who'd been a good chap. I felt responsible for both their deaths, although, rationally, I knew that neither was my fault.

I went into the village to seek oblivion in a bottle, and came upon Madeline being harassed by a group of drunken soldiers – boys, really. She was working in an estaminet as a waitress. The boys didn't speak any French and seemed to assume that all French women were whores, there being a legal brothel nearby. I sent them on their way. She was grateful and we started talking. She had evacuated from a village then behind German lines, but had lost both her brothers and father in the initial fighting. Her mother had died years earlier, so she was completely alone, the rest of her relatives being still behind enemy lines. She was only eighteen, the same age as you were then.

We weren't married when I met her, and I was convinced I would never see you again. She was lonely and frightened. So we consoled one another. It didn't seem wrong at the time. I have no other excuse.

But once I found out about our baby, and that you were coming over, I felt as if I had been given an extension on my death sentence. Perhaps a reprieve. I stopped seeing her, and although I never loved her – how could I when I loved you? – I did feel terribly sorry to have misled her and hurt her, as it seems that she fell in love with me. What I hadn't expected was that she was with child as well. She told me just a few days before you were to arrive. I gave her money to care for the child, and have since set up a trust fund for him, as you now know from my will, but told her that there could be nothing more between us. I realized then that I had behaved dishonourably toward you both. And I felt that I had indeed been punished for my sins when our baby died, and I almost lost you. Forgive me, my darling.

You may think the words empty now that you have heard my story, but I love you more than I can ever express, except to say that I would gladly have given my life for yours. Our days together have been the most treasured and joyful of my life. You enthralled me, inspired me, gave me a purpose, made me happy. I hope that you can remember me with love, and not just bitterness. What was a small, insignificant interlude in my life should not become the focus of yours.

I had to do what was right for my son, for he is mine. I met him once, and I see the resemblance. He should have been ours, but that wasn't to be. Perhaps one day you can find it in your generous heart not only to forgive me, but to see that young Charles knows something about his father. I had intended to tell you about him, but the time was never right. At first you suffered so terribly from your ordeal, and losing our son. Then, when we were so happy, I didn't have the courage to tell you, and risk spoiling our brief but idyllic times together.

So now forgive me, my darling, for deserting you yet again. I would gladly sell my soul to the devil to be able to stay with you, and grow old with you.

How I wish I could be with you now to comfort you, to tell you how much I love you, to hold you once more in my eager arms. Perhaps I am with you. Perhaps I shall be one of those dragonflies that worship and protect you.

And I hope that you can find some happiness in this life. Don't close your heart to a new love that may come your way. There are better men out there than I, but surely none who could love you more deeply and passionately than I have.

If Edelina is right and we are soul mates, then we will meet again in another life. Until then, take care, my darling Ria.

Your loving and devoted Chas

Ria thought she must be in a nightmare. Or going mad. What the hell was this letter all about? It couldn't be real. But it was too brutal to be someone's idea of a joke.

The letter addressed to her "in the event of my death" had fallen out of Jack's jacket pocket when she had moved it from the chair where he had carelessly flung it before going into the garden. She had thought it odd that Chas would have left her a letter that she couldn't read while he was alive, and had been afraid that it might mean he knew somehow that he was going to die. From the consequences of injuries he hadn't told her about? Or some disease? She had been concerned about his mental state, although he always denied there was a problem, rarely sharing with her his experiences beyond the banal or humorous.

So she had opened the letter, thinking that it would bring them closer, that she would tell him afterwards that he shouldn't have been afraid to open his heart to her.

But this was devastating. More powerful than a bomb, those words had just ripped her world apart.

Chas had a son. By another woman.

Their relationship was a lie. What did it matter that they hadn't been married when he'd had his affair? They had pledged themselves to each other at the Shimmering Sands months earlier. For her it had been a lifelong commitment. Their wedding ceremony had been merely a formality.

Chas had betrayed her.

She crushed the letter in her hand just as Jack and Justin walked into the sitting room.

At the deathly pale, shocked look on her face, Justin immediately thought that she had received a dreaded telegram. "Ria, what's happened?"

Glaring at Jack she held the letter toward him and hissed, "What the hell does this mean? Tell me it isn't true!"

Jack was dumbfounded when he realized what she held. Chas had given him the letter to leave with his lawyer in London. Jack knew more or less the gist of it. Bloody hell and damnation!

Before he could say anything, she said, "Don't tell me I shouldn't have read it! Chas shouldn't have any secrets from me. He's betrayed me!" She hugged herself and turned away from them in anguish. "Oh, God! It's all been a sham."

Justin realized what she must have discovered. He went to her side and put his arm about her, but she brushed him off angrily. "Did you know as well?" she demanded, for he hadn't asked her what was wrong. "That my beloved, cherished, perfect husband has a mistress and a son?"

Reluctantly, Justin said, "Chas asked me at Christmas to be a trustee, if necessary. Along with Jack and Rafe. He told me the affair was over. He truly loves you, Ria, and deeply regrets his actions." Justin had once again been surprised and disappointed in Chas, although he did understand some of his excuse for having had a fling with Madeline. The daily struggle for survival on the front lines made conventional morality seem insignificant in comparison. He wouldn't have succumbed to the temptation if Ria were awaiting him at home, but he didn't know, if he were in Chas's shoes, whether he could have told her either. But for her, finding out in this surreptitious way made things even worse.

A memory suddenly came to Ria of Chas and Rafe arguing, of Rafe grudgingly agreeing to do something. A trust fund for Chas's son. And his friends would administer it if he couldn't.

She remembered, too, the mysterious letter Chas had received at Christmas. Had that been from Madeline, informing him of the baby's birth, since the timing would have been about right? The military was most efficient about forwarding mail. So it may not have been from the sister of his blinded Oxford friend after all. Lies upon lies.

Jack said, "Chas didn't betray you, Ria. He was in a funk when he met Madeline. I'd been worried about him, because he'd lost his concentration and that's usually fatal when flying. So she was actually good for him. Perhaps saved his life."

"What a bloody perfect excuse! Should I feel grateful to her? Why couldn't he have shared his feelings with me instead?"

"You weren't there. You couldn't know, and none of us can or want to find the words to explain what we go through. We see friends die every day. Chas needed something to keep the darkness at bay. A lot of men use alcohol and sex, but most of them have to buy their women. Madeline was alone and frightened. He gave her some comfort as well."

"The knight in shining armour!" Ria said bitterly, "Chas likes vulnerable women, doesn't he?"

"It's you he loves, Ria. And he's been faithful to you since your marriage."

"He's obviously seen her again, since he's seen the child."

"Only to give her information about the trust fund."

"He lied to me about having no choice in staying at Upavon. He engineered that beautifully, didn't he, making it seem as if he was just following orders! Was he so anxious to get back to France to be with her?"

"She had nothing to do with it."

"I don't believe you!"

"Why should I lie?"

"Because you're his friend. And you men stick together. Besides, what's different about his life now?"

"The fact that you're here. He no longer feels like he's doomed. He's had amazing success. I think it's his way of dealing with his own grief. Losing the baby and almost losing you affected him profoundly. You and Chas have something special, Ria. We're all envious of you. Try to forgive him."

"I can't. Being faithful is a commitment to someone you love, whether or not it's a legal union. I was at home, miserably lonely, worried sick about him, carrying his child, and he was consoling another woman!"

"You never told him you were pregnant," Jack said. "You weren't exactly honest with him either."

"So now it's my fault that he had an affair! Because I didn't want to add to his worries!"

"I'm not saying that, Ria. I just want you to understand the circumstances."

"I can't see how that makes a difference! I can't bear to think of Chas being intimate with her like he is with me. And I really can't bear to think that she has his child, while I lost ours!" She broke into heart-rending sobs. "I loved him so much. Why has he made me hate him?"

"You don't hate him, Ria," Justin said. "You're just angry and hurt at the moment. Give Chas a chance to explain..."

"Oh, he has. But too late. Protestations of love seem rather empty compared with deeds. The rock upon which my love was based has just been shattered. How can I ever believe him or trust him again?"

"But he married you, despite..." Jack began, realizing he had just made a terrible mistake. Christ almighty, he was making a balls of this.

"Despite what?" she demanded.

"Nothing. It's not important."

"No more secrets! No more evasions! I want to know what you're talking about! Despite what? That he was in love with the mother of his child?"

Looking at her with compassion and regret, Jack said, "The doctor may be wrong, but it's possible that you may never be able to bear children. Because of the infection."

Justin was surprised at this, and concerned that it was another stunning blow to Ria, which might push her over the edge.

She was barren, useless. And Chas had married her anyway. To appease his guilt? "So all this time he let me go on hoping, planning, dreaming of our children and our future. Nothing has been real. It's all been based on some convenient fantasy." Coldly she said, "So he will be glad of his son."

When she started to leave the room, Justin once again tried to comfort her, but she turned to him in fury and said, "Don't touch me! You are all a part of this conspiracy of silence and deceit!"

He followed her into the hallway. She grabbed her handbag and swept out of the house. "Where are you going?" he asked with concern. She seemed too icily in control of herself, but he knew that she was about to explode in anger and grief. He didn't want her doing it somewhere where she could hurt herself.

"That is no concern of yours."

"Ria…"

"Leave me alone, Justin! I don't want anything to do with any of you just now: This is not something that can be changed or forgiven with slick words. The betrayal cuts too deep."

"Chas didn't know how to tell you, and it wasn't our place to do so."

She turned and fixed him with a hostile glare. "Because you're his friends, not mine."

"Ria…"

She ran to her car and slammed the door. Justin tried to stop her, but she spun out of the drive, the loose gravel shooting up behind the wheels.

"Bloody hell," Jack said, joining Justin. "I couldn't have handled that any worse if I'd tried! You don't think she'll do something foolish?"

"We'd better call Peggy and make sure Ria doesn't take an aeroplane up. And send Chas a telegram."

But Peggy reported back an hour later that Ria never came to the aerodrome. Nor had she gone to the Club. When she didn't show up for dinner, they began to worry.

Beatrice, who had been filled in on the shocking details, said grimly, "Ria's a romantic, sensitive soul, despite her brashness. This has surely devastated her. Dear God, but this is a mess!"

"It's my fault," Jack said. "Chas handed me the letter at the last moment, and I just shoved it into my jacket. And forgot about it."

Beatrice said, "Chas should have found the courage to tell her long ago. And the fact that he obviously never planned to tell her until after his death must surely make her feel even more betrayed."

By the time darkness fell, all three were on edge. Then the telephone rang. Beatrice jumped to answer it. "Ria, thank God! Where are you, my dear?"

"London."

Beatrice breathed a sigh of relief and said, "You've been frightfully hurt. Come home and let me help you."

"Thank you, Cousin Bea, but nothing that anyone can say or do will change the facts. That's what I have to learn to live with. Or not. I just didn't want you to worry about me. I know that *you* care."

"My dear, wounded child we all care! I know that you don't want to hear this just now, because you want to be angry with Chas, and justifiably so. But I have never seen a man so truly devoted to anyone as Chas is to you. Whatever you do, remember that he really does love you. He's not perfect. In fact, he's a dashed fool! But he's only human. And he's been hurt, too. He needs a bit of compassion and understanding."

"You think I haven't noticed, that I haven't tried to give him that? But he shuts me out of so much of his life. Obviously! I need to be alone, Cousin Bea. I can't face excuses and justifications right now. I'm still damaged from my own experiences. I want to lash out. So I think it's best if I go and do that productively."

"What are you saying, dear child?"

"Good night, Cousin Bea."

Ria put down the phone and burst into tears yet again. She hadn't had any real plan when she'd left Bovington, other than to escape the people who knew her and Chas, and were embarrassed and would try to influence her to put it all behind her. So she had driven around aimlessly for a while, negotiating her way through her tears, and had found herself on the outskirts of London. She had brought nothing, but would buy herself some things tomorrow.

She had toyed with the idea of going back home, to Wyndwood. It was a place where her spirit might heal. She longed to sit on the sun-warmed granite of her rock at the Shimmering Sands in the early morning, looking out at the serene lake, to hear the lonely cry of the loons, to feel the silkiness of the clear water on her naked skin, to see the multitude of stars against a midnight-deep sky or the moon dancing across the water. But all those images were intimately entwined with Chas. How could she go back without him?

She received a telegram from him first thing in the morning. "Life has no joy or meaning without you, my darling. What can I do to earn your forgiveness? Please give me a chance to redeem myself."

She didn't respond.

Beatrice arrived after breakfast, which Ria hadn't touched. "I've brought you some things," she said, as the cab driver deposited a large suitcase in the hallway.

"Thank you, Cousin Bea. It wasn't necessary," Ria replied, meaning that Beatrice shouldn't have bothered to come. But it was her home after all.

"On the contrary. Much as I love you, my dear, I think you have the unfortunate habit of running away when things get tough."

Ria's anger flared. "Perhaps this time I'm running *to* something, not away. I've always wanted to play a more direct role in this war. The Club is pretty well self-sufficient with Grayson at the helm and Enid Robertson so competently taking over my duties. I've had an inner rage ever since the *Lusitania*. Which is probably why I still have nightmares and panic attacks. Ask Blake! But that flame has been fanned by all this deceit. I need to do something for myself."

"Meaning?"

"I'm going to go overseas. Drive an ambulance."

"But why?"

"To try to release the vengeful demons within me. Does anyone question men's motives when they enlist? Why shouldn't I be allowed to go and fight against the monsters that killed my baby and my friends?"

"Putting yourself in danger won't help them."

"But it may help me. And I hope I can help others. I need to see more of Chas's world, and try to understand how he could have betrayed me, before I can even begin to think about forgiving him. I can't stop loving him, Cousin Bea!" She burst into tears. "But I can't bear what he's done to me!"

She allowed Beatrice to hold her as she wept.

Beatrice said, "Don't shut him out of your life, Ria. He made a stupid mistake, but he's learned from it. Your relationship is precious. It deserves a second chance. Love isn't easy. Successful marriages require work. Loving someone means forgiving him as well."

"But surely marriages require honesty. And why didn't he tell me I can never have children?" She choked on the words.

"We weren't convinced that the village doctor was right. It was better for all of us to hope. Chas wanted to give you time to heal emotionally as well as physically, and then planned to take you to a specialist in London if you didn't conceive. Not telling you yet was meant as a kindness. Don't think of it as deceit."

The next telegram from Chas said, "I can't live without you, Ria. Am trying to get leave."

She cabled back saying, "Don't. I need time. I don't know if love can survive without trust and integrity."

Later that day, after many more tears, she wrote him a letter.

*Dear Chas,*

*I loved you so much. You were my world, all that I needed or wanted, other than your children.*

*But now my world and my soul are in fragments. My love is raw, painful, bleeding. Words can't stitch the pieces back together.*

*Your friends say that I should try to understand, but you never gave me a chance. Planning to tell me only after your death was cowardly and cruel. Perhaps I would have hated you if you had told me sooner, but I think my love would have been strong enough to forgive you. I'm not sure it is now, because you didn't trust me enough to share your fears and weaknesses, your mistakes.*

*But was it a mistake? Perhaps we have a fundamental difference of opinion about what constitutes love and loyalty and devotion and faithfulness. You call your affair an 'insignificant interlude'. That seems rather callous. Are women just to be used for your pleasure? Have you learned well from your father? Can I have sex with another man because if I claim I don't love him, it's insignificant? Would you still feel the same about me afterwards?*

*Perhaps those words were just for my benefit. I can't believe that you have no feelings for the mother of your child. Compassion, tenderness, affection – you must have felt all these and more. And undoubtedly still do, which amounts to emotional adultery. Do you now think yourself a faithful husband for restraining yourself from physically expressing your feelings for her? How long will that last? What excuse will you have the next time? I can't live with that.*

*Jack seems to think it was noble of you to marry me despite my barrenness. I don't want your pity! Will you, like my father, decide in a few years that you need to father sons to build a dynasty? What* use then a sterile, aging wife? Is it even possible for us to grow happily old together?

Reggie is now all my dead children. I feel such a rage that I can no longer stay in England, pretending that all is well, that we can play tennis before tea as if the world and our lives weren't completely insane. And feeling that you have shut me out of a large part of your life. By trying to protect me from the truth, you have driven us apart. I can no longer live with illusions.

I love you too deeply to stop loving you in an instant. But my heart is too battered to be entrusted to you just now. Perhaps time can heal. I can't believe that all your protestations of love were just empty words. If they were, then please be honest with me now. Perhaps I expected too much of you, and am, as Cousin Bea seems to think, too idealistic and naïve about true love.

So I need time to come to grips with all this, and I need to take a more active role in this war.

You can end this marriage now, if it is just a mockery. I can't bear any more deceit. And I won't settle for just those parts of your life that you choose to share with me. If you can't commit your heart, mind, and soul to me then we truly have nothing.

Take care, my love. I wish you well.

Ria

The story continues in Book 2 of "The Muskoka Novels".

# Author's Notes

Trying to create a realistic portrait of a bygone era requires lots of research. I drew heavily on biographies, journals, memoirs, letters, and other sources to create believable characters and incidents in all aspects of this novel, from the lavish lifestyle of privileged summers in Muskoka to aerial battles in the skies over France. My extensive bibliography is listed on the website www.theMuskokaNovels.com.

I have anticipated some readers' questions with the following information:

- The cover photo is of a Disappearing Propeller boat, commonly known as a "Dippy". These were built in Port Carling, Muskoka, beginning in 1915, and were popular for more than a decade. Dippys and other fine water craft, like the Ditchburns mentioned in the novel, can be seen at the annual Antique Boat Show in Gravenhurst, Ontario, in July.
- Although we may think these more modern than pre-WW1, expressions like "hot dog!", "not on your life", "frigging", and "OK" were already in use at that time. All the slang in the book was verified through the *Oxford Dictionary of Slang*. The term "flapper" was used before the first war, and not confined to the 1920s.
- There was a "clothing-optional" beach for naturists at Hanlon's Point on the Toronto Islands from 1894 – 1930. Naturists occasionally visited one of the islands on lake Rosseau in Muskoka.
- "Indians" was the term used at that time to refer to First Nations People.
- For the story of Megan and Keir Shaughnessy, the grandparents of Justin, Vivian, Lydia, and Simon Carrington, see *A Place To Call Home*, my first novel.
- Canada's Prime Minister, Sir Robert Borden, was in Muskoka on holidays until July 30, 1914, when European events escalated – indicating that Canada, at least, wasn't anticipating the war that was declared only a few days later.
- Waldorf=Astoria is how the name was written historically. At the time of this novel, the hotel was located on Fifth Avenue at the site of the present Empire State Building. The new hotel was built on Park Avenue in 1931.

- The incidents surrounding the *Lusitania* are all based on those of real survivors. For an excellent account, see Diana Preston's book, *Lusitania: An Epic Tragedy*. Unbelievably, many of the survivors were in the frigid waters of the Irish sea for well over 2 hours before being rescued. Some victims were actually thought to be dead, but were able to be revived.
- Captain Turner's quotes are almost verbatim from accounts given by survivors of the *Lusitania*.
- The King George and Queen Mary Maple Leaf Clubs did exist in London – although started by Lady Drummond – and enjoyed the patronage of the Kiplings and others, as mentioned. The one at Thameshill Park is fictional.
- 8000 men died in Britain during pilot training for the Royal Flying Corps. In addition, more RFC pilots died from accidents and equipment failures than from enemy action.
- 1/ 3 of all RFC pilots were Canadians.
- RFC scenes and incidents are based on the experiences of real pilots, especially the aces.
- "He was [killed] by shrapnel in his hotel room, while standing at the window watching the bombing" – as quoted from my grandfather-in-law's memoirs. This happened to an acquaintance of his who was on leave in London during a Zeppelin raid. He had just mentioned to his friends how ironic it would be to die in an air raid on London after surviving so well at the Front.
- My British grandmother-in-law and her friend, Vi, actually managed to get to Marseille in 1916 to be with their husbands before the men departed for Salonika, their Company having just been transferred from the Front. The officers were allowed to stay at the hotel with their wives, one of them needing only to go to the camp daily for a bit of work. "How Vi engineered the whole thing – permits, passports, and all the other details and forms, I never discovered.... And so, instead of being probably killed on the Somme, here we were with our wives for a blissful week!"
- Reports from the Somme were positive in the newspapers throughout the summer of 1916, and although there didn't yet (Aug. 1916) seem to be any knowledge among the populace about how many casualties there really were, I included that information to show what a callous waste of young lives the Somme had been – nearly 60,000 British casualties on the first day alone.

- So many Canadian families followed their men to live in Britain during the war that the Canadian government made special arrangements to repatriate them in 1919. One source states that 30,000 women followed husbands and sweethearts to England.
- With nearly half a million Canadian soldiers and their families in England during the war, it was not at all unusual for people to constantly run into acquaintances in London or elsewhere. Diaries and letters home to Canada often mention meeting up with old friends.
- France had legalized brothels, but separate ones for officers and men.
- Some officers, like Lieutenant Colonel John McCrae, kept their own horses behind the lines for their leisure hours.
- There were some women aviators before and during the Great War. A few taught fighter pilots, while a very few Russian women and one Belgian actually flew in combat missions. The American Stinson sisters trained over 100 Canadian pilots from 1915-1917 at their Texas flying school.
- Zeppelin bombing raids during the four years of the war killed 557 people, injured 1358, and caused £3 million damage. During the last two years of the war, the new German Gotha bombers killed an additional 836 people, injured 2,000, and caused a further £1.5 million damage. This first "Battle of Britain" served to terrorize the population, disrupt factory production, and draw pilots and resources away from the front lines for Home Defence.
- Several sources, including autobiographies, mention the frenetic, desperate party atmosphere of wartime London. Excessive drinking actually led to reduced pub opening times, which lasted well into the later part of the century. There were frequent newspaper reports about the problems of cocaine and other drugs.
- People can once again cruise the three large Muskoka lakes on the restored steamship, *R.M.S. Segwun*, built in 1887, which sails out of Gravenhurst, Ontario.
- Book 2 of the Muskoka Novels will take the story through the rest of the Great War and the 1920's – and perhaps beyond.

Questions and comments are always appreciated at
books@mindshadows.com